T0072442

Praise for
THE ADVENTURES OF AMIR HAMZA

"Farooqi's *The Adventures of Amir Hamza* is for a seasoned, patient, and curious reader.... Students of world literature and Eastern languages will absolutely swoon if they are fortunate enough to receive this new translation." —*The Austin Chronicle*

"A spectacular and literally marvelous Islamic epic that ought to be almost as often spoken of as the *Tales of the 1,001 Nights*." —*The Buffalo News*

"As the first complete English translation of a medieval classic that has been in danger of neglect, this is a landmark work in its very conception—invaluable to students of Islamic heritage and Arabic literature—but the excellence of its execution makes it a fantasy-adventure that can be relished by readers of all backgrounds." —*Business Standard*

"It is indeed a wonderful book, replete with poetry, elegant turns of phrase, choice abuses, jokes, drama and suspense.... Quite simply, this *dastaan* in any language is an antidote to the cares of this world." —*India Today*

"The Indo-Islamic *Dastan-e Amir Hamza* is a rip-roaring, bawdy, magical journey into the fantastic life and exploits of Amir Hamza, the paternal uncle of the prophet Muhammad.... The story is reminiscent of the tales of Homer and King Arthur and *The Arabian Nights*. Farooqi's ... English translation from the Urdu is masterful.... Destined to become a classic." —*Library Journal*

"Captivating ... A must-have for serious Near Eastern collections and fans of epic literature from any culture." —*Booklist*

"A refreshing and eminently readable translation, a gem of exceptional brilliance ... a piece of fantastic literature."
—MUHAMMAD UMAR MEMON, professor of Urdu, Persian, and Islamic studies, University of Wisconsin

"There is simply no other book in the history of literature quite like *The Adventures of Amir Hamza*. Part romance, part morality play, part trickster fable, this is traditional story-telling at its poetic height."
—REZA ASLAN, author of *No god but God: The Origins, Evolution, and Future of Islam*

"Extraordinary. Farooqi has translated into English what most of us thought was untranslatable. The adventures of Hamza have beguiled readers in many languages for centuries. This translation from Urdu should interest all students of Eastern literatures."
—C. M. NAIM, professor emeritus of
Urdu Studies, University of Chicago

"Possibly one of the most important fantasy events of the year... Farooqi's energetic and stylish translation... captures brilliantly the insouciant delights of the storyteller's voice, and gives us a highly readable version of a major work of world literature that few of us even knew about. The Modern Library has done us a big favor." —*Locus*

"What a find it is! Farooqi's translation is both elegant and earthy.... One is tempted to think that only a malevolent enchantress of great power could have kept *The Adventures of Amir Hamza* from a mainstream American audience for so long."
—*The Magazine of Fantasy and Science Fiction*

"The translation by Musharraf Ali Farooqi is a bravura performance.... Nothing that readers in India, or elsewhere, have read would have prepared them for its lightness, deftness and frothiness."
—*Hindustan Times*

"Stupendous... a major achievement... Farooqi has opened a window to a very different world." —Calcutta *Telegraph*

THE ADVENTURES OF
AMIR HAMZA

GHALIB LAKHNAVI AND
ABDULLAH BILGRAMI

THE ADVENTURES OF
AMIR HAMZA

LORD OF THE AUSPICIOUS
PLANETARY CONJUNCTION

SPECIAL ABRIDGED EDITION

Translated, with an Introduction and Notes, by
Musharraf Ali Farooqi

THE MODERN LIBRARY

NEW YORK

FOR AZHAR ABIDI
SORCERER OF THE ANTIPODES

CONTENTS

INTRODUCTION

Musharraf Ali Farooqi

I grew up in Hyderabad, Pakistan, whose climate during summertime closely resembles that of Hell. Temperatures can reach 50°C (approximately 120°F), and in the absence of air-conditioning, a three-hour nap is considered the best answer to nature's excesses.

My younger brother Arif and I came up with another, more entertaining alternative. We would improvise a spear by affixing a butter knife to the tip of a bamboo pole and go into the courtyard to hunt the lizards and chameleons that lived in the crevices of the brick walls and the wind catchers on the roof of our house. The authorities never learned of the carnage, because we always eliminated all signs of it. The corpses were fed to Mano—a fellow hunter and a fine specimen of a marmalade cat. That was how we passed our afternoons before we discovered books.

Everyone from my generation is familiar with the children's titles published by the house of Ferozsons. A few of these were translations of English-language classics, but the rest were written in Urdu. My older sisters had accumulated about a hundred of these titles, and in a city lacking in public libraries, this was a considerable treasure. After inheriting the collection from our sisters, Arif and I developed an unhealthy appetite for these stories. The schoolwork suffered, and I was often caught under the covers with bound paper and a pencil light. All this was probably enough to send my parents into a panic, and they decided to remove the temptation from the path. The storybooks were put in an iron chest, which was locked up and placed in the storage room. We tried but were unable to find the key during our periodic searches.

While sadly lacking in lock-picking skills at the time, we had not entirely wasted our time at school. Here was an opportunity to put our book learning to use. It was the principle of the lever that we applied—inserting a heavy shish-kebab skewer between the lid and the top of the trunk and giving it a little lift. The physics were flawless. The lid rose, then twisted, becoming almost dog-eared. Sliding our hands in and grabbing a book each was what we did next, before covering the lid with an old quilt and stealing away.

Our parents never suspected we had burglarized the iron chest. It was a little unimaginable for two quiet boys living a protected life to have committed such a heinous deed (may that be a lesson for parents not to put a limit on their children's imaginations). In that trunk, among other books, was the juvenile edition of the *Dastan-e Amir Hamza,* in a set of some eight or ten books. That was my first introduction to the *devs,* jinns, *peris,* cow-footed creatures, horse-headed beasts, and elephant-eared folks.

I remember that after spending an hour or two reading these stories my brother and I would undergo a transformation. One of us would become Amir Hamza, the other the king of India, Landhoor bin Saadan, or some other such mighty champion. We would head for the courtyard. Our arms and armor were ready and we would gird ourselves: swords improvised of hockey sticks, spears made of bamboo, body armor fashioned of sofa cushions. Mattresses would be spread on the courtyard floor to break the fall, and hostilities were declared. Once we tired of fighting with weapons, it would be time to wrestle. When that too was insufficient to dissipate the adrenaline rush, our focus would turn to the lizards. While our parents slept, Amir Hamza and Landhoor would indulge in the pleasures of the chase. Death to the infidel lizards and the faithless chameleons!

Meanwhile, at school I was having an existential crisis—or perhaps it was one of the spiritual kind. Often during the classes I would have an unworldly awakening. I would look around and find myself surrounded by uniformed creatures sitting in rows while an older person chalked something on a blackboard. I would try but could never figure out how I had ended up with them. I would have preferred to be a *dev,* running around swinging a tree trunk and clobbering humans with it. Or a jinn, throwing humans from the heavens into the mountains and seas. Thus, at a young age I had my first experience of alienation. I returned home worn, exhausted, and a little stupider, and sneaked away to the storage room where my real and true friends awaited me—the *devs,* jinns, and so forth. I felt one with them. In their company I never had any of my spiritual or existential dilemmas. I was back under the covers with bound paper and a pencil light. This time I took care not to be caught. And so the years passed.

Let me now fast-forward six years, to a time when I was having another crisis. I had ruined my eyes from reading with the pencil light and disqualified myself from my natural calling as a soldier. Then I had moved to Karachi and ended up in the electrical engineering program, where both the induction motor and the synchronous motor refused to reveal their secrets to me. I decided not to force the issue. But my parents were not prepared to hear of my dropping out. So I carried on, going in the morning to the university, where some considerate person had provided very comfortable sofas in the dining lounge. While the future builders of the country made their parents proud and strove mightily against the curriculum in rooms adjacent, a lonely truant grappled with his very own curriculum of assorted fiction scrounged from secondhand bookshops.

Most of the books I read at that time were in English, many of them classics. A story is a story, and I was too busy enjoying the books to pause and wonder where all the classics of the Urdu language were hiding. One did not see them in the bookstores.

After dropping out of engineering studies in the late 1980s, I spent a few years experimenting with learning languages, working as a journalist, and making films—and failing at all of them. During this time, I also made new friends who introduced me to good contemporary Urdu fiction. However, the fiction writers were unable to keep pace with my reading consumption and I soon ran out of Urdu books. In their absence I read in English, and later, when I tried to write fiction myself, I found it easier to structure sentences in English than in Urdu. Still, for a very long time, I needed to read something in Urdu before I could go to sleep.

Then I got married, and in 1994 I moved to Toronto. One day at the University of Toronto library I came across *Urdu Ki Nasri Dastanen.* It was a record of Urdu's classical literature compiled by Gyan Chand Jain. It contained information about a large number of classics written in the Urdu language in the nineteenth century and earlier. Most of this literature had originated in the oral narrative genres of *dastan* and *qissa*. They were packed with occult, magic, and sorcery. I realized that if I could find them, I would have more than a lifetime's supply of reading.

I also discovered the *Dastan-e Amir Hamza* a second time. I learned of one version of the *Dastan-e Amir Hamza* (1883–1917) that existed in forty-six volumes, each of them approximately a thousand pages long. It can no longer be found and exists only in one or two special collections in the form of microfilm. Another version of the *Dastan-e Amir Hamza* (1801) was compiled by Khalil Ali Khan Ashk. It was one of the many texts written at the Fort William College in Calcutta to teach Urdu to the officers of the British colonial administration. I obtained an undated reprint of this book but found Ashk's language rather insipid. It also lacked a large portion of Amir Hamza's adventures in Qaf. This Ashk fellow was probably some freedom fighter who had infiltrated the Fort William College to sabotage the education of the colonial officers. He must have feared that if the Brits began enjoying these stories too much they might become very difficult to get rid of. I could appreciate his motives, but I did not appreciate the fact that in the process he had also killed many of my friends. That was just not right. Finally, I discovered the most popular one-volume version of the *Dastan-e Amir Hamza*, first published by Ghalib Lakhnavi in 1855 and amended by Abdullah Bilgrami in 1871. Neither one of them were "authors" in the sense we understand today. They were compilers of this oral *dastan*, and in the process they rewrote and expanded the story.

When I started reading about the *Dastan-e Amir Hamza* in greater detail, I also discovered a family connection to its social history. My great-grand-uncle Ashraf Ali Thanvi (1864–1943) was a religious scholar and one of the spiritual leaders of the Indian Muslims. He found the story's ribald passages unsuitable for the sensibilities of proper women and in his book *Bahishti Zevar*, which is an introduction to social norms for women, he declared that they should avoid reading it. Now that I have read these passages, I have the same advice for proper women. Taking modern-day sensibilities into account, I would just add that men, too, must not sit down with this book without a bottle of smelling salts close at hand.

Through the writings of *dastan* scholar Shamsur Rahman Faruqi, I began to understand the significance of this legend, its complex theme of predestination and its thousand-year history in the South Asian subcontinent. At first, while reading the Lakhnavi-Bilgrami *Dastan-e Amir Hamza*, I had difficulty understanding the ornate passages. I had to look into classical dictionaries to understand what was being said. Three generations ago, those considered truly literate in our culture could read and write with equal facility in Arabic, Persian, and Urdu. My father's generation had lost Arabic and the ability to write in Persian. In my generation, reading classical Urdu had become an issue, too. With our literary heritage becoming inaccessible to us at this rate, it seemed reasonable to assume that—let alone being able to share it with other cultures—we would soon find ourselves alien to it.

This was a complex and weighty problem that lay far beyond my capacities to resolve. I worried about my friends—the *devs*, the cow-footed creatures, the horse-headed beasts, the elephant-eared folks. If the world ever forgot their existence I knew I would not be able to bear the tragedy.

I checked to see if the *Dastan-e Amir Hamza* had ever been translated into English or one of the European languages. I found out that in 1892, Sheik Sajjad Hosain published an abridgement of Book One titled *The Amir Hamza: An Oriental Novel*. By his own admission he tried to make a novel of it, but the results were disappointing, the experiment was left unfinished, and he was not heard from again. In 1895 Ph. S. Van Ronkel published his Dutch study of Amir Hamza's legend, titled *De Roman van Amir Hamza*. Then, in 1991, Frances Pritchett published *The Romance Tradition in Urdu: Adventures from the Dastan of Amir Hamzah,* which contained excerpts translated from a 1969 edition. That was it. The complete *Dastan-e Amir Hamza* had never been translated into English or any other Western language.

Someone simply had to be found who had enough time on his hands to translate a thousand-page book. Ideally, this person should not be bright enough to anticipate the distinct likelihood that the book might never be published. As the whole thing was to be done without any grant money, it also had to be someone whose spouse had a reliable job. Since everyone I knew seemed to have a purpose in life, and their spouses would not hear of any such nonsense, the search soon drew to a close. And the matter would have rested there but for a most eventful dream, which should be recounted here in its entirety due to its historic significance.

It was a wintry night. I was fast asleep when suddenly I heard galloping noises and woke up. A horse-headed creature appeared from the darkness. Behind him walked an elephant-eared lady carrying a candle. The horse-headed gent greeted me with a sly smile, congratulated me, and said that I had been chosen to do the translation. Then the elephant-eared lady came forward and said that everyone was counting on me. Before I could say anything or ask any questions, they plunged back into darkness. I heard sniggering, galloping sounds, and then all was quiet.

It is not every day that one receives such distinguished visitors in dreams and is declared their chosen one. Naturally, I could not forget the dream. And didn't the lady tell me that *everyone* was counting on me? I could not ignore that, for sure. I finally told my wife what the horse-headed gent and the elephant-eared lady expected of her, and threw myself wholeheartedly into the task.

I had thought that with such auspicious beginnings the translation itself would be a breeze. But I ran into major problems with the very first passage. It took me several hours and left me somewhat disillusioned and embittered. I persevered and tried not to think too much about the meaning of my dream visitor's sly smile. After Book One the language becomes simpler, the ornate passages shorter, and the poetry less frequent. I also had more practice. A few years earlier, I had translated the Urdu poetry and fables of Afzal Ahmed Syed. This exposure to translating one of our contemporary masters helped me. But I think the real breakthrough came when I learned to keep three fat dictionaries open in my lap at the same time.

Because I visited the text over and over again, the structure of the tale began to reveal itself. I was happy that I was beginning to see structure in fiction, but I could not say the same about my life. I was piling up rejection slips for my own writings. Naturally, I felt jealous of Ghalib Lakhnavi and Abdullah Bilgrami, who had found publishers in their time and were important enough to be translated. The evil thought often crossed my mind to stop the translation. That would teach Messrs. Lakhnavi and Bilgrami a nice lesson! But my friends began calling to inquire when the book would be ready. For the last few years I had constantly bragged to them about it, and they had remembered. Now I had to finish it just to save face. Later, when the Modern Library decided to publish it, it became a contractual obligation as well. In short, as always I was caught in a web of my own follies, and the only way out was to finish the thing.

Now that the translation is done, after seven years of intermittent work, I hope that *everyone* is satisfied. If they feel a need to express their gratitude I would very much prefer it if they did not appear in my dreams and communicated instead by e-mail.

I also have a message for all young boys and girls. They should take warning from my example and get themselves a good education. I now realize its virtues. If I had had one, the horse-headed fellow and the elephant-eared lady could not possibly have made such a capital fool out of me.

—Toronto, July 3, 2007

A NOTE ON THE TEXT

In 1855, the obscure press Matba-e Hakim Sahib in the Indian city of Calcutta published a book titled *Tarjuma-e Dastan-e Sahibqiran Giti-sitan Aal-e Paighambar-e Aakhiruz Zaman Amir Hamza bin Abdul-Muttalib bin Hashim bin Abdul Munaf* (A Translation of the Adventures of the Lord of the Auspicious Planetary Conjunction, the World Conqueror, Uncle of the Last Prophet of the Times, Amir Hamza Son of Abdul Muttalib Son of Hashim Son of Abdul Munaf).[1] Its writer, Navab Mirza Aman Ali Khan Bahadur Ghalib Lakhnavi, identified himself as the son-in-law of Prince Fatah Haider, the oldest son of Sultan Tipu of Mysore. According to one account, the writer was a new convert to Islam and a public official.[2]

This book by Navab Mirza Aman Ali Khan Bahadur Ghalib Lakhnavi (Ghalib Lakhnavi, for short) was one of the earlier versions of the *Dastan-e Amir Hamza* (Adventures of Amir Hamza) printed in India in the Urdu language. It already existed in multiple handwritten manuscripts and was a long-established legend in the South Asian oral narrative tradition of *dastan-goi* (*dastan* narration). It was a narrative of composite authorship, and different versions of the same event existed in different narrative traditions.

Ghalib Lakhnavi's use of the term "translation" is confusing. Unless it was a translation from a Persian-language version of the *Dastan-e Amir Hamza* originally composed in South Asia, it is difficult to explain the overwhelming number of references particular to the social life and culture of South Asia found in the book. Certain passages which are in regional Indian dialect could not possibly have originated in any foreign language. It is more probable that Ghalib Lakhnavi compiled the text from various versions and attributed it to an older source to give his story an ancient pedigree, a practice common among *dastan* writers.

Ghalib Lakhnavi's text became the basis of a very popular edition that remained in print until recently, although these later editions were drastically abridged. In November 1871, sixteen years after Ghalib Lakhnavi published the book, the Naval Kishore Press in Lucknow brought out its own version of the *Dastan-e Amir Hamza*.[3] The book was identified as an amended version of a tale previously published in Calcutta, Bombay, Delhi, and Lucknow.[4] However, the author of the text of the Naval Kishore Press version was not acknowledged, only the man who amended it: Abdullah Bilgrami, an instructor of the Arabic language in Kanpur. We now know that it was, in fact, Ghalib Lakhnavi's text, modified by Abdullah Bilgrami by adding ornate passages and poetry to it. This translation is made from Abdullah Bilgrami's 1871 edition of the *Dastan-e Amir Hamza*.

The oral narrative tradition of the *Dastan-e Amir Hamza* heavily influenced its written version. The text of the *Dastan-e Amir Hamza* was used both for reading and as a guide for the narrator of the *dastan*. In a few places, instructions appear to guide the person narrating the story. A *dastan* narrator knew more than one version of a particular episode of the *dastan* and used the one most suited for the audience being addressed. In addition, a *dastan* was never narrated in its entirety during a session. Only certain episodes from it were narrated. Therefore, considerations of continuity and structural integrity were not important. The histories of multiple versions of the same event and the loosely woven oral tradition sometimes intervene in the text. In some places parallel traditions and discrepancies have crept in (see notes 13 and 14 to Book Two, notes 5, 6, and 8 to Book Three, and notes 12, 13, and 18 to Book Four).

I have not tried to straighten out these inconsistencies, not only because to do so would compromise the story, but also because they allow for a comparison of different traditions and texts, which can be very helpful in the study of the *dastan* genre. These inconsistencies reveal that this text was compiled using at least three variant traditions (see note 13 to Book Two, note 6 to Book Three, and note 18 to Book Four).

Consistent with the classical *dastan* literature, the Urdu text of the *Dastan-e Amir Hamza* is unpunctuated and has no text breaks except where a new chapter is marked. While this offers a translator great flexibility in structuring a sentence, it is a challenge to identify and isolate individual phrases and sentences in a continuous text before translating them. In some instances, the print was not legible and an approximation was made in choosing the missing text. Such instances have been marked with a question mark following in brackets.

The title *amir* (meaning "commander" or "leader") has become an inseparable part of the hero's name and has been used as such throughout the text. The title *khusrau* (meaning "king") has likewise become part of Landhoor's name and is similarly used.

The characters and the numerous legendary kings, warriors, sorcerers, historical figures, deities, and mythical beings mentioned in the story are grouped together in the List of Characters, Historic Figures, Deities, and Mythical Beings.

NOTES

1. The Library of Congress has a microfiche of this title (Control Number: 85908676; Call Number: Microfiche 85/61479 [P] So. Asia).
2. Shamsur Rahman Faruqi, *Sahiri, Shahi, Sahibqirani: Dastan-e Amir Hamza ka Mutalaa,* Volume I, *Nazari Mubahis* (New Delhi: National Council for the Promotion of Urdu Language, 1999), 209.
3. The only known copy of this text is in the British Library (Reference No. 306.24.B.21).
4. *Dastan-e Amir Hamza Sahibqiran* (Lucknow, India: Naval Kishore Press, 1871), 752.

ACKNOWLEDGMENTS

My understanding of the many facets of the *dastan* literature has been shaped by the Urdu language's foremost writer and critic, Shamsur Rahman Faruqi. His unparalleled insight into the poetics of Urdu's classical literature in his monumental study *Sahiri, Shahi, Sahibqirani*, which analyzes the known Urdu and Persian versions of the *Dastan-e Amir Hamza* and their sources, has laid the foundations of a serious study of the *dastan* genre and was immensely useful during my work.

In the course of translating this text, I have been fortunate to have had the help and encouragement of many other friends as well. At a very early stage of this translation, Professor Muhammad Umar Memon published an excerpt from it in the *Annual of Urdu Studies*. Mr. Salimur Rahman read that excerpt and offered his valuable advice. Professor C. M. Naim's testimonial underlined the importance of this book's publication. Ms. Elham Eshraghi helped in translating the Persian verses and phrases. My wife, Michelle, put up with me during the time it took to finish the translation and let me clutter up the living room with dictionaries and printouts.

The publication of this work owes a great deal to Frances and Bill Hanna of Acacia House Publishing Services, who placed this work with the Modern Library. My editor at the Modern Library, Judy Sternlight, deserves special thanks for her thoughtful editing advice and all her help in seeing this project to completion. Thanks are also due to Rebecca Shapiro and to production editor Evan Camfield. Lastly, a big thank-you to Medi Blum for her truly marvelous copyediting work. For any remaining shortcomings in the translation, I alone am responsible.

BOOK ONE

The First Book of the Dastan *of the Sahibqiran,
Amir Hamza bin Abdul Muttalib, and of the
Events Preceding His Birth*

The florid news writers, the sweet-lipped historians, revivers of old tales and renewers of past legends, relate that there ruled at Cte-siphon[1] in Persia (image of Heaven!) Emperor Qubad Kamran, who cherished his subjects and was a succor to the impecunious in their distress. He was unsurpassed in dispensing justice, and so rigorous in this exercise that the best justice appeared an injustice compared to his decree. Prosperity and affluence thrived in his dominions while wrong and inequity slumbered in death, and, rara avis–like, mendicants and the destitute were extinct in his lands. The wealthy were at a loss to find an object for their charity. The weak and the powerful were equals, and the hawk and the sparrow roosted in the same nest. The young and the old sought one another's pleasure, neither ever deeming himself the sole benefactor. The portals of houses remained open day and night like the eyes of the vigil, for if someone stole even the color of henna from the palm,[2] he was ground in the mill of justice. The thief therefore did not even dream of thieving, and if perchance a wayfarer should come upon someone's property on the road, he took it upon himself to restore it to its owner.

In the same city there also resided a savant by the name of Khvaja[3] Bakht Jamal, who traced his lineage to the prophet Danyal (God's favors and mercies be upon his soul!). He was unrivaled in learning and the sciences of *hikmat*,[4] *ramal*, astrology, and *jafar*, and was truly a successor beyond compare of the ancient philosophers. Malik[5] Alqash, the emperor's vizier who had often made use of the divinations of this sage, offered himself as a pupil to Khvaja Bakht Jamal, and before long, Alqash, too, became adept at *ramal*.

One day Alqash said to Khvaja Bakht Jamal, "The other night as idleness weighed on my heart, I decided to cast lots in your name. Reading the pattern, I discovered that your star is in the descendent, and some vicissitude of fortune will befall you. Your star shall remain in the same house for forty days. Thus it would not bode well for you to step out of the house during this period, or trust anyone. Even I must suffer under this burden of separation, and not see you!"

Following Alqash's advice, Bakht Jamal secluded himself from the world. Of the foretold days of ill-boding, thirty-nine had passed without mishap. On the fortieth day, Khvaja felt wretched to be shut inside his house, and set out carrying his staff to see vizier Alqash, to bring his only faithful and affectionate friend the news of his health and welfare.

By chance, instead of the thoroughfare, he followed a deserted road to the riverside. As it was summer he took refuge from the burning sun under a tree's shade. While he sat there, his eyes suddenly beheld a building most imposing, save for its outer walls that had fallen to ruin. Some curiosity led him toward it, and as he drew near, he found most of the apartments inside in a state of decay, and the vestibules in ruins, but for one that had survived ravaging and still stood—in desolation and disarray like a lover's heart. In that vestibule there was an antechamber whose entrance was bricked up. Removing the bricks he found to his right a door with a padlock. When he held the padlock in his hand, it came open of its own accord and fell to the floor. Stepping inside Khvaja discovered a cellar. There he found buried Shaddad's seven boundless treasures of gold and jewels. Seized by fright, Khvaja was unable to take anything, and retraced his steps out of the cellar, then hastened to Alqash's house to give him the propitious news.

Alqash's face brightened at the sight of Khvaja. He made room for him on his throne, and after expressing joy at seeing his friend, said, "Today was the fortieth day. Why did you take such trouble and inconvenience yourself? Come tomorrow, I had intended to present myself at your door." After making small talk Khvaja mentioned the seven treasures to Alqash, and recounted the windfall, saying, "Though I was blessed in my stars to have come upon such an untold fortune, it was found on royal land, and lowly me, I cannot lay claim to it! I resolved in my heart that since you are the emperor's vizier, and an excellent patron and friend to me, I should inform you of this bountiful treasure. Then, if you saw fit to confer a little something upon your humble servant, that bit only would I consider warranted and rightful!"

Alqash was beside himself with joy when he heard of the seven treasures, and ordered two horses to be saddled forthwith; then he mounted one, and Khvaja the other, and they galloped off in the direction of the wasteland. By and by, they arrived at their destination. Alqash became greatly agitated and ecstatic the moment he set eyes on the seven hoards, and while murmuring gratitude to his Creator for bestowing such a windfall on him, the thought suddenly flashed across Alqash's mind that Khvaja Bakht Jamal was privy to this secret. Alqash reasoned that if some day Khvaja Bakht Jamal chose to betray him to the emperor in order to gain influence at the court, the vizier would find himself in a sorry plight. It would be by far the lesser evil, Alqash thought, to kill Khvaja right there, and then lay claim to the boundless treasure without the least anxiety that someone might one day reveal the secret.

Once resolved, he immediately bore down upon Khvaja and put the dagger to his throat. Confounded by this turn of events, Khvaja cried out, "What has got into your head, Alqash? Is that how a favor is returned? What injury have I done you that you resolve to punish me thus?" And much did the poor old man groan in the same vein, and seek compassion, but to no avail. The heart of that villain did not soften.

When the frail man saw that it was only a matter of a few breaths before the candle of his life would be snuffed out by Alqash's hands, he entreated in despair, "O Alqash! I see that you are bent upon my murder. But if you could find it in your heart to act upon my last words, I shall entrust them to you and die with at least this debt toward you." The ungrateful wretch shouted back, "Make haste! For the cup of your life is now ready to overflow, and the thirst of my inclement dagger is ordained to be quenched in your blood!" The poor man spoke: "There is hardly any money in my house to last my family beyond tomorrow, and even less food. I would to God that you might send them enough to survive. And inform my wife, who is expecting, that if a boy is born to her, she must name him Buzurjmehr, and if a girl is born, she may follow her own counsel." After saying this he closed his eyes and began reciting the *kalma*.[6] Whereupon that heartless villain cut off Khvaja's head with his dagger, destroyed his horse, too, and interred the two of them in the same vault where the treasures were buried.

After sealing the door, Alqash went to the river to cleanse the blood from his hands and the dagger, and then he rode away to his house, glad in his heart and thrilled. The next day, he returned to the place with great pomp, and after surveying it, ordered the prefect to build a garden for him on the site, bound by walls of marble, and a turquoise chamber erected over the vestibule. In a matter of days, the garden, the marble walls, and the turquoise chamber were ready, all of which delighted Alqash greatly, and he named the place Bagh-e Bedad.

Then he called at Khvaja Bakht Jamal's house, and told the family that he had sent Khvaja off to China to conduct trade, and he should soon return after turning a profit. He then communicated to them Khvaja's wishes. He consoled and comforted the family, and bestowed on them a rich purse, mentioning that more would be available whenever there was need, and that they ought not entertain any fears of adversity. Then Alqash returned home, with the grim truth buried in his heart.

OF BUZURJMEHR'S BIRTH, AND OF THE CONTENTS OF THE BOOK BECOMING CONSPICUOUS

The singing reed of the knowers of tales of yore, and the mellifluent quill of claimants to past knowledge thus luxuriously modulate their song, and in a thousand voices delightfully trill their notes to proclaim that by the grace of God Almighty the auspicious day arrived when, at a propitious hour on a Friday, a boy of high fortune was born to Khvaja Bakht Jamal's wife.

Remembering Khvaja's wish, she named him Buzurjmehr, and the child began to blossom in her care. His stately forehead bespoke nobility, and his princely face shone with the light of eminence.

When Buzurjmehr was five years of age, he was taken to an instructor who had been a pupil of Khvaja Bakht Jamal. He was told he could repay Khvaja's debt and earn acclaim by imparting knowledge to his son. The man very gladly accepted the charge, and put all his heart into educating Buzurjmehr.

It was Buzurjmehr's routine to spend the whole day at his teacher's side, learning, and to return home when a few hours remained before the close of day, to partake of whatever his mother had provided for him with her labors. One day, it so happened that there was nothing to eat. Buzurjmehr said to his mother, "I am perishing with hunger. Please give me something that I might sell it and buy some food." His mother replied, "Son, on the shelf there lies an ancient book, belonging to my father, and written long ago. Many a time, when your father was in need of money, he resolved to sell it. But every time he reached for it, a black serpent would dart out hissing from the shelf, and your father would turn back in fright. See if you can fetch it from there and sell it."

Buzurjmehr went and fetched the book as his mother had bid, but he did not find the serpent. As he turned a few pages and read them, he at first began to wail loudly, and cried copious tears; then, having read a little further, he burst into riotous laughter.

Those present were greatly astonished, and marveled at what might have caused such a reversal of humor in him. Suspecting a fit of lunacy, his mother beseeched some of the witnesses to send for a bloodletter to bleed him, and others to get an amulet to put around his neck, wailing all the while that he was her only son and if he were seized by madness she would have no support in her adversity.

Noticing his mother's agitation, Buzurjmehr comforted her, and said, "Do not grieve, Mother, and stop worrying in your heart. I have become neither deluded nor taken with delirium. The reason I cried and laughed was that from reading this book I have learned all that has gone before and all that shall come to pass. I cried to discover that the vizier Alqash had murdered my innocent father. And I laughed upon finding out that I will avenge my father's blood, and shall become our emperor's vizier. Vex yourself no further! We shall have enough for ourselves—and to feed ten others besides."

Having said this, Buzurjmehr took a handmaiden to the grocer's and asked him to weigh out daily as much in victuals, butter, and sugar as she might ask for, without bothering about payment. The grocer asked, "But when would I be paid?" Buzurjmehr said, "Do you ask payment of me? Perhaps you have forgotten how you poisoned the farmer Chand along with his four sons to avoid payment for the several thousand *maunds*[7] of wheat you had bought from him." Hearing this the grocer was seized with fright and pleaded in a trembling voice, "My son, whenever you desire anything, send for it from here, but pray keep to yourself what you have just uttered."

From there Buzurjmehr took the servant girl to the butcher's shop, and asked him to apportion one Tabrizi *maund*[8] of meat to her daily. The butcher asked, "And when shall I be paid and the account settled?" Buzurjmehr answered, "Remember shepherd Qaus, whom you slaughtered and buried in your shop's cellar, and appropriated thousands upon thousands of rupees from that innocent man. Have you taken leave of your senses that you demand payment of me?" Upon hearing that, the meat vendor began to tremble like a cow at the sight of a butcher, and threw himself violently at Buzurjmehr's feet declaring, "As much as Your Honor's girl shall desire shall be weighed out to her, and never even in my dreams would I desire compensation. But please safeguard my life and honor, and keep your lips sealed!"

Buzurjmehr dealt with the jeweler similarly, unnerving him by telling him of his past heinous deeds, and settling at the jeweler's expense a daily stipend of five dinars for himself. Then he returned home and bided his time in happy anticipation.

OF THE EMPEROR'S VISIT TO ALQASH'S BAGH-E BEDAD, AND OF THE FESTIVITIES HELD IN THAT HEAVENLY ABODE

Gardeners of annals and singers of the nursery of articulation plant the trees of words row after row, and thus embellish the brightness of the page with the flowers and redolent blossoms of colorful contents, making it the envy of Mani's tablet, telling how when Bagh-e Bedad was ready, and the form of Shaddad's Heaven realized, the euphoric Alqash, in his giddiness, forgot all cares of this world and the next.

Enthralled and enchanted at the sight, and beside himself with joy, he submitted to the emperor, saying, "By virtue of Your Highness's blessings, your slave has built a garden. A host of rare plants has been collected at great expense, and choice landscapists, past masters of the art, have been employed to tend to them. But none of it brings any joy to your follower, for whom it shall remain a figure of autumn, until Your Eminence sets his blessed foot there.

"I desire Your Excellency, Emperor of the World, the Immortal Soul of the Age, to crown it with your presence. Then shall the garden taste of spring, and every bud and flower sprout in majestic splendor. And should Your Highness deign to partake of a fruit or two, this slave's prayers will be granted, and his trees of hope will bear fruit." The emperor consented to his request. Gratified, Alqash bowed low and after making his offering, departed to busy himself with preparations for the feast.

Before long, everything needed for the feast was provided. And presently there arrived, exalted as the heavens, bright as the sun, most just and clement, His Imperial Majesty, attended by his retinue of nobles and viziers, to increase the beauty of Bagh-e Bedad with his presence.

At the approach of the royal procession, the lookouts and riders posted by Alqash to gather intelligence proclaimed the emperor's arrival.

Alqash, escorted by his sons and aides-de-camp, came out with a majestic procession to welcome his sovereign lord. Alqash went to the entrance of the house at the head of this procession to make his offering. Then, holding a post of the royal litter, he escorted the emperor into the garden. When he entered that heavenly sphere, the emperor found the garden an indulging and alluring retreat.

In the nave of the garden stood a chamber, unrivaled in architecture, made of turquoise and surrounded by canopies of variegated gold leaf fixed on gold-inlaid posts. A platform made of seven hundred thousand gold pieces was built in the courtyard of the chamber, on which sat a bejeweled throne.

At this platform, the emperor ascended and graced the throne, and received offerings. Alqash was in seventh heaven and felt himself most extraordinarily distinguished. When the emperor regarded the splendor and glory of Bagh-e Bedad, he praised it to high heavens. Alqash the wretch relished every last word of his praise. For twenty-one days the emperor indulged in convivialities and merriment. On the twenty-second day he conferred on Alqash the Jamshedi robe of honor.[9] The royal litter arrived presently, and the emperor then repaired to his palace, fully content. He was soon occupied in matters of state.

Of Alqash Taking the Innocent Buzurjmehr Prisoner, and of His Deliverance from Alqash's Clutches, and of the Emperor's Assembling His Prudent Ministers to Ask Them of the Dream, and Vowing Punishment on Them

Such is the decree of Destiny's Gardener that every instant a new flower should bloom in Life's Green. The farsighted one regards in it His transcendent art, and disengages his mind from this world and all things worldly. No sooner does one laugh than he feels some grief prick his side. The bough that bows in humility procures forthwith desire's fruit. A branch that overreaches, the Gardener's hand promptly prunes.

Regard what new blossom flowered in that garden, and what fresh colored bud sprouted there. We return to Buzurjmehr and his story. Regard how times change and fortunes ebb and flow.

Thus narrate the legend writers and the raconteurs of yore that since Buzurjmehr was wise, sagacious, virtuous, and discerning, he had given himself to a solitary life, and the hours of his nights and days were spent venerating the Almighty. One day his mother said to him, "Son! Of a sudden I am taken with a longing for some greens. If you were to inconvenience yourself, your mother's craving would be fulfilled." Buzurjmehr gladly acquiesced to his mother's wishes, and bent his legs toward Bagh-e Bedad.

Arriving at the gate he found it locked. He called the garden keeper, who came directly. As he was about to unlock the gate, Buzurjmehr said to him, "Do not touch the lock. The female of the snake you killed the other day is secreted away in the catch of the lock to bite you and avenge her mate." When the keeper looked closely he did indeed find a female snake in the catch. He killed her, too, and opening the gate, threw himself at Buzurjmehr's feet declaring, "It was your forewarning that saved me! Otherwise nothing stood between me and my death, and certainly I would have breathed my last. What is your pleasure, my dear boy? What was it that brought you here today?" Buzurjmehr answered, "I needed some greens. I will pay for them with pleasure." The keeper replied, "I will fetch the greens directly. But I cannot accept payment from my savior, and shall make a present of them to you."

When the gardener went to get the greens, he noticed a goat plundering the saffron fields with great abandon. He struck her with his mattock in irritation, and her chapter of life soon ended with her throes. Buzurjmehr called out, "O cruel man! Why did you take the blood of three innocent lives on your neck?" The gardener smiled and said, "Here I killed one goat, son, and you count her as three! Are you in your right mind?" Buzurjmehr told him that the goat had two kids of such and such color inside her womb, and when the gardener killed her, they died with her, too.

Unbeknownst to them, as they stood there talking, they had attracted Alqash's ears. He called the garden keeper over, and inquired what they had been discussing. When Alqash ordered the goat's belly cut open, it did reveal two kids of the same color as Buzurjmehr had described. Greatly surprised, Alqash called Buzurjmehr over, and asked him to introduce himself.

Buzurjmehr said, "I am Buzurjmehr, Khvaja Bakht Jamal's son, and the grandson of Hakim Jamasp. Afflicted by fortune, as some tyrant has murdered my father, I long for revenge. "

Alqash asked, "Did you find your father's killer, then?" Buzurjmehr said, "One of these days some mark will be discovered, and the blood of the innocent victim shall call out." Alqash asked, "Could you divine what was in my heart that night?" Buzurjmehr replied, "You had it in your heart to divulge to your wife the treasure that you had discovered but something decided you against telling her, and you resolved to maintain your quiet."

Alqash's wits took flight at these words. He began trembling like a willow. This boy has the gift of clairvoyance, he thought, and anyone who would eat the vital organs of such a one would become all-seeing, too. He decided to kill Buzurjmehr and devour his heart and liver. That would nip in the bud any evil that might be afoot, he thought.

Thus decided, Alqash called for his Nubian slave, Bakhtiar, and secretly told him that if he were to slaughter Buzurjmehr, and bring him kebabs of his heart and liver, he would grant him his heart's desire. The slave took Buzurjmehr to a dark cellar, and there he bore down upon Buzurjmehr and was about to slit open his throat with a knife, when

Buzurjmehr involuntarily broke into laughter, and said to the slave, "The hope for which you sully yourself with my murder shall never be fulfilled by Alqash's false promise. However, if you refrain from killing me, you shall find success with me, God willing!" The slave said, "If you were to reveal to me my motive, I would set you free this instant!"

Buzurjmehr replied, "You are in love with Alqash's daughter, but he will never give you her hand. I, however, shall arrange for you to marry her. Set me free now! Ten days from now, the emperor will have a dream that he shall forget. He will assemble all his viziers to quiz them and ask them of the dream and its interpretation. Then your master will come asking for me. But beware, not until he has slapped you thrice should you divulge the truth about me." The slave said, "He had sent me to bring him kebabs of your vitals. If I took him some made from an animal, he would discover it at once and punish me." Buzurjmehr said, "At the gates of the city a woman is selling a kid raised on human milk. Take money from me and slaughter it and take Alqash its vitals."

At length the slave relented. He did not kill Buzurjmehr but did as he had told him. Alqash ate the kid's kebabs, and believing that he too had now become oracular and sapient, rejoiced exceedingly.

Delivered from death, Buzurjmehr returned home and narrated all to his mother. That poor, star-crossed woman offered many thanks to God for her son's safe return home and said, "My son, confine yourself to the safety of our house, and do not step out. The enemy lies in wait! God forfend that he should set in motion any evil, and God forbid that your enemies should come to any harm."[10] Buzurjmehr replied, "You must not torment yourself with thoughts of disaster. Wait and see how God manifests His will!"

It so befell that on the tenth day, the emperor had a dream that he in no way remembered. In the morning, he said to his wise counselors and viziers: "Last night I had a dream that I do not now recall. You must narrate it to me and tell me its interpretation to ingratiate yourselves with me!"

All of them replied that they would oblige him with an interpretation if they only knew the dream. The emperor replied: "The wise men in Sikander's times would often narrate to him dreams that he could not recollect and tell him their interpretations. I have employed you for similar offices. If you fail to narrate the dream and tell me what it signifies, I shall have every single one of you put to the sword, and order your wife and children to be pulverized in the oil press and your households plundered. For mercy's sake, I give you a reprieve of forty days.

After forty days had passed, the emperor again assembled the company and asked them if they had succeeded in finding out the content of his dream. Everyone remained silent, but Alqash spoke: "This slave has divined from geomancy that Your Majesty dreamt of a bird that swooped down from the heavens and dropped Your Eminence into a river of fire. Your Excellency started in your sleep in fright, and woke up without remembrance of the dream."

The emperor replied angrily, "O vile and brazen-faced liar, a fine story you have concocted. Never did I have such a dream that you relate to be mine. I shall allow you two days more of respite. If you have not related the dream by the end of that time, I swear by Namrud's pyre that you shall be the first to be buried alive."

Greatly distressed at the emperor's words, Alqash returned home, and immediately sent for Bakhtiar and asked him, "Tell me verily where the boy is hidden!" Bakhtiar answered, "I killed him just as I was ordered." Alqash replied, "As he was most wise and sapient, I am convinced that he escaped from your hands. Bring him to me that my life, and the life and honor of countless other innocent people shall be spared."

When Bakhtiar reiterated his statement, his master in annoyance slapped him three times so hard that Bakhtiar's eardrum was ruptured and spurted blood, and Bakhtiar fell on the floor in pain. When he came to in a few moments, he replied, "Do not punish your slave. I shall go and bring Buzurjmehr as you command!" Alqash said, "I wonder at your foolishness! How many times did I ask you for him, and so kindly, but got nothing except denial." Bakhtiar said, "He had strictly forbidden me to disclose his whereabouts to you until you had struck me thrice." Thereupon Alqash embraced Bakhtiar, and said, "Hurry and bring him at once!"

Buzurjmehr came out directly when Bakhtiar knocked at the door, and accompanied him to Alqash's house. The vizier showed Buzurjmehr much respect and deference, and excused his past conduct. Then, to inform him of his present predicament, Alqash spoke thus: "The emperor had a dream that he forgot and we are made to bear the brunt of it. If you would be kind enough to relate the dream to me, it would be as if you granted us all a reprieve from death."

Buzurjmehr replied, "Come morning, tell the emperor that you had only been testing the wise and learned counselors and viziers to see if they had any claim to omniscience. And that you would like to bring forward your pupil, that if His Highness were to send for him, he would presently relate the dream and all its particulars. Then, when the emperor shall send for me, I will relate the dream and its interpretation."

Of Buzurjmehr's Relating the Emperor's Dream at
the Appointed Hour, and of Alqash's Life
Being Claimed in Retribution

The world is the abode of retribution. Oftentimes every deed is accounted for here, and occasionally something remains in abeyance, to be settled on Judgment Day. What this adage verifies and where the discourse drifts is the story of unworthy Alqash, tyrant and malefactor, who at long last reaped the harvest of his sins.

The next day Alqash presented himself before his sovereign, narrating verbatim Buzurjmehr's words. Orders were given that Buzurjmehr be produced and presented before the emperor.

A mace bearer called at Buzurjmehr's house and said, "Come at once! The Imperial Highness wishes to see you!" Buzurjmehr said, "What conveyance have you brought me from his Highness?" The mace bearer replied, "I did not bring a conveyance. But I shall return and request a conveyance for you from the nobles."

The mace bearer was ordered to take a steed, and bring him forthwith. When the mace bearer arrived with the horse, Buzurjmehr said, "In its essence the horse is made of wind, and I am fashioned of clay. Wind and clay are manifest opposites, and I shall not, therefore, ride the horse. But if you bring me a conveyance that is suited to me, I will presently go with you."

The mace bearer returned with Buzurjmehr's reply, whereupon the emperor ordered all kinds of conveyances to be sent to Buzurjmehr's house. Buzurjmehr looked at them and said, "I cannot possibly ride the elephant, as it is reserved for the emperor. And only the sick ride litters. The camel is seraphic in nature, and I am but an insignificant mortal. The mule is misbegotten, and I am of noble birth. Therefore it does not behoove me to ride it. As to the ox, corn-chandlers and launderers ride it, and I belong to neither trade but am of gentle birth, learned and discerning. And the ass is reserved for the guilty and the culprits, and I am innocent of any crime. Return them all, and convey my words to the sagacious ears of the emperor."

The messengers again returned without Buzurjmehr. The emperor said, "Whatever he wishes for shall be provided." The royal pages took the emperor's message to Buzurjmehr, who said, "If His Highness wishes me to narrate his dream, he should send me Alqash saddled. Because as the saying goes, everyone tends toward his own, and I will ride him and present myself before His Majesty and describe his dream in its entirety. Again, as I profess to be wise, and Alqash is the Mount of Wisdom,[11] it is only meet and proper that I ride only him."

When the messengers brought back Buzurjmehr's reply, the emperor broke into laughter, and ordered that Alqash be saddled and sent to bring back Buzurjmehr. No sooner was the order given than Alqash was bridled and saddled, and he trotted over to Buzurjmehr's house to carry out Buzurjmehr's wish. Buzurjmehr mounted Alqash and spurred him on, proclaiming every step of the way, "I have redeemed myself this day, because I caught the one who had murdered my father!"

Whoever saw them along the way—young and old alike—found the sight a curiosity and followed them in the train.

When Buzurjmehr was presented before the emperor in such state, he said, "You must explain what Alqash has done to you that caused him to be treated so scandalously at your hands." Buzurjmehr replied, "In the first place he is an embezzler, who had for his master Your Highness—and yet he stole from Your Highness!

"In the second place, he studied geomancy with my father. And my father in his great generosity imparted to him every word of the knowledge at his command. He never concealed any useful knowledge from this miscreant nor kept any secrets. When my father came upon the seven treasures of Shaddad,[12] he never took anything, and due to the camaraderie that he felt for this man, divulged to him the find. And this man here murdered my innocent father and consigned him to the cellar where the treasure is buried. Thus, at the same place lies my father's cadaver still, half buried in gravel, without coffin or grave. I now beseech Your Majesty, my equitable sovereign, for justice in the hope that I shall be dealt with fairly."

When he heard these words, the emperor cast a fiery glance at Alqash, and said, "What injury did his father do to you that you ruthlessly killed him in disregard of all obligations due him? If you did not fear me, did you also not fear God?

"But regard now, O villain, what just punishment you shall receive for this unjust deed! If I do not have you riddled with the arrows of Justice, I shall have the blood of equity on my head."

Alqash replied, "Your Majesty, he calumniates me and plots my undoing for no reason!" Buzurjmehr spoke: "Put me to the proof! Whoever cares to come with me, I shall prove what I profess." The emperor accompanied Buzurjmehr with his royal cortege to the place where Khvaja Bakht Jamal lay murdered. He had ordered that Alqash be brought on foot in chains, and led behind a horse like a prisoner.

All these developments caused much stir in the city, and the populace turned out to see what the villain had been brought to. By and by, surrounded by officers of law and the public, Alqash was brought to the gates of Bagh-e Bedad.

Buzurjmehr guided the emperor to the cellar and showed him the site. The emperor saw the seven treasures consigned there and also saw lying in a corner Khvaja Bakht Jamal's withered corpse. The dead man's steed, too, lay murdered beside him.

The emperor was delighted to see the treasure, and ordered that it be removed without delay to the royal treasury. His orders were carried out, and thus came true the proverbial saying that "In the world gold attracts gold, and treasure, more treasures!"

The emperor then ordered Khvaja's last rites performed with ceremony according to the custom of his people, and a shrine built to his memory. Then he granted Buzurjmehr forty days' leave to pass in bereavement and conferred on him thousands of rupees from the imperial treasury. Buzurjmehr brought home elephant-loads of money and placed them before his worthy mother, and told her all that had transpired.

After forty days, Buzurjmehr appeared before the emperor and began attending the court every day. One day he found occasion to say to the emperor: "If it is Your Majesty's pleasure, I shall now narrate your dream to you." The emperor said, "Nothing would be more opportune! If you describe the dream properly, you shall be richly rewarded."

Buzurjmehr thus spoke: "Your Majesty dreamt that forty-one dishes of all varieties were laid out on a spread. Your Eminence took a morsel of halva from a dish and raised it to your mouth, when a black cur darted forward, snatched the piece from Your Majesty's hand, and devoured it."

The emperor declared, "I swear by Namrud's pyre, it is indeed the very dream I had. Now interpret it, too, and gladden my heart!"

Buzurjmehr replied, "Allow your slave to be conducted to your palace, and order all your harem to be assembled. Then I shall tell you the interpretation of this dream." The emperor took Buzurjmehr to the palace and ordered his harem assembled. After everyone had congregated as ordered, there arrived, walking with dignity and state in the cortege of her consorts and mates, a damsel of comely features and great pride, wearing a most exquisite robe adorned with lustrous gems and jewels.

Among her consorts there was also a black woman. Buzurjmehr caught her hand, and said to the emperor, "This is the black dog, Your Honor, who took the morsel away from Your Majesty's hands. And that morsel was this princess, who is guilty of the most grievous ingratitude to the emperor."

The emperor was transfixed with wonder upon hearing this and when he asked what it all meant, it came out that in reality it was a man who lived in great luxury with the princess, disguised as a woman, and imbibed, unrestrained, the wine of her charms at all hours of night and day. The emperor raged most wonderfully when he discovered this. The black man was thrown before the hounds, and that ill-starred princess's face was blackened, and she was paraded around the city mounted on an ass and then bricked-up alive in a tower on a thoroughfare. A robe of honor was conferred upon Buzurjmehr, and that same day Alqash was taken outside the city walls and, before a crowd of onlookers, buried up to his waist and riddled with arrows by expert archers. All the goods and chattels belonging to Alqash, with the inclusion of his wife and daughter, were awarded to Buzurjmehr.

After making his offering to the emperor, Buzurjmehr took the slave Bakhtiar to Alqash's palace and said to Alqash's wife, "I do not desire this estate and its riches. However, I did promise Bakhtiar that after avenging my father, I would arrange for him to be married to your daughter. I would that you give him your daughter's hand in marriage for my sake. I promise you that if a boy is born to your daughter from Bakhtiar, I shall educate him myself and, when he comes of age, shall prevail upon the emperor to have him instituted as a vizier in Alqash's stead."

Alqash's wife acted on Buzurjmehr's request gladly, and married her daughter to Bakhtiar the Nubian.

When these tidings reached the emperor, he was overwhelmed by

Buzurjmehr's act of generosity. After many days, when all the emperor's viziers, privy counselors, learned men, commanders, and sovereigns were assembled in the royal court, he spoke to them thus: "I have found Buzurjmehr to be pious and devout, of noble blood, courageous, and unrivaled. And he is oracular, moreover. Therefore, I desire to make Buzurjmehr my vizier, and confer upon him the robe of ministerial rank."

The courtiers unanimously sounded their praise and approval of the emperor's propitious opinion. The emperor conferred the robe of ministerial honor on Buzurjmehr and granted him a seat to the right of his throne. Thereupon, the court was adjourned.

Buzurjmehr returned home with great pomp and ceremony, lavishing gifts and offerings, and dispensing alms. Witnessing this, his mother offered thanks to the Omnipotent King. Before long Buzurjmehr occupied himself with ministerial affairs.

OF DIL-AARAM'S EXPULSION FROM THE EMPEROR'S FAVOR AND OF HER RETURNING TO HIS GOOD GRACES

How man is reduced to a mere trick in the hands of the celestial juggler! What enchanting antics does this trickster world play on man! Here a beggar is made king! There a whole empire is wiped from earth's face! Those who once longed for dry bread now distribute alms and food! Those who never saw a farthing today command untold wealth! Such is the story of the poor man here told.

Reliable chroniclers report that, once exposed to the culpable princess's deceit, the emperor became wary of all women—with the exception of Dil-Aaram—who, apart from her natural beauty and grace, and chastity and virtue, was most accomplished in musical arts and a lute player par excellence.

One day the emperor rode out to the chase with a troop of game-keepers in the train. Not too far from the seat of his empire there stood a sky-high mountain. At the foot of the mountain was a game reserve, most worthy and fair beyond description. The place abounded with birds and beasts of game, and, covered with lush growth, the ground stretched like an emerald carpet for miles. Several miles across in width, a grand river flowed on one side. Its banks were bounded by green fields, and the lagoons swarmed with blue water lilies.

There the emperor dismounted to admire the landscape. By chance, his eyes espied an old man carrying a load of bundled sticks on his head. He was most feeble and decrepit and staggered at every step. Pitying his plight, the emperor asked members of his party to inquire after the woodcutter's name. It emerged that the miserable old man was also named Qubad. Upon hearing this the emperor marveled greatly, and asked Buzurjmehr, "How do you account for this variance in fortunes?

Despite our having the same name, I am the Emperor of the Seven Climes,[13] and he is all but a beggar!" Buzurjmehr answered according to the established codes of his knowledge, "Your Highness and this man were born under the same star, but at the moment of your auspicious birth, the sun and the moon were together in the constellation Aries, while upon his birth they were in Pisces."

Dil-Aaram, who was present there, could not help but remark: "I cannot for a moment subscribe to these notions! It seems that his woman is a slovenly frump, and this poor man is an ignorant simpleton. Otherwise, he would not have fared so ill."

Already virulently set against women, the emperor was incensed by Dil-Aaram's words. He said, "Her words suggest that all our wealth and riches are indebted to her good management! That we rule an empire simply because she has arranged it so! Strip her naked, and let the woodcutter have her! Drive this insolent wench from before our presence this instant!" Then and there before thousands of onlookers, Dil-Aaram was dishonored and disgraced. She declared, "I submit to whatever fate ordains!" and then said to the woodcutter, "God has shown you favor by bestowing upon you a woman such as myself. Offer thanks to the Beneficent Succor that your adverse days are now over, and hard times lie behind you. Do not worry how you shall provide for me, or that in your advanced age you are further encumbered. I shall provide for myself and a thousand others, and earn you honor and acclaim." Upon hearing that, the old woodcutter was very well pleased and took Dil-Aaram to his house.

When they arrived near the house, the woodcutter's wife saw that her man had brought along a fresh blossom. And he took long strides, beside himself with joy. She came out flying like a fiend, and screamed, "Doddering fool! Have you become senile that you bring a rival on my head in my dotage?" Speaking thus she gave the old man such a powerful blow that he fell to the floor in pain, and began thrashing around like a ground-tumbler pigeon.

Dil-Aaram said to the woman, "O *houri*-faced mistress of chosen virtue! I consider our relationship as that of mother and daughter! I shall not be a burden on your hearth but a support to you." At Dil-Aaram's words, the old woman relented, and was ashamed of herself and her behavior. She said, "My daughter! I make you the keeper of my life and domestic realm. You are now in charge of everything in this household."

It was the old man's custom to sell his wood in the bazaar every day for bread. His twelve or thirteen children, who were all blind and handicapped, swarmed over him when he returned home and wolfed down the bread amongst themselves, without the food ever satisfying their hunger. Dil-Aaram saw this on the first day and kept quiet. But the second day she could no longer contain herself, and said to the woodcutter, "Dear father! Today sell the wood for wheat, and under no circumstances must you buy bread from the bazaar." He replied, "My daughter, I shall do as you say."

That day the woodcutter sold the wood for grain and brought it home to Dil-Aaram. She took it to the neighbor's to grind it and made enough bread from it to suffice them all for three days. With the money saved from two days Dil-Aaram bought wool, strung it into ropes, and gave them to the old man to sell in the bazaar. In the days that followed, it became her custom that she would barter the wheat saved from several days for wool and string it and sell the ropes. In a few days she gradually saved enough money to buy the old man a mule for carting wood from the forest.

To cut a long story short, in a matter of just two years, Dil-Aaram bought some five or six mules and several slaves, and put together enough money from renting them out to buy an estate. By this time the circumstances of the woodcutter's household had undergone a complete reversal and adversity had given way to prosperity.

When it was summertime, Dil-Aaram said to the old man, "Ask your slaves not to bring wood into the city from now until the end of summer but to store it instead in some mountain cavern. During the rains and in the winter, they will fetch a better profit." The patriarch did as Dil-Aaram had advised him. And when the rains ended and it was the outbreak of winter, there was a great demand for wood in public baths and other places.

The weather completely changed and the winter started in earnest. One day the emperor returned to the mountainside to hunt. The following night it suddenly snowed so hard that tongues froze inside people's mouths. The emperor's cortege came very near to dying from frost. They began scouring the forest and plains for wood and, by chance, they happened upon Qubad's store in the mountain cavern. Their spirits revived upon finding the wood. They made a great big fire and began warming themselves, repossessed of their senses and breathing easily.

In the morning the emperor finished hunting and returned with his great entourage to the seat of the empire. And Qubad the woodcutter returned to remove the wood from his cavern. When he arrived there and found a great heap of coal instead of wood, he was so shocked that he collapsed on the ground clutching his sides, and began lamenting his fate and crying at his ruin.

Once the workings of fortune were brought into play, Qubad's lot then changed for the better. It turned out that where the wood was stored in the cavern there was a gold mine. Heated by the fire, the ore melted and gathered in one place. The old man began excavating the coal. Thinking that the scorched floor was also coal, he dug it up when underneath he found some slabs. Not knowing that he had found gold, Qubad loaded up two mules with coal, threw a few slabs in with it, and brought it all home to show Dil-Aaram and with tears coursing down his face told her the whole story.

When Dil-Aaram scratched a slab with the point of a knife to see what it was, she discovered it to be gold, and then prostrating herself before Allah and offering thanks, she said to the woodcutter, "Return immediately with the mules and cart back all the slabs that are there!" The patriarch did as she had bid him.

Dil-Aaram then wrote out a note to the goldwright Faisal and, after loading a mule with as many slabs as it could carry, said to Qubad, "Take the mule to Basra and hand this note and these slabs to the goldwright Faisal. Tell him that I have sent you and what I desire is written in that note. He will melt these slabs into gold pieces and give them back to you."

While Qubad headed for Basra, Dil-Aaram had a large, deep hole dug in the courtyard and buried the rest of the slabs there. Then she sent a slave with a message to the goldsmith Suhail, who sojourned in Ctesiphon, which read, "For several years I was in disfavor with the emperor. But God willing, I shall very soon regain prestige and acclaim at the imperial assemblage. You must immediately come here with craftsmen, masons, laborers, and carpenters. I wish you to supervise the construction of a building in the image of the royal palace. If it is built under your care and is to my liking, I shall forever remember your loyalty and diligent exertion and God willing, I shall reimburse you very soon to the last farthing."

As Suhail put great store in Dil-Aaram's words, he hired skilled masons and accomplished carpenters as soon as he received her message and set to work and laid the foundation of the building at an auspicious hour.

Thousands of masons and workmen and sculptors busied themselves with the construction. Before long a splendid building was made ready. The borders of all of its gates and walls were painted with portraits of Dil-Aaram and the emperor.

In the meanwhile, Qubad had arrived from Basra with the gold pieces. Dil-Aaram had him sent to the baths. Then he was decked out in a stately robe. Dil-Aaram announced that from then on everyone must call him Qubad the Merchant. After a few days Dil-Aaram furnished Qubad with choice gifts and curiosities from all over the world and sent him to see Buzurjmehr.

By and by Qubad arrived at the ministry. When Buzurjmehr was informed, he greeted him with an embrace. After the exchange of greetings and words of gratification, Qubad, in accordance with Dil-Aaram's advice, asked permission to wait upon the emperor. Buzurjmehr said, "I shall mention you to His Imperial Highness today and arrange for an audience. Tomorrow is an auspicious day and the emperor shall also be at leisure. Present yourself in the early hours of the morning and you shall be ennobled by waiting upon His Majesty."

Qubad took his leave, returned home, and narrated to Dil-Aaram all that had passed with Buzurjmehr. The next day Dil-Aaram sent him for his audience with the emperor. Qubad first called on Buzurjmehr, who took him along to the royal court as he had promised.

Dil-Aaram had explained to Qubad before he left how he should put his right foot forward in the court of the Shadow of God, and make seven low bows. Qubad soon forgot all about it. But when he laid eyes on the emperor, he suddenly remembered Dil-Aaram's injunction. He collected his feet together and leapt; but slipping on the polished marble floor, landed flat on his ass.

The emperor smiled at this caper, and the courtiers, too, grinned when they noticed their sovereign smiling. The emperor accepted Qubad's offering, and as a mark of singular favor, conferred upon him a piece of sugar candy from his own hand. Qubad took the candy and put it in his mouth thus making his impudence and ill-breeding manifest to everyone assembled there.

When the court adjourned Qubad went home and narrated to Dil-Aaram how the emperor had given him the sugar candy and how he bolted it down. Feeling ashamed at his folly, she felt greatly embarrassed in her heart and said to him, "The next time the emperor gives you something, make three low bows and put the gift on your head. And where making offerings is warranted, you must not be unmindful either."

Qubad committed these injunctions to memory and the next day again presented himself at the court.

The emperor was having his meal, but as he had found Qubad's antics amusing, when the presenter of petitions announced Qubad, the emperor ordered him to be shown in directly. Then, when Qubad presented himself, the emperor accorded him a most uncommon preference by giving him a bowl of curry. Qubad made a low bow upon receiving the bowl and, remembering Dil-Aaram's words, poured it over his head, besmearing not only his clothes, but drenching as well his beard, whiskers, and his whole body with the gravy. The emperor said in his heart, *His every deed is a marvel of folly. And then he also calls himself a great merchant! Wonders never cease!*

That day Dil-Aaram had asked Qubad to invite the emperor to a banquet, using the good offices of Buzurjmehr. Acting on Dil-Aaram's advice, Qubad mentioned the banquet to the emperor. Buzurjmehr, who indulged Qubad, petitioned in his favor, too. The emperor, already amused with Qubad's antics and simple ways, granted his request. Qubad returned home joyous and elated and communicated the news to Dil-Aaram, who immediately busied herself with arrangements for the banquet.

Of the Emperor's Arrival at Qubad's House and His Restoring Dil-Aaram to Honor, and of His Feasting and Drinking

When the diligent orderlies of faultless Nature unfurled the bright spread of morn across the heavens, and with great excellence decked them with the golden dish of the world-brightening sun, the emperor, accompanied by Buzurjmehr and his viziers, arrived at the woodcutter's palace. Qubad received him in the approved custom and made an offering.

When the emperor looked around he saw portraits of himself and Dil-Aaram staring down at him from every wall. Remembering his courtesan, the emperor expressed great remorse at her loss.

Then the emperor moved to the bejeweled throne in the summerhouse, where the tabla began to play and the dancers to perform. Presently the meal was ordered. The table deckers laid out the spread and the head cook started bringing out all kinds of sweet and savory delights. Qubad put choice delicacies before the emperor with his own hand. After the emperor had finished the meal, Dil-Aaram, appareled exquisitely, showed a beloved view of herself to the emperor from behind a lattice. The emperor asked Qubad, "How are you related to the woman behind the lattice and what is her name? She appears to have excellent taste, and to my mind it seems all these preparations are owing to her organization and industry!"

Respectfully folding his arms before him, Qubad responded, "She is your slave's daughter! And all that you see is indeed the fruit of her diligence and industry. If Your Eminence were to grant the women the charity of visiting their quarters, Your Honor's slaves would be most exalted. Your Majesty's slave girl, my daughter, is herself most desirous of audience and eager to wait upon Your Eminence!"

When the emperor went into the women's quarters, from a distance he thought his eyes were deceiving him. And when Dil-Aaram approached nearer and made an obeisance, the emperor exclaimed, "What do I see here, Dil-Aaram? Is that you?" Dil-Aaram flung herself at the emperor's feet and began to unburden her heart by way of shedding copious tears. The emperor raised her head and embraced her.

Dil-Aaram revealed that it was the selfsame woodcutter, Qubad, to whom she had been given away, handed over in utter disgrace. And that by virtue of His Highness's prestige he had risen in the world to be called the Prince of Merchants and was so honored that the Emperor of the World had directed his august and distinction-bestowing feet thither to grace his house with his presence.

The emperor was most embarrassed to hear this and, taking Dil-Aaram by her hand, brought her to the summerhouse. Praising her industry highly, he seated her near the throne.

The emperor invested Qubad with a robe of honor and confirmed him as Prince of Merchants. Then, to show Dil-Aaram his former favor, he asked her to play on the lute. Acquiescing to his wish, Dil-Aaram began strumming on the lute and played it more wondrously than she had ever played before. Some time having passed in these regalements, the emperor invested another robe of honor on Qubad. Then, taking Dil-Aaram alongside him, he repaired to the royal palace. The emperor's misogyny having thus changed into fondness for women, he was royally wedded to his uncle's daughter, Mohtram Bano, before long.

REGARDING THE BIRTH OF NAUSHERVAN AND BAKHTAK, AND BUZURJMEHR'S PREDICTIONS, AND OF NAUSHERVAN'S FALLING IN LOVE WITH MEHR-ANGEZ

A year after the emperor's marriage the empress showed signs of expecting a boy, and by God Almighty's grace, when the gestation was over she went into labor. The emperor sent for Buzurjmehr, and asked him to prepare an account of his heir's fortunes and draw the horoscope.

By the grace of the Incomparable Progenitor, a sun of magnificence and prestige, and a luminary of grandeur and dignity, to wit, a worthy son arrived securely into the midwife's arms under the constellation Aries at an auspicious moment. Drawing the horoscope, when Buzurjmehr matched the forms, he found the sun and the moon in Aries, and discovered Venus, Jupiter, Mercury, Saturn, and Mars also in auspicious constellations.

Beside himself with joy, Buzurjmehr went to the emperor and announced: "This glorious child will grow up to reign over countless kingdoms and realms. He will be just and equitable, and the sovereign of a bountiful land, and shall rule for seventy years. However, from the knavery of one of his counselors he will often find himself in dire straits." Having said this Buzurjmehr was about to propose a name, when two *ayyars*[14] presented themselves and pronounced to the emperor: "The chosen spring for royal consumption that had dried up long ago has begun to flow of itself today, and gushes with water." Deeming it a propitious augur, Buzurjmehr named the prince Naushervan.[15] Some chroniclers have written that at the moment of the child's birth the emperor was holding a cup of red wine, and Buzurjmehr said to him in Persian:

Qibla aalam jam ra nosh-o-ravan ba farmayid
Pray imbibe from the goblet, O Guide of the World!

It is said that the emperor was so pleased at Buzurjmehr's words that he invested him with a robe of honor, and named the prince Naushervan.

On the eleventh day after the birth, even as the emperor was occupied with the festivities, informers brought word that a boy had been born to Alqash's daughter. The emperor turned to Buzurjmehr and said, "It would do well to do away with Alqash's grandson forthwith. If allowed to live, this boy would bestir great evil. However, I leave the matter to your esteemed opinion, and shall give it precedence over mine!"

Buzurjmehr protected the infant and persuaded the emperor against murdering him. Then he took his leave of the emperor and went to Alqash's house. And he named Bakhtiar's son Bakhtak.

When Naushervan reached the age of four years and four months, the emperor put him under Buzurjmehr's care to be educated. A week later, Buzurjmehr arranged for Bakhtak to make an offering to the emperor, and used his good offices to have him appointed the beneficiary of Alqash's estate. Then he began educating Bakhtak alongside Naushervan.

As Naushervan was intelligent and bright, he very soon mastered all the sciences of council and he excelled as well in martial sciences, making a name for himself in those fields, too.

It so happened that merchants from China arrived in the city one day. After they had made their offerings to the emperor, they presented Naushervan with gifts and curiosities and lavished many delicate and wondrous marvels on him. Naushervan desired that they tell him about the emperor of China.

Having discoursed at length about the Chinese emperor, the merchants said, "The emperor of China also has a daughter, Mehr-Angez of name, whose face is like the moon, whose forehead is bright as the sun, and whose bearing is as elegant as a flower's, who is jasmine-bosomed, whose waist is thin as hair, and who is *houri*-like and fairy-limbed. The renown of her beauty has traveled the world from one end to the other."

These words about Mehr-Angez's charms evoked a passionate longing in Naushervan's heart and the flame of love kindled in the prince's breast. Naushervan was overcome by passion's potent spell. By degrees his verve and endurance gave way and his patience and composure took their leave. Eating and drinking became things of the past and Naushervan was struck silent. He gave up merriment and society altogether and soliloquized night and day in his heart thinking of Mehr-Angez. And sometimes, imagining himself before her, he would passionately intone love verses to proclaim his passion.

However much Naushervan tried to disguise his condition, he was betrayed by his wan appearance, his chapped lips, and the cold sighs flowing from the well of his ailing heart. As his condition began to deteriorate with each passing day, well-wishers declared to the emperor: "We do not know what malady has befallen the prince (from the good fortune of his foes!) that he has stopped eating and drinking altogether. He neither listens to anyone nor speaks his heart and sits by himself transfixed by wonder." Upon hearing this, the emperor became agitated and distraught, and sent Buzurjmehr to inform him of the prince's condition.

Buzurjmehr comforted the emperor and went to see Naushervan. After arranging a private audience with Naushervan, he said to him, "What is it that has weighed you down? You would be well advised to confide in me, so that I may busy myself in finding some cure for it!"

Naushervan replied, "Dearest Khvaja! I have become enamored of the daughter of the emperor of China, Princess Mehr-Angez, just from hearing of her charms. Claimed by the arrow of her love, I am fully confident that I shall not survive if I do not wed her."

Buzurjmehr said, "My dear Prince! One must not become derelict and let go of one's reason so completely, as it does not behoove the high-minded! What you are out of sorts about, and unnecessarily distressed over, is not something that lies beyond the realm of possibility. Set your mind at ease! I shall take charge of this affair myself and fill your cup of longing with the wine of desire!"

Comforted by Buzurjmehr's compassionate words, and with his hopes of union with Mehr-Angez now revived, Naushervan leapt out of his bed. After having a bath and sending for his friends and companions, he changed clothes and sat down to have his meal.

After speaking with Naushervan, Buzurjmehr went to see the emperor and conveyed to his ears the amorous affliction of the prince. The emperor said, "Khvaja, this matter will not be resolved without your agency."

Through their mutual counsel it was decided that Buzurjmehr would go with an embassy to the emperor of China, and undertake to arrange Naushervan's marriage to Mehr-Angez. Arrangements were made to this effect, and Buzurjmehr proceeded to China at the head of fifty thousand foot soldiers and cavalrymen.

―――――

Now we return to Bakhtak, who, ever since he had come of age and heard about his grandfather, would daily say to his mother, "Whenever I lay eyes on Buzurjmehr, blood rushes into them; and thinking of my poor grandfather, my heart becomes overcast with grief. I shall remain restless until I have avenged his blood. Once Buzurjmehr is in my snare, he will find no escape. I only wait for the day when he falls into my power!" But Naushervan always censured and reproved him.

OF BUZURJMEHR'S JOURNEY TO CHINA WITH TROOPS AND RETINUE, HIS RETURN WITH PRINCESS MEHR-ANGEZ, AND THE NUPTIALS OF THE SEEKER AND THE SOUGHT

The singers of the pleasure garden of ecstasy and the melodists of the assembly of discourse thus create a rollicking rumpus by playing the dulcimer[16] of delightful verbiage and the lute of enchanting story, and thus warm the nuptial assembly most exquisitely. Having taken leave of his emperor, Khvaja Buzurjmehr proceeded with his retinue in wondrous pomp, state, and grandeur, and traversed league after league, bridging stretch after hazardous stretch, until he entered the frontiers of China.

The emperor of China was greatly taken with Buzurjmehr's fine manners and refined ways. When the emperor asked Buzurjmehr the purpose of his visit, he explained the matter in so courteous and refined a manner, that the emperor agreed to Naushervan's marriage with his daughter with all his heart.

He then ordered his subjects to commence the preparations for the princess's departure forthwith, and no sooner were the preparations ordered than Mehr-Angez's entourage was made ready.

After a journey of many months, Buzurjmehr arrived near Persia safe and happy. A jubilant and exulting emperor and prince greeted the cavalcade. Imperial arrangements were then set afoot for the nuptials, and at a propitious hour Naushervan was married to Mehr-Angez.

It is said that when the emperor gracefully broached with Buzurjmehr his heart's desire to step down in Naushervan's favor, Buzurjmehr replied, "You may vacate the throne for him after forty days have passed. Until then, give the prince into my power to do with him as I see fit, and have no one interfere in this matter!" The emperor acquiesced to Buzurjmehr's wishes and gave him the powers he desired.

Buzurjmehr ordered Naushervan to be shackled and consigned to the jail forthwith, where he remained for forty days. On the forty-first day, pulling a running Naushervan behind his steed, Buzurjmehr brought him to the royal palace and lashed his back with his whip three times so severely that Naushervan cried out from its violence. Then Buzurjmehr unsheathed his sword, and presenting it to Naushervan, lowered his neck and humbly said, "I deserve to be beheaded for this outrage, for such is the punishment for this contumely!" Putting his arms around Buzurjmehr's neck, Naushervan violently embraced him, and said, "Khvaja! There must be some logic behind what you did, or else you would not have put me through this trial and suffered yourself at my pain!"

According to Buzurjmehr's advice, the emperor stepped down from the throne in Naushervan's favor. But he enjoined Naushervan again and again before his coronation: "Do not take any step without first consulting Buzurjmehr, and do not heed Bakhtak at all or allow him to have any say in the state affairs, lest the empire slip into the hands of ruin and the sun of your prestige become clouded."

But when Qubad Kamran died two years later, Bakhtak gained influence in Naushervan's court and rose to command great authority. There was no audacity or evil but that wretch had forced Naushervan's hand to commit it, and at Bakhtak's inciting the emperor let loose all manner of grief and injury on his subjects.

One day a convict was brought before Naushervan on the charge of banditry. He was the chief of highway robbers and a most bloodthirsty and consummate rascal. Naushervan ordered him to be put to the sword. When the executioner arrived to drag him to the execution ground, the convict submitted: "I understand that I shall be killed and awarded my due punishment. But I have a wondrous gift and knowledge. If I were to be given forty days' reprieve from death, and besides that grace period the emperor also were to allow me the pleasures of food, wine, and women, I shall impart that knowledge—after forty days have passed—to the one in whom Your Excellency reposes his trust. Then my life would be entirely at your disposal!" Naushervan asked, "What is this knowledge?" The convict replied, "I know the language of all beasts, but I am particularly versed in the speech of birds."

Granting him the desired reprieve, Naushervan put the convict under Buzurjmehr's charge. Buzurjmehr provided him a mansion furnished with every last comfort and amenity that he desired. And there the convict lived in great luxury for forty days.

On the forty-first day, Buzurjmehr said to the convict, "Now instruct me in the language of animals, as you promised." The thief replied, "I am a complete stranger to all learning, and never crossed ways with any kind of knowledge. But, all praise to the bountiful God and His amazing ways, even His donkeys feast nobly! It was His will to save me from impending doom, and keep me in food and drink most wonderfully, and thus apportion these pleasures to my lot. I craved that luxury and by this ruse my longing was fulfilled. Now I am at your mercy, to be beheaded, lynched, or put to death in any which way you find seemly!"

Buzurjmehr laughed heartily upon hearing his speech, and after securing a pledge from him that he would never again rob or steal, set the man free.

One day Naushervan separated from his hunting party, with only Buzurjmehr and Bakhtak remaining by his side. They came upon two owls perched atop a tree hooting and screeching, and Naushervan asked Buzurjmehr, "What is it that they confer and argue about?" Buzurjmehr replied, "They are discussing the plans for their children's wedding, and argue regarding the settlement. The boy's parent says that he will not give his consent unless the girl's parent agrees to give three wastelands in her daughter's dowry. He says that only then would he let his son marry her; otherwise he will arrange for his son's match elsewhere. The girl's parent replies that if Naushervan were to live and continue in his cruel and audacious ways, he would give Naushervan's whole empire, not just three wastelands, as a bridal gift."

Naushervan said, "Now our despotism has become so widespread that the word of our injustice and tyranny has reached even the animals!" Naushervan took warning from this. Upon his return he had a bell hung from the Court of Justice fitted out with a chain,[17] and had it proclaimed throughout the country that any petitioner might ring the bell without having himself announced or being routed through mace bearers and functionaries. From that day forward Naushervan's justice became legendary, and to this day he is remembered by the young and old as Naushervan the Just.

But why go into these details! After many years the emperor was blessed with a daughter and two sons from Mehr-Angez. He named his daughter Mehr-Nigar, and his sons Hurmuz and Faramurz. They were raised in the imperial custom and their instruction and education was entrusted to Buzurjmehr's care. Two sons were born to Buzurjmehr. He named the one Daryadil and the other Siyavush, and applied himself to their breeding and supervision. God also sent a son to Bakhtak, who named him Bakhtiarak.

Storytellers relate that one night the emperor had a dream that a jackdaw came flying from the east and flew off with his crown; then a hawk appeared from the west and killed the jackdaw and restored the crown to his head. Naushervan woke up from the dream and in the morning narrated it to Buzurjmehr, then asked for its interpretation. Buzurjmehr said, "Toward the east there is a city called Khaibar. From those regions a prince by the name of Hashsham bin Alqamah Khaibari will rise against Your Highness. He will rout the imperial armies and claim Your Highness's crown and throne. Then a youth named Hamza will come from the city of Mecca in the west. He will kill that villain and restore the crown and throne to Your Majesty."

Naushervan became jubilant upon hearing these words, and sent Buzurjmehr to Mecca to announce that when the boy was born he should be proclaimed the emperor's protégé.

Carrying numerous gifts, jewels, and riches, Khvaja Buzurjmehr repaired to Mecca to seek out that worthy boy, and went searching for signs of his birth in every house.

The gazetteers of miscellanies, tale-bearers of varied annals, the enlightened in the ethereal realms of legend writing, and reckoners of the subtle issues of eloquence thus gallop the noble steed of the pen through the field of composition, and spur on the delightful tale. Arriving near Mecca (the hallowed!) Khvaja Buzurjmehr sent a missive to Khvaja Abdul Muttalib, chieftain of the Banu Hashim tribe, which read: "This humble servant has come on a pilgrimage to Mecca. He hopes to enjoy your audience, and awaits permission to partake of your hospitality."

Khvaja Abdul Muttalib was most pleased to read Buzurjmehr's communiqué, and proceeded, together with all the nobles of Mecca, to welcome Buzurjmehr. Buzurjmehr first went with Khvaja Abdul Muttalib to pay homage to Kaaba.[18] Then he greeted the elite of Mecca with great propriety, and conferred riches and gold pieces on every last one of them.

Sending for the town crier, Buzurjmehr had it announced that the next boy born from that date would be raised in the service of the emperor of Persia; and that as soon as he was born, his parents should bring him to the vizier, that he may be named and bequeathed his legacy from the emperor.

Some fifteen or twenty days had passed since Buzurjmehr's arrival in Mecca, when on one of his visits, Khvaja Abdul Muttalib said to the vizier, "The Eternal God conferred upon me a firstborn, yesterday!"

Buzurjmehr immediately had the boy brought to him, and discovered that it was the selfsame boy destined to exact tribute from the emperors of the Seven Climes and humble all the great and mighty on Earth and on Mount Qaf.[19] Buzurjmehr kissed the child's forehead and named him Hamza, and congratulated Khvaja Abdul Muttalib most warmly.

Khvaja Abdul Muttalib was going to offer sherbet to the assembly according to the Arabian custom when Buzurjmehr said, "Wait a while! Let two others arrive, whose boys shall be your son's companions and peers." Even as Buzurjmehr spoke, Abdul Muttalib's slave Basheer brought in an infant, and said to his master: "Your slave has also been blessed with a son!" Buzurjmehr named the boy Muqbil Vafadar, and conferred a purse of one thousand gold pieces on Basheer, prophesying, "This boy will be an accomplished archer!"

As Basheer was returning home after seeing Buzurjmehr, he crossed paths with the cameleer, Umayya Zamiri and gave him all the details. Then Umayya went home all excited and happy, and narrated the whole episode to his wife. He said to her, "You keep telling me you are with child; now quickly bear me a son that we may take him to receive gold pieces, and begin a life of luxury."

His wife said to him, "Are you mad? I am hardly into my seventh month! Heaven forfend I bear the child now!" Umayya said, "Just begin straining and I am sure the boy will drop! We need him hatched between today and tomorrow. Plenty of good it will do me if he is born two months from now!"

His wife, who had worked herself into a rage, shouted, "The brains of this wretch have gone woolgathering! How wantonly he forces me into labor!"

In a fit of rage, Umayya kicked her in the abdomen with such violence that she fell to the floor. The boy burst out of the womb from the impact, and the woman's spasms ended soon afterward.

Umayya quickly wrapped up the infant in the sleeves of his coat, took him to Buzurjmehr, and declared, "Propitious fortune has smiled at your slave and blessed him with a son! I have brought him here to present before you." Khvaja Buzurjmehr laughed when he looked at the boy's face, and remarked, "This boy will be the prince of all tricksters, unsurpassed in cunning, guile, and deceit. Great and mighty kings and champions of the order of Rustam and Nariman will tremble at his mention and soil their pants from fright upon hearing his name. He will take hundreds, nay, thousands of castles all by himself, and will rout great armies all alone. He will be excessively greedy, most insidious, and a consummate perjurer. He will be cruel, tyrannical, and coldhearted, yet he shall prove a trustworthy friend and confidant to Hamza!"

After speaking, Buzurjmehr took him into his arms, and the boy fell to screaming and yelping lustily. To quiet him Buzurjmehr gave him his finger to suck. The boy slipped off the ring from Buzurjmehr's finger into his mouth and fell silent. When Buzurjmehr noticed the ring missing from his finger, he searched the pockets of his robe and, not finding it there, remained purposely quiet. When sherbet was brought for every-one, Buzurjmehr put a few drops in the infant's mouth, too, and as he opened his mouth the ring fell out of it. Buzurjmehr picked it up, and remarked jestingly to Khvaja Abdul Muttalib, "This is his first theft, and he has chosen me as his first victim!"

Then Buzurjmehr said, "I name him Amar bil Fatah!" Thereupon he conferred two chests of gold pieces on Umayya, and enjoined him to raise the boy with every care. Umayya first secured the chests of gold coins, then said, "How can I raise him? How does Your Honor propose that I care for him, when his mother died in childbirth!" Buzurjmehr said to Khvaja Abdul Muttalib, "Hamza's mother died in childbirth too, as did the mothers of these two boys here. It would be best that all three of them stay under your roof. Presently, there shall arrive at your door Aadiya Bano, the mother of Aadi Madi-Karib, whom Prophet Ibrahim has con-verted to the True Faith in the realm of dreams and sent here to be Hamza's wet nurse. Go forth to greet her and let her nurse Hamza on her right breast, and Muqbil and Amar on her left."

Following Buzurjmehr's advice, Khvaja Abdul Muttalib gave the three boys into her care and appointed her their wet nurse.

When six days had passed after Hamza's birth and he had been bathed, Buzurjmehr said to Khvaja Abdul Muttalib, "Come morning, have Hamza's cradle removed to the roof of your house and do not despair if it goes missing! The inhabited part of the earth is bounded on all sides by a great sea beside which lies Mount Qaf, the domain of the dormant folk and the jinn, *peris, devs, ghols, Shutar-pas, Gao-sars, Gosh-fils, Nim-tans, tasma-pas, Ghur-munhas*, and others. The emperor of those dominions is Shahpal bin Shahrukh. His vizier, Abdur Rahman, will send for Hamza's cradle for his emperor, and have it returned after seven days. Many advantages will be gained from this." Then Buzurjmehr took his leave and returned to his encampment, and Khvaja Abdul Muttalib began biding his time in anticipation of the augured moment.

Hamza's Cradle Is Carried Off to Mount Qaf, and That Sun of Excellence Shines on the Mount of Brilliance

The zephyr-paced sojourner, the stylus of fascinating accounts of the expert chroniclers, and the flying arrowhead—to wit, the pen that must detail the messages of intelligencers—also records a few words concerning events on Mount Qaf, and regales those enamored of fables and legends of the past with some choice phrases from this wondrous tale.

One day the sovereign lord and potentate of Mount Qaf, Shahpal bin Shahrukh, was giving audience on King Suleiman's throne. The monarchs who ruled the eighteen realms of Mount Qaf were receiving royal audience, when the porter of the harem presented himself, and communicated the propitious tidings that a princess, like the Sun in beauty, and in nature the like of Jupiter, had risen forth to shine over the emperor's house by gracing the cradle from her mother's womb.

Emperor Shahpal turned to his vizier, Abdur Rahman—a most eminent jinn who had seen the court of Suleiman and served there, and was a past master of all sciences—and asked him to name the girl and cast her horoscope to see what it foretold. As per his sovereign's wishes, Abdur Rahman named the girl Aasman Peri. Throwing dice, casting the horoscope, relating the shapes together, and rejoicing greatly at what he had deciphered, he conveyed the news to Emperor Shahpal: "My felicitations to Your Honor! This girl will rule the eighteen realms of Mount Qaf. But eighteen years from this day, the mighty jinns shall rise as a body in rebellion. In those days a human will come from the inhabited quarters of the Earth, and will rout those rebels and conquer the occupied countries by his might and return them to Your Majesty's rule!"

Emperor Shahpal greatly rejoiced and told Abdur Rahman, "See if that boy has been born yet." Vizier Abdur Rahman cast the dice and said,

"Today is the sixth day since his birth and this day his father has sent his cradle to the roof of his house." The emperor ordered four *perizads* to bring the cradle to him.

When the *perizads* brought Hamza's cradle before him, all those present were amazed and spellbound as they gazed upon Hamza's beauty. The emperor lifted Hamza from his cradle, kissed his forehead, and had his eyes lined with the collyrium of Suleiman.[20] Then he had Hamza nursed by *devs, peris,* jinns, *ghols,* lions, and panthers for seven days.

Khvaja Abdur Rahman then said, "My knowledge of *ramal* tells me that Aasman Peri shall be betrothed to this boy, and the ties of man and wife shall be established between the son of Aadam and the daughter of Jan." The emperor rejoiced at the news, and sent for a cradle from his palace encrusted with various costly jewels. He placed Hamza in it and hung the cradle with several lustrous carbuncles,[21] woven into red and green silk, and lined it with all sorts of rare and expensive jewels. Then he ordered the *perizads* who had brought him to conduct him back safely, upon which the *perizads* took Hamza's cradle back to Khvaja Abdul Muttalib's roof.

The swift-paced traveler of the quill hastens through its journey along the stretches of the ream, and thus diligently passes the landmarks of this new history with its digressions, revealing that a week later Buzurjmehr sent word to Khvaja Abdul Muttalib to inquire if Hamza's cradle had returned from Mount Qaf, and whether or not he had been reunited with his lost Yusuf.[22] Khvaja Abdul Muttalib sent a man to the roof to verify, who was startled upon setting eyes on the cradle. Khvaja Abdul Muttalib was informed that Hamza had brought back a cradle the likes of which even the eyes of Heaven had not seen.

A joyous Khvaja Abdul Muttalib immediately sent for Buzurjmehr, who arrived directly upon receiving the news to procure bliss for his eyes by gazing upon Hamza.

Then Buzurjmehr said to Abdul Muttalib, "I shall beg your leave now! Pray do not be neglectful in raising Hamza, Muqbil, and Amar. Proclaim Hamza the protégé of the Emperor of the Seven Climes, and have this fact announced in all regions to all men."

Khvaja Abdul Muttalib acquiesced to these requests and wrote out a note of gratitude to Naushervan.

Buzurjmehr then returned to Ctesiphon with Khvaja Abdul Muttalib's letter. Immensely pleased to read the letter, the emperor invested Buzurjmehr with a robe of honor.

One day, many months later, Naushervan was seated on his throne when the report of the gazetteer from China came to be read out. It brought intelligence that Bahram Gurd, the son of the grand emperor, had been enthroned as the emperor of China and had become the master of crown and power. Besides the whole empire of China, several cities had also fallen to his sword. He was loath to submit his due part of the four years' tribute and averse to remitting land taxes to the emperor's auspicious coffers. As his force and might had made him arrogant, he brazenly averred that the Emperor of the Seven Climes would do well to forget about his unpaid debts, but pay him some tribute instead, or else he would devastate and plunder Ctesiphon.

Naushervan became greatly alarmed upon hearing this news, and said to Buzurjmehr, "What do you advise we do regarding this menace?" Buzurjmehr replied, "As Bahram Gurd has yet to consolidate his power and resources, I would suggest that you detail some fierce and seasoned warrior to apprehend and bring Bahram Gurd before Your Highness alive or dead." Naushervan said, "I authorize you to appoint whomever you find worthy of leading this campaign and crushing this recreant!"

Buzurjmehr chose Gustham bin Ashk Zarrin Kafsh Sasani for the task. He was sent at the head of twelve thousand troops for the correction and chastisement of Bahram Gurd.

Of Amar Stealing the Ruby, and the Three Boys Being Sent to the Academy

Children on their reed horses gallop about the pages inscribing with ink drops the delightful episodes of Hamza and Amar's time at the academy. It was Aadiya Bano's custom to nurse Hamza on one breast alone and have Muqbil and Amar share the other one. But with every passing day Hamza grew thinner and Amar fatter.

One night Aadiya Bano started in her sleep and woke up to find Amar sucking the milk from both her breasts with great abandon, having pushed both Hamza and Muqbil from the bed. In the morning she recounted the episode to everyone and said, "This boy will grow up to become an infamous and notorious thief, that such are his deeds at birth!"

After some time when Amar began to crawl on his hands and knees, he made it a custom to go crawling into the vestibules at night after everyone had gone to bed. Slipping away with women's rings and bracelets, he stowed them away in Aadiya Bano's betel box or under her pillow, and quietly went to sleep. In the morning, when people searched for the lost objects, they were recovered from Aadiya Bano's betel box or found under her pillow. Aadiya would be most puzzled and embarrassed, but could offer neither any explanation nor voice a suspicion.

One day, Amar stole a carbuncle from Hamza's cradle and put it into his mouth. Khvaja Abdul Muttalib was informed that there was one ruby less in the cradle. By chance Khvaja Abdul Muttalib caught a glance of Amar's face, and noticed that one of his cheeks was swollen. When he pressed Amar's cheeks, the carbuncle fell out of his mouth. Khvaja Abdul Muttalib exclaimed, "Heaven's mercy! If such are his deeds in infancy, what will he grow up to be? There will be no outrage that he will not commit!"

When Hamza, Muqbil, and Amar were five years of age, Khvaja Abdul Muttalib sent them to study with a mulla. Hamza and Muqbil read as the mulla instructed them, but Amar expressed great wonderment and perplexity, and his mischievous nature found play. However much the mulla admonished him, Amar paid him no heed. Sometimes Amar would say to Hamza, "You are free to waste your time with the mulla and continue with your lessons. But I shall have nothing further to do with it."

One evening the mulla called on Khvaja Abdul Muttalib, and after bitterly complaining about Amar, spake thus: "He neither studies nor lets Hamza or anybody else learn anything! If you wish me to continue teaching Hamza, you should give Amar into someone else's care." Khvaja Abdul Muttalib resolved to send Amar elsewhere, but Hamza would not hear of it. Khvaja Abdul Muttalib found himself helpless, and desisted from separating the boys.

It was the custom that the parents of these young scholars sent food for them to the academy. One day, the food had arrived from the homes. Except for Amar, who was wide awake, everyone had fallen asleep, including the mulla. Amar bolted down everything he could eat, and hid away the rest under the mulla's gear. When everyone woke up and looked for food, it was nowhere to be found. The mulla said, "Who else could be behind this except Amar?" Amar replied, "O Master, first conduct a thorough investigation into the matter. The guilty party is the one from whose possession the food is recovered." The mulla said, "Why don't you search for the thief yourself?"

Amar first frisked all the boys most thoroughly. Then he looked this way and that, and began searching under the mulla's mattresses and pillows. Then everyone saw the food hidden inside, whereupon Amar immediately raised a great hue and cry.

Abashed and embarrassed, the mulla gave Amar a few tight slaps, and when that failed to silence him, dealt him the whip. But Hamza intervened and did not let the mulla have his way with Amar.

The next day, when the mulla and the boys went to sleep in the afternoon, Amar took the mulla's turban to the sweetmeat vendor. He pawned it for five rupees' worth of sweets and stored them in the academy, then curled up in a corner to sleep. When the mulla woke up and saw such a huge amount of sweets, he rejoiced in his heart, but also feared lest it should turn out to be one of Amar's pranks. He inquired of every single boy the occasion for those sweets, and who had brought them, but all of them expressed ignorance as none of them knew the truth.

When the mulla woke up Amar and asked him, Amar replied, "Father brought these sweets as an offering he had pledged. He left instructions with me to have you say the *fateha*[23] on the sweets when you wake up, and to distribute them." In the end the mulla said the benediction, and gleaning the choice morsels from the top of the bowl partook of them himself. Amar distributed the rest among the boys and also ate some himself.

Now, Amar had laced the inviting *peras*[24] the mulla ate with croton oil, and presently the teacher began experiencing cramps and tenesmus. His stomach began to churn and his bowels to grumble. Stricken with a severe case of diarrhea, he rushed to the toilet every few moments. Soon he was unable even to bear himself to the toilet, and his hands began to shiver and tremble. He groaned, "O Amar! What was in those sweets that has brought me to this?"

Amar replied, "You are so fluent in the primer of insinuation that it has become a refrain in your speech. All of us here had the sweets, and we did not suffer the least belch or burp. How are we to blame if you have come to this end from eating them? There is always the possibility, as the saying goes, that some consume the eggplant and some are by the eggplant consumed."

Hamza discovered Amar's hand in this and sent for buttermilk for the mulla, and having it administered to him, said, "It must be the sugar's warmth that caused your body to become heated." The mulla barely escaped with his life.

Some hours then remaining until the close of the day, the mulla sent the boys home. After everyone had left, the mulla also prepared to leave, but he could not find his turban. Giving it up for lost, the mulla wrapped his cummerbund around his head and set out for home. When he approached the sweetmeat shop, the vendor came running out with the mulla's turban and said, "You did not have to insult me by pawning your turban if you wanted to buy sweets from my shop! Consider it your own shop and settle the account whenever you are paid."

The mulla made up a reply, and was obliged to pay him five rupees from his own pocket to ransom his turban. He said in his heart, *Those were the same sweets that Amar made me say the* fateha *on! Very well! Let the night pass! Come morning, it will be Amar and myself, and his back and the whip in my hand!*

Now hear of the next morning when Amar arrived before anybody else had entered the academy. He spread out and tidied up the mulla's mattress. Then he opened up the primer and began reading it with great engrossment. When the mulla arrived and saw Amar in the academy, he said in his heart, *My terror has plainly overwhelmed him. That is the reason why he arrived before everybody else today. Rather than chastise him, today I must seize the opportunity to show him some indulgence!*

After setting them the lesson for the day, the mulla said to the boys, "I am going to the baths and shall be back presently. Read and learn your lesson while I am away!" The mulla then set out for the baths, having already prepared his hair dye and sent it ahead of him with Amar. On the way Amar found time to mix a *tola*[25] of very fine ground ratsbane into the dye. In the baths, after he had applied the dye, the mulla rinsed it with warm water, and his beard and whiskers were washed away, too, along with the dye.

Come night, he presented himself before Khvaja Abdul Muttalib clad in a burqa[26] and said to him in a voice choked with tears, "This is what I have been brought to in my old age, at the hands of Amar. Now I cannot show my face for the shame, and while I am in this state, I must remain hidden from my friends and acquaintances!" The mulla also narrated the episode of the turban and sweetmeats.

Khvaja Abdul Muttalib sent him away after comforting and consoling him, and then he punished Amar and banished him from the house. He then said to Hamza, "I shall be angry with you if I ever hear you mention Amar's name again." But Hamza could not think of parting with Amar and he went without food and drink for two days. When Khvaja Abdul Muttalib learned of this, he found he had no choice but to send for Amar, forgive his conduct, and reunite him with Hamza. Khvaja also wrote a note to the mulla, interceding on Amar's behalf. The mulla forgave Amar, and he was allowed into the academy as before.

One day food was sent to the mulla from a pupil's house. The mulla said to Amar, "Take it to my house, but see that you do not play any tricks on the way, as there is a chicken inside that will fly away if you open the pot." Amar replied, "I am not bitten by a mad dog so that I'd do such a thing! I shall hand it to your wife and bring back a receipt." Speaking thus, Amar set out carrying the tray over his head.

Approaching the mulla's house, Amar found a safe spot and put down the tray. Upon opening the pot he found it full of sweet rice. Hungry to begin with, he now sat down with the bowl and ate to his heart's content. Then throwing the remainder before the dogs, he tore off the tray cover and the wrapping cloth, and went forth and knocked on the mulla's door, calling for his wife. When she came to the door, Amar handed her the tray, and said, "The mulla has forbidden you from opening it. He has asked you not to cook anything, and to ask your friends in the neighborhood not to cook anything either, as food will be sent to them from your house today!" That poor woman knew nothing of Amar's treacherous and deceitful ways. She did not cook anything, and kept her two close friends in the neighborhood also from cooking that day.

It so happened that when the mulla finished at the academy, he decided to stop by a friend's house to talk and inquire after his welfare. Obtaining his friend's leave much later, the mulla returned home and said to his wife, "I put you through a lot of trouble today by keeping you waiting for me. Bring whatever you have cooked today!" His wife replied, "How was I supposed to cook anything today, as you forbade me from cooking yourself. Then you returned home so late, and the two women in the neighborhood I had invited because of you, were also kept waiting along with their sons and husbands! However, the food that you sent is here. First send some to our neighbors, and then we can have some ourselves too."

The mulla's heart sank upon hearing this, and he said to himself, *God have mercy! There is more to Amar's prank than meets the eye!* And sure enough, upon opening the pot, the mulla found it empty. That night the mulla's whole family slept on empty stomachs, and when their neighbors heard what had happened, they did likewise.

After scraping together some breakfast in the morning, the mulla went to the academy and asked Amar, "Whatever became of the food that I had sent home with you yesterday?" Amar replied, "I know nothing about any food, but the chicken you sent flew off on the way, after tearing the tray cover and its cloth." The mulla then asked, "Why did you forbid my wife from cooking anything, and when did I ask you to invite the neighbors?" Amar replied, "In doing that I was indeed in the wrong!"

At this, the mulla bound Amar's hands and feet and punished him severely. But Hamza again interceded, promising that Amar would never again do such a thing or trouble him in any way. But now Amar swore enmity against the poor mulla, and waited for a chance to even scores with him.

Abu Jahal and Abu Sufyan studied in the same academy. One afternoon, when the boys were asleep, Amar slipped Abu Jahal's ring from his finger, and sneaking inside the mulla's house, hid it inside the mulla's daughter's betel box. Then he called on the mulla's daughter, and asked her to give him her earring in the mulla's name. Returning to the academy, he slipped the earring onto Abu Jahal's finger, and lay quietly in a corner without stirring.

When the boys woke up and returned to their studies, the mulla gave a start upon noticing his daughter's earring on Abu Jahal's finger. But he did not challenge him outright, but asked him instead, "How did you come upon the earring on your finger?" Greatly startled himself upon noticing it on his finger, Abu Jahal became frightened and replied, "I cannot say who slipped the ring onto my finger!" Thereupon Amar interjected, saying, "Ask me, respected master, for I have become privy to this secret." The mulla said, "I bid you speak!"

Upon that Amar said, "In the afternoon when yourself and the boys go to sleep, Abu Jahal visits your house. It was his ill luck that just when he was stealing out today, I woke up and quietly followed him. Upon arriving at your house he shook the door chain and your daughter came running out. They first exchanged kisses, arranged future trysts, and then indulged in loving prattle. When they parted, Abu Jahal gave her his ring and himself took her earring. I returned after witnessing the whole episode and pretended to be asleep."

When he heard these words, blood rushed to the mulla's eyes. He snatched the earring from Abu Jahal and, spreading him on the floor on his face and securing his limbs, gave him such an unmerciful thrashing that Abu Jahal forgot he had ever partaken of any comfort since the day he was born. Fuming, the mulla then went home, and told his daughter to bring out her betel box. When the mulla looked inside, he found Abu Jahal's ring. Immediately upon discovering the ring, the mulla lay violent hands upon his daughter and, seizing her by her hair, slapped her until the girl cried out in pain and fainted. Her mother came rushing to her rescue, shouting abuses at the mulla at the top of her voice: "What has come over you? What devil has taken possession of you that you are bent upon murdering her?" She then landed a powerful blow to the mulla's back and the mulla let go of his daughter and turned upon his wife. Soon the mulla was pulling at her plaits and she was hanging from his beard.

The racket reached even the neighbors, who came running and demanded of the mulla, "Who has instructed you in molesting a woman? Show us the book that commands that a man beat his wife!" In the end the neighbors intervened between the mulla and his wife, after heaping many rebukes on his head.

The next day being a Friday, the boys had a holiday and they were busy in recreation and play. Amar had an idea, and he went to the haberdasher's shop and said to him, "Your wife is on her death bed, and I have come to inform you at the pleading of your family!" Immediately upon hearing this, the haberdasher rushed home, crying and lamenting and pulling at his beard.

Amar accompanied him a short distance, then retraced his steps to the haberdasher's shop, and said to his apprentice, "Your master has sent for the large box of needles. He has a buyer willing to pay a good price for them. As your master cannot come himself, he sent me in his stead." The apprentice looked at Amar's face and, thinking that he looked truthful, handed Amar the box of needles. Amar headed straight for the academy and riddled the mulla's bed and bedding with the needles, and went home.

As the mulla and his wife had quarreled that day and come to blows, the whole house was in turmoil, and nothing had been cooked. Estranged from his wife, the mulla headed for the academy and spread out his mattress. The moment he set foot on the mattress, needles pricked the soles of his feet. Screaming with pain, the mulla sank onto the mattress. The needles now bore into his rear, piercing him painfully. As he lay down to allay his anguish, his back and stomach were all run through, and he began rolling about in fits of agony and his whole body swelled up like a crocodile's. As the children were away on holiday, there was no one in the academy who could remove the needles from the mulla's body.

When the pupils arrived on Saturday, they found the mulla groaning and rolling on the floor. They began plucking the needles out, and they had a hard time of it with the mulla screaming loudly every time one was removed and becoming inconsolable with pain. Meanwhile, Amar arrived at the academy late on purpose, and called for a litter, and had the mulla carried on it to the surgeon's.

When the litter passed by the haberdasher's shop, the shopkeeper recognized Amar, and came rushing out, saying, "O vile boy! Indeed you are a wanton seditionist! Duping me and sending me home by claiming my wife to be on her last breath, you cheated my apprentice in my name, and made away with the box of needles! But now I have caught you." The mulla pricked up his ears when he heard mention of the needles, and asked the peddler, "When did he make away with your box of needles?"

Realizing that the secret would be out before long, Amar gave them both the slip, and returned to the academy posthaste. Addressing Hamza and Muqbil, he said, "So long, my friends! My time is up as this city has become too small for me!" Hamza could not think of a life separated from his friend. He asked, "What is the matter?" Amar said, "I cannot at present make answer. But I will convey the entire story to your blessed ears when I am a little more composed!"

Hamza said, "Come, take us where you will, as I shall be miserable without you!" Hamza, Muqbil, and other boys who had become attached to Hamza, followed trembling with fear in Amar's train. Amar brought them to a pass in the hills of Abu Qubais where they hid for a night and a day.

After they had gone hungry for a whole day, Hamza said to Amar, "Now we are consumed with hunger and dying of starvation." Amar replied, "Wait and see what wonderful delicacies I shall provide for you in this wasteland!"

Thus having spoken, Amar went into the town, and bought a length of clean intestine from the butcher. Then he headed for the dunghill in the backyard of an old woman's house, where her pullets were pecking. Amar tied a knot on one end of the intestine and threw it on the dunghill. When a pullet swallowed it, Amar blew into the intestine from the other end and it inflated and choked the bird. Then Amar quickly slaughtered it, and wrapped it in a kerchief.

In this manner Amar had caught some fifteen or sixteen pullets, when he began to think of stealing something else. He showered a hail of stones on the old woman's roof and then lay in wait. Frightened by that barrage of stones, the terrified crone rushed out shouting and screaming from the front entrance, and Amar sneaked into her house by the back door. He stole some eggs lying there in a pot, then headed out.

Farther down the road was a kebab shop where Amar had the chickens roasted and a *khagina*[27] made of the eggs. He also bought *shir-maals*[28] and *nihari*.[29] After putting all the food on a tray, Amar asked the kebabist to send a man with him to Khvaja Abdul Muttalib's house, and told him that he would be paid for the food there.

After they had gone a little way, Amar said to the man, "Go ahead and wait for me at Khvaja Abdul Muttalib's guesthouse. I shall be there soon and will pay you for your trouble!" The man headed toward Khvaja Abdul Muttalib's house, and Amar for the hills of Abu Qubais.

When Amar returned to his companions, they marveled greatly at the package of food that he put before them. All his companions fell upon the food.

In the meanwhile, the man sent by the kebabist arrived at Khvaja Abdul Muttalib's house and said, "My master has sent this humble servant to request of you the payment for the *shir-maals* that you had sent for by Amar!" Now, the mulla had already arrived and detailed his woes, and a bewildered Khvaja Abdul Muttalib was listening to the kebabist's man when suddenly crying and wailing was heard, and the old woman presented herself. She petitioned Khvaja Abdul Muttalib: "Oh, poor me! With what treachery Amar deprived me of my chickens and eggs, and in so foul a manner tricked an invalid old widow like myself!"

Khvaja Abdul Muttalib now asked the kebabist's man, "Did you see where Amar went?" He replied, "I saw him heading toward the hills of Abu Qubais."

Khvaja Abdul Muttalib paid him, compensated the old widow, too, and said to the mulla, "I ask that you take the trouble to go to the hills of Abu Qubais with your pupils to apprehend Amar and bring him before me!"

His ill luck drove the mulla to lead his pupils to the hills of Abu Qubais to catch Amar. When they drew near the hilly pass, Amar said to Hamza, "Here comes the mulla with his novices to catch us! They will have Hell to pay for this!" Overhearing this, the mulla stopped in his tracks, but urged Abu Jahal and Abu Sufyan and some others to go forward and capture Amar.

When Abu Jahal and the other boys closed in upon them, Amar cried out, "Do not call this calamity upon your heads! It would be best for you to return in one piece to your folks!" But Abu Jahal mustered his courage and went forward. When he came close, Amar let fly a barrage of pebbles at him with such violence that his whole face was cut and bruised, and the sharp points of the pebbles lacerated Abu Jahal's whole body. Rubbing his eyes and screaming with pain, Abu Jahal turned tail. And when they saw Abu Jahal's state, the other boys dared not take a step forward either.

The mulla, imagining that Amar would give up in terror if he saw him coming, went boldly ahead. But as soon as he drew close, Amar hurled a stone at the man with such savage fury that it broke open his head and a stream of blood came gushing out from his wound. Finding his business done there, the mulla also beat a retreat and headed back to town drenched in blood. He went straight to Khvaja Abdul Muttalib's house and recounted the whole episode, and said, "I have had enough of teaching and educating Amar, as he makes me wonderful recompense for all my pains!"

Upon hearing this, Khvaja Abdul Muttalib himself rode out to the hills of Abu Qubais. Amar recognized Khvaja Abdul Muttalib from far away, and said to Hamza, "I see Khvaja Abdul Muttalib coming. There is no knowing what punishment he will mete out, if he finds me. Now I must go my way!" Arriving at the pass, Khvaja Abdul Muttalib did not find Amar. He sent Muqbil and the other boys to their homes and returned home with Hamza.

Once they were home, he said to Hamza, "Never must you utter Amar's name again! Boys from good homes do not mingle with such vicious liars and cheats. He will earn you a bad name, and sully the honor of your forefathers!"

But when was Hamza ever comforted or consoled without his friend? He began to sob most uncontrollably and did not touch food or drink for seven days. Then Abdul Muttalib panicked. Worried that his son might forfeit his life over a trifle, he was forced to send people to look for Amar and bring him back.

But at the same time, Khvaja Abdul Muttalib also enjoined Hamza, "Never must you follow Amar's bidding, my son! And never again lend your ears to what that rascal says. And remember to adhere strictly to my words!"

Of Amar Leading Hamza into the Neighbor's Garden, and of Amar Stealing Dates and Hamza Pulling Down Three Trees

One day Amar persuaded Hamza to visit the garden. At Amar's incitement, Hamza took him and Muqbil to his garden. From there Amar sneaked into a neighbor's garden. He came back after having his fill of the fruits and said, "My lords! There is such a paradisiacal garden close by, before which the blooming splendor of this garden is reduced to an image of autumn!"

With Muqbil and Amar alongside him, Hamza headed there. When they reached the garden, they found date palms laden with fruit.

Hamza sat down while Amar went around, climbing over the trees and stealing fruit. Presently he returned with his hands and mouth full of dates. Hamza said to him, "Let me have some, too, that I may also taste and enjoy these delicious dates!" Amar replied, "Why must I give you a single fruit, after all the trouble I have undergone in picking them? If you are so consumed with greed, help yourself!"

As Hamza got up to climb the tree, Amar chided him, and said, "Such labors become thin people like your humble servant! Fat people are well advised not to climb trees! If I had a physique like yours, I would have pulled down this tree from its very roots!" Hamza felt the challenge in Amar's words, and he dealt a blow to the tree in his rage. It broke from the base, and came crashing down. Amar said, "What is so great about bringing down a sapling of a tree like this one?"

Upon hearing that, Hamza grew even more furious and pulled out a second tree from its roots. Amar said, "Now, this is what I call a proper tree! However, the real test of strength would be to fell that big, strong, firmly rooted tree over yonder." In his anger Hamza felled that tree as well. At this point, Amar said, "O Arab! Why are you set upon destroying someone else's property? Have you no fear of God?"

Amar then ran to inform the garden's owner. He also called the gardener over, saying to him, "A while ago such a strong storm blew that it brought down three of your trees." The gardener said, "There was hardly enough wind here to stir a leaf, let alone bring down trees!" Amar replied, "Go and see for yourself! Once you are in the garden, you can judge for yourself."

When the gardener went over to investigate, he did find three trees, the pride of his garden, lying on the ground. He began to cry and lament loudly, as the subsistence of his whole family depended on them. Hamza took pity on the gardener, and comforted and consoled him by promising to give him three camels in lieu of the three trees. Beside himself with joy, the gardener blessed Hamza from his heart.

But Amar said to the gardener, "Do not for a moment think that you can dupe boys and trick them into parting with camels! Or do you believe that I would allow you to benefit from this arrangement, and let you have a moment's peace until you have shared the spoils with me." The gardener was frightened out of his wits by Amar's dark and ominous threats, and gave one of the camels to Amar.

Of Hamza, Muqbil, and Amar Becoming Blessed and Acquiring Occult Gifts

The fingers of ancient scribes straddle the provident dark reed, galloping their mount in the sphere of rhetoric, and in this enchanting wise, speed the fleet gray steed of the pen in the domains of the page. One day Hamza was seated with his friends Muqbil and Amar in the vestibule of his mansion, when Hamza noticed a stream of people heading in one direction. Regarding this activity, Hamza said to Amar, "Find out where these people are going in droves!" Amar brought news that there were horses on display in a merchants' caravan. And if Hamza so desired they, too, could join them and view the steeds on show. The three friends set out on foot. Upon arriving there they found horses of fine breeds and one stallion, heavily restrained with chains.

Amar made contact with the horse's owner and asked, "What is this horse's crime that you have chained and fettered him thus?" The merchant replied, "This horse is a great biter, and has all five vices[30] defined in the sharia.[31] Nobody can go near him, let alone mount him. He is fed with the muzzle on, and eats and drinks with much ado!" Amar said, "What senseless talk is this that nobody can mount this horse. Tell me what you wish to wager for someone to ride this horse." The man answered, "If someone could mount this horse and manage him even a few paces I would present him with this horse worth thousands and never ask for a farthing!" Amar returned to Hamza and repeated the terms of the wager to him, inciting him to ride the horse.

Hamza went forth to have the horse saddled and brought to the grounds with its fetters and blinders removed. The unchained beast began to display its vile temper the moment Hamza put his hands on its mane with the intention of mounting him. But Hamza closed in and with one leap seated himself upon the animal's back. Hamza made him amble, then trot, then break into a gallop. As he was a headstrong stallion, no matter how much Hamza tried to rein him in, the beast could not be controlled, and he bolted and ran at a gallop for fifty leagues. Finally, Hamza weighted himself down in the saddle and broke the horse's back in retribution for his wickedness and malevolence. The horse collapsed to his death, and Hamza turned homeward. As he was not used to traveling on foot, the soles of his feet got blistered and imperiled his safe return home. He tried to lift his feet but they failed him. Exhausted, Hamza sat down to rest under a tree.

Presently he espied an approaching rider, his face veiled, leading a parti-colored horse adorned with a jewel-encrusted saddle.

As he drew nearer, the veiled rider greeted Hamza and said to him, "O Hamza! This horse here is the mount of Prophet Ishaq (may the blessings of God be upon him!), and answers to the name of Siyah Qitas. He has properties of the zephyr, and at God's bidding I have brought him to be your mount. I make you my favored one, and pronounce this blessing that no warrior will ever overcome you, and the height of your prestige shall forever remain ascendant over your opponent's. Remove that stone standing on the heap over yonder, and dig into the earth underneath. It will reveal a chest containing the arms and armor of the prophets. You shall find therein an endless array of choice weapons. Decorate yourself with them, and test their mettle when the occasion presents itself!"

Hamza directly removed the stone and doing so discovered such power and force in his limbs that he had never suspected himself of possessing even a fourth part of it. He removed the earth, and upon uncovering the reliquary, found within the vest of Ismail, the helmet of Hud, the chain mail of Daud, the arm guard of Yusuf, the ankle guards of Saleh, the cummerbund and dagger of Rustam, the swords Samsam and Qumqam of Barkhia, the shield of Garshasp, the mace of Sam bin Nariman, the scimitar of Sohrab, and the lance of Nuh. Hamza took them out, and dressed and decorated himself with these arms and armor, pronounced the name of the Almighty, and mounted Siyah Qitas.

The veiled one was gone within the blink of an eye, and had vanished from Hamza's sight. It is recorded that the veiled ancient was none other than the angel Jibrail (may the blessings of God be upon him!). Then Hamza turned the reins of his mount toward Mecca.

Now we turn to Amar, who followed Hamza on foot for ten leagues and did not let up but kept him within sight. When the soles of his feet became as porous as a beehive from acacia thorns, he could carry on no longer, and collapsed unconscious under a tree. As per God's decree, the prophet Khizr reached his side, and offered him words of encouragement and solace. He lifted Amar from where he lay on the ground, and made him his favored one.

Then Khizr declared: "Rise, O Amar! I bless you by the command of Allah, and declare that no one shall outpace you in this world!" With this proclamation, Prophet Khizr vanished. Amar got to his feet and, in order to test the veracity of what Khizr had pronounced, sprinted a short distance. He learned that he could indeed run swifter than the wind itself. He prostrated himself to say thanks to the Almighty, and set out in search of Hamza.

He had gone but a few paces when he saw Hamza coming. Amar marveled greatly at the horse and armor, and said to Hamza, "O Arab! Tell me verily, whom did you waylay to come into this horse and armor?"

Hamza replied, Murdering people is an office best suited to the likes of you! God has ordained that I be blessed by the angel Jibrail! This horse named Siyah Qitas was the mount of the prophet Ishaq, and the arms and armor you see are the belongings of the prophets that are a gift from God!" Amar said, "I would believe your word as true, if your horse would outrace me."

Hamza thought Amar was speaking like a buffoon as was his wont. He said to Amar, "Here! Come show me how you fare alongside my horse."

Hamza spurred on the horse, and Amar, too, set off. They both raced for ten leagues, and remained shoulder to shoulder and head to head. Hamza was amazed at Amar's speed and marveled greatly. Amar then admitted, "Hear this, O Hamza, that I, too, have been blessed by Prophet Khizr and made his favored one!"

———

When Muqbil heard that Hamza and Amar had been blessed and proclaimed favored ones of the angel Jibrail and the prophet Khizr (may God bless their souls), he said in his heart, *Now I cannot possibly hope to prevail alongside these favored personages. It would be best to offer myself into Emperor Naushervan's service and become his courtier. In the emperor's service, all are equals and coevals!*

Engrossed in these fancies, Muqbil set out toward Ctesiphon. He had barely gone some five leagues when he sat down under a tree from exhaustion, and said to himself, *Death is far better a prospect than a life such as mine! It is better to give up my life than to continue in this wretched existence, with neither a farthing for traveling provisions, nor a mount for transport.* Giving in to despair, Muqbil climbed up the tree and tied one end of his cummerbund to a branch. Then making a noose of the other end and putting it around his neck, he let himself go, and his limbs began to flail from suffocation.

The avis of his soul was on the verge of fluttering out of his body and flying heavenward, when there arrived the Lion of God, the Exalted One, *Sahib-e Hal Ata*,[32] the Feller of Khaibar's fort, the Second of the Five Holies.[33] He called out to him, whereupon Muqbil fell to the ground. That holy personage helped him to his feet and, presenting him with a bow and five arrows, proclaimed, "I bless you with the art of archery, and pronounce you peerless and unmatched in this skill."

Muqbil replied, "If someone were to ask me by whom I had been blessed, how must I answer, and make reply?" The Exalted One said to Muqbil, "Say that you have been blessed by the Triumphant Lion of God." Hearing these words Muqbil turned toward Mecca jubilant and happy, carrying his bow and arrows.

Upon learning of Muqbil's adventure, both Hamza and Amar expressed great joy.

Of Hamza Exacting Tribute from the King of Yemen, and of the Fortunate King's Conversion to the Folds of the True Faith

The inkwell's closure is opened by the reed's key, manifesting to the connoisseurs' eyes a treasure store of florid locutions, and the trinket box of the ocean floor is pried open, revealing pearls of eloquence that thus decorate the ears of the listeners. Hamza was into his seventh year when one day he happened by the bazaar in the company of Muqbil and Amar. There they came upon some deputies of Suhail Yemeni, the commander under the king of Yemen, exacting treasury revenues from the shopkeepers by their king's orders. Those shopkeepers who had nothing to give them pleaded with them and made pledges, but those tyrants would not have mercy, and cuffed and buffeted them and used them ill.

Hamza took pity on the victims and asked Amar to tell the deputies to desist, but nobody would listen to a boy. Then Hamza himself went forth, and ordered Amar to tell the shopkeepers not to pay anything, and to seize from the deputies all they had collected. At this command Muqbil and Amar at once confronted the deputies. Thinking of them as mere boys, the deputies tried to disperse them. At this, Hamza severely punished some of the deputies, breaking their arms and legs and cracking open their skulls. They soon turned tail and sought refuge in Suhail Yemeni's pavilion, and recounted to him how a seven-year-old boy[34] interfered with the collection of taxes and charged at them along with two other boys, battering them into this state and confiscating all they had collected.

Even as they were narrating, Hamza arrived astride Siyah Qitas outside Suhail Yemeni's pavilion, flanked by Muqbil on his right and Amar on his left side. Suhail Yemeni came out of his pavilion and addressed Hamza. "Hear, O youth, that I greatly admire your mount and armor.

Waste not a moment and forthwith make a present of them to me, that I may forgive your trespasses and pardon your transgression."

Upon hearing this, Hamza laughed loudly and replied, "Convert first to the True Faith if you value your life. Submit to my allegiance, or else you will grievously lament your ways!" Suhail Yemeni thundered, "What is come over this boy that he utters threats so far beyond his scope! Pull him down from the horse and snatch all his arms and armor!"

At these orders his soldiers surrounded Hamza, and resolved to lay violent hands upon him. Hamza killed some on the spot with a hail of arrows, beat a few more to pulp with his mace, and dispatched some to Hell with his sword. Some others were trampled under the horse's hooves and found in the Erebus of Hell[35] a permanent abode. Then arrows began to fly from Muqbil's bow and claimed many lives.

When Suhail Yemeni regarded thousands of his men lying murdered,[36] he grew livid with rage, and himself came charging at Hamza. Catching hold of his cummerbund, Hamza raised him over his head, and resolved to smash him against the ground. Suhail Yemeni then begged for mercy. At this, Hamza put him gently on the ground, and Suhail Yemeni converted to the True Faith with one thousand of his champion warriors.

Then Muqbil, Amar, and Suhail Yemeni—and the thousand champion warriors who had converted with him—declared Hamza their amir,[37] in tribute to Hamza's ferocity and grandeur.

Upon entering the city Hamza said his prayers of gratefulness to Allah. Then presenting himself before Khvaja Abdul Muttalib, Hamza kissed his feet and narrated how he had battered, routed, and massacred infidels. Khvaja Abdul Muttalib said, "The king of Yemen commands forty thousand fierce mounted troops and hundreds of thousands of foot soldiers. Should he advance against Mecca, drawn here by this incident, the citizens of this city would hold you to blame!"

Hamza replied, "God willing, I shall keep the king of Yemen from attacking Mecca. Indeed, yours truly will himself advance against him and visit his head with a calamity, should he refuse conversion to the True Faith!"

After a few days Amir Hamza took leave of Khvaja Abdul Muttalib and left the city with Muqbil, Amar, and Suhail Yemeni at the head of one thousand mounted warriors.

The first leg of their journey over, Amir Hamza was riding at some distance from his entourage, conversing with Amar, when he beheld a youth of ten or eleven, dressed like a mendicant. He sat with his head on his knees, looking all distracted and distraught. Taking pity on the boy's condition, Hamza expressed a desire to know what had caused him to suffer such a state. When the youth did not answer, Hamza persisted all the more.

Before Hamza's perseverance the youth could not hold and, heaving a cold sigh, he exclaimed, "Hear, O kind friend, that I am afflicted with that pain to which the world offers no cure! A malady of which there is no remedy in this life!"

Hamza said, "There is no malady save death but has a cure in this world!"

In view of Hamza's compassionate indulgence, the youth opened his heart to him and, told his story thus:

"I am the heir to the throne of Maghreb, which is the country and domicile of my fathers, and Sultan Bakht is my name. I have been brought into this terrifying wilderness by my love for Huma-e Tajdar, the daughter of the king of Yemen. It is my passion that has shown me this day in this reduced state. As I could not meet the demands of my beloved, grief-stricken and helpless I have turned my back to the world!"

Hamza replied, "It is neither a difficult undertaking, nor an occasion to despair! One must not take leave of one's senses and despair, becoming derelict after such trivial considerations!

"Anchor your hopes in the bounty of your Lord. Exercise patience and restraint. Renounce this wasteland and accompany me back into civilization. God willing I myself shall bring your wishes to fruition."

That day Amir Hamza camped at that place, and converted Sultan Bakht Maghrebi to the True Faith. The attendants and menials were ordered to wash and clean the prince and exchange his beggarly garb with a princely attire.

After they had gone a long way and traversed many fathoms, Amir Hamza beheld a youth wearing a cap and robe of lion skin seated in their path with a fierce lion tethered by his side. Hamza went forward and asked him, "Who might you be, O youth? And why is that lion chained by your side?" The youth answered, "I am a robber and a highwayman, and my name is Tauq bin Heyran. Whenever someone happens by and when a wayfarer takes this path, I let my lion loose at him. After the lion has killed him, I seize his goods and chattels, while my lion here devours him and feeds on the carcass!"

Amir Hamza said to him, "O youth! Repent from this carnage of the innocent, or you will find yourself a loser in this world and the next. The highwayman replied, "O stranger! Your beauty and graceful airs move me to have pity on you. It would bode well for you to surrender your horse and your arms and accoutrements and peaceably go your way, with my promise of safe conduct!" Amir Hamza said, "What great swagger, and what an impetuous speech! Let loose the lion and behold a little show of my divinely gifted might!"

Immediately the man let the lion loose at him. As the lion leapt at Amir Hamza, he skewered him with his spear and flung him back at the bandit. That man was amazed at Hamza's might, and unsheathed his sword and attacked him. With one blow from the shaft of his spear, Amir Hamza made him bite dust. Then dismounting and catching him by the scruff of his neck, he lifted him over his head and would have gladly crashed him against the ground, when Tauq bin Heyran asked for forbearance, and pleaded for mercy. At this, Amir Hamza gently put him down. Amir Hamza converted him to the True Faith and appointed him the standard-bearer of his army.

When they neared the end of their journey, and the fortress of Yemen lay just five leagues farther, Hamza gave the order to set up camp, and they bivouacked with ease and comfort in a verdant pasture.

Now we return to Munzir Shah, the king of Yemen. Those from Suhail Yemeni's army who had escaped with their lives during their skirmish with Amir Hamza returned to their homeland and narrated all the details of Amir Hamza's battle with Suhail Yemeni. Thereupon Munzir Shah left his son Noman with ten thousand troops to guard the fortress, and himself advanced toward Mecca at the head of thirty thousand mounted troops. But the paths of Munzir Shah and Amir Hamza did not cross, as they had taken separate routes to and from Mecca.

Amir Hamza sent an embassy to Noman with a missive stating that he represented a friend who sought the hand of Huma-e Tajdar, the daughter of the king of Yemen, in marriage. He conveyed to Noman his desire to find out Huma-e Tajdar's terms for marriage, so that he might fulfill them. When Noman communicated Amir Hamza's message to his sister, she said, "Very well! Let the ground be made ready. After routing Hamza at the game of horse-shinty,[38] I shall behead him and spike his head over the fort parapet!" Noman wrote back to Hamza, "We express our deference to your wish. Tomorrow we shall play at horse-shinty, and the mettle of each combatant will be thereby tested. If you should bear the ball away from the field, you shall also bear away the princess. Otherwise, your head shall be spiked at the fort parapet."

Amir Hamza was delighted to hear of a match of horse-shinty. The whole night battle drums pounded, and kettledrums were played in the two camps.

When the kingly sun ascended its heavenly throne, Noman marched to the battlefield at the head of his army, and took position in the field. The august king, Lord of the Auspicious Planetary Conjunction of the Age, the distinguished Amir—to wit, Hamza the Illustrious, also armed himself and mounted Siyah Qitas.

When it was time to seek combat after the battle lines were drawn on both sides, Amir stood opposite Noman bin Munzir Shah. Suddenly, a rider hidden by a green veil and covered from head to heel in a sea of jewels like his steed, leapt onto the battlefield astride his horse, and sauntered into the arena with a stately and graceful air, carrying in his hand the horse-shinty stick. Addressing Amir Hamza, he declared, "Here is the ball and here the field. Show what you have got to offer of your skill!" The moment Amir heard the challenge, he spurred on the charger of the prophet Ishaq. Advancing the ambling stallion into the arena, he declared, "O youth, take heed!"

The opponent's attendants threw the ball into the field, and that veiled youth urged the horse with strong legs, and struck the ball with the stick and bore it away. Amir Hamza took the stick from Amar's hands, and spurred his horse forward. He swung the pole and struck the ball with great precision, displaying his divinely gifted might. When that youth saw the game slipping from his hands, he directly threw back the veil from his face and displayed a luminous aspect, making the whole field resplendent with a damsel's world-ornamenting charm. For it was no other than Huma-e Tajdar.

As Amir sat thunderstruck by her beauty and confounded by this display of the Creator's handiwork, Huma-e Tajdar again nudged the horse and struck the ball. She was on the verge of carrying it away, when Amir steeled his heart and proclaimed, "There is no power or might save in Allah!" Then he urged his horse forward and declared, "I see your fraud and deceit. This explains how you bear the ball away from the field, and how you win the wager to spike men's heads on the fort parapet. I will show you the essence of courage and valor and how the ball is borne away from the field! Behold! Beware! Be warned! Here I take the ball and, with the attendant grace of God, win this game!" He bore away the ball and handed Huma-e Tajdar a resounding defeat.

Then Amir Hamza addressed her thus: "O Huma-e Tajdar! Speak if you have anything to say! Are you satisfied, or do you wish to put yourself to further test?" She replied, "Let us match ourselves once more!" In honor of her request Amir threw the ball once more into the field and, again flourishing the stick, he won the game with his superior speed and skill. Recognizing that she had lost the competition, Huma-e Tajdar sought retreat and spurred her horse to reach her brother Noman and the safety of her camp. Amir Hamza also spurred his horse forward and, catching her by her cummerbund, lifted her up from her saddle and threw her like a ball toward Amar, who fastened her arms with his lasso, and headed toward his camp.

Upon noticing this turn of events, Noman shouted to his soldiers, "Make haste and cut him off."

Upon his call, ten thousand armed troops besieged Amir Hamza and attacked him from all sides. Amir fell upon them and, every which way he lunged, he cleared the field of men and their bodies of their heads.

At his approach that malevolent host scattered away like moss on water's surface. The slain carpeted the battlefield, and villains who had before made bold claims now all meekly laid down their arms. At this point, Noman bin Munzir Shah Yemeni came with his sword raised over Amir's head, and brought down his villainous arm to unleash his vigor. Amir took the blow on his shield, and then plucked Noman clear off his saddle by his cummerbund. Like an intrepid hawk clutching a timid sparrow, he thus gave him into Amar's custody. As the rest took to their heels in terror, the crocodile of the saber continued his attack, also dispatching to Hell those in flight.

Amir Hamza returned glorious and victorious to his pavilion. At night when the revelries began, Amir sent for Noman, and said to him, "Speak your mind and let your tongue unburden your heart!" Noman relented, "It was not given to one among mankind to come before my numerous host of swashbucklers and dagger fighters and escape with his life! I have nothing further to say but that I convert hereby to the True Faith!"

Amir embraced him, and had a seat spread out for him by his side. Then drinks were passed in rounds; Noman became one of the legion of the faithful; and Amar began to croon a festive song.

In the morning, Noman summoned his army and extended to them the invitation to convert to the True Faith. All of them lowered their heads as one in acquiescence. All the commanders of Noman's forces found the ennoblement of the True Faith and were presented before Amir Hamza, who conferred upon every one of them a robe of honor.

When the tidings reached Munzir Shah Yemeni, a blaze of rage flared up in Munzir Shah's breast. Aborting his advance on Mecca, he returned posthaste and, upon his arrival in the fort, sounded the war drums. Amir also ordered kettledrums to be sounded in his camp.

At the crack of dawn the two armies marched into the arena. Munzir Shah sauntered into the arena astride his horse, and bellowed out thus from the ranks of his heathenish horde: "Declare thyself who is Amir Hamza, the commander of the army. Where hides he? Let him show himself and his wits, and display the might and stature he claims as a man. Let him test his mettle with me."

In response, Amir Hamza rode up to him and said, "Why bark so boastfully, and brag thus? In just one stroke, God willing, you shall bite dust. I shall give you the first blow so that all your heart's desires may be realized and they do not die unrequited with you!"

As Munzir Shah aimed his spear, Amir urged his horse alongside Munzir Shah's, wrested the spear from his hands, and threw it over his shoulder after breaking its shaft. Munzir Shah attacked with his sword, but Amir Hamza parried that, too, and grasping him from behind, lifted him off his saddle and snatched his sword from him. He would have dashed Munzir to the ground, but the latter asked for mercy. Amir released him lightly to the ground. Munzir Shah kissed Amir's feet, and converted to the True Faith with all his heart by reciting the Act of Faith.

For a whole month Munzir Shah hosted Amir Hamza. From the first day Munzir Shah began preparations commensurate with his status for the wedding, and in accordance with Hamza's wishes arranged for Huma-e Tajdar to be wedded to Sultan Bakht Maghrebi. Then Bakht Maghrebi pleaded before Hamza, "Huma-e Tajdar is now affianced to me. I will marry her and set up house, God willing, on the day when Your Honor shall celebrate his own nuptials."

Thereupon Amir said their engagement sermon and had the ceremony grandly solemnized. When the festivities ended, Amir Hamza said to Munzir Shah, "Now I shall take my leave and head back home, where my father shall be anxiously awaiting my return." Munzir Shah replied, "I shall be your riding companion." Thus speaking, he appointed his deputy to run the affairs of the state and, along with Noman and thirty thousand fierce grapplers in his train, rode toward Mecca with Amir.

Thus unfolds the account of authentic historiographers and this tale of great import and moment, that Hashsham had turned twelve when he set foot out of doors with lofty aspirations, and heard a great tumult in the marketplace. People told him that collectors sent by Naushervan were exacting taxes, and punishing anyone who offered the least excuse for not promptly submitting the levy. Galled by anger, Hashsham had a few collectors arrested, and banished them from the city after cutting off their ears and noses. Then he proclaimed a ban declaring that no one should pay even a farthing in tribute, and should submit an equivalent amount into Hashsham's coffers instead. He set about enlisting an army, and before long he assembled an intrepid force and marched on Ctesiphon.

The emperor assembled the ministers of state and sought Buzurjmehr's counsel. Buzurjmehr said, "In my judgment it would be improper that your Excellent Highness skirmish with the offender yourself. There is no glory to be gained in vanquishing such a one as he. And should the results be otherwise, your enemies shall have the occasion to say that the Emperor of the Seven Climes was humbled by an abject fellow. Your Highness should depart on a hunting expedition before his ingress, leaving some commander in charge of affairs in Ctesiphon. That way, when that wretch (deserving to be beheaded!) should arrive, he will be accorded such a chastisement that the wind will be taken out of the sails of all, high and low, and they never again will raise their heads from your obedience and vassalage."

The emperor found Buzurjmehr's advice to his liking, and highly commended his well-intentioned counsel. Then deputing the celebrated champion Antar Filgosh with a force of fifty thousand troops to guard

Ctesiphon and rout Hashsham, the emperor took himself to the hunting fields. In a matter of a week or ten days Hashsham bin Alqamah Khaibari descended with forty thousand ruthless troops, besieged the fort, and threatened the populace with his tyranny.

Antar Filgosh proved worth his salt; his hot cannonade did not allow a soul to approach the protection moat, nor a single trooper from the enemy host to advance an inch. One day a thought crossed Antar Filgosh's mind: *I am fortified within, and Hashsham bin Alqamah Khaibari continues his siege of some days. Why not give him combat outside the city walls, rout him speedily, and earn myself renown in the world and receive rank and estate from the emperor!*

Thus resolved, Antar departed from the city with five thousand troops. Upon catching sight of him, Hashsham laughed with contempt, and said, "Death flutters above his head seeking a perch, since he has come forth to skirmish and dares show me his face!" Then urging his rhinoceros alongside Antar's mount, Hashsham said, "Why do you desire the massacre of your troops, and wish to lay down your life!"

Antar answered, "O infidel, perfidious dog! You dared raise the flag of rebellion and dared bite the hand that fed you! Did you not realize that a humble slave of the Emperor of the Seven Concentric Circles could call you to account!" Hashsham replied, "O ignoramus! Take heed! In matters of conquest and statecraft when did anyone ever show any consideration to who is a master and who is his subject and vassal? With this sword I shall claim tribute from your emperor and lay claim to all his lands and treasures soon!"

As Hashsham made this utterance, Antar couched his spear, then thrust it at Hashsham's evil bosom. The point of the spear piercing Hashsham's breast, it exited from the back. But despite receiving this deadly wound, Hashsham yet cleaved Antar in two with his sword, and then attacked his army. Deprived of its commander, Antar's army retreated toward the gates of the city. Hashsham gave them chase with his troops and, following them into Ctesiphon, pillaged the whole city, took seventy thousand prisoners, and secured the crown and the throne. Spending the night in festive revelries, he then set out toward Khaibar with his grandees.

After traversing many leagues, they arrived at a forking path, whence one road led to the Kaaba, and the other toward Khaibar. Hashsham's companions counseled him that having earned victory and triumph this once, he must fight on for benediction, and earn a high laurel by marching further, and razing the Kaaba to the ground. Hashsham's luck now being exhausted, his misfortune thus ordained that these improvident words inveigled him to advance toward Mecca.

This news circulated in Mecca, that Hashsham bin Alqamah Khaibari was headed there, bent upon violating the Kaaba.

That very day Amir Hamza the Renowned arrived triumphant and victorious in Mecca with his intrepid army. Khvaja Abdul Muttalib embraced him with exceeding affection, and then he broke into a cascade of tears.

Amir Hamza cried, "O Father! This is a day for rejoicing. What is the occasion for your grief and sorrow?"

Khvaja replied, "O my illustrious son! The reason I shed tears is that in just a few days we will face a great terror. Hashsham bin Alqamah Khaibari, having ravaged Ctesiphon, is now headed to destroy the Kaaba. As he is a fierce and mighty warrior, I wish to send you off quietly to Abyssinia on some pretext."

Amir responded, "O Father, have no fear that Hashsham will ever set foot in Mecca. I will intercept him outside the city, and dispatch him speedily to Hell." Having spoken thus Amir took short leave of his father. He went to the Kaaba where he offered prayers, with a view to soliciting victory. Then arraying his army, Amir Hamza set out to overtake Hashsham.

After traversing many stretches expeditiously, the scouts brought news that Hashsham's army was encamped two stations away, and his forces were strung out for miles. Upon receiving this news Amir halted and arranged his army. And four hours into the night, Amir chose several thousand soldiers from his army, and advanced to ravage the enemy force.

Before long Amir's troops alighted like an unforeseen calamity at the enemy's camp. Hashsham's troops were thrown into turmoil, and before it was daybreak, ten thousand men of Hashsham's army lay slain.

Hashsham lay sleeping in his tent when cries of "Slay and Slaughter! Slay and Slaughter!" reached his ears, and a cry of "God is Mighty!" rang out. Hashsham immediately awoke from his sleep, and asked his men the cause of all the pandemonium and stir. His people told him that some Arab named Hamza had made a night assault and if the carnage continued a few hours longer, neither man nor beast would be left alive in the army.

Hashsham rode his rhinoceros forthwith into the camp and witnessed his whole army in trepidation and disarray. Just then the kingly orb ascended the throne of the heavens; the night melted away and the day shone bright upon the field.

Riding his rhinoceros into the field, Hashsham regarded Hamza and declared, "O Arab lad! Whose horse and weapons are these that you borrowed to use them as your mainstay to dare challenge me? You showed little regard for your life, indeed. But my compassion is stirred by your youthfulness. Were you to make me the offering of this horse and armor and supplicate my forgiveness for your crime, I should yet forgive your trespass."

Upon hearing this babble Amir could not contain his rage any longer, and bellowed out, "O abject dog (who deserves decapitation!), little do you know who I am, and to which noble house I belong—I am the son of Abdul Muttalib bin Hashim! Has the renown of my sword not reached your ears? Come to your senses, you hellbound dog, and do not commit such reckless words to your tongue! Why do you wish to throw away your life?"

Hashsham raged marvelously upon hearing this speech, and attacked, thrusting the spear he was wielding at Amir's unpolluted breast. With the point of his javelin Amir blocked Hashsham's spear, and then they sparred on with lances. After a hundred thrusts of their spears had been exchanged without injury to either party, Hashsham threw away his spear in vexation and unsheathed his sword to close in and strike Amir. But Amir wrested the sword from his hand and, throwing it to his companions, spoke to Hashsham thus: "You had your chance, now take my blow and watch out for your weapons and mount."

Hashsham covered his head with his shield, but when Amir landed his sword on that refractory's head with the cry of "None but God Alone Is Powerful!" it cleft his shield in two, splitting his steel helm and smashing his cranium into splinters. Carving up his neck, the sword descended through the felt saddle and cleaved the rhinoceros's back.

Thus dispatching Hashsham to Hell, Amir broke into his army flanks and before long heaped up piles of the slain. Many a blackguard then turned tail and fled, and several converted to the True Faith. Amir sanctioned full rights to pillage to his army—with the exception of Naushervan's crown and throne—and set free the prisoners, conferred a robe of honor upon each according to his status, and equipped each of them with a mount and money for the journey. Thereafter, Amir wrote out an epistle to Naushervan, which read:

God's grace accompanied me, and by virtue of Your Eminence's Majesty I dispatched the tyrant Hashsham to the Erebus of Hell, and seventy thousand of your subjects and vassals were freed from his captivity. I hereby send that rebel's head by the agency of Muqbil Vafadar to your illustrious presence, and await orders regarding the restoration of the crown and throne of Kaikaus, whether I must bear them into your presence myself, or entrust them to one designated by Your Royal Highness.

Then charging Muqbil Vafadar with the delivery of Hashsham's head and the letter, Amir Hamza sent him to Naushervan's court, and himself embarked toward Mecca, triumphant and victorious. It is related that after this one time, Amir never again made a night assault.

The Philomel of the pen sings a new story and thus makes the expanse of the leaf a flower bed, narrating that after forty days of absence, when Naushervan returned to Ctesiphon from his hunting expedition, he found the city an image of desolation, and his crown and throne plundered. With moist eyes he said to Buzurjmehr, "Your interpretation of the dream has thus far come true; time alone will tell when the rest shall come true." Buzurjmehr replied, "It is ordained that some hour between today and tomorrow, God willing, your spirits shall revive and there will be reason to celebrate."

Meanwhile, the Sassanids who had survived carnage and enslavement said to Bakhtak, "All our troubles stem from the doings of Buzurjmehr. Had he not inveigled the emperor away from Ctesiphon on a hunting expedition, we would have been spared the terrors Hashsham unleashed upon us. Indeed Buzurjmehr's religious prejudice against us became our undoing. Pray plead our case before the emperor and have justice done to our cause."

While this commotion was rising, Sabir Namdposh Ayyar presented himself before the emperor, and declared how Hashsham was checked in his retreat and killed by Hamza's hand, who had dispatched the head of that villain with his companion and liberated the emperor's subjects.

The emperor became ecstatic upon receiving this delightful intelligence and ordered that all nobles should go forth to welcome Muqbil Vafadar and escort him into his presence with the utmost honor. When Muqbil produced Hamza's epistle, the emperor first read it himself, then handing it to Buzurjmehr, said, "Read it aloud and advertise well its contents."

Thereupon the emperor conferred a most sumptuous robe of honor upon Muqbil Vafadar, and ordered that during the length of his stay in Ctesiphon Muqbil would have the freedom of the court in order to bestow the honor of his daily attendance.

The scribe has recorded that on the day Muqbil presented himself to wait upon the emperor, people witnessed a ringdove perched on a cypress branch[39] in the court of Jamshed,[40] with a black snake curled ringlike around her neck. The informers conveyed these details to the righteous ears of the emperor, who said, "It appears she has come to seek redress. Is there such a clever archer in the assembly whose arrow will not falter, nor fail to pierce the serpent? For it would cause me inexpressible grief if the ringdove were harmed!" No one came forward for this undertaking. Then Muqbil rose from his station, and kissed the foot of the emperor's throne, and then ventured forth having obtained his leave.

Positioning a mirror at the point of a javelin, he appointed a man to hold it steady before the snake's head. The serpent lifted his hood when he saw the image appear in the mirror, and lunged at it, darting his tongue. Finding his chance, Muqbil drew the bow to his ear and let loose death's bird of prey at the bird of the serpent's soul. The arrow lodged itself into the serpent's head, and not a feather of the ringdove was harmed. The serpent fell to the ground, Muqbil withdrew his arrow, and the bird flew away to its nest striking her wings. A spontaneous chorus of "Bravo!" and "Well done!" rose from the assembly. The emperor kissed Muqbil's hands and decorated him with a golden robe of honor.

Then he wrote out the reply to Amir's letter and, along with a robe of honor, entrusted it to Bakhtak to stamp it with the royal seal. Bahman Sakkan and Bahman Hazan were ordered to hasten before Amir Hamza's presence and to present these items with great decorum and esteem. It is reported that the emperor had written the following words in his reply to Hamza:

O Indomitable Champion and Wringer of Rebellious Necks of the World, you showed excellent regard to your status as my protégé and, fighting my foe whose head was filled with the wine of sedition, effaced his existence from the face of the world. I herewith send Bahman Sakkan and Bahman Hazan to you with a robe of honor as a token of my regard. Send with them the crown and the royal assets that you recovered from that villain's possession, and also present yourself at my court without further delay, so that my longing eyes may be brightened by the light of your beauty, and my heart regaled.

But Bakhtak the wretch did not send that note. He changed the sumptuous robe with a shabby one, and wrote out a letter to this effect: "O Arab stripling! Before I was intent on inflicting a wholesale slaughter on the Arab race, and exterminating every single soul among the Banu Hashim, but you performed a deed that regaled my heart. Therefore, I forgive your trespass and send Bahman Sakkan and Bahman Hazan with this robe." Then having included a similar message for Khvaja Abdul Muttalib, Bakhtak sent the emissaries to Mecca.

Of Amir Hamza's Encounter with Aadi Madi-Karib

On the way to Mecca was the fortress of Tang-e Rawahil where tarried the mighty swashbuckler Aadi Madi-Karib. Upon hearing of the rise and exploits of Hashsham bin Alqamah Khaibari, he vacated his residence and, with a force of eighteen thousand men, laid an ambush at the foot of the hills with the intent of devastating and ravaging Hashsham bin Alqamah Khaibari when he should pass by that place. While he lay in wait a scout brought Aadi the news that Hashsham was put to death by one Hamza, who was heading toward the fortress on his way to his homeland, Mecca, with his booty. Upon hearing this news Aadi chose a commander of his fortress as the emissary, and sent him to Hamza's camp with this message:

> I had marked Hashsham as my prey. But you snatched my prey for your own, and my desire thus remains unfulfilled. Therefore I enjoin you to amiably share your booty with me. Then you may carry on safely toward your destination with your share. Otherwise, longing and bitter grief will be your sole inheritance.

Amir Hamza laughed heartily upon receiving this message and, conferring many honors upon the messenger, said to him, "Report this to Aadi after conveying to him my blessings: Should peace be to his liking, he will find me ready to celebrate it with a goblet of wine; but should he desire to venture forth on the path of confrontation he will not find me lagging.

Greatly taken with Hamza's courteous manner, the ambassador carried Aadi the reply to his message. Aadi made preparations for battle upon the receipt of Hamza's message, and the next day rode into the field with eighteen thousand mounted warriors to clarions of war.

Aadi entered the arena in such an impressive array that many a heart sank in Hamza's army. They regarded a giant twenty-one cubits high, with a girth and bulk to match, wonderfully corpulent and of surpassing power and strength. His waist—which may only be called superhuman—measured a full twenty-one yards. When Amar Ayyar laid eyes upon Aadi's form, he said to Hamza, "You put great store in your might, but today the truth will out, and even your teeth will pour sweat!" Amir laughed, and replied, "The One in whom I put store is far more powerful."

Amir Hamza then turned his heart to his Creator in prayer and urged his steed forward until the horses stood touching ear to ear. Immediately thereafter Amir gave such a powerful blow of his shield to the forehead of the enemy's mount that it staggered back some steps. When Aadi saw this show of Hamza's strength, he called out: "O youth! I see that you, too, have a claim on might! Give your name so that a champion of your stature does not die at my hands unsung!"

Amir answered, "Do you not know that the name of a brave man is engraved on the hilt of his sword, on the notch of his bow, and on his arrow's point? Be warned that I am Abul-Ala.[41] Show what power you have—and do not hold back what your arm can deliver!"

Aadi couched his massive mace in his hand, closed in on Hamza, and raising it over Hamza's head with great might, he struck Amir's head with his bludgeon and unleashed wonderful vigor and might.

Amir parried the blow, then said, "Now give another blow, too, so that all your heart's desires are fulfilled. If I survive it, I shall deal one blow in return, whose memory will accompany you all your living days!"

Upon hearing these words Aadi waxed ever more wrathful, and returned the mace to its hold in the saddle. He unsheathed his sword and, locking the stirrups together, made to land a blow on Hamza's head. But Amir laid hold of Aadi's hilt with one hand, and with the other grasped his cummerbund.

As Aadi tried to break loose of Hamza's clasp, Amar approached and said, "O warriors! While you are at each other's throats, your combat takes its toll on your mounts. If you wish to match your might against each other, then dismount and skirmish, and display your vigor and valor to the world!"

Amir Hamza and Aadi broke off their combat, dismounted, and stood facing each other. Aadi then said, "O Hamza! We were both evenly matched in armed combat. Now let us try Maghrebi wrestling,[42] and exert our skill and vigor in this discipline! Whoever is victorious shall command the obedience of the vanquished!"

Amir replied, "I am willing to test and be put to trial!" Amir then sat down cross-legged. Aadi exerted himself mightily, so that sweat coursed from every pore on his skin. Yet he could not move Hamza an inch.

Then Aadi spoke thus: "O Hamza! I exerted myself all I could, now it is your turn to exert yourself." Hardly had Aadi squatted on the ground than Amir in his first attempt lifted Aadi's massive ass above his shoulders. Wheeling him several times around his head, he said, "What do you say now, and what are your intentions?"

Aadi answered, "I shall be faithful to you, and swear allegiance with all my heart!" At this, Hamza set him lightly upon the ground. Aadi kissed Amir's feet and, reciting the Act of Faith, was ennobled in the True Faith. Aadi brought Amir with all his army to the citadel of Tange Rawahil and arranged for a great feast and presented his brothers also into Hamza's service.

When the feasting and the celebration were over, Amir spoke to Aadi thus: "Farewell now, I am headed to my homeland to show my face to my compatriots, and to kiss my dear father's feet!" Aadi replied, "When was I ever such a crapulous glutton that you would be unable to feed me, and would refuse to take me along?" Amir laughed, and replied, "The one who feeds both you and me is the True Provider, even as he is responsible for feeding all his creatures."

Aadi mustered his eighteen thousand troops, and accompanied Hamza.

OF AMIR HAMZA'S ARRIVAL IN MECCA AND HIS RECEIPT OF NAUSHERVAN'S EPISTLE

Sweet-lipped narrators and historians of honeyed discourse report that when Khvaja Abdul Muttalib received the news of Hamza's arrival, he took the nobles of the city with him and went forth to welcome Amir. The meeting of the father and son took place along the way. Amir kissed his father's feet, who in his turn raised him and embraced him to his heart.

Khvaja returned to his house with Hamza, and they reposed in the Hall of Audience.

One day in the course of the conversation Amir chanced to learn that Aadi was Aadiya Bano's son. Amir rejoiced upon discovering that Aadi was his foster brother, and on that very day Amir appointed him the commander in chief of his armies and commander of his vanguard.

Following Amir's directions, Amar said to Aadi, "Let us know what quantity of rations and other victuals you require." Aadi answered, "I just need food enough to keep body and soul together. Inform the Master of the Kitchen, then, that I eat a *nihari* of twenty-one camels in the morning; and in the afternoon the kebabs of twenty-one deer and as many fat-tailed sheep, with twenty-one flagons of grape wine to wash it all down. For dinner I have a fricassee of twenty-one camels and as many deer, fat-tailed sheep, and buffalo; and for the two principal meals, I have by my side a pile of bread made from twenty-one *maunds* of flour. As to the sweetmeats, they are never enough to my liking, but somehow I manage to ward off the pangs of hunger!"

When Amir was informed of Aadi's demands, he said, "Direct the Master of the Kitchen to have twice this amount—neither more, nor less—sent daily to Aadi's camp!"

After several days Amir heard of the arrival of Naushervan's emissaries, and the news that they had brought him a letter and a robe of honor from Naushervan.

Amir Hamza was greatly vexed upon reading the letter they had brought and regarding the shabby robe, and gave himself to disquiet and distress.

The next day when Nature's Table-Layer produced the blazing hot sun from the Heavenly Oven, Khvaja Abdul Muttalib held a feast in honor of Naushervan's emissaries. After the ambassadors had been plied with meat and drink, they handed to Khvaja the letter addressed to him. Upon reading the letter, Hamza bitterly resented his fidelity toward Naushervan.

The appellations of the emissaries, as written in the letter, greatly intrigued those assembled. They misspelled the dot in Bahman Hazan's name, rendering it Bahman Kharan, or Bahman the Ass; and misusing the Arabic letter *kaaf* as written in the Persian convention, spelled Bahman Sakkan's name Bahman Sagan, or Bahman the Cur.

Upon learning of the content of Naushervan's letter, Amar waxed even more furious than Hamza. When food was laid out on the spread, he brought before the assembly two salvers covered with pack cloths, and said, "I have prepared this feast for our two honoured guests!" He then laid the two salvers with great ceremony before the emissaries, and said, "Here is food worthy of your palates!" and undid the pack cloths, producing a salver piled up with grass. Amar put this before Bahman Hazan; and the other one filled with the bones of the dead he put before Bahman Sakkan.

All those assembled were astonished by Amar's deeds, and said, "What is meant by this?" Amar replied, "What other delicacies are fit for the ass and the cur? This is what these creatures crave. I did my utmost to indulge their pleasure!"

The two emissaries could only grind their teeth at Amar with rage, as to say a word against him would have been indecorous. When the meal was over and everyone was well sated, Amar ordered two trays of robes placed before the ambassadors. Then removing the cover from the first, he produced a golden packsaddle and laid it on the back of Bahman the Ass; and producing from the other tray a jewel-studded halter and wrap, he draped them over the shoulders of Bahman the Cur. Unable to restrain themselves any further, the two emissaries drew their daggers, and ran after Amar to savage him. But Tauq bin Heyran wrested the daggers from their hands, and with well-aimed fists knocked them flat on the floor. Confounded by this turn of events, the emissaries escaped with their lives as fast as their feet could carry them.

Amir now wrote a letter to Naushervan, which read:

> Your humble servant received wonderful recompense for whatever service he had rendered you and for all the fidelity that he manifested toward Your Highness. Indeed the services of your faithful merited just such a letter and robe as he got, and the note of disapprobation he received instead of a worthy letter of exaltation!

Along with his epistle, Amir also returned the letter and the robe he had received from Naushervan by the agency of Mehtar[43] Aqiq.

Meanwhile, the two emissaries arrived in Naushervan's court and narrated their woes amid great lamentations, making a great to-do about their treatment. Upon hearing all this Naushervan became vexed, and addressing Buzurjmehr, said, "These Arabs are a most rebellious lot. It is manifest from the emissaries' account that they have embarked upon the path to revolt!"

Buzurjmehr replied, "Your Honor! No one more courteous, civil, courageous, or valiant, generous or polite was ever born in this world than Hamza. There is no one like him in prudence and precocity, in learning and intellect. If the account of the emissaries is true, and not adulterated with calumny, then there must be a good enough reason for it. The true picture of things will emerge before long!"

Even as this conversation was in progress, Muqbil presented himself with Hamza's letter delivered by Aqiq, as well as the note and robe received from Naushervan.

Upon reading Hamza's letter, and discovering the false note and the robe, the emperor raged marvelously, and severely rebuked Bakhtak.

The emperor then wrote out an apology with his own hand, then, handing Khvaja Buzurjmehr this letter and a far costlier and more resplendent robe of honor than before, the emperor bid him send them with Khvaja Buzurg Ummid.

After returning home, at an auspicious moment Khvaja Buzurjmehr constructed a dragon-shaped standard of such subtlety that when the wind entered its mouth and filled its cavity, it resounded thrice with the cry of "O Sahibqiran!" The sound was designed to reach friend and foe alike. Along with this standard, Buzurjmehr also sent Hamza the tent of the prophet Danyal.[44] He also vouchsafed to Buzurg Ummid's care four hundred and forty-four devices of manifold virtues packed inside a costume of trickery meant for Amar.

At a distance of four leagues from Mecca, Buzurg Ummid halted and set up camp. It so happened that that day Amar chanced by those environs during the course of his daily exercises. From the runner's physiognomy, Buzurg Ummid ascertained him to be Amar and called him over. He embraced Amar, and said, "You and I are like brothers. In the name of Allah, stop here and rest a while, as my honorable father has sent you a present in this costume of trickery that I have brought you. Take off your Arabian vestments that you may be decked out in this livery." When Amar took off his clothes, Buzurg Ummid handed them to his companions, and left Amar standing naked. Then Buzurg Ummid said, "Never strip again in vain expectations! Clothed in your nakedness, now resign yourself to the will of God, and remain thus denuded and carefree like a child!"

Hearing this speech Amar became greatly alarmed, and cried abundant tears pleading movingly, "Return my clothes to me, and don't leave me in this disarray." Buzurg Ummid burst out laughing, and said, "O Father of the Racers of the World! You, Amar, will thus consternate many by stripping them naked, and will steal the mantles and robes of many a person. I left you standing naked for a while so that the memory of this humiliation may accompany you on those occasions."

Then Buzurg Ummid sent for the parcel from the wardrobe, and fitted Amar with all the gifts.

Buzurg Ummid also gave Amar a cloak of *ayyari* of vast length and breadth that covered his entire body from head to foot, reticulated like a bird net so that one wrapped in its folds would not feel his breath strangulated and would neither agitate nor suffocate; a pair of shoes decorated with broadcloth tassels, softer than cotton, light, and weightless; and two *hava-mohra*[45] plaited in silken cords for tying around the thighs so that even a thousand mile sprint would not tire out his legs nor would his legs ever falter.

Amar then took his leave of Khvaja Buzurg Ummid and presented himself in this array before Amir, providing him a detailed account of his encounter. Amir rejoiced greatly upon receiving these glad tidings, and rode out to greet Khvaja Buzurg Ummid who received Hamza with affection, and presented the apology and the costly robe that Naushervan had sent for him. Then Buzurg Ummid presented him the dragon-shaped standard and Danyal's tent.

Amir was greatly taken with Buzurg Ummid's ways. He escorted Buzurg Ummid into the city, presenting him before Khvaja Abdul Muttalib and other nobles.

One day Buzurg Ummid said to Amir, "The emperor will be expecting you. It would now be appropriate that you present yourself in Ctesiphon!"

Amir rendered homage to the Kaaba with Buzurg Ummid and, having taken his leave of Khvaja Abdul Muttalib, headed toward Ctesiphon with his companions at the head of thirty thousand sanguinary foe-slayers. They made regular stops on their journey, then setting out again toward their destination, admiring the scenery on land and water.

One day they came upon a forked path, and Amir asked Buzurg Ummid where those roads led. Buzurg Ummid replied, "Both these paths lead to Ctesiphon. The one does not offer any perils, but it takes a longer journey of six months' duration; the other shall bring you to your destination much sooner, but this road has lain forsaken for the past five years as it passes the den of a lion who comes out of the thicket when he catches the scent of man, and deals death to even the hardiest and most intrepid man with just one blow." Then Amir said, "That villainous beast torments God's creatures, therefore it is incumbent upon me to put an end to his mischief!"

And with that, Amir embarked on the perilous road to Ctesiphon, taking only Amar Ayyar along, and sending Buzurg Ummid to Ctesiphon with his companions and army from the safe road, enjoining them to travel expeditiously.

On the afternoon of the second day, Amir Hamza and Khvaja Amar arrived at the reed thicket adjoining the forest and dismounted by a spring. Amir spread his saddlecloth by the spring and sat down to rest. Amar took the horse for grazing. Of a sudden a rustling of leaves was heard in the forest, and the snapping of twigs announced the arrival of a beast. A great lion emerged soon thereafter. Amar, who had never beheld even the clay effigy of a lion, was frightened beyond measure and climbed up a tall tree, and called out, "O Hamza! A great big lion has emerged out of the thicket and is headed toward you! For the sake of God leave your place and take refuge in the branches of some tree!"

Amir laughed heartily upon hearing Amar's words, and said, "O rascal! Why have you become aflutter all of a sudden? I took this path for the sole purpose of exterminating this beast, having separated myself from my army! And now you wish to turn me from my purpose."

Amir pursued the lion and discovered him to be a magnificent beast of terribly ferocious aspect, some forty cubits in length from nose to tail, and a full head taller than an ox. Amir challenged the lion and called to him: "Whither are you fleeing, O jackal-face? Behold here your adversary!"

Upon these words the lion leapt on Hamza, but Amir foiled his charge. Then Amir bellowed "God is Mighty" with such clamor that the whole forest rang out with the cry. Catching hold of the lion by his hind legs, Amir shook him with such violence that the column of the beast's spine was shattered from the impact. Roaring with anguish, the lion soon breathed his last. Then Amar climbed down from his tree and kissed Amir's hands.

The next morning, Amar skinned the beast, cleaned it thoroughly inside, and stuffed it with straw. He made a pedestal with the branches and installed the stuffed lion on it, so that whoever might see it would take it for a live beast. Then Amar hired a laborer to carry the contraption on his back, and accompanied Amir. Amir made frequent stops during his journey. Thus it was that Amir Hamza and Buzurg Ummid arrived at Ctesiphon on the same day. And while Amir went to visit his army, Amar set up the lion at the side of a hillock near the castle's gates.

The gates of the city opened the next morning, and a group of scythemen issued forth to do their day's work on the hillock. By chance, the eyes of one of them alighted on the stuffed lion, and screaming in terror, he began trembling violently and then fell to the ground in a faint. His companions, too, discovered the lion and thereupon ran helter-skelter into the city in a state of great alarm.

A great stir was created in the city by this news, and everyone became aggravated and perturbed. When the emperor heard the news he sought shelter in the royal tower, escorted by his ministers, commanders, and champions. They witnessed that a ferocious lion indeed reposed in a corner of the hillock.

It happened that at that time Muqbil Vafadar was headed to the royal court from his camp outside the city, when arriving near the hillock he saw the lion. He saw no signs of life in the lion when he drew near, and quickly discovered the subterfuge. Immediately it occurred to Muqbil that no one but Amar could have pulled such a prank. He reasoned that Amir Hamza must have taken the path through the dense forest upon hearing of the lion, and once the lion was slain, Amar must have stuffed him and installed him here to play this trick and frighten the people.

Muqbil narrated these thoughts to the emperor. Rejoicing at the news, the Refuge of the World then conferred a robe of honor, precious jewels, and three chests of gold pieces upon Muqbil Vafadar, and said to him, "Go forth and find out where Amir Hamza is camped and send me intelligence at once." Muqbil took his leave of the emperor and headed for the forest path.

Coincidentally, Amar was headed up that path toward the city. Upon recognizing Amar, Muqbil asked him where Amir had pitched his camp. It displeased Amar that Muqbil neither greeted him nor asked of his welfare.

Addressing Muqbil he said, "O pitch-faced one! Did Amir send you here to wait upon the emperor, or to go gallivanting?" Muqbil replied, "O Amar! Have you become crazed that you address me as an equal?" Amar, who was looking for just such an excuse, said with vexation, "O slave of slave stock! The three chests of gold pieces that Naushervan has conferred upon you have so robbed you of your reason that you deem yourself a Khvaja!"

Thereupon, Amar instantly undid the sling from his headdress and produced from his trickster's girdle a carved and chiseled stone and let fly. Blood gushed immediately from Muqbil's forehead.

Muqbil hastened before Amir Hamza's presence in this wounded state, and raised a hue and cry. Amir seethed with rage imagining that the people of Ctesiphon had thus bathed his friend in blood. But when Muqbil blamed Amar, Amir sent for the *ayyar* and said to them both, "What is this that I see? Why do you harbor such malice toward each other?" Amar replied, "Hear me out, too, before you assign the blame." Amir then replied, "Let us hear what you have to offer in your defense!"

Then Amar said, "In an alien land one expects even a stranger to greet him and make him welcome. And in this instance I had met my old companion after a long separation, but he did not greet me, nor did he show the least token of fidelity by dismounting and embracing me. And what was the first word he said? How dare I claim an equal footing with him! Now, I ask that you do justice and redress the wrong he did me."

Upon hearing Amar's address, Amir said to Muqbil, "Indeed the fault is yours that your pride made you keep reserved with Amar. Come now, and embrace each other!"

Muqbil readily stepped forward, but Amar refused, saying, "My lord! He is a man of riches and effects, and I am but a common trickster without any means! Where is the parity between us?" When Muqbil saw that Amar was unwilling to bury the hatchet, he offered him one of the chests of gold pieces, and said, "Now, forgive my wrong and wipe all spite from your heart!" Guided as he was by greed in all things, Amar readily accepted the chest of gold pieces and embraced Muqbil.

When the emperor, heeding Buzurjmehr's counsel, made ready to go forth with his nobles to welcome Amir, Bakhtak incited the Sassanids to persuade the emperor not to go, and they cried that indeed an unhappy hour had descended upon the honor, majesty, and glory of the empire when the Emperor of the Seven Climes should go forth to greet a vulgar Arab lad and confer such prestige and honor on a common vassal and a ward!

Then Khvaja Buzurjmehr said, "Besides the fact that Hamza enjoys the honor of being the emperor's protégé, you are indebted to him, too, for the great favor he showed you, securing the release of your kith and kin from the clutches of the foe. It shows that all of you are utterly shameless, wretchedly ungrateful, and blind to all sense and intelligence!" At Buzurjmehr's words, all conspiratorial babble immediately died out.

Then the emperor had his throne mounted atop four elephants and, escorted by his nobles and ministers, he went forth with great royal splendor to greet Amir. The procession had advanced two leagues when a dark cloud appeared on the horizon. The scissors of the billowing wind cut asunder the veil of dust, and there then appeared on the horizon twenty standards, with a force of thirty thousand mounted warriors marching underneath. Hedged by a body of troops, Amir Hamza was seen riding Siyah Qitas in the shadow of the dragon-shaped standard. To his right rode illustrious kings, and to his left renowned warriors.

When the emperor trained his eyes on Hamza, he beheld a youth of fifteen or sixteen whose cheek was covered with down, and before whose beauty the sun in the heavens was a mere worthless speck. With manifest courage, valor, grandeur, majesty, and glory he rode Siyah Qitas. The powerful and mighty champions in the emperor's cortege, upon beholding this sun of majesty and glory, were thrown into great despondency.

Amir dismounted upon beholding the emperor's throne, and came forward to present himself, kissing the legs of the emperor's throne. Amir Hamza bore on his head the Throne of Kai-Khusrau,[46] which the hellbound Hashsham had plundered from Ctesiphon, and submitted it into the emperor's presence, along with the crown and other regalia of the empire. Amir had borne the throne on his head because when Emperor Kai-Khusrau had vanquished Turan[47] and then occupied Iran, to render homage to the emperor, Rustam bin Zal had walked thirty steps bearing this throne on his head. In like manner Amir showed regard for Nau-shervan by carrying the throne on his head for forty steps—to declare that he was ten times more powerful than Rustam, the Champion Warrior of the World, and the Reigning Lord of the Powers of Time.

Naushervan was mightily pleased by this deed of Amir Hamza, and signaled to his attendants and minions to transfer the burden from Amir's head to their own. Then he himself dismounted and embraced him.

Narrators who illuminate the assembly of discourse, and storytellers
who relate ancient tales, recount that Buzurjmehr then presented Khvaja
Amar Ayyar before the emperor. Amar kissed the emperor's feet and
pressed the emperor's hands, and with wonderful artistry slipped the
signet ring from the emperor's finger, and when he was introduced to
Bakhtak, he quietly slipped the signet ring into Bakhtak's pocket.

The emperor then mounted his steed and, taking Hamza the Lord of
the Auspicious Planetary Conjunction by his side, headed for Ctesiphon.

When the emperor's procession arrived at the city gates, he ordered
that the army of the Lord of the Auspicious Planetary Conjunction
might camp at Tal Shad-Kam.

Then Hamza entered the city gates with the emperor. The whole
populace had turned out to set eyes on the Lord of the Auspicious Planetary Conjunction, and young and old alike were rejoicing because Amir
had secured their freedom and shown them great favor. They arrived in
the royal court accompanied by the companions, counselors, and noble
champions of both groups.

The emperor ordered that the nobles belonging to the True Faith be
seated to the right of his throne, and that the rest take their allotted stations. The emperor then addressed Hamza, saying, "Consider this your
own house, and find a seat for yourself where you will!" Amir said in his
heart, *One must nip evil in the bud! I should set a lasting precedent by finding
myself a station that will not be contested!*

By the throne was a chair inlaid with jewels, which traditionally had
been the seat of Rustam. Amir made obeisance to the emperor and
stepped thither. The moment he lifted the insignial covering of the chair

and made to sit on it, a shaft of grief pierced the hearts of the Sassanids. But they held their tongues, realizing that it would be futile to contest this privilege that day.

At a signal from the emperor, richly adorned, fairy-limbed, and sweet-lipped youths brought goblets of sherbet and offered cups of the rose and sugar concoction. Then the emperor requested Amar to sing.

Producing the prophet Daud's *do-tara*,⁴⁹ Amar began to strum at it, and his music attracted the ears of all assembled, young and old alike. From every corner of the assembly rose cries of "Marvelous!" and "Well done!" Naushervan thought of conferring his signet ring on Amar as a token of royal praise for his gift of song. But finding his finger bereft of the ring, he asked in all surprise, "Who took Our ring? Has it fallen somewhere?"

Amar responded with folded arms, "Your Honor! Except for those present in this assembly, no stranger has set foot here who could be suspected of this infraction. If you allow me, I shall search everyone present and recover the ring by the blessings of Your Honor's glory!"

Then at the emperor's signal, Amar made a pretense of searching people and looking into their pockets. After Amar had finished searching the warriors and commanders, the emperor ordered Buzurjmehr to search all the philosophers and nobles. Following the emperor's orders, Buzurjmehr searched well their robes, girdles, and mantles, and upon Bakhtak's turn, discovered the signet ring in his pocket. Buzurjmehr was greatly surprised and all the nobles bit their fingers in astonishment. And Bakhtak was sunk into the mire of shame.

Then Amar declared with folded arms before the emperor in a loud voice: "*Ayyars* have been known to play such capers, but until today we neither saw or heard of a vizier thieving. Yet now that Bakhtak's example is before us, we can assume that viziers, too, are embezzlers. Indeed he is a worthy grandson of Alqash, and molded in his cast."

Naushervan blazed into a rage against Bakhtak, and heaped rebuke on his head before the whole assembly. Then Amar said, "The just punishment for a thief is to cut off his hands." Bakhtak said in his heart, *Confound this trickster! He clamors to have my hands severed! What retribution he has served me!*

At Buzurjmehr's interceding, Bakhtak's hands were not severed, and the infliction of that punishment was removed from his head. But ever more abuse and defamation was bestowed on him. That very moment Bakhtak was shamed before the court, and thrown out.

After some time had passed, Amir Hamza told the emperor that Bakhtak was innocent of the theft and that it was Amar's roguery. The emperor was astonished at this display of Amar's sleight of hand and, at Amir's intercession, Bakhtak was allowed into the court as before. The emperor conferred the ring on Amar, and was mightily pleased by his sharpness and deceit.

The writing finger of the storyteller shows its might and exerts itself in the arena of the paper in this majestic manner, relating that while Amir returned from the court to Tal Shad-Kam, there arrived a note addressed to Khvaja Amar from Bakhtak. It read:

> I hereby send an offering of five hundred *tomans,* and a promissory note for an equal amount. Other offerings will be made in the future at all suitable occasions in the hope that you shall never again play such jokes on me that threaten to condemn me to grievous insults.

Upon receiving this money and promissory note, Amar rejoiced greatly, and said in his heart, *God be praised that a little fortune has come my way of itself.* Amar wrote out an apology to Bakhtak, and sent with it the receipt for the money and the note.

The next day Amir Hamza presented himself in the court with his companions, and as before seated himself at the same station. The Sassanid nobles prickled with jealousy at this gesture, and schemed to reduce Hamza in the emperor's esteem.

One day Amir Hamza was seated at this spot when a towering youth presented himself before the emperor, clad all in armor. He made an obeisance to the emperor and after he sat down, he regarded Hamza with a sideways glance and submitted to the emperor: "Your Honor sent my father on a campaign to Zabul, and in his absence seated an Arab lad in his chair. Is this fair consideration of my father's estimation in the emperor's eyes? Soon, when my father returns in all triumph, it will be seen how this contumacy bodes for this Arab's merriment!"

Amir could not abide listening to this idle swagger, and said to the emperor, "What is the name and rank of this youth? His words smell of rebelliousness and sedition!" Nausherwan said, "He is Faulad bin Gustham. I sent his father to chastise the rebellious emperor of China, Bahram Gurd, and he will soon return successful from having captured Bahram Gurd. The chair in which you are seated belongs to him."

Amir replied: "I am desirous, then, that his father test his mettle against mine. And may the vanquished then forever pledge obedience to the victor!"

Upon hearing this, Faulad entered a wild rage and said with knitted brow, "O Arab! Wrestle my father later, when you have first wrestled down the hand of his son!" Amir responded, "As you please!" Then Faulad sat alongside Hamza and they interlocked their hands and exerted their strength. Before long Amir wrestled the boy's arm down, and Faulad fell from his seat. Embarrassed beyond measure, he drew his dagger and came rushing at Hamza. When Amir then wrested the dagger from his hands, Prince Hurmuz said to Faulad, "O Faulad! Do you wish to disrupt the royal court? You have been suitably humiliated and yet you remain relentless in your conceit. Take yourself quietly to a seat, and then do not stir or say a word."

Some ten or twelve days had passed when news reached the emperor that Gustham was nearing Ctesiphon, with Emperor of China Bahram Gurd and four thousand of his Uzbek warriors as captives, and had halted four leagues from the city. Now, Bakhtak's heart was full of rancor toward Hamza, and he was always seeking a pretext to abase Amir. The emperor had gone in person to welcome Hamza, and this fact rankled Bakhtak's heart and he resolved to use the precedent to Gustham's advantage.

In short, Bakhtak managed to prevail upon the emperor to ride out and welcome Gustham, and Bakhtak, too, went riding alongside. On the way Buzurjmehr said to the emperor, "Amir Hamza must needs ride in the royal cortege, too, as the escort of such a noble, valorous, and renowned champion would augment the prestige of Your Highness's retinue no end!" The emperor immediately sent word to Hamza's camp.

The emperor's procession had gone a league outside the city when they saw Gustham bin Ashk Zarrin Kafsh approach, clad in mail and armor, twirling his whiskers, and riding a rhinoceros under the shadow of a wolf-shaped standard.

Upon coming close, Gustham dismounted, kissed the leg of the royal throne, and with great eloquence narrated the account of his bravery in taking captive Bahram Gurd and of the skirmishes of the battle. The emperor then made a gratuitous prostration to his one hundred and seventy-five gods, and turned back toward the city. But Gustham lagged behind at a sign from Bakhtak. On his return the emperor crossed paths with Hamza and said to him, "Go forth and meet Gustham, and please yourself for a while listening to his adventures!"

Now we turn to Bakhtak, who bitterly complained to Gustham about Amir, and said, "Besides committing other misdemeanors that Arab lad had such pride and haughtiness in his valor that he committed the grave disrespect of couching himself in your chair. Then he grossly humiliated and disgraced Faulad before the whole court. But God be thanked that now you are finally here! When embracing him, press him in your grasp so that all his bones are set out of joint and he learns to reckon with your strength, and does not commit any further acts of pride and contumacy in your presence." Gustham replied, "I shall see to it!"

In the meanwhile Amir's party arrived. As he embraced Amir, Gustham pressed him with his arms for all he was worth, offering him sweet words of welcome expressing his pleasure and delight. Amir returned his compliments and pressed him back so powerfully that Gustham's rear trumpeted many a note from an abundant release of wind. Greatly confounded by this mishap, Gustham whispered in Amir's ear, "O Amir! I trust to your chivalry never to breathe word of this to anyone. Let that forever remain a secret between us!" Amir said, "Have no fear in this regard."

Then Gustham returned to the fort with his army in train, and Amir occupied himself with admiring the scenery with his friends. Amir noticed a chest being brought forward, heavily secured with chains, with four thousand menacing troops marching in the rear. When he inquired of the guards about the contents of the chest, they replied, "Within is enclosed Bahram Gurd, the emperor of China, whose chivalry and valor are famous to the whole world!" Amir exclaimed, "Who has ever heard of champions and kings transporting a prisoner in this manner?"

He ordered the chest put on the ground, and when his attendants opened it they beheld within a beautiful youth wrapped in chains and lying in a faint. Amir had him taken out of the chest, released him from his prison.

When the youth regained consciousness, Amir asked him, "Who might you be, O brave one?" He replied, "I shall give a detailed account once I have reached your camp. At present my strength fails me from speaking a single word." Amir forthwith provided a horse for him and released his imprisoned men, and brought them all with great honor to his camp.

When Bahram Gurd regained the command of his faculties, he said to Amir, "Your auspicious aspect betokens nobility and majesty. I request that you tell your pedigree and lineage and satisfy me regarding the title and station of the one whose hand warded off certain death from my head. Many a day I lay entombed in that coffin without food or drink, and had all but resigned myself to death when God put my destiny in your path and showed me this happy day!"

When Amir had satisfied Bahram regarding his particulars, Bahram rejoiced exceedingly and exclaimed, "Oh, happy hour! That I incurred a debt of gratitude toward one peerless in the Seven Climes!" Then Amir asked him, "O Bahram, how did Gustham manage to overwhelm you?"

Bahram replied, "After I had overpowered him in the battle, ravaged and destroyed his army, and taken him prisoner, he vowed fidelity to me, and for four whole years he remained constant in his devotion and servitude. On a hunt one day, I rode far away from my army and, as I was dying of thirst, I asked him for some water. He found the opportunity to drug it, and offered it to me. When I fell unconscious, he sent for his companions and abettors in my army, who had until now kept up the pretense of loyalty to me. They put me in irons, shut me in that chest, and inflicted all manner of torture and suffering upon me!"

Upon hearing this, Amir Hamza offered Bahram Gurd many words of consolation and solace.

When the news reached Gustham, he hurried before the emperor with rage blazing in his breast and detailed the whole episode to him. The emperor was also greatly vexed upon hearing Hamza's conduct in this matter, and forthwith sent for him, and said to Amir, "O Abul-Ala! You knew well that in the Seven Climes I have no greater enemy than Bahram Gurd, yet you showed no regard for this consideration. Why did you grant him his freedom?"

Amir said, "Your Majesty being the Emperor of the Seven Concentric Circles, if champions and brave men are to be taken captive by wile in your time, there will be no stopping people from uttering inauspicious words about you. History will bear witness and to all eternity it will be mentioned in the assembly of Kings that Naushervan was such a coward that champions were subdued with guile in his reign—and that his retainers and ministers and warriors were ever skillful with the weapons of chicanery and fraud! When was Bahram Gurd ever such a mighty champion that he could not have been subdued in fair combat or prevailed against and vanquished by a valiant warrior?"

Hearing this the emperor said, "Where is Bahram Gurd? Send for him forthwith and bring him into my presence so that I may verify the circumstances of his capture and hear his account with my own ears!"

Amir had left Bahram in Naushervan's antechamber and immediately sent for him. Addressing Bahram, the emperor asked, "Did Gustham take you prisoner in the traditions of valor, or were you captured and imprisoned by treachery?" Bahram replied, "Your Honor will judge the facts with your own eyes, and will weigh the veracity of my account when I say that I have been kept on starvation rations for four months and have been denied food and water until today. If Amir was any later in securing my release from those confines, that chest would have served me for a bier. But were I to encounter Gustham even in these reduced circumstances, I could still wrest the sword from his hand, or else I should gladly forfeit my head to the executioner's sword!"

Gustham was present in the court with the Sassanid army. The emperor turned to him and said, "Do you hear what he states?" Embarrassed, Gustham hung his head and made no reply for his shame. The emperor then said to Bahram, "Would you be ready to wrestle with Hamza?" Bahram answered, "Most willingly! Once I have proclaimed myself a champion, I cannot disregard a challenge."

Then Amir said to the emperor, "O Guide of the World! At the moment he lacks any real vigor and strength. But were he to be plied with nourishment for forty days, it would afford some joy to see a display of his strength against mine."

The emperor highly commended Hamza's suggestion and said, "O Hamza, I trust Bahram to your care. You may then wrestle together and we shall judge the power and skill of both of you!"

Amir returned safe and happy to his camp with Bahram, and fed him on choice food for forty days. On the forty-first day, with Bahram alongside, Amir presented himself before the emperor, and said, "I am ready now to be matched with Bahram, as he is now well nourished and restored to his previous strength."

Both Amir and Bahram clad themselves in loincloths and caps of lion skin and girded themselves. Striking their arms with their hands in challenging postures, they were soon locked in combat.

Clasping each other's necks, they butted so mightily that a mound of steel would have turned to powder from the impact, but neither one even shed a hair. For a full three hours they wrestled together, without either having any success in lifting the other over the shoulder, to say nothing of stretching the adversary on his back.

Finally, Amir yelled out "God is Mighty!" and lifted Bahram over his head. Bahram cried, "O Amir! You are clearly endowed with a might that is divinely gifted. I surrender and vow submission."

Amir set Bahram lightly on ground. Then Amir said to Bahram, "Now, O Bahram, enter into the folds of the emperor's service, and ennoble yourself with the prestige found in his servitude." Bahram replied, "I shall never commit myself to anyone's service save yours!" The emperor said to Hamza, "To be admitted into your service is the same as to be brought into Ours!" He then conferred robes of honor on both Amir Hamza and Bahram.

———

Now to the Sassanids, who in Bakhtak's company went to visit Gustham, lamenting and clamoring for redress. They related how the emperor conferred increasing honors upon Hamza, and how with every passing hour their esteem and worth diminished as a result.

Gustham said to them, "Nobody can best Hamza in strength. But soon I will work a stratagem in the guise of amity and concord, and will put paid to Hamza and erase all vestiges of his name from this land!" The next morning Gustham rode out to present himself before Amir, and ingratiated himself with great deeds of flattery. That day they both rode side-by-side to the court, with many words of conciliation and friendship exchanged between them.

When the court adjourned, and Amir left the palace to return to his pavilion, Gustham was on hand to escort him to his camp. Gustham presented himself before Amir twice a day, performing new feats of fawning and cringing, and outdoing himself in his avowals of fidelity and servitude. Slowly Amir developed a fondness for Gustham, and all traces of his former spite were cleansed from his heart.

It was the emperor's routine to hold court for one week, and spend the next carousing with moonfaced beauties. When the emperor next retired to attend to his private commerce, Gustham announced to Amir, "We have leisure this week. It would be a great boon to your orderly if you would deem it proper to set foot in his garden and spend this week there in feasting and revelry!"

Amir took Bahram Gurd and Muqbil and a few other associates, and arrived in all happiness and joy at the garden gates.

Gustham had spread out a floor covering of satin, brocade, and gold tissue from the gates of the garden to the summerhouse. Amir was greatly pleased with Gustham's exertions, and praised his fine taste to his companions. Fresh and dried fruits were put before them, and then Gustham sent for the silver-limbed cupbearers, and they began to drink in rounds.

Before Amir's arrival, he had secreted away four hundred trusted intrepid warriors, with instructions that when he clapped his hands thrice they must come in force, and with relentless swords fall upon Hamza and all his sympathizers.

In short, when Gustham saw the night spread its dark shades, and Amir and his companions had become befuddled and robbed of their senses by drink, he stepped into the corridor of the summerhouse and struck his hands in succession three times. His accomplices emerged from their hideout and followed Gustham's lead to where Hamza and his companions lay in the summerhouse.

Gustham looked squarely into Hamza's eyes, and spoke thus: "O Arab lad! You displayed great rebelliousness, and deemed the nobles of the empire insignificant and worthless! Now behold the death that stands above your head!" He closed in, and dealt Amir a blow from his sword. Although Bahram was himself addled by drink, he threw himself on Hamza to act as his shield. Gustham's blow was thwarted and it landed on Bahram's back, cutting him open from back to front. The wound caused his intestines to fall out from his abdomen.

Muqbil had been prudent and had imbibed very little wine, and when he saw these events unfold before him, he secured his bow and arrows without further delay. He unleashed a hail of shots, riddling so many bodies with shafts that he brought down one hundred-odd men, and heaps of the slain were piled up in the garden. Gustham escaped with his companions, mistakenly believing that he had killed Hamza.

Upon regaining his senses, Amir Hamza saw Bahram lying on the ground and groaning with his stomach slit open, and more than a hundred men scattered around stuck with shafts. Upon inquiring of Muqbil, Amir discovered that all of this was the doing of the redoubtable Gustham.

The emperor became inconsolable with grief upon hearing the news and sent the crown prince Hurmuz, along with Buzurjmehr and Bakhtak, to attend to Hamza and administer him aid and relief; with the promise of rich reward, he dispatched Alqamah Satoor-Dast at the head of three thousand troops to arrest Gustham. Gustham absconded from the city in great disarray.

Hurmuz, Buzurjmehr, and Bakhtak prostrated themselves in gratitude upon finding Hamza intact, and expressed great remorse at Bahram's injury. Amir said to Buzurjmehr, "You are a learned physician. Make haste to attend to Bahram's wound, and cure my cherished friend. For mark well that should Bahram die (perish the thought!), I vow by Holy Mecca that I will put every last Sassanid to the sword!" When Buzurjmehr investigated Bahram's wicked wound, he was thrown into a great doubt, and was brought to his wits' end by anxiety and dread.

In the meanwhile there arrived Khvaja Amar bin Umayya Zamiri, who narrated to Hamza the joyous news of Khvaja Abdul Muttalib's welfare. But when Amar beheld Bahram's state, he shed many a tear, and said to Amir, "O Lord of the Auspicious Planetary Conjunction, is this the treatment one metes out to his associates?" Amir replied, "O Amar! This is not the time or the occasion to make injunctions or to revile and reproach me with these thinly veiled words!"

Amar turned to Khvaja Buzurjmehr and said, "What do you suggest, as you are by the grace of God the most learned of physicians?" Buzurjmehr replied, "The wound is grave and past all art and modes of surgery. It could not be stitched up without the intestines first being returned inside and restored to their place; but to return them to the stomach cavity will be the devil's own work! The viscera are a most delicate affair, and just touching the artery of the heart would kill him—then nothing whatsoever could save him! And it is well-nigh impossible to stitch up the wound without handling the viscera!" Amar said, "Indeed Khvaja! You are a great, astute physician! Yet truth be told the province of medicine is a most abstruse domain, and none may claim command over it."

And having thus spoken, Amar produced a razor from his pocket and, pressing Bahram between his legs, reached for his gut. Khvaja Buzurjmehr asked Amar, "What is your intention?" Amar replied, "With a nimble hand I will first crop the intestines that are protruding out, so that they may be used to sew up the wound. Then I will apply a salve and make him well." Confounded beyond belief, Buzurjmehr cried out, "What is this disastrous course that you have embarked on? Do you wish to do away with this miserable man?"

Bahram was mortified by Amar's speech, and lost all hope for his life. He heaved such a deep sigh of resignation that it caused his viscera to return to the cavity of his abdomen. Then Amar said to Khvaja, "There you have it! The problem stands resolved. Now apply the sutures and sew up the wound." Buzurjmehr commended Amar highly for his judgment, and all those present broke into fits of laughter and praised the clever stratagem employed by Amar.

Buzurjmehr sutured Bahram's wound, and ordered that he be plied with sherbet so that the corrupted blood could be purged and all other contaminated matter expelled. Khvaja Buzurjmehr, Crown Prince Hurmuz, and Bakhtak then took leave of Amir and retired.

When Buzurjmehr detailed all these events to the emperor, he responded, "Khvaja! There is no dwelling more sumptuous in Ctesiphon than the Bagh-e Bedad. I wish to invite Hamza to stay there for some days, and make him the recipient of my best hospitality. For he might think ill of me, imagining that Gustham committed this pusillanimous, dastardly act at my behest.

When Buzurjmehr went to see Bahram again, he said to Amir, "The emperor offers many thanks that you escaped unhurt from the hands of that villain. He sends the message that it would afford him great delight if he could have your company for a weeklong sojourn at Bagh-e Bedad. However, Bakhtak and Amar must be excluded from the company, as they are both the very essence of knavery, and their hearts are bitter toward each other!" Amir acquiesced and accepted the wishes of the emperor.

Amir brought Muqbil Vafadar and Aadi along, and presented himself before the emperor.

Amir Hamza sat to the emperor's right, and Buzurjmehr and the other commanders took their stations to the emperor's left. Then musicians of alluring art and singers of enchanting voice appeared, regaling and rejoicing this reveling assembly.

———

Now a few words about the yearning of the Lord of the Cunning Ones, Khvaja Amar Ayyar. When Amar did not see Hamza for a whole night and day, he set out worriedly, and his search and curiosity brought him to the gates of Bagh-e Bedad. There he found Aadi installed in a sumptuous chair, guzzling wine, with attendants at regular intervals plying him with delicacies. Amar began to inquire among his friends and companions as to why Aadi was keeping watch outside, while Amir was occupied within. Someone told him that the emperor had ordered Amar and Bakhtak to be kept out of the garden and that this was the reason why Aadi was deployed there.

Then Amar went forward and, after greeting Aadi, took a seat next to him. Aadi said, "O Khvaja! How did you happen to come here?" Amar replied, "I bought a ruby today, and I believe I made an excellent bargain! But you take a look at it, and assure me that I was not duped." Greatly flattered, Aadi puffed up with happiness thinking that Amar considered him a connoisseur of jewels. He said, "Khvaja, no jeweler in the world could claim your astute judgment. But allow me, in obedience to your wishes, to have a look at it." Amar put his hand in his pocket, took out a handful of earth, and shoved it into Aadi's eyes. Aadi began rubbing his eyes, crying, "Confound you, Amar, you have blinded me!"

All those around them worriedly turned to attend to Aadi. In one leap Amar got inside the garden, and reached the courtyard. When Aadi washed his eyes and cleared them of dirt, he asked those about him where they had seen Amar go. But when nobody could tell him where Amar had disappeared to, Aadi thought that Amar had run away for fear of him.

Amar sauntered off toward the palace where the emperor and Amir were assembled and sat under the tree, and, strumming, began a prelude on his *do-tara*.

When the voice reached Hamza, he said to Muqbil Vafadar, "I believe that I hear Amar singing, and my ears recognize the strumming of his *do-tara*! How did he gain entrance since I had enjoined Aadi not to let Amar set foot in the garden? Go and bring Aadi before me forthwith!" When the emperor noticed Hamza's discomfiture, he said, "Do not send for Aadi as I exonerate Amar! But instead send for Amar by the mace bearer, and invite him here to join us!"

When the mace bearer called on Amar, he answered, "In such august company where the emperor and Amir preside, there is no place for a common, worthless *ayyar* like myself!"

The mace bearer returned alone and narrated Amar Ayyar's speech to the emperor. The emperor then stepped out of the palace holding Amir's hand, and they made their way to where Amar sat singing. When Amar saw them coming toward him, he made a leap and fell before the emperor, kissing his feet, and said, "I never once imagined that Your Highness, too, would consider my person as a nuisance and would forbid my presence! As to Hamza, his singular devotion and faithfulness to his friends is amply manifest in the fact that he indulges in feasting by himself, and in no time forsakes old friends in pursuit of the least pleasure!" The emperor laughed at this speech and, leading Amar by the hand, brought him to the Qasr-e Firoza-Nigar. When he was seated on the throne, the emperor ordered Amar to be the cupbearer.

Now a few words regarding Bakhtak, that listeners may be afforded some mirth.

———

When Bakhtak heard that Amar had found his way into Bagh-e Bedad, he was greatly chafed and vexed. Bakhtak left for the garden, carrying with him salvers laden with bales of velvet, brocade, and gold-worked satin, and arrived at the gates of Bagh-e Bedad, where he greeted Aadi with a great show and avowal of friendship.

At this, Aadi said to him, "Where are you headed and what has brought you here?" Bakhtak replied, "I have brought some gifts for you, and I will be forever indebted, if you would accept these tokens of my gratitude and allow me into the garden!" At these words Aadi flew into a rage, and with great anger exclaimed, "O Bakhtak, did you think me a bribe taker, that you could gain admittance to the garden by thus luring me? If you do not wish to be publicly chastised, you would do well to take yourself from my presence!"

Thwarted and downcast, Bakhtak returned home and bided his day in weeping and gnashing his teeth. But come evening, he donned a felt mantle and, carrying his clothes under his arm in a bundle, arrived under the walls of Bagh-e Bedad after giving the slip to the guards. There, he threw the bundle over the wall into the garden, and made himself ready to enter by way of the sewer.

Now, Khvaja Amar was performing the services of cupbearer in the Qasr-e Zarrin by order of the emperor, filling up the crystal goblets with crimson wine, when all of a sudden the notion that some roguery was afoot took powerful hold of him. He said in his heart, *Gustham, too, had arranged a similar feast in Hamza's honor, and for all appearances showed him similar hospitality and warm indulgence. I must go investigate and sniff around, lest some mischief should stir as before and some devilry be enacted!*

On the pretext of going to the toilet, Amar stepped out of the Qasr-e Zarrin and arrived near the gates of the garden, where at that very moment Aadi was telling someone, "Bakhtak came today to bribe me, taking me for one as unfaithful as his own grandfather, Alqash!" Amar started upon hearing these words, thinking that if Bakhtak had approached Aadi with that intention, he would certainly attempt to get inside the garden by all means fair or foul. Then Amar applied himself to examining every promenade and grove, in order to find some sign of Bakhtak's entry.

Suddenly Amar caught sight of the bundle lying under the garden wall heavy with robe and regalia. He hid the bundle in a nook under some leaves, and then sought the place where Bakhtak would stage his entry. Amar's eyes fell on the sewer and when he looked closely he saw a man's head emerge from the hole and withdraw after looking around here and there. Amar decided that it could be no one but Bakhtak.

Amar hurried to Khvaja Alaf Posh, who was the chief garden keeper, and said to him, "A thief is about to break into the garden by way of the sewer! When I heard him stirring I came to alert you. Now it is up to you and your sense of duty to decide what to do."

Khvaja Alaf Posh became duly alarmed and bandied together some gardeners. Armed with mattocks they took up positions at the sewer by the garden wall. The moment Bakhtak crept out, the gardeners fell upon him and tied him up in no time. Although Bakhtak shouted, "I am Bakhtak!" they paid absolutely no heed to his declarations, and began beating him after suspending him from the branch of a tree.

When Bakhtak had been beaten to a pulp, Amar called out to ask Khvaja Alaf Posh, "What is all this noise that I hear, Khvaja Alaf Posh?" Khvaja Alaf Posh replied, "We have caught a thief, and tied him to a tree."

When Bakhtak heard Amar's voice, he called out to him, addressing Amar in the language of *ayyars*. "O Khvaja Amar! In God's name, release me from the clutches of these ruffians. I shall remain indebted to you all my life for this!"

Amar then spoke to Khvaja Alaf Posh and interceded on Bakhtak's behalf, telling him that this man was indeed Bakhtak the emperor's vizier. When he asked Alaf Posh to release Bakhtak he accosted Amar in a thousand ways, and said, "O Khvaja Amar, what is this that you propose? Why would Bakhtak call such a calamity on his head when he is a close associate of the emperor? And should the real Bakhtak himself be caught in this manner, we would not let go of him either."

Amar then returned into the emperor's presence to resume his duties, and remained occupied thus for the course of the night.

When day broke, Amar declared before the emperor, "There is a spicy gale and the air is sweetened by the zephyr. The dawn is breaking and it is a fit time to promenade in the garden."

Thus was the emperor inveigled, and leading Hamza by the hand, he headed to the flower garden for a jaunt, with his attendants in the train. Amar led the emperor to the place where Bakhtak was tied up against the tree, naked as the day when he emerged from his mother's womb. Bakhtak raised a hue and cry when he saw the emperor and began to shout, "O my guide and mentor! I was brought to this state at the hands of the gardeners!" Then Khvaja Alaf Posh presented himself before the emperor and admitted, "Your Honor! Last night this thief tried to break into the garden by way of the sewer. When we thrashed him he made claims to be Your Honor's vizier, Bakhtak!" When the emperor and Amir Hamza looked closely, they discovered that it was indeed Bakhtak who was tied to the tree.

Then Amar stepped forward and said, "Bakhtak is most astute and discerning. Why in the world would he take it into his head to break into the garden and invite this calamity on his head? In all likelihood it is some demon who has come in Bakhtak's guise and now enthralls Your Honor with this prank." Beholding Bakhtak in this state, the emperor blossomed into laughter, and those in his retinue split their sides laughing.

After Amar had spoken and the emperor made to move onward with his stroll, Hamza determined in his heart that the episode bespoke Amar's hand. He pleaded for Bakhtak's release and delivered him from that unforeseen scourge.

The emperor then headed for Bagh-e Hasht Bahisht, which was situated in the center of Bagh-e Bedad, set like a precious stone in a ring.

In this manner, the emperor conducted Hamza into a new palace every day and regaled him there in numerous ways with feasting and revelry. When it was morning again, the emperor removed himself to Qasr-e Chahal Sutoon. As the emperor had not closed his eyes even for a moment for the past five days and nights, he was overtaken by sleep, and Amir stepped out of the palace to retrieve a change of livery, accompanied by his associates and attendants.

During their stroll, they came upon a stream in a corner of the garden, where Amir occupied himself with bathing.

It so happened that at that time Princess Mehr-Nigar, the daughter of Naushervan the Just, was looking out the window from the palace roof.

When she laid eyes on Hamza, the shaft of Amir's love pierced her heart, and she fell into a swoon. Thus love-struck, she said in her heart, *Those arched eyebrows have shot my heart with love's arrow. It would be a fitting response to give him a taste of his own medicine.* She took the *ambarcha*[50] from her neck and threw it at Amir. It fell on Amir's shoulders, and upon looking upward, he beheld the handiwork of the Perfect Artist. Presently Amir was overwhelmed and he fell on his back in the water. Muqbil jumped in to rescue him and helped him out of the water in his arms.

Then Amir heaved such a soul-searing sigh that his garden of pleasure was set ablaze, the flames of love conflagrated his heart, and tears of longing began to issue forth from his eyes. And he began reciting love verses.

At this, Muqbil counseled Amir, "Now is not the hour to become derelict or cultivate the familiarity further! You must change into your new livery and return to the assembly!"

Acting on Muqbil's advice, Amir changed and returned to Qasr-e Chahal Sutoon. But his senses were in confusion. And likewise Princess Mehr-Nigar was in no better state. Her nannies, domestics, and female attendants surrounded her. The princess stopped partaking of all food and drink, and her eyes were robbed of sleep. When she recovered and realized that her secret might leak out and her passion compromise her, she said to her attendants, "Do not give yourself to disquiet, as it was a momentary giddiness that overtook me. Stop all this rumpus and speaking, and allay your anxiety!"

Amir Hamza, meanwhile, bided his time by vacantly staring about and waiting for the day to come to a close, so that he might find some remedy for his disconsolate heart, and the pangs of his yearning might be softened by the prospect of the evening drawing nigh. He passed his day somehow, and restrained himself until the evening hour, but then his restive heart prevailed upon him to say to the emperor, "If I may be granted leave, I would take some rest and remove myself to a garden nook for a little repose!" The emperor replied, "By all means!"

Then Amir stepped out with Muqbil and arrived under Mehr-Nigar's lattice window, but he found no foothold there save a great tall tree that stood by the palace wall, its canopy spread over the palace roof and touching the coping. Amir left Muqbil standing under the tree and climbed up himself.

OF AMIR HAMZA'S FIRST TRYST WITH THE APOGEE OF ELEGANCE, PRINCESS MEHR-NIGAR

The melancholic pen fathoms the affliction of lovers and discerns the humors of those languishing in parting; and with the tip of its tongue the love-stricken reed records the history of yearning and desire, and narrates this tale of separation and meeting thus: Hamza saw from the palace roof that Mehr-Nigar sat with a cluster of her moonfaced and fairy-limbed companions, with a flagon of crimson wine placed before her, and a full crystal goblet held in her hand.

But pearls of tears rolled down ceaselessly from the tips of her eyelashes onto the skirts of her dress. The fire of love blazed in the chafing dish of her bosom; cold sighs abundantly issued from her lips.

That morning Amir had beheld her from afar. When he regarded her now in proximity, he witnessed that the resplendent sun confessed its inferiority before her beauty; and the luminous moon borrowed its radiance from a single ray emanated by her dazzling aspect.

Amir's senses fled when he beheld Mehr-Nigar's ravishing beauty, and in his heart the flames of love raged ever more furiously. Princess Mehr-Nigar, too, was counseled by her companions and confidantes, who did all they could to bring solace to her heart. They would say, "Who is to know what further ruin these lamentations would invoke? Become not derelict. Show some restraint, and control your passion! The one after whom you long so violently has also regarded you, and separation from you indeed will never give him peace! He will contrive some way to see you, and find a ruse to obtain a tryst with you."

At long last all those many counselors prevailed, and Princess Mehr-Nigar ceased her crying. Then Fitna Bano, the daughter of Princess Mehr-Nigar's nanny, handed her a goblet of wine to drink.

The princess said, "I shall drink in a little while, after all of you have sipped first and made toasts to the ones who have captured your hearts!" Before anyone else, Fitna Bano raised a cup filled to the brim, and drank it in one swig, toasting the name of Amar Ayyar.

Hamza was confounded upon hearing Amar's name, and wondered how Amar had found his way there. While he was occupied in these speculations, yet another beauty, Tarar Khooban, raised her goblet and drank the roseate wine, announcing the name of Muqbil Vafadar. And in like manner, one after another, the companions and mates of the princess made toasts in their turn.

Then the princess raised the goblet of crimson wine and brought it to her lips, exclaiming, "I drink this to the memory of the slayer of Hashsham bin Alqamah Khaibari, who secured the release of all of you present here!" At these words Hamza was thrown into transports of joy.

After six hours had passed, the assembly adjourned and the princess retired to her bed, but though she tossed and turned, her eyes found no sleep in memory of the Sahibqiran,[51] and she cried on without cease until she was exhausted. Hamza saw that at last the princess had fallen asleep, and all her attendants had retreated, too, and were taken with slumber. He came down the palace roof from the stairwell, and stole quietly toward the princess's bedstead. He beheld that her eyes were closed in sleep, but the eyes of her longing had remained open.

For a long while Hamza stood there admiring her luminous face. As the Sahibqiran rested his hands on the pillows to lean over and kiss her sweet lips and also plant a token of his love on her rosy cheeks, his hands accidentally slipped down to the princess's bosom. The princess started and, having no suspicion of Amir's presence, screamed lustily with cries of "Thief! Thief!" Her attendants rose immediately and rushed to her aid from all corners of the palace. Then Amir said, "O sweetheart! The slayer of Hashsham bin Alqamah Khaibari stands before you—in love with, and all but slain by, the coquetry of the fairy, Princess Mehr-Nigar!"

Upon recognizing Hamza, the princess was embarrassed by her screaming and offered him many excuses and apologies. Without delay she hid Amir under the bed. Then she said to her attendants, "I screamed as I started in a nightmare. You may go back to sleep now!" After they were gone, Amir came out from under the bed and sat beside Princess Mehr-Nigar. Upon regarding him in proximity, she fell into a greater swoon and took leave of her senses. But after a while she revived when

Amir joined his mouth to hers and she inhaled his scent. The roseate twilight having appeared, Amir said to her after filling his narcissus eyes with dewlike tears of longing, "Farewell, O sweet one. The slayer of Hashsham bin Alqamah Khaibari can stay no longer! I fear lest the secret come out, as I had taken my leave of the emperor on the pretext of getting some sleep. Should I live, I will return tonight, after warding off and averting all hazard!"

The princess sighed deeply and with tears in her eyes spoke thus: "How I shall while away this dismal day and bring solace to my heart remains to be seen!"

Thereafter Amir took his leave, climbed down from the palace roof the same way he had climbed up, and returned to the royal assemblage in Muqbil's company.

At that time the emperor exited his bedchamber to give audience and make his appearance in the assembly. When the morning breeze freshened up the flower of the sun, the emperor arrived in Char-Chaman holding Amir's hand. But Amir was all restless like quicksilver in fire, and he no longer had any control on his heart.

Every so often Amir would venture outside the assembly to behold again the sight of Princess Mehr-Nigar's palace.

When Buzurjmehr noticed Hamza's restiveness, he surmised that Hamza must have become enamored of someone's charm. He signaled to Amar, who said, "I had come to this conclusion long before you did, and the caprices of his heart are responsible for his state!"

Amir Hamza's restlessness had not escaped Bakhtak's notice either, and he concluded, too, that Hamza was in love. Bakhtak submitted to the emperor, "Your Honor! People disturb the assembly with their constant coming and going. Pray declare that whoever shall now step out of the assembly without cause will be made to pay a fine of a hundred *tomans* for the disruption!"

The emperor found the counsel to his liking, and said to Amir, "If anyone now wanders out, he will invite a fine of a hundred *tomans* for doing so!" Amir acquiesced, yet his impatience made him rise twice from the assembly, and he was obliged to pay two hundred *tomans* in fines.

Buzurjmehr now said to Amar, "We must arrange it so that somehow Bakhtak is made to leave the assembly, or is ejected on some pretense!" Amar replied, "Nothing could be simpler!" Having said this, Amar approached the emperor and conveyed the following to the royal ears: "The festive assembly is now at a new height of elation. Should Your Highness so decree by your order, this slave would present a few cups of wine to Your Majesty!" The emperor answered, "Nothing would be better!" After passing three or four cups to the emperor in quick succession, Amar filled a cup for Prince Hurmuz and another for Hamza, and after serving them, presented one to Buzurjmehr. And going around in this manner he then put a wine cup to the lips of the Lord Swine of Faith, Bakhtak.

Then suspicion arose in Bakhtak's heart that something foul and villainous was behind this and Amar's request to be made the cupbearer hid some nefarious intent. He said to Amar: "The past day I gave up drinking, and therefore I shall abstain!" At this, Amar announced loudly for everyone to hear: "It is a prodigious thing that all the cupfellows of the emperor, and even His Highness himself, would deign to drink out of my hand, but Bakhtak deems it unworthy of his station."

The emperor included, all those present laughed heartily at Amar's quip, and the courtiers said to Bakhtak, "Indeed it is a signal honor to have Amar for one's cupbearer. It is most remarkable that you spurn this honor in your insistence not to drink!" Helpless, Bakhtak was left with no choice but to take the cup from Amar's hand and reluctantly drank it like one imbibing hemlock.

Now, Amar had admixed Bakhtak's drink with a drug that was a most potent purgative. Hardly a moment had passed when Bakhtak felt a great turmoil in his bowels. Bakhtak submitted to the emperor, "Your born slave seeks leave to attend to the call of nature, and will return presently!" But hardly had he returned after relieving himself than he again felt a grinding in his bowels, and he was again obliged to rise. Amar said to him, "Whither go you now, as you ventured out only a moment ago!" Bakhtak said, "I am going to the toilet!" Amar replied, "You just returned from the toilet!" Bakhtak then paid a hundred *tomans* in fine and attended to his need. No sooner had he returned when he again felt the urge to go. But the fear of incurring the fine kept him rooted to his station, until the urge became unbearable and, unable to control it any longer, Bakhtak relieved himself in his chair. The scat filled up his pants and flooded out from its cuffs.

Amar, who had been waiting for that moment, put down the goblet in his hands, and declared to the emperor, "Your Highness is now pleasantly intoxicated. Your pleasure would double if Your Highness were to take a stroll in the garden." The emperor replied, "O Amar! At this moment I would like it very much indeed!" The emperor took Hamza's hand and directed his steps to the garden, and those present also rose and followed in the emperor's train.

As Bakhtak, too, was obliged to rise, people soon noticed that his whole chair was smeared with excrement, which also flowed from the bottoms of his pants. Amar bore the news to the emperor, who was already tipsy from drink. Naushervan sent for Aadi, and said to him, "This uncouth, ill-mannered man is not fit for our company! Throw him out of the garden and drive him from our presence this instant!" Aadi, who was already furious with Bakhtak, immediately took him away, dragging him along by his beard.

Then Buzurjmehr said in his heart, *Bakhtak was gotten rid of by this stratagem, but Hamza's restiveness grows by the moment. If the emperor should discover it, some new misgiving might find way into the emperor's heart!* Therefore, he declared with folded arms before the emperor, "Hamza is greatly indebted to the honor Your Majesty has accorded him. The Guide of the World may now ascend the throne of the empire, as God's creatures await him for the dispensation of justice, and the royal subjects are waiting to receive his audience!" The emperor greatly appreciated Buzurjmehr's counsel and, after investing Amir Hamza with a sumptuous robe of honor, gave him leave to retire, while he himself repaired to the court.

Scribes of love chronicles and cherishers of tales of love, passion, and
desire write that the Lord of the Auspicious Planetary Conjunction
returned to Tal Shad-Kam to count the moments and hours left until
night, and in this manner bided the day of separation with prospects of
the night meeting. When the sun's simurgh[52] returned to its nest in the
West, and the moon's partridge dove[53] sauntered out to display its gait
across the expanse of the heavens, Amir sent for his nocturnal livery.
Then covering his luminous aspect in a veil of black silk, he stepped out
from his pavilion with Muqbil, and in this array headed for the palace of
Princess Mehr-Nigar.

Amar lay in hiding along the way, and as they passed by he leapt out
and shouted, "Beware, O thieves! Whither go you, and why do you hide
your faces from me? How would you enjoy the prospect of my summoning the guards on duty and putting you under incarceration until morning?" Amir responded, "O rogue and ruffian! Why must you needs thrust
your nose in this affair?"

Amar answered, "It is now become amply manifest to me that I am not
among your confidants, and so you kept this affair a secret from me and
deem me unworthy of your trust!"

Amir replied to him, "There is no one worthier of my confidence
than yourself! I did not confide this matter in you for the reason that you
would counsel me against this undertaking, and I have no control over
my passion and no power over my heart. Come follow me, as I am headed
for the alley of my sweetheart to bring solace to my heart with a tryst
with my beloved!" Amar said, "O my lord and potentate! Who might she
be, and what is she like—is she of the human kind, or is she a *houri* or a

fairy creature—that she has thus melted a man of tenacious persever-
ance like yourself?" Amir replied, "It is better to behold than be told.
Come and witness with your own eyes!" After thus conversing with
Amar, Hamza bent his legs toward Bagh-e Bedad.

———

Now hear how miserably Princess Mehr-Nigar fared, and how she
passed her day in separation from Amir. Grief and lamentation filled up
that morning, and she clung to her bedstead the whole day. Neither
getting up nor getting out of her bed, she did not do her toilette, she neither ate a morsel nor drank a drop, nor raised her head from the pillows;
she did not change clothes, nor brush nor plait her hair. The whole day
she washed her face with tears, and cried from the pain of separation. For
food she gnawed on morsels of her heart; for water she shed rivers of
tears, and restrained them only when she felt someone's presence near.
Her only combing and plaiting was to ruffle her hair with her dainty paw.
She hid her face in the coverlet, and when she noticed someone
approach, she stared wild-eyed, heaved cold sighs.

When her female attendants noticed Mehr-Nigar in this state, they
said to Fitna Bano, "It appears that the princess has lost her heart to love,
as she neither eats nor sleeps, and neither in day nor in night finds any
peace! Go take these tidings to your mother the nanny, so that she may
busy herself in effecting a remedy."

Fitna Bano said, "It would carry more weight if you carried this message to her and heard what she recommended and counseled!" In the
end, some female attendants went in a body to narrate the whole situation to the nanny, who rushed before the princess in a state of great anxiety and beheld that indeed the princess was entirely out of sorts, caring
neither for food nor drink, nor attending to her toilette or adorning herself. The nanny lifted the coverlet from her face, and said, "O my lady,
what is the matter? Hide nothing from me, but confide in me your heart's
grief without fear or inhibition! I shall lay down my life for you, and scat-
ter it away to bring you cheer."

The princess said to her nurse, "Though considerations of modesty
forbid me, yet there is no recourse left to me but to confide in you, as the
fire in my heart sears also yours! Hear then, O Nanny, that the love dart
of the slayer of Hashsham bin Alqamah Khaibari has shot my heart.
There is scarce hope this wound will heal except by the medicine of a
tryst!" The nanny replied, "Consider this proposition well, O Princess!

He is a follower of the True Faith, someone who shares neither your faith nor your language. In my view it is improper for you to attach and tie yourself to him!"

The princess replied, "O dear Nanny! When did love ever have scruples about coreligionists or those who are not coreligionists! Bear it well in mind that I shall not have long to live if I am not united with the Sahibqiran!" She then took off her *ambarcha* worth three thousand rupees, and conferred it upon the nanny, promising that hag many additional rewards from the Sahibqiran, as well as many rich gifts that she herself would bestow.

The greed of the nanny was no less voracious than Khvaja Amar's own. Her mouth watered when she set eyes on the *ambarcha,* and she agreed to do the princess's bidding. She said to the princess, "Once the night has spread its dark shades, I will dress you in nocturnal livery and take you to visit the Sahibqiran."

Her anxiety a little allayed, the princess became pacified, and at once went to bathe and put on lavish vestments. When the court timekeeper gonged with his mallet and rang the third hour of the night, the nanny dressed the princess in night attire. Donning a manly garb herself, she and the princess climbed down a rope tied from the tower on the palace roof, and headed for Tal Shad-Kam.

Amir Hamza's encampment was still some distance farther from them when they saw three persons clad in black coming toward them from their destination. Upon espying them the princess and the nanny took cover behind a tree and set about making themselves inconspicuous.

Amir Hamza, as it was none other than he and his companions, saw these two dark-clad figures seek cover. He remarked in a loud voice, "Behold, O Muqbil, these ladies clad in black who have ventured out of their house without the escort of men."

When Muqbil neared the tree, he saw it was the selfsame dainty, silver-bosomed, rosy-cheeked, and moonfaced Princess Mehr-Nigar, and he shouted joyously to Amir, "Bring yourself here, sire, and behold and recognize these personages!"

When Hamza saw the princess he was beside himself with joy, and grinned from ear to ear. Holding Princess Mehr-Nigar's hand, he returned to his pavilion.

Soon Amar presented himself before them and, after making salutations, declared with great deference, "O Princess! Indeed it was a signal honor you bestowed on us by being attracted to this place by your love for my dear friend."

The princess asked Muqbil, "Who is this man and what are his name and particulars?" Muqbil replied, "He is none other than Khvaja Amar, who is renowned to the ends of the world for his roguery!" The princess was much fascinated by Amar's general cast.

Upon entering his court, Hamza had seated Mehr-Nigar by his side and poured crimson wine for her into crystal goblets. The princess, too, picked up a ewer and cup, and plied Hamza with wine while Amar sat and sang.

Before the dawn appeared, Hamza, accompanied by Muqbil and Amar, escorted Princess Mehr-Nigar to her palace, and parted from her with the firm promise to meet again.

Some eunuchs lay awake when the princess and the nanny entered the palace and, sighting these two dark-clad figures, they raised the roof with cries of "Thief! Thief!" But when dawn broke, no sign even of the thief of henna could be descried.

In the morning the head of the eunuchs sounded his drum, and submitted to Empress Mehr-Angez: It would be seemly to appoint some commander at the princess's palace on night watch who will do the rounds of vigil with adroitness and skill!" The empress found his counsel to her liking, and informed the emperor who delegated the warrior Antar Teghzan with a contingent of four hundred troops and foot soldiers to watch over the princess's palace.

Now to Hamza who waited for Princess Mehr-Nigar until the middle of the night. But when the princess did not arrive and he learned of the deputation of Antar Teghzan's guard to the princess's palace, he became most inconsolable from the pangs of his heart, and sent for his nocturnal costume.

When Amar noticed Amir in this state, he broke into tears and threw himself at Hamza's feet, imploring him thus: "O Hamza! I would to God that you not set foot from your pavilion this night. May God forbid even the likelihood that Antar should see you, and inflict some harm upon you!"

Hamza, who was in tears until now, involuntarily burst out laughing, and said, "O Amar! What has got hold of your senses that you frighten me with the prospect of death? I do not give the least thought to the day of my dying. But indeed, if you should put a premium on your life, you are at liberty not to accompany me." Having said this, Hamza took Muqbil and headed for the palace of Princess Mehr-Nigar. And as Amar could not help but accompany him for better or for worse, he followed in his train.

Approaching Bagh-e Bedad, they saw Antar's night patrol armed with torches doing their rounds. Amir Hamza and his companions hid themselves in a dense coppice that was close by, and after the night patrol had passed, Hamza left Muqbil to stand guard as before under the palace wall, while he climbed up with Amar. Hamza found Princess Mehr-Nigar sitting dressed in her finery awaiting him, with all the paraphernalia of the assembly laid before her. She was surrounded by a profusion of wax tapers, and flanked on one side by Tarar Khooban, the lover of Muqbil Vafadar, and on the other side by Fitna Bano, the nanny's daughter and Amar's faithful beloved. The princess's eyes were riveted on the roof, and cheerfully but with yearning eyes she kept watch for Hamza's arrival.

The nanny said, "O Princess. Today it is well-nigh impossible for the Sahibqiran to find his way here, as Antar is on night vigil with four hundred troops and foot soldiers." The princess replied, "O Nanny! If the Sahibqiran is at all constant in his love, then even if the emperor's whole army had been put on vigil duty he would yet make sure to visit before long! Indeed, I have a premonition that he shall be here soon!"

At these words Hamza rejoiced in his heart and came down from the palace roof. Then the princess said to the nanny, "Witness now how I had told you that the Sahibqiran would be here any moment!"

The princess rose and led the Sahibqiran by the hand to her throne, and the two exchanged many words of mutual longing and desire. The princess filled cups of roseate wine with her own hand and plied Amir with them, who drank with his arm around the princess's neck. Presently their lips joined, their bosoms pressed together in the frenzy of passion, and Amar began to sing and prelude.

Greatly taken with Amar's pleasantries, the princess said to him, "Do you feel a desire for any of these beauties?" Amar said to her, "I dare not broach this subject as she is one of your boon companions and enjoys precedence over all your other attendants. There is no likelihood of her welcoming my advances. Nay, she will answer the very mention of my name with abuse and vilification!" The princess gave her pledge that Amar was at liberty to seek the company of the one he preferred. Then Amar nimbly leapt over to snuggle next to Tarar Khooban, and began making sheep's eyes at her. She began to abuse Amar at once, and with knitted brows rose in great indignation from his side.

The princess asked Amar, "What says she? Does she dare to revile and imprecate you?" Amar responded, "What has she to say? She indulges in dalliance and plays the coquette, but rejoices in her heart of hearts!"

The princess rolled down laughing. Then she said, "O Amar, tell me truly what attracted you to her!" Amar answered, "She is laden with jewels, and first and foremost that was what attracted me to her."

At this reply the princess and the assembly again burst out laughing. As Tarar Khooban began to feel the teasing, the princess said to her, "Indeed you are a veritable jade and a grump! Amar is of the same rank as Amir Hamza, and he is the Lord of Tricksters and Rogues. I swear by your head that you shall find no better man to attach yourself to!"

After these pleasantries had passed, Amir taught the princess the vow of fidelity to the One God and instructed her in the Act of Faith. The princess converted to the True Faith and said to Amir Hamza, "I shall remain faithful to you, and never step out of your authority for as long as I shall live!" Amir replied, "And until I have taken you as my wife with betrothal, I shall never have eyes for another woman!"

While these vows were being mutually exchanged, the morning star rose in the heavens. Amir Hamza took leave of the princess, and climbed down from the palace roof along with Amar and Muqbil and headed for his encampment.

On their way they were challenged by Antar's night patrol, and the guards gave them chase. Amir drew his sword and dispatched a dozen or so of his pursuers to Hell, and then returned safe and sound to his camp.

When it was daylight, Antar Teghzan found only his own men among those slain and discovered no stranger among them. He narrated the details to the emperor and gave him a complete account of what had passed in the night. As per custom, when the Sahibqiran presented himself at the court that day, the emperor said to him, "O Abul-Ala, I would like that you take the trouble to guard the palace so that the thief who visited it last night is captured or put to death, since your men are renowned for their vigilance!"

Amir replied, "I am faithful as ever, and I hear and obey!"

But Bakhtak said in his heart upon hearing these tidings, *The emperor has given the lamb into the guardianship of the wolf. Alas and alack, and a thousand plagues on such sagacity!*

After receiving the royal orders, Hamza delegated Muqbil with a strong force of two hundred for the night vigil and, at the third hour of the night he took Amar along as before to pay a visit to the princess, and they spent the whole night drinking and listening to Amar's songs. At the approach of dawn Amir took leave of the princess, after biding the whole night in great merriment, and returned to Tal Shad-Kam.

When the court assembled that day, Amir presented himself and submitted to the emperor: "Your humble servant stood vigil the whole night, but never did I see even the ghost of a thief!" The emperor said, "It was from fear of you that nobody set foot there." The emperor then conferred a robe of honor on Hamza.

Bakhtak then begged of the emperor, "Pray deputize Qaran Deoband today to night patrol as he is a Sassanid commander of noble birth, and this shall test his skill and diligence!" The emperor agreed to Bakhtak's counsel.

When the court adjourned, Amir returned to Tal Shad-Kam accompanied by his friends and companions. Qaran Deoband picked three hundred warriors from among his troops and deployed his night patrol at the onset of evening. The princess was most perturbed upon hearing the news of Qaran's deputation, and said to her nanny, "Today Qaran Deoband is appointed on night vigil. It is nonetheless certain that Amir will not be deterred in his resolve to pay me a visit. I wish somebody would take my message to him that he must not plan on visiting today, or even give it a thought!" The nanny replied, "Amir is not such an arrant fool: He will master his passion, as he puts a premium on his name and honor."

Now hear of Hamza who sent for his nocturnal livery when the night was a little advanced in hours. Amar beat his head at this, and said, "O Hamza! What devil has possessed you that your patience runs short for the length of a night?"

Amir said: "O Amar! Indeed love and patience have no affinity with each other. Who has the wherewithal to deter me from this undertaking?" Amar said in response, "But Qaran Deoband is not one to show any qualms in confronting you and he will not look the other way!" Amir replied, "If I should let the fear of Qaran prevail upon me I might as well give up all thoughts of love and desire now!" Thus, he donned his nocturnal livery and headed out of his pavilion toward the princess's palace, with Muqbil and Amar alongside him.

From far away they made out small coveys of guards patrolling the place, and upon arriving near Bagh-e Bedad, Amir saw Qaran installed in a chair, commanding his troops to be on the alert and look sharp.

Leaving Muqbil to stand guard, he climbed up with Amar and gained the roof.

When he beheld the princess, Amir was beside himself with joy and hurried to embrace her. They passed the night in great merriment and, at the approach of dawn, Amir sought to leave, making preparations for his departure while bidding the princess adieu. Amar climbed down the rope first, and when it was Hamza's turn, Qaran rushed upon him and dealt him a blow of the sword.

Amir escaped the blow, which fell on the rope instead, cutting it in two. Although Muqbil tried to break Hamza's fall, he never stood a chance under Hamza's weight, and the Sahibqiran's head struck against the wall, wounding him enough to bleed. Muqbil then unleashed a barrage of arrows and Amar a hail of stones from his slingshot, and they injured several of Qaran's companions. When Qaran realized that the thief was Hamza, he did not pursue him. Instead, he took the rope, which was marked with Hamza's name, and presented it to the emperor.

The emperor flew into a rage when he saw this evidence. He sent for Buzurjmehr and said to him, "Regard this deed of Hamza, O Khvaja! Tell me if it is commensurate with the profession of nobility, or fair recompense for my hospitality!" Buzurjmehr replied, "This evidence is fabricated! Hamza is not one to commit so indelicate an act, and raise his eyes at the royal harem with nefarious intent!"

Qaran responded to this, saying, "Hamza's head struck against the wall and he was wounded and bloodied. You may send for him and witness it for yourself!" The emperor dispatched a mace bearer with the summons to bring back Amir.

Now hear how after Hamza had reached his pavilion, and was back among his confidants, he thought in his heart, *Qaran will surely give an account of my injury before the emperor and then I will be held up to shame and my name will be made to bear the greatest ignominy!*

He supplicated without cease to the Shielder of Blemishes and Hearer of Petitions.

Hamza was occupied with prayers when sleep at last overcame him and he was suddenly lost in dream. He beheld that he was in the presence of the prophet Ibrahim who stroked his head gently with his hand, and said to him, "Rise, O Hamza! The injury of your head is healed, and not the least sign of a wound now remains!" When Amir opened his eyes, he discovered that indeed no sign of injury was left on his head.

Presently he was informed of the emperor's summons, and brought himself to the emperor's presence accompanied by his companions. By a clever stratagem the emperor made him uncover his head, and upon looking closely he could not find even a sign of a swelling, let alone a wound. Then the emperor held Buzurjmehr's words as true, and severely rebuked Qaran for casting malicious aspersions on Hamza. He conferred a rich robe of honor on Hamza, and had Qaran driven away from the court.

———

One day Buzurjmehr said to the emperor before the whole court, "Ever since the Khusrau[54] of the dominion of India, King Landhoor bin Saadan Shah, has ascended the throne, the royal treasury has not received the required tribute from his dominion. The emperor's response was: "What is to be done about this menace?"

Now, as Buzurjmehr was a most sagacious man of great address, and well versed in the ways of the world, he had quickly determined that Hamza's beloved could be none other than Princess Mehr-Nigar. And when the thief could not be apprehended, Buzurjmehr became further convinced in his view that these night exploits were indeed Hamza's doings. He said in his heart, *Amir's head is filled with the wine of adolescence, and he is blind to all considerations of what is seemly and what is aberrant! If this leads to an untoward incident, nothing will be gained but disrepute. And as I am Hamza's aid and abettor, I shall also be vilified, and my name will be sullied.* He therefore resolved on a course of action, and thought of bringing up the matter of Landhoor's revolt. He well knew that nobody would consent to undertake this perilous adventure, except for Hamza.

Thinking that Hamza would be cured of his calamitous love if he were sent on a campaign for a while, Buzurjmehr said to the emperor, "Have it declared that arrogance in his might has led the Khusrau of India astray from obedience to you, and that he assumes that the world has nobody to offer as his equal. Let us then see who pledges to undertake the campaign against Landhoor and subjugate that rebel."

OF KING SAADAN SHAH'S BROTHER SHAHPAL SENDING AN EPISTLE IN CONDEMNATION OF LANDHOOR, AND OF HAMZA'S RESOLVE TO DEPART FOR INDIA TO CHASTISE HIM

The steed of all riders of the arena of narrative, that charger of horse breakers of the field of ancient legends, thus springs with ardor and gallops through the expanse of the page, revealing that talk of King Landhoor's refractory ways had not yet been brought up in court when cries of "Redress!" and "Succor!" were heard, and a plaintiff's lamentations and pleadings for mercy were conveyed to the righteous ears of Naushervan the Just.

Following the emperor's orders, Bakhtak emerged from the court and received a memorandum from the plenipotentiary of the king of Ceylon, King Shahpal, who had written:

> May it be known to the discerning regard of the Emperor of the Seven Climes, that in the past my brother, Saadan Shah, used to be the master of crown and writ.
>
> One day he was separated from his party while chasing a quarry. He arrived near a fountain half dead with thirst, and beheld a woman of extraordinary stature about to lift three filled water skins on her shoulders. Saadan Shah said to her, "I have gone thirsty for three days: Give me some water." Immediately that woman threw out the water in the water skins and set about refilling them. Greatly vexed by her deed, Saadan Shah resolved in his heart that once he had quenched his thirst he would spill the blood of her life as she had spilled the water of the water skins.
>
> Later, that woman filled up a bowl with water and put it before Saadan Shah. But hardly had he taken a few draughts when she stayed his hand and began to ask him who he was, what his name was, and from which land and city he hailed. Saadan Shah said to her, "Allow me to

quench my thirst, and then ask me what you may!" But the woman did not desist. King Saadan Shah had a few sips more, and drew his sword with the intention to murder the woman. She said, "O stranger, what is my crime that you are bent upon my murder?" Saadan Shah replied, "First, I had told you that I had gone thirsty for three days and was dying for a drop of water! But you drained away the three water skins. Then you began refilling them, purposely indulging in procrastination. And when at last you did give me some water and I began drinking, you did not let me have my fill, but interrupted my drinking every few sips.

Upon hearing this the woman laughed out, and then said, "First give me your name and particulars, then I will answer your questions!" Saadan Shah said, "I am the king of these dominions, and my name is Saadan Shah." She answered, "Fie on you that even though you are the potentate of twelve thousand isles, you are bereft of all sense and reason." To this Saadan Shah said, "Can you prove what you say, or do you speak idly?"

She replied, "I kept you from drinking too quickly for the reason that you were thirsty of many days, and in your greed you would have drunk with excess. I reasoned that if you drank the water swiftly, and it affected the lungs, you would die to no purpose!"

When Saadan Shah heard the rationale for her conduct, he marveled to the limits of marveling at her sagacity, and became hopelessly enamored of her propriety and sense. He said to her, "Do you have any dependents or do you live by yourself?" She replied, "I have no protector but God. I have no guardian to speak of."

Saadan Shah brought her with him to the city and betrothed her, and after some days the woman was with child. And then Saadan Shah died and I ascended the throne.

After the period appointed for gestation the woman bore a son who measured five yards in height. After some time the woman also died, and I named the boy Landhoor and busied myself with his caring. God had also blessed me with a boy the day Landhoor was born, and I named that boy Jaipur.

When the boys were five years old, one day in the way of disciplining him, a dry nurse slapped Landhoor, which caused his cheek to swell. Landhoor picked up that dry nurse and smashed her to the ground, and she soon grew cold and met her end. The guards escaped in terror of Landhoor, and gave me a detailed account of the incident. I ordered that Landhoor be thrown before a rutting elephant. When the elephant made to pick up Landhoor with his trunk, Landhoor caught hold of it and gave it such a violent pull that it tore from the root. Roaring with agony, the elephant ran amok causing great upheaval in the city.

I ordered that Landhoor be put in chains and led straight to jail, but no one found the courage to come forward, except for one vizier, who took a big dish of halva for Landhoor, and placed it before him. After Landhoor had eaten the halva, the vizier made him follow him into my presence.

Upon beholding me, Landhoor asked the vizier, "Who is this man, and what is his name?" The vizier said, "This here is your venerable uncle, who is the king and master of these lands!" Landhoor said, "And who was the king before him?" The vizier answered, "It was your father!" Then Landhoor said of me, "Then who is this man when I am the heir to the crown and throne?" The vizier said, "Indeed you are our lord and master." Landhoor said, "Depose him then! I shall ascend the throne, and issue writs from today onward, and govern the kingdom." The vizier said to me, "It would be expedient to oblige, and step down from the throne!" Then I stepped down from the throne, and Landhoor was enthroned.

After a while Landhoor asked for food, and the vizier laid out drugged food before him. Once Landhoor was unconscious, I ordered that Landhoor be put in irons from head to foot, and given into the charge of Aurang and Gaurang, the princes of Lakhnauti. They took Landhoor away and, after throwing him into the well of Lakhnauti, sealed its mouth.

For twenty-five years Landhoor remained imprisoned in that dark well. As Landhoor's mother was the progeny of Prophet Shis, one day the sister of Aurang and Gaurang had a dream in which she saw a throne come down from the heavens with Prophet Shis seated on it. And after informing her of all the particulars about Landhoor, the prophet said to her, "I have made you and Landhoor a pair, and from him you will be borne of a child who will grow up to be the sun of glory!" She started from her dream, and went to the prison well carrying a salver of food.

The guards asked her, "Who are you, what have you brought, and whence do you come at this hour?" She said, "I have brought food for Landhoor and come to convey to him the annunciations of a saint."

She climbed down the well and fed Landhoor, and filed away at his fetters with a rasp. After narrating her dream to Landhoor, she went away. Landhoor put the chain irons to his side, and released from that encumbrance after such a long while, fell asleep like a log. The guards wondered why they did not hear his wailing and lamentations, as Landhoor never was wont to let up his cries. When one of them went to investigate the matter, he found Landhoor sleeping peacefully with his feet outstretched, with the irons that chained him lying broken by his side.

Aurang and Gaurang were forthwith informed. They rushed to the well. As they made to take him unaware Landhoor woke up and pinned the two princes to the ground. Then Landhoor narrated to them their sister's dream. The two princes rejoiced upon hearing these auspicious tidings, and led Landhoor out of the dark pit.

Landhoor ordered a war club to be made for him weighing one thousand and seven hundred Tabrizi *maunds,* and he mounted a giant elephant wielding that club. He began to make inquiries as to the way to the land of Ceylon. Aurang and Gaurang submitted to him with folded arms: "O Refuge of the World! Wait a while! You may march on Ceylon once you have enlisted an army!" When an intrepid army was raised, he advanced toward Ceylon and soon arrived at the fort of Ceylon.

I sent Jaipur at the head of a force of two hundred thousand to battle Landhoor. Then battle lines were drawn on both sides, and the two armies skirmished.

Jaipur observed that with each blow of Landhoor's war club, scores of his champions were macerated. Jaipur retreated and fortified himself. Landhoor advanced to the gate of the fort and gave a mighty blow with his war club, which shattered the gate to pieces. The moment the gate fell, Landhoor entered the fort and indulged in wholesale carnage.

I saw no recourse left to me but to present myself before Landhoor and ask for mercy. Landhoor said, "With what intention do you bring this plea before me?" I said, "I rule this kingdom in trust for Naushervan the Just, the Emperor of the Seven Climes. He appoints the one who ascends the throne. Wait a while until a reply to my epistle has arrived from his court!" Landhoor said, "Remove yourself to some isle until your pleas and entreaties are answered, What do I care about Naushervan or yourself?

Helpless, I escaped from the city with my life, and Landhoor was enthroned. As I was duty bound to inform you, I have made my report. Now I leave it to the judgment of Your Highness. If Landhoor is not speedily routed as he deserves, he will not stop short of committing the gravest outrages against Your Highness!

After listening to this message the emperor sought Buzurjmehr's counsel in private, and also sought the advice of his viziers and nobles.

Buzurjmehr said, "First, order Gustham to advance on Ceylon. Then announce before the whole court that you will pledge the troth of Princess Mehr-Nigar to the one who brings Landhoor back a prisoner to Your Majesty. In my view there is no Sassanid warrior who will undertake to bring Landhoor's head. But Hamza is ever enamored of renown and honor, and it is certain that he will make this pledge. And this plan is also not without ingenuity in that, should Hamza be killed in the undertaking, you will be saved from humiliation; and should he prevail against Landhoor, all of the lands of India will fall to your lot!"

Upon hearing Buzurjmehr's thoughtful opinion and counsel, the emperor rejoiced in his heart. And that very moment he sent a precept by a camel rider to Gustham, who was in hiding in Zabul. Through this messenger, he ordered Gustham to proceed to Ceylon with his forty thousand troops and bring back Landhoor's head, in order that his past misdemeanors might be pardoned.

The next day in the court, the emperor said, "O renowned warriors and champions of time! The Khusrau of India has raised the flag of rebellion and foments sedition against me. Whoever among you will bring me his head, I shall adopt him as son, and he shall be proclaimed my kin. The head of the Khusrau of India would be considered the jointure of Mehr-Nigar."

No one came forward to accept this undertaking, thinking in their hearts that it was well-nigh impossible to escape with one's life from the Indian Ocean, and even should one survive it, nobody would find the courage to fight such a powerful enemy.

But Sahibqiran rose from his seat and spoke thus: "Should you order this faithful servant, he will produce the Khusrau of India before you in person! Should I be killed in the undertaking, I shall become a sacrifice of Your Majesty!"

The emperor rose from his throne and embraced Amir, and said, "O Abul-Ala! How could you have laid claim to the august station you hold if you did not have such courage and valiancy!" Having said this, the emperor conferred a royal robe of honor on Amir, and ordered thirty ships carrying a thousand men each to be furnished for the campaign.

Amir Hamza ordered his troops to march that very day and to wait for him in Basra. Then he sent for Amar, and said to him, "O Amar, if I could have had a glimpse of the princess before I left, I would have left with a pacified heart!"

Amar said, "Write a note to Buzurjmehr, for such an arrangement could only be made by the intercession of the nobles. He would be the one to consult in this matter!"

Hamza therefore wrote a note to Buzurjmehr with his own hand, and Amar took it to Buzurjmehr's place.

Buzurjmehr took Amar along before the emperor, and said to him,

"From Ctesiphon to the dominion of India, Hamza will be proclaimed your son-in-law. But what is to be said about such a relationship when not even a drop of sherbet was imbibed to celebrate it?"

Naushervan said, "Indeed there is no harm in what you suggest."

Then Khvaja Buzurjmehr said, "It would be improper to hold the ceremony in the men's quarters, in the absence of Her Highness the Empress!" Naushervan said to Buzurjmehr, "You may accompany Hamza into the palace. Instruct them to perform all the rituals of engagement, and to feast Hamza after the drinks and inform him that we will keep Mehr-Nigar for him in trust." Buzurjmehr went into the palace without Amir, and conveyed all that the emperor had just said to Empress Mehr-Angez.

When Bakhtak received these tidings he said in his heart, *If Hamza goes inside the palace, it is certain that he will view Princess Mehr-Nigar. I should go there, too, so that he is denied even a glimpse of the princess!* Directly Bakhtak mounted a mule and rode to the palace gates.

When he saw Bakhtak coming, Hamza said to Amar, "One must somehow ward off this bird of ill omen at this time! I will give you two hundred *tomans* and other rewards besides if this is so arranged!" Amar replied to Hamza in the language of *ayyars,* "You may go forth and enjoy yourself at the palace without the least worry. I shall deal with him presently!"

The moment Hamza left, Amar stopped Bakhtak by catching hold of his mule's reins, and said to him, "O Khvaja Bakhtak, I am headed for India, and God alone knows whether I shall return safe and sound or whether my grave shall be made there! Here is your promissory note of five hundred *tomans:* Please make good on the payment!" Bakhtak responded, "At the moment I am accompanying Hamza on an assignment, and proceeding in the cortege of your master. And you make yourself an obstacle. Go lodge your complaint in the royal court of appeals. I shall make the payment duly if the debt is proven against me!"

Amar cried, "I would move the royal court if I did not find it in my power to extract my debt myself. You are warned not to take a step forward without first clearing my debt."

Riled upon hearing these words, Bakhtak said to his slaves, "Move Amar aside! Push him away from before my mule!"

In one leap Amar mounted the mule behind Bakhtak. Drawing his dagger and pressing it into Bakhtak's side, he said, "I will bring you to your final rewards before your time if you so wish, and pile up your entrails right here!" Bakhtak was terrified and made fervent pleas to

Amar, who then let him go, but first clouted his head with the dagger's hilt so that blood issued out.

Bakhtak rushed before the emperor drenched in blood to complain about Amar. Displeased at this spectacle, Naushervan sent for Amar, and asked him, "What harm did you receive at Bakhtak's hand that you perpetrated this felony against him?"

Amar replied, "Your Honor, I, your slave, have a duly signed and sealed promissory note for five hundred *tomans* against Bakhtak, but he dithers in making good the payment! I asked him to kindly redeem this promissory note. But he became angry at my words, and ordered his slaves to use violence to throw me out and drive me away from before him. I then became vexed and clouted him with my dagger's hilt, so that his crown swelled up a little." Then Amar produced the promissory note from his pocket, and laid it before the emperor, seeking justice.

The emperor said to Bakhtak, "Your high-handedness is now proved beyond a shadow of the doubt. Yet you have the cheek to present yourself before me as the aggrieved party! Make haste to pay the money due on the promissory note to Amar, or else you will be held guilty and thrown into the mire of ignominy upon failing to make good the payment!" Bakhtak was obliged to bring every last bit of money from the treasurer that very moment. Then, while he returned home moaning and groaning, Amar headed for the emperor's quarters in the harem to join Hamza.

While Amar was thus entangled, Hamza and Muqbil had entered the palace and arrived in the royal gallery. Empress Mehr-Angez seated Hamza on a throne in the gallery, and called for all the paraphernalia of festive revelry to be set up. The empress herself sat in the annex with Princess Mehr-Nigar. The festive assembly began in a most regal manner and sherbet was soon served, with the company drinking it in rounds.

When Amar reached the gallery's threshold and made to enter, the porter barred his way with his staff, and said to him, "Who might you be that you dare to enter the palace in this impetuous manner, and set foot on the royal threshold without permission?" Covering his eyes with his hands, Amar fell to the floor crying and rolling, and screaming all the while, "Confound you, Porter, that you have poked out my eyes and blinded me, depriving me of my sight!" At this, the porter was dumbfounded and began pleading with Amar profusely.

When Empress Mehr-Angez heard the noise, she said to her attendants, "See what the row is all about, and who is crying at the gates!" Upon discerning Amar's voice, Hamza himself ran out in great trepidation with Buzurjmehr at his heels. They found Amar on the floor, rolling around with his eyes covered, exhibiting signs of great suffering. Hamza said, "O Amar, open your eyes and tell me if, God forbid, some harm has come to your eyes. Khvaja Buzurjmehr will treat you and prescribe some cure!" But Amar would not open his eyes, and said nothing but "Gone are my eyes, alas, gone!"

Finally Hamza forced Amar's hands from his face, and saw that his eyes twinkled like stars and showed no sign of having come to any harm. Hamza then said, "O Amar! Why did you make Khvaja and myself come rushing to no purpose with this prank and roguery of yours—and also distressed the empress?"

Amar replied, "I swear by your life that the porter had raised his staff to hit me, and had I been hit, it is a foregone conclusion that my eyes once wounded would have lost their sight!" Hamza and Khvaja Buzurjmehr laughed out loud at this, and brought Amar into the palace.

Hamza was seated on a throne and was served sherbet according to the royal custom, and shouts of "Congratulations!" and "Salutations!" rose to the skies. The companions and confidantes of Princess Mehr-Nigar began frolicking and making merry. Then Empress Mehr-Angez said, "O Sahibqiran, we shall hold Princess Mehr-Nigar in trust for you. When you return triumphant and victorious from India, she will be married to you!"

Amar exchanged glances with Buzurjmehr at this speech, and addressed the empress thus, "While we head for India and wager our lives at the orders of the emperor, you deny us even a glimpse of the princess. If God returns us alive and triumphant with our mission accomplished, there is no knowing to whom Hamza will be married off! We know not whether the emperor's daughter is dark or fair, lean or plump! If we were allowed a glance of her now, we will not be sold into some deception later. Indeed, we shall not set foot out of doors before we have been granted a view of Princess Mehr-Nigar!"

Empress Mehr-Angez laughed at Amar's speech, and said, "Now that the princess is become your honor, you are free to view her whenever you may desire!" Then she said to Khvaja Buzurjmehr, "O Khvaja, pray bring Amir inside and let him view the princess!"

Buzurjmehr stepped forward with Hamza, who made obeisance upon beholding Empress Mehr-Angez, and made an offering himself, too. Princess Mehr-Nigar sat by the empress's side with her head lowered. Upon beholding the princess, Hamza was beside himself with joy and rejoiced exceedingly.

Buzurjmehr said to Princess Mehr-Nigar, "Hamza is about to embark on a journey of great length. Pray confer some memento on him that keeps him engrossed with your memory! Mehr-Nigar took an emerald ring from her finger and gave it to Hamza, who put it on. Then exchanging for it the ring from his finger, he said to Princess Mehr-Nigar, "Take this as a memento from me, so that it may always remain with you, in order that you shall never become forgetful of me but instead think of me often!"

Then Amar submitted before Empress Mehr-Angez with folded arms, saying, "God willing, when Hamza is married to Princess Mehr-Nigar, the nanny's daughter, too, *nolens volens,* shall be married to me! Therefore, have some memento conferred on me, too, and request that respected nanny to serve me the sherbet of nuptials with her hands!" Then Empress Mehr-Angez said to Fitna Bano, "You, too, must give Amar some memento of yourself!" She gave Amar a scent box worth several hundred *tomans.* Empress Mehr-Angez said, "Now, O Fitna Bano, receive from Amar a memento for yourself!" Amar put a date and two walnuts into Fitna Bano's palm, and said, "Here! Keep them with you, and safeguard them well!" At this new caper of Amar's all those present collapsed in a fit of laughter.

When Hamza took his leave from these revelries and went to present himself before the emperor, Khvaja Buzurjmehr said to Amar, "My son, proceed to the camp of the faithful, and I shall escort Hamza myself, so that he is seen off by the emperor and granted a robe of honor!"

While Amar headed off to perform the task, Buzurjmehr seated Hamza and Muqbil in his house, and then went before the emperor and reported that Empress Mehr-Angez, too, had accepted Amir Hamza as her son-in-law with open arms, and had invested him with the robe of the son-in-law. Then Buzurjmehr took Amir and Muqbil to his office and after imparting some instructions to Amir regarding the mission, served sherbet to him. Upon drinking this, Hamza fell unconscious immediately. Buzurjmehr cut open Hamza's side, and after planting the Shah Mohra[55] inside him, sutured up the wound and rubbed it with the salve of Daud.[56] Witnessing this, Muqbil asked, "What was that physic, O venerated Buzurjmehr?" He replied, "A man scheming to work Hamza's death (may such be his enemies' fate!) will poison him in India, and for that poison this is the sole antidote! But you must not divulge this secret to Amar, until you are beaten with his hand first!" Buzurjmehr then dribbled a few drops of some liquid into Hamza's mouth, whereupon he immediately came to his senses. And as the wound had completely healed by then, he never discovered a thing.

In the meanwhile Amar also returned from his errand, and Buzurj-mehr bade them all adieu. Hamza arrived in his camp and soon rode out to the sea in the manner becoming a commander. Arriving at the port with his triumphant army, Hamza boarded the ships with his thirty thousand men, and made ready to sail.

At this point, Amar got off the ship, calling up to Hamza, "As yours truly is most frightened of jinns, magic, and water, I will not sail for India, but will head for Mecca instead, where I will pray for your victory before the True Triumphant One. Hamza said, "O Amar, I would not force you into an undertaking that is not in accordance with your pleasure, but do wait a while so that I may write you a note for my father!"

Amar went aboard to Hamza, who wrote out a letter, handed it to Amar, and then said: "Come, Brother, let's embrace once, for God alone knows when we shall meet again!" Tears filled Amar's eyes at these words. Then Hamza caught Amar in his embrace and said, "Dearest friend! How could I bear separation from you in this campaign when you have never left my side in the most trying of times!"

Next thing, Hamza called out to the captain, "Weigh the anchor!" No sooner were the orders given than the ships weighed anchor. It was only after they had left the shore behind that Hamza released Amar, who began running on the deck in confusion, muttering with dismay, "I was always true in my camaraderie toward this Arab, but he has become my mortal foe!"

After some time had passed they sighted an isle some thirty yards in both length and breadth, and upon spotting it Amar said in his heart, *I will jump on it and from there find some way to return home!* But what Amar had mistaken for an island, was in fact a great fish that had swum to the surface of water to bask in the sun. When Amar jumped on it, the fish felt the thump of his feet and dived; and a panic-stricken Amar began to flounder in the open sea.

The sailors threw ropes and tackle into the ocean, fished Amar out of the sea, and seated him next to Hamza.

Many days later they arrived on the shores of an island, and the ships dropped anchor. Amar was the first one to leap onto shore. By chance, he espied a man with a strap around his waist sitting under a tree. Upon beholding Amar the man began to smile from ear to ear, and called to Amar, "Come hither, my nephew! It is a wonder of wonders that the two of us have been brought together! I had become convinced that I would die and all my riches would go waste, but God sent their rightful owner!" At hearing the mention of riches, Amar kept quiet; otherwise, he would have objected to the old man's calling him his nephew.

When Amar inquired about his particulars, the old man said, "You were a mere toddler when I left for Ceylon. When I had accumulated a great fortune there, I resolved to leave that place and return to my home-land. On my return passage, a contrary wind took hold of the ship. A storm began to blow and the sea began to rage, and the ship capsized at this place. I laid hold of my chest of jewels and jumped overboard, and swam to the land. But in that undertaking my foot was injured and it ren-dered me an invalid. A surgeon who is a past master of his trade lives on this island. People took pity on me and carried me to him. My condition is now improved to the extent that when I felt my heart becoming over-cast, I brought myself here. I have been trying to muster the strength to return to my house. If you were to carry me to my house on your back, I would be doubly indebted to you, and shall also vouchsafe to you what by rights is yours! That is to say, I would hand over that chest of jewels to you."

Amar's mouth watered upon hearing this talk of the chest of jewels, and without further thought, Amar loaded up that *tasma-pa* on his back.

The moment the *tasma-pa* climbed on Amar's back, he strapped his legs tightly around Amar's waist, then goaded him forward with his knees, exclaiming, "Come, my ambler! Now trot along, and show me how you gallop!" Amar was thoroughly tied up and howsoever he tried to free himself, he was unable to do so, as his arms were also secured. The old man began to slap Amar's cheeks and clout his head. Cuffing his face and kicking him in the ribs, the old man said, "Run! Why don't you run? Do you wish to obtain all the riches without taking a single step, and estab-lish yourself as an heir without the least labor?" Amar was taken with a great panic and alarm, and all his roguery and trickery left him.

In all helplessness, Amar ran toward the ship, thinking that Hamza would grant him release from this monster. But upon arriving near the ship Amar beheld that Hamza and all his companions were caught in the same calamity. Helpless, Amar drew away from Hamza but kept consid-ering some way to secure his release.

Every so often the *tasma-pa* would command Amar to jog, then order him to leap and gambol. When he saw others of his race likewise fur-nished with mounts, he said to them, "Race your mounts, and show how your chargers stride and gallop! I will race my mount, too. After having our fun we will kill them and roast them on skewers!" Upon hearing these words, Hamza's companions began heaving cold, despondent sighs. Their riders again spurred them on and started forward.

At one place in that wilderness, Amar saw a profuse growth of grapevines from which clusters of fruit were hanging. Adjacent to this was a growth of gourds, with hundreds of goblet-shaped fruits hanging down, their tendrils spread over a great expanse. Amar approached the gourd vine, and said to the *tasma-pa*, "Pick me a big gourd and fill it up with the juice that drips from the grape clusters. Give me sips from it along the way, so that after drinking it I can stride even more nimbly."

That dolt did as Amar had bade him and, plucking off a gourd, filled it up with grape juice. Then he dripped some into Amar's mouth and gave him also some grapes to eat. Amar broke into an air and carried his rider sprinting at ever greater speed. That rascal was mightily pleased, and said, "Oh, my charger! I will never release you from between my legs, as you lighten my heart with your pranks and by running so swiftly!" Amar said to him, "Mind that you drink none of this liquid, but leave it all for me!"

The *tasma-pa* now thought in his heart, *It seems that this juice is some sovereign elixir! That is why he forbids me to drink it.* Thus thinking he took two sips from the gourd and, immensely enjoying the taste, he put the gourd to his lips and guzzled down its entire contents. Now when the forest breeze billowed against the *tasma-pa*'s face from the giddiness in his head he fell down unconscious from Amar's back. Then Amar took out his dagger and slit open the *tasma-pa*'s belly.

From there Amar returned to Hamza and said, "You imperiled the lives of the followers of the True Faith for the sake of an infidel's daughter, and put me to great distress!" Hamza said, "Indeed I am guilty of the charge, as well as inexperienced. But you now have the chance to earn great recompense by delivering us from this scourge!" Amar replied, "What is in it for me if I kill this multitude of *tasma-pas* and have the blood of these invalids on my neck?" Hamza said, "Their blood will be on my neck, and I shall give you two hundred gold pieces for every one of them that you kill!"

Amar killed every single *tasma-pa* by picking them clean off their mounts with well-aimed slingshots, and made piles of the dead. After everyone had been released from the clutches of those beings, Hamza ordered the ships to weigh anchor without further delay and set sail.

After many days a speck of cloud appeared on the horizon, and in no time a tempest began to rage and a storm to brew. Everything drowned in pitch darkness.

After three days the tempest gradually blew away. The pall of this calamity was not yet cast from their hearts when it was discovered that the ships of Emperor of China Bahram Gurd could not be accounted for. All four of his ships had disappeared without sign or trace, and no sign of them could be found. Upon hearing these tidings Hamza immediately drowned in the abyss of sorrow, and cried out, "A great leviathan of the sea of courage and valor has drowned!" His companions said, "They have perhaps found a port and the Sailor of Fate has taken them to shores of safety. By virtue of His great beneficence He will bring us together again!"

OF ANOTHER STORM, AND HAMZA'S SHIPS BEING
DRIVEN INTO THE WHIRLPOOL OF SIKANDER, AND OF
THE DELIVERANCE OF THESE POOR SOULS FROM THE
TEMPEST; AND OF THEIR ARRIVING IN THE LANDS OF
CEYLON AND EXACTING TRIBUTE FROM THE KHUSRAU OF
INDIA, LANDHOOR BIN SAADAN SHAH

The divers of the ocean of historiography and the excavators of the sea of ancient tales bring up the pearls of legends, and thus display them by stringing them into prose, that after the storm had blown away, the fleet found favorable winds for a few days and the travelers remained safe from any catastrophes, and the captains gave full sails and sped on their vessels. Then one day the lookout of the ship shouted, "Hear, O friends! A great storm is about to engulf us, and a greater calamity still is the Whirlpool of Sikander that lies a short distance from here. Should the ships be led into it (perish the thought!), they will founder in no time. Then every man will find himself at the mercy of the open sea!"

Upon hearing this news Amar was terribly frightened and was thrown into a great panic.

Soon the storm came upon them, and the sea began to rage, and before long the ships were driven into the Whirlpool of Sikander. As Hamza peered into the storm, he beheld a stone obelisk of great length and breadth that rose from the center of the whirlpool. Affixed to it was a tablet of white stone. When he looked closely, Hamza saw words in Arabic letters chased on it in black stone, which read:

> There will come a time when the fleet of the Sahibqiran shall arrive at this place and be caught in the Whirlpool of Sikander. Then the Sahibqiran must climb up the obelisk and sound the Timbal of Sikander that is kept here, or else order his deputy to climb up, and do what is needful. Then the ships will find escape from this whirlpool, and the Sahibqiran shall be delivered from this difficulty.

Hamza said to Amar, "Adieu, my brother! I shall head for the obelisk and sound the timbal!" Amar said, "The same command applies also to your deputy. And thus, as I am your deputy, I shall climb this obelisk and sound the Timbal of Sikander!" But in his heart Amar thought, *Once I have climbed to the safety of the column, I will be saved from the raging sea, and when some ship happens by, I will board it, and go anywhere it will take me!*

Then he turned to Hamza's commanders and said, "O noble chiefs! I am now become your sacrificial lamb! Prithee show the generosity of your pockets, in order that I may reap the reward of my perilous labor should I survive!" Everyone present there wrote out promissory notes and handed them to Amar, who took them, held his breath and leapt. But he landed short of the obelisk, and fell into the sea with a splash.

As he began to sink, he saw a mighty leviathan awaiting with open jaws to make him his fodder. Amar rallied his senses, and using the jaws of the beast as leverage he jumped up and landed on the summit of the obelisk.

Amar saw that a timbal was indeed placed there and the name of Sikander Zulqarnain was inscribed on its head. Proclaiming, "In the name of Allah!" Amar hit it with a mallet, whereupon a most deafening rumble was created, and for sixty-four leagues the sea was thrown into a turmoil. All the marine life appeared on the surface, and all the seabirds within a circumference of ten miles suddenly cried and drummed. The wind from the constant fluttering of their wings filled the sails of the ships, and they sailed on. Amar stayed on the obelisk as he had planned.

In a few days the ships dropped anchor in the isles of Ceylon, and the Sahibqiran landed on the island with his armies. Amar, however, was in great distress from solitude. Finding the violence of the sun unbearable, he supplicated before the True Lord and wept for his deliverance when suddenly he heard someone say, "Blessings of Allah be upon you!" Upon hearing this, Amar looked to his left and right with great surprise. Then the holy Khizr appeared to him, and said, "I am Khizr and have brought you deliverance." Amar kissed Khizr's feet, and made a prostration of gratitude.

But the scurrilous trickster who was famished with hunger had no qualms telling Khizr impertinently, "O venerated sir! I now put my store of hope in your hospitality as I am consumed with hunger!" The holy Khizr offered him a bread-cake, and said, "Eat this! Then I will also give you water to drink." Amar grew wrathful and said, "How can I eat my fill with this bread-cake?"

Khizr answered, "Start eating in good faith and then you shall judge for yourself whether you are able to finish it, or if you spoke prematurely from your impetuosity!"

Then Amar began eating the bread-cake, and even after he had eaten his fill, the bread-cake remained whole as before. Next Khizr produced a water flask and gave it to Amar to drink from, asking, "How is it that you did not finish the bread-cake, since you were so hungry to begin with?" Amar saw that the flask also remained full as before, although his thirst was fully quenched. He thought up a ruse to keep them both, and expressing his gratitude to Khizr, said to him, "Thirst and hunger follow a man everywhere. When I am again consumed by the pangs of hunger, there will be nobody I can petition for relief! I would be most indebted if you would confer this bread-cake and water flask upon me!"

The holy Khizr granted Amar's request, and said, "Give this Timbal of Sikander to Hamza along with all its regalia, but mind that you keep none of it yourself!" Amar said to the prophet, "How will I carry this great load, and travel under its burden?" The holy Khizr gave him a sheet of cloth, and said, "Wrap it all in this, and you shall feel no weight whatsoever." Amar said to himself, *This sheet is also a good thing to have. It will come in handy, and keep me warm in the winter besides!*

Wrapping all the goods and the Timbal of Sikander in the sheet, Amar carried the bundle on his head, and climbing onto the instep of Khizr's feet he closed his eyes and began to recite the Most Great Name—as Khizr had instructed him—and he was carried away from one place to another in just an instant. When Amar opened his eyes he found himself standing on land.

Now hear of Hamza, how when he landed in the port of Ceylon and reached the safety of its shore with his troops, he said to his men, "We shall sojourn here and occupy ourselves in grieving and mourning Amar's death. Indeed I held Amar as dear as my own life, and in the end he laid down his life for me!" Then all the commanders and their troops dressed themselves in black, and occupied themselves with grieving and lamentations.

We return to Amar's account.

In a few days Amar approached the Sahibqiran's camp. He noticed that everyone there was clad in black, and appeared grief-stricken. Pretending to be a stranger, he asked a passerby, "Whose army is this, and why are all of them dressed in mourning?" The man answered, "This is the army of the Sahibqiran, who set up camp here some time ago. Amir had a brother, Amar Ayyar by name, who died in the Indian Ocean, and the Sahibqiran dressed himself in black to mourn his death. His entire entourage are also clad in black since they, too, are in mourning. Today being Amar's *chehlum*, food and victuals over which *fateha*[57] has been said are being distributed among the beggars and the indigent."

That night put Amar on the mantle given him by Ilyas and entered Madi-Karib's pavilion. He found him lying fast asleep. Amar clambered over his chest, whereupon Madi-Karib woke up, and said, "Who are you, and what is your issue with me?" Amar replied, "I am the Angel of Death! Today when Amar's soul was bidden to enter Paradise, he refused, and told the keeper of Heaven that Madi-Karib was his bosom friend, that he would not enter Heaven without him, and in the end I was ordered to extract Madi-Karib's soul."

Madi-Karib replied, "I am most certainly not Amar's friend! Indeed I was his mortal foe!" Amar now said, "If you were to offer me a little something, I would spare your life, and take your words to God Almighty!" Madi-Karib said, "A chest of gold pieces is kept over yonder. Pray take it and refrain from taking my life!"

After securing the chest Amar left. In a similar manner Amar visited all the commanders that night, and received gold pieces from all of them after leading them into deception.

Come morning, when Aadi first narrated what had passed with him the previous night, Amir Hamza laughed heartily, reckoning that Aadi had probably had a nightmare. But then other nobles as well related identical details. Then Amir said, "This place is under the influence of the devil: How else could all the men have an identical dream? Our troops should be moved elsewhere, lest they fall into the power of the devils!"

The next day Amar played the trick on Hamza, pulling the same prank. Hamza said aloud, "It is a marvel that I hear the voice, but do not see the man who speaks!" When he groped with his hands, Hamza felt a body. Thinking it was a jinn, Hamza caught hold of it by one hand, and made to clout it with the other hand when suddenly Amar called out, "Beware, O Arab! Don't hit me!" Amar then threw off the mantle. Hamza had recognized his voice and now embraced him with great delight. Amar narrated all that had passed with him, and handed the Timbal of Sikander and other effects to Hamza.

The next morning Hamza moved his camp to the foot of Mount Ceylon, and at last arrived at his destination.

Amir had arrived at Mount Ceylon at the time of the festival commemorating the day Prophet Aadam's expiation was accepted by God. On the mountain was a stone that bore an imprint of Aadam's foot, and the Hindus and the True Believers made their pilgrimage to that site.

Amar made his way to the place. By chance, he spied a hut and went toward it, and he found an ancient praying inside. When the old man visited blessings on Amar, and addressed him by his name, Amar frowned and reached for his dagger, thinking this was a *tasma-pa*. The ancient smiled, and said, "O Amar! I am not of the race of the *tasma-pas* but of the line of Nuh, and my name is Saalim! I recognized you by virtue of receiving annunciation about you last night in a dream, otherwise I would know nothing of you or your name!" He handed Amar an iron club, and said, "Go to that nook, and dig in the ground to this club's length, and there you will find what is apportioned your share. Mind not to give in to greed!"

Amar dug up the ground to the measure, and found a bright grain of ruby. He kept digging, but found nothing else. He felt embarrassed, and returned to Saalim. The old man said, "Now go to the mountain and make pilgrimage to the imprint of Aadam's foot!"

Amar took the trail the old man advised to the mountain, and came upon a most sumptuous enclosure. When Amar drew close, he saw there a white stone with the imprint of Aadam's foot. Amar's mouth watered when he saw tall heaps of jewels piled up around the stone. Then his heart was possessed by a powerful greed.

Amar spread the mantle on the ground and gathered up all the jewels inside it, but when he neared the door of the enclosure carrying his burden, the door disappeared from before his eyes. He retraced his steps and put the jewels back, and now when he looked toward the door, he found it there as before. Amar said in his heart, *Now it is becoming plain to me that grandfather Aadam was not one to leave anything to chance! His riches shall forever remain before his eyes and nobody may swallow or plunder them!*

Amar made his ablution with water from the spring and offered his prayers. He broke into tears thinking of his mercenary act and, deeming that this holy site was a place where prayers would be granted, he supplicated to God with all sincerity. In the midst of his weeping and importuning he was overtaken by sleep of a sudden, and beheld a group of ancients standing around him, regarding him with affection.

One among them who was tall of stature gave Amar a lion skin, and said, "Put this on! It is called the *dev-jama*.[58] Once you have dressed yourself in it, you shall become immune to any and all calamities and will be safeguarded from the harm of all demons and malignant jinns. The *zam-bil*[59] that you see with it can accommodate the entire contents of the world in it, will produce all that you may wish for, and will safeguard what you vouchsafe to its care. Such is the miraculous power of this *zam-bil* that when you place your hand on it and recite, 'Grandfather Aadam! May I acquire such and such an aspect!' you shall presently convert to that form. Moreover, you will be able to speak and comprehend all the languages of the world. Learn ye now that I am Aadam!"

The second ancient gave Amar a goblet, and said, "Commit to memory the Most Great Name written on this, as it will be of great value to you! Learn ye now that I am Ishaq, the prophet of God!"

The third ancient introduced himself as Prophet Daud. Giving Amar a *do-tara*,[60] he said to him, "When you shall play this *do-tara* and sing, you will surpass even the greatest musician, and even if your audience is alien to the science of music, their hearts will be overwhelmed by your singing, and they will adore you and love you with a great passion!"

The fourth ancient gave his name as Prophet Saleh and, stroking Amar's back with his hand, said to him, "Nobody will ever outpace you, and the finest charger will be unable to match your speed! You shall run faster than the wind, and never tire!"[61]

As Prophet Saleh was saying these words, a throne descended from the heavens on which an ancient was seated. Amar's eyes were bedazzled upon beholding the face of this ancient, and he was awed and overcome by his majesty. The other four prophets greeted him with great reverence and honor. Amar asked them, "Who is this personage?" And they replied, "He is the Last Prophet of Time, Muhammad the Messenger of Allah (peace be upon him)!"

Amar made obeisance, and with folded arms spoke thus: "Sire! I plead you to grant my wish that the Angel of Death not extract my soul, that I may not die until I myself ask for my death three times!" Then Prophet Muhammad (peace be upon him!) said, "Should it be Allah's pleasure, your wish shall be granted!"

Then Amar woke up, and saw lying around him all the gifts that he had received from the prophets. Amar gathered all those gifts and displayed them before Saalim, who said, "Send Hamza here, too, Amar, so that he may also receive what is apportioned to him by destiny!" Then Amar left, and on his way back, he put his hand on the *zambil* to try it out, and called out, "O Grandfather Aadam! Make me tall and change the color of my skin to a hue darker than pitch."

Immediately Amar noticed that he had risen in height, and when he held a mirror to his face, he was himself terrified by his features.

He entered the camp of the faithfuls and started playing on his *do-tara*. Whoever heard its sound left their work unattended, and followed in his train. People brought news to Hamza who ordered that the Indian be presented before him, and found him to be of a form exceedingly strange. Riveted by his singing and music, Hamza and all his nobles became so engrossed that they lost command of their senses and were thrown into reverie as if somebody had cast a spell over them.

After Amar finished his song and stopped playing, Hamza asked him, "Where have you come from, stranger, and what is your name?" Amar answered, "I go by the name Mahmud Siyah-Tan! I am a denizen of this very land, and am known to the Khusrau of India, who rewards me according to his liberality, albeit always short of my expectations, thus obliging me to solicit before other princes!" The Sahibqiran ordered his men, saying, "Take this Indian to our treasury, and allow him to take all he can carry!" Thereupon Sultan Bakht Maghrebi took Amar to Hamza's treasury, and asked him to collect his reward.

Amar started bringing each and every chest out of the treasury, whereupon Sultan Bakht Maghrebi said, "All this is worth hundreds of cart-loads. Take only what you can carry!" Amar replied, "Rest assured that I am only doing what I was bid!"

Thinking that the Indian was perhaps a lunatic, Sultan Bakht Maghrebi kept quiet. The other employees of the treasury also watched in silence, while Amar spread his net and piled up all those chests on it. When he slung the entire load over his shoulder and made to head out, those assembled became bereft of their senses from marveling.

Sultan Bakht Maghrebi stopped Amar from leaving, saying, "Wait a while until I have informed my commander." Amar put down his load and sat there to wait. Sultan Bakht then narrated the whole episode to Hamza, and said, "O Sahibqiran, he seems to be some jinn or a *ghol* of the desert, or else he is some wizard. He tied up all the chests in the treasury in a net and, carrying them all upon his shoulders, walked with a light foot! I held him up with the ruse of obtaining your leave before he departs."

Hamza discerned that this could only be Amar, returned with some new artifice. He then went himself, and said to Amar, "What a surprise, my friend, that you picked us to be the target of this trickery!" Amar could not hold back his laughter then. Amar related his whole adventure, and said, "Saalim has sent for you, and he has put away gifts for you as well!"

Hamza rested that night, and in the morning headed for the vale with Amar and other nobles. He came upon an arena where a body of men were guarding exercise equipment. When Amir asked them to whom the arena belonged, they replied, "It is the arena of the Khusrau of India!" Hamza turned to Amar and said, "Let me show a display of my strength to these people!"

Then Hamza stepped into the arena, but when he could not lift the mace, Hamza became most distraught and cried out, "O Almighty God! When I am unable to lift up Landhoor's mace, it is certain that combat with him will be most perilous!"

Then Hamza left the arena despairing, and after visiting Saalim, went to the mountain and made his pilgrimage to Aadam's footprint and offered prayers at that site. In the course of his penultimate prostration, all of a sudden he was overtaken by stupor and fell into a deep sleep.

In his sleep he witnessed a throne descending from the heavens and lighting up the place with its brilliance. On that throne a group of ancients of illuminated aspects were seated. One among them, who was of a tall stature, greeted Hamza by his name and said, "O Hamza, take this armlet and wear it. Your arm will never be lowered by your adversary then, nor will anyone ever prevail against your arm's might. And even should your adversary be a thousand yards tall, by virtue of this blessed armlet your sword will yet surmount his head. But do not ever be the first to sound the war drums, never take precedence in seeking combat, and not until your adversary has first dealt you three blows should you deal him one yourself! Never kill one of noble soul, offer reprieve to the one who asks for it, do not pursue a retreating enemy, and never break the heart of one down in spirits! Never turn a mendicant empty-handed from your door. Never give yourself airs of vanity, and never be a braggart, nor let yourself be the agency through which the least injury is inflicted on the weak and humble. And take heed when you bellow your war cry, as its sound will travel sixteen *farsangs,* and instill great fear in the hearts of those who hear it!"

After imparting these injunctions Prophet Aadam embraced Hamza, and other prophets showed him their favor also, whereupon Amir's eyes opened in ecstasies of joy. He returned to Saalim, who congratulated Amir and said, "This traveler to the land of Death awaited you only, as guiding and initiating you on your destiny was entrusted to me[?]. Adieu, as I must now depart for the final leg of my journey!"

Having said this, Saalim recited the Act of Faith, and was entered into Heaven.

After Amir had attended to Saalim's burial, he headed to Landhoor's arena. He lifted up the mace weighing one thousand and seven hundred Tabrizi *maunds* with ease upon reciting, "In the name of Allah!" as if it were a twig, and removed it to another corner of the arena. Then he returned joyously to his camp.

The guards carried news of this incident to Landhoor's ears, who presently arrived at the arena. He marveled greatly upon finding the mace placed in another corner, and reasoned that someone who was his equal in might had arrived on the island.

Now hear of Amar, who entered Landhoor's camp in the guise of a Khorasani, with the *do-tara* in his hand. The mace bearer asked him, "Who are you, what is your trade, whence have you come and from what land?" Amar answered, "I have come to these lands with the son-in-law of the Emperor of the Seven Climes, and the fame of the liberality of the Khusrau of India has brought me to his august threshold." The king ordered that the Khorasani be brought into his presence.

Amar's appearance greatly intrigued Landhoor. He asked Amar, "What is your name, of which country are you a native, and where are you domiciled?" Amar made answer: "I am known as Baba Zud Burd, and I call Khorasan my home!" Landhoor said, "A matchless name you have, and it appears that you assault men and plunder their property!" Amar replied, "The only strikes this vassal makes are with a plectrum on the cords of my instrument; and I plunder only the hearts of my audience, and make them mellow!" Landhoor was greatly delighted by this quip and ordered Amar to sing, and Amar complied with his request

As Amar began to sing, the whole assembly was thrown into raptures. While the assembly was engrossed in his song, Amar's greedy eyes were glued to the four emerald peacocks affixed to the four corners of Landhoor's throne.

Greatly pleased by Amar's singing, Landhoor said, "Ask me for anything, O Baba Zud Burd! Speak what you most desire!" Amar replied, "Naushervan's son-in-law has bestowed much on your vassal, and freed me from all material concerns!" After a while, Landhoor again said to him, "You must ask for something, as I wish to reward you for bringing such delight to my heart with your singing!" Amar answered, "Your slave does not crave gold and riches, but desires instead to be your cupbearer, should the permission be granted!"

Landhoor signaled to the head cupbearer who handed Amar the goblet and ewer. After the cup had been passed for some two or three rounds, and Amar saw that Landhoor's eyes showed the effects of intoxication and signs of losing control of his senses, he stretched out his hand and plucked out one of the emerald peacocks, and hid it under his arm. Landhoor saw him from the corner of his eye, and said, "What is this you are doing, O Zud Burd! Why did you put the peacock in your bag?" Amar winked at him, and said, "Be quiet lest someone hear this and the thing become known!"

Then Landhoor laughed out loud and said to Amar, "O Baba Zud Burd! Little do I care should someone hear me, since the goods belong to me and it is not I who steals them! But since even your theft is so deliciously audacious, I willingly grant you the other three peacocks as well."

Amar made obeisance and, after putting away the peacocks, thought of lining his pockets further. Without the Khusrau catching him this time, he mixed four *mithcals*[62] of an inebriant in the wine ewer, and poured out two cups each for Landhoor and all his courtiers. Hardly a moment had passed before the eyes of all those present became glazed, and with resounding thuds they fell unconscious on the floor. Without loss of time Amar began his pillaging and looting. Then he made his way out, and reaching his camp before long, sat dragonlike upon all the treasure he had gathered.

It so happened that just then Amir Hamza ordered a search to be made to determine Amar's whereabouts. The members of the search party said to Amar, "Come along with us as the Sahibqiran has sent for you, and ordered us to produce you before him, however and wherever we find you!"

When Amar was led before Hamza with all these goods and effects, Amir laughed, thinking that Amar must have robbed someone again. He asked his friend, "How did you come into these possessions?" When Amar replied that everything was a gift from the Khusrau of India, the Sahibqiran did not believe him, and had all the effects put away into safekeeping for the night.

The following morning, Hamza said to Aadi, "Convey my regards to the Khusrau of India and take to him all these things, in addition to the other gifts that I shall also give into your care. Also, give the Khusrau this message from me: 'Amar visited your court last night in disguise and he maintains that the Khusrau of India made him a gift of all these effects, but as I do not believe his account I am returning all these goods back to you. And should you deign to accept my small token as a gift—it would afford me great joy. And I beseech you to inform me if Amar is guilty of any offense, so that I may chastise him accordingly!'"

In Landhoor's court, meanwhile, the Khusrau of India and the nobles of his court regained their senses when the sun of the new day rose. Upon beholding the whole court looted bare, they looked for Baba Zud Burd, and made inquiries as to his whereabouts. As Landhoor was busy conducting these inquiries, he noticed a note tied to his neck. After reading its message, he discovered that it was in fact Amar who had visited him the previous night in the guise of Baba Zud Burd.

When Aadi arrived, Landhoor received him with honor and seated him above all his nobles, and accepted from him the gifts sent by the Sahibqiran. As to the things stolen by Amar from his court, however, he declared that he had conferred their possession to Amar.

Landhoor said to Aadi, "After offering him my humble greetings, convey this message to Amir Hamza: 'Even if the tiniest shadow of spite passed over my heart against Amar, it has now been forgotten. I request that he, too, not let it cloud his heart. I would be beholden to Hamza if he would send Amar to visit me without a disguise!'" After speaking, Landhoor conferred a robe of honor on Aadi and gave him leave to depart.

When he returned, Aadi narrated all that he had seen and heard, and upon hearing this Hamza was greatly pleased, and said to Amar, "O Baba Zud Burd! The Khusrau of India desires to see you in your real person, and has returned your booty as a gift." Amar was in seventh heaven when he heard these words, and headed for Landhoor's court after stashing away all the goods.

Along his way Amar saw a group of merchants who were also headed for the Khusrau's court. They were carrying very many excellent and choice objects, and one of the merchants had a crown, which was studded with such a marvel of jewels that nobody had seen or heard the likes of them. Amar donned the garb of a merchant, and followed along in their entourage. When the party reached the threshold of Landhoor's court, they were ordered to enter and display their goods.

Landhoor was most delighted when the crown was presented before him, and said "Reward these merchants over and above the cost of the crown! I shall wear this crown on my head this instant!" When Amar overheard this, he said, "We must first be paid the price of the crown, then the Khusrau may freely put it on his head!"

At these words, Landhoor instantly returned the crown and said to the keeper, "Bring it to me once its price has been paid to the merchants. I would never dream of acquiring anyone's property by force!" The broker took the crown to the merchants, and asked them to name its price.

Amar took the crown from his hand, and said, "I shall judge its worth once I have appraised it in the sunlight—as one must speak judiciously regarding business matters in the court of kings!"

Amar stepped out of the Hall of Audience and, peering intently in the sky, spoke thus, "What a dark cloud is rising in the skies! I imagine it is the harbinger of a severe dust storm, as a great mist is upon us!" Thus speaking Amar stepped to one side, and then made away, giving them all the slip.

The news was immediately conveyed to the Khusrau who mounted his elephant and went in pursuit, and intercepted Amar, who tried to hide himself in a thicket. But finding no escape from there, he was distressfully looking around when he beheld a hut, with a man inside grinding a hand mill. Amar immediately barged into his house, and said, "The Khusrau has had a dream, and philosophers have interpreted that the king will be delivered from the evil boded in his dream, if he beats a drum with a head made of a miller's scalp. A party is on their way here to catch you, and they bring the executioner along!"

When he heard that, the poor man almost died of fright. He asked Amar, "How can I escape from the power of these tyrants?" Amar replied, "Give me your waistcloth so that I may wear it and sit here grinding the hand mill in your stead. You must dive into this pool here. If someone comes looking for you I will divert them from your house by some trick!" The miller immediately handed his waistcloth and dress to Amar, and dived into the pool stark naked and settled there without moving.

Soon Landhoor arrived and told Amar that a man of such and such a description had entered his house and to tell him where he was hiding. Amar replied, "That man jumped into the pool and has been hiding there!" Landhoor then undressed and jumped into the pool after him, and Amar picked up his dress and headed to the office of the royal treasurer.

When he found the treasurer, he showed him Landhoor's dress, and said to him, "The Khusrau of India has sent me with this token to collect two hundred *tomans* from you and return to him posthaste to bring him the money!" The treasurer handed him the two hundred *tomans* without asking any questions, and Amar headed for his camp.

Now, when Landhoor tried to get the miller out of the pool, the miller banged his head against the stones of the pool. After inflicting this injury on himself, he said to Landhoor, "Now my scalp is damaged and shall be of no use! You must look for another miller now, and fit out the drum with *his* scalp, and present it to the Khusrau so that he may drum it and ward off the evil boded by his dream!" Landhoor wondered what insanity might have come over him to utter such crazy words.

When the miller got out of the pool Landhoor saw that he was not the person he had been looking for. Landhoor stepped from the pool and asked the people gathered outside if they had seen anyone come out of the house and pass their way. They replied, "We did not see anyone pass here except for the man whom Your Excellency sent with his robe to collect two hundred *tomans* from the treasurer. He passed by here again after collecting the money from the treasurer. But we know not where he lives!" At this, Landhoor understood that it was Amar, and he marveled at his ingenuity. After changing into a new robe, he mounted his elephant, and headed in a straight line toward Hamza's camp by himself.

Hamza received and welcomed him and seated him on his own bejeweled seat. Landhoor became greatly enamored of Hamza's manners and, thanking him profusely for his kindnesses, he said, "Where is Amar? Please send for him! But do ask him to appear in his own person."

Upon these orders, Amar immediately presented himself and took a seat after making obeisance to Landhoor. Fair-bodied cupbearers, clad in gold finery, arrived carrying goblets and ewers. With his own hand, Hamza offered the first cup to Landhoor, and then drank one himself. Landhoor requested Amar to sing and asked him to send for musical instruments. Amar sent for the *do-tara* and after tuning it, sang a song of such subtlety and elegance that the whole assembly sat enraptured, and Landhoor involuntarily called out "Bravo!" and "What excellence!"

The Sahibqiran and Landhoor next conferred together privately. Landhooor said to Hamza, "I wish that you would renounce your plans for war, and take me along with you. I shall kill Naushervan and seat you on his throne."

Amir answered, "I gave my pledge to Naushervan to efface your existence from this world. How could I go back on my word and break my pledge?" Then Landhoor drew his sword and, presenting it to Hamza, lowered his neck before him, and said, "If this is your pleasure, go ahead and behead this unworthy one, and take my head and present it to Naushervan without subjecting yourself to the least labor or toil on my account!" The Sahibqiran embraced Landhoor and greatly extolled his manliness and courage.

Then Amir said to him, "Such an act is suited either to a coward or an executioner! Sound the war drums and let us descend tomorrow into the arena, and let the course of events be determined by the results in the battlefield!" Landhoor answered, "Adieu, then! If this is what you desire, you must sound the clarion of war today from your camp!"

Amir replied, "You may sound the drums in your camp and take precedence! Then I shall also give orders to that effect and answer your call!" The Khusrau was obliged to sound the war drums. While the courageous and valiant warriors busied themselves in supplications to the Almighty God to safeguard their honor in the field of combat, many a coward slipped away, taking advantage of the dark night, and others suffered bouts of diarrhea from fear.

In the morning none had yet come forward from either side to seek combat when the horizon was darkened by a great cloud of dust that arose in the sky. When scissors of wind cut the skirts of this dark cloud and blew away the dust from the face of the land, forty new standards came into view. It was soon revealed that this approaching host numbered forty thousand troops.

When this unannounced army came to a halt, the Sahibqiran saw Gustham bin Ashk Zarrin Kafsh standing in the front row under his swine-headed standard, busily arranging his troops. Hamza brought this scene to Amar's attention, who thought of a stratagem. Separating from his army, he headed toward Gustham's camp. Having arrived there he made a profusely humble salutation to Gustham, who said, "How are you, Khvaja Amar?" Amar replied, "What is there to be said about the existence of such a one as I! It was an evil day when I entered the service of that Arab." Gustham asked, "What is the matter?"

Amar replied, "Since you ask me, everything is falling apart! Thinking that he is already Naushervan's son-in-law, Hamza is riding such a high horse these days that he cares not a whit for anybody else! Gone are the days when he would beg me to sit on the throne by his side. Things have come to such a pass now that he begrudges me even a seat in his court! If I cannot find myself an equally illustrious service, I will willingly settle for one half as august, in order to save myself my present degradation."

When he heard this, Gustham replied, "If you would condescend to enter my service, I would hold you dear as my own life, and ensure that you are accorded all due care and comfort!"

Then Amar said, "Indeed this was the reason for my leaving behind that camp and approaching you! But you must first ensure that Hamza does not engage in combat with Landhoor. You would do well to be the first to seek combat with Landhoor, in order that Hamza will seem a fool and his army put to shame. Landhoor has absolutely no might or power. I inspected his mace and found it to be nothing more than a lump of wood covered in iron shell for appearances! As to Landhoor himself, he is the worst coward in the whole world. Thus, if Hamza were to kill him, he would become Naushervan's son-in-law. And then any excesses that he might commit will be too little!"

Gustham said, "It was a happy moment when you came to me! I shall put to sword both Landhoor and Hamza and dispatch them to Hell! Gustham rode his rhinoceros forward, and called out, "Let Landhoor bin Saadan emerge from hiding and present himself here! The day of reckoning is come!" Landhoor spurred his she-elephant Maimoona forward, and said to Gustham, "What rot do you speak, O wretch? Give your blow, and deal what you have to present!" Then Gustham drew his sword from his scabbard and aimed a blow to Landhoor's head, but Landhoor blocked it with his mace. Then Landhoor dealt him a strike with his mace. As Gustham was destined to live yet some more days, the mace did not come down squarely on him, but the shaft brushed his side, breaking his ribs and mixing all his courage and valor into dust. He fell face forward from his rhinoceros and lost the power of his senses. His comrades rushed in and carried him away by stealth, and soon sounded the drums of retreat.

Then Landhoor turned toward Hamza with a smile, and said, "Come tomorrow, we two shall settle our account, and witness how your sword shall fare and what it has to offer!"

After the drums of retreat were sounded, the two armies withdrew from the battlefield.

Of Landhoor Doing Battle with the Sahibqiran, and His Surrendering to the World Conqueror

The might of the reed is tested by the narrative's power, and the vigor of the swashbucklers of colorful accounts is now manifested in the arena of the page. Hear now this history of the war of the clime of India, and an account of the combat between two lions of the forest of courage and valor.

When the seraph of the morning routed the night's foe in the arena of ascendancy and raised the standard of light in the clime of the heavens, the Sahibqiran mounted his steed Siyah Qitas. The Khusrau of India, King Landhoor bin Saadan, came forth from the other side, armed to the teeth and mounted on his she-elephant Maimoona. The two armies descended into the arena and arranged their forces for battle.

The Sahibqiran spurred his steed and stood face to face with Landhoor and delivered these words with his graceful tongue: "O King Landhoor! I have issue with you, and you with me! Nothing shall be gained from the carnage of God's creatures, and therefore we must needs abstain from it! Deal me a blow with your greatest claim, and thus fulfill your heart's desire!" Landhoor replied, "O Sahibqiran! If I were the first to deal the blow, you would perish with all the desires of your heart unrequited! I ask that you deal the first blow yourself!" The Sahibqiran replied: "I would not give you a blow myself until you have given me three blows first!"

As Landhoor was much taken with Amir, he did not touch his mace but attacked Sahibqiran with his lance instead. The Sahibqiran blocked the point of Landhoor's lance with the point of his own lance, and they sparred this way for a while. After a hundred thrusts of the spear had been made and foiled on each side, the Sahibqiran locked Landhoor's spear with his own, and gave a blow with its shaft which sent the lance flying out of Landhoor's hands into the air. Landhoor's face turned deathly pale from mortification, but he quickly regained self-possession and said to Hamza, "O Sahibqiran! The cloak of spearsmanship sewn by the Seamstress of Death befits you alone! If I were to deem myself a champion in the arena of valor, never ever would I touch a lance again."

Thus having spoken, he weighed his mace in his hands, and said, "O Sahibqiran, the opportunity for making peace is not yet lost. I request that you spare me the grief of having to kill you!" Amir replied, "This is a time for seeking combat and dying, not a time for making exhortations and establishing bonds of love! Come, I would like to see what your mace has to deliver."

Then Landhoor sat back on his haunches and, weighing his mace in both his hands, brought it down with great force on the Sahibqiran's head. Amir received Landhoor's blow on the shield. Even though sweat broke from every pore on Hamza's body, still his arm did not flinch from the grace of Prophet Aadam's armlet.

Then Landhoor dealt a second blow with greater might, and even though the Sahibqiran remained steadfast as Sikander's rampart,[63] he was suddenly reminded of the taste of the milk on the day he was born. Irritated, Landhoor now brought down his mace with such force that had it landed on the *Koh-e Besutoon*,[64] it would have caused water to flow from it. The Sahibqiran blocked this blow on his shield again, but from the impact of the blow the legs of his steed Siyah Qitas were driven into the ground to the shanks, and Amir himself was enveloped in a cloud of dust.

The hue of Landhoor's face underwent a sea change upon beholding this scene, and involuntarily these words escaped his mouth: "What a disgrace that a youth such as the Sahibqiran was killed!" Landhoor then dismounted his elephant and called out, "O august and illustrious lord! Answer me if you are alive so that I may rejoice; and if you are dead, we shall meet again on the Day of Reckoning!"

Having regained possession of his senses, the Sahibqiran struck Siyah Qitas with the whip of Prophet Daud, whereupon Siyah Qitas extricated his legs and jumped up from the pit and emerged clear of its depression. Amir said, "O Khusrau! I do not see the one whom you killed and laid low! Give another blow and satiate every last desire of your heart! Our combat has just begun."

Landhoor was most astonished and, mounting a horse, he drew the steel blue Bardwani[65] sword from his belt and dealt a blow to Amir's head with it. Amir raised his bejeweled shield and blocked that devastating blow. Then he spoke thus: "O King Landhoor! I blocked all your five strikes, and indeed the best of all blows were arrayed in them! It is my turn, and now I shall return your blows."

Amir now locked his stirrup with Landhoor's and, drawing his sword Samsam, dealt a blow to Landhoor's head. The Khusrau attempted to block the blow with his shield and lock Amir's arm, but Amir's sword cut through Landhoor's shield as if it were made of fresh cheese. Landing on his horse's neck, the sword severed his head from the neck and felled it. The Khusrau of India was obliged to empty his saddle and, flying into a fierce rage, he drew his sword and came charging furiously at Hamza. Amir, too, emptied his saddle and, wresting Landhoor's hand and wrenching the sword from it, threw it toward his camp. Then Landhoor locked his arms around Amir's neck in a tight clasp, and the two of them began to wrestle.

When the wrestler of the day retired for repose to its Westerly pavilion, and the night's master began to take up his daily exercise rituals with his celestial novices, torches were lit in both camps. They burned continuously through the following nights, for Amir and Landhoor remained locked in combat for three nights and three days. On the fourth day Amir bellowed "God is Mighty!" and heaved Landhoor up, lifting him to the height of his breast, and maintained his stupendous weight above the ground but failed to hoist Landhoor over his head.

Hamza resolved to release Landhoor and plunge the dagger chivalrously into his own breast and put out the lamp of his precious life. But Landhoor stayed his hand and submitted to him thus with folded arms: "O Sahibqiran! It was not given to anyone besides yourself to lift me or even to heave me up from the ground! I declare my allegiance and fealty to you from the bottom of my heart!"

Amir embraced Landhoor and said, "O Khusrau! I pronounce you my right arm! I shall treat you like a brother, and hold you more dear than my life. But I desire that you accompany me before Naushervan, and help me fulfill my promise to him." Landhoor replied, "I shall be obedient to your wishes and go anywhere that you command me to!"

Landhoor accompanied Amir to his pavilion, and the Sahibqiran ordered an assembly of merriment arranged. Then he set about filling his eyes' goblets with tears of blood in remembrance of Princess Mehr-Nigar. Noticing this, Landhoor surmised that thoughts of the princess occupied him, and he wiped at Amir's blood-red tears with a kerchief, saying, "The days of parting are coming to an end, and the day of meeting is approaching! Why cry now?" Then the Sahibqiran regained the control of his heart, and asked Amar to sing.

Landhoor presented the keys of his treasury to Amir, and conferred many choice objects from the lands of India on him as gifts. Landhoor then ennobled himself by converting to the True Faith.

Amir sat down for the meal with Landhoor by his side, and after they had finished the meal, Landhoor said to him, "I long to be blessed by a visit from you. And for a long time I have nursed this desire."

Amir answered, "This proposition is most agreeable to me!" Landhoor then retired to his palace and ordered preparations for a royal feast. Then he escorted the Sahibqiran with all his renowned nobles and august champions to the feast, and the assembly began to warm up and the tabla to play.

———

Now we leave Amir and Landhoor occupied in these revelries, and turn to Gustham. The *ayyars* brought him intelligence that Hamza had prevailed over Landhoor, and that for several days festivities had been celebrated in which Landhoor had supped with Hamza. The *ayyars* also informed Gustham that aside from Muqbil Vafadar there was no commander present in Hamza's camp and no one left to defend the army, as all the champions and nobles were occupied along with Amir in the festivities.

Gustham had brought with him two attendants of Princess Mehr-Nigar, whom Amir knew by sight. He filled up two flagons with the choicest grape wine, and mixed it with four *mithcals* of such a potent poison that were a drop of it to fall into the Indian Ocean it would suffice to kill all marine life. After counterfeiting Mehr-Nigar's signet, and sealing the flagons with it, Gustham dressed her attendants in travelers' attire, and then forged an amorous missive from the princess. Handing the letter to the attendants, he explained in detail that they must first present themselves before Muqbil Vafadar and announce that Princess Mehr-Nigar had sent them in utmost confidence and at great risk of exposing herself. This would put Muqbil under obligation to take them to Amir whereupon the attendants were to convey to Amir a great deal of love talk from Mehr-Nigar, and present him the wine and the letter. Gustham made it known to them that if they succeeded, he would induct them into his harem and take them as his wives.

Then those two vixens garbed themselves in manly clothes and set out. When they entered Amir's encampment and were announced by Muqbil, Hamza rose from his seat excitedly and said to the Khusrau, "I must needs attend to a matter of utmost importance, and shall soon return. In the meanwhile pray continue with the festivities!" Then he commanded Amar to regale Landhoor and keep him company in his stead.

Amir ordered privacy and sent for the attendants the moment he arrived in his pavilion. Upon hearing their account, Amir kissed the princess's seal on the letter and pressed it to his eyes. Beside himself with joy, he threw all caution to the wind. Breaking open the seal of the flagon, he made a toast to Princess Mehr-Nigar's name, and drained its contents.

No sooner had the wine traveled down his throat than Amir fell into a daze. He began to foam at the mouth, his limbs began to convulse, and he was taken unconscious.

Thinking that Amir was at death's door, and that his life was only a matter of a few more breaths—and that their mission had been accomplished—those two strumpets pulled out a peg of the pavilion by some artifice to escape unseen, and happily made their way out of there to take these tidings to Gustham.

It so happened that at that moment, Landhoor mentioned to Amar that the absence of the guest of honor had deprived the assembly of all joy. He promised Amar a gift if he would bring back Hamza that instant. Once Amar heard of the reward, he immediately set out on his errand.

He found Muqbil guarding the entrance to Hamza's pavilion, and asked him what Amir was occupied with. Muqbil said, "Two female attendants sent by Mehr-Nigar arrived, and Amir is conferring with them." Amar's heart skipped a beat from some unknown foreboding, and exclaiming, "May God have mercy on us!" he entered Amir's pavilion where he found all the tapers extinguished. Without loss of time Amar lit up one of his trickster's flares and witnessed that Hamza's whole body was covered with blisters, his coloration had turned dark, spume flowed from his mouth, and he was writhing in convulsions while unconscious on the floor. One flagon of wine stood upright while the other lay shattered on the floor. Where its contents had splashed, the earth had cracked. When Amar looked around, he found nobody there, but discovering that one peg of the pavilion had been pulled out from the ground, he immediately followed where the footprints nearby it led him.

Those slogging and plodding bawds were no match for Amar's superior speed and reach. They were still on their way when Amar caught up and descended upon them. One of them was saying, "Come friend, let us go and receive the reward that Gustham had promised us!" when Amar called out from behind them, "O villainous witches! Behold here your Angel of Death! And I will send you to the House of Death as you deserve!" Thus speaking, Amar drew his dagger from his waist, and relieved their shoulders of the burden of their heads.

Then Amar retraced his steps and returned to his camp. He took Muqbil along to show him Hamza's state, and said, "It all came about thanks to your negligence and lax guard! Now tell me what is to be done about it!"

When Muqbil began to beat his head in remorse, Amar said, "Quiet! Lest word of it leak out and the armies of India revert upon us! Guard Amir and do not set foot outside the pavilion until I have returned."

Then Amar went before Landhoor, and privately addressed him thus: "Amir Hamza is unable to return at present, as two commanders have arrived from Naushervan's court. They have brought word that should Hamza wish to remain true to his promise to the emperor, he must immediately take Landhoor prisoner! Amir has requested that if you oblige him by pretending to be taken prisoner for the sake of appearances, not the least harm will come to you, and it will promote his cause!"

The Khusrau replied, "Let aside such a thing as imprisonment, I would have thought nothing of it even if Amir had asked for my head! Never in the least would I dither from obedience to him!" Amar said then, "I fear lest your camp take offense and rebel." The Khusrau replied, "There is no one who would even contemplate such a thing!" Then Landhoor gave out orders to the commanders of his camp and, with his hands bound by a kerchief in the token of willful surrender, he entered the camp of the Faithful.

Amar removed Landhoor to a secluded place and had him attended to with great honor, and offered him a goblet of drugged wine. The moment Landhoor was taken unconscious, Amar put him in chains and confined him in a chest perforated with holes for air, so that he would not suffocate. Then Amar attended to his army and set out from there to find some cure for Hamza.

He spotted two horsemen, and much though Amar tried to escape notice, the encounter could not be avoided. Amar boldly went forth and confronted them. The two riders dismounted, and inquired after Amar's well-being. When Amar asked them to introduce themselves, they replied, "We are the sons of Shahpal Hindi. Our names are Sabir and Sabur, and we have undertaken a long journey in search of you. Our father professes to the True Faith, but at heart he has remained an infidel! Last night, when he heard the news of Amir's poisoning, he went over to the side of Gustham. Thus we have come to remove Amir to our fort, and to treat him with all due diligence!"

Amar was mightily glad upon hearing these words, and exclaimed, "Make God a witness to your pledge of his safety, to dispel the doubts of treachery and fraud from my heart!" They readily swore by God.

Amar brought Sabir and Sabur into his camp, and when the time-keeper announced the middle hour of the night, Amar had Hamza carried in a litter to the fort of Sabir and Sabur. After making all arrangements to his satisfaction, he said to the brothers, "Now, tell me what must be done to cure Amir?" They answered, "Ten days' journey from here is the isle of Narvan, where Hakim Aqlimun lives. He can restore Amir to health, as he is veritably possessed of the breath of the Messiah! We shall write out a note for him. If you were to bring the hakim here, Amir would be cured before long!"

At first Amar thought he might lose Hamza by the time the hakim arrived, but then he realized that he would not get well without the hakim being present. Thus he resolved to go and fetch the hakim.

Sabir and Sabur sent Darab the trickster to accompany Amar and guide him on the way. A little distance farther on was a garden where they both sat down to take rest after traveling some distance. Amar offered Darab drugged food, and when Amar saw Darab's eyes becoming glazed, and noticed that he was growing all torpid and limp, Amar tied him to a tree trunk and went forth with great dispatch.

When Amar arrived at the house, the porter sent him before the hakim. The hakim took the letter from Amar's hand, but bristled upon reading it, and said to Amar, "How royally Sabir and Sabur have written that if I come posthaste and make Hamza well, they will fill up my pockets with jewels that would afford me great joy. They take me for an avaricious man to address me thus. I would have certainly gone if they had not mentioned it, but now I would never go!"

Amar said, "O reverend sage! They were clearly in the wrong and made a mistake by thus addressing an ascetic puritan like yourself. But pray overlook their error, and send for a conveyance!" The hakim flew into a rage, and said, "What business have you poking your nose in, suggesting how I must reason! You shall gain nothing by your insistence!"

Amar said, "Sire, I fail to see what great hurdle blocks your accompanying me. We must needs find some way that you do!" Hakim Aqlimun replied, "What melancholy is it that drives a base creature like yourself to reason with the Pride of Creation in this manner?" Amar answered, "Sire, if I were a madman of any sort, no doubt I would have been followed to your door by shouting and abusing urchins. As it is, during my long journey here no one even snapped a finger at me!"

Then Hakim Aqlimun called out to his slaves, "Secure this man's hands and feet as he suffers from contumaciousness of speech. And then bastinado him, for it is a sovereign remedy and a veritable cure for madmen like him!" Amar saw the matter getting out of hand and realized, too, that while Aqlimun would not come with him, he would be punished to no purpose, and thus he set to weeping and wailing, and submitted to the hakim thus with folded arms: "Sire, I spoke idly! The speech that I made before you was put into my mouth by Sabir and Sabur. However, now I cannot leave as the dark of the night has fallen, and I would not be able to find my way out of here! If you would be so kind to give me permission, I will lodge myself in the servants' quarters for the night, and go my way come morning!" Then Aqlimun ordered his slaves to conduct Amar into the kitchen, feed him something, let him sleep the night over, and send him on his way in the morning.

Once he found his way into kitchen, Amar drugged the cook. Amar dug a deep hole underneath the kitchen's kiln and interred the cook there. After covering him up with a great pile of billets, he kindled a fire and put a cauldron of water to boil on top of it. Then he dressed himself in the cook's garb and began to prepare the hakim's breakfast with great skill, and drugged it before serving it to the hakim.

The hakim was most satisfied by his sumptuous meal and began to burp out loud once he had finished eating. Addressing Amar, he said, "You have a most sublime talent! I shall dictate other recipes to you as well, and share many a trick of preparing the food with you!"

Amar now took a few steps back, and said, "Indeed, O hakim! When it comes to recipes, you are another one! Look at all your knowledge and learning, and how it has been totally lost on you!" Hakim Aqlimun flew into a great passion, and as he rose, saying, "What is this buffoonery, you fool!" Amar gave him a shove and the hakim fell flat on his face on the floor. Amar tied him up in his mantle, and took the leftovers and fed them to the servants. When those unsuspecting fools, too, lost the power of their senses, Amar put the hakim into the *zambil* along with his whole library and pharmacopoeia, and all the goods and chattels of his house. He then wrote out a bill of passage, which stated that it was incumbent upon the ferryman at the wharf to take the carrier of the bill across the river with great care and dispatch. Then sealing the document with the hakim's signet, Amar cheerfully made his way out of the house.

In a few moments he arrived at the wharf carrying the bundle on his back, and handed the note to the ferryman. The ferryman set diligently to work, and ferried Amar across the river in a trice. And in a few hours Amar reached the spot where he had tied Darab to the tree. Amar untied Darab and gave him a physic that restored him to his senses. Then Amar narrated his adventure from the beginning to the end of how he had come to bring back Hakim Aqlimun. Darab was so utterly confounded upon hearing the account that he threw himself down at Amar's feet exclaiming, "You are the master!" and became Amar's professed pupil.

Amar said to him, "Follow me at your sweet pace, as I must now speed away." Before long he approached the fort, and there a wonder of wonders awaited him. Gustham stood before the fort with his own host, and with the armies of the Khusrau of India arrayed opposite his. Amar speedily threw his rope ladder on the crenelations, and shot upward like a rocket, but as he climbed an archer on the ground took aim and shot at him. The arrow pierced the bundle but its progress was stopped by the golden mortar and pestle inside. Amar jumped inside the fort and laid the bundle before Sabir and Sabur.

Amar then gathered all of Hakim Aqlimun's goods and possessions around the hakim, and administered him a drug to dispel his faint. The hakim looked around and was utterly perplexed and confounded to find that while all the goods and paraphernalia of his trade were there, it was not his house, nor was it the city and the people of his land, as he could well see. During this time Sabir and Sabur presented themselves, and greeted the hakim, and busied themselves in making him welcome. Hakim Aqlimun asked them, "How do I happen to be here with all my things?" Amar replied, "Sire! It was yours truly who brought you here, after traversing such a long journey!" When Aqlimun found out that it was Amar, he rose to embrace him, and said, "O Khvaja! Had I known that it was you, I would have come without arguing in the least!" Amar replied, "I am still indebted to you for the kindness you showed me. Pray now make haste and find some way to exude the poison from the Sahibqiran's body!"

When he examined Amir, Hakim Aqlimun wrung his hands in great anguish, and said remorsefully, "Alas! Except Naushervan no one has a cure for this illness on the face of the Earth!" Amar said, "O sage, what is this sovereign elixir that is like the rara avis in its properties?" The hakim replied, "The name of this antidote is Shah Mohra. Amir will not recuperate without it, as the toxin has invaded the veins, and every single organ in his body has been affected by the deadly poison!" Amar then said, "How will Hamza survive by the time the Shah Mohra is sent for, and brought back from Ctesiphon?" The hakim replied, "Indeed, I see no other way to cure Hamza"

Amar went weeping and wailing and throwing dirt on his head to the gates of the fort, where Muqbil Vafadar was standing guard. He asked Amar, "Say, O Khvaja, what was it that the hakim prescribed as a remedy for Amir?" Amar said, "I put myself to all that hazard in bringing the hakim here, only to hear that bird of bad omen tell me that there is no cure for Hamza's affliction except for the Shah Mohra, which can be found neither in the perfumeries of the world nor anywhere else but the coffers of Naushervan!"

When Amar had taken a few steps, Muqbil called out from behind him, "O Khvaja! If you go to Ctesiphon, give my salutations and regards to the old woman of Ctesiphon[66] who dwells by Naushervan's palace!" Amar turned upon him in great vexation, and struck him on the head with his staff so hard that Muqbil was bathed in blood and fell to the ground in a swoon. Then Muqbil addressed Amar gently thus: "O Khvaja, do not be angry with me. The Shah Mohra is right here!" Then Amar became even more wroth with Muqbil, and began to rebuke him, and said, "Then why did you not say so right away instead of sending me off on a wild goose chase?" Muqbil replied, "O Khvaja! When Hamza's side is opened, the Shah Mohra will be revealed! It will be there where Buzurjmehr secreted it before my eyes!" Amar then embraced Muqbil joyfully and went to see Hamza.

When Hakim Aqlimun saw him, he said, "O Khvaja! I thought that you would have left for Ctesiphon to fetch the Shah Mohra, but I see you are still here!" Amar said, "How would it please you if I told you that I have already returned from Ctesiphon, and have possession of the Shah Mohra?" Aqlimun replied, "Knowing you, I would not be surprised if you have indeed accomplished what you claim. Come, hand me the Shah Mohra now if you have it on your person!" Amar replied, "It is buried in Amir's side, and had been in his possession all along!" When Aqlimun examined Amir's body, he discovered that while the rest of it had turned crystal blue, the poison had not affected the part where the Shah Mohra was embedded, and there the skin had retained its natural color. Aqlimun said, "Amir would not have survived this long for his body is all darkened, and would have died long ago if the Shah Mohra was not buried in his side."

Then Aqlimun ordered that a large cauldron be filled with several hundred *maunds* of milk. After opening Amir's side with his blade, he removed the Shah Mohra, wrapped it in silk, and inserted it into Amir's stomach by way of his mouth. And after leaving it inside for a while, the hakim extracted it and dipped it into the cauldron of milk. The milk began to change color and turned rusty. In this manner, the hakim lowered the Shah Mohra some five or six times into Amir's stomach, kept it there for a few moments, and then dipped it into the milk. Then the milk stopped changing color, and showed no further variation in its hue, and the coloration of Amir's skin began to turn natural, and he sneezed. Aqlimun covered him with *katan* sheets, and busied himself in restoring him to his senses.

When he regained control of his senses, Amir sat himself up with the help of pillows, and asked, "Where is King Landhoor, and what became of all the festivities?" Amar immediately restored Landhoor to consciousness, and took him to Amir, on the way recounting all the events that had transpired to Landhoor, and saying, "My fear of your reverting was the reason I was guilty of this contumely!" Then Landhoor and all the illustrious nobles presented themselves before Amir.

In the meantime the news reached them that Shahpal Hindi, who was aiding and abetting Gustham, had attempted to storm the battlements, but his elder son, Sabir, had dispatched him to Hell with a fiery missile, and because of the incident Gustham had resolved to charge the fortress. Hamza said to Amar, "Go and convey to Gustham on my behalf the message that I have shown restraint until now for the sake of Naushervan. But he has been blind to my consideration and is unable to desist from his malevolent ways! Tell him to make his dark face scarce soon, or else he will receive the deserts of his deeds and be taken to task before long!"

When Amar conveyed Hamza's message to that man of evil-omened aspect, Gustham replied thus: "O cameleer's son, play these tricks on someone else! It has been a long time since Hamza died, and no mark remains even of his grave. If Hamza is alive, as you claim, then go and ask him what secret of mine he is privy to! I will believe the veracity of your claim if you bring me the right answer."

Amar returned to Hamza and narrated word for word what Gustham had told him, and then said, "O Sahibqiran, I would never have believed that you were on such intimate terms with a cad like Gustham! First it was Bahram who barely survived his villainous plot, and then he poisoned you! May God recompense Buzurjmehr, who hid the Shah Mohra in your side, or else there would have been no hope of your escaping with your life."

Then Hamza narrated the incident of Gustham breaking wind in his embrace, and said to Amar, "This is the secret that he alluded to. Go and tell him this." Amar returned to Gustham, and said to him, "Hear this, you dolt! Amir replies that just from the force of his embrace you broke wind three times! If you were to receive a blow from his arm you would fill up the whole arena with your scat!"

When Gustham heard Amar reveal the secret, he knew that Hamza was alive and well, and that some new calamity now lay in store for him. For which reason he decided that the wisest course of action would be to turn tail. He headed for Sindh without further loss of time and, unable to give up his seditionist ways, he obtained the severed heads of two men in Sindh, and sent them by messenger to Naushervan, and wrote this in the accompanying note:

> Landhoor has defeated Hamza in battle, and by the grace of Your Highness I managed to kill Landhoor, and many an adventure befell me in the undertaking. I am herewith sending you the heads of both Hamza and Landhoor!

Gustham also wrote a detailed note to Bakhtak in which he gave him a true account of the event, and his future plans.

When the two severed heads and the note were presented to Naushervan, his eyes filled up with tears, and he said to Buzurjmehr, "Alas for the youth of Hamza! I know it for a fact that if the vaults of the heavens were to turn for a thousand years, one who is Hamza's match would never be born!" Buzurjmehr said, "I cannot say anything, as Hamza's horoscope testifies to his well-being—although it does clearly manifest and attest to great physical suffering. However, the knowledge of the future is only with Allah!"

The reins of the steed of the pen are turned and it is spurred into a gallop to traverse the stations of the narrative, thus revealing that when Hamza's strength was a little recovered, his heart again began to pine in the memory of his charming beloved, and he said to Landhoor, "Now I wish for us to proceed to Ctesiphon!" The Khusrau replied, "As Your Honor pleases!" The Khusrau appointed his uncle's son, Jaipur, as his deputy, and then Landhoor himself with his army in his train accompanied the Sahibqiran as his riding companion.

Although the violence of the poison had reduced Amir to little more than skin and bones, yet his desire to set eyes again on Princess Mehr-Nigar made him persevere station after station of all-day journeying, and the ardor of his love and passion propelled him forward.

———

Now hear of the machinations of Bakhtak, who applied himself to devising a strategy after reading Gustham's note. It occurred to him that Aulad bin Marzaban, the relative of Zhopin who traced his lineage to Kaikaus, might be inveigled to ask for Princess Mehr-Nigar's hand, and therefore must be sent for without delay. In his letter to Aulad, Bakhtak wrote,

> Princess Mehr-Nigar has passed from adolescence into nubile age. An Arab named Hamza had sought her hand, but he was sent to India on the campaign against Landhoor and was killed at Landhoor's hands. Therefore, it is my well-intentioned counsel that you proceed here posthaste. I will arrange to have you married to Princess Mehr-Nigar and have you declared Naushervan's son-in-law!

Upon reading this letter, Aulad bin Marzaban was near to bursting with joy, and he left Zabul with thirty thousand troops, arriving in Ctesiphon within a few days. Upon receiving the news of his arrival, Bakhtak began making preparations for his welcome. Aulad was received with great fanfare, and after some days had passed, Bakhtak found an opportunity to speak privately with the emperor, and said to him, "Now that Hamza is dead, we must needs attend to the marriage of Princess Mehr-Nigar. As to Your Highness's considerations of Gustham, he is well advanced in years. It would be more suitable to marry her to someone young and honorable."

Naushervan said to him, "Then, why do you not propose someone yourself?" Bakhtak replied, "In my humble opinion, there is no better match than Aulad bin Marzaban."

Most satisfied with Bakhtak's counsel, the emperor informed Empress Mehr-Angez of the proposition. As no one in the female quarters of the royal palace yet knew the news of Hamza's death, it brought Empress Mehr-Angez great distress to hear it, and she strictly forbade anyone from conveying the news to the ears of Princess Mehr-Nigar. But the news soon circulated and reached Mehr-Nigar, who was struck with such violent pains of grief that her woe and sorrow and fury were the cause of great anxiety for all of them. Empress Mehr-Angez herself went and offered her many words of consolation, but the princess paid no heed.

Finding herself helpless in this matter, the empress informed Naushervan of their daughter's state, who said to Buzurjmehr, "Go to the princess and bring her around to the prospect of marrying Aulad bin Marzaban!" Then Buzurjmehr took Mehr-Nigar aside, and said to her, "O Princess! Amir is safe in all ways, and is secure and unharmed by the grace of God! However, Amir did undergo great physical suffering after being poisoned by Gustham. You shall see him on the fortieth day from today. In the meanwhile, reasons of expediency dictate that you accept Aulad bin Marzaban's suit. But make him pledge that until forty days have passed Aulad must not present himself before you or be admitted in hours of seclusion." At Buzurjmehr's counsel, the princess agreed to the proposition.

The following day Naushervan conferred the robe of son-in-law on Aulad bin Marzaban before the whole assembly, and told him that the nuptials would be celebrated forty days hence. Bakhtak said to Aulad, "This delay does not bode well for your plans, as news has reached here that Hamza is alive and well and headed for Ctesiphon! If he were to arrive here during this period, it would unravel the whole scheme. I suggest that tomorrow you should declare to the emperor that you wish to celebrate the nuptials in Zabul, and that by the time the princess's procession reaches Zabul, the forty days will have elapsed, and your kith and kin will be afforded an opportunity to participate in the celebrations."

The next day Aulad made his plea before Naushervan, and Bakhtak also petitioned on his behalf. The emperor consented and ordered the dowry and all such preparations to be made ready.

The emperor sent Mehr-Nigar off with great pomp and ceremony, and himself accompanied the procession for a day.

Aulad made progress toward Zabul happily and joyously, but at Mehr-Nigar's instructions, his pavilion was always pitched three leagues away from her own, and her tent was guarded by twelve thousand slaves. When thirty-nine days had passed, the princess knew that the day of her meeting with Amir had come.

Aulad ordered his camp to be set up at a picturesque hillside and said, "Tomorrow we shall remain camped here, as it is also the day when my promise to the princess will be fulfilled. We shall celebrate the nuptials at this very spot!"

Mehr-Nigar had resolved in her heart that the moment Aulad entered her pavilion, she would kill herself and put an end to her life.

Of Aulad bin Marzaban Being Taken Captive, and a Grief-Stricken and Remorse-Bitten Aulad Being Sent as Prisoner to Naushervan at Amir Hamza's Orders

Regard this marvel of the work of the Gatherer of the Separated that a new flower blossomed in the wild. The nightingale of the pen thus chirps that the Almighty God ordained that the Sahibqiran would arrive in that neighborhood the same day, and he, too, set up his camp on the acclivity of that hillside.

Hakim Aqlimun said to Amar, "Go to the pasture with your hunting gear, and bring me a deer! The smell of the roast will serve to invigorate Amir's heart, and the two of us will do it justice thereafter." Immediately upon hearing Aqlimun's words, Amar took his lasso and sling, and set forth. He caught a stag near a hill. Amar then tied his legs and buried him under a rock and climbed up the hill to enjoy the scenery.

Amar beheld a pavilion by the rivulet that bordered on the royal encampment. Two men, who for all appearances seemed to be waiting on someone, were standing by the rivulet, holding in their hands a ewer and basin made of gold and silver. Amar hung one of his arms loose and, swinging it from side to side, he approached them, limping with one foot, and addressed them in a most sweet and affable manner thus: "My friends, whose camp is this, and who are you, and what are your particulars?"

They replied, "This is the encampment of Princess Mehr-Nigar, the daughter of the Emperor of the Seven Climes. We are her slaves."

They gave Amar a complete account of Mehr-Nigar's hardships and said, "Today the fortieth day will come to a close, and if the Sahibqiran should arrive by this evening, the princess will live; otherwise, tomorrow, the moment Aulad steps up to the threshold of her pavilion, she will swallow the dose of deadly poison in her possession!"

Amar replied, "Sirs, have faith in the Provident God! It is not beyond His power to send the Sahibqiran here this very day, and grant the princess's desire despite all odds! I only have this to ask of you: My arm and leg are paralyzed, and a hakim had told me that if I were to wash my arm and leg with a ewer and basin made of gold and silver, my limbs would become well again. It appears I have some days of happy life remaining to my lot to have come upon such kindly folk as yourselves, who have the possession of such utensils. If you were to lend them to me for a moment, I shall wash my arm and leg before your eyes with the water of this rivulet."

These men took pity on Amar, and handed the ewer and the basin to him.

After washing his limbs and pretending to have recovered, Amar leapt away from them, and said, "I may have regained the use of my limbs, but if the ailment were to relapse, who would lend me this ewer and basin?" And with these words Amar fled toward Aulad bin Marzaban's camp. Realizing that it would be futile to try to catch him, the two men did not give chase.

Amar reached Aulad's encampment, where he made his way disguised as a geomancer. Mehr-Nigar's attendants decided they, too, should solicit his help in tracing the thief. With that intent they drew near to see him at work, and observed that the geomancer would most miraculously relate the secret of a man's heart. They asked him to tell them what might have occurred to them. The geomancer said, "It appears that you have lost some utensils made of gold and silver!" Now the two attendants became convinced that the geomancer was entirely genuine, and one of them stayed behind and the other went to the princess's pavilion to inform her.

The princess reasoned that nobody but Amar could display the cheek to steal her goods so close to her encampment, and then make his way out, dodging thousands of guards. It would be little wonder, she thought, if the geomancer, too, was Amar in disguise. Immediately she sent out a train of messengers and mace bearers to have the geomancer conducted into her presence. After arranging for privacy, she had him seated by the curtain and said, "O geomancer, pray narrate to me the secrets that I hide in my bosom and give an account of my grief-stricken heart!" Amar replied, "Your ladyship should know that I am not initiated in the art of recounting the secrets in people's hearts without examining their aspects, as I never learned the art of divining secrets from behind a curtain!"

The princess had the curtain lifted from between them, and showed her face to Amar who held out the dice to Princess Mehr-Nigar, and said, "Take these dice and throw them over the charts. Then I will interpret them and narrate the secrets of your heart."

After she had thrown the dice, Amar narrated the whole story of her love from its beginning up to that moment, and told her that she would receive tidings of Hamza's arrival that very day. Then deducing that this was indeed Amar, Mehr-Nigar reached out and pulled at his false beard, which came off in her hands to reveal Amar's face. Unable to contain herself any longer, the princess fell crying at Amar's neck, and with tears coursing down her cheeks in a flood, she asked him, "Tell me verily where Amir is now. Amar replied, "This very morning Amir set up camp on the slope of this hill. By the grace of God he is alive and out of danger, but he is foundering in the depths of the sea of grief and sorrow because of his separation from you."

Just at that moment messengers arrived to announce that Aulad had requisitioned the geomancer to ascertain the proper hour and moment for the nuptials. Amar said to Mehr-Nigar, "My ladyship may now breathe easily, and not fall prey to any worries. Observe what terrible calamities I shall now visit on Aulad's head in lieu of the bliss he anticipates!" With these words, Amar took his leave.

Then Amar went before Aulad and beheld a Gueber[67] stripling seated on a bejeweled throne, covered from head to foot with gold and jewels, with all the paraphernalia for the nuptials strewn about him. Aulad asked Amar, "Why did the princess send for you?" Amar replied, "She inquired of me regarding one who is deceased, and lamented his loss a great deal. I told her that the man was dead and departed, but that she had great happiness in store in a marriage with Aulad bin Marzaban. At first she would hear nothing of it but she softened after I advised and counseled her, and thus made her reconciled to her lot."

Upon hearing these words Aulad began to grin from ear to ear, and conferred a costly robe of honor on Amar, and asked him, "When should I celebrate the nuptials and consummate my troth with that moonfaced beauty?" Amar replied, "Arrange it at your earliest pleasure!" Aulad was even more delighted by this reply and further conferred a purse of red gold on Amar.

Amar visited blessings on Aulad, and said to him, "This humble servant of yours has four sons. One of them indulges himself with plying the mace, another excels in the art of cudgeling, my third son is a great drummer, and the fourth is a legendary master of the hautbois. It would afford you the greatest pleasure, and delight you no end if you were to see a display of their talents!" Aulad replied, "Come morning, send your sons into my presence."

Amar took his leave and, having reached the hillside, got rid of his disguise and brought the deer to Hakim Aqlimun, who slaughtered it and had Hamza smell the roast to invigorate his spirits. From there Amar headed straight for Landhoor's pavilion. On the way he met Muqbil, whom he asked to come posthaste to Landhoor's pavilion and bring Aadi with him. Once they were assembled Amar counseled with them and took them into his confidence regarding his plans.

When the master of the sky stood at the framework of the vaults of the heavens wielding the cudgel of the sun's beam, Amar hung a big drum from Aadi's neck, furnished Muqbil with a hautbois, and asking Landhoor to take along his mace, and with Amar himself dressed as a fair youth sporting a cudgel, the four arrived at the threshold of Aulad's pavilion.

Aulad sent for them and ordered them to display their talents in his court. Amar produced eleven brass cudgels from his bag of trickery, and plied them so dexterously that the whole assembly sat entranced and praised his talent to the skies. Muqbil on the hautbois and Aadi with the drum also delighted the company, and they as well received robes of satin and many other gifts and rewards besides. When Landhoor began to swing his mace around, it caused such powerful blasts of air that the onlookers started to be blown to the ground from their seats and thrones, and they shouted from all corners "Stop!" and "Enough!"

Then Amar gestured to Landhoor, who swung his mace and brought it down on the supports of the pavilion whereupon Aulad was buried inside with all his courtiers. Then they turned to attack his army, and a battle ensued. Landhoor raised the mace over his head and bellowed, "Anyone who does not know, learn that I am Landhoor bin Saadan, the Khusrau of India!"

Upon hearing Landhoor's war cry his twelve thousand warriors, who had lain waiting in their positions, fell upon Aulad's army with drawn swords. Ten thousand men from Aulad's host died in the battle, another ten thousand were taken prisoner, while five thousand escaped with their lives.

Now we turn to Aadi, to whom it suddenly occurred in the midst of the battle that food must have been cooked in great abundance in Aulad's

camp that day and the finest delicacies would have been prepared to celebrate the nuptials. And this thought convinced Aadi that he ought to
break into the pantry and gorge on and gobble up all that he could lay
his hands on, and so he headed for the kitchen with that intent. On his
way Aadi noticed a man crawling out from under Aulad's pavilion. Aadi
squashed him with his drum, which caused the drum's skin to rupture
and the man to be transported inside it. Aadi quickly secured the drum's
mouth tightly, and barged into the kitchen. And it was indeed the case
that food had been prepared there in great plenty, and Aadi helped himself to whatever took his fancy without the least anxiety of having to
share it with anyone.

Amar searched for Aulad high and low, but could find no trace of him.
Looking for Aulad among the slain, Amar happened by the kitchen and
saw Aadi sitting before a great pile of delicacies, bolting them down like
there would be no tomorrow. Casting an angry glance at him, Amar
addressed him thus: "O drum-bellied one! In Hamza's camp you give
yourself the airs of a great champion, but when the time comes for skirmishing, you shirk your duty and hide in this nook to nurse your glut-
tonous gut!" Aadi replied, "I have taken a man prisoner, and that justifies
my freedom to have my meal!" Amar said, "I would like to be blessed by
the sight of him!" Aadi replied: "He is trapped inside the drum. Go and
take a look at him, and leave me to have my food in peace!" Stealing a
glimpse of the captive, Amar said to Aadi, "This one man alone is worth
a hundred thousand prisoners! Indeed, O Aadi, you accomplished a great
deed, and acquitted yourself most honorably!"

Thus speaking Amar had Aadi carry the drum to Landhoor, and put
it before him with great fanfare and triumph. Then Amar said to him, "O
Khusrau! I have brought you a veritable bird of paradise, and solicit your
munificent indulgence!" Landhoor replied, "Show me whom you have
caught." The moment Aadi opened the drum's mouth, Aulad emerged
from it with a drawn dagger, and came charging at Landhoor, who
wrested the dagger from Aulad's hand and slammed him against the floor.
Amar tied him up like a skein of yarn with his lasso, and took these glad
tidings to the princess. From there he went to Hamza and narrated from
the beginning to the end all that had come to pass. Hamza embraced
Amar, and then said to Landhoor, "Indeed our prestige and honor are
now one! Who would come to the defense of my honor if not you yourself!"

It was decided that Sultan Bakht Maghrebi would escort Princess

Mehr-Nigar back to Ctesiphon, and Aulad would be sent back in chains to the emperor. Hamza then wrote a missive to the Emperor of the Seven Climes, which read:

Your humble servant had taken himself to Ceylon as per Your Excellency's orders. I prevailed over King Landhoor and Almighty God preserved my name and honor. I am bringing Landhoor along and shall soon present him before Your Highness, the Shadow of God.

In the meantime, my enemies had circulated the rumors of my death, and propagated this falsehood far and wide. Your Honor believed it to be true and pledged Princess Mehr-Nigar to Aulad bin Marzaban at the instigation of shallow and perfidious counselors. Your Majesty did not pause even for a moment to show the least sympathy for my cause, nor attempted to research the veracity of these rumors. On my way back from battle Aulad and I crossed paths, and I am now sending him as a prisoner to Your Honor. What passed has been recompensed now, and Your Highness may deal with him as you see fit.

I am also sending back Princess Mehr-Nigar, who shall be kept there in trust for me. God willing, I shall soon present myself and celebrate my nuptials with her and put paid to the mischief of all seditionists and calumniators!

Mehr-Nigar then sent for Amar, and said to him, "I made all preparations and arranged for festivities, but Amir did not once send for me and has ordered that I be forthwith dispatched to Ctesiphon! What great crime is mine that I am no longer worthy of showing my face before him?" Amar went to Hamza and told him that Mehr-Nigar had sent this message from the depths of grief and sorrow. Amir said, "You see that the poison has disfigured me, and my body has been stripped of all its glory! It is not my desire to present myself before the princess in this reduced state. God willing, I shall be restored to my natural looks and health by the time I arrive in Ctesiphon. Then the True God, the Gatherer of the Separated, will arrange for us to meet in happiness! Go and gently advise the princess that she must not take offense at this arrangement nor give herself to any anguish."

Hakim Aqlimun said to Amar, "Khvaja, since you are headed for Ctesiphon, pray bring some *noshidaru*[68] with you. But do not ask for it in Hamza's name because then you will be denied it!"

Then Amar took his leave of Hamza and went before Mehr-Nigar and delicately advised her and offered her consolation. He then had her carried in a litter toward Ctesiphon. In a few days the princess's litter arrived in Ctesiphon, and Naushervan came out to receive her and escorted her into the palace. He conferred a robe of honor on Sultan Bakht Maghrebi, and expressed great delight upon receiving news of Hamza's well-being.

Now hear of Amar, who dressed himself as a peasant and went and moved the chain of justice, whereupon the emperor sent for him, and asked him what it was that he sought. Amar took two farthings from his pocket and, putting them on Naushervan's throne, said, "Your Honor, I require two farthings' worth of *noshidaru*, as my son was bitten by a snake, and the village doctor said that he would make him well if I were to bring him three *mithcals* of *noshidaru* from Ctesiphon. I have been to the butcher, the grocer, the spice merchant, and the greengrocer, but none of them know of it. A man I met on the way told me today that I would find it at the emperor's court, so I present myself before Your Highness, and throw myself at the feet of my Lord. Take this money and give me a three *mithcals'* measure of *noshidaru*, but if it is even a grain short of three *mithcals*, it will not serve the purpose! I will have the full three *mithcals'* measure, or I will not pay!"[69]

Upon hearing Amar's speech the emperor and all the nobles in the court broke into laughter, and were most amused by his mien and air. The emperor said to Buzurjmehr, "Take him to the royal treasury, and give him three *mithcals* of *noshidaru!*"

Buzurjmehr did as he was ordered. Then Buzurjmehr took out another three *mithcals*, and quietly slipped them into his pocket, for since discovering Hamza's poisoning at Gustham's hands, he knew that Amar would arrive there any day to ask for *noshidaru*. On the way back to the court, Amar said to Buzurjmehr, "It is a thing to marvel at, sire, that you steal even though you are the emperor's attendant! Hand me the *noshidaru* that you have stolen and secreted away in your pocket." Buzurjmehr was obliged to give the *noshidaru* to Amar for fear of inviting scandal.

Now we turn to Bakhtak who also knew of Hamza's poisoning. The knowledge gave him no peace but constantly worried him that Buzurjmehr would certainly reserve some *noshidaru* from the pharmacopoeia for Hamza. Unable to overpower his base nature, Bakhtak said to the emperor, "Regard Buzurjmehr's status, and then consider his theft of *noshidaru*! Behold his prestige and honor, and see how he has crowned it with his embezzlement! If he needed the *noshidaru*, why would he not ask Your Majesty for it?"

Incited by Bakhtak, the emperor gave orders that Buzurjmehr be subjected to a full search. But nothing at all was found on Buzurjmehr, and Bakhtak was taken to task and penalized, and the emperor offered an apology to Buzurjmehr. When Buzurjmehr learned that it was Amar himself who had expropriated *noshidaru* from him in the guise of a peasant, he rejoiced exceedingly that Amar had saved him the humiliation of being branded a thief.

Once Amar was outside Ctesiphon, he took off his disguise and headed for Hamza's camp. Hamza had fallen into paroxysms of tears one day, distressed by suffering this weakness that had reduced him to the last extremity. He cursed himself, thinking that death would be far more preferable than a life such as his, since he became increasingly decrepit with each passing day. Then Prophet Ibrahim appeared to him in the realm of dreams and offered him consolation and many words of solace.

In the morning Hamza offered prayers in gratitude, and had propped himself up in his bed, when Amar arrived. Amar handed the *noshidaru* to Hakim Aqlimun, who began administering Hamza several *mashas*[70] of that confection.

Now hear of what passed with Bahram Gurd, the emperor of China. After his four ships had been separated from Hamza's fleet by the storm, he was tossed around in the turbulent sea for six months. After the storm abated, he anchored near Sindh and thought of stocking his ships with provisions, and went ashore with that intent.

He had gone a little distance when he saw a bow and a purse of a thousand gold pieces lying on a pedestal under a great tree. Bahram asked some passersby, "Why are this bow and this purse of gold kept in this place?" The people answered, "This bow belongs to Koh Bakht Hindi, who is the brother of our ruler Sarkash Hindi, and one who has a title to great strength. He put the bow and the purse here as a challenge, so that the one who could draw the bowstring might claim the purse of gold!"

Bahram walked up to the pedestal and drew the bowstring, pulling its notch up to his ear. Then he picked up the purse of gold pieces and placed the bow back on the pedestal, and made to leave after handing the purse over to his attendant.

The guards took the news to Koh Bakht Hindi. By chance, an *ayyar* had also witnessed the incident and, like an arrow shot from a well-strung bow, he hied before Sarkash Hindi and narrated the whole incident to him. Sarkash Hindi ordered him to produce the merchant and the bow before him at once. Immediately upon receiving these orders, people rushed to fetch Bahram, proclaiming, "The ruler of the city has sent for the merchant, and expressed the desire to see him!"

Bahram went as demanded by traditions of chivalry, and Sarkash Hindi received him with great kindness and showed him much honor. When the men sent by Sarkash Hindi had returned with the bow, and the nobles had also assembled, Sarkash Hindi asked Bahram, "Were you the one who handled this bow?" Bahram replied, "Indeed it was I, God's weakest creature, and I thank God a thousand times for endowing me with the strength to do it!" Sarkash Hindi said, "I wish you to draw it once more in my presence!"

Bahram grasped the handle of the bow, and pulled at the bowstring with such force that the bow snapped into two. Then as a token of his respect Sarkash Hindi gestured to Bahram to be seated, and Bahram stepped up to the gold-inlaid steel chair next to Sarkash Hindi's throne.

Hardly had Bahram seated himself when Koh Bakht Hindi walked into the court like a fierce lion. When he saw his bow lying broken, and Bahram seated at his station, he flew into a great passion. Brandishing his dagger, he charged at Bahram, bellowing, "Not only did you break my bow, but you dared also to sit in my seat! Now you shall taste the deserts of your presumptions!"

Bahram twisted Koh Bakht Hindi's arm and, wresting the dagger from his hand, he threw him to the floor by catching him from behind. Then Bahram said to him, "Is this all the strength you had to show or is there some left in you still?" Sarkash Hindi apologized to Bahram, obtained pardon for Koh Bakht's contumacious behavior, and then addressing Bahram, spoke thus: "In the name of your creed and your people, I ask you to tell me verily who you are, what is your appellation, of which land you are denizen, and where is your homeland!" Bahram gave a complete account of his particulars, and told Sarkash Hindi all that had led him to this land.

Upon hearing Amir Hamza's name, Sarkash Hindi heaved a cold sigh, and said, "I forever nursed a desire to some day kiss Amir's feet, but may the devil take Gustham, who killed such a peerless youth and champion without match!" At these words Bahram let out a cry, and was taken unconscious.

When he was restored to his senses, he said, "Pray tell me in detail who is your source for this news, and how these tidings reached you!" Sarkash replied, "Gustham himself was here, and although he tried to obtain an audience with me, I would not grant it. He sent the heads of Hamza and Landhoor to Naushervan's court from here by the agency of one of his companions. His destination upon leaving this place I could not determine."

Bahram said, "Now that you have mentioned Gustham's name, I no longer doubt the truth of his claim. Surely, that wretch (deserving of beheading!) must have killed Hamza by deceit. I cannot stay here a moment longer, but must needs head immediately for Ctesiphon! If I do not rout Naushervan's army with these selfsame four thousand troops and do not quench my dagger's thirst with the blood of Naushervan's life, I shall never again show my face among brave and valiant men, and will eat poison or extinguish my life with this very dagger!"

Bahram boarded his ship lamenting and grieving, and they reached the port of Basra in six months and from there Bahram headed for Ctesiphon at the head of his four thousand Uzbek warriors, giving orders to pillage and plunder and raze to the ground every village, town, city, and tract of land, and burn down every last hut and hovel on the way to Ctesiphon.

The news reached Naushervan who sent Faulad bin Gustham with ten thousand mounted troops to go and comfort Bahram with the news that Hamza was alive.

Faulad bin Gustham encountered Bahram on the way, but try as he would to convince him of Hamza's well-being, Bahram did not believe him. In the battle that ensued, Bahram killed Faulad and half his army. The other half fled and went before Naushervan to give a complete account of the encounter.

On the fourth day, while the emperor was still occupied with thoughts of somehow dispelling this calamity, Bahram's Uzbek troops arrived within sight of the fort.

Bahram used a clever stratagem to advance to the parapets of the fort, whereupon Naushervan underwent ecstasies of fear, knowing that it was only a matter of time before Bahram would enter the city after felling the gate.

Bahram was about to bring his mace down on the gates of the fort when a dust cloud rose on the horizon. Bahram beheld that the dragon-shaped standard had manifested itself from the cloud of dust. Bahram spurred on his steed and rode at a gallop to kiss the stirrup of Amir Hamza, who introduced Bahram to Landhoor, and said, "Just as you are my one arm, he is the other! He is an illustrious person, a valiant warrior, and a faithful friend!"

They had not yet mounted their steeds when a camel rider dispatched by Naushervan arrived with the message that Amir should camp at that station that day, and the following morning, His Majesty would come himself to welcome him and to escort him in his cortege into the city.

When the King of the Four Climes[71] ascended the throne of the heavens and filled the whole world with the grace of his luminance, the Sahibqiran mounted his steed and rode out to kiss the royal threshold in the cortege of the Khusrau of India, Landhoor bin Saadan, the Emperor of China, Bahram Gurd, and other illustrious nobles. When Amir sighted Naushervan's throne draw near, he dismounted and kissed its leg. Naushervan ordered his throne to be put down, and embraced Hamza, and then the two headed toward the city, regaling each other with clever repartee and conversation.

Upon entering the court of Kai Khusrau, the emperor ascended the imperial throne to give audience, and Amir was seated on the throne of Rustam.

And while Amir was thus occupied, the malicious Bakhtak declared to Naushervan, "Before, everyone was in awe of Hamza and there was no one but was terrified of him. Now that he has Landhoor and Bahram by his side, no one dares look him in the eye or stand against their combined might! I fear that they may overthrow Your Majesty and usurp Your Highness's crown!" Bakhtak's words smote terror in the emperor's heart, and becoming panic-stricken, he asked, "What must be done about it?" Bakhtak answered, "You must dispose of them one by one! Tomorrow when Hamza presents himself into Your Honor's presence, Your Majesty must tell him that he had been ordered to bring Landhoor's head, not to bring Landhoor alive, contradicting Your Majesty's commands!" Naushervan said to Bakhtak, "I give you the authority to speak to Hamza as you deem proper."

In the morning when Amir arrived in Naushervan's court, Bakhtak addressed him in a loud voice even before greetings had been exchanged: "His Majesty states that he ordered you to bring him Landhoor's head!" Amir took offense at these words, and replied, "Rather than beheading people unwarrantedly, gaining their fidelity should be the desired end. Landhoor has come here with his army to offer servitude." Bakhtak replied. "His servitude has no meaning! Today he may lay down his head at the emperor's feet, but who would answer for him should he revert tomorrow?"

Amir replied, "For as long as I live, he will not have the gall to raise his head from His Majesty's servitude or rebel or go against the emperor's orders. But should the emperor so desire, I will presently go and bring his head, as His Majesty's pleasure is my command!"

Bakhtak said, "How could you claim with any certitude that he will not rebel and display his headstrong ways?" Amir replied, "At a word from me Landhoor shall willingly submit his head to the inclement sword and would not show the least hesitation!"

Bakhtak said, "Then why this delay? What is it that you await? Send for Landhoor and tell him what you must!"

The Sahibqiran ordered Amar to bring Landhoor to him. Amar went before Landhoor, and said, "Come along! The emperor has ordered you to be put to death, and Amir has sent for you to fulfill the emperor's wishes!"

Then Landhoor rose, and said to Amar, "My sole consideration is a life that is spent seeking the Sahibqiran's pleasure! What do I care whether my head stands on my neck or rolls? Come, tie my hands with a kerchief and lead me to the emperor's court!"

Hearing Landhoor's words, Amar embraced him, and spoke warmly thus: "O Khusrau! No power on Earth could cast an evil glance at you or even presume to harm a single hair on your body. Come along with me. Hamza's head shall fall before any injury will come to you! And after him all the nobles, the champions, and I myself will lay down our lives before your person is exposed to the least detriment! Decorate yourself with all your arms and armor, and follow me on your she-elephant Maimoona." Then the Khusrau placed all his arms on his person and, carrying his mace resting on his shoulder, rode his she-elephant to the Hall of Audience.

Amar went into the court, and said to Hamza, "Landhoor who is to be executed has arrived!" In the Hall of Audience Landhoor began playing with his mace by tossing it into the air. It occasioned a great uproar, and people cried, "If the mace should slip from his hands, some ten or twenty lives will be lost immediately, the bones of hundreds will be crushed and they will lose the use of their limbs!" Upon hearing the hue and cry the emperor asked, "What has caused this din to erupt all of a sudden?" When the people explained the reason, the emperor was struck silent.

Then Hamza said, "Go and show Landhoor in!" Amar went outside and brought Landhoor with him to the Hall of Assembly. Landhoor submitted to Hamza with folded arms, saying, "What is your pleasure, my lord?" Amir replied, "The emperor wishes to have your head, as he has become distrustful of you." Landhoor replied, "I will obey whatever you shall command, and submit to it fully!"

Amir said: "Very well then! You must take leave of His Majesty, and wait outside in the yard of the Hall of Audience with bowed head. The one who shall receive the orders to behead you will be sent there."

Landhoor made obeisance, went into the yard, and sat there resting against his mace. Amir then ordered Aadi to go and bring him Landhoor's head. When Aadi expressed his duty to Landhoor, the emperor of India lowered his neck and said, "I am most grateful to God that my submission to Amir does not show the least variance even as I am being beheaded at his command!" Struck by the degree of Landhoor's devotion, Aadi sat down next to him, saying, "Before anyone could cast an impious glance at Landhoor, he would first have to behead me."

Upon hearing of this turn of events Amir Hamza bid Bahram to behead Landhoor with his own hands. But Bahram, too, became enamored of Landhoor's noble sentiments, and sat down by Landhoor's other side himself, pronouncing, "My head will also fall with Landhoor's head! If Amir wishes to behead us with his own hands, he has the freedom to do so!" When the Sahibqiran heard Bahram's words, he sent Sultan Bakht Maghrebi, who also sat down next to Landhoor, and said, "A fine thing is this purposeless slaughter that Amir has taken into his head. But if he is set upon this course, my head will also roll with my friends' heads!"

The emperor was notified of these men's comments by spies who narrated the speeches of these nobles before him. Bakhtak said to this, "Why is the royal executioner not ordered to go forth and bring His Majesty the heads of all of the men that His Highness desires, and put an end to this scandalous state of affairs instantly?" Hamza replied, "You are at liberty to send whomever you choose!"

Bakhtak immediately signaled to an executioner. Amar quietly shadowed the executioner when he noticed him walk up to Landhoor wielding a Bardwani blade, dressed in a lion skin robe, with a bloodied butcher's towel stuck at his waist. The executioner arrived at Landhoor's head, and called out, "Who is the one whose life's sun is become pale? Who is the one whose sun of life is about to set?"

All of a sudden a great clamor arose when a carriage passed by, and the cries of crowd dispersers and the shouting of the royal proclaimers began to fill the air at intervals. It was revealed that Empress Mehr-Angez and Princess Mehr-Nigar were passing by in a litter on their way to the palace. The empress looked out from the curtains of the carriage, and asked Mehr-Nigar, "Who is this man, and what is all this bustle about?" When Mehr-Nigar told her that it was Landhoor, the empress ordered the eunuchs to report to her why a throng was gathered at the royal threshold.

When the eunuchs had made queries and brought the details to Empress Mehr-Angez, she said, "A fine bloodlust this is that prompts the emperor to shed the blood of innocent men! Go and conduct Landhoor to our palace!"

Landhoor was released from that scourge, and taken to the empress's palace, where the empress conferred a robe of honor on him and gave him leave to depart. Then Landhoor retired happily and joyously to Tal Shad-Kam, alongside Bahram, Aadi, and Sultan Bakht Maghrebi. When spies took this intelligence to the emperor he said, "The empress would not have acted in this manner without good cause! She must have seen some wisdom in so doing. I shall come to learn the reason before long and then this mystery will unfold." He then adjourned the court and retired to his palace.

OF RUMORS OF PRINCESS MEHR-NIGAR'S DEATH BEING SPREAD BY BAKHTAK'S MOTHER, SAQAR GHAR BANO, OF HAMZA BECOMING DISTRESSED UPON HEARING THEM, AND OF AMAR KILLING SAQAR GHAR BANO AND BURYING THE BAWD IN THE LEAVES

The ebb and flow of time is proverbial, and the juggling of the heavens is ever evident and fully manifest. At times grief will strike amid transports of joy; sometimes in the depths of sorrow the face of hope will gleam. Similar is the course of the story here told.

The connoisseurs of the tale recount that when the emperor entered the royal harem, he asked Empress Mehr-Angez, "What was the reason that you granted pardon to Landhoor?" The empress answered, "In the first place, Landhoor was not guilty and did not put up the least resistance despite all the power and might at his command, for his hands were tied by his love for Hamza. In the second place, Landhoor is also the sovereign of a clime, and monarchs do not mete out such treatment to their equals. My third reason was that if the news of this incident had been carried abroad, your reputation would have been forever lost, people would have heaped rebuke on your head, and never again reposed faith in your word or believed in your promises. Again, if Landhoor had died in this manner, in retribution for his blood, Hamza himself would have laid your whole empire to ruin. Did you not consider that if Landhoor had not submitted his neck himself at Hamza's bidding, no one among your royal retainers could have dared cut off his head? These were the reasons why I conferred a robe of honor on Landhoor, and sent him away in safety!"

Then the emperor praised to the skies the empress's reasoning, and greatly lauded her judgment. But then he became listless, and said, "Alas, no ruse has yet been found to dispel Hamza's menace!" Bakhtak's mother, Saqar Ghar Bano, who was present there, submitted before the emperor with folded arms saying, "If Your Majesty would so order, I could rid you of Hamza's life in a most suitable way." Naushervan asked, "How do you propose to go about it?"

She answered, "Tomorrow Your Majesty should tell Hamza before the whole court that he will be wedded to Mehr-Nigar after a week. This slave will hide Princess Mehr-Nigar in a cellar on the pretext of her *maiyoon*[72] ceremony. After two days news of Princess Mehr-Nigar's being ill will be spread, and then on the sixth day her demise (may such be her enemies' fate!) will be proclaimed. When Hamza hears this sorrowful news, he will kill himself and thus die at his own hands!"

The emperor was greatly taken with Saqar Ghar Bano's plan, and the next day before the assembled court he ordered Hamza to make preparations for the wedding, whereupon Amir retired to his camp rejoicing.

Then Saqar Ghar Bano went and congratulated the princess in the palace, and using the *maiyoon* ceremony as an excuse, removed her to a cellar, where she spoke to her thus: "My lady! Now, you must not set foot outside this cellar for an entire week, because such are the formalities of this ritual!" Mehr-Nigar's companions gathered around her, and they all began to frolic and make merry.

After two days that harridan, Saqar Ghar Bano, spread the news that Mehr-Nigar had taken ill (may such be her enemies' fate!), and four days later, the palace rang out with lamentations that Mehr-Nigar had moved out of the confines of the Garden of Night and Day to promenade in the Copse of Paradise.

Amir was struck with the most violent anguish from hearing merely of the Princess's sickness. Now that he heard the news of her death, he made to plunge his dagger into his bosom. But Landhoor and Bahram took away his dagger.

Amar said, "Let me go and confirm the news of the princess's death." Amar set out with great dispatch and he saw every last person there dressed in black, and found both young and old in mourning. But a while later he caught sight of Saqar Ghar Bano walking up to the empress and then retiring whence she had come after whispering something into her ear. Amar said in his heart, *There is some mystery behind this.*

Night had fallen and the whole palace was covered in darkness. Looking around and making sure that nobody saw him, Amar disguised himself as an old woman. Then Amar followed Saqar Ghar Bano at a slow pace. The harlot halted at hearing a sound when she entered the back garden of the palace, and called out, "Who is there?" Amar replied, "It's only me, and only a matter of time before the Angel of Death carries you off instead of the princess!" The moment Saqar Ghar Bano took a forward step, Amar caught her neck in the loop of his lasso and pulled it, knocking her flat on her back. Then Amar throttled her, and buried her body under a pile of dry leaves, and after disguising himself in her person, he went up the promenade. He stood there perplexed, unable to decide which direction to take, when a young courtesan came up to him from a corner of the garden holding a taper, and addressed Amar thus: "O Saqar Ghar Bano, the princess has sent for you!" Amar said nothing in reply, but followed the courtesan to the cellar.

There Amar beheld Princess Mehr-Nigar sitting all made up on the bridal throne, making repartee with her attendants in perfect bliss and happiness.

Seeing Amar, Mehr-Nigar said, "Saqar Ghar Bano, How long must I wait before the bridegroom will arrive?"

Then Amar took her aside, and said, "A wedding procession, indeed! The whole palace is ringing with lamentations on news that you have died (may such be your enemies' fate!). Now I shall return posthaste to Hamza, and bring him the happy tidings of your well-being so that he may find a new lease on life."

Mehr-Nigar was overjoyed upon hearing this news, and sent Amar away after conferring five purses of gold pieces on him. So that Hamza would believe the veracity of the news Amar also made Mehr-Nigar write a note in her own hand. He brought the note to Hamza whose spirits revived upon reading it, and he, too, conferred a reward of ten thousand gold pieces on him.

Amar then said, "Now, if you would grant me leave, I will let the cat out of the bag with such marvelous subterfuge that the bastards who have colluded in this plot will themselves be most fittingly humiliated." Hamza replied, "I shall do as you bid me."

Amar said, "Then proceed to the Kai Khusrau's court, dressed in black, and prevail on the emperor that he must bring out the funeral procession of Princess Mehr-Nigar without delay, to stop malicious tongues from speculating why the daughter of the Emperor of the Seven Climes lies unburied so long after her demise!"

Hamza went to the Kai Khusrau's court escorted by Landhoor, Bahram, and the others. They saw that the emperor along with all his Sassanid and Kianid grandees was also wearing black.

Amir said to the emperor, "The decree of fate is now passed, and no appeal can overturn it. But keeping the princess's corpse in the palace so long will invite scandal. Pray order that the funeral procession is brought out now." Empress Mehr-Angez, sent the reply that the funeral procession would be brought out that night.

When darkness fell, hundreds of Brahmins began ringing wooden gongs and rattles and chanting the names of their one hundred and seventy-five gods and goddesses.[73] When people searched for Saqar Ghar Bano in the palace, they discovered her body buried under leaves, and her corpse was placed in a casket at Empress Mehr-Angez's orders and taken in a funeral procession from the palace.

The path was lit with hundreds of thousands of torches, and thousands of mourners followed the bier. Amar dressed himself as a Brahmin and, carrying a rattle in his hand and singing the praises of Lat and Manat, he, too, began embracing the fire worshippers.

Slowly Amar made his way toward Bakhtak, and after dropping a squib[74] inside Bakhtak's collar, he caught him in his embrace. Realizing that only Amar could have done such a deed, Bakhtak involuntarily cried out, "Oh! Oh! I burn! Oh, Amar! For the sake of Hamza, let me go as my stomach and my breast are burning!" Amar replied, "Since it is your own mother who has died it would reflect most nobly on your filial love if you were to burn in her memory!"

At this, Amar let go of the ill-starred Bakhtak and moved back. The firecracker flew out of Bakhtak's collar after it had scorched his whole stomach and breast and thoroughly scalded his skin. To bring himself relief, Bakhtak plunged headlong into a nearby water hole, and lost power of his senses.

When the crowd returned after burying Saqar Ghar Bano they found the emperor weeping and grieving in the Hall of Private Audience, and they, too, broke into a flood of tears at the sight. When Amar regarded closely, he saw that the emperor held an onion root in his kerchief, and when he applied it to his eyes the burning sensation caused the eyes to bring forth tears. Amar stole close to the emperor, and in a whisper spoke to him thus: "Never has the world known or heard of a more treacherous emperor who so grossly violates his promises to men willing to lay down their lives for him!"

The emperor laughed this off, saying, "The one who wrought the deceitful plan has received his just deserts!" But even though the emperor dismissed Amar's comment, he was mortified with shame in his heart.

Now hear of Bakhtak, who smoldered in the fire of envy. When he

learned that the emperor had written a letter to Hamza, giving consent
to his marriage to Princess Mehr-Nigar after twenty days, he mustered
enough strength despite his condition to present himself before the
emperor in order to vent his inconsolable grief.

Naushervan answered, "I could not help but give my consent, even
though I was in great anguish myself, as all my strategies have come to
naught." Bakhtak replied, "Your Honor need not worry any longer, as I
have thought of a most disingenuous and artful scheme!" Naushervan
asked, "What plan is it that you have devised now?"

Bakhtak replied, "Tomorrow, when the nobles and the royal attendants assemble in the court, Hamza will also present himself escorted by
his companions and associates, as is his wont. I will send some men who
will rattle the chain of justice. Then Your Majesty will send for them as
per custom, and demand to know their grievance. They will identify
themselves as Your Majesty's faithful old servants, and relate that every
year they collect the revenue from the Seven Climes and send it to the
royal treasury. But this year not only were they kept from collecting a
single farthing in revenue, they were also rebuked, and told that the
Emperor of the Seven Climes was no longer worthy of receiving land
revenues because as a fire worshipper he had shown utter disregard for
the name and honor of his forefathers by marrying off his daughter to
Hamza—an adherent of the True Faith. And that the monarchs throughout the Seven Climes have declared that should the emperor's son-in-
law dare, he can come and collect the revenue himself! When Hamza
hears this speech, he will fly into a passion and seek Your Majesty's leave
to depart on a campaign against them!" This counsel immensely pleased
the emperor and then the villainous Bakhtak took his leave and departed.

In the court the next day, when the emperor ascended the throne to
give audience, and Amir also presented himself someone was heard to
rattle the chain of justice. When the noise reached Naushervan's ears, he
sent for the petitioners. He soon beheld some men with severed ears and
noses enter the court presenting a picture of great distress and with all
their senses in complete disarray.

Then the petitioners gave a complete account of the events, as
instructed by Bakhtak, in a most effective manner, whereupon every single hair on Amir Hamza's skin bristled with rage, and unable to control
his fury he avowed, "I swear by the God of Kaaba, that I shall not marry
the princess until I have exacted revenge on those recalcitrants!"

Naushervan said, "O Abul-Ala, if such is your desire, then attend first to the matter of your nuptials, and then you may embark on the campaign to punish the rebels." Amir replied, "I, your humble servant, have avowed not even to think about marriage until I have exacted revenue from those rebels!" The emperor said, "If this is the course you are resolved on, leave behind Landhoor or Bahram to attend to the princess's safety in your absence." Amir appointed Bahram to remain in attendance at Naushervan's court.

The emperor conferred a robe of honor on Amir, gave him seven epistles addressed to the seven monarchs of the Seven Climes, and gave him injunctions that in making terms with the monarchs, he should use force only as a last resort. The emperor then appointed Qaran Deoband at the head of twelve thousand Sassanid troops to accompany Amir, giving him express orders to obey Amir in all matters. Amir said to the emperor, "Pray accompany me with some other Sassanid noble, and let Qaran remain in Your Honor's presence, as we have crossed paths at times, and it would not bode well for him should he pick a feud with me along the way. For even if I were to forgive him, he would die at the hands of my companions." Then Qaran wrote out a letter of obedience to the effect that if he were guilty of any wrong, he would forfeit his life to Amir without recourse to any appeal. Then Amir said, "I shall forgive you two offenses, but your third offense will not go unpunished!" Amir then took his leave, and retired to Tal Shad-Kam.

Then the emperor wrote out and handed Qaran another set of seven missives addressed to the monarchs of the Seven Climes stating that reasons of expediency made him send Hamza toward their dominions. They must ensure that he is not allowed even to trespass the boundaries of their lands, let alone collect any land revenues. And they must see to it that Hamza is beheaded and his head sent to the court. The emperor also gave seven *mithcals* of the deadliest poison to Qaran, with instructions that he administer it to Hamza at the first opportunity. Then the emperor conferred a robe of honor on Qaran and sent him off.

Qaran presented himself at Hamza's camp, who ordered the march drums to be sounded, and headed toward his destination with his triumph-incarnate host.

Then Amar said to Hamza, "Your love for Mehr-Nigar is only a pretense, and your true love lies in the skirmishes of the battlefield! However, you are your own master and may go wherever you will. Yours truly has whiled away a great many days of his life accompanying you in your adventures and overcoming all manners of perils. Now I am headed for

Mecca. If you would like to send a letter for your honorable father, I would most gladly carry it for you."

Then Hamza wrote out a letter to his father, and gave it to Amar, who departed for Mecca.

• • •

All praise is merited for God alone, through Whose agency Book One came to an end and reached its culmination with facility. Should it be the will of Allah (Whose aid we solicit and in Whom we trust!), the second book shall detail the bravery and the munificence of Amir Hamza (a thing to try the limits of the pen's expression!), the departure of the Sahibqiran (the world conqueror, Uncle to the Most Holy Prophet of God, the Last Prophet of the Times—upon whom be peace!) toward the Seven Climes with his companions, and the adventures that befell them.

Completed this day, Thursday, dated the 29th day of the holy month of Moharram, Anno Hegirae 1288, corresponding to the 20th day of April, Anno Domini 1870.[75]

BOOK TWO

The Second Book of the Dastan *of the Sahibqiran,*
Amir Hamza bin Abdul Muttalib,
and of His Departure for Mount Qaf

The imperious pen departs to conquer the dominions of rhetoric, girding itself to trek the blank stretches of paper, and delivers the account of Amir's journey, painting a host of new episodes and choice encounters before the mind's eye.

Amir had put seven days' journey under his belt after embarking on his campaign to the Seven Climes, when Qaran Deoband pulled up his steed at a forked path. Upon Amir asking his reason for stopping, Qaran replied, "From here two roads lead to the Seven Climes. The first one is lengthy and full of peril, and it would take us at least a month before we arrived at our destination. The other road is shorter and would get us there within a week or ten days' time, but while there is no hazard to be met on the way, we shall not find any water for three days." Amir said, "Store enough water in the water bags to last three days, so we do not have to take the longer route!"

The army loaded enough water on the camels and set out upon the shorter route. Not a single drop remained in the water skins, after three days had passed, and on the fourth day the whole army suffered from severe thirst.

Amir asked Qaran, "Where is the water source you said we would find on the fourth day?"

Qaran replied, "I had passed this way twelve years ago and it seems that the springs, rivers, and rivulets have silted up in the interim. However, I have in my flask enough water to quench your thirst. You only have to say the word and it will be yours!"

Amir replied, "Very well, then! I am beside myself with thirst!"

Qaran poisoned the water and offered it to Amir, who took the goblet in his hand and said to himself, *It would be most unbecoming if I were to quench my thirst while a friend like Landhoor remained thirsty.* He handed the goblet to Landhoor and said, "I am a denizen of Arabia and have much greater resilience against thirst compared to you. Drink this and afford some solace to your mouth and lips!"

Khusrau thought, *It would be contrary to all the norms of camaraderie if I were to quench my thirst while Amir remained thirsty!* Thus Landhoor did not drink it and offered it instead to Aadi who had been struck silent, with his mouth dried of all moisture.

Aadi reasoned that drinking the draught of water would only make the thirst worse. He offered the goblet to Muqbil, and said, "This water is enough to quench your thirst. Drink it and moisten your dry tongue!" Muqbil deemed it against all considerations of fidelity that Amir should remain dry-lipped while others drank up that water. Thus the goblet passed from hand to hand without anyone drinking it.

In the end, all of them handed the goblet back to Amir and said to him, "It would be unseemly for us to drink without your drinking first."

Of the Mysterious Voice Enjoining Amir from Drinking, and of Amar Keeping Hamza from Imbibing the Poisoned Water by Prophet Khizr's Injunctions

Divers of the sea of traditions extract treasures of discourse from the oyster of imagination, and bear forth the luminous offering of the pearls of narrative thus, telling that Amar was on his way to Mecca when he beheld an old man in the distance. He considered that the journey would pass amiably if they were to strike up a conversation together. When Amar tried to catch up with the old man, he was unable to bridge the distance between them. Amar began importuning and beseeching the man in God's name.

The moment that old man stopped Amar saw that he was the holy Khizr. When Amar asked him the reason for his haste, Khizr replied, "O Amar! At this moment Hamza is thirsty and Qaran has offered him a goblet of water mixed with a deadly poison. Rush and take it from him. Hasten forth, crying, 'Drink it not! Drink it not!' The True Protector shall cause your words to be carried to Hamza's hearing!" Amar hurried from there in a state of great despair, crying out every step of his way: "Beware! Drink it not! Here I come! Drink it not!"

Hamza had raised the goblet to his lips when his ears heard a voice calling out, "Drink it not! Drink it not!" He lowered the goblet and looked around. When he could not see the one who forbade him, he made to imbibe the drink. Someone warned him again in the same manner.

He was still caught in this bewilderment when a dust cloud rose on the horizon, and Amar appeared from it shouting, "Drink it not! Drink it not!" The moment Amar reached Amir Hamza's side, he took the goblet from his hand and smashed it to the ground. Wherever the water splashed, the earth bubbled and broke open. At beholding this sight, the faces of the onlookers were drained of all blood in horror.

Qaran ran with all haste toward his army. He had already instructed them to stand at the ready. Immediately, that twelve thousand-strong host fell upon Hamza's camp. Qaran aimed his lance at Landhoor's chaste chest. Wrenching the lance from his hand, Landhoor struck a blow with its shaft and sent Qaran rolling in the dust. The rest of Qaran's troops removed that coward from the scene, carrying him off to the forest.

Amar took Hamza's army to a spring whose location the holy Khizr had disclosed to him, where he quenched his thirst and drank to his heart's content along with the rest of the soldiers. Amir and Landhoor embraced Amar with gratitude. Then Amir said, "Now we must look for a way to exit from this arid valley."

Amar left the army behind and went into a nearby village, where its people ran from his sight. Amar chased and caught hold of one of them and, after comforting him, asked, "What is the reason for this mad flight?" The man replied, "A host of troops descended on our town a few days ago, took us captive, and appropriated our riches. The memory of that terror made all of us flee to save our lives at your sight!"

Amar said, "It is not our wont to show injustice and cruelty to anyone. Go with confidence to your people to ask them to return."

The man went and comforted and reassured the others and led them before Amar, who took them to Amir Hamza and had their needs liberally provided for. Then Amir asked the man, "Tell us, how far do we have to go before we discover a source of potable water? Tell us also, what is the name of the first land of the Seven Climes, and who rules over it?"

That man answered, "After you have emerged from the forest you will come upon a sweet-water ravine. The first city lies a day's journey from there. It is known as Antabia and the name of its governor is Haam. Beside Antabia is the city of Antaqia, which is joined on its border by another city, Antakia. Haam's younger brother, Mehd Zarrin Kamar, rules over Antaqia, and their youngest brother, Saam, is the ruler of Antakia. Should you wish it, I would willingly lead you along your way there and see you to safety!"

Amir richly rewarded him, and they charted their way out of that place with the man as their guide. After they had exited the forest and reached the banks of the ravine they discovered that its water had turned green. Amir asked the guide, "Has this water recently turned green or did it always have this coloration?" He replied, "It seems that someone has contaminated it with poison grass and now this water has become a deadly poison itself and is no longer potable!"

Amir's army then dug out several wells, and quenched their thirst. The next day they pitched their tents near the fort of Antabia.

———

Now hear of Qaran, that viper who poisoned all the ravines and wells in Amir's path with poison grass. He presented himself before Haam, gave him Naushervan's letter, and said, "If Hamza asks you for tribute, you should refuse it and instead kill both Hamza and Landhoor or take them captive in any manner you see fit. No tribute will be levied on you for three years as a reward for producing their heads." Qaran later communicated the same message to Saam and Mehd Zarrin Kamar, and then marched away with his troops.

Haam sent a communiqué to his brothers asking them to join him urgently for deliberations.

Saam and Mehd Zarrin Kamar arrived at Haam's fort, and after they had consulted together, Haam said, "I propose that we call on Hamza with mementos and gifts. It would be little wonder if Hamza showed us favor and received us nobly in accordance with the traditions of hospitality. Kings and illustrious men comprise his entourage, and brave men always show honor and esteem to those who are valiant."

Saam and Mehd Zarrin Kamar found Haam's counsel to their liking. The following day they presented themselves in Amir Hamza's court carrying mementos and gifts, and ennobled themselves with his audience.

OF HAAM, SAAM, AND MEHD ZARRIN KAMAR CONVERTING TO THE TRUE FAITH AND SWEARING ALLEGIANCE TO AMIR, AND OF THEIR PAYING THE TRIBUTE AND BECOMING HIS FOLLOWERS

The charging pen gallops forth in the domains of composition, and thus recounts with great ardor Amir's journeys through the stations and stages. Amir Hamza received the three brothers in the finest traditions of hospitality.

They recited the Act of Faith and converted to the True Faith. Then Haam and his brothers showed Amir the letters that Qaran had brought them. Thinking that perhaps the letters had been forged by Qaran, Amir did not allow them to cloud the mirror of his heart, and drew no conclusions.

He said to the brothers, "Tell me what the name of the land we shall come upon next is, who its ruler is, and how long a journey will take us there." Haam replied, "Fifteen days' journey will bring you to Alania, whose ruler goes by the name of Anis Shah."

Amir then said to the brothers, "Adieu now! You may return to your affairs of state while I head for Alania." They replied, "We have sworn ourselves into your slavery now! Pray grant us leave to be your riding companions!"

Thus all three brothers joined Amir's entourage.

When Anis Shah learned of Hamza's arrival, he drew battle arrays with the intention to skirmish with them. Then he reasoned that he would be wiped out of existence by an encounter with Amir's powerful force. He recited the Act of Faith and converted to the True Faith in fear for his life.

Amir welcomed him into his camp and that knave remained in Amir's presence for several days, fawning on Amir and flattering him. Finding the opportunity one day, he said to Amir, "Your slave has constructed a most pleasant and agreeable bathhouse. I desire that you visit it some day and divest yourself of both the fatigue of your journey and your bodily pollutions." Amir Hamza could not prevail against Anis Shah's insistence and, finally acquiescing to his wishes, paid him a visit.

That bath attendant's child (deserving to be burnt!) had constructed a bathhouse of a marvelous design. The roof was raised on iron pillars and suspended by a contraption [?] with four chains minded by four slaves. If they let go of the chains the roof collapsed on the bathers below and they were buried underneath without even a winding-sheet. That day Anis Shah appointed four sturdy Nubian slaves to mind the chains and instructed them that the moment he struck the drum and they heard its sound, they should let go of the chains and flee. Amir Hamza had brought Landhoor, Muqbil, and others along with him and they occupied themselves with bathing. Amir invited Amar and Aadi to join, but they would not consent to set foot in the bathhouse.

It suddenly occurred to Amar to investigate the bathhouse from the inside. He entered by the back door disguised as an old man. The Nubians took pity on him and called out, "Run for your dear life, old man! We will let go of the chains at the sound of the drum and then, as the saying goes, the weevils will be ground in the mill with the wheat, and we will have your innocent blood on our necks!"

Upon hearing these words Amar immediately retraced his steps and, arriving at the gate of the bathhouse, communicated the whole story to Amir Hamza, who stepped outside and got dressed. Anis Shah said, "There is an adjacent private chamber where I have laid out fruit both fresh and dried for Your Honor!" Amir replied, "Pray arrange for everyone to be served. Then we will do justice to those delicacies and enjoy your hospitality."

The moment Anis Shah set foot into that private chamber, Amar struck the drum with the mallet with all his might, whereupon the Nubian slaves let go of the chains. The roof of the bathhouse collapsed on Anis Shah. And thus Anis Shah landed in the pit he had dug with his own hands.

Hamza greatly extolled Amar's wisdom. He converted Anis Shah's underage son along with his whole army to the True Faith and gave him to the tutelage of Mehd Zarrin Kamar.

The commanders of Anis Shah's army then disclosed that Qaran had brought a note from Naushervan ordering the deaths of Hamza and King Landhoor. After delivering the letter that perjurer had left for Aleppo, to the kingdom of Hadees Shah. Upon hearing this, Amir's heart filled with rage and he dispatched the advance camp toward Aleppo the same day.

———

Now hear of that unsurpassable Qaran. Upon arriving in Aleppo Qaran filled up Hadees Shah's ears with all manner of gossip and after poisoning his mind sufficiently toward Hamza, prepared to depart for Greece.

Hadees Shah said to him, "Wait and see how I kill Hamza before your eyes and relieve that rebel's neck of the burden of his head!" Qaran replied, "It is mere wishful thinking that you will conquer Hamza in the battlefield and hand him a resounding defeat!"

Hadees Shah replied, "If you advise against open combat, I will have a pit dug in the arena filled with pointed arms and sharp-edged weapons. I will play horse-shinty with Hamza and lead him to it, and put paid to his existence before long."

Qaran replied, "Indeed this is a much preferable strategy, and one certain to yield results!"

———

When Amir's army arrived near Aleppo, Hadees Shah came to them with gifts and mementos and made an offering of three years' land revenue to Amir. He willingly recited the Act of Faith, and to all appearances acted out the rituals of obedience and allegiance. Amir Hamza arranged a feast in his honor, and conferred a costly robe of honor upon him.

One day Hadees Shah said, "This slave had come to learn that you hold your own in the arts and crafts of the war. I nurse a desire in my heart to match my talent with yours, and be initiated in the finer points of the game of horse-shinty!" Amir Hamza replied, "I am at your command."

The next morning Hadees Shah addressed his troops and gave them these stern orders: "Disguise the pit by skillfully covering its mouth with grass so that nobody will harbor the least suspicion that a pit or a moat has been dug there. The moment Hamza falls into it, fall upon the armies of the True Faith and put them to the sword!"

When the horse-shintier of the heavens bore away the ball of the moon and the world-illuminating sun descended on Earth sporting its lance of rays, Hadees Shah and Amir Hamza stepped from either side into the arena. Amir said, "My preceptor instructed me against taking the lead in any matter. You should strike the ball first and then I shall handle the stick next!" Hadees Shah made a bow and spurred his steed.

When he had advanced by a distance of a bow shot, Amir grabbed his stick and urged his horse onward. Hadees Shah was left behind, and Amir went forward toward the pit without entertaining the least suspicion of that knave's treachery. Amir's horse, Siyah Qitas, vacillated at approaching the pit whereupon Amir gave him a cut with Prophet Daud's lash. While the horse did its best to clear the chasm it could not fully escape it, and its hind legs landed on the inner walls of the pit. Amir exited the saddle and, holding the reins and clucking his tongue, brought the horse out and leapt back into the saddle. Suddenly Amir found himself face-to-face with Qaran, who was standing close by keeping an eye on things. At the sight of Amir, Qaran fled toward the nearby mountain range and Amir gave him pursuit.

Thinking that the waters of death had closed over Amir Hamza in the pit, Hadees Shah fell upon the armies of the True Faith with his twenty thousand troops, and many a follower of the True Faith met martyrdom at the hand of the infidels. In the end, however, Hadees Shah died at Landhoor's hand, and his army took flight.

Amar set out to took for Hamza following the tracks made by Siyah Qitas.

Qaran reached a field of melons and, taking a melon from the field's farmer and lacing it with poison, addressed him thus: "Make an offering of this melon to the rider who comes behind me, and accept what he gives you in return! If he eats it, I will give you a hundred gold pieces as a reward!" The wily Qaran then headed for the mountain pass.

When Amir reached the field in pursuit of him, the farmer made him the offering of the melon. Amir accepted it and asked him, "A rider passed this way before me. Which direction did he take?" The man replied, "He went toward the mountain pass over there, but the path offers no refuge to the one who travels there as a ferocious lion stalks those parts!"

As he was extremely parched, Amir made to eat the melon and quench his thirst. The farmer stopped him and submitted, "O youth! That first rider laced this melon with something, and I am certain that it was some kind of poison. He told me to feed it to the one who comes following him, and he would give me a hundred gold pieces as a reward if you died through this device!" Amir threw the melon from his hands, and conferred jewels worth a thousand gold pieces on the farmer. Then he spurred his horse toward the mountain pass.

He had hardly entered the pass when a lion leapt at him with a mighty roar. Amir dealt him a blow of his sword and the beast fell in two parts to the ground. When Amir entered the mountain pass he saw Qaran hiding behind a rock. Amir was of a mind to strike him with his dagger and cut off the rogue's neck when Qaran said, "O Hamza! If you spare my life I will confer three things on you!" Amir Hamza answered, "Give me whatever you have to offer and thus take out another short lease on your life!" Qaran produced a dagger from his belt and presented it to Amir. He said, "This dagger belonged to Tahmuras Deoband!" Then he took off his armband, which sported twelve carbuncles, each weighing three *mithcals*. After handing Hamza these objects, Qaran said, "The third object is kept in a cavern in this mountain. Come, let me lead you to it and make a present of it to you as well!"

Amar arrived there in the meanwhile. After securing Qaran's hands, Hamza delivered him to Amar and said, "See what treasure it is that he was going to divulge, or if it was one of his fibs." Amar bound a rope around Qaran and led him out of the pass. As Qaran tried to escape from Amar's clutches, Amar said to him, "Why do you exert yourself needlessly? Lead me to the treasure and I shall plead on your behalf to Hamza. You will surely be freed!" Qaran replied, "I mentioned the treasure only to purchase more time. However, if you were to set me free I would confer two hundred thousand *tomans* on you when I reach Ctesiphon!"

Amar answered, "O tyrant! Now that you are in my power, do you expect me to let you go free?" Amar drew out his dagger and killed Qaran then and there.

OF AMIR MARCHING ON GREECE, AND OF HIS BETROTHING HIS HEART-RAVISHINGLY BELOVED NAHEED MARYAM

The beautifiers of discourse adorn their rhetoric with the ornament of narrative, and evoke in multitudinous new ways the beauty of the story. With Amir's heart filled with pleasure from his triumph, he returned to the fort of Aleppo and indulged in festivities and celebrations for seven days. He sent Muqbil Vafadar to Naushervan's court with the tribute from the five lands, along with a missive describing events with Qaran and other incidents. Then he marched toward Greece and, having arrived at the frontiers of that land in a few days, pitched his tents.

Faridun Shah, the potentate of Greece, had already come to learn of Hamza's exploits through his chroniclers' reports, and upon hearing of Amir's arrival he gathered together a worthy offering and came forth with his brothers to meet him, and ennobled himself by converting to the True Faith along with his brothers.

One day Faridun Shah said to Amir Hamza, "O Amir! I am faced with three challenges, each of which I find most daunting! If you were to help resolve them, it would be a supreme token of indulgence from you toward this slave!" Amir said, "What are these challenges?" He replied, "The first is posed by a dragon on whose account whole lands have been depopulated! The second challenge is Shankavah, a pitch-faced Nubian, who raids the surrounding area every hundredth day, putting thousands of people to the sword. Once these two challenges have been resolved, I shall tell you the details of the third!"

Amir answered, "Accompany me in the morning, and lead me to the dragon's lair. Then you may stand aside and witness what unfolds." Land-hoor said, "It would not become Your Honor's eminence to challenge the pitch-faced Shankavah! Pray order me to produce his rebellious head to you!"

When the pitch-skinned dark night was laid low by the Turk of the bright morn, and the Emperor Sun routed the armies of the stars, the Sahibqiran sallied forth to kill the dragon, taking along Faridun Shah and some of his devoted followers. Landhoor marched against Shankavah with Faridun Shah's brother, Asif.

Three *farsangs* from the dragon's lair, Faridun Shah dismounted his horse and said to Amir Hamza, "Pray witness that the whole expanse of the mountain and the forest has been scorched! When that abominable creature awakens from his slumber and exhales, the tongue of flame reaches as far as this spot from his hiss."

Amir also dismounted and, taking Amar and Faridun Shah with him, went toward the dragon's lair. When they approached, they beheld a dark hillock and upon closer inspection discovered it to be the dragon himself. Amir said, "It is contrary to the traditions of chivalry to kill an enemy in his sleep, let alone a despicable worm!" He broke the dragon's sleep with a loud cry, and the dragon raised his head, which was the size of a Palmyra palm. Seeing Amir there, the beast rushed hissing and charging at him. Amir took out his bow and let fly a two-pronged arrow at the dragon's eyes, which soon became the arrowhead's nest. As the dragon pounded his head against the ground in agony, Amir stepped close and dealt him a blow of his dragon-slaying sword so that one hillock became two, and all signs of life departed the monster. Faridun Shah rushed forward and kissed Amir's hands.

Amir then headed back. The moment he entered the fortifications of the city, he saw Landhoor arrive there bearing Shankavah's head and treasure. Faridun Shah arranged for an assembly of revelry, where they all remained occupied with festivities and celebrations for a long time.

Toward the end of the night, Faridun Shah said to Amir, "Two of my troubles have ended. My third petition is that Your Honor take your slave's daughter, Naheed Maryam, as his handmaiden and make her an attendant in your harem, so that I may gain eminence among my peers." The Sahibqiran replied, "I shall be unable to agree to it because I promised Princess Mehr-Nigar that until I have married her I will never have eyes for another woman."

Faridun Shah was thwarted in his plan. After he found privacy, he said to his brother, Asif, "Now the whole world will come to learn that Amir refused Faridun Shah's daughter's hand because he deemed the king unworthy of such an alliance. They will think that to be the real reason he did not betroth my daughter. Death would be a far better prospect than a life such as mine!"

Having said this, Faridun Shah made to disembowel himself with his dagger, but his brother stopped his hand and said, "Send for Amar and I will see to it that Naheed Maryam is married to Amir Hamza."

Faridun Shah sent for Amar and showed Amar much favor and honor, and after making him an offering of five thousand gold pieces, said, "O Khvaja! In God's name pray find some way to resolve my problem, and have the Sahibqiran marry my daughter. After their betrothal I promise to make you a further offering of ten thousand gold pieces!"

Amar said, "I shall see to it that the betrothal takes place before the day is past. Have no worries in this regard, and begin the preparations for the wedding privately." Amar took the gold pieces and returned to his camp and when privacy was arranged, he broached the subject of Naheed Maryam's beauty and fair looks with Amir and planted the seed of desire in Hamza's heart.

Amir said, "O Khvaja, I would readily marry Faridun Shah's daughter, but how would I show my face to Princess Mehr-Nigar afterward?" Amar replied, "How can the Lord of the Auspicious Planetary Conjunction repress his desire and devote it singularly to Mehr-Nigar's person alone? Pledge your troth to Naheed Maryam freely and take your pleasure of her. Leave it to me to deal with Princess Mehr-Nigar. If she reproaches you later, tell her that you did it at my bidding. Then it will be my responsibility to bring her around!"

Amar at last assented to betroth Naheed Maryam on the condition that he would not consummate their marriage until he had first married Princess Mehr-Nigar. Faridun Shah gladly consented to that condition and was greatly beholden to Amar.

In addition to the promised ten thousand gold pieces, Faridun Shah conferred a most sumptuous robe of honor on Amar along with priceless gems. From there Amar went to Hamza. He sang such praises of Naheed Maryam's beauty to him that Amir's desire was fully aroused.

Amir pledged his troth to Naheed Maryam and for the length of a fortnight remained in his harem occupied with the exercise of nuptial pleasures. On the sixteenth day Amir sent Landhoor and Amar with the tribute from the five lands and the goods and chattels of Shankavah to Naushervan, and ordered his advance camp to move toward Egypt.

The historians of kingdoms and metropolises, and the account bearers of provinces and cities report that, after traversing many *farsangs* and miles, King Landhoor bin Saadan approached Ctesiphon, and Naushervan sent many a Sassanid noble to welcome him and inquired at length about the Sahibqiran's welfare.

Landhoor made an offering to the emperor of the gold received in tribute and presented him with the letter and gifts sent by the Sahibqiran. The emperor had the gold tribute removed to the royal treasury and conferred two luxurious robes of honor upon Amar and Landhoor. He ordered them to remain in daily attendance at the court and wait upon him as before. Then, while Landhoor took himself to his camp at Tal Shad-Kam, Amar called upon Princess Mehr-Nigar. He gave her Amir's letter of fond remembrance and said to her, "O Princess! The Sahibqiran thinks of aught else but you." The princess replied, "Khvaja! The night of parting and the day of separation weigh so heavily upon my soul that from the burden that it was before, my life has become a veritable curse!"

Amar replied, "Princess, you have shown exemplary patience thus far. Hold on a while longer, and do not lose your poise and equanimity. None but the Almighty God shielded Amir from calamities, and freed him from the power of a despot. By the decree of the same Omnipotent Lord the day will come when you shall be blissfully reunited with Hamza."

Then Amar called on Bahram Gurd and Muqbil Vafadar. Amar addressed Landhoor, Bahram, and Muqbil, saying, "Remain in daily attendance at Naushervan's court, but do not for a moment drop your guard. Because of Bakhtak's presence, there is no knowing how the emperor will act toward you from one day to the next as he has shown himself to be irresolute and fickle." Afterward, Amar headed toward Mecca.

———

Now to satisfy those seeking the news of more adventures, a short account of Amir Hamza. The Sahibqiran arrived near Egypt's frontiers and set up Prophet Danyal's pavilion and pitched his tents by the banks of the Nile.

The king of Egypt, Abdul Aziz, had learned that Hamza had been sent there by Naushervan to levy tribute on him. The king had a wise counselor in the person of his vizier, Karvan. He sent for him in private and sought his opinion about the course of action they must follow.

Since Karvan was a prudent and sagacious man, he said to the king, "It would be wise in my humble opinion to call on him and make him a royal offering. It is well-known that just as he is without match in courage and valor, he is peerless, too, in fortitude and generosity of spirit. He would show an equal degree of preference and partiality should your excellent manners and sincerity be revealed to him!"

Abdul Aziz was incensed by his vizier's counsel and said irritably, "Your advice in this matter is most injudicious. The preferable course of action is the one I have resolved upon in my mind!" Karvan decided to hold his tongue and let the king hang himself with his own rope.

Early the next morning, Abdul Aziz called on Amir with the three years' tribute and many gifts. During his audience, he said to Hamza, "Why did Your Honor choose to camp in a field when the comforts of the city are available to you? Pray come into the city and ennoble my humble abode by setting foot there." Amir conferred a robe of honor upon him and said, "I have no objections to accompanying you to your place!" Amir stood up and leaving his army stationed at that place, headed for the city in the company of some of his illustrious nobles.

When Amir set foot in the city, every last person came out to feast their eyes on his face.

Amir gave audience on a bejeweled throne in the royal court and the eminent nobles of his entourage occupied seats and thrones according to their established ranks. The king of Egypt ordered moonfaced cupbearers to bring goblets and ewers and directed the Venus-like dancers and exquisite musicians to dance and sing.

All this while, Abdul Aziz employed himself in officiating and looking after the party's arrangements. When Amir insisted that he should rest and let others take care of the arrangements, he replied with folded arms, "It is a signal honor for me to wait upon the son-in-law of the Emperor of the Seven Climes." Amir was greatly pleased by his talk, and the glib tongue of that wily man led Hamza into such deception that he threw all caution to the wind.

When evening drew to a close, that deceitful devil went into the wine cellar and drugged the wine with his own vile hands. After drinking the very first cup of that wine, the Sahibqiran said to the king, "It tastes different and unlike the one served earlier!"

That malevolent king replied, "Indeed it is a different wine, and a finer one it would be impossible to find. Your Honor's visit is a fit occasion to bring out this wine, which is much headier and stronger than the first."

Amir, who had never tasted drugged wine in his life, believed the king's word. After the wine had made a few rounds, one after another, Amir's companions began to swoon, falling down from their stations. Amir, too, fell unconscious to the floor.

The king of Egypt said to his vizier, "Send for the executioner this moment to behead Hamza and his companions, and have their heads dispatched to Naushervan's court!"

Karvan humbly replied, "Indeed Your Honor overpowered the adversary with great facility but I see good reason why you must not act hastily in executing Hamza. Hamza has powerful friends who would wipe the kingdom of Egypt from the face of the earth if they heard of his murder. Therefore I deem it advisable that you put Hamza and his companions in chains and send this news to the Emperor of the Seven Concentric Circles. If he writes back to sanction Hamza's execution, then you may proceed to fulfill your heart's desire!"

The king of Egypt said, "Indeed in this matter I deem your advice most judicious and propitious, O Karvan! But I fear that if Amar arrives here before the courier can return from his two thousand *farsangs* journey to Ctesiphon, all my labor will come to naught. Then there will be no punishment that Hamza would consider too harsh for me!"

Karvan replied, "I could arrange for the emperor's reply to be received here within two days. Pray hand me the letter and I shall dispatch it in the morning by tying it to a courier pigeon's neck. By evening it will have reached Ctesiphon, and if the emperor immediately grants a reply, it should arrive here the next day!"

The king greatly praised Karvan's counsel and highly commended him, and that very moment he sent for blacksmiths and had Amir and his companions put in irons and imprisoned in a well. Then the king summoned Sarhang Misri, the chief of his *ayyars*, and said, "Keep strict watch on these prisoners with your men. Have it proclaimed in the city that anyone who utters Hamza's name is to be killed on the spot!" His edict was so severe that the denizens of the city refrained from even uttering the name of the followers of the True Faith. The next day, the king of Egypt wrote out a missive to Nausherван and the bird was sent toward Ctesiphon.

Of the Pigeon Bringing the Missive into Ctesiphon; of the Conspiracy to Kill Landhoor, Bahram, and Others; and of Amar Making an Unexpected Appearance

The dove of the narrative is entrapped in the cage of these lines by lovers of sweet discourse and admirers of high-flying fancy, who expound on all manner of singular and propitious subjects thus.

The pigeon reached Ctesiphon and the pigeon keeper took the letter to Bakhtak.

Beside himself with joy upon reading it, Bakhtak hurried before the emperor. Upon reading it, Naushervan, too, came very near to bursting with joy. Bakhtak declared, "Your Honor must send a reply forthwith sanctioning Hamza's death. This humble slave of yours has in his possession a pigeon from Egypt. He shall be dispatched early in the morning with the reply!" Naushervan replied, "I must needs, however, take Buzurjmehr's advice in this difficult matter." The emperor summoned Buzurjmehr and gave him the letter to read.

Buzurjmehr summoned his senses to his aid and said, "Congratulations! Your greatest anxiety was addressed without your becoming involved yourself. However, it will not bode well to sanction Hamza's death this instant. I counsel this for the reason that if the news is leaked to Landhoor, Bahram, and Muqbil neither bird nor beast will be found alive in Ctesiphon before the pigeon has even reached its destination. You should first address these matters. Then you may give the orders for Hamza's death!"

Bakhtak replied, "It can be arranged with facility. Tomorrow, when these men present themselves in the court, Your Honor must arrange for wine and meat to be served and then take them unconscious with drugged wine. Thereafter, the sanction for Hamza's death may be dispatched and when Hamza's head arrives in the court, Your Honor may have Landhoor and the others beheaded at your pleasure!" Naushervan was delighted by Bakhtak's counsel and greatly praised his wisdom.

Bakhtak counseled the emperor not to let Buzurjmehr go home that night and stayed over at the court himself, too. When it was morning, Landhoor, Bahram, and Muqbil arrived in the court according to their custom. The emperor gave orders for an assembly of revelry to be arranged and drugged wine began to circulate. Buzurjmehr tried to warn the men by making signs with his eyes in vain.

After Muqbil had had two cups, he sensed some mischief. He rose from the assembly on the pretext of a headache, and headed straight for Buzurjmehr's house where he fell unconscious on the floor. Landhoor and Bahram had had four and five cups each and, once fully drugged, they tumbled from their seats and thrones and collapsed to the ground. At the emperor's orders they were manacled and put in leg irons, and thrown into the jail. Then Nausherван wrote these words to the sovereign of Egypt:

> Indeed, you showed great loyalty toward me by taking Hamza captive. You should behead him and dispatch me his head upon receiving this letter, and carry out this order with the greatest expedience!

After writing this note Nausherван said to Bakhtak, "Seal it with the royal seal and send it early tomorrow morning." After giving these orders the emperor adjourned the court and retired to the royal bedchamber.

Buzurjmehr took his leave and returned home, where he found Muqbil lying unconscious on the floor. He administered him a physic that dispelled the effects of the drugged wine. Then Buzurjmehr gave him a detailed account of all that had come to pass. Upon hearing it, Muqbil began wailing and lamenting and was fully disposed to put an end to his life. Buzurjmehr said to him, "This is not the occasion to indulge in wailing and lamentation. I have a camel that can traverse eighty *farsangs* in a day. Ride him full tilt and when you catch sight of the pigeon, kill him at the first opportunity."

Muqbil set out astride the camel that very moment. After he was gone, Buzurjmehr learned through *ramal* that all obstacles would be removed and the dilemma resolved only with the help and participation of Amar. He wondered how and where he could track down Amar that moment. He was engrossed in these meditations when he learned of Amar's arrival at his doorstep.

Khvaja Buzurjmehr ran out barefoot and brought Amar into the house, and narrated the whole story to him.

Amar said, "How do you think that I can travel a thousand *farsangs* in one day, since I do not have a bird's feathers and wings?" Buzurjmehr replied, "O Amar, I have learned from studying your horoscope that during your life there will be three occasions when you will run so swiftly that the feat will surpass those of great men who have gone before, and remain unequaled by those who will come after!"

Amar replied, "O Khvaja! Indeed a pretty picture you paint of my fate where my lot is to spend my life running errands and playing the courier." Khvaja Buzurjmehr replied, "Now make haste and be off, for this is not a time to make delays. I have also dispatched Muqbil by camel whom you will surely meet on the way."

Amar then went to Tal Shad-Kam and said to the nobles of India and China, "It is not advisable for you to camp here, as Naushervan might pick a quarrel with you in finding you without a leader. You should move camp to the forest, and wait and pray for God's favor and see what fate unfolds!"

Of Amar Setting Out for Egypt in Pursuit of the Pigeon and Killing Him Close to Its City Gates, and of His Securing Hamza's Release After Much Toil and Affliction

The dove of the stylus trills its notes inside the vestibule of the page and the pen's homing pigeon makes circles around the pigeon tower of the ream. When the hour of dawn struck, Amar decked himself in an *ayyar*'s attire and stationed himself under the royal pigeon house. The moment Bakhtak took the bird out of the pigeon house and released him, Amar locked his gaze with Bakhtak and said, "Mark it well that if, God forbid, even a single hair of Hamza or his companions is harmed, I will pluck clean the avis of Naushervan's soul[1] and annihilate those party to this treacherous counsel along with their kin. What an unenviable lot yours will be you cannot even imagine!"

Amar, the Father of Racers and Tumblers, sped on under the pigeon's shadow reciting "Help, O Immortal One! Help, O Imperishable One!" At every step of the way his eyes remained transfixed on the bird like a hawk chasing a pigeon.

————

Now to those eager to hear a brief account of Muqbil Vafadar. He dismounted at a rivulet and ate a little. Letting his camel graze in the forest, he lay down a while to rest himself. It so happened that this forest abounded in poisonous grass, and upon eating it the dromedary fell dead. Muqbil set out from there on foot feeling completely at a loss, and trekked onward for several *kos* until his feet became swollen. Feeling completely powerless, he sat down under a tree and fell unconscious from a paroxysm of tears.

Amar, who had been following the pigeon, found Muqbil lying unconscious under a tree. Amar immediately dripped some water into his mouth. Muqbil opened his eyes and began crying upon finding Amar there. Amar said, "This is no time to waste in crying tears. Make haste and climb on my shoulders, and let us find some way to hunt down that pigeon!" Muqbil fitted the notch of an arrow in his bowstring and climbed atop Amar, who set out at a comet's pace.

The westbound bird[2] had not yet retired to its nest when the pigeon approached the ramparts of the castle of Egypt. As the pigeon was about to fly over the castle walls into the city, Muqbil released the falcon of his arrow from his bow's nest and the talons of the death's hawk caught the pigeon at once. The pigeon came spiraling down and fell dead into the moat, where Amar fished him out. He opened the letter and, after reading it, put it safely into his *zambil* to show to Hamza.

Amar then accompanied Muqbil into the camp of the followers of the True Faith. As Amar was exhausted by the day's journey he slept like a log the whole night and when the first light of the morn appeared, he went into the city disguised as an Arab, but never heard anyone so much as mention Hamza's name.

Around the time of the *maghreb* prayers,[3] he saw a water carrier. When Amar asked him where Hamza was imprisoned, that infidel (marked for hell fodder!) caught hold of Amar's arm and began screeching, "Hasten to my aid, friends, for I have caught Amar!"

Amar wondered how the man had recognized him. He bit the water carrier's hands, and won release from his grip. He climbed atop the upper story of a nearby house in one leap, and sped away. When Sarhang Misri could not find a trace of Amar he ordered his men to arrest any stranger they came upon.

Amar found his way into another bazaar in due time and saw a blind beggar resting against a pillow by the roadside. When Amar drew near him and inquired about Hamza's whereabouts, the beggar caught the skirts of Amar's robe and began to scream loudly for Sarhang Misri. Amar wondered endlessly how a man born from his mother's womb blind could have recognized him. As people began gathering in throngs from all sides to apprehend him, Amar again escaped.

Night fell in the meanwhile and Amar hid himself in a temple in a priest's garb for the fear of being spotted by the chief vigil. In the morning, he went out disguised as a merchant and passed the magistrate's chair where he saw Sarhang Misri sitting. Sarhang Misri saw him and walked up to Amar and asked, "Who are you and what is your name? Where have you come from and what has brought you to this city?"

Amar replied, "I am a merchant and have arrived from China. My name is Khvaja Taifus bin Mayus bin Sarbus bin Taq bin Tamtaraq Bazargan." Sarhang Misri called two of his *ayyars* and said to them, "Go with Khvaja here and see what goods are there in his caravan and what kind of merchandise is stocked in his shop!"

Amar said, "I see that it is a city reigned over by turmoil, where the ruler's deputies expose tradesmen to the hardship of searches!"

Sarhang Misri replied, "I am sending you to your camp accompanied by my men so that they may post a night vigil in the evening to guard you and attend to your comfort and needs!"

Amar replied, "In that case I appreciate your offer!" He then set out from there taking the two *ayyars* with him.

OF AMAR SWINDLING AND DUPING
SARHANG MISRI'S *AYYARS*

Truthful spies and wise and cunning scribes recount that Amar took along the two *ayyars* and marched about the city's neighborhoods. He paraded them all over town until afternoon, keeping them constantly occupied in conversation. In the end Amar led them to a baker's shop where he feasted at their expense and then escaped, leaving them to settle with the baker.

———

Amar roamed around until evening and then went to a grain parcher's kiln to sleep there. In the morning he disguised himself as a beggar and began reciting verses and asking for alms outdoors. By chance, Sarhang Misri happened by that place along with two of his *ayyars*. The moment their eyes met, Sarhang was convinced that this was none other than Amar. He sidled up to Amar, and after giving him a gold piece from his pocket caught hold of his hand. It was Amar's wont to always wear an *ayyar*'s greased gauntlet. When Sarhang Misri called out to his *ayyars*, Amar laughed loudly and withdrew his hand from the gauntlet. Leaving it in Sarhang Misri's hand, he escaped, leaping and bounding from roof to roof as before.

Amar hid in a ravine the whole day and trotted out from his hiding place in the evening disguised as a dervish. Two hours of the night had passed when he presented himself at a kebab seller's shop. The kebab seller asked him, "Where do you come from, venerated sir?" Amar replied, "What business do you have with the name and domicile of a dervish?" When the kebab seller realized that he had the privilege of hosting a holy man, he led Amar upstairs, seating him with great cordiality and affection and then serving him meat and wine.

After a while he said to Amar, "If it is not offensive to you, there is no harm in giving out your name and domicile!" Amar replied, "I am the son of a beggar and have arrived from Ctesiphon." The kebab seller said, "Did you ever come across Amar Ayyar?" Amar answered, "I stayed at his house for several days before coming here!" The kebab seller said, "Indeed he is a most ungrateful wretch."

Amar asked, "What harm has he done you that you are so bitterly set against him?" He answered, "I am angry with him because he earned all his prestige, honor, and fame on account of Amir Hamza and yet he is oblivious to the welfare of Hamza, who has been held prisoner by the king of Egypt for so many days!" Amar replied, "Even if he did arrive here, what could he possibly do, as every traveler who arrives here is taken prisoner on suspicion of being Amar in disguise!" The kebab seller answered, "If he came to me, I would lead him straight to Hamza!"

Upon hearing this, Amar said, "O kebab seller! Amar presents himself before you! Now take me to Hamza!" The man replied, "What resemblance do you have with Amar? Even though I have not seen Amar, still his appearance is well-known to me. In the bygone days of my youth, I was also an *ayyar.*"

Amar took off his disguise and said, "Judge for yourself whether or not I am Amar!" Upon regarding this, the man embraced Amar and said, "The king of Egypt has imprisoned Hamza in the well where Yusuf was incarcerated by his brothers. Come, let me lead you there!"

The kebab seller also donned the trappings of trickery and set out alongside Amar. They had gone a short distance when they saw a man sitting outside a shop. On drawing close he noticed that it was none other than Muqbil Vafadar.

The three of them then headed for the fort and in good time arrived under its ramparts. They gained the wall with a rope and climbed up the ramparts.

On the roof they saw a person wearing a veil standing in wait. As Amar approached, the masked one came forward and placated him and kissed his hand and said, "My name is Zehra and I am the daughter of the king of Egypt! Prophet Ibrahim converted me to the True Faith in the realm of dreams and betrothed me to Muqbil. He gave me your whereabouts, and told me that Muqbil and Amar would come from such and such a tower and I should employ myself in ministering help and hospitality to them. I have been standing here since evening in anticipation of your arrival!"

She took off an *ambarcha* worth five thousand rupees and gave it to Amar as an offering, and promised him a further reward of five thousand gold pieces. Amar kissed her forehead and, securing the *ambarcha* in his possession, congratulated Muqbil and said, "Consider this a good omen. God willing, we shall soon find what we seek!" Then Zehra came down from the ramparts of the fort with these three companions, and they headed for the well of Yusuf where Amir was incarcerated.

Of Amir Hamza's Release from the Well of Yusuf, and of His Regaining His Freedom with Zehra Misri's Assistance

The pen draws out new fictions from the pit of nothingness, and the fingers exert themselves to unfold this wondrous tale on the paper's bright expanse. When the four of them arrived near the well of Yusuf, Sarhang Misri appeared there, and said, "O Khvaja Amar! I was deep in my slumber when Prophet Ibrahim appeared to me in a dream and showed me visions of Heaven and Hell. He converted me to the True Faith and bade me to hasten to join the four of you to secure Hamza's release!" Delighted, Amar embraced Sarhang Misri.

Sarhang Misri rendered unconscious the guards at the well of Yusuf and then beheaded them. Next he conducted Amar and his companions to the mouth of the well. Amar dropped a rope down and lowered himself into the well.

The captives heard a noise and reasoned that the king of Egypt had sent his executioner to execute them. Then Amar approached them and asked, "O believers in the True Faith, who among you is Aadi?" Aadi was frightened out of his wits. He pointed toward Munzir Shah Yemeni and said, "That's him!" All the other prisoners laughed at his words. Amar said to Munzir Shah Yemeni, "O Aadi! The king of Egypt has ordered your release!"

Aadi bitterly repented his words then and cried out, "Sire! Aadi is, in fact, my name." Amar said to him, "Indeed you were described to me as one with a tremendous gut, who has defiled the well from his excessive defecating. You should be taken out of the well, executed, and flung away as a corpse!" Upon hearing these words, Aadi's blood curdled in his veins.

It became obvious to Amir Hamza from the conversation that the visitor could be none other than Amar. Amir sat on his haunches and bellowed, "God is Great!" whereupon all the links of his chains and the collar on his neck snapped open as if made of gossamer. To give Amar a good scare, Amir charged at him swinging the chains. Amar cried out, "O Arab! Is this how one conducts oneself with friends? Mark that I am your old faithful!" Amir Hamza embraced Amar and removed the chains of his companions. Then he climbed out of the well with them.

Amir headed straight to the king of Egypt's palace, companions in his train. They searched for the king, but did not find any trace of him. Amir's companions entered the back garden and began feasting on the guavas, apricots, and mulberries they found there.

Aadi presently felt an overpowering urge to empty his bowels, since he in his bovine greed had eaten several *maunds* of fruit. He took himself to the royal toilet chamber and began attending to nature's call. The ill-starred king of Egypt had hid in the toilet for some reason, and he was soon sunk up to his head in Aadi's ordure. Realizing that he would have no refuge there, he caught hold of Aadi's testicles and hung from them for dear life. Feeling the terrible pain in his balls, Aadi jumped up and ran out of the chamber without washing himself, dragging the king of Egypt along with him. He ran raising a great hue and cry, shouting, "Terrible is the effect of this city's air and water that it causes a man to excrete men!" Munzir Shah Yemeni and others came rushing to him and, upon seeing the king of Egypt dragging from Aadi's testicles, rolled on the floor in fits of laughter. They had the king bathed and then conducted before Amir in his sorrowful state.

Amir Hamza said to him, "O King, you were meted out your just deserts! I have no desire for your kingdom, and you may possess it with joy, but convert to the True Faith you must, or else it will not bode well for you!" Then the king of Egypt made vile imprecations, whereupon Amir's attendant dealt him a blow of his sword and beheaded him.

Amir put Zehra Misri on the throne of Egypt and bestowed the charge of public offices on Sarhang Misri. Then Amir asked Muqbil to marry Zehra Misri. Muqbil replied with folded arms, "Until Your Honor marries Mehr-Nigar, this slave shall also remain unwed!"

Later Amar gave Amir Naushervan's letter that he had recovered from the pigeon's neck. Upon reading the letter Amir let out a cry of anguish and wept, and then addressed his eminent nobles, saying, "Consider, my friends, that I underwent all kinds of ordeals and trials on Naushervan's account but he always played me false. Now, God willing, I shall march on Ctesiphon and reduce it to ruins, and give every single

Sassanid's wife and daughter to the equerries and cameleers to do with them as they please, as sure as my name is Hamza."

Everyone present replied with one voice, "Your Honor speaks the very truth in maintaining that you fulfilled every last bidding of that ungrateful wretch! You must not countenance his evil further."

Amir rode back to his camp and gave orders to prepare to march. Zehra Misri said to Amir, "I wish you to command me to ride alongside you as your riding companion and to wait upon the princess until she is married to Your Honor!" Amir acquiesced to her wishes and, leaving vizier Karvan behind as their deputy in the city, marched on Ctesiphon.

———

Now hear of Naushervan, who was seated on his throne one day when he suddenly proclaimed, "Go fetch Landhoor and Bahram from the prison and hang them on the scaffold before my eyes!" Buzurjmehr said, "From the divination of *ramal* it appears that Hamza is still alive and Your Honor's star is in the house of bad omen. It would be judicious for Your Honor to go with the nobles of your court and harem on an excursion by arranging a hunting party. When the news of Hamza's death reaches here, Your Honor may hang Landhoor and Bahram and rid the world of their existence!"

Naushervan agreed to this counsel and, leaving his commanders Harut Guraz-Dandan and Marut Guraz-Dandan behind with forty thousand troops to guard the city, he himself headed for Egypt at the head of a vast force.

Now hear an account of Hamza. He arrived at Ctesiphon within a matter of days to set up camp at Tal Shad-Kam as before. There many of his troops who had bivouacked in the woods in his absence also joined him. Two *ayyars* presented themselves to Amir and reported that Naushervan had left behind Harut and Marut Guraz-Dandan to guard the city and the prisoners with forty thousand troops. Amir then said to Amar Ayyar, "Go and tell Harut and Marut to send Landhoor and Bahram over. They will have not the least blame in the matter for I myself shall answer to the emperor!"

As Harut and Marut wished to invite an untimely death, they answered, "What authority does Hamza have that we should release the prisoners at his bidding? If he has any wherewithal he may come and take them himself!" Amar returned to Hamza and recounted their exact speech.

Amir passed the night in ecstasies of grief and rage, and early the next morning he charged the fort, besieging and attacking it from all sides. When Harut and Marut tasted Hamza's wrath they immediately led Landhoor and Bahram from their prison to the ramparts of the fort and proclaimed, "O Hamza, your companions shall pay with their lives if a single troop advances from your army."

Apprehensive that Landhoor and Bahram would die pointlessly, Amir commanded his army to advance not one step nor launch any attacks without his express orders. Then he said to Amar, "O Khvaja, think of some ruse to save their lives and punish those bastards at the same time." Amar replied, "It is hardly a challenge beyond my scope. Those bastards and eunuchs are certain to fail in their strategy!"

Amar jumped across the moat, and addressed Harut and Marut, calling up to them, "Amir Hamza asks you not to kill Landhoor and Bahram. In return we shall retreat and not extend a single hand of molestation toward your city!" Then addressing Landhoor in Hindi and Bahram in the Chinese language, Amar said, "Amir states that the two of you are unfit to be called men, and are indeed nothing but craven cowards, the way you stand idle without moving a muscle!"

Landhoor and Bahram both felt the sting of these words and, bellowing "God is Great!" exerted themselves so that the links of their fetters snapped open like so many crude linkages. Upon this sight Harut and Marut Guraz-Dandan charged at them with drawn swords, but Bahram and Landhoor wrested the swords from their hands and dispatched them to Hell. They also killed those doing duty on the ramparts before Amar gained the wall and joined them. Some twelve or thirteen thousand Indian troops stormed the ramparts and rivers of blood flowed in the battle that ensued. Amar flung the fort gates wide open immediately and the army of the True Faith entered the city and handed a humiliating defeat to the royal army.

Then Amir Hamza entered the royal bedchamber accompanied by Amar and began searching for Princess Mehr-Nigar. Amar searched for the princess in the palace's back gardens and in the gardens of Qasr-e Chahal Sutoon and Bagh-e Hasht Bahisht, but could catch no trace of her. He was almost out of ideas for her search when his eyes suddenly beheld a marble well in the foyer of one garden. When Amar approached the well, he found it covered with a slab weighing several hundred Tabrizi *maunds*. To move that slab was beyond Amar's strength so he called Amir Hamza over to help.

Amir slid the slab over to one side and lowered himself into the well. He saw Princess Mehr-Nigar sitting there with her head cradled on her knees filling the skirts of her robe with tears. Raising her head at the sound of approaching steps, she caught sight of Amir and ran to him, falling upon his neck and proclaiming in a cascade of tears: "O Hamza! Do not tear me away from you again for I will be unable to withstand the pain of separation!"

Amir wiped her rose-tinted tears with his sleeve and said, "O soul of Hamza! The night of separation is over and the day of union has arrived." Amir first helped Mehr-Nigar out of the well, then had all her attendants conducted out of there, and then he climbed out himself. He forthwith sent for a gold-inlaid litter for Mehr-Nigar's conveyance, and headed for his camp at Tal Shad-Kam.

Mehr-Nigar said to Amir, "O Abul-Ala! For my sake now release the men of Ctesiphon, and restore the prisoners to freedom as your sacrifice." Amir replied, "Your wish is my command!" He ordered all the prisoners to be set free instantly and all pillaged goods to be returned.

———

Now hear of Aadi, who was posted by the kettle drums when Amir gave his earlier orders for assault. While at his post, he espied a damsel, barely twelve years of age, who was like the sun in beauty, wandering in great confusion. She stumbled at every step from daintiness as she was clearly unused to such exertions. Aadi was greatly charmed by her ways and rushed from his post to catch her. He soon found out that she was Bakhtak's daughter. Aadi thought, *It is meet and proper that the Sahibqiran should have Naushervan's daughter and I should have Bakhtak's!* He took her into his pavilion. That night, when he tried to ravish her, she was unable to bear the pain and cried loudly. Aadi desisted from his pursuits fearing that Amir would visit the most terrible chastisement upon his head should the alarm reach his ears.

But after so many days of hard austerity he was unable to keep his hands off such succulent fruit. Throwing all modesty to the wind, he ordered the Timbal of Sikander to be sounded. Then he returned to his pavilion to renew congress with the girl. Lust prodded him on, and the devil was his counselor. She was too frail to receive Aadi's phallus without injury, and the moment he squeezed her rear, her mouth opened like a sparrow's and the avis of her soul flew from the confines of its corporeal prison.

When they heard the Timbal of Sikander, Landhoor, Bahram, Muqbil, and other commanders armed themselves and gathered in the Hall of

Audience. Amar found all the illustrious nobles and kings armed to the teeth and in their saddles, and the entire army arrayed outside the hall ready for battle. Amar asked Landhoor and Bahram, "Why do you stand here armed, and who ordered you out?" They replied, "You should know the details yourself as you were with the Sahibqiran."

Amar marveled greatly, wondering what had caused the alarm and what fresh mischief and new devilry was afoot. He kept his quiet for the moment and went to the assembly of trumpeters and said to Kebaba Chini and Qulaba Chini, "Amir demands to know at whose command the Timbal was sounded. Who brought you the orders?" They replied that it was Aadi who had ordered them to sound the Timbal.

Perplexed, Amar went to Aadi's pavilion where he saw a most peculiar scene. Having killed a dainty damsel in her pubescence by forcing her maidenhead, Aadi sat with her corpse before him, contemplating his deed. Amar asked Aadi about the circumstances of her death, whereupon Aadi shamefacedly narrated the whole account.

Amar returned to Amir Hamza and narrated to him the entire account. Amir was enraged and said, "Have Aadi arrested so that I can bury him alive in the same grave where that girl is interred!" Mehr-Nigar interceded with Amir to pardon Aadi, and Amar added to her petition by saying, "Just imagine that in the same way Your Honor took a fortress by storm, he, too, forced open a citadel of virtue!"

When it was morning, Amir ordered a weeklong period of festivities. After that merrymaking was over, Amir Hamza was about to give marching orders to his army when Aadi presented him a letter from Jaipal Hindi, whom Landhoor had left behind to look after the affairs of his land in his absence. Jaipal Hindi had written:

> Firoz Shah the Turk has attacked us with an army of three hundred and fifty thousand troops and foot soldiers. We have already had a few encounters, but because Firoz Shah came with a vast army, he has returned victorious from the battlefield after each skirmish. If the Sahibqiran or the Khusrau of India should fail to come to our aid, we shall all become Your Honor's sacrifice by the good fortune of your foes.

Amir said to Landhoor, "I want you to advance on India and chastise that headstrong rebel."

Amir dispatched Mehr-Nigar and Zehra Misri toward Mecca escorted by Amar and Muqbil with forty thousand troops, and said to them all, "I shall have the pleasure of your company as soon as I have seen off Landhoor on his campaign." Then Amir ordered Aadi to move the advance camp toward Basra for the purpose.

In a few days Amar and Muqbil arrived in Mecca with Mehr-Nigar and Zehra Misri, and the Sahibqiran reached Basra accompanied by Landhoor and Bahram and his army. After Landhoor and his army had boarded the ships and set sail, Amir said to Bahram, "O Bahram! I had no choice but to send Landhoor on the campaign to India, and now I count on you to proceed there and assist him in his undertaking. From one end Landhoor shall visit scourges on Firoz Shah and from the other you shall despoil his land and spring a surprise on his rear. Once you have accomplished your mission, I will send for you along with Landhoor. Until the two of you have joined me, I promise not to marry Mehr-Nigar."

That same day Bahram also boarded a ship with his army; and after seeing him off on his campaign, Amir himself headed for Mecca with his victory-clinching army. On the way to Mecca Amir Hamza bivouacked in the pasture of Alang Zamarrud. A day later, two *ayyars* presented themselves to him. They announced that the warrior Zhopin Kaus was headed there to challenge him at the head of a seventy-thousand-strong intrepid army.

While Naushervan was on his way to Egypt to murder Hamza he received intelligence that Ctesiphon had been sacked and ruined by Hamza, who had absconded with Mehr-Nigar. Naushervan hastily retraced his steps to the seat of his empire where he saw the devastation.

Presently Bakhtak also returned to the court from his home and, flinging his turban on the floor, wailed that after Amar had killed his mother, now his daughter had died at Aadi's hands. Naushervan replied that he was at a loss to find a remedy for the plague that was Hamza. Bakhtak answered that none but Gustham might be pitted against Hamza. Then Naushervan immediately sent a communiqué summoning Gustham to his presence.

The next day intelligence reached the emperor that Zhopin Kaus had issued forth with forty thousand troops and was encamped two *kos* from the city in order to present himself and wait upon the emperor. When Zhopin presented himself before Naushervan, he vowed to punish Hamza and bring back Mehr-Nigar. The emperor asked him to bring back Mehr-Nigar so that he might give him her hand in wedlock, and moreover appoint him as his heir. Naushervan then accompanied him with two nobles of his court, one of whom was Ayashan Malik, with a force of thirty thousand warriors.

Upon hearing this account Amir smiled and said to his men, "Zhopin shall be dealt with when he arrives."

Around the time of *asr* prayers, the horizon was darkened by a foul dust cloud rising to the heavens, and an army was seen approaching. When the scissors of wind tore apart this collar of dust, Hamza's men beheld seventy standards and many detachments of one-thousand-strong troops marching under them. By and by Zhopin's army settled down before them and set about making preparations for battle.

Before long, King Sol routed the Potentate of the First Heaven[4] along with his army of stars, and Zhopin entered one end of the battlefield with his seventy-thousand-strong army, and the Sahibqiran arrayed his five hundred thousand valiant troops at the other. Zhopin Kaus spurred his horse from out of the center of his army. He brought him to a halt in the middle of the field and called out, "O worshippers of the True God! May the one who yearns for death come forward to face me." Unable to countenance this vain and boastful talk, Amir spurred on Siyah Qitas and descended like lightning on Zhopin's head, ramming his steed so powerfully against Zhopin's own that the latter was thrown back a full twenty paces. Zhopin said, "It seems to me that you are the one who goes by the appellation of Hamza!" Amir replied, "Indeed, I am Hamza, an abject servant of God!"

Zhopin said, "O Hamza! Surrender Princess Mehr-Nigar to me so that I may take her as my wife, and follow me yourself with your hands tied in voluntary submission, so that I may intercede for you!"

The Sahibqiran answered, "O wretch! Fulfill your heart's desire and deal me a blow if you have any claim to valor!"

Upon hearing this Zhopin thrust his spear at Amir's immaculate chest. Amir pulled the weapon lightly from Zhopin's hands. Enraged, Zhopin next attacked with his mace, but Amir received its blows on the shield of Garshasp, foiling every single one of his strikes. Zhopin brought down his mace ceaselessly and repeatedly, yet Amir foiled every blow, which landed on the ground causing a cloud of dust to rise over their heads. As that dust cloud screened Amir, Zhopin fell to boasting and swaggering and said, "There! I have killed him and made him dust."

When Amir heard his bragging, he spurred on Siyah Qitas like a blinding bolt of lightning and advanced on his adversary, saying, "O dastard! Who do you claim to have killed, and boast to have made into dust? The Angel of Death stands before you in my person seeking your soul. Come, I shall give you another blow, so that your desire is fully requited!"

Zhopin weighed his mace in his hands and attacked again. Amir again foiled the blow and wrested the mace from his hands. He plucked Zhopin off his saddle as a hawk picks up a wagtail, or a kestrel a pigeon, and slammed him against the ground.

After dismounting his steed, Amir pinned Zhopin down by sitting on his chest. Zhopin pleaded for mercy, and made a pretense of conversion to the True Faith. Amir got off his chest and stepped away. Drums of victory were sounded in the camp of the followers of the True Faith.

Amir returned triumphant and victorious to his camp along with Zhopin. When the cloth was spread and food served, Amir broke bread with him. Later, Zhopin said to Amir, "I ask your leave now to return to my camp and convert my army to the True Faith." Amir was immensely delighted by his words and said, "Go forth with my blessings!" Then Zhopin departed and went back to his men, and busied himself in spawning deceit and subterfuge.

Of Zhopin Conducting a Night Raid on Amir Hamza's Camp, and of Amir Disappearing Wounded from the Battlefield

Those who are pure of heart do not nurse grudges once they have made peace, and never brood on what lies in the past nor think of settling old scores. Hear what Zhopin the wretch planned and plotted in his camp. Upon entering his own camp Zhopin comforted and consoled his army, and said, "I converted to the True Faith upon finding my life in peril. Now, gird yourselves for ambushing Hamza's camp tonight and routing and scattering his army speedily." When night fell Zhopin headed for Amir's camp with his seventy thousand men to conduct the night raid.

On the way he ran into Amir Hamza's commander, Shis Yemeni, who beheld Zhopin advancing with hostile intent at the head of seventy thousand troops and foot soldiers. He challenged Zhopin, and the two parties drew swords and were locked in fierce combat. Shis Yemeni met his martyrdom at Zhopin's hands. The enemy then fell upon Hamza's camp.

Amir's army was deep in peaceful slumber when Zhopin's seventy thousand troops took them by surprise. The men snatched the first thing they laid their hands on, and faced the enemy. The cling-clang of swords, the rattle of weapons, and cries at last interrupted Amir's serene repose. His spies informed him of Zhopin's night raid on their camp. Fearful lest some harm should come to his mount, Amir headed for Siyah Qitas's stable from his pavilion and bridled the horse and rode out bareback.

Naushervan's commander, Ayashan Malik, attacked Amir with a bloodied sword, but Amir foiled his blow and, wresting the sword from Ayashan Malik's hand, dispatched him to Hell with his own weapon. Ayashan Malik's younger brother then attacked Amir who parried his blow and returned it with such a blow to his back that it sliced him in two like a cucumber.

In the meanwhile, Zhopin stole up behind Amir and, calling all his power to his aid, landed a lethal blow on Amir's head. Nevertheless, Amir turned back and answered with a blow to Zhopin's head that left a four-digit-deep impression in the skull of that brainless ape. Amir's second blow cut through his ribs on one side, and his next blow wounded him similarly on the other side. Disconcerted by these blows, Zhopin swung forward in his saddle, and his derriere presented itself to Amir, who drove the point of his sword nearly a handspan's measure into Zhopin's ass, causing it to burst forth in a veritable fountain of blood. As Zhopin fell unconscious from his horse, ten thousand men from his army rushed to his aid and carried him off to Ctesiphon.

Of Zhopin's seventy thousand men, sixty thousand made their permanent abode in Hell. Several thousand men in the camp of the followers of the True Faith entered the gates of Paradise after attaining martyrdom in the night raid. Amir lost consciousness from the continuous bleeding of his head wound. Noticing that his master had been injured, Siyah Qitas carried him into the forest and away from the battlefield.

Aadi and other commanders from Amir's army looked for him among the dead and searched high and low the surrounding area of the battlefield for some trace of him, but they found none. Then the clamor of the mourners rose from the camp of the followers of the True Faith, and all the commanders and their men ripped open their collars in grief and clad themselves in sable. On the third day following the incident, Aadi arrived in Mecca with his entire army and gave news of the tragedy to Khvaja Abdul Muttalib and Amar. Stunned by grief, Khvaja Abdul Muttalib clutched his heart. Amar and Muqbil tore the collars off their garments. Mehr-Nigar slapped her rose-colored cheeks purple as the iris, and pulled out her locks until she was far from all cares of combing and plaiting them, and her face looked like that of a woman recently widowed.

Amar said, "Believe me when I tell you that by God's grace the Sahibqiran is alive and well and safe. If the least harm had come to him, Siyah Qitas would not have failed to return to camp." Then, clad in the livery of *ayyars,* Amar embarked on his search for Amir Hamza, and headed toward that field in Alang Zamarrud which had been the scene of the battle.

Of the Arrival of Abdur Rahman Jinn, Minister of the Emperor of Qaf, for the Purpose of Carrying Away Amir Hamza to His Dominion

The chroniclers of news and the copyists of traditions relate that at the appointed time the infamous *devs* of Qaf rebelled against Shahpal bin Shahrukh, the emperor of the realm of Qaf, and wrested control of his dominions. The emperor was reduced to taking refuge in Gulistan-e Irum, where he and his family hid in a fort.

One day the emperor of Qaf sent for his minister Abdur Rahman and said, "Find out what became of that boy Hamza, about whom it was foretold that after the rebellion of the *devs* of Qaf, he would arrive and root out the rebels, and return the land to our control."

Abdur Rahman cast lots and said, "He has lately seen action in a fierce battle and received a wound from a poisoned blade! If Your Honor so desires, he can be presented before you!" Shahpal forthwith sent for the salve of Suleiman[5] and gave it to Abdur Rahman along with plentiful fruit from the lands of Qaf, saying, "Go forth without further delay and apply this tincture to Hamza's head so that his wound is healed, and feed him these fruits so that he regains his lost strength. Then bring him along once he has recuperated!"

Abdur Rahman left the realm of Qaf mounted on a throne, accompanied by an entourage of several hundred jinns, and departed in a flash to fulfill his mission. Arriving in the pasture, he looked around and discovered Amir Hamza lying on the grass, unconscious. Abdur Rahman carried Hamza away on the throne and moved him to a cave in the hills of Abu Qubais.

There he cleansed his wound gently and carefully, and bandaged it after applying the salve of Suleiman. When Amir opened his eyes, Abdur Rahman offered his blessings to the Sahibqiran, whereupon

Amir returned them and said, "Who are you, whence have you come? Tell me if it was you who brought me here and laid me on this throne!"

Abdur Rahman then narrated the entire history to Hamza. Amir said, "How and by what signs did you recognize me?" Abdur Rahman replied, "By the exercise of deduction, from remembering your dark mole, and by your curled locks, which are the telltale mark of Prophet Ibrahim's progeny!"

Abdur Rahman's manners greatly pleased Amir Hamza. Then Abdur Rahman introduced the several hundred jinns who had accompanied him and entered them into Amir's service. Next he told Amir, "I have a favor to ask of you, and I put my hope in your manly courage! Once you are fully recovered, I shall wait your pleasure to grant it!" Amir replied, "I grant you your request without your asking for it!"

———

Now hear of Amar. He happened upon a pasture where he saw Siyah Qitas grazing. Amar kissed the horse's forehead and said, "Lead me to your master!" Siyah Qitas neighed and pointed with his muzzle toward the cave. But the gesture was lost on Amar and, unable to comprehend it, he made a futile search of the surrounding area. Amar decided that he would resume his search after taking Siyah Qitas home. Amar led Siyah Qitas back to his camp and headed back to find Amir.

This time his path led him to the slope of Abu Qubais where his ears picked up the buzzing of human speech. Upon entering the hill's cave he beheld Amir seated on a throne, partaking of a variety of fruits the likes of which Amar had never before seen. He rushed forward and fell at Amir's feet. His friend raised him and embraced him affectionately, and asked news of Mehr-Nigar's well-being.

Amar narrated all that had happened up to that point, and then stood with folded arms before Amir. Because Amar's eyes were not lined with the collyrium of Suleiman, he could not see any of the jinns present there. The jinns were greatly amused by Amar's mien and appearance. One of them pulled Amar's feet out from under him, and Amar fell flat on his face. When Amir laughed at the caper, Amar said to him, "Do not laugh at me O Sahibqiran, since I am exhausted after wandering in the forest and hills in search of you. I fell down because there was no strength left in my legs!" Then Amir asked him to draw near, and as Amar stepped forward one of the jinns sat down on his haunches in front of him. Amir Hamza again broke into laughter as Amar stumbled over the jinn and fell.

Another jinn removed Amar's headgear with such a light hand that he never felt a thing. Amar felt his head with his hand and, finding his headgear gone, raised a great hue and cry, and gave vent to his anger.

Seeing Amar become so nettled, Hamza told him what had come to pass. He had Amar's eyes lined with the collyrium of Suleiman as well. Amar was then able to see everyone present there, and the Sahibqiran introduced him to Abdur Rahman. Afterward, Hamza said to Amar, "You may go back to Mecca and take news of my well-being, but do not breathe a word to anyone about my whereabouts!" After Amar had departed for Mecca, the Sahibqiran said to Abdur Rahman, "Now you may relate the matter regarding which your lord and master sent you here!"

When Abdur Rahman presented his case before Amir and gave account of Ifrit *dev*'s ravages, Amir replied, "O Abdur Rahman! The prospect of that *dev* dying at my hand and the emperor's land being freed and restored to him by the dint of my arm affords me immense delight. I will accompany you most willingly!" Abdur Rahman answered, "I have already divined the certainty through *ramal*—and I am convinced of it in my heart as well—that you are the slayer of Ifrit!"

———

The next morning when Amar again presented himself, Amir said to him, "Dear friend, I am obliged to undertake a journey that will last a number of days." Then Hamza repeated all that Abdur Rahman had told him. Amar said, "What leads you on this fruitless endeavor to that far-off place, after you went to all that trouble to rescue Mehr-Nigar?"

Amir answered, "I am obligated to Abdur Rahman because he healed my wound and tended to me as I lay injured. You well know that the mightiest *dev* or *ghol* or sorcerer holds no terror for me because the True Savior is my protector."

At that point, Abdur Rahman said, "O Sahibqiran! The journey to Qaf will take you three days. Allowing another three days for the return journey, one for rest, one for killing Ifrit, and another to celebrate your victory, the entire trip will last nine days." Amir said, "I would still agree to your request even if the journey took twice that time, and a full eighteen days!"

Amar said to Hamza, "Do as you wish! I shall guard Mehr-Nigar for another eighteen days. But my responsibility will end on the nineteenth day, and I shall go my way, leaving you the master of your own affairs!" Hamza answered, "You have my consent! Bring me my inkstand, so that I may write out my instructions to Mehr-Nigar and the commanders of the army, enjoining all of them to obey your orders and seek your pleasure and consent in all matters."

Amar left the cave with tears in his eyes, and headed for Mecca. When he arrived there, and Khvaja Abdul Muttalib learned Hamza's intent of journeying to Qaf, he became greatly alarmed. Khvaja wrote out a letter to Hamza counseling him against undertaking the journey to Qaf, and handed it to Amar.

From there Amar went to his camp, where a pandemonium like the Day of Judgment broke out when the commanders heard the news of Amir's impending journey. Mehr-Nigar fell to the floor crying, and tossed and turned and writhed in agony. Amar said to her, "Princess! All this crying and wailing will serve no purpose! Write a letter to Amir as Khvaja Abdul Muttalib has done and see what he writes in reply!"

As Amar counseled, Mehr-Nigar wrote a letter. At the end of the letter she asked him to allow her to accompany him, in the event that she was unable to prevail upon him to reconsider his decision.

Amar put her letter together with Khvaja Abdul Muttalib's and carried them secretly to Hamza. Amir first answered his father's letter and then addressed one to the commanders of his army. In reply to Mehr-Nigar's letter, Amir wrote:

> I am going away for a mere eighteen days. I ask that you accept another
> eighteen days of separation for my sake, and resign yourself patiently and
> contentedly to the will of God. It is not the custom of soldiers to take their
> women on campaigns with them. I shall adhere to this rule. I would have
> had no qualms, however, in taking you along if I were embarking on an
> excursion or hunting expedition. Until my return you must act on Amar's
> advice, and always consider him a well-wisher and as someone devoted to
> you with his life.

Amir gave these letters to Amar to deliver to the addressees, and asked him to return with his arms and armor. Amar returned to Mecca and gathered Amir's arms and armor for him, but he did not deliver any of the letters. Satisfied, Amir Hamza decorated himself with his weapons and made preparations for his departure to Qaf.

Regard how fate displays its machinations and how death calls out to the one whose end is nigh. Now the battle with Gustham and the encounter between jinn and men shall be related.

After Amir left for his homeland, along with his intrepid army and Princess Mehr-Nigar, Naushervan's summons to Gustham was dispatched. Receiving them, that wretch set out and presented himself in Ctesiphon expeditiously. Naushervan narrated to Gustham Amir's sack of Ctesiphon and his abduction of Princess Mehr-Nigar.

Gustham then left for Mecca with thirty thousand troops and led his army forward with great speed. As he approached Mecca, Gustham learned that Hamza had received a fatal wound at Zhopin's hand and that nobody had heard any news of him since. However, a small contingent of followers of the True Faith had arrived in Mecca and were said to be in a sad plight. Gustham was mightily pleased upon receiving this intelligence. He pitched his camp three *kos* from Mecca and ordered the drums of war to be sounded.

Hamza, who had not yet departed for Qaf, heard the sound of these war drums. But since there was no army within sight, he said to Amar, "Dear friend, go find out who has sounded these drums." Amar went out, and he beheld an army of several thousand troops. Amar learned upon making inquiries that Naushervan had sent Gustham with thirty thousand troops to kill Amir and take back Mehr-Nigar.

First Amar went to the walls of the city and delegated soldiers to man the towers and the ramparts. In the meanwhile, Gustham attacked the fort with his thirty thousand men. Amar answered their assault with a thunderous hail of Greek fire whose burns caused a great many enemy deaths. Terror seized the rest and they did not dare move a step, and became rooted to their spots. Gustham sounded the drum of retreat for the day and said to his men, "Rest for today and, come tomorrow, we shall settle scores with them!"

Then Amar found his chance and went before Amir to tell him the details. Amir said, "Go and sound the drums of war, and lead your army out into the battlefield. I shall come and settle this menace."

Amar returned to the city and conveyed the fortuitous news to all and sundry, saying to everyone he met, "Come tomorrow morning, you shall see the Sahibqiran." Once they heard the auspicious news, the whole camp passed that night in celebrations.

In the morning Amar rode a handsome mule into the battlefield, and arrayed his troops. Gustham also rode his rhinoceros into the field ecstatically and joyously, and was about to bark out his vain war slogans and order his army to charge into battle, when Amar espied the Sahibqiran's throne in the sky borne aloft by the jinns. Amar called out to the commanders of his army, "There! See the Sahibqiran coming to ennoble you with his magnificent presence!"

When the throne approached, everyone saw Amir Hamza seated on it fully dressed for battle, and observed that his face did not appear the least bit transformed by any sign of illness. Beholding this, his followers hastened to dismount their steeds, and in their joyful eagerness to rush forward to kiss Amir's feet, some of them even fell over, as their feet were caught in their stirrups.

While Gustham laughed out loud and made jests with the commanders of his army at this sight, Amar called out to him, "Laugh not so hard, O sniveling one, for you shall soon be crying harder when you are dispatched to Hell! Mark that the Angel of Death has come to claim you!" The Sahibqiran's throne descended from the sky in the meanwhile, and Gustham and his companions marveled greatly when they beheld this sight. They wondered how and from where Hamza descended like some heavenly calamity.

The Sahibqiran alighted from the throne and challenged Gustham forthwith, saying, "O worthless knave! Come now and face me, for which reason you made your long journey!" As Gustham was drunk on the wine of pride and vanity, he made a thrust with his spear at Amir's immaculate chest. Amir wrested the spear from his hand and brained the rhinoceros with a mighty blow of its shaft. The beast fell dead to the ground. Relieved of his mount, Gustham unsheathed his sword and came charging at Amir on foot. Gustham's sword broke as Amir parried his blow, and he was left holding the hilt. He ducked his head the first few times Amir dealt him blows, but then his luck ran out. An excellent thrust of the sword from Amir's hand cut Gustham in two like a raw cucumber and sent him to Hell. Witnessing this scene, Gustham's army charged the followers of the True Faith.

Then Abdur Rahman said to the jinns, "Do not stand idly thus! Fall upon Amir's enemy!" Each of the four hundred jinns who had accompanied Abdur Rahman caught two men in his arms, flew heavenward, and then smashed the soldiers against their companions on the ground. In this manner they killed twenty thousand men from Gustham's army and sent them to keep their master company in Hell. Three thousand had already become Hell fodder on the first day of the battle, when Amar had let loose his fireworks after Gustham's attack on the city walls. The remaining seven thousand realized that they must not sell their lives cheaply, and headed for Ctesiphon carrying Gustham's cleft corpse. With Amir's triumph secured in his battle with Gustham, Abdur Rahman carried him off toward Mount Qaf, leaving his army bivouacked in that place.

Of Amir's Journey to Mount Qaf and the Beginning of His Eighteen-Year Stay

The *dastan*⁶ writer's pen traverses the vast expanse of the page as a journey to a far-off land is afoot. The circumstances of Gustham's death and the routing and retreat of his army have all been related. After Hamza departed for Qaf, Amar gathered the booty the enemy had left behind. Then Amar handed out the letters Amir had written earlier to Khvaja Abdul Muttalib, Mehr-Nigar, and the commanders of the army, and announced to everyone the news of Amir's departure for Qaf.

Khvaja Abdul Muttalib laid the burden of patience on his heart and busied himself in prayers for Amir's safe return. The commanders of the army said to Amar, "O Khvaja, we always deemed you worthy of the same honor as the Sahibqiran himself. We shall not dither or vacillate in obeying you."

Amar embraced all of the commanders. He then told them, "All of you are companions of the Sahibqiran. Do not speak of obedience to my person, for I shall be happy only if we share the obligation brothers have toward one another. I declare that I would lay down my life for you. I am afraid that when Naushervan hears of Amir's departure to the realm of Qaf, he will not leave any stone unturned to have Mehr-Nigar back."

The commanders replied, "Khvaja! If one of his commanders, nay, even if Naushervan himself, should descend on us with his army, God willing, he will take back nothing but humiliation and defeat as long as a single one of us keeps drawing breath!"

Amar replied, "Indeed I have even greater faith in your courage!" Amar conducted the army inside the fort, ordered them to lift up the drawbridge, and after fitting out the whole city, flooded the moats around the fortifications.

After giving audience, Amar went before Mehr-Nigar, and spoke to her of Amir's victory over Gustham. Mehr-Nigar said to him, "O Khvaja, I consider you the same as my father, and therefore obey you in all matters. Amir wrote to admonish me not to act vainly or take any step without first securing your counsel and advice. God forbid I ever take into my head to act in defiance of your wishes."

Upon hearing that, Amar praised Mehr-Nigar for her probity and noble nature and said to her, "O Princess! You can be sure that if I ever request anything of you it will be in your own best interest. Amir asked you to obey me in his absence because he knows that women are unsophisticated and are not privy to the devious ways of men. Except as it regards your father—who nurses a grievance and is bent upon settling the score—I shall remain your faithful servant at all times!"

Amar bought enough provisions to last for six months and then said to himself, *Now even if the armies of the entire world should congregate here in an effort to drive us out of the fort, they are sure to leave empty-handed. We have taken refuge in the House of the Almighty and the favor of the Most High God is with us!* He deployed his commanders and champions to guard the ramparts, and cladding himself in a regal robe waited in his pavilion for the Sahibqiran's promised return.

Now an account of the Sahibqiran's journey and the continuation of this singular tale. The jinns carrying the Sahibqiran's throne soared so high that all the mountains and fortresses on land were lost to view. Around the time of *zuhr* prayers,[7] they descended and set the throne in a pasture. Amir asked Abdur Rahman, "What is the name of this place where we have landed?" He replied, "We are still within the dominion of man. A human reigns over this land and it is the place where the arena of Rustam bin Zal is situated."

After saying his *zuhr* prayers, Amir headed toward Rustam's arena for an excursion accompanied by a few close aides of Abdur Rahman. There they beheld a dome, and upon entering it, found a huge locked iron chest hanging from the roof, which no ordinary mortal could have brought down. Amir retrieved it and put it gently on the ground. When he opened it he discovered lying within a cummerbund, a dagger, a bow, and a stone tablet that read: "These artifacts belong to Rustam, and nobody may lay hands on them. But the Sahibqiran will acquire them and will be made our beneficiary heir.[?]" Overjoyed, the Sahibqiran brought the artifacts and stone tablet to Abdur Rahman, who said, "This is an auspicious augur that has been bestowed on you from the future state."

They rested in this place that day and in the morning Amir again mounted the throne and resumed the journey. At night they descended to a spot where an iron wall of indeterminate antiquity rose to the high heavens and stretched for miles on end. No doors were marked in the wall, and there were no signs there of bird or beast or human. Upon Amir's orders the jinns searched, and discovered a door hidden in the wall. Amir opened it and gained entrance to the other side, where he beheld a saintly man saying his prayers inside a dome in a pasture.

When he caught sight of Amir, the man visited blessings on him and said, "O Sahibqiran! I have waited for you for two hundred years!" Amir returned his blessings and asked, "How did you learn my name, and know that I am the Sahibqiran?" The man answered, "I heard from my elders that in this domain of Qaf no human would set foot except for a man called Hamza! Now the time has arrived for me to return to my Lord, and I request that you give me my funeral bath and bury me with your own hands!" The man then recited the Act of Faith and died, and set out for the land of the Future State. Amir was grieved to behold that scene, and carried out the saintly man's last wishes. After the funeral rites were over, Amir had his meal and again mounted the throne.

Abdur Rahman's entourage flew continuously for a night and a day and around the time of the *zuhr* prayers they again descended into a desert. Amir said to him, "Only a quarter of the day has elapsed as yet. Why alight here now?" Abdur Rahman answered, "A little distance from here is the abode of Rahdar the *dev*, who plies the trades of banditry and murder. Anyone who escapes his notice escapes with his life. I descended here so that we could renew our journey in the middle of the night. Then we will have no fear of attracting his eye, and will be relieved of all dread and anxiety regarding him."

Amir replied, "I wish you to lead me to his den so that I may kill him to free God's creatures from his depredations." Abdur Rahman remarked, "O Sahibqiran! He is a veritable monster. It would be best to wait here for night to fall!"

Amir demanded, "I would like you to tell me if Rahdar Dev is an even greater menace than the dastardly Ifrit!"

Abdur Rahman responded, "Rahdar is of absolutely no significance before the monster Ifrit! Indeed, he stands nowhere in relation to Ifrit, and any comparison between the two would be idle!"

Amir replied: "It begs reason then that while you are conducting me to Qaf to slay the mighty Ifrit, you forbid me an encounter with a smaller menace like Rahdar!"

Abdur Rahman was at last convinced by this argument and said, "There is yet another monster who infests these grounds." Amir asked, "What is this monster?" Abdur Rahman replied, "This monster is a most feral two-headed lion!"

Amir at once headed for the desert. When the scent of Amir reached the lion he left his desert lair to search for its source. Amir beheld a mighty beast, some sixty cubits in length from head to tail. As the lion charged him with a mighty roar. Amir leapt to one side and brought down his sword on the lion's back, cutting it in two. Abdur Rahman kissed the hilt of Amir's sword, and from there they carried Amir's throne to Rahdar Dev's den.

The whole night Amir did not sleep a wink from anxiety that the jinns' concern for his safety and fear that he was not a match for Rahdar would force them to divert him from the encounter. Dawn was breaking as they arrived at the *dev*'s abode, but the jinns became panic-stricken from fear and, putting the throne down, they rushed away into any nook or corner that offered them refuge. Amir dismounted his throne and set out in search of Rahdar Dev.

Now hear of Rahdar Dev. One day, a *dev* brought him news that the emperor of Qaf had dispatched his minister, Abdur Rahman, to the dominion of men to bring back a human who would slay the *devs* of Qaf and reinstate Emperor Shahpal on the throne. Ever since he had caught wind of this news, Rahdar Dev had lain in wait for that human to pass his way so that he could sink his fangs into Hamza's tasty and luscious flesh.

It so happened that Rahdar was sitting on the summit of the mountain when he espied the Sahibqiran. Seeing him from afar, Rahdar reasoned that the anticipated human must have arrived, and the man he saw was probably one of his companions. Rejoicing in his good luck to have found such a delicious tidbit, Rahdar ordered one of his *devs* to bring the human being alive into his presence. As the *dev* approached Amir and extended his arm to take him to Rahdar, Amir caught hold of his hand and wrenched it so mightily that the *dev*'s knees buckled and he came very near to dying from the violence of the tug. Amir then clouted him so powerfully over the head that his brains were smashed into his neck and he departed forthwith from the Qaf of the present to the Qaf of the Future State. Watching all of this, Rahdar decided that this must be the selfsame champion whom Abdur Rahman had gone to fetch. Feeling certain of this fact, he descended upon Amir's entourage with a force of three hundred *devs*. Amir bellowed "God is Great!" so powerfully that the entire expanse of the desert reverberated with the sound and the jinns very nearly died from fright.

Rahdar arranged his three hundred *devs* opposite Amir and made preparations for combat. Rahdar swung a box-tree branch tied with several millstones and brought it down on Amir with full force, but he foiled the blow. Then stepping to the *dev*'s side, Amir dealt him such a fierce blow with Rustam's dagger that it exited clean from Rahdar's other side. With the link to his senses permanently severed, the *dev* gave up the ghost from just that one blow. Amir put his dagger in its scabbard and, unsheathing the sword, he fell upon the three hundred *devs* that stood by. Whoever received a blow from his hand that day did not draw another breath.

Abdur Rahman said to the jinns in his entourage, "Go forth and help the Sahibqiran!" At this command, all the jinns fell upon the *devs* and fought mightily. A great many *devs* were dispatched to Hell and entered the dominion of the Future State. Amir did not pursue the few who managed to escape with their lives but allowed them to flee. Then Amir went to Rahdar's abode with Abdur Rahman, where there were heaps upon heaps of countless priceless jewels and valuables. Amir said to Abdur Rahman, "All these goods here are the property of Emperor Shahpal bin Shahrukh, and I am not going to touch these ephemeral riches or be tempted by them."

All the jinns present there warmly lauded Amir's gestures of courage and munificence, and commented to each other that they little knew that such noble men were born among the sons of Aadam. From there Amir set out again mounted on his throne. Four jinns brought up the rear carrying Rahdar's head.

When they reached the castle of Ghaneem, Salasal Perizad, who was one of the companions of Emperor Shahpal, came out with an entourage of forty thousand *perizads* to welcome Amir. The next day Amir set out again with Salasal Perizad toward Gulistan-e Irum. His throne was flanked by Abdur Rahman on the right and by Salasal Perizad on the left. They were making their way, discoursing together, when scores of *perizads* of such luminous aspect that they overwhelmed one's vision materialized before them. They came flying toward them mounted on hundreds of thrones, chanting and playing musical instruments. They were followed by several thousand more carrying bouquets of flowers, incense, and aromatic unguents, which fragranced the whole desert. They all clustered around Shahpal's throne. Spotting them in the distance, Abdur Rahman and Salasal Perizad said to the Sahibqiran, "What a marvel! The emperor himself has come out to receive you!" When Shahpal's throne approached, Amir ordered that his own throne be set down on the ground, whereupon Shahpal said to the *perizads*, "Set down our throne, too, next to Amir's so that we may derive wholesome bliss from our meeting!"

When Emperor Shahpal's throne alighted, Amir dismounted and kissed its foot. Shahpal embraced Amir and kissed his forehead. Amir presented the emperor with Rahdar's head, along with all the jewels and valuables.

Then seating Amir by his side, the emperor repaired to Gulistan-e Irum, where he conducted Amir into the Hall of Suleiman, offering him a bejeweled throne for his station and scattering precious jewels as a sacrifice to Amir. All the illustrious *perizads* stood with folded wings before Amir and said to one another, "Who would have thought that the Creator endowed feeble humans with such beauty and might, and made them so courageous and suave?" The emperor ordered that wines of Qaf be served in order to break the timidity of Amir, who sat quiet with his gaze lowered.

This scribe now returns to the realm of Earth to discourse on what passed there until the wine is brought out for Hamza.

The historians of chronicles of yore relate that Naushervan was already floundering in a sea of sorrow after hearing of the reverses suffered by Zhopin and Ayashan Malik, when Gustham's corpse was brought before him, and the companions of this slain commander narrated how Hamza's throne had descended from the skies like an unforeseen calamity after Gustham had arranged his army for battle. They recounted how Hamza killed Gustham and their troops were lifted to the high heavens by some unseen force that then hurled them at their compatriots on the ground, and how, in that manner, twenty thousand troops died without anyone finding out who or what had killed them.

After these tidings, Naushervan looked askance at Buzurjmehr, who from his foreknowledge narrated the entire account of the realm of Qaf to the emperor and told him that Hamza will remain held up in Qaf for eighteen years.

Naushervan rejoiced upon hearing Buzurjmehr's account, thinking that eighteen years were an eternity, and that Hamza would certainly die at the hands of some *dev* or another. It occurred to Naushervan that now was a most opportune time to settle the score with the followers of the True Faith and wipe them out of existence when they least expected an attack. Thus resolved, he ordered Wailum and Qailum, who were the mightiest warriors among the Sassanids, to advance on Mecca with thirty thousand troops and bring back Princess Mehr-Nigar. Having received their orders, the two commanders took their leave and headed for Mecca.

Now hear an account of Amar Ayyar, the exterminator of all infidels. After eighteen days had come and gone, and another few days had passed beyond the period stipulated by Hamza, Amar broke into loud cries and began to wash his face with tears. When he went to see Mehr-Nigar, he found her also in a state of great agitation. She said to him, "O Amar, Amir Hamza has not returned, and separation from him weighs heavily on my heart. God alone knows what passed with him. I can think of nothing else but taking poison to die, and removing from life's page the mark of my existence. Then you may bury me wherever you deem proper, and inter me where you will."

Khvaja Amar responded, "O Queen of Heavens! What is this I hear? When did you ever hear of anyone taking poison due to separation from his beloved? Why do you not put your hopes in God's aid and assistance? I am now headed to Ctesiphon to seek Buzurjmehr's opinion on this matter."

After counseling Mehr-Nigar, Amar put on his *ayyar*'s attire and set out for Ctesiphon by way of the forest. He accomplished the journey in a few days and arrived at Buzurjmehr's door in the guise of a farmer and informed him of his concerns.

Khvaja Buzurjmehr said, "It is true that Hamza promised to return after eighteen days. You will see him at the Castle of Tanj-e Maghreb, but not until eighteen years have passed. He shall slay all the rebellious *devs* of Qaf and come to no harm himself. In the meanwhile, you will have to undertake and surmount many challenges. You will be assailed from all sides by kings and warriors. But rest assured that none of them shall prevail against you. Have no fear of anybody now. Repair to Mecca posthaste, and employ yourself in fortifying your defenses, because Naushervan has dispatched Wailum and Qailum at the head of thirty thousand troops to kill you and bring back Mehr-Nigar."

Amar replied, "I will not mind it in the least even if I should lose my life in Hamza's service. Pray write out a letter of instruction to Mehr-Nigar, so that she may find some solace from your words and act upon my counsel."

Buzurjmehr sent for his inkstand and wrote a letter. Amar set out toward Mecca by way of the forest. Passing all of the stations of the journey without taking rest night or day, Amar reached his fort and gave Buzurjmehr's letter to Mehr-Nigar. Reading it, she shed tears without cease and cried out, "Alas, such was my destiny that I should burn in the fire of separation from Hamza for eighteen years, and waste away like a taper by the flame of disunion from him."

Amar consoled her and said, "O Queen of Heavens, may you live long! God willing, these eighteen years will pass like eighteen days. The Almighty God is the Unifier of the Separated. He will ease your separation until the day you meet Hamza."

After comforting Mehr-Nigar with these words, Amar went into the camp and mustered the army, and addressed all of them thus. "My friends, I have learned through Buzurjmehr that Hamza will remain in Qaf for eighteen years. Therefore, anyone among you who desires to leave may leave now, and those who wish to stay may stay in the spirit of fraternity."

Regardless of rank, the whole camp replied with one voice, "O Khvaja! We have vowed to be true and faithful to Hamza with all our hearts! Now that you are with us in place of Hamza, we will never leave you, or ever dream of setting foot outside the bounds of obedience due you!" Rejoicing at their words, Amar embraced every one of them. He delegated the necessary force to the ramparts of the fort, deputized Muqbil Vafadar with his faultless archers to man the defenses, and sat waiting for Wailum and Qailum.

Hardly a few watches had passed when a dark dust cloud rose on the horizon, enveloping the whole expanse. As it drew closer, and the wafts of air dispersed it a little, Amar's army saw a host carrying thirty standards. At its head rode two mighty and valiant champions clad in armor, whom Amar reasoned to be Wailum and Qailum.

In their greed to receive robes of honor and rich rewards from Naushervan, those fools made the blunder of ordering their forces to surround the fort and to take away Mehr-Nigar by force after slaying the followers of the True Faith.

When they came within range, Amar let loose a hail of Greek fire that burnt alive all those who had advanced close and stopped the rear ranks in their tracks. When Wailum and Qailum saw that the day was nearing its end and their army had suffered a reverse, they sounded the clarion for the cessation of hostilities, and set up camp beyond the fort's firing range.

The next day Wailum and Qailum again sallied forth with their army and when their troops were opposite the fort, Amar again fired salvos of Greek fire from the fort. Wailum and Qailum revived the spirits of their troops and confronted those retreating with accusations of cowardly behavior. Wailum and Qailum covered their heads with their shields and spurred their mounts forward until they reached the edge of the trenches around the fort and their army charged in to fight beside them.

Amar immediately took out a missile filled with naphtha and, setting it afire, let it fly at Wailum's breast. The naphtha soaked Wailum when the missile burst on impact, and set him ablaze. When Qailum saw Wailum burning and tried to help, he fared the same as Wailum, and writhed in agony from the pain of burning. Both brothers began rolling on the ground like tumbler pigeons. Catching sight of their commanders burning away and unable to put out the fire, their army covered them with mud and dirt. The fire was at last put out, and the fight called off for the day, their army retreated to its camp.

When about an hour remained until the close of day, Amar disguised himself as Naushervan's *ayyar,* Aatish. Then he brazenly entered the pavilion of the enemy commanders and, calling on Wailum and Qailum, spoke to them with great warmth. They said to him, "Brother Aatish! See how ill we have fared at Amar's hands!"

The fake Aatish replied, "Mark my words well: Only an *ayyar* can be an *ayyar*'s match. Now that I have arrived here, you shall see how Amar fares at my hands, and what a terrible retribution I will visit on him."

At that moment the agony of their pain again overwhelmed Wailum and Qailum, and they resumed crying and wailing. Again the false Aatish spoke: "You should both imbibe a few goblets of the finest wine to recuperate your energy and allay the pain." Amar handed out two rounds of pure wine to the brothers and the rest of the assembly, but then drugged the wine when serving the third round. Every one assembled became bereft of his faculties and fell unconscious to the floor. Amar went to the entrance of the pavilion and served the same wine to all the servants and menials as well. Then he stripped everyone naked and put all the furnishings of that pavilion, carpet and all, into his *zambil.* Then shaving one side of each man's face of its mustache and beard, and tying small bells to the mustache on the other side, he marked each bare cheek with lime, catechu, and kohl,[8] and blackened the other cheek entirely. After that Amar tied a note around Wailum's neck that read:

> It was I, Amar in person, who visited you today. I spared your lives this once and saved you the fate of the dead. You had better wind up your circus tomorrow and depart for Ctesiphon, or else I will slaughter all of you and exile you from the realm of the living.

Then hanging them upside down and naked from the posts of the pavilion, he headed out.

In the morning, when Wailum and Qailum's discovered that it was Amar Ayyar who had visited them in disguise as Aatish, they veiled their faces out of mortification, and immediately broke camp and headed for Ctesiphon, returning to Naushervan's court in their sorry state.

OF NAUSHERVAN SENDING HIS ELDER SON, HURMUZ, TO CHASTISE AMAR AYYAR

The narrator writes that after Wailum and Qailum departed toward Cte-siphon with their tails between their legs, Amar packed the fort with enough provisions to last his army for six months, and bided his time in peace.

Now, to return to the account of Wailum and Qailum: When they arrived battered and beaten in Ctesiphon and complained to Naushervan of Amar's ravages, he sent for Hurmuz and said to him, "I would like you to go and bring back Mehr-Nigar after killing Amar. Proceed with great pomp and array, as many a battle is won from the propitious presence and good fortune of kings and princes." In addition to forty thousand armor-clad warriors, he dispatched Hurmuz with several mighty, swash-buckling champions, and provided them for all eventualities. Naushervan also sent Bakhtak's son Bakhtiarak to accompany them, and obtained a promise from him to exert his utmost for the success of the mission.

But while they head toward Mecca, let me narrate what passed with Amar. One day Amar realized that he had not enjoyed a good sprint for some time. Deciding not to put it off any longer, he exchanged his regal clothes for the attire of an *ayyar*, and headed in the direction of Cte-siphon. He had gone some twenty-odd *farsangs* in that direction when he beheld a great dust cloud on the horizon. Thinking that he should inves-tigate the cause and learn what new calamity lay hidden therein, Amar disguised himself as a water carrier, and went toward it with a water skin slung over his shoulder.

When Amar drew near the cloud he beheld crown prince Hurmuz marching forward with a grand and intrepid army. The soldiers, however, were unable to open their mouths from the violence of their thirst. Upon catching sight of a water carrier, they rejoiced. Amar witnessed the prince's tongue hanging out of his mouth and his eyes all clouded. A few of his men stood around him, holding a sheet over him for shade, wondering if he would survive.

Amar dripped a few drops of water into his mouth whereupon Hurmuz opened his eyes. When Hurmuz regained his senses he cried out, "O water carrier! Pray put aside a little water for me, and serve the rest to my army, and resurrect them, too."

Amar had with him the gift given him by Prophet Khizr, which worked the miracle that even if ten million people were to drink from it, the source never dried and it remained as full as before. Amar satiated the thirst of the whole army including its beasts. Hurmuz gave him several hundred gold coins in reward and said, "O water carrier! I am headed at the emperor's orders toward Mecca. If I am successful in killing Amar, I will make you the ruler of that city. Now show me a way to Mecca that has some water sources so that my army can advance without suffering."

Amar led Hurmuz and his army deep into the heart of a forest where for miles around there was not a drop of water to be found, and exclaimed, "O Hurmuz! Little did you know that I am Amar in person! Even though I am by myself in the midst of your whole army, there is nothing you can do to harm me!"

Amar then dove away and made off after taking away Hurmuz's crown. The troops gave him chase, yet none could catch even the cloud of dust he raised in his wake. Then some battered and ravaged troops from Wailum and Qailum's army whom they had met on the way led Hurmuz's army out of that pass after many a false start, and put them on the right path to Mecca.

On the fourth day, around evening, they arrived within sight of Mecca, and pitched their tents. Come night, when the commanders of the army presented themselves before Hurmuz, he said, "I want a plan that will put an end to the menace of the followers of True Faith without imperiling us in the least. It would bring me no end of ridicule and shame to have battled with a lowly *ayyar*."

Bakhtiarak praised Hurmuz's judgment and said, "If you were to command me, I would be willing to counsel Amar and persuade him to surrender before Your Honor." Hurmuz replied, "Nothing would be more to the purpose."

Come morning, Bakhtiarak mounted his mule and trotted up to the trenches around the fort. Bakhtiarak made a low bow and greeted Amar, calling out, "O Khvaja! Since I consider you as my cousin and have the greatest regard for your person, I have come to counsel you as a well-wisher. Hamza has left for Qaf, and to imagine that he will escape the clutches of the *devs* is against all reason. You would do well to hand Princess Mehr-Nigar over to Prince Hurmuz, and receive from him in exchange the authority to rule Mecca."

Amar replied, "O coward! Do not make sport of my beard. Know that if Naushervan, the Emperor of the Seven Climes, should himself advance here with all his army, he would not be able to lay hands on Mehr-Nigar. So save your loquacious tongue its gymnastics for someone else's ears. The *devs* of Qaf will soon find out to their peril where they stand with Hamza. Now leave before I put you to the sword in retribution for your words!"

Upon hearing this, Bakhtiarak said despite his better judgment, "O cameleer's son! You'll see now how your unbridled manner lands you in untold calamities and afflictions. I shall have lived to no purpose if I do not soon put a halter through your nose!"

At this, Amar swung his sling and let fly a stone at Bakhtiarak with such fury that it inflicted a two-digit-deep wound on his brow. He arrived before Hurmuz covered in blood. After he had recovered command of his faculties, Bakhtiarak narrated the words exchanged between Amar and himself, whereupon Hurmuz flew into a towering rage and rebuked Amar in harsh and severe terms.

The Pen's Charger, Coerced by the Reins of Discourse, Renders an Account of the Lord of the Auspicious Planetary Conjunction, the Conqueror of the World, the Most Munificent and Bounteous, Amir Hamza the Magnificent

The nurturers of narrative relate that when the *perizads* brought out the grape wine, Shahpal served Amir a goblet with his own hands, and the flower bud of Amir's fancy opened up in delight from the amiable effect of that pleasant and temperate wine.

Let it be known that Emperor Shahpal's daughter, Aasman Peri, who was one of the comeliest fairies and unsurpassed in charm and beauty, was screened off sitting on a throne behind Shahpal's station. She was able to catch sight of the Sahibqiran from behind the screen. Upon beholding his peerless, youthful beauty she became enamored of him, smitten by love to the very core of heart and soul. Becoming disconsolate, she began to pine away that very instant.

After one night and one day had passed in feasting, Shahpal said to Hamza, "O Sahibqiran! I cannot even begin to tell you how I have suffered at the hands of these *devs*. I will live under a debt of obligation to you all my life and will offer my whole empire in your service if you would do me the kindness of eliminating them!"

The Sahibqiran replied: "It is no great favor that you ask. By the grace of Your Excellency, and God willing, I shall behead every single one of these rebels and restore your lands to your control."

Shahpal rejoiced at Amir Hamza's words and said to Abdur Rahman, "Bring out the four swords of King Suleiman so that from among them he may choose the one to his liking!" Abdur Rahman produced the swords without delay. Shahpal put them before the Sahibqiran and said, "These are Samsam, Qumqam, Aqrab-e Suleimani, and Zul-Hajam.[9] You may pick the one that you prefer!" Amir chose the Aqrab-e Suleimani and girded himself with it, whereupon all the *perizads* broke into joyous cheers.

When Amir asked Abdur Rahman what it signified, Abdur Rahman replied, "O Sahibqiran, these four swords once decorated the belt of King Suleiman who is reputed to have said that after his days were done, the heads of the contumacious *devs* would be severed by the Aqrab-e Suleimani. You must have chosen it by divine prescience since you were unfamiliar with its legend!"

Then Abdur Rahman said, "One last test remains in this matter. "There is a poplar tree that the *perizads* consider to match the height and dimensions of Ifrit. It is also a legend known all over Qaf that the one who brings down the poplar with one blow of the Aqrab-e Suleimani will be the one to dispatch Ifrit to Hell."

Amir then went to this tree and, reciting the name of Allah, dealt one blow to its trunk, which sliced through the wood as if it were made of soap.

As the tree fell, Shahpal kissed Amir's hand and arm and, embracing him with great joy, said, "O Hamza! Indeed you have been blessed by King Suleiman and for that reason you command such power and might."

Amir replied, "Pray order your army to sally forth from Gulistan-e Irum and pitch their tents in the battlefield. Have the drums of war sounded!"

Ifrit received the tidings that Emperor Shahpal had sent for a man from the realm of Earth to assist him, and heard that this man had reached Qaf with great pomp, array, and acclaim, and that by dint of his help Shahpal had come to the battlefield and arrayed his troops to give fight. Ifrit roared with laughter upon hearing this news and then said, "How could there ever be a match between a human being and a *dev*? It is well, I suppose, that it brought Shahpal out of his hole!" He ordered his side to answer the drums of war, and commanded his armies to prepare for battle and carnage.

Emperor Shahpal ordered his army to beat the battle drums and the rumble of twelve hundred pairs of golden and silver drums rose like reverberations of thunder. In Ifrit's camp the *devs* struck stones together, and by way of drumming thumped their asses. In short, the whole night the two camps engaged in clamoring and shouting. The next morning, Ifrit stepped into the battlefield with hundreds of thousands of *devs*.

When the *devs* beheld the Sahibqiran they indulged themselves in all manner of foolish capers and horseplay. Amir could not help but laugh watching their antics. He found them fatuous and, watching their unbridled horseplay, formed a low opinion of their shameless lot.

The first to seek combat was Ifrit's father, Ahriman, who stood five hundred yards high. He stepped out of the ranks to confront Shahpal's army, holding a box tree in his hands. He let out a war cry and bellowed, "Where is the Quake of Qaf, the Latter-day Suleiman who puts great store in his valor and gallantry? Let him come forward and face me so that I can make him taste death's relish!"

Amir, descended into the battlefield without allowing the least fear or terror to find foothold in his heart. He bellowed "God is Great!" so lustily that the whole desert reverberated with the sound. Ahriman said, "O Quake of Qaf! You make a big squeak for one your size! Come deal me the great blow that you have!" The Sahibqiran replied, "Deal me a blow first, and then I shall return it!"

Ahriman replied: "How would all the *devs* judge me if I were to attack a diminutive being like you whose very creation is tainted with infirmity."

Hamza said to this, "You got your fill when nature was distributing stature and height, and I got mine when it distributed power and might! Little do you know that I am your Angel of Death." At this, Ahriman brought down the box tree on his opponent. Amir foiled the blow and, unsheathing the Aqrab-e Suleimani, said, "O vile creature! Now you cannot say that you were killed without due warning, for I am about to smear my shining sword with your foul blood."

Even as he finished speaking those words, Amir struck a blow that cut that carrion-eater in two. Shahpal prostrated himself before God in gratitude and ordered the *perizads* to play festive music. Ifrit Dev heaved a searing sigh and said, "O human! You committed a terrible deed in killing a great warrior like my father. Witness what terrible calamity shall visit you!" He sent a *dev* of even more imposing stature than Ahriman to combat with the Sahibqiran. Amir Hamza dispatched him to Hell as well. In short, within no time Amir destroyed nine mighty *devs* who were the pride of Ifrit's army, leaving their master confounded and baffled.

Then Ifrit shivered and groaned and immediately had drums sounded to announce the cessation of hostilities for the day. He had his father's corpse carried away, and returned to his camp crying and wailing in ecstasies of grief and fear. Emperor Shahpal retired to Gulistan-e Irum and was most pleased by Amir's valor and courage.

The Dastan Changes Course to Give an Account of Khvaja Amar Ayyar

Now hear a short account of the father of racers of the world, the King of *Ayyars*, Khvaja Amar bin Umayya Zamiri. When Bakhtiarak returned to his camp wounded by Amar's hand, Hurmuz ordered that ladders be prepared to climb the fort walls on the day of the battle. It took four months before the ladders were ready. A day before the attack, Amar Ayyar managed to set them afire, destroying all of them.

Hurmuz then ordered his army commander Zura Zarah-Posh to charge the fort. Amar used deceit to kill him and inflicted heavy losses on Hurmuz's army. Then Bakhtiarak counseled retreat and Hurmuz sent a report to Naushervan's court.

The emperor sent the warrior Akhzar Fil-gosh with seventy thousand troops to aid Hurmuz. As well, he dispatched Mehr-Nigar's childhood attendant Khvaja Nihal. It was his mission to use subterfuge to enter Amar's graces, poison him at the first opportunity, and then throw open the castle gates to admit Hurmuz's army.

OF KHVAJA NIHAL'S DEPARTURE FOR MECCA TO BRING BACK MEHR-NIGAR, AND OF HIS DYING AT AMAR'S HANDS

Narrators of sweet discourse have passed down that in three months' time Akhzar Fil-gosh and Khvaja Nihal reached Hurmuz's camp. When Amar got the news of their arrival he entered the enemy camp in disguise and learned of Khvaja Nihal's secret mission to kill him. Amar then called on Khvaja Nihal without any disguise and deceived him with talk of his hardships in Hamza's absence and his desire to pay allegiance to Naushervan. Khvaja Nihal believed him. Amar gave him drugged dates to eat, then killed him and took his place. When Hurmuz gave a feast in the honor of Akhzar Fil-gosh and the false Khvaja Nihal, Amar drugged the wine and, once everyone had fallen unconscious, he robbed the court and left, carrying Hurmuz in his *zambil*. He also left Bakhtiarak and Akhzar Fil-gosh together in a highly compromising state.

Back in his fort, Amar Ayyar took out Hurmuz from the *zambil* and secured a pledge of non-aggression from him until Hamza's return from Qaf. When Akhzar Fil-gosh tried to attack Amar's fort, Amar used Hurmuz as a hostage. When Hurmuz returned to his camp after his release, and announced his decision to cease warfare with Amar Ayyar, Akhzar Fil-gosh took exception to it, and called the prince a coward. While Hurmuz returned to Ctesiphon after an altercation with Akhzar Fil-gosh, the latter prepared to attack Amar's fort. The night before the assault, Amar infiltrated Akhzar Fil-gosh's pavilion and rendered him unconscious. Then Amar left him hanging upside down and naked, in a most degrading and shameful state from a post on a crossroads in his camp. Amar also left behind a message to reveal that he was the author of Akhzar Fil-gosh's disgrace. After his soldiers freed Akhzar Fil-gosh, he could not bear his shame and killed himself. His men returned to Ctesiphon carrying his body.

Upon hearing of Hurmuz's capitulation before Amar, Naushervan severely rebuked him but Buzurjmehr commended his actions since according to him, Hurmuz had refused to fight a lowly *ayyar* which was commensurate with the dignity of a prince. Naushervan had still not recovered from this reverse when Akhzar Fil-gosh's corpse was brought before him, causing him even greater distress.

After the return of Akhzar Fil-gosh's army, Amar Ayyar went to Mecca to offer thanks to God. Khvaja Abdul Muttalib advised him not to stay in Mecca lest the citizens of Mecca were made to bear Naushervan's wrath for harboring him and his men. Aadi Madi-Karib suggested to Amar that they move to the castle of Tang-e Rawahil. However, Tang-e Rawahil was now under the rule of Humran Zarrin-Kamar, who was one of Naushervan's commanders. Amar took on the disguise of Humran's shepherd and went before him to report that a party of Arabs had attacked him and stolen his animals.

Upon hearing this, Humran went in pursuit of the raiders, convinced that they could only be Amar Ayyar and his men. While he was away, Amar dressed Sultan Bakht Maghrebi as Humran who then led Amar's army into the castle of Tang-e Rawahil. Amar secured control of the castle, and deputed his men to the defenses. When Humran returned to his castle after his fruitless pursuit, he was attacked by Amar's men on guard. Realizing that he had been fooled by Amar, Humran returned to Naushervan's court and narrated the account of his folly before the emperor.

Naushervan ordered Buzurjmehr to jointly lead a campaign against Amar with the princes Hurmuz and Faramuz and Zhopin Kaus of Zabul with a large army.

After leading an unsuccessful assault on Amar's position at the advice of Bakhtiarak and suffering the loss of many men, Naushervan's forces laid siege to the castle.

Amar busied himself in finding another safe fort where he could move his army. He came upon the fort of Kurgistan, which was jointly ruled by two brothers, Sohrab and Darab. Amar deceived Sohrab into believing that he was ready to marry off Princess Mehr-Nigar to Sohrab since he resembled Amir Hamza, and that the princess, too, had given her consent. Sohrab offered Amar and his camp shelter in the fort of Kurgistan. Darab was also fooled by Amar's seemingly earnest statements and it was ordered that Amar be allowed to enter the fort at any hour with his army. When Sohrab insisted on accompanying Amar Ayyar to bring Mehr-Nigar into Kurgistan, Amar thought of a scheme to get rid of him and enlisted Buzurjmehr's help.

Amar then went and told Sohrab that Buzurjmehr had arrived from Ctesiphon to take away Mehr-Nigar and that he needed armed help to safeguard the princess from Naushervan's army. With Amar's counsel, Sohrab decided to make a night assault on Buzurjmehr's forces. However, as pre-arranged between Amar and Buzurjmehr, the latter had emptied his camp. When Sohrab attacked, he found the camp empty and soon thereafter was ambushed by Naushervan's army and taken captive.

While Sohrab was sent to the emperor as a prisoner, Amar led his army into the fort of Kurgistan and secured its control. Darab converted to the True Faith.

Finding that Amar Ayyar had again fooled him, Hurmuz wrote a note to the emperor, apprising him of the circumstances, and sent it to Ctesiphon with Buzurjmehr.

Enraged by his constant humiliation at Amar's hands, Naushervan next sent the warrior Qaran Fil-Gardan on the campaign against Amar.

The narrator has related that when Qaran Fil-Gardan arrived in Hurmuz's camp, he derided the prince's efforts against Amar, and vowed to take the fort of Kurgistan speedily.

Initially unsuccessful, Qaran Fil-Gardan managed to reach the gates of Kurgistan and was about to break them down when Naqabdar Naranji-Posh, a rider whose face was covered by an orange veil, came to Amar Ayyar's aid with forty thousand troops. He killed Qaran Fil-Gardan and routed his army. Then the mysterious Naqabdar went away with his army without revealing his identity to Amar Ayyar.

Now Amar decided to play a trick on Hurmuz. By the miraculous power of the *zambil*, he turned himself into a forty-yard-tall giant. Pretending to be Sa'ad Zulmati, a messenger from Qaf, he went to Hurmuz's camp and announced that Hamza had been killed in Qaf at the hands of Ifrit Dev and Emperor Shahpal had sent Hamza's bones in a lionskin sack to Earth for the burial. When Hurmuz, Zhopin, and Bakhtiarak heard the noise of lamentations rising from Amar's camp, which Amar had orchestrated as a part of his plan, they believed the news.

Not long afterwards, Amar presented himself before Zhopin and told him that he had received the news of Hamza's death from the *perizads* and he was willing to surrender Mehr-Nigar to Zhopin. Bakhtiarak warned him not to believe Amar's words but Zhopin ignored his advice. He invited Amar and his companions to his camp and arranged a feast for them. After having their fill Amar and his companions returned to their fort after telling Zhopin to prepare for his nuptials with Mehr-Nigar. Amar also took a good quantity of gold from Zhopin to prepare for the wedding, which he spent on stockpiling food in his fort, and strengthening its defenses. When Zhopin did not hear from Amar after seven days and sent his *ayyar* to inquire the reason for the delay, Amar sent him back a curt reply that he was loath to have any commerce with Zhopin for the next six months. Zhopin realized that Amar had made a fool of him but could do little.

Next, Amar set fire to a nearby forest in such a manner that the direction of Zhopin's camp was the only exit for the wild beasts fleeing the fire. As the animals stampeded through Zhopin's camp in the darkness of the night, his army took them for night raiders and in their confusion fought and killed one another all night long. The following night Amar made a night raid on Zhopin's camp. Aadi Madi-Karib confused the enemy further by sounding the war cries of Landhoor.

A few hours before morning, Amar received intelligence that Zhopin's brothers were on their way with a vast army to aid Zhopin. Amar had it proclaimed that the approaching army was a force led by Bahram Gurd. Hearing this, Zhopin and Hurmuz's men turned tail despite Bakhtiarak's warnings that it could be another deception orchestrated by Amar Ayyar.

The nimble scribes of fancy inform us that the army of the infidels lost its nerve and was in full retreat. After some time, when they learned that it was in fact an army that had come to their aid, they bitterly lamented their error.

Jahandar and Jahangir then sallied forth to attack the fort of Kurgistan. Before they could break down its gates, however, Naqabdar Naranji-Posh arrived to Amar's aid and routed Jahandar's and Jahangir's army.

Soon the provisions ran out in Amar's fort and Darab suggested that they move to the fort of Nestan, which was ruled by Quful Nestani.

Amar managed to enter the fort of Nestan and after rendering Quful Nestani unconscious, he put him into his *zambil* and took his place. The next day he announced in the court that Mehr-Nigar had pledged him her love and he had invited her into the fort with her entourage. To deceive Zhopin, Amar had arranged for palanquins hiding wild beasts to be sent out in plain view of Zhopin's camp in one direction, while Mehr-Nigar and Amar's army left from the back door of the castle for Nestan.

Zhopin was deceived and followed a palanquin carrying an animal. Upon discovering that there was a bear inside, he realized how he had been duped. He followed Mehr-Nigar's procession and caught up with her before she could reach the fort of Nestan. Repulsed by his advances Mehr-Nigar assaulted him, and as he turned his back and fled, one of the arrows shot by Mehr-Nigar got lodged in his derriere.

Amar Ayyar took Quful Nestani from his *zambil* and persuaded him to convert to the True Faith.

Amar now disguised himself as a surgeon and arrived at Zhopin's pavilion. He was taken to Zhopin and asked to minister to his wound.

Amar Ayyar made Zhopin undergo many tortures in the name of surgery and, after leaving him in a worse condition than before, Amar headed out after looting his pavilion. When Naushervan sent aid in gold and riches with Hakim Majdak for the princes, Amar intercepted him, and stole that hoard as well.

Upon finding out that it was Amar who had deceived them the princes raged against him but found that there was little they could do.

Of Ifrit Dev Seeking Refuge in Tilism-e Shehristan-e Zarrin at the Counsel of His Mother, Maloona Jadu

Before I resume the narration of the events mentioned above, let me give a few sentences to relate an account of the Quake of Qaf, the Latter-day Suleiman, the World Conqueror, the Lord of the Auspicious Planetary Conjunction, Abul-Ala, Amir Hamza.

Emperor Shahpal ordered a week of festivities in honor of the Sahibqiran. On the eighth day of festivities the Sahibqiran said to Shahpal, "Your Majesty, Ifrit's intentions remain uncertain. Your Honor should take precedence and imprint your awe and dread on his heart. I came here on the promise of an eighteen-day sojourn. That period is long past, and God knows what became of my relatives and dear ones."

Shahpal ordered the war drums to be beaten. This was the Music Band of Suleiman whose report reached even far-off places that lay a distance of three days' journey from there.

Ifrit himself was not too far away from there. Upon hearing the war drums and their thunderous, cacophonous noise, he became agitated and his senses were thrown into disarray. He said to his accomplices, "I am still in mourning for my father. While my heart has yet to find solace and comfort from this terrible loss, Hamza has already sounded war drums. I am sure he is my slayer." Then Ifrit broke into sobs and washed his face with tears of anguish.

He dispatched a swift *dev* to fetch his mother, Maloona Jadu, a matchless sorceress. Immediately upon receiving these tidings, she arrived flying like a whirlwind. Ifrit fell upon her neck crying loudly. Giving her a detailed account of the Sahibqiran, he informed her of all the occult details about him. She replied, "Indeed, this human who has arrived to assist Shahpal is your sworn enemy. It would be best for you to retire to the *tilism*[11] I have created in Shehristan-e Zarrin. We will settle our account with Shahpal once that human being has returned to the realm of men!"

Along with his accursed mother, Ifrit departed forthwith for the *tilism* of Shehristan-e Zarrin. Many of his warriors went their own way; many others consulted together and decided to present themselves before Emperor Shahpal and repent.

Upon hearing these happy tidings the emperor bestowed gold and jewels to Amir Hamza as the sacrifice for his life and the favorable news that Ifrit's army had come to pledge obedience to him gave him great joy. The celebrations continued for many days on a grand scale. After the revelries had ended, Amir Hamza said to Emperor Shahpal, "Kindly give me leave to depart, and send me back, as many obligations have been lying in abeyance and await my return."

Emperor Shahpal replied, "O Sahibqiran, it was our agreement that you would leave Qaf after slaying Ifrit. Once this task has been fulfilled, you will be given leave to return. As you know, Ifrit is still at large. It would be far better for you to return to the realm of men after putting an end to his menace."

Amir lowered his head and, after a moment's silence, said to Shahpal, "I am willing to oblige. However, I would like to find out where Ifrit Dev is now hiding so that I may go there myself, kill him, and bring you his head." Shahpal replied, "His present abode will not be revealed until we have reached Qasr-e Bilour." Amir said, "Then we must not delay in starting for Qasr-e Bilour."

Shahpal sent his advance camp at once to Qasr-e Bilour and the next day departed for Qasr-e Bilour in Amir Hamza's company. When they arrived, the nobles of Qasr-e Bilour reported, "Ifrit along with his mother, Maloona Jadu, is hiding in Tilism-e Shehristan-e Zarrin."

At this, Amir said to Shahpal, "As he is hiding at the *tilism* by himself, I shall also confront him alone." Shahpal looked toward Abdur Rahman who replied, "I have discovered by the calculations of *jafar* and astrology that Amir will triumph over Ifrit and defeat him immediately upon his arrival."

Shahpal seated Amir on a throne and ordered four swift *perizads* to carry him to Shehristan-e Zarrin. The *perizads* immediately flew off with the throne, and after three nights and three days alighted atop a green mountain known by the name of Zehr Mohra, and said, "O Sahibqiran! We have come across an impediment! Magical *tilisms* created by Maloona Jadu are strewn all along the path from this slope to the boundaries of Shehristan-e Zarrin. If we were to take a single step farther, we would be combusted by magical devices. Behold that radiance in the distance: It is the same Shehristan-e Zarrin where that reprobate *dev* has made his abode!"

The Sahibqiran camped for the night on the mountain. After saying his prayers in the morning, he said to the *perizads*, "Pray stay here without anxiety or fear and remain alert to my call. I am now headed toward Shehristan-e Zarrin. I forewarn you that I shall make three war cries: the first one when I encounter Ifrit; the second during combat; and a third cry upon my victory. If you do not hear the third war cry, you should understand that I have been beheaded and have died at the hands of Ifrit. You may then take the news of my death to Emperor Shahpal."

Amir Hamza girded himself and descended the mountain. However, when he suddenly could not take a step forward for the darkness, he was forced again to climb the mountain. From there he saw light all around as before, and wondered why it had disappeared when he descended.

When the same thing happened five or six times and he had to climb up again the *perizads* said, "These wonders are due to the *tilisms* created by Ifrit's mother, Maloona Jadu, which are spread from here to the castle where she lives." Amir said, "Come what may, I shall now head into this darkness with God as my guide!" He climbed down the mountain and had gone some distance when someone invisible called out to him, "O Sahibqiran! Pray do not advance! Have patience until I come!" Amir stopped and saw Salasal Perizad appear there who handed him an emerald tablet inscribed with the names of God and said, "Abdur Rahman has sent this tablet for you and instructed you not to take a single step without first consulting it or else you will fall into great error and suffer terribly!" After handing him the tablet, Salasal Perizad disappeared whence he had come. As Amir looked at the tablet, he saw written there:

IN THE NAME OF ALLAH

O Destroyer of *Tilisms*, the Exalted and Illustrious God showed you unique favor that you have come into possession of this tablet and secured the key to victory and triumph. Read the word written on the margin and blow at the sky. Then the darkness will part, and the path will become illuminated.

The Sahibqiran recited that word and blew at the sky. His yearning was fulfilled and the darkness was completely cast away. Amir made a prostration of gratitude before God and stepped onward, carrying that tablet.

When he arrived close to the castle, he saw a dragon whose lower jaw touched the foundation of the gate and whose upper jaw sat atop the portals, as if he held the door to the castle in his mouth. As Amir was looking upon that sight in wonder, the dragon called out to him, "O Destroyer of *Tilisms*, walk into my mouth and entertain not the least fear or anxiety in your heart!" When the Sahibqiran consulted the tablet, it read:

> Recite this word and breathe on yourself and jump into the dragon's mouth without fear of it. It is neither a real dragon nor is it a ghost.

The moment the Sahibqiran jumped into the dragon's mouth, a loud and mournful cry rose to the heavens and a thunderous clamor was heard, as if doomsday itself had burst upon him.

When Amir opened his eyes after a moment, he saw no signs of the dragon or the castle but instead a garden in full bloom that was the very envy of the garden of Paradise. Birds made of jewels were chirping in the trees, creating a most angelic music with their caroling. Amir Hamza sat down beside a lake and suddenly heard a most doleful voice calling out from the summerhouse in the garden, "Alas, there is no man of God to release me from my dreadful prison and receive from the Almighty the reward for this deed!" He followed the voice to its source and beheld a nubile maiden of great beauty sitting prisoner on a throne.

Amir felt great pity for her and asked her with compassion, "O maiden, tell me who you are and who has imprisoned you here." She answered, "I wish for you to take precedence in introductions and give me your particulars." Amir replied, "I am the Quake of Qaf, the Latter-day Suleiman, Lord of the Auspicious Planetary Conjunction, World Conqueror, Slayer of Sly Ifrit, and a believer in God Almighty."

She said, "And I am Susan Peri, the daughter of Saleem Kohi. Ifrit became enamored of me and asked my father for my hand in marriage. Upon my father's refusal, Ifrit descended on us with his army. I said to my father, 'Marry me to Ifrit and have not the least trepidation or anxiety regarding my welfare. I shall drug him with deceit and throw him in prison.' My father then married me to Ifrit. One day the *dev* drank himself unconscious. I immediately tied up his hands and feet but before I could carry out my plans, someone took the news of these proceedings to Ifrit's mother, Maloona Jadu, who arrived instantly. She released him and left me imprisoned here. If you were to liberate me from my prison now, I would conduct you very easily to where Ifrit is hiding."

The Sahibqiran released her and gave her a new lease on life. She led the Sahibqiran into another garden and showed him Ifrit's dwelling. The Sahibqiran saw that twelve hundred armed *devs* were standing guard there, alert in their vigil.

After reciting magical incantations Susan Peri suddenly rose before Amir's eyes into the air, and called out loudly to the *devs*, "O *devs*! The Slayer of Ifrit and the Destroyer of *Tilisms* is standing within your sight. Put him to death in any manner you see fit."

The *devs* surrounded Amir on all sides, brandishing their weapons to kill him. Amir drew the Aqrab-e Suleimani from its scabbard and any *dev* to whom he dealt a blow he cut in two and dispatched to Hell. The *devs'* blood fell on the ground and quickly created new *devs*. Amir's hands and arms became worn from the fatigue of fighting them. Amir then remembered the tablet, and therein he saw written:

> O Destroyer of *Tilisms*, do not be duped by the chicanery of Susan Peri or release her from captivity. If by chance you commit this error and the *devs* attack you, read the Most Great Name on the point of your arrow and shoot at her so that the scourge of her existence vanishes!

Amir carried out the tablet's instructions and directly a great hue and cry arose: "There he is! The Slayer of Ifrit has arrived at the *tilism*. Kill him without mercy!" After this clamor subsided, Amir looked around, and saw neither Susan Peri nor any *devs*.

From behind the garden wall he heard *perizads'* voices and when he went to the other side to investigate, Amir saw another garden, and a fourteen-year-old comely beauty sitting in chains in the summerhouse. An ancient sat beside her with his head hanging down from grief. Some four hundred jinns and *perizads* were also imprisoned there. When she beheld Hamza, the girl called out, "O Sahibqiran! Release us from this confinement." Amir Hamza reasoned that this was a case like the one he had encountered earlier. Drawing his sword, he advanced to kill her.

The old man accompanying her interceded with a thousand solicitations and said, "O dear friend! Have some fear of God and show mercy on our sorry plight. I am Junaid Shah Sabz-Posh, the elder brother of Emperor Shahpal, and this girl is my daughter, Rehan Peri. When Ifrit defeated Shahpal, he asked me to give him my daughter's hand in marriage. I did not give in to his threats, but he defeated me in battle, and imprisoned me with my daughter and our four hundred companions. Now you know my story. Do as you wish!"

When Amir consulted the tablet it corroborated the old man's account. That very instant he freed them and sent them to their home.

Amir went ahead in his mission and came upon a most magnificent building that was sumptuously furnished. He marveled, however, to see its courtyard inundated with water. In the nave of the courtyard he saw a chest lying with its lid open. When he put his foot in to judge the depth of the water, Amir Hamza discovered that it was not water but an illusion created by a crystalline surface. He wished to look into the chest but the moment he peered down to look, he found himself in the clutches of a *dev* who was hiding inside. With one hand Amir held on to the edge of the chest and used the other hand to consult the tablet, on which was written:

> O Trampler of *Tilisms,* do not enter the chest. If you do, you will never find release from this *tilism.* There is a hair like a thick rope on the chest of the *dev* to which a tablet is attached. Pluck this along with the hair so that you find release from the hands of the *dev.* Afterward, recite the Most Great Name on this tablet, then strike it on the *dev*'s head and witness what transpires by the marvels of God.

Amir did as he was instructed and the *dev* was dispatched to Hell directly with a blazing flame rising from his head, and the wooden chest began to burn. Terrible cries rose to the heavens, echoing, "Kill him! Do not let the Slayer of Zaraq Jadu escape!"

When that pandemonium subsided, Amir saw only a desolate wasteland with a pool of blood with a pulley hanging above at its center. The blood was conducted by means of the pulley into a big pond. He proceeded forward and came upon a garden where a boy stood guard at the entrance. Amir asked him repeatedly to tell him his name, but the boy stood quiet without offering Amir any answer. However, the moment Amir stepped into the garden, the boy called out, "Beware, O *dev*, the Destroyer of *Tilisms* has turned all your marvelous devices to naught and gained entrance into the garden!" Amir turned and dealt him a powerful blow of his sword, which cut the boy's head off like a corncob.

When Amir advanced he witnessed that the boy's head flew back through the air and became fixed again to his torso at the neck. He came back to life immediately. Surprised, Amir consulted the tablet and found the following written there:

> O Destroyer of *Tilisms,* beware not to attack Darban Jadu as he will not die until the end of time, and no weapon will prove successful against

him. However, if you were to recite the Most Great Name on the point of your arrow and then successfully lodge it in his breast, he will die from it. Congratulations to you for closing in upon Ifrit and arriving at his lair.

When Amir followed the instructions, a dark dust storm bore down upon him. It was as if the entire world were plunged into darkness. Thunderbolts began falling and sparks of lightning started dancing all around. A clamor greater than thunder was heard. Amir huddled down with the tablet, covering his eyes.

After the clamor had subsided and the gale had blown away, Amir Hamza looked around and beheld beds of tulips stretching for miles on end and flowers and fragrant plants in full bloom. Some *perizads* were there singing harmonious notes and when the *perizads* spotted him, one of them came rushing toward him with a goblet of wine, cooing, "O Sahibqiran, you are all exhausted. Come, drink this and wash away all your woes and revive your spirits. You may spend a few hours listening to our music and songs, which will bring joy to your heart."

Amir consulted the tablet and, following its instructions, took the goblet from her hand and reciting the Most Great Name poured it over her head. Directly, a flame rose from her body, and she thoroughly combusted in just a few moments. Even greater clamor was heard then, and voices called out, "The Destroyer of *Tilisms* has killed Asrar Jadu as well!"

After a moment, Amir's eyes fell upon a mountain of unfathomable height and a riverbank, with the hill of Koh-e Besutoon[12] between them. From its cave emanated the enchanting peal of kettledrums. Amir stepped into the cave and beheld Ifrit sleeping like a log, and saw that it was his snores that sounded like kettledrums. The Sahibqiran thought, *It would be a heartless act and the worse kind of pusillanimity to kill someone in his sleep.* He drew Rustam's dagger and struck Ifrit Dev with such great force that the blade sunk up to its hilt into his foot. Ifrit thumped his foot irritably and grumbled, "What troublesome mosquitoes!" The Sahibqiran thought, *If he considers that blow a mere mosquito bite, how shall I ever wake him up?* Amir caught Ifrit's neck and arms in a lock and bellowed "God is Great!" so mightily that mountains and deserts were thrown into turmoil.

Terrified, Ifrit arose. As he rubbed his eyes and looked around, he saw the face of the Quake of Qaf. A great fear seized Ifrit then, he was all atremble and said, "O son of Aadam! I know and recognize only too well that you are my Angel of Death. I am determined that whether I live or die, I shall not turn away from the encounter, and you will meet your death at my hands." Ifrit Dev came at Amir Hamza swinging a box tree tied with millstones and attacked Amir Hamza. Amir stopped the blow with the Aqrab-e Suleimani and cut the tree in two. Without wasting another moment Amir dealt Ifrit a blow of the sword that struck his back. It cut Ifrit in two, but the halves remained attached by a cord of flesh and kept his soul enchained.

Ifrit cried out, "O son of Aadam! Now that you have killed me, sever this last cord, too, with another blow so that my soul shall be released from this receptacle and be freed of its pain and misery." The Sahibqiran did as requested. The moment the cord was severed, the two halves of Ifrit's body flew toward the heavens and fell down before the Sahibqiran as two Ifrits, each fully alive as before. In short, within a few hours thousands of Ifrits were produced and *devs* surrounded the Sahibqiran. He was utterly confounded and marveled at this turn of events.

At that moment Amir received divine help. When Amir turned to look he found holy Khizr. Amir kissed his feet and pleaded with him: "Sire, my arms are numb from plying the sword. The situation I find myself in is a marvel to stupefy reason."

The holy Khizr replied, "O Sahibqiran! You know well that this is a *tilism*. You act here as it pleases you, without consulting the tablet. Do as I tell you now, and recite the blessed word I instruct to you in the manner I suggest. Then bless an arrow with that word and aim for the head of the *dev* whose face glows like a ruby and on whose forehead you see a mole like a carnelian. Then this calamity would be dispelled." The Sahibqiran acted upon Prophet Khizr's directions and saw not one single *dev* and found Ifrit lying dead before him. Amir saw that Ifrit's head was missing. When he could not find the head, holy Khizr said to him, "Ifrit's mother, Maloona Jadu, is sitting in this cave holding Ifrit's head. It was that harridan who set in motion this sorcery. Now go into the cave and kill her as well so that the *tilism* can be finally conquered." The Sahibqiran went with holy Khizr into the cave, the two of them stepping into it together.

When Maloona saw Khizr along with the Sahibqiran, she began reciting some incantation. Prophet Khizr recited an incantation himself and blew it on her head. She was dispatched to Hell in the flash of an eye. All signs of the *tilism* then dissolved away.

Holy Khizr congratulated the Sahibqiran on the conquest of the *tilism*. Amir said, "I feel famished, O sire! Perform another miracle and provide me with something to eat!" Holy Khizr produced a small loaf from his leather bag and offered it to Amir. He had his fill of it and found relief from the pangs of hunger, but the loaf remained the same size as before. The holy Khizr also gave Amir a flask of water to satisfy his thirst.

After many days of hunger Amir had eaten his fill and became a little torpid. He stretched himself out to rest on the same rock where Ifrit lay in the sleep of death. Amir forgot to make the third war cry, and the *perizads* returned to Shahpal to give him the news of Amir's death.

When Shahpal heard the news of Amir's death from the *perizads*, he involuntarily broke into tears, and the pain of his grief threatened to endanger his life. He turned to Abdur Rahman and said, "Alas, the blood of one of Ibrahim's descendants will now be on my neck, for it was I who sent him on the errand to search and kill Ifrit Dev!" That very moment Abdur Rahman made calculations by *jafar* and astrology and said, "The Sahibqiran has already slain Maloona Jadu and Ifrit Dev. He has severed their necks and relieved the land of their filthy burden! However, a little iniquitous influence of the stars yet prevails, which is the reason why he forgot to make his third signal. That evil influence shall be dispelled soon, too, and his heart's desire fulfilled. Let us go, so that we may bring him back and everyone here can receive great bliss from the sight of him, and any misgivings regarding his welfare may be dispelled."

Shahpal ordered his musicians to start playing festive tunes and made elaborate preparations for the journey. Then, along with the nobles of Qaf, he rode out to Shehristan-e Zarrin and the *perizads'* hopes were revived.[?]

When Aasman Peri heard the auspicious tidings of Amir's victory, she could not contain her joy and hastened there herself to indulge herself with the sight of the Sahibqiran.[?] She found him asleep in a cave with his face exposed to the sun. With her one wing Aasman Peri shaded Amir's face from the sun, and with her other wing she began fanning him.

Feeling relief from her ministrations, Amir Hamza opened his eyes and saw Aasman Peri earning great blessings in her labor of love. Amir rose and embraced her and kissed her upon witnessing such ardor and love on her part. He said to her, "O life of the Sahibqiran! I wonder about the reason for your presence." Aasman Peri replied, "I arrived upon hearing the news of your victory. I have brought the happy tidings that the emperor himself is on his way here."

Amir was most gratified to hear this. He seated that beauty beside him and showed her much affection. While he was still making love vows, the conveyance of Emperor Shahpal arrived there. Amir rose to his feet.

The emperor stepped down from the throne to kiss Amir's victorious hand and arm, and seated Amir on the throne by his side, and flew him back to Gulistan-e Irum. A most sumptuous royal assembly was arranged to celebrate the festivities on a grand scale.

Then the *perizads* began to dance and unburden their hearts with the strains of song and music. The emperor said to Abdur Rahman, "I recall you telling me that Hamza has the ability to couple with Aasman Peri, since he is superior to the whole race of human beings in all matters. I cannot think of any time more auspicious than the present for the occasion."

Abdur Rahman got up and said to Amir, "The emperor has accepted you as his son-in-law!"

Amir replied, "I cannot accept this honor. If I married Aasman Peri, my return to the realm of Earth would be deferred. I would become occupied with her here in pursuit of pleasure seeking. The other qualm I have is that I promised Mehr-Nigar, the daughter of Emperor Naushervan, that until I married her, I would never even look at any woman with the eye of desire."

Abdur Rahman then said, "O Sahibqiran! You made that promise on the realm of Earth and this is the realm of Qaf. Your actions here will not contravene your compacts there!" Amir asked, "How long will it be before you see me off and return me to Earth?" Abdur Rahman said, "O Sahibqiran, this is a promise made in the land of Qaf. Pray do not press me in this matter. One year from now I shall take you back to Earth!"

Amir saw no recourse except acquiescence. Emperor Shahpal busied himself with preparations for the wedding. The kings of the realms of Qaf joined that festive assembly.[?]

The news of Amir Hamza's defeat of Ifrit and Maloona Jadu had spread all over Qaf. When it reached the ears of the *dev* Samandoon Hazar-Dast, he became angry and rueful, and a blaze of fury burned his heart to ashes. He said to himself, *The emperor of Qaf sent for a human being called the Quake of Qaf and the Latter-day Suleiman from the realm of Earth, and had mighty* devs *such as Ifrit and his parents murdered. The Tilism-e Zarrin was destroyed and then the emperor himself conducted him to Gulistan-e Irum and betrothed his daughter to him. Now it is incumbent on me to avenge Ifrit's blood!* He dispatched his commander in chief, Sufaid Dev, a brave and intrepid warrior, along with four hundred *devs,* to speedily produce that human being before him.

Amir Hamza's marriage to Aasman Peri was being celebrated when Sufaid Dev burst in upon the assembly along with his four hundred *devs,* and delivered Samandoon Hazar-Dast's message. Greatly enraged by the speech of that vile creature, the Sahibqiran said, "O wretch deserving of beheading! Rein in your loose tongue! Go and tell your master that if he has a desire to meet Ifrit, he should come here himself and I will dispatch him to the same abode!"

Sufaid Dev said, "O dark-haired, white-toothed creature! Come with me as my commander has sent for you!" Sufaid Dev then extended his hand toward Amir. The Sahibqiran turned his mind to thoughts of God and, catching the *dev*'s arm, gave it such a violent tug that he fell to his knees. Then, drawing his dagger, Amir stabbed him in the breast with a powerful thrust from which the *dev* gave up the ghost with just one cry.[13] The *devs* who had accompanied Sufaid Dev fled from there with their tails between their legs.

All the kings and nobles of Qaf applauded the Sahibqiran's power. The Sahibqiran was led from the Court of Suleiman to the royal harem. All articles and accessories necessary for the festivities were amply provided. The Sahibqiran proceeded in the circle of the kings, nobles, *perizads,* and mace bearers of Qaf like the moon surrounded by clusters of stars. The bridegroom's procession reached the bride's house and Abdur Rahman tied the nuptial knot between Amir Hamza and Aasman Peri. Then the Sahibqiran entered the bedchamber. After the necessary rituals and ceremonies were finished, he took Aasman Peri in his embrace and took his pleasure of her. By the grace of God, that same night, his seed was planted in Aasman Peri's womb, and by the work of God the union between the man made of clay and a *peri* whose essence was fire bore fruit. In the morning, Amir arrived in the court and a festive party was held in which the newlyweds cast off all inhibitions. In short, night after night the revelries continued for Amir Hamza.

However, Amir still counted the days and nights of his sojourn in Qaf, waiting for the year to be over so that he could return to the realm of men and enjoy once again the company of his near and dear ones.

———

Leaving the Sahibqiran thus busy in enumerating the years, months, days, and hours, I shall now give a few words regarding the Khusrau of India, King Landhoor bin Saadan. Let it be made clear that when King Landhoor took leave of Amir Hamza and boarded the ship, he was tearful at the prospect of separation from his friend. The next day Landhoor's vessel crossed paths with Bahram's ship and the two of them exchanged news. Upon learning that Amir Hamza had sent Bahram Gurd to his assistance, Landhoor was very gratified.

On the fifth day a storm brewed in the sea. For three whole days the raging sea tossed their ships about. It returned to calm on the fourth day. However, before long they learned that the ship carrying Bahram had gone missing.

Now hear of Bahram. His ship was driven away by the tempest and after traveling some distance it broke apart from the violence of the sea. Bahram caught hold of a wooden board and drifted upon it toward shore. He then set out on foot. One day, he saw a caravan of merchants encamped at some distance from him. Bahram feared that if someone in the caravan happened to recognize his identity, he would lose his honor in the eyes of men. He sat down far away from them under a tree.

Fate ordained that the leader of the caravan passed by the very spot where Bahram was sitting. He said to Bahram, "O youth, who are you and whence have you come?" Bahram replied, "I am a merchant. My ship capsized in the tempest and I await the decree of fate now to see what new hand it will deal me." The leader of the caravan said to him, "Dear friend, I do not lack for riches. What I do not have, however, is a son and heir. I hereby declare you my son and give you the status of my heir. Come along with me and you shall never again see a hard day."

Bahram went along with the man, who gave Bahram control of the entire trade. Bahram asked the merchant, "Where will you travel from here?" The man answered, "I will travel next to the land of Mando, which is the seat of governance of Malik Shuaib and is close to the land of Ceylon." Bahram was glad to hear this and he thought that he would soon have occasion to meet Landhoor again.

After several days the caravan arrived in the land of Mando. The next day the merchant visited the baths with Bahram and they changed and went into the bazaar and saw a bow and a purse of gold coins lying on a small table. When Bahram asked the guards about the bow and the purse of gold, they answered, "This bow belongs to the commander in chief of our king's forces, Zaigham. Because he finds himself unable to draw the bow, he has declared that anyone who is able to draw the bow can claim the purse of gold coins."

Bahram said to a guard, "I would like to draw the bow, and display my strength!" The guard said, "A mere cotton merchant? What do you know about drawing bows and such?"

While Bahram was arguing with the guards, Naik Rai, Malik Shuaib's vizier, happened to pass by with his entourage and allowed Bahram to draw the bow. Bahram picked up the bow and, securing the bow's grip in his hand, pulled the bowstring to his ear and flexed it seven times. Everyone there cried out "Bravo" and "Well done" except for Zaigham's servants, who took offense at Bahram's success. They began barking inanities at him and Bahram clouted some of them on their heads, causing their brains to flow from their noses. Naik Rai warned the rest and took Bahram to his house.

When Zaigham heard the news, he armed himself and headed for Naik Rai's house. When he found Bahram, he drew his dagger and rushed at Bahram to kill him. But Bahram hit him on the head with such force that his brain flowed out of his nose. When this news reached Malik Shuaib, he immediately sent for his vizier Naik Rai along with Bahram and when Bahram presented himself, the king said to him acidly, "O contumacious man, how dare you kill my commander in chief?" Bahram answered, "O King, you must not keep such men as the commanders of your forces who depart from the world with just one blow of the fist!"

Bahram's retort went straight to the king's heart and pleased him immensely. Then and there he offered the robe and office of commander in chief to Bahram, and appointed him to that august post. Bahram then drew that bow a few times before the king and then ordered it to be placed on the same platform as before with a purse of gold, with the instructions that he should be notified if anyone was able to draw the bow. The king was convinced of Bahram's rectitude. That very day he married his daughter to Bahram and made lavish arrangements for the nuptials as were demanded by the occasion. He also said to him, "I make you the lord of one half of my kingdom, and make you its absolute ruler. For two quarters of the day you may sit on the throne and administer the law and redress the needs of your subjects. For the other two quarters I shall rule, and administer all affairs."

Now hear a few words regarding Landhoor, the Khusrau of India, and hear an account of that king of lofty eminence who arrived in Ceylon and dropped his ships' anchors. Along with his army he came ashore and after resting for a few days he headed for the fort of Sabir and Sabur.

Of the Arrival of King Landhoor bin Saadan, the Khusrau of India, at the Gates of the Fort of Sabir and Sabur

The narrator relates that Jaipur had been left behind by Landhoor on the throne of India when he went to Ctesiphon with the Sahibqiran, and had been named his vice-regent in charge of all administration and defenses. He had been forced to seek refuge in a fortress after suffering reverses at the hands of Malik Siraj, Firoz Turk, Ajrook Khwarzami, and Muhlil Sagsar. All those imprisoned in the fort had become weary of their lives on account of the siege. In the end, the army said to Jaipur, "If you were to order us, we would march out to encounter the enemy and either kill them or die fighting so that our suffering might end in some manner." Jaipur said to them, "I shall do as you ask." That very instant he sent a messenger to the enemy camp to say that if they were to remove their armies from the gates of his fort, his army would then arrange itself for a final encounter.

Malik Siraj and his accomplices assented to the request and the two forces arrayed against each other.

Before anyone else, Muhlil Sagsar urged his rhinoceros forward into the arena to do battle and slaughter the foe. From the other camp Jaipur spurred on his mount to answer the challenge. No one had yet dealt a blow or raised his arms against the adversary when a great dark cloud rose on the horizon and seventy gleaming standards emerged over a force of seventy thousand. Marching ahead of those standards was Landhoor on his she-elephant Maimoona.

Landhoor killed Muhlil Sagsar and two of his renowned champions, Maghlub Fil-Zor and Haras Fil-Dandan. A large number of the enemy forces were also killed by Landhoor.

King Landhoor entered his court regaled by the sound of festive music. However, Malik Siraj's daughter snared Landhoor by deceit when he was diverting himself in the forest afterward. She put him in a chest and threw him into the sea. It was picked up by a merchant ship and sold to a trader who was a follower of the True Faith. Upon learning of Landhoor's identity, he promised to conduct him to Ceylon in safety. When the ship arrived in Mando, Landhoor went ashore and found the bow and purse of gold coins put there by Bahram. Landhoor also showed his might with the bow and was taken before Bahram and united with his friend. Malik Shuaib finally learned of Bahram's true identity. He ordered a feast in Landhoor's and Bahram's honor. Afterward, Landhoor and Bahram gathered an army and headed for Ceylon.

An Account of the Events That Passed with the
Sahibqiran, the Conqueror of the World, the
Quake of Qaf, the Latter-day Suleiman,
Amir Hamza the Magnificent

The narrators of past legends thus continue their tale: When the year
neared completion and the days of gestation were over, a girl whose visage was as resplendent as the sun was born from the womb of Aasman
Peri, and everyone was greatly taken with her charm and beauty.

The emperor was most pleased at the news of her birth. However, the
Sahibqiran was extremely unhappy and apprehensive. Upon learning this
the emperor said to him, "O Amir, it was the will of God that it should be
so, and nobody is to blame for this event! It is not an occasion for you to
be sad!"

Abdur Rahman said, "O Sahibqiran, this girl shall prove very fortunate and will overpower all the rebellious *devs* of Qaf. She will earn the
title of the Sahibqiran of Qaf." Amir's sadness was dispelled upon hearing these words. The emperor celebrated the birth of his granddaughter
for several months.

One day when the girl was six months old the Sahibqiran said to the
emperor, "I have carried out all that you asked me to do. Now pray return
me to the realm of Earth and honor your promise to me!" The emperor
answered, "O Sahibqiran! Indeed I am most indebted to you and have no
objection in granting you leave to depart but the fort of Simin, which is to
the north of Qaf, has been taken over by two malicious *devs*, Kharchal and
Kharpal, who lead a force of ten thousand *devs*. As that is my ancestral castle, I hope that you will liberate the fort from their hold before you leave.
If not, we will be most happy to acquiesce to your pleasure."

Amir replied, "I am bound to obey your wishes." The emperor sent
for a throne for Amir Hamza. Then Amir seated himself on the throne
and took command over ten thousand intrepid *devs*. The Sahibqiran then

set out from there on his new adventure. At a distance of some five *kos* from the castle of Simin, Amir saw a vast field and ordered the *devs* to descend there.

The news of Hamza's arrival reached Kharpal and Kharchal and they arrayed themselves opposite Amir Hamza's camp with a force of twenty thousand *devs*. Amir observed two *devs* of most singular appearance standing some distance from the enemy ranks. One of them had ears like an ass, and the other had the face and features of that beast. Amir learned that they were the commanders of the enemy forces, Kharchal and Kharpal in person.

Kharchal entered the arena wielding a box tree and called out, "Where is the slayer of Ifrit and the murderer of Ahriman? Come forward and demonstrate your valor, so that I may avenge the death of the *devs* of Qaf!" When Amir stepped out to meet him, Kharchal laughed uproariously and said, "Surely I would not ruin my reputation by attacking a puny creature like yourself!"

Amir replied, "It was with this small stature that I prevailed over those of mighty stature, like Ahriman and Ifrit, and sent them into the sleep of death. Your death is as truly written on my sword as it is in your destiny!"

Kharchal was infuriated by this, and dealt a blow to the Sahibqiran with the trunk of the box tree. Amir foiled this blow and countered with a thrust of the Aqrab-e Suleimani and Kharchal stretched himself on the bed of death.

When Kharpal saw his brother lying dead, he rushed at Amir. Amir foiled his attack and, securing a hold on him by his cummerbund, forced the *dev* to the ground. Amir Hamza then drew his dagger with the intention to kill Kharpal who cried out, "If you spare my life, I will pledge obedience to you for the rest of my life!" The Sahibqiran then stood up from the *dev*'s chest once he had secured Kharpal's word, and asked him, "O Kharpal, would you carry me back to Earth and take that duty upon yourself?" The *dev* answered, "I would do so with the greatest pleasure, but pray rest a while in the castle of Simin. Then I will carry you wherever you command me to!"

Amir dispatched four *devs* to Shahpal to convey news of the victory to him, and himself sojourned in the fortress of Simin.

One day Amir fell asleep in a summerhouse. When Kharpal saw that deep slumber had wrapped the Sahibqiran in its arms, he decided that it would prove an easy task to kill him. He picked up the Aqrab-e Suleimani from Amir's side and unsheathed it and dealt Amir a blow. It is proverbial that no one can kill the man who is in the protection of God: The sword struck instead one of the room's arches and, by chance, Amir also turned over at the same moment. Thinking that the Sahibqiran had awakened, Kharpal sheathed the sword and fled in terror. The circumstances appeared ominous to the Sahibqiran when he awoke. Not a single soul was around, nor could he find the Aqrab-e Suleimani anywhere. He assembled the *devs* and said, "Where is Kharpal?" They answered, "He is in the Bayaban-e Mina, but no other *dev* can gain admittance there to find the way to him." However much Amir pleaded with the *devs* to carry him to the Bayaban-e Mina, none of them would consent. Amir therefore gave them leave to depart and set out on foot by himself.

On the seventh day he arrived in the Bayaban-e Mina, where he beheld a mountain. At the foot of the mountain, in the middle of the fields, there was a crystalline platform on which Kharpal lay in deep slumber like his fortune and the Aqrab-e Suleimani lay beside him like an omen of death. The Sahibqiran secured the Aqrab-e Suleimani. Then Amir bellowed so mightily that the whole mountain shook. Kharpal awoke to this and attempted to escape, but Amir stepped forward and dealt a blow of the Aqrab-e Suleimani to his waist. Kharpal fell to the ground in two like a withered poplar. After killing him, the Sahibqiran rested on the same platform.

In the meanwhile, the *devs* returned to Shahpal and after they had given him a detailed account, Shahpal became troubled and said to Khvaja Abdur Rahman, "We must hastily get news of the Sahibqiran and hurry to his aid." Khvaja mounted a throne and set out in search of Amir Hamza. After several days' journey, he finally arrived in the Bayaban-e Mina. There he beheld the corpse of Kharpal lying in two pieces. Abdur Rahman saluted Amir, kissed his hand and arm, and conveyed to him the emperor's message. Then Abdur Rahman returned to Gulistan-e Irum with Amir Hamza. The emperor embraced the Sahibqiran, showed him many tokens of kindness, and said, "Let six months pass and then I shall certainly send you back to the realm of Earth." Amir returned to his chamber and sat there counting the days, while trying to restrain his yearning to return to his world.

Of the Notorious Khvaja Amar, the Prince of *Ayyars*, and of the Princes Hurmuz and Faramurz

Artful storytellers and crafty narrators thus record the account of these men: When the fort of Nestan also ran out of provisions, Quful Nestani told Amar of the well-fortified and impregnable castle Rahtas Gadh, which was jointly ruled by Tahmuras Shah and Sabir Shah.

Amar said to Muqbil Vafadar, "Be watchful of our fort's defenses while I think of some scheme to capture the fort of Rahtas Gadh." Amar changed from his royal robe to the *ayyar*'s attire and, sporting his weapons, set out from his fort. In a few hours, he arrived at Rahtas Gadh. However, despite making several rounds of the fortifications, he saw no means to gain entrance. Amar fooled a grass cutter and rendered him unconscious by appearing before him in the guise of a saintly man. Then Amar managed to enter the fort, and took up residence in the grass cutter's guise.

After one half of the night had passed, he donned his night livery and entered Tahmuras Shah's palace. He saw Tahmuras Shah lying asleep on a bed of lapis lazuli. When Amar lifted the fold of a shawl to uncover Tahmuras Shah's face, the man caught Amar's hand. Amar usually wore a greased glove for such occasions and pulled out his hand. Tahmuras Shah said to him, "Khvaja Amar, pray have no fear! Just now Prophet Ibrahim appeared to me in the realm of dreams to convert me to the True Faith and gave me tidings of all the efforts you have made and news of your arrival."

Finally Amar drew near again, and Tahmuras Shah embraced him and promised Amar every help. He invited Amar to move Mehr-Nigar and his army to Rahtas Gadh.

Amar returned happily to his fort and with his army in train, headed out by way of a tunnel in the direction of the fort of Rahtas Gadh.

Meanwhile, news of Tahmuras Shah's conversion to the True Faith spread by word of mouth. Upon learning of this from his vizier Shamim, Sabit Shah, Rahtas Gadh's co-ruler, murdered Tahmuras Shah. Then Sabit Shah went together with Shamim to the gates of the fort to await Amar's arrival and murder him, too.

Oblivious to these machinations, when Amar and his companions approached the walls of the fort they were targeted by soldiers in the battlements, and Sabit Shah called out to him, "O cameleer's son! Tahmuras Shah fell to your tricks and paid for it with his life. Be warned that you will receive your just deserts if you take a single step forward."

Amar was troubled by this trick played on him by the contemptible heavens. He said to himself that if Hurmuz and Faramurz were to follow him, all his months of hardships would come to naught.

The following day Sabit Shah sent a letter to Hurmuz by Mehtar Sayyad who was the chief of Tahmuras Shah's *ayyars*. As Mehtar Sayyad had secretly mourned his master's murder by Sabit Shah, he brought the letter to Amar instead. Amar was greatly pleased and returned with Mehtar Sayyad in the disguise of Katara Kabuli, the commander of the princes' *ayyars*. He told Sabit Shah that the princes had ordered him to guard the garrison himself until they arrived with their armies.

When night fell Amar murdered the other guard and flung open the fort's gates, admitting his army. He hanged Sabit Shah and his vizier Shamim and installed Mehtar Sayyad as the king of the castle. When the princes learned of Amar's *ayyari*, they took the real Katara Kabuli to task for not performing his *ayyar's* duties as Amar Ayyar had done. After being rebuked, Katara Kabuli sneaked into Rahtas Gadh, made Amar Ayyar unconscious, and kidnapped him. When Amar was produced before the princes, they ordered that he be put to death without delay.

OF NAQABDAR NARANJI-POSH'S *AYYAR* SECURING AMAR'S RELEASE FROM HIS CAPTIVITY

The narrator states that the executioner took Amar along, seated him on a sand platform, and approached him after drawing his sword. Seeing his death approach, Amar Ayyar prayed for divine help. Then Naqabdar Naranji-Posh's *ayyar* presented himself before the princes disguised as a messenger and helped Amar escape.

Although Amar escaped with his life, his fort ran out of rations. Amar Ayyar then learned of the fort of Salasal Hisar, which was ruled by Salasal Shah. Amar used cunning and disguise to gain control over Salasal Hisar. He was also helped by Mansoor Ayyar, who was in the employ of Salasal Shah. Afterward, when Salasal Shah and his son Bahman refused to convert to the True Faith, Amar had them killed and installed Mansoor Ayyar as the ruler of the fort.

Hurmuz was most upset upon receiving this intelligence and sent a message to the emperor, detailing their circumstances, the story of Amar escaping to Salasal Shah's fort, and the many factors responsible for the *ayyar*'s success.

It has been narrated thus far that after slaying Kharpal and Kharchal, Amir spent another six months in Qaf at the pleading of Emperor Shahpal. One night he was lying with Aasman Peri when Mehr-Nigar appeared in his dreams looking gaunt and withered. As she cried bitter tears, she accosted him thus: "O Abul-Ala, indeed I must be culpable of some terrible sin, that you find it fit to burn me in the fire of separation while you yourself take pleasure in the company of *peris*. I suffer a hundred thousand bitter woes that the heavens do not release me from this horrible existence."

Amir cried out in his sleep and became inconsolable with anguish. Upon hearing Amir's cries, Aasman Peri woke up and asked, "What terrible grief has gripped your heart that you make such heartrending complaints?" Amir replied, "I feel so weary and downtrodden that I wish to end my life with my own hands." Aasman Peri said, "Pray tell me about your sad state of affairs, and share this with me." Amir answered, "O Aasman Peri, I implore you to send me back to the realm of men. Just now I saw Mehr-Nigar in my dream, who appeared in a most wretched state brought on by the pain and agony of separation from me."

Aasman Peri asked, "How is Mehr-Nigar related to you?" Amir replied, "She is my beloved and the daughter of Naushervan. There is none who surpasses her in beauty, and she is in love with this wretch who has lost his heart to her." Upon hearing this, Aasman Peri said, "So why didn't you plainly admit to me that there was someone from the race of humans whom you love? Listen, O Amir, and speak the truth to me: Is she more beautiful than I?" Amir could not hold back his words, and said, "You cannot be compared with Mehr-Nigar; you cannot even hold a candle to the charm of her maids."

Turning crimson with rage upon hearing these words, Aasman Peri said, "O Hamza, woe to you that you put me below her maids and prefer them over me! I swear that for as long as I live you will never find your way back to the world of humans!" As Amir Hamza was already eaten by frustration, he replied, "I will find my way there all the same! And if you become an obstacle, then I shall have to travel upon your dead body." Aasman Peri said, "O Sahibqiran! Do not let the facts that you are the Lord of the Auspicious Planetary Conjunction, the progeny of Prophet Ibrahim, and superior to the race of jinns cause you to entertain any illusions about me. If you are the Sahibqiran and descended from the line of prophets, I also am highborn and come from the line of a mighty prophet, Suleiman. Nor indeed am I any weaker than you. When you think of killing me, know well that I can also kill you."

Amir was most vexed by her words, which sent him into a mad rage. He drew his sword and leapt at Aasman Peri, who also drew her dagger and charged at him. The *perizads* swarmed over them to break up the fight and separated the warring parties. Someone took this news to Emperor Shahpal. It caused him great distress to hear about it. He rushed to the scene and rebuked his daughter, saying, "O impudent girl! How dare you talk back to your husband and fight with him?" After admonishing his daughter, Shahpal said to Amir, "Come morning, I will send you off and say farewell to you."

In the morning, the emperor sent for a throne for Amir, and ordered four swift *devs* to take him immediately to the world of humans. When Aasman Peri received the news, she took their daughter, Quraisha, into her arms and went to see Amir Hamza. Upon seeing Amir Hamza sitting on the throne, Aasman Peri began crying and said, "O Sahibqiran! I can understand if you do not love me, but do you not feel any pity for this girl? For God's sake forgive my offense."

Amir replied, "I am not angry with you and I do love the girl, but I must needs return to the land of the humans. I shall return to you when you invite me. You can also come to see me whenever you wish, and also bring Quraisha with you!" Amir then ordered the *devs* to carry his throne aloft and set out toward his homeland.

Aasman Peri returned to her quarters and gave herself over to fits of sorrow and grief. Salasal Perizad became sorrowful upon finding her in that state. Aasman Peri said to him, "It is my wish that you go to the *devs* and caution them not to carry Hamza to the world of men but to abandon him instead in the Bayaban-e Heyrat."

Salasal Perizad carried out Aasman Peri's orders and instructed the *devs* as he was told. The *devs* consulted together and concluded that if they went against Aasman Peri's wishes, it would be impossible for them to inhabit the lands of Qaf in peace. They decided at last to leave Hamza where Aasman Peri had ordered. Having settled on this course of action, they descended with the throne into the Bayaban-e Heyrat and lay down there to rest their backs. When Amir asked why they had alighted there, they replied, "We are hungry and would like to go hunting." Amir said, "Very well!" Amir sat down on the throne to wait for the *devs'* return. But he saw neither hide nor hair of any *dev* after keeping wide awake the whole night. When it was broad daylight and there was still no sign of the *devs'* return, Amir reasoned that it must be fear of Aasman Peri that caused them to deceive and abandon him. He decided to submit to fate and go forth on his own on foot.

Around noon he reached another bleak desert where neither grass nor any shrubbery grew and there was no sign of any life, plant, animal, or human. Wherever he looked, mounds of sand shone like mercury and flames danced on the sand from the blazing sun. The armor Amir wore on his body became so hot that merely touching it burned his hands. Amir threw his weapons on the ground. From the pain of thirst he came very near to dying. He dug a pit in the sand and pressed his breast against the cool, moist sand underground. When that sand became hot, too, he dug even deeper and lay there. Amir had dug under a dune, and it collapsed over him. Amir was buried underneath, making it impossible for him to extricate himself as he was unable to move his limbs.

Meanwhile, one day Emperor Shahpal asked Abdur Rahman, "Tell me how Hamza has fared in his journey." From drawing the horoscope Abdur Rahman determined that Hamza lay buried under the sand. He sighed, then said, "A hundred thousand bitter woes that Hamza's youth and his life were thus squandered for nothing!" Then he narrated Hamza's circumstances.

The emperor sent for the *devs* who had been ordered to carry Amir's throne and angrily asked them, "Where did you take Hamza?" The *devs* replied, "We left him in the Bayaban-e Heyrat as Aasman Peri commanded."

This propelled the emperor into a fit of passion. He looked toward Aasman Peri and said, "How do you explain yourself?" She replied, "I have no desire to send Hamza to the world of humans. But I will go in search of him now and shall bring him back myself." The emperor replied, "Don't waste your time. Not knowing where to find him you will torment yourself in vain." The emperor set out on the quest taking his *devs* along.

One *perizad* happened upon the dune where Amir lay buried under mounds of sand. The *perizad* saw the glow of the *shabchiragh* jewel in Amir's headgear. He removed the sand and discovered Amir lying unconscious in a sorry state. He called out, "The Quake of Qaf lies here!" After extricating Amir, Shahpal had him carried to his throne.

After some hours, Amir woke up and found Shahpal sitting near him. He gathered his strength and rose and addressed the emperor thus: "What wrong have I done you that you acted in this manner toward me?" Shahpal replied, "O Sahibqiran! I swear by the name of King Suleiman and by your life that these actions were not carried out at my behest. It was all done at the command of my thoughtless daughter, Aasman Peri."

Upon these words Aasman Peri rushed in and threw herself at Amir's feet, and said, "O Sahibqiran! Indeed I am the guilty one. Pray forgive me this once. Come with me to Shehristan-e Zarrin to rest and enjoy yourself. I promise to send you to the world of men after six months." Amir answered, "I trust neither your words nor your actions." Aasman Peri swore upon the name of King Suleiman and finally prevailed on Amir to return with her to Shehristan-e Zarrin.

However, the appointed time came and passed, and Amir did not receive leave to return to the world of humans. He again saw Mehr-Nigar in his dreams one night and discovered her in the same anguish and torment as before. The Sahibqiran started in his dream and when he opened his eyes he saw that he was still languishing in Qaf. He began to weep and cold sighs issued from his lips.

Aasman Peri opened her eyes and saw Amir inconsolable with despair. She got up and wiped the tears from his face and said, "What has caused you such grief at this hour?" Amir kept absolutely silent, drenching kerchief after kerchief with his tears and weeping without cease.

In the morning Amir said to Shahpal, "Grant me leave now to depart!" The emperor immediately consented and ordered four *devs* to transport him to the world of humans with comfort and bring back a receipt from him of his arrival at his destination. The *devs* departed carrying the throne on their shoulders and Aasman Peri abandoned herself again to the same state of lamentation and grief.

She told Salasal Perizad to take a message to the *devs* that if they valued their lives at all, they would abandon Amir on the enchanted Jazira-e Sargardan, where he might wander around for a few days by himself and have some time to reflect on his fate. Salasal managed to communicate Aasman Peri's message to the *devs* and persuaded them to carry out her wishes.

The *devs* flew the whole day and, come evening, they alighted in the arid plains of Jazira-e Sargardan to carry out Aasman Peri's orders. The *devs* made an excuse and departed, promising to return in the morning. When it was morning and the *devs* did not return, Amir reckoned that they, too, had deceived him. He embarked alone on the journey, but in the evening he ended up in the same place where the *devs* had left him. He underwent the same trial for three days even though he took a different direction each time. On the fourth day he took a new direction and traveled well into the afternoon. When the desert began to burn with heat, he saw a few green trees in one spot and headed there to lie down to rest his back. Amir saw an octagonal marble building there and he sat on the floor and rested his back against its columns.

Hardly an hour had passed when a great din was heard from the direction of the forest, from which a most singular creature now appeared. It was a *dev* with the head of a peacock who was as tall as a tower and wielded the trunk of a box tree. Upon arriving before Amir, he said, "O son of man! Woe to the ill will and the hand that sent you here! Now you will not escape with your life!" He swung the tree and brought it down on Amir. The Sahibqiran answered with a strike from the Aqrab-e Suleimani, which cut the tree trunk in two but produced not even a scratch on the *dev*'s body. The *dev* escaped in the blink of an eye, but before long he reappeared and attacked Amir again. Once again Amir failed to injure him.

When the same thing happened a third time, Amir pleaded to the Almighty God and his eyes welled up with tears. Suddenly Prophet Khizr materialized there. After reciting the Most Great Name, Khizr himself killed the *dev* and disappeared whence he had come. Amir sat down and occupied himself with admiring the expanse. A cold breeze suddenly picked up and lulled him to sleep. Amir had a dream in which he saw Mehr-Nigar crying in his love. When he awoke, it occurred to Amir Hamza that he should trust his fate and follow the path of the river that flowed there to find his way out of that wasteland. Thus determined, Amir cut down tree branches to make himself a raft, and then he put it in the water. The raft had traversed half the length of the river when suddenly a great current came over the water and sent the raft back to the shore where Amir had embarked. Amir put the raft in the water seventy-two times and each time when the raft reached the middle of the river, either a great turbulence or a great storm returned it to the shore where it had begun its journey. Amir spent a whole week trying his luck but was foiled every single time.

Finally Amir was once again on shore and said his prayers in preparation for taking to the water, supplicating with passionate fervor to the Captain of the Ship of the World. At once Amir was overtaken by sleep, and in a dream he saw Prophet Nuh, who helped him ford the river by disclosing its secret. Amir travelled on the river in his raft for twenty days.

On the twenty-first day he arrived along a pleasant expanse of field. Amir disembarked and walked inland a little ways. Before he had gone two or three *kos*, he came upon seven great wolves. The largest among them was white. It is said that these were the Seven Wolves of Suleiman. When the wolves saw Amir, they surrounded him on all sides. The Sahibqiran unsheathed the Aqrab-e Suleimani and killed all seven of them. He skinned the wolves and draped the pelts around his shoulders and traveled on.

One day Amir came upon a garden and saw in it a throne of emerald luxuriously decorated with bolsters and cushions. Amir stepped up and reclined on the throne. Amir was comfortably seated on the throne when a two-headed *dev* named Ra'ad arrived there thundering and roaring. The commotion and tumult he created were the same as if an ensemble of a thousand musicians had suddenly started playing simultaneously. He first attacked Amir but witnessing his might, went and hid himself into an empty well. Amir waited at the mouth of the well but the *dev* showed no signs of emerging. Then Amir fell asleep and Amar Ayyar appeared to him in a dream. Amar guided Hamza to inundate the well to force the *dev* to emerge from it. When Amir woke up he followed the instructions received in the dream and presently Ra'ad emerged and tried to escape, but Amir leapt forward and dealt him a blow of his sword which sliced Ra'ad like a cucumber, and he fell to the ground in two halves. The flames of Hell immediately engulfed his corpse.

A female *dev*, Sharara Jadu, who was a monument to old age arrived there before long. She said to Amir, "O human child! You have murdered my child who was only three hundred years of age! You never feared that someone in his family may survive him? I am here to avenge his death now." Sharara Jadu began to call out an incantation whereupon Amir recited the Holy Names for counteracting enchantments, which made Sharara Jadu forget all her magic. Amir stepped forward and struck her with his sword and dispatched that harridan to Hell. He spent the night there and started out again in the morning.

On the thirteenth day of his travels, his feet became blistered and he was forced to stop. Not too much time had passed when a dust cloud rose on the horizon. When it settled Amir saw a black stallion heading toward him. Upon approaching Amir, he came to a standstill. Amir got to his feet and mounted the horse.

He had hardly seated himself in the saddle than the horse reared like Burraq, shot forward, and then flew away like a *peri*. Amir tried to rein him in, but he did not stop and flew on for three days and three nights. On the fourth day Amir espied the wall of a garden in the distance. His steed entered the garden, where a herd of horses of the same color were grazing. Amir's horse joined them to forage on the grass, which was of a quality superior even to sweet basil and hyacinth. Amir was amazed by the spectacle. When he looked closely he saw a fourteen-year-old girl, whose beauty was the envy of the sun, riding one of the horses. She herded and guided the horses and laughed and cried in turns.

Amir asked her, "Pray tell me now who you are, and what is this place and its name." She answered, "This is the Tilism-e Shatranj-e Suleimani. To this day nobody who has entered it has left it alive."

The girl had disclosed this much when her horse carried her away to the other side of the garden and she was unable to say more. When Amir Hamza looked to his right he noticed that Prophet Khizr had appeared to bring him aid. "O Sahibqiran, there's an emerald tablet embedded with great skill in the neck of your mount. Remove it and keep it in your possession. I urge you to act wisely and never act without first consulting the tablet." Having imparted this advice, the holy Khizr disappeared.

Amir took the tablet from the horse's neck and upon inspecting it found the following written on it:

O Traveler and Voyager to *Tilisms*! When you see the woman who laughs and cries in turn, recite the Most Great Name, and shoot an arrow at her face. Then you will see what unfolds.

Amir shot an arrow at the girl when her mouth opened in laughter. It shot through her face like lightning and came out of the back of her neck. A ball of fire shot from the hole and began burning the horses' manes and tails. All the horses there were burned in the conflagration. Only the horse on which Amir was mounted survived the blaze and no harm came to the animal.

Amir saw that along with the horses, the garden also disappeared and there rose a tumult of wailing voices that struck the heart with dread and terror. Amir found himself in a vast and desolate desert. Amir's horse had traveled just a few paces when Amir saw the boundaries of another garden, even more beautiful and scenic than the first. When Amir entered this garden it was as if he had entered a replica of the garden of Paradise, for verily it was one in spirit with the Garden of Eden. In the middle of the garden stood a great tree, with signs of enchantment written all over it. Each of its branches was as wide as a tree trunk. All manner of different colored animals were perched on its branches singing in their own manners and talking in their many voices. In the middle of those animals sat a woodpecker wearing a pearl necklace. When it beheld Amir, it rose five hundred yards in the air along with all the other birds and wailed in a human voice. Amir cried upon hearing the lamentations of these birds; however—once bitten, twice shy—he said to himself, *What if these animals are also made by sorcery?*

When Amir consulted the tablet, he found the following written there:

Be warned and beware! Do not stand under this tree or you will be snared by its enchantments and will never find release from it. These animals are a part of the *tilism.* Recite over your arrow the word inscribed herein and kill the enchanted woodpecker with it!

Amir drew his bow and rose to his feet. The enchanted woodpecker had just perched to rest when Amir shot his arrow, which pierced the woodpecker's breast. The bird began to flutter and a flame darted out of its breast that engulfed in fire the entire garden with all its birds. When all of them had been burned to death, the heaviness was lifted from Amir's heart.

Now becoming aware of more noise and commotion, Amir discovered he was in a different garden where a frenzied *ghol* of outlandish appearance stood before him holding a golden spade. Upon beholding Amir he said, "O human-born, of black head, white teeth, and frail body, how did you manage to find your way in?" Then the *ghol* attacked Amir with the spade. Amir dealt him a blow of his sword, killing the *ghol* who fell to the ground in two pieces. Every piece that fell to the ground became another *ghol,* however, and then Amir was faced with two *ghols,* each mightier and more prodigious than the first. Both of them attacked Amir and surrounded him. In a matter of hours the garden became full of *ghols* that kept multiplying in the same manner. They appeared every moment in a new guise to frighten Amir, with their heads embedded in their chests or their arms extended from their torsos like horns. Finally, Amir remembered the tablet he carried and read upon it the following message:

> The *ghols* will not die by sword and your blade will inflict no harm on them. On the forehead of the white *ghol* is a red mole that shines like a carnelian. This *tilism* will be conquered when an arrow hits the mole; and only then will you be rid of their menace.

Amir looked around and discovered that indeed there was a white *ghol* among them with a red mole on his forehead. Amir recited the name of Allah and shot an arrow at the mole. Suddenly, a great clamor arose from all sides. It thundered and hail began to shower from the sky. In a short while, however, all that evil subsided and all the furniture of that *tilism* disappeared from view.

When Amir looked about he saw another dwelling, most magnificent and imposing, and found a most refreshing and invigorating garden. He saw that in the center of the garden was a well full of water. At the foot of the well a luxurious throne was set, where a *dev* sat propped up on pillows. A woman lay prostrated in front of him with her hands and feet tied, and a jinn sat atop her wielding a dagger, keeping her pinned down with great force. Upon seeing Amir, the woman cried out, "O Destroyer of the *Tilisms,* pray release me from his power and secure my freedom from the hands of this tyrant!" The moment she let out this cry, the jinn cut off her head and threw it into the *dev*'s lap, who threw it into the well. In this manner the woman was dispatched to her fate by the *devs.* But then the head bounced out of the well and again connected itself to the woman's body, and again the same sequence of events repeated itself. When Amir looked at the tablet, it read:

> When the jinn throws the woman's severed head into the *dev*'s lap, recite the Most Great Name and shoot an arrow into his gullet, and destroy all the wizardry in this place.

Amir fired the arrow at the *dev*'s throat. A great commotion broke out the moment the *dev* died and a tremor like the tremors of the Day of Judgment shook the ground.

When it subsided, Amir beheld that he was surrounded by a desert and a boundless wasteland. He went forward and before long arrived at a marvelously constructed fortress made of jet stone. He could hear noises coming from within its walls. When Amir entered the fortress he found it indeed fully inhabited. Shops were open with shopkeepers in attendance but all of them were stock-still. Amir addressed them, but none of them offered a single word in reply to him. From the marketplace, Amir turned toward the Hall of Announcements and found it also crowded, but as before the throngs stood motionless. A little farther along, Amir found luxurious residences, and saw heralds, attendants, mace bearers, guards, and servants at their stations—all in a similar state of stillness.

A few steps ahead was the court, which contained a jewel-studded chamber in which Amir found a king seated in full regalia, surrounded by his courtiers and circled by warriors at their respective stations. Amir approached the king and greeted him, but when he did not receive an answer, he became irate and testily asked, "Is it your custom to disregard a person's salutations and disdain even a reply by way of common courtesy?" He received no answer to that either, and turned in anger to go back, but discovered that neither the door through which he had entered nor any signs of its presence could be seen anymore. Disappointed, when he returned to relate his woes to the king in the hope that he might get an answer this time, Amir saw a piece of paper in the king's hands. He took the paper and read the note, which said:

> O visitor to the *tilisms,* this court is a replica of the Court of Suleiman.
> All the figures that you see in the fortress were people who used to live
> here in the time of Suleiman. It is useless to seek replies from effigies
> and figures who do not have the power of speech.

Amir was pondering over the contents of this paper when he saw another throne next to Suleiman's. He found a fourteen-year-old beautiful coquette sitting there covered in jewels, whose beauty was such that even *peris* could not hold a candle to her charms. Four hundred *perizads* stood behind her throne with arms folded in obedience. Amir approached her throne and greeted her, whereupon she returned his salutation and said, "O friend, how did you find your way through these enchantments and gain admission where no human is allowed?" Amir answered, "I know not how to tell my never-ending tale. It would be simpler if you were to tell me first who you are, and how you came to settle in this remarkable place?"

She answered, "I belonged to the harem of Suleiman and my name is

Salim Shairan. When Suleiman bid adieu to this transitory world and Shah-pal took over command of the jinns, he made me the sovereign of the realm of Zulmat. After Ifrit rebelled and extended his influence to Zulmat he told me to give myself in concubinage to him. I considered, therefore, that I would be putting my honor in jeopardy by continuing to live in Zulmat. Thus I decided to escape and willingly became a prisoner of this *tilism*. The four hundred *perizads* that you see here are my attendants, whom I brought with me. Now tell me who you are, and how you happened upon this place."

The Sahibqiran gave her a complete account of himself and his adventures and told her that now she was free to leave that *tilism* and return to her land.

Queen Salim Shairan said, "No one who arrives here is allowed to go in freedom from this place." Hamza answered, "I make you my pledge that I will destroy this *tilism* as well and release you from here, provided you promise that you will take me to the realm of the humans!" Salim Shairan replied, "I make you this promise with all my heart and soul!" Then Amir took out the tablet to read its instructions, but he could not discern a single letter on the tablet. Amir was gripped by apprehension and put away the tablet and made his ablutions, and then said prayers outside. He was soon overcome by sleep and in that state he saw Prophet Suleiman press Amir's head to his breast and speak thus:

My son! Do not grieve! One of your sons, Badi-ul-Mulk,[14] will conquer this *tilism*, for the destruction and unraveling of this *tilism* is written in his name. To escape this *tilism*, walk toward the door reciting the words that I instruct you, and a path will appear to lead you out of here. As you step outdoors, a stag will appear and then flee from you. You must give him chase while continuing to recite these words. When you cannot see him anymore, know then that you have come out of the boundaries of the *tilism*.

Upon coming out of this reverie, Amir raised his head and offered another prayer of gratitude for divine help.

Then he related the dream to Queen Salim Shairan and said to her, "When I walk out of here, you should also hurry out behind me and do as I tell you." Reciting the words taught him by Prophet Suleiman, Amir and Salim Shairan followed the stag along with her companions. Immediately a great hue and cry rose from the palace as if the Day of Judgment had arrived, and loud cries were heard: "Seize them! Detain them!" None of Amir's party paid any heed to those cries, and running and scampering, all of them exited that prison.

They arrived near two hillocks. The stag disappeared between them, and Amir realized that he had come out of the boundaries of the *tilism*. For a full seven days Amir and his companions remained occupied with assemblies of music and dance.

On the eighth day, Queen Salim Shairan sought counsel from her companions and said to them, "I have promised Hamza that I will take him back to the world of men. Advise me in this matter and tell me what means will secure an auspicious result."

They replied, "Beware that if you fulfill your promise to Hamza, Aasman Peri will dishonor and defile you and revoke your sovereignty over the realm of Zulmat. You would do well to leave this man where he lies sleeping and never think of defying Aasman Peri." Salim Shairan found their advice in her own best interests. Leaving Amir asleep there, she flew away toward Zulmat with her *perizads*.

When Amir woke up the next morning he saw no signs of Salim Shairan or her entourage and realized that she, too, had succumbed to fear of Aasman Peri. Amir said to himself that he should put his faith in God whose will alone could accomplish his return to his world. Having made up his mind, Amir continued forward. It is said that Amir walked for nine nights and nine days, and when he felt hungry he took a bite from the bread-cake given him by Prophet Khizr. On the tenth day he stopped under a clump of box trees to spend the night and in the morning he headed into the open field. He had not gone far when he espied at the foot of a hill a flame that rose every so often. When Amir approached, he saw it was a most scenic hill. Water spouted from springs and greenery covered the entire expanse. A magnificent palace constructed of bricks of gold ingots stood atop the hill, whose breaches were blocked with jewels. All kinds of fowl and beasts abounded there.

At the foot of the hill on the huge mouth of a cave a *dev* sat roasting a buffalo, camels, and elephants over a pyre and gobbling them down with abandon. The flame that rose from the spit and traveled to the heavens was the fire of that pyre. It is told that the *dev* Arnais who was the master of that land had declared himself God and thus brought damnation on himself. He had designated the palace as his heaven and the pyre and the cave as his hell. He had also appointed four hundred *devs* who kept guard on it as the keepers of that hell. Amir thought of approaching them to ask what were these marvels when one of the *devs* suddenly caught sight of Amir and said, "My skewers were all bare, but the God of Qaf has sent me a tasty morsel!" The *dev* rose and gestured to Amir to approach and, speaking softly, said to him, "O human child, come trotting here softly, and let no one hear your footsteps lest another *dev* nab and gobble you up first."

Amir began to laugh upon which the *dev* took offense and wielding the skewer rushed forward to strike Amir and catch and eat him. Amir drew the Aqrab-e Suleimani from his scabbard and dealt him a blow. The *dev* fell to the ground in two pieces along with his skewer. Witnessing that their companion had been slaughtered, all the *devs* wielded their weapons and attacked Amir. He stood in the middle of them with the shield of Garshasp in his left hand and the Aqrab-e Suleimani in his right, putting his trust in God, and fighting dexterously and displaying his Rustam-like might and belligerence. Whoever received a blow by his hand fell to the ground in two. Many were killed and the few who survived fled.

When Amir saw that none of the *devs* remained, he climbed the hill to Arnais's heavenly garden and saw an emerald throne, where he seated himself and thought of taking a few hours of sleep. Then he abandoned the thought realizing that the *devs* who had fled would inform their leader, who would certainly return with them to kill him.

As it happened, the *devs* who had fled went as a group to the castle of Aqiq Nigar to inform their god, Arnais Dev. Arnais demanded to know where Amir had gone and asked them his whereabouts. The *devs* answered that the human being had trespassed into his heaven.

Arnais flew from the castle of Aqiq Nigar along with several thousand *devs* and immediately laid siege to the palace occupied by Amir. He ordered the *devs,* "Storm the palace and apprehend that black-headed, white-toothed one!" They answered, "It is not in our power to step inside and challenge and apprehend him. You are our god; you should kill him by some ruse. Then we will witness how mighty you are!" Arnais waxed even more furious upon hearing their reply, and their jeering words rankled in his heart. Wielding a box tree, he barged inside, and said to Amir, "O child of man, why did you attack my angels? Didn't my fear and terror deter you in your actions?" With these words Arnais brought the box tree down on Amir to show him his power and might. Amir jumped to one side to foil his attack and, catching hold of the *dev* by his cummerbund, lifted him over his shoulders and slammed him to the ground. Arnais rolled away and attempted to escape, but Amir leapt up and came down on his chest, and drawing his dagger from his cummerbund pressed it against the *dev*'s neck.

Then tears came to Arnais's eyes and fearful of losing his life, he pleaded, "O courageous man and the Quake of Qaf, spare my life!" Amir answered, "I will do so on two conditions: First, you must confess to me about your person and your origins, and second, you must convert to the True Faith and pledge allegiance to me!" Arnais Dev sincerely converted to the True Faith.

Then he related this story to Amir: "O Amir! I was employed among the mace bearers in the time of Suleiman! When Suleiman passed away, anarchy took root and everyone laid their hands on whatever they could secure. I occupied this place and declared myself the god of *devs*. Now you have arrived to show me the righteous path and the wealth of the True Faith. I shall do what you order and through it receive grace in this world and the next."

Arnais next stepped out of his palace and said to all his *devs*, "I have converted to the True Faith and those among you who wish to convert to my new faith may stay; and the rest may go their own way." Some of them converted, but most of them refused and turned away to follow their own path. Upon hearing his account, Amir said to him, "You acquitted yourself well in this matter, but it would be a greater service to me if you conduct me back to my world."

Arnais replied, "Nobody undertakes the task for fear of Aasman Peri, as everyone is scared of her tyranny. Indeed she is a despot, but I agree to bear the brunt of her cruelty, and defy her will for your pleasure, provided you help your faithful servant fulfill his desire and obtain what he covets." Amir asked, "What is it that you so ardently desire?" Arnais replied, "Close by is the castle of Zamarrud Hisar, whose sovereign, Lahoot Shah, is a mighty and majestic king. He has a daughter called Laneesa, whom I love. Without her I find no pleasure in this world. If you could help me get her, and make efforts on my behalf, I will undertake to take you to your world and put myself in opposition to Aasman Peri's wishes."

Amir answered, "I will do my best to join you with your beloved and take up this task to please you!" Arnais said, "Come then, climb on my neck and get ready to embark!" Amir adjusted his mail and armor and clambered upon Arnais, who sprang into action and headed toward Zamarrud Hisar, the city and land of his beloved Laneesa.

• • •

The second book of the tale of Amir Hamza, Lord of the Auspicious Planetary Conjunction and Conqueror of the World, is ended. The rest of the story will be told in Book Three, if it be the pleasure of Allah, whose aid and succor we seek.

BOOK THREE

The Third Book of the Dastan *of the Sahibqiran, Abul-Ala Amir Hamza,
the Conqueror of the World, the Quake of Qaf, the Latter-day Suleiman,
and Uncle of the Last Prophet of the Times*

Be it known that Arnais Dev carried Amir Hamza toward Zamarrud Hisar and descended around sunset to a resting place. Amir asked Arnais about his plans. He replied, "Zamarrud Hisar is not too far from here, but you see that the night is pitch dark. It would be best for you to spend the night here." Amir answered, "The holy Khizr has given me instructions never to trust the word of the *devs* of Qaf. Therefore, I will sleep only after I have tied you to a tree." Arnais Dev answered, "O Amir, if you do not have faith in my word, do what puts your mind at ease." Amir tied Arnais to a giant tree. Then he spread the wolves' skins and settled down for a good night's rest.

Arnais said to himself, *In Qaf I claimed the station of a god, but the one at whose persuasion I abandoned my claim considers me so unreliable that he tied me to this tree. He cares not a whit about my suffering. It would be a folly to remain in the company of such a man whose selfish needs are his only concern.* Thus resolved, Arnais flew away along with the tree.

When Amir woke up the next morning, he saw no trace of the *dev* or the tree. Amir reconciled himself to the event, and headed onward. When the sun climbed the skies, a blistering hot wind picked up. Amir saw a clump of trees and longed for their shade.

He sat down under the trees. Hardly a moment had passed before a *dev* arrived wielding a millstone and said to him, "O child of man, before making this place your resting post, were you not at all troubled with fear of me?" Amir answered, "The *devs* of Qaf do not frighten me." Upon hearing that, the *dev* brought the millstone down on Amir's head. Amir foiled this attack with the Aqrab-e Suleimani, and cut the *dev* in two. When the heat had subsided, Amir went forth. He heard sounds of weeping and wailing from the direction of the forest, and beheld Arnais Dev being prodded forward by some four hundred jinns who kept severely lashing and tormenting him. Upon spotting Amir, Arnais cried for help. Amir took pity on him and released him from the clutches of the jinns.

Then he asked Arnais, "What passed with you that you ended up in this plight?"

Arnais answered, "I was seen by Lahoot Shah, who put me in the power of these jinns. He ordered them to take me into the forest and kill me. I must have a few more days remaining to my life, for I saw you." Amir asked, "Why did you flee from my service?" Arnais responded, "I was duly rewarded for my deeds. I shall never again betray you!"

Amir again clambered onto his back and the two went forth toward Zamarrud Hisar. In the evening, they rested at another station. Amir again fastened Arnais to a tree, and again Arnais escaped. In the morning when Amir did not find him, he journeyed on alone. After seven days he espied a fortress and saw some four hundred mighty and stalwart jinns guarding the ramparts. A force of four hundred armed *devs* surrounded the fortress, as if they were assembled there for battle. Amir also observed a *dev* about to break down the fortress gate.

When Amir challenged him, the *dev* answered "What makes you think I harbor any fear or dread of you?"

The Sahibqiran countered, "Do you not know me? I am the Quake of Qaf, the Slayer of Ifrit, the Killer of Ahriman!" The *dev* replied, "It appears that you were sent to me so that I could exact revenge on you for the blood of all the *devs* of Qaf."

At this, the *dev* landed a blow of his *zangala* on Amir, which he foiled and cut down the *dev* with a single blow of the Aqrab-e Suleimani. At once, all the *devs* attacked Amir. Amir killed a great many *devs* and the remainder escaped with their tails between their legs.

Lahoot Shah now came out of the fort and conducted Amir back inside with great honor. Amir said to him, "I have a favor to ask of you." Lahoot Shah replied, "Pray express your wishes so that I may carry them out!" Amir said, "You have a daughter, Laneesa of name. I ask that you marry her off to Arnais. I have given him my word to champion his suit."

Amir's words rankled Lahoot Shah's heart. Keeping up appearances, however, he said to Amir, "Arnais is after all a king. If you wished, I would give her in marriage even to a slave!" He led Amir by the hand to a chamber and insisted that he sit on a throne there that was suspended in the air above a well. The moment Amir sat down, he sank into the well, along with the throne, and fell into the hole. Then Lahoot Shah placed a stone on top of the well and ordered two hundred jinns to stand guard around the prison chamber.

When news of this reached his daughter, Laneesa, she went to her father trembling with rage and exclaimed, "Indeed you have no fear of God! You have returned the favor to the Sahibqiran—through whose exertions your life and honor were saved—by scheming to kill him." Lahoot Shah replied, "He wished me to marry you off to Arnais. That was why I have punished him thus!" Laneesa did not respond to her father.

When it was night, she went to the well and exerted herself in releasing Amir. She descended into the well. Amir saw before him a fourteen-year-old damsel whose beauty was the envy of the moon. He asked who she was, to which she answered, "My name is Laneesa, and I have come to release you from this prison." Amir then climbed out of the well with the help of the rope. When the guards tried to thwart Amir's escape, Laneesa unsheathed her sword and many a jinn was killed in the skirmish.

As Amir bid farewell to Laneesa, she said to him, "Now I cannot think of an existence except in your service. I will remain beside you wherever you go." She thus came to accompany Amir.

After several days' journey they saw a crystal mountain bright as a flash of lightning. Fields of saffron spread for hundreds of miles around it, and in the middle of those fields there flowed a lake. As Amir sat by the lakeside to regard the scenery, a wild bull materialized and came straight toward him. When Amir tried to catch the bull, he ran off toward the forest. Amir chased the bull and caught him. He then said to Laneesa, "It seems that God sent this animal to be your mount." Amir put Laneesa on the bull's back. After they had traveled some distance, the bull suddenly bolted toward the forest, and flying like the wind he disappeared with Laneesa without a trace. Lamenting the loss of Laneesa, Amir headed in the direction where he had seen the wild bull disappear, but he could not track them farther.

Toward the end of afternoon Amir arrived near a hill where he saw a captivating and enchanting garden in which there was a jewel-studded golden dome. When Amir arrived at the door of the dome, he found it locked from within, and heard two people talking within. One of them made pleas and exclaimed, "Accept my love and do not break my heart by spurning me!" The other person replied, "I would sooner eat manure than have you for my life partner! I'll never have it!" Amir called out, "Who is inside?" When nobody answered, Amir kicked in the door, and his eyes met a marvelous sight: Laneesa was sitting on a throne and Arnais stood before her, heaving cold sighs from his ardor.

When Arnais Dev saw Amir, he threw himself at his feet, and said, "Pray witness how I beseech Laneesa endlessly but she does not accept my suit. If you were to have me betrothed to her with your persuasion, I shall remain loyal to you and conduct you anywhere you desire." The Sahibqiran said to him, "You have deceived me twice!" Arnais countered, "You tethered me and went to sleep, and I ran away as it made me suffer. But pardon my misdemeanor now and never again shall I repeat what I did."

Taking pity on the *dev* the Sahibqiran said to Laneesa, "O Laneesa, Arnais promises to conduct me to my world, and he also languishes in his love for you. I wish that you would accept his suit for my sake." Laneesa replied with folded arms, "He is, after all, a *dev*! If you had wished to marry me off even to an ass, I would have accepted it. But I, too, will now set a condition that he must transport you to your world and not again deceive you like a cad!"

Arnais Dev accepted her condition, whereupon Amir wedded them together. After making his salutations to Amir, Arnais said, "Pray give me leave to take her with me to my castle Aqiq Nigar, to satisfy the desires of my heart. Aasman Peri will certainly come to hear that I transported you to your world against her wishes, and she will undoubtedly put me to death. Thus I wish to satisfy all my desires during the life that I have left. I will present myself in your service three days from today and will do as you command!"

Amir said to him, "I shall wait for you for three days." Arnais placed Laneesa atop his neck and together they set out for the castle of Aqiq Nigar.

Midway in the journey they came upon a scenic grassland. Arnais set Laneesa down under a pear tree by the side of a pond and said to her, "Laneesa, my soul! Take rest here a while. I go to arrange a conveyance so that I may conduct you to the castle of Aqiq Nigar with fanfare and honor." At once, he left for Aqiq Nigar.

When Laneesa grew oppressed by the heat of that place, she cast off her clothes and stepped into the pond to bathe. Hardly a moment had passed when a horse resembling a wild bull appeared from the fields and came to stand at the side of the pond. Because its aspect was most strange and frightful, Laneesa was scared by its sight and rushed out of the pond to retrieve her clothes. The horse gave her chase and the terrified Laneesa fell flat on her back. The horse then took his pleasure of her and satisfied his carnal desire. As God had willed, Laneesa became impregnated in that act.

Now, that horse was none other than Arnais, and after he had relieved himself and satisfied his letch, he rolled around on the ground and returned to his original form. Be it known that Laneesa would bear a colt, and a wonder of the Progenitor's work would thus become manifest. He would be named Ashqar Devzad and was to become Amir's favored mount.

Laneesa said to her husband, "O Arnais, what pleasure did you derive from this exercise?" Arnais replied, "God alone knows what tomorrow holds. For that reason I satisfied myself today. He lifted Laneesa onto his shoulders as before, and carried her to Aqiq Nigar and held celebrations.

———

Let me now say a few words about Aasman Peri. One morning, dressed in a red costume and with a frown playing on her forehead, she sat on her throne to give audience. She sent out summonses to all the nobles of the state, ordering them to present themselves. Then Aasman Peri turned toward Abdur Rahman and said, "Khvaja! I had Amir cast into the Bayaban-e Sargardan. Pray see what passes with the Sahibqiran these days and whether he is alive or dead."

Abdur Rahman made his calculations by geomancy and gave all the particulars of Amir's arrangement with Arnais.

Aasman Peri raged like a flame from the fury of her anger at this news. She said, "How dare Arnais have the gall to separate me from my husband! Watch how I shall punish him now!"

She immediately flew toward the castle of Aqiq Nigar in the retinue of thousands of jinns, *devs,* and *perizads,* and she had both Arnais and Laneesa arrested and taken to Gulistan-e Irum as prisoners. She had them severely thrashed and then imprisoned them in Zandan-e Suleimani.[1]

———

Now hear of Amir. After three days passed and Arnais did not return, Hamza cursed Arnais and, remembering Mehr-Nigar again, cried bitter tears.

Suddenly he heard someone say, "Peace be with you!" Amir looked up and saw Prophet Khizr before him. He said, "O Prophet of God, am I fated to languish in Qaf and remain forever lost in this wilderness? Nobody who makes me a promise ever fulfills it." The holy Khizr told Amir what passed between Arnais and Aasman Peri. Then he asked Amir to exercise patience and left.

Amir went forth, and after completing a journey of seventeen days arrived under a hill that held a crystal dome at its peak. Hamza surmounted the hill after great struggle and came to the dome's boundary wall but found the door locked and saw nobody around. Amir broke open the lock and stepped into a beautiful garden. When he studied the cupola again he found it surmounted with an inestimably precious *shabchiragh* ruby. Using the miracle granted him by Prophet Aadam, Amir reached up and took the jewel from the cupola. Upon comparing it with the one in his headpiece, he found not the least disparity between the two.

When Amir went inside the dome, his eyes caught upon a jewel-studded throne, and rarities and marvels of astonishing quality. He thought of resting there for a few moments but then thought the better of it, realizing that it was entirely likely that the custodian of the place was some *dev* who would become enraged to find him there. He stepped out of the dome and sat down on a promenade. Hardly a moment had passed when a mighty blast of wind issued from the forest and Amir saw Sufaid Dev, who was some five hundred yards in height, enter the garden shouting and making the heavens and Earth alike ring with his clamor.

Sufaid Dev called out, "Where is the thief who has taken the *shabchiragh* jewel from the cupola of the dome that was the relic of Prophet Suleiman, and thus extinguished the light of life in Gumbad-e Suleimani?" Amir said, "You towering fool of hideous form and amorphous shape, your search has now ended! I wonder if you know me, and recognize the Slayer of *Devs* and Destroyer of *Tilisms*! If not, then approach and learn that I am the Quake of Qaf, the Latter-day Suleiman, the Killer of Ifrit, and the Destroyer of Ahriman."

Sufaid Dev's eyes filled up with tears, and he said, "O Quake of Qaf! Do not kill me, for I will prove of much help to you!"

Amir said to him, "No harm will come to you if you convert to the True Faith. Otherwise this very dagger will take your life."

The *dev* replied, "I have some enemies who dwell on the slope of this hill. If you were to kill them, I would convert to the True Faith." The Sahibqiran said, "Tell me where I would find them."

Sufaid Dev answered, "At the bottom of this hill in the scenic fields of saffron, dwell the seven *Nasnaases* of Suleiman who are considered by all *devs* to be of unsurpassing might. If you were to kill them, it would be an extraordinary favor to me." Amir said to him, "I wish you to take me to their dwelling!"

Sufaid Dev accompanied Amir to the bottom of the hill and showed him the home of the *Nasnaases.* When Amir called out to the *Nasnaases,* all seven *Nasnaases* came out en masse and stood in a row at Amir's side. He regarded their singular form and bodies: They resembled humans, but they had sharp front teeth, keen as the point of a spear. Amir drew the Aqrab-e Suleimani and jumped into their midst. He killed all seven of them with his gleaming sword. Then Amir said to Sufaid Dev, "Now all your enemies have been killed and your wishes fulfilled." Sufaid Dev was so pleased that he placed one hand on his head and another on his ass, and began dancing with joy. Then he said, "O child of man, although you killed all my enemies, I remain sworn to your enmity! It is a rule with our race that we do evil to those who do good unto us without fear of God's retribution."

Sufaid Dev then lifted a heavy slab of stone and threw it at Amir's head. Amir dodged it, and then drawing his sword, attacked Sufaid Dev, who turned tail and said, "I will come after you whenever I find you unawares." At this, he flew away. The Sahibqiran reasoned that it would not bode well for him to stay there longer and he immediately departed from that place.

For seven nights and seven days, fear of Sufaid Dev drove Amir onward. On the eighth day Amir came upon a city whose denizens each possessed only half a body. When two of them stood together, they formed one person. It was on this account that those people were called *nim-tans.* Their king was Futuh Nim-Tan. When he heard of Amir Hamza's arrival, he came to welcome him and conducted Amir with honor into his city. He kissed Amir's feet and said, "I was told by Prophet Suleiman that a child of man would arrive in Qaf to lay low the *devs.* I was told that he would be called the Latter-day Suleiman and would carry the signet of Suleiman.[2]

Amir asked him, "Is it possible for you to conduct me to my world?" The king answered, "We *nim-tans* cannot set foot beyond the boundaries of our city." Then Amir took his leave and traveled onward.

The *dastan*'s narrator tells that the Sahibqiran passed through a desolated stretch for ten days straight with great hardships. On the eleventh day, he reached the shores of a turbulent sea, but saw no sign of any ship or boat there. Amir sat down upon a rock and, recalling Mehr-Nigar and his companions, began crying. In the course of his wailings, Amir was overtaken by sleep.

Sufaid Dev, who had lain in wait for just such an chance, saw his opportunity. He flew away with the rock on which Amir lay sleeping. After the *dev* rose some two hundred *kos* into the sky, the blasts of wind finally awoke Amir. He saw Sufaid Dev flying away with him. Amir called out to him, "O Sufaid Dev! The kindness I have done, you return with wickedness. Have you no fear of God?" Sufaid Dev replied, "I already told you that it is the custom of *devs* to reward good with evil. Now, tell me what is your pleasure—shall I throw you into the sea to drown or smash you against the mountains below?" Amir reasoned that since the *devs* have twisted minds, Sufaid Dev would do the very opposite of whatever he told him. Therefore, Amir said to him, "Throw me into the mountains to avenge yourself!" Sufaid Dev said, "O human child! I will throw you into the sea instead."

Having said this, the *dev* threw him and the stone into the sea and flew away. At God's orders, the holy Khizr and Prophet Ilyas caught Amir in their arms in midair and carried him to safety to the shore. Amir greeted and thanked both prophets and said to them after much weeping and wailing, "Sires! Aasman Peri persecutes me severely. She prohibits my returning to my world and does not allow me to seek a remedy for my distress."

The holy Khizr said, "O Amir! A few more days of hardship remain and, God willing, they, too, will pass."

———

Now hear an account of Emperor Shahpal and Aasman Peri: One day Emperor Shahpal was giving audience in his court when Aasman Peri arrived dressed in the color of Mars[3] and looked full of fury.

At that moment, Abdur Rahman arrived. Addressing him, Aasman Peri said, "Khvaja, pray tell us of Amir's whereabouts at this moment, and whether he is alive or dead, happy or miserable!" Upon studying the horoscope, Khvaja Abdur Rahman beat his head and shed many tears, and at last said to Shahpal, "What evil did Hamza do you that you take your revenge in this manner?" Shahpal was greatly alarmed and replied, "I hope all is well, Khvaja! How does Amir fare?" Khvaja Abdur Rahman answered, "Where evil thrives, no good ever takes root. You are oblivious to his fate and not in the least concerned about his welfare. Sufaid Dev has thrown Amir into the Caspian Sea. It remains to be seen whether Hamza will live or die."

When Emperor Shahpal heard this inauspicious news, he dashed his crown on the ground. Aasman Peri, too, began pulling out her hair by fistfuls and uttering many plaintive cries. That very moment the emperor departed for the Caspian Sea. The *devs* of Qaf bore his throne heavenward, and in the flash of an eye they arrived over the waters of the Caspian.

The Sahibqiran had just finished saying his prayers with the prophets Khizr and Ilyas when Emperor Shahpal arrived with Aasman Peri. Amir showed not the least favor to either of them. Both Emperor Shahpal and Aasman Peri threw themselves at Prophet Khizr's feet and said, "O holy Khizr! We swear and pledge that six months from this day we will send Amir Hamza back to the world of humans. Pray intercede on our behalf with the Sahibqiran just this once."

Holy Khizr then advised and convinced Amir to trust their word. Amir took leave of Khizr and Ilyas, and sitting on the throne alongside Shahpal and Aasman Peri, returned to Gulistan-e Irum.

Of the Khusrau of India, Landhoor bin Saadan, arriving at the Fortress of Ceylon and Routing Muhlil Sagsar and Malik Ajrook; and of the Departure of Bahram Gurd, the Emperor of China, Toward the Clime of China, and His Giving Audience at the Seat of His Kingdom

The narrator now tells that many days had passed since Muhlil Sagsar and Malik Ajrook Khwarzami laid siege to the fortress of Ceylon, and they had had many skirmishes with those within the fortress walls. One day they sounded the battle drums, charged the fortress, and assailed the followers of the True Faith yet again.

Suddenly a dust cloud rose from the direction of the forest. When those in the fortress gazed upon the horde with spyglasses, they saw Landhoor bin Saadan, riding his she-elephant Maimoona with great pomp and glory.

Those inside the fortress sounded notes of jubilation. As Malik Ajrook and Muhlil Sagsar looked around with surprise upon hearing these jubilant notes, Landhoor bin Saadan fell upon the Sagsar army with his warriors. When Jaipur saw Landhoor leading the charge, he flung open the gates of the fortress and led his army out to join the battle.

Malik Ajrook led his elephant next to Maimoona and dealt a blow of his mace to Landhoor. While Landhoor successfully foiled the blow, it landed on the head of Maimoona, and the she-elephant's brains immediately gushed out her trunk, her life extinguished with great pain. The Khusrau jumped off his mount, and as Malik Ajrook landed a second blow on him, he foiled it and caught hold of the trunk of his enemy's elephant. He pulled it mightily, sending Malik Ajrook's elephant tumbling on its face, with a river of blood issuing from his trunk. The Khusrau caught Malik Ajrook by his cummerbund and slammed him to the ground.

Malik Ajrook tried to rise to his feet and escape, but Landhoor pressed one leg of his adversary under foot and, securing the other in his hand, tore him apart like an old rag. Landhoor then turned his attention toward the Sagsar army. But just at that moment a cloud suddenly appeared in the sky, and it thundered so loudly that it seemed the heavens would come crashing down to Earth. Everyone was blinded by the lightning and traumatized by terror.

Then a claw came down from the heavens and carried Landhoor away, just as a squall carries away a twig. Upon witnessing this the Sagsars fell like ferocious lions upon the armies of India. The armies of India again sequestered themselves in the fortress. The Sagsars encircled them and laid siege on the fortress as before.

Before I give their full account, let me say a few words about King Landhoor.

The claw that carried Landhoor from the battlefield was Rashida Peri, daughter of Rashid Jinn, the distinguished and celebrated king of the lands of Abyez Min Muzafat, one of the realms of Qaf. When Rashida Peri witnessed Landhoor's demonstration of power and might, she resolved in her heart to carry him away to slay Sufaid Dev. That blackguard *dev* had become enamored of Rashida Peri, and demanded of Rashid Jinn his daughter's hand in marriage. When Rashid Jinn did not accept his suit, the *dev* captured Rashid Jinn and imprisoned him in a cave. He then pursued Rashida Peri so that he could capture her, too, and ravish her.

Upon getting wind of the *dev*'s plans, Rashida Peri had escaped to Gulistan-e Irum so that she might find succor and a protector in Aasman Peri. But upon arriving in Gulistan-e Irum, she discovered that Aasman Peri was visiting another land, so then Rashida Peri traveled to the world of humans to divert her mind. She witnessed the display of Landhoor's power in Ceylon, and carried him away, enamored of his appearance and comely aspect. She placed Landhoor in her garden, and then bedecked with the seven adornments, she presented herself before him. When Landhoor beheld Rashida Peri he fell head over heels in love, and asked her, "Who has brought me to this garden, and what land is it where I find myself?" Rashida Peri narrated her circumstances and said, "Our emperor avenged himself on his enemies with a human's assistance, and gave him the hand of his daughter in marriage. I have brought you here likewise to avail myself of your aid and succor. If you kill this *dev*, I will give myself to you in slavery for the rest of my borrowed existence."

Landhoor asked, "Where is that wretched *dev*?" Then Rashida Peri conducted him to the domicile of Sufaid Dev. The *devs* who stood guard at Sufaid Dev's dwelling ran to their chief Saqra-e Barahman with news that a human had appeared. When Saqra-e Barahman saw Landhoor, he thought of capturing and making a present of him to Sufaid Dev. As he approached and extended his hand to grab Landhoor, the Khusrau caught it and torc it from Saqra-e Barahman's shoulder with one mighty tug. Saqra-e Barahman was knocked out by the pain, and all his pomp and might were made dust. The *devs* fell upon Landhoor, who slaughtered many with his sword. The rest of them escaped with their lives.

Landhoor then brought Rashid Jinn with him to Qasr-e Abyez. The latter arranged a royal feast for him. In the midst of the revelries, the Khusrau turned to Khvaja Abdur Raheem, who was one of Rashid Jinn's ministers, and said, "Pray inform your king that I have fallen in love with Rashida Peri, and I desire that the king give me his daughter's hand in marriage." Khvaja Abdur Raheem conveyed his message to the king whereupon Rashid Jinn replied, "I would be honored to give him my daughter's hand in marriage. My only conditions are that he first kill my mortal enemy Sufaid Dev, and then clear the Qasr-e Marmar of the scourge of the *devs*." Landhoor accepted these conditions. It being night, he then went to sleep, after making ready to leave the next morning to kill Sufaid Dev.

Now hear of Sufaid Dev. The *dev* named Palang-Sar informed him of Landhoor's arrival and Rashid Jinn's release. Sufaid Dev flew into a passion and shouted, "I drowned the Quake of Qaf in the Caspian Sea and put an end to his existence! Whence has this second human come?" When Sufaid Dev went to look, he saw a gigantic youth cavorting with Rashida Peri. She sat in his lap, and he was kissing and fondling her and having a merry time of it. Upon seeing this marvel, Sufaid Dev rushed at Landhoor wielding a box tree and brought it down upon him. Landhoor foiled his attack and, snatching the box tree from his hands, smote the *dev* so powerfully on his head that Sufaid Dev was laid out flat on the ground. The Khusrau pinioned him and flushed out all the *devs* from the palace. He produced Sufaid Dev before Rashid Jinn, who incarcerated Sufaid Dev in a cave and appointed several thousand *devs* to guard him.

Rashid Jinn now again ordered festivities in Landhoor's honor and married off his daughter to Landhoor with great fanfare.

After the marriage Landhoor skirmished with the *devs* occupying Qasr-e Marmar, drove them out, and took over control of that palace as well.

One hot day, Landhoor was enjoying a deep sleep on a marble platform under the shade of trees, when Palang-Sar Dev released Sufaid Dev from his prison, and informed him of the place where Landhoor lay sleeping and told him to take him unawares.

Thus, Sufaid Dev carried Landhoor away and imprisoned him in a cave. Then he left to capture Rashida Peri so that he might avenge himself on her.

From fear of her enemy Rashida Peri cast herself into the Tilism-e Anjabal, which was a creation of the Seh-Chashmi Dev, and hid herself there from his wrath. Upon learning this news, Sufaid Dev resolved to enter that *tilism* and secure control over it. His companions, however, prevailed on him to banish such thoughts and told him that anyone who entered that *tilism* never left alive but brought on an end to his life. Sufaid Dev's heart became full of dread upon hearing the details of that *tilism*. He laid siege around it instead, and settled down to bide his time.

———

Now let me narrate a few words about Jaipur who was forced to ask Muhlil Sagsar to grant him thirty days' reprieve so that he might make a decision about surrendering the castle. Jaipur wrote a missive to the emperor of China, Bahram Gurd, soliciting help.

Upon receiving this missive, the emperor of China headed for Ceylon with his army.

Now hear of the Sagsars. When thirty days had passed, the duration of the reprieve requested by Jaipur, they again attacked the fortress and were about to breach it when the armies of the emperor of China arrived on the scene, and routed them.

Bahram entered the fortress of Ceylon amidst great jubilation. Bahram was concerned about Landhoor's fate. He sent his *ayyars* out in all directions to bring him back some intelligence of Landhoor.

Now hear of Rashida Peri. At the time she cast herself into the Tilism-e Anjabal, she was with Landhoor's child. After nine months a son was born to her. Rashida named him Arshivan Perizad. She inscribed his name and the complete account of his birth on a piece of paper, and after attaching it to the point of an arrow, shot it out of the *tilism* in an attempt to convey her news to her father.

It so happened that a *perizad* found this arrow and carried it to Rashid Jinn, who instructed the *perizad* to carry it to Ceylon and deliver it to an elder of Arshivan Perizad. Upon arriving in Ceylon, the *perizad* put the letter in the lap of Bahram Gurd who made every attempt to learn the contents of the letter, but because it was written in Jinni, the language of the jinns, no one could read it. Bahram could do aught else but safely put away the letter, in the hope that one day he would find someone who knew the language and it would prove of use.

———

Now hear of Arshivan Perizad. When he turned eight, he noticed his mother's sorrow and dejection, and said to her, "Why do you remain so grief-stricken? And why do you not confide to me the cause of your melancholy." Rashida Peri told him her whole story. Arshivan said, "Someone must have the tablet of this *tilism* in his custody. I must find him and take possession of it!" Upon that Rashida Peri wrote a letter to her father asking him to search for the tablet, and dispatched that letter out of the *tilism* with an arrow as before.

After an unsuccessful search, Rashid Jinn sent a message that the tablet was probably inside the *tilism* itself.

Arshivan now cried copious tears at the helplessness of his mother and himself. During his lamentations he was suddenly overtaken by sleep. He saw an old holy man in his dream, who said to him, "My son! Open the gate of the dome that is opposite your abode and there you will find a *dev* from whose neck hangs a tablet made of carnelian inscribed with bold letters. You must act according to the dictates of that tablet. The *dev* will depart after handing you the table and you will conquer the *tilism* through the assistance of God."

Arshivan did as he was told and afterward carried out all the instructions on the tablet, and then he went forth to discover the secret of the *tilism*. He came across a great empty desert. In the middle of the desert was a cedar tree covered in delicately patterned foliage. He saw a giant crane,[4] which was the size of a mastodon, sitting atop the tree. Its mandible was like a beam, and its pouch was the depth of Amar Ayyar's *zambil*. Arshivan consulted the tablet and then recited the Most Great Name over the point of the arrow, aimed it at the bird's pouch, and let fly. No sooner had the arrow hit the bird than it fell to the ground and there arose a dark storm, which made the bright day darker than the *Shab-e Yalda*. A hue and cry arose of: "Catch him! Do not let him escape! Don't let him get away! The Destroyer of *Tilisms* is escaping after killing the *dev* of the cedar tree! Let us see who puts him to the sword!"

Arshivan began reciting the words on the tablet loudly, and when the commotion ended, he saw a black hill before him. Arshivan headed toward it and saw a marble staircase there that led to a huge pond. Standing there were twelve- and thirteen-year-old damsels who were the envy of the sun and the moon in beauty, carrying goblets of roseate wine in their hands. The moment they beheld Arshivan Perizad, they said with one voice, "O Destroyer of *Tilisms*! Indeed you have made us wait too long for you! We have stood here for an eternity, suffering the pangs of expectancy!"

Arshivan found himself in a quandary as he could not possibly drink up all the wine they offered him. Wondering whom he should favor, Arshivan looked at the tablet. Acting on the tablet's instructions, Arshivan took the goblet from the hand of the woman in the red dress, and after reciting the Most Great Name over it, threw it in her face. The moment the wine touched the face of the sorceress, it caught fire. The fire raged so potently that all the women standing around the pond began to burn like a candelabra and they wrung their hands with grief at their destruction. Within an hour they had completely burned away.

Arshivan offered his thanks to God and looked to the tablet again, and acted as he had been commanded and destroyed the *tilism*.

Rashida Peri embraced Arshivan and exited the *tilism*. Rashid Jinn forthwith arrived on his throne and embraced Arshivan fondly. Then seating both Rashida Peri and Arshivan on his throne, he returned to Qasr-e Abyez scattering gold and jewels as their sacrifice.

Arshivan then asked his grandfather, "Where has Sufaid Dev imprisoned my father?" Rashid Jinn took Arshivan with him to the domicile of Sufaid Dev.

———

Now hear of the Rustam of His Age, King Landhoor bin Saadan. One day he was bemoaning his helplessness when he heard someone say the words, "Peace be with you!" He answered the greeting and saw that his interlocutor was Prophet Khizr. The prophet removed the fetters from Landhoor's arms and legs, and then disappeared.

When Landhoor left the cave, he beheld Rashid Jinn and Rashida Peri sitting on a throne outside, looking in his direction. Rashida Peri held a boy in her lap. After kissing Rashid Jinn's feet and embracing Rashida Peri, Landhoor asked, "Who is this boy? Give me all the details and tell me the truth about the whole matter!"

Rashida Peri told Landhoor all about his son and then made Arshivan kiss Landhoor's feet. Landhoor embraced Arshivan and they returned to Qasr-e Abyez in the company of Rashid Jinn.

Of Khvaja Amar Ayyar's Moving to the Castle of Devdad from the Fort of Salasal Hisar Along with Mehr-Nigar and the Followers of the True Faith

After a year had passed, the fort of Salasal Hisar ran out of provisions. Mehtar Sayyad advised Amar that they move to the castle of Devdad which was constructed by Jamshed and was stronger than any fort in the world. Amar set out to find some way of capturing the castle.

After his attempts to find a way into the castle were unsuccessful, Amar saw a water carrier in a turret of the castle who was drawing water from the lake. Amar climbed into the bucket and when the water carrier had pulled him up, he drowned him and took his place. Pretending to be sick Amar had other water carriers lead him to his house. In the night, Haam Devdadi, the commander of the king's *ayyars* knocked on the house and confessed to Amar that he was a follower of the True Faith, and offered Amar full support in his mission. Together they entered the palace of King Antar Devdadi but before Amar could drug and overpower the king, Devdadi called out to Amar that Prophet Ibrahim had converted him to the True Faith in the realm of dreams and ordered him to help Amar.

At the king's invitation, Amar moved into the castle of Devdad with his whole camp. When the princes Hurmuz and Faramurz learned this news, they sent a message to Naushervan asking him to personally lead the campaign against Amar. However, Buzurjmehr advised Naushervan against it when he asked his opinion. Then Naushervan heard news that Zhopin's brother Bechin Kamran was on his way to enter his service with two hundred thousand troopers. Naushervan received him with honor and narrated to him his woes. Upon learning of the emperor's troubles, Bechin offered to join the campaign against Amar and vowed to defeat him.

Upon his arrival Bechin Kamran criticized Zhopin, Jahandar, and Jahangir for failing to defeat Amar. Zhopin asked him to test the waters for himself and the next day Bechin assaulted the castle. His army retreated with many losses after Amar showered them with Greek fire. However, Bechin and Zhopin reached the gates of the castle and were about to break them down when Naqabdar Naranji-Posh arrived to Amar's aid. In the pitched battle that was fought, eighty thousand infidels, including many of Naushervan's renowned commanders, lost their lives. Again the Naqabdar Naranji-Posh went away despite Amar entreating to him to reveal his identity.

When Naushervan received the news of the new defeat suffered by his army, he was wroth with Bakhtak, whose son Bakhtiarak had not proved himself at all useful against Amar. Bakhtak wrote a note of reprimand to his son whereupon Bakhtiarak used a forged letter to convince Khvaja Arbab, one of King Antar Devdadi's sons, that Naushervan would richly reward him if he helped in Amar Ayyar's capture. Khvaja Arbab proposed to the princes that they use a tunnel which opened in his house to enter the castle with their armies and then capture Amar and take control of the castle.

However, Khvaja Arbab's daughter, Dil-Aavez, felt dismay that her father was willing to barter away the lives of innocent men because of his avarice. She immediately informed Amar Ayyar who arrived at Khvaja Arbab's house some hours before the arrival of Hurmuz's men and put him under arrest.

After partaking of the feast Khvaja Arbab had prepared for the princes, and having Aadi Madi-Karib stuffed with choice dishes, Amar deputed him to sit at the mouth of the tunnel and capture all the men who might come out of it. In this manner Amar was able to capture four hundred enemy commanders.

When none of his commanders returned to make a report, Zhopin became suspicious and took caution before he put his head out of the tunnel. As a result Aadi was unable to get a good hold on him. Zhopin got away with the sacrifice of his ears, which Aadi presented to Amar. After Zhopin raised the alarm, Amar fired many fiery missiles into the tunnel, which burnt ten thousand troops who were in there. The princes Hurmuz and Faramurz returned to their camp with only a handful of men.

The next morning Amar hanged Khvaja Arbab and all four hundred of Naushervan's commanders. Then he had molten lead poured into the tunnel and sealed it.

Hurmuz and Faramurz sent the news of their defeat to Naushervan with Sabir Namad-Posh Ayyar.

———

Now for some news of the Sahibqiran. When six months had passed, Amir said to Aasman Peri, "Now the time has come to fulfill your promise. Send me back to my world and carry out your pledge." Aasman Peri said, "I will send you back after one year has passed." Upon hearing these words Amir was enraged and said irately, "O Aasman Peri, do you have *any* fear of God in your heart? Six months ago you swore before two prophets that after this period you would send me to my world!" Aasman Peri answered, "The retribution for breaking my word will be mine alone, so have no worries on that account!"

Amir took his complaints to Emperor Shahpal, who comforted Amir, showed him much favor, and offered him words of consolation. Seating Amir on a throne that very instant, he ordered four *devs* to carry Amir to his world. When Aasman Peri received this news, she arrived there holding Quraisha in her arms and said to Amir, "O Abul-Ala, have you no love for your daughter either? If I have wronged you, what is her crime?" Amir answered, "When you come to visit me in the world of humans, bring her with you. But now I must depart." Thus speaking, Amir ordered the *devs* to carry his throne aloft and departed from there.

Aasman Peri returned to her quarters tearful and heartbroken from Amir's departure. She sent for Rizwan Perizad and said to him, "Go to the Sahibqiran on the pretext of bidding him adieu to convey my orders to the throne bearers. Tell them that they are to travel no farther than the Dasht-e Ajaib, where they should leave Amir and then return here." Rizwan Perizad flew away and speedily approached Hamza's throne. Amir saw his arrival as an ominous sign. He said to the *devs* who were bearing his throne, "Return to Shahpal and do as I command you!" When the *devs* resisted, Amir grasped the hilt of his sword and said, "If you do not return, I will kill every single one of you!" The *devs* were thus forced to return Amir's throne to Shahpal's court. When Shahpal accosted the *devs* after hearing Amir's account, the *devs* told him that they would not act in defiance of Aasman Peri's orders. When the emperor confronted Aasman Peri she told him to keep out of her conflict with her husband.

Hearing this, Amir dismounted the throne and heaved such a terrible sigh of anguish that the whole castle shook from its impact. Then he said, "O Aasman Peri, you made the prophets witness your promise to me and then you betrayed your word. God willing, His wrath will overtake you." With these words, Amir headed for the wilderness crying with the frenzy of a man deranged and distraught.

Amir Hamza had traveled in this wise for fifteen days when he came upon a castle where jinns with unbraided hair were busy praying, soliciting the court of heavens. It appeared that a towering *dev* with ears like an elephant was forcefully and relentlessly besieging them. Amir felt pity for those inside the castle and he challenged and routed the *devs*.

Half of the *devs'* army was slaughtered and the rest turned tail and ran. The king of the castle embraced Amir and seated him on the throne with great honor and said, "I am the same jinn, Junaid Shah Sabz-Posh, the elder brother of Emperor Shahpal, whom you freed from the Tilism-e Shatranj-e Suleimani." He took Amir into the castle of Sabz Nigar, asked about his welfare and said, "If my life can be of some service to you, I am willing to sacrifice it at a word from you." Amir replied, "Do me the kindness of having me transported to my world. For as long as I live, I will remain indebted to you."

Upon hearing this, the king contemplated for a while. Then he sent for his vizier Khvaja Rauf Jinni and said to him, "Tell Amir that if he marries my daughter, Rehan Peri, who is enamored of him, I will have him conducted to his homeland on the ninth day from today." After an initial refusal, Amir accepted the proposal. Sabz-Posh married Amir to Rehan Peri with great fanfare.

However, on the first night Amir slept with a sword between Rehan Peri and himself. She thought that it was perhaps a human custom to sleep with a sword between man and wife. That night Amir encountered Mehr-Nigar in his dreams yet again, and saw her suffering on account of their separation. He woke with a start and took to the desert like a frenzied man.

In the morning, Rehan Peri's mother, Durdana Peri, saw her daughter sleeping by herself. She woke her up and asked, "Where is the Sahibqiran?" She replied, "I do not know. In the night he slept with a sword between us. Then I do not know where he went because I, too, went to sleep."

Durdana Peri was upset upon hearing this account and reported it to Sabz-Posh. He said, "Why did Amir agree to marry my daughter if such was not his desire? Everyone will say that there must be some fault with my daughter that caused Amir to leave her after marrying her, for nobody would turn away from a day-old bride without good reason." He immediately sent for the *peris* and *devs* and ordered them to find Amir Hamza and to bring him into his court.

———

Now hear of Aasman Peri. One day she bedecked herself in a crimson dress and went to the court of her father. She turned toward Abdur Rahman and said, "Pray check where Amir is now and discover his whereabouts." After interpreting the geomancy pattern, Abdur Rahman did not give the whole account. He said only, "On account of you Amir tarries all distressed and distraught, and he suffers many a hardship." As Aasman Peri was sitting next to Abdur Rahman and was well versed in geomancy herself, she glanced at the calculations of the horoscope and said, "How wonderful it is to see that Sabz-Posh, despite being my uncle, still married his daughter to my husband, and showed neither regard for my prestige and honor nor any fear of my burning wrath. I have learned today that he is not an uncle to me but a rival. I shall no longer call myself by the name of Aasman Peri if I do not burn his land down to cinder and punish him most severely." She then mounted a throne and, taking along an intrepid army of *devs,* headed for the castle of Sabz Nigar.

The narrator says that when Aasman Peri arrived at the castle of Sabz Nigar, she ordered her attendants to restrain Junaid Sabz-Posh and Rehan Peri at once. Then Aasman Peri laid to ruin the city of Sabz Nigar and returned to Gulistan-e Irum. For many days she punished Sabz-Posh and Rehan Peri with a thousand strokes of the lash each day. Then she had them thrown into the Zandan-e Suleimani.

The news of Aasman Peri's ravages reached Shahpal. He tore his collar in grief and rushed bareheaded and barefoot to the prison. He threw himself at his brother's feet crying copious tears, and made every apology to attempt to wash away Sabz-Posh's rancor. Although Shahpal said all this and more, he did not console Sabz-Posh in the least.

Sabz-Posh opened his lips to entreat the Court of Heaven and said, "O Almighty Lord! Visit your wrath and retribution on Aasman Peri for the harsh treatment I suffered at her hands. Cast her lot among the damned!" He went away in tears to return to his land and cursed Aasman Peri without cease.

Now hear some news of that fickle creature, Aasman Peri. There lived in the seventh realm of Qaf a *dev*, Ra'ad Shatir, whom everyone considered peerless in courage and valor. When Prophet Suleiman departed from this world, Ra'ad Shatir, who was a nephew of Ifrit Dev, constructed two castles in the Seven Enchanted Seas of Suleiman, which he named Siyah Boom and Sufaid Boom, furnishing the castles with luxurious trappings and devising a *tilism* to guard them.

The news of Amir Hamza's exploits enraged Ra'ad Shatir and he immediately flew from the castle of Siyah Boom carrying Suleiman's net, which he had acquired by some devious means after the prophet's death.

Ra'ad Shatir imprisoned everyone in Gulistan-e Irum and ordered the guards of the jail to put them to torture. Only Abdur Rahman escaped imprisonment, for he had left earlier for his home on some errand. When Abdur Rahman learned of this, he cast lots and discovered that Amir Hamza was to the north of the city, and he departed immediately upon a throne in search of him.

Now hear of the Sahibqiran. When he stepped out of the city of Sabz Nigar, he walked for several days in the desert, and after crossing it, rested at the foot of a hill that was situated not too far from the abode of Abdur Rahman. Hardly a moment had passed when he saw Abdur Rahman approaching on a throne. Amir received him very kindly and Abdur Rahman gave him a complete and detailed account of his chance escape and the capture of Shahpal, Aasman Peri, Quraisha, and the chiefs of the races of *devs* and jinns and all the hardships that they were undergoing. Amir Hamza replied, "It was on account of their swearing false oaths and tormenting me that they were overtaken by God's wrath!" Abdur Rahman said, "All that Your Honor states is true, but I still entreat you to devise some way of securing their freedom in consideraion of your relationship to them."

Abdur Rahman was finally able to persuade Amir to undertake the mission despite great reluctance on his part, and told him that only Shah Simurgh could convey him there. He then took him to his home and ordered a celebratory feast in Amir's honor.

After the feasting was over, Abdur Rahman seated Amir on a throne and ordered four jinns to take it to the abode of Shah Simurgh with the utmost diligence. The four jinns carried Amir's throne aloft and rose as high as the stars. Amir looked down but could see only an expanse of water stretched beneath him. The jinns carried his throne for seven days and seven nights. On the eighth day, a few hours had passed before sunrise when they placed Amir's throne on the seashore.

Huge tall trees grew by the shore whose branches almost reached up toward the lofty tree of Tooba in Paradise. On top of those trees was a wooden castle of great expanse and vastness, adorned with all kinds of trappings. Amir asked the jinns, "Who has constructed this castle?" They answered, "O Sahibqiran! This is not a castle but the abode of Shah Simurgh."

After the messenger jinns returned to their city, Amir heard a clamor arising from a tree. When Amir looked up, he observed that Simurgh's young were making the noise. Each one of them was bigger in size than an elephant. They cried continuously. When Amir looked around to see what had terrorized and frightened them, he beheld a dragon climbing their tree. Amir killed the dragon by shooting arrows at him and saved the young ones from the beast. Then he cut the dragon into pieces and fed his meat to the chicks with the point of his pike. Having had their fill, the young ones retired into their nest to sleep. After a few hours a pair of Simurghs returned carrying food for their young. The Simurghs saw Amir Hamza sleeping under the tree and they said to each other, "It seems that this man who lies sleeping under the tree is the one who has long caused us much grief by eating up our children. Today as well he ate our young, and this is why they did not come out of the nest. We must kill him without delay."

Upon hearing these words, the Simurghs' young emerged from their nest. They told their parents about the dragon and how Amir had slain him. Shah Simurgh was very grateful to Amir Hamza. Witnessing that Amir was exposed to the sun, he shaded him with one wing and with the other began fanning him. Feeling this pleasant sensation Amir opened his eyes. Witnessing the Simurgh standing over him, he reached for his bow and quiver when the Simurgh said, "O Quake of Qaf! First you put me in your debt and gratitude, and now you are bent on killing me. Those were my young whom you saved from the dragon!" Amir asked, "How did you learn my name?" The Simurgh replied, "I heard from Prophet Suleiman that a man would arrive here some time in the future and save the Simurgh's young from the dragon. His name would be the Justice of Qaf and his mission would be to slay the *devs*." Amir asked, "What is the name of this frontier?" The Simurgh answered, "It is called the Baisha-e Qaza va Qadar and it lies outside the dominions of Qaf."

The Sahibqiran said, "I have come to you in need and in a most distressed state." The Simurgh replied, "Your word is my command!" Amir said to him, "I ask that you carry me to the castle of Sufaid Boom where Ra'ad Shatir has imprisoned Shahpal and his court." The Simurgh answered, "I will take you there and do you this service. But make sure to bring seven rations of food and seven portions of water to carry on my back. When I feel hungry and thirsty you should give me a morsel to eat and a sip to drink!"

Amir caught seven blue antelopes on the plain and skinned them and made water skins of their hides and filled them with sweet water. Then he climbed on the Simurgh's back carrying the water skins and blue antelopes. The Simurgh said to him, "O Sahibqiran, do not carry on your person any weapons of steel lest the mountain of magnet that lies in the middle of the Magnetic Sea draw and claim them." Amir took the dagger of the champion warrior Sohrab and tucked it away in his shoe with great care. The rest of the weapons he handed to the Simurgh who hid them in his feathers.

The Simurgh then reached for the heights of the heavens and when Amir looked down he saw that the earth was the size of a small jewel. For as far as he could see there was only water to behold. As they were flying over the Magnetic Sea, Amir lost his weapons which were attracted by the magnetic force.

Amir fed one antelope to the Simurgh each time they flew over a sea. When flying over the Sea of Fire, however, Amir put the blue antelope in the Simurgh's mouth, but he withdrew his hand quickly because of the heat of the blaze and the antelope fell into the Sea of Fire. The Simurgh's strength soon began to decline and Amir saw that it was only a matter of a few breaths before they would both fall into the Sea of Fire and drown. He immediately put the bread-cake given him by Prophet Khizr into the Simurgh's mouth and freed him of all hunger. The simurgh landed on the other side of the Seven Seas and congratulated Amir.

However, the loss of his weapons weighed heavily on Amir's heart. Suddenly someone called out, "Peace be with you!" Amir saw it was holy Khizr. He restored to him all the weapons. Then holy Khizr went away, and Amir decorated himself with his weapons and gazed upon the expanse before him. Amir saw before them two hills: One was as white as the dawn and the other as dark as the night of lamentations. Amir said to the Simurgh, "Are these white and black hills or something else?" He answered, "These are the castles of Sufaid Boom and Siyah Boom." Amir said, "I now bid you adieu, and you will always have my gratitude for helping me reach this place!"

The Simurgh pulled out three feathers from his wing, gave them to Amir, and said, "If, God forbid, you ever fall into difficulty, you should burn one of these feathers and I will come to your help that very instant. The second feather you should put in the aigrette of your horse and adorn him with it. Give the third feather to Khvaja Amar Ayyar as a gift from me!"

Then the Simurgh flew away to his nest and Amir headed toward the castles. He had gone some distance when a lion appeared and attacked him. Amir cut him in two and skinned him and draped the hide on his shoulders. When Amir arrived at the castle of Siyah Boom, he saw four hundred *devs* seated at the gates to make sure that no stranger should enter or trespass there.

The commander of those *devs* caught sight of Amir, let out a cry, and said, "Aaargh! My friends, woe unto us that the Quake of Qaf has reached this place!" He ran at Amir and smote him with a box tree so mightily that from its shock the Earth cried out, "Have mercy on me!" Amir managed to foil his attack and dealt him a mighty blow with his sword. The *dev* received such a vicious cut from its blade that he fell to the ground in two pieces. When the *devs* saw that, they ran off to inform Ra'ad Shatir.

Amir was standing at the gates of the castle when he heard a voice exclaim, "O Amir! Shahpal and Aasman Peri are imprisoned in the castle of Sufaid Boom."

Amir headed for Sufaid Boom, and when he reached its gates he saw that the castle had a hundred towers and each tower was manned by *devs* in different forms. Some had heads of lions, some of horses, others of peacocks, crows, or wolves. The gates of the castle were manned by a dragon that spewed fire profusely. His mouth was wide enough that it extended to the portals of the castle and was like a trap laid around the entrance. Then Amir heard the same voice again, saying, "O Hamza! The destruction of this *tilism* is not given to you. Your grandson instead is destined to break it, and he will be titled the Latter-day Rustam."

Amir said to himself, *I am a boy myself yet! Those who are imprisoned here will certainly not remain incarcerated until then and spend the rest of their lives in jail!* The voice again called out, "Beyond undertaking to secure the prisoners' release, do not take it into your head to destroy this *tilism*. Recite the Most Great Name and then blow on the dragon, and he will turn away and you will prevail over him."

When the Sahibqiran recited the Most Great Name over the dragon, he turned away and left. Amir went inside and found a garden where Emperor Shahpal was sitting with his companions, lamenting his wretched fate. Hamza released them, broke open the door of the castle's dome and found Aasman Peri hanging there upside down, close to her death, and Quraisha sitting and crying. The Sahibqiran reunited them with Shahpal.

Aasman Peri was most remorseful and greatly mortified at her deeds. She threw herself at Hamza's feet and said, "O Hamza, forgive me my trespasses. I will send you to your world for certain six months from now."

Amir made no reply. He gathered all the prisoners he had freed and headed out of the castle. As they exited they saw Ra'ad Shatir Dev coming toward them with several thousand *devs* whose footsteps made the whole world tremble with terror. He lifted a heavy stone and threw it at Amir's head. Amir eluded his attack and dealt him a sword blow that felled him. The *devs* who accompanied Ra'ad Shatir carried off his corpse to Samandoon Hazar-Dast Dev.

Amir meanwhile brought Shahpal and his entourage back to Gulistan-e Irum and all of them relaxed upon reaching their homeland.

Six months later, Amir again had a disturbing dream. When he asked Aasman Peri to send him to his world, she asked him to wait yet another year. When Amir complained to Shahpal he arranged to send Amir back but Aasman Peri again arranged things that stopped Amir from leaving.

Some transcribers write that Amir Hamza divorced Aasman Peri that day, while some contradict this account and consider it a false tradition.[5]

The narrator has it that Emperor Shahpal was so troubled by Aasman Peri's disobedient speech that he gave up his crown and throne. Aasman Peri inherited his kingdom. She had it broadcast throughout Qaf that whoever dared to take Hamza to his world would be punished severely. Then Aasman Peri said to Khvaja Abdur Rahman, "Find out who the woman is whom Hamza loves, what she is like in her appearance, and where she lives!" Khvaja Abdur Rahman made calculations by geomancy and declared, "Indeed Hamza is justified in his passion. Her beauty is such that even her attendants surpass you by far in comeliness! The woman herself is secured within the walls of the castle of Devdad." Aasman Peri had a map made of the castle of Devdad, and then sent for the *perizads* and said to them, "Go to the world of humans and fetch Mehr-Nigar from this castle!" Immediately at her orders, the *perizads* departed to fetch Mehr-Nigar for Aasman Peri.

———

Before I continue in this tale, let me first give an account of Landhoor bin Saadan.

Be it known that after Landhoor was released from prison and returned to the city, one day a *perizad* brought him the news of the approach of Sufaid Dev. Landhoor went out to encounter Sufaid Dev. He killed him at once and did not let that blackguard draw another breath.[6]

Landhoor's war cry resounded throughout the whole expanse of Qaf and was also carried to the ears of Amir Hamza, who was at that moment skirmishing with Ra'ad Shatir. Amir's war cry was likewise carried to the ears of Landhoor. Hearing a familiar war cry, they both marveled and wondered at the incident. Hamza said to himself, "It can't be Landhoor. Surely, there is no likelihood of his being in Qaf!" And Landhoor convinced himself of the same.

After Landhoor had killed Sufaid Dev and relieved that wretch's accursed body of the burden of its unclean head, he said to the king, "I have slain your enemy. Pray send me to my home now and fulfill your promise." The king immediately ordered a throne for Landhoor and Arshivan Perizad, and ordered the *devs* to carry them to the world of humans.

Now hear of Bahram Gurd, the emperor of China. After prevailing over the Sagsars, he was again lamenting the loss of Landhoor one day when Landhoor's throne descended from the skies into Bahram's castle.

Bahram rushed to embrace him. Festive music played in the castle. In the midst of the celebrations, Bahram said to Landhoor, "I was fighting the Sagsars when someone threw a letter before me, which I picked up. A palm was imprinted on the letter, and it was written in strange characters!" When Bahram sent for the letter and handed it to Landhoor, Arshivan revealed that it was the letter dispatched by his mother.

Of Zehra Misri's Disappearance from the Roof of the Castle and of Her Being Presented Before Aasman Peri

Now hear a few words of the story of one afflicted by separation, who had become a human incarnation of the longing gaze: to wit, Princess Mehr-Nigar. Night and day she occupied herself with mourning her separation from Amir. She would lie disheveled and unkempt in her bed and bore alone the burden of her boundless grief and countless sorrows.

Her companions worried that Mehr-Nigar would slowly slide into a state of frenzy and that the extremes of her passion would overwhelm her senses. They assured her that Amir would return in a few days and that her grief would be allayed by the grace of the munificent God. One day they persuaded her with their entreaties to accompany them to the roof of the castle, where they showed her the greenery of the pastures and diverted her humors with gossip.

They had not been standing there long when a little cloud appeared in the sky along with a dark mist. Slowly that small cloud glided over the castle and covered its whole expanse. Blinding bolts of lightning began striking then, and deafening claps of thunder sounded. Suddenly and unexpectedly, a claw materialized in the sky from nowhere. This claw came down from the cloud and grabbed Zehra Misri, who was standing next to Mehr-Nigar, carrying her off in the flash of an eye. The terrified attendants and companions of the princess collapsed unconscious. They raised a great hue and cry, and the very image of doomsday was replicated in the shouting and chaos that ensued. Everyone, young or old, was distressed by this tragic disappearance.

Now hear a little of what passed with Zehra Misri. When she saw that she was sitting on a throne that was bearing her away in the sky and nothing but darkness could be seen all around her, she asked the *devs* carrying the throne, "Who are you and where are you taking me?" They answered, "Aasman Peri, who is Hamza's wife, ordered us to bring her Mehr-Nigar, the daughter of Naushervan. Therefore we are taking you to Aasman Peri."

Zehra Misri reasoned that Hamza must have made a marriage in Qaf and that his new wife had sent for Mehr-Nigar so that she might kill her. She understood then that since the *devs* did not recognize Mehr-Nigar, they mistook her for Mehr-Nigar.

When Zehra Misri reached Gulistan-e Irum, her eyes were lined with the collyrium of Suleiman so that she might see all those present. When Zehra Misri was presented before Aasman Peri, she was crestfallen to behold Zehra's beauty. Addressing Zehra Misri, she said, "Are you Mehr-Nigar, the daughter of Naushervan?" Zehra Misri made obeisance and said, "My name is Zehra Misri and I am the daughter of Abdul Aziz, the king of Egypt, and the wife of Muqbil Vafadar. Even in my dreams I cannot seek an equal footing with Mehr-Nigar."

Aasman Peri asked her, "Speak the truth, Zehra Misri, am I more beautiful or is Mehr-Nigar?" Zehra Misri yielded with folded arms, saying, "I regret any disrespect to you, but there is greater beauty to be found in the soles of the feet of the attendants who wait on Mehr-Nigar than in your face!"

Aasman Peri was enraged by her reply and said to her slaves, "Send her to the executioners and have them behead her!" At once, the executioners carried Zehra Misri to the execution grounds.

It so happened that Quraisha was headed at this time for the court. Seeing a crowd gathered, she went where Zehra Misri was sitting and asked the executioner, "Who is she and what is her crime?" He answered, "I do not know. The sovereign of *peris* has ordered her beheading!" Quraisha then asked Zehra Misri and upon hearing the story, Quraisha began trembling with rage. She took Zehra Misri along with her to the court and said to Aasman Peri, "What was her crime that you sent for her from the realm of men and ordered her killed? It appears that if Mehr-Nigar had been brought here she would have suffered the same fate. You would have cared neither for the feelings of the Sahibqiran nor for the wrath of God. Mehr-Nigar is also someone in whose person the honor of the Sahibqiran resides, and she is a hundred thousand times worthier of respect and reverence than you because she is the Sahibqiran's first wife. My hands are tied because you are my mother; otherwise, with a single stroke of my dagger I would cut you in two without fear of consequences."

Aasman Peri trembled to witness Quraisha's fury. Quraisha sent for a throne for Zehra Misri and ordered the bearers to carry it back to where they had caught her.

Now, Samandoon Hazar-Dast Dev's dwelling was along the path they took. When he saw the throne flying away with a woman, he ordered the *devs* to bring it down and asked Zehra Misri, "Who are you and where are you headed?" Zehra Misri submitted her detailed account to him, where-upon he had the *devs* killed and said to Zehra Misri, "I am setting you the duty of rocking my son's cradle and making sure that he sleeps comfort-ably." Dealt this new hand by fortune, Zehra Misri was forced to accept the duty of tending the baby *dev*'s cradle.

———

Now hear of Khvaja Amar. When he heard the hue and cry in the women's quarters, he went there and learned that a claw had come down from the skies and taken away Zehra Misri. Amar trembled with rage and said to Mehr-Nigar, "I counseled you a hundred thousand times not to do anything without first seeking my advice, but all of that was to no avail. If that claw had carried you off, how would have I shown my face to Hamza or have ever found you? My twelve years of labor would have come to naught!" Having said this, he lashed Mehr-Nigar three times so hard that she was unable to bear the violence and fell to the floor writhing like a tumbler pigeon from the ecstasies of pain. Amar's treat-ment of her rankled in her heart. She felt loathing for him and said in her heart, *It was all because I fell in love with Hamza that I was lashed today at the hands of a lowly cameleer's son and had to bear this humiliation.*

After night had fallen she scaled down the walls of the castle with a rope and headed toward the camp of her brothers. Then she had a change of heart and decided that she must not appear before her brothers or pre-sent herself at their court. She saw a horse that belonged to Hurmuz. Donning a man's disguise and throwing a veil on her face, she rode the horse into the forest and removed herself from Amar's guard and vigil.

Now hear of Amar. When he left the women's quarters after lashing Mehr-Nigar, he felt too ashamed at his actions to return there. He decided that he would apologize to Mehr-Nigar in the morning and make every effort to win her over. At the end of the night, Amir Hamza appeared to Amar in his dreams and addressed him thus: "O Amar, was it a seemly manner in which you treated Mehr-Nigar and gave her such pain? Because of your treatment, she has now taken to the forest and fallen into a thousand hardships!" Amar awoke from that distressful dream, and when he rushed into the women's quarters, he discovered that Mehr-Nigar was not in her bed. Amar became very anxious for her safety. When he climbed to the top of the castle he saw the rope hanging there. Amar climbed down by the same rope and followed Mehr-Nigar's footprints. Tracing them, he approached Hurmuz's pavilion and learned that Mehr-Nigar had been there and had ridden away. Amar followed the hoofprints of the horse in the hope of discovering her path.

Now hear of Mehr-Nigar. Before daylight she had traveled a distance of fifty *kos* when suddenly a sovereign of that land, King Ilyas[?], arrived there on horseback. Mehr-Nigar hid herself behind the trunk of a tree but the king saw from a distance that a veiled rider had hidden from him. He approached her and said, "Tell me who you are, and what has brought you into this jungle." Mehr-Nigar answered, "I am a traveler and have been sent here by the revolutions of the heavens and a fated misfortune!" The king asked, "Would you like to enter my service?" She replied, "I have no need to enter anyone's service!" From her voice, the king suspected that the veiled rider was a woman. He extended his hand and pulled off her veil and beheld a woman whose beauty would have blinded the sun itself. He immediately brought her down from her horse, put her into a litter, and comforted her with many sweet words. King Ilyas carried her to his abode and put her in excellently furnished quarters. He provided her with every item of luxury and comfort and gave her much in which to find delight and pleasure. When he tried to enter her quarters and ravish her, Mehr-Nigar said to him, "Beware not to take another step forward or you will receive a grievous injury!" Frightened by her threat, the king returned to his quarters gnashing his teeth with anger.

It so happened that Khvaja Nihal[7] arrived in the service of King Ilyas, who told him that he had caught a fairy-faced creature in the forest who spurned him and rejected his advances.

Khvaja Nihal said, "If I could see her, I would say a charm over her that would make her surrender before you." The king immediately led Khvaja Nihal to her quarters. Nihal recognized Mehr-Nigar and called her loudly by name. Mehr-Nigar recognized him as well and opened the door. After learning the whole story from Mehr-Nigar, Khvaja Nihal counseled her and told her that she must not give herself to distress as he would release her from the clutches of the king. After allaying Mehr-Nigar's worries, he returned to the king and declared to him, "Pray order the guards to allow me to come and go freely to see her at any hour of night or day. I will be able to persuade her on the third day from today."

After taking his leave, Khvaja Nihal bought two horses and brought them to the door of the house where Mehr-Nigar was kept. That same night he rode out of the city with her.

The next day the king sent for Khvaja Nihal, but he was not found at his dwelling. Then the guards arrived to report that the woman the king had kept in the house was no longer there. The king reasoned that Khvaja Nihal had eloped with her, and he went in pursuit of him at the head of an intrepid army.

It was getting close to afternoon when Mehr-Nigar saw a dust cloud rising behind them and said, "O Khvaja! Spur on your horse, for the king's army is approaching!" While Khvaja Nihal stood still watching the approaching dust cloud, Mehr-Nigar entered the forest to hide from the eyes of that rascal and escape from his clutches. In the meantime, the king reached Khvaja Nihal. The king killed him, and then began searching for Mehr-Nigar. After he had been thwarted and disappointed in his search, King Ilyas returned grieving to his palace.

By the next day Mehr-Nigar was feeling famished when she came across a field of melons. She asked the man who tended the field for one melon. He brought several melons and Mehr-Nigar ate every single one of them. That dotard, who was well into his nineties, said to Mehr-Nigar, "O life of the world! If you agree to live with me, I will make sure that whatever you wish for is provided." Mehr-Nigar thought that perhaps he suffered from melancholy.

After she had eaten her fill of the melons, she asked him, "Do you have any family?" He answered, "I have ten sons, eleven daughters, and one wife." Mehr-Nigar then said, "How would I live with you when you already have a wife?" He answered, "I will divorce my wife for your sake." Mehr-Nigar replied, "Very well, then, go and divorce her while I wait for you here!"

That simple man rushed home, and Mehr-Nigar left him money for the melons and rode away. When the melon grower returned to the fields after divorcing his wife, he did not find Mehr-Nigar there and began crying out loudly, "Oh, my *peri*! Ah, my *peri*! Where have you gone?"

Mehr-Nigar continued riding until evening when she reached a forest that abounded in wild beasts. Mehr-Nigar dismounted her horse and climbed a tree. In the morning a lion killed her horse. Mehr-Nigar tied all his trappings to a tree trunk and started out from there on foot.

That evening she reached the outskirts of a small village where there were some farms and a big pond where a huge tree stood. Mehr-Nigar climbed up that tree and spent the night in its branches. In the morning the head of the village sent his handmaiden to fetch him water from the pond for his bath. Looking into the water of the pond she saw the reflection of Mehr-Nigar's face and imagined that it was her own reflection. The sense of her own beauty made her so vain that she refused to carry water for anyone. Her master gave her a good thrashing and sent her back to carry the water but again she saw the reflection and her vanity was stirred. When her master sent her back a third time, Mehr-Nigar, who had noticed the handmaiden coming there more than once, figured that some mischief would now transpire. She climbed down from the tree and rushed away.

The handmaiden's master went with her to the pond to learn the truth, taking others along. When she saw her hideous reflection in the water, however, she still insisted that she was beautiful which convinced everyone that she had become possessed.

Mehr-Nigar continued onward and on the second day arrived at a mendicant's abode. He was the chief of a group of beggars. Upon encountering Mehr-Nigar he asked her story. Mehr-Nigar replied, "I am a weaver's daughter. My father has taken a wife in his old age and this stepmother has driven me away from the house. Now I wander around in a state of ruin and distress." When he heard Mehr-Nigar's account he said to her, "I declare you my daughter. Just do me the favor of distributing the food and the collection among the mendicants and make this your daily duty." Mehr-Nigar offered thanks to God and expressed her gratitude to the mendicant.

———

Now hear of Amar Ayyar, King of All Tricksters. In his search for Mehr-Nigar, he followed all the clues and and finally found his way to the abode of the head of the mendicants. He recognized Mehr-Nigar from afar, doling out food to the mendicants. Amar disguised himself as an old man and approached her. When Mehr-Nigar started serving him, Khvaja Amar became tearful and said to her, "O princess, I am not a mendicant but your slave, Amar. I am remorseful for what I did and I profess myself your humble slave." When Mehr-Nigar recognized Amar she rushed into his embrace and began crying. Hearing her crying the chief rushed there, calling out, "What has happened, my child, that you cry so inconsolably?" Mehr-Nigar told him, "This man is my father." The beggar gave Amar five hundred rupees and told him to use that for her dowry. Amar then left with Mehr-Nigar.

On the way back to his fortress, he put the money in his zambil and drugged Mehr-Nigar to render her unconscious. Then he made her into a bundle and carried her on his back to the fort.

Hurmuz and Faramuz had received intelligence from their *ayyars* that Mehr-Nigar had come into their camp one night dressed as a man and had ridden away for some unknown destination on one of their horses tied at the post. They also learned that Amar had gone in search of her. The princes conferred and decided that there was no way for Amar and the princess to return to their fort without entering the mountain pass. They ordered the *ayyars* of their camp to lay an ambush there and when they saw Amar returning with Mehr-Nigar, they should snatch her from him.

They ambushed Amar when he entered the pass and Jahandar and Jahangir Kabuli also joined them with their armies. Then Amar prayed to God for help.

All of a sudden Naqabdar Naranji-Posh arrived there with his forty thousand troops to assist Amar by the order of God Almighty. He killed Zhopin's brothers, Jahangir and Jahandar Kabuli, and routed the entire army of Hurmuz and Faramurz. Many an infidel was killed and Hurmuz and Faramurz returned to their camp in a state of dejection. Meanwhile, Naqabdar Naranji-Posh returned to his abode after seeing Amar to his castle. Later, Amar apologized to Mehr-Nigar all over again and had his offense pardoned by her.

———

Before we return to their account, a few words from the story of the Sahibqiran, the Conqueror of the World.

Amir Hamza frantically forged a path through the plains for forty days and forty nights after leaving Gulistan-e Irum. On the forty-first day, when he came to his senses, he saw before him a castle that was under siege by *devs* who were standing at its gates. Amir bellowed his powerful war cry and challenged their commander. He killed him and routed the army of *devs*.

A race of *gao-pas* inhabited that castle and their king's name was Tulu Gao-Pa. He came out of the castle, embraced Amir, and took him inside the fort with great respect and deference. He organized a feast in Amir's honor and waited upon him with great awe and reverence. After the feast was over, Amir said to him, "Would you be able to take me to my world?" He answered, "I am willing to defy Aasman Peri and take the risk if you agree to take my daughter in marriage." Amir answered, "I am not inclined to marry anyone as I am not attracted to the people of this land!" Tulu Gao-Pa answered, "If you refuse my daughter's hand in marriage, then pray instead kill for me the monster Rukh who is my enemy." Amir replied, "I agree to the second condition. Take me to the beast who is your enemy." King Tulu Gao-Pa sent his men to accompany Amir Hamza to show him this creature from afar and give him the directions to his abode. When they arrived at a white hill Amir asked them, "What regal and majestic personage is it who lives here?" His companions answered, "This is not a hill but the egg of the selfsame Rukh. It seems that he has gone away to feed."

When the bird returned to sit on the egg and spread his wings to settle down on his perch, Amir said in his heart, *This is a mighty and powerful bird and it would be well-nigh impossible to overpower it. It is also certain that this creature travels to the world of humans. I should catch his legs and scream loudly to frighten it into flying away, and he will head for the world of humans.* Deciding on this course of action, Amir caught hold of Rukh's leg and made a cry that frightened the bird into flying away with him. However, when the bird reached the Caspian Sea, he pecked at Amir's hand with his beak so hard that Amir's hold weakened and he lost his grip on the bird's leg.

The prophets Khizr and Ilyas caught Amir in their arms before he could fall into the sea. They carried Amir, who had lost consciousness from the fall, out of harm's way and laid him down safely on the shore to let him rest.

———

Now hear of Aasman Peri. One day she inquired of Abdur Rahman, "Pray find out where Amir is, and whether he has returned to his world or is still within our dominions."

Abdur Rahman drew the horoscope and wrote down the results, and then read them out. Upon hearing Abdur Rahman's account, Aasman Peri cried bitterly. She sent Quraisha at the head of an intrepid army toward the fort of the *gao-pas* with orders that no living creature should be left alive in their city. Aasman Peri herself flew toward the Caspian Sea, but finding holy Khizr and Ilyas there she turned away mortified with shame and hid herself from their sight.

When Amir came to, he complained to Khizr and Ilyas about Aasman Peri. They said, "O Amir! Though a lot has transpired of the decree of fate, more yet remains! Do not worry and torment yourself." Amir said to them, "O holy personages! Pray send me back to the castle of the *gao-pas*!" Prophet Khizr conveyed Amir to the fort of the *gao-pas*, carrying out his wishes. Amir saw that the whole city was deserted: A deathly quiet prevailed there and not even a bird was to be seen. Amir Hamza asked Khizr, "O holy one, where have the inhabitants of this place disappeared? Verily, the very sight of this city makes me shudder with fear." Khvaja Khizr replied, "Whatever passed with you here was discovered by Aasman Peri and she sent Quraisha here with an army to lay ruin to this fort and kill every single inhabitant." Khizr then disappeared and Amir stayed all by himself in that city for three days.

On the fourth day he headed out of the city and into the plains. After another four days of traveling he saw a fort with some signs of life. As he approached, it looked as if it were the fort of Ctesiphon. When he went inside he saw the same buildings that he had seen in Ctesiphon but did not see any people and found every building empty of human presence. He encountered a towering *dev* of mighty build standing there who sniggered upon catching sight of Amir Hamza and said, "O human! It is my greatest wish to populate this city. I have had it constructed on the model of the city of Ctesiphon in the world of humans. I have already brought two humans to populate it and will bring more of them in the future. Because you have come here by yourself and God has sent you into this city I will appoint you the king of this city."

Amir asked him, "Do you at all recognize me or know my name?" The *dev* answered, "How could I recognize you when I have never before set eyes on you?" Amir said, "My title is the Quake of Qaf." The *dev* asked, "Were you the one who killed Ifrit and Ahriman?" Amir answered, "I have killed scores of *devs*, not just Ifrit and Ahriman!" The *dev* said, "I will avenge the blood of the *devs* of Qaf on you." He flung a millstone at Amir's head. Amir deflected his attack and with one mighty blow of his sword, dispatched that unfortunate soul to Hell.

After killing the *dev* Amir went into the courtyard, where he saw two beautiful and comely boys whose names were Khvaja Aashob and Khvaja Bahlol. When Amir asked their particulars, they replied, "Our father was a merchant. When he died, a *dev* who lived here kidnapped us and the tyrant kept us incarcerated here. Now tell us, who are you?" Amir answered, "I am called the Sword of God, the Hand of God, the Proxy of the Beneficent, the Quake of Qaf, and the Latter-day Suleiman. I have come from the world of men and have killed many a *dev*—including the one who kidnapped you. Have no worries now, for I shall take you to the world of humans."

Amir Hamza left the castle along with the boys and sat down under a leafy tree to eat the bread-cake given him by Khizr. Some time had passed when a *dev* carrying a box tree on his shoulder came up to Amir and challenged him. Amir found out that his name was Maymar Dev and he had constructed the replica of Ctesiphon and all the buildings of Qaf. When he learned of Amir's identity, he attacked Amir and brought the box tree down on Amir's head. Amir foiled this attack and dealt him an unwavering sword thrust that sliced him in two like a cucumber, with not a fiber remaining attached between the two parts.

The boys were delighted to see this display of Amir's might and valor, and said jocularly, "Bravo, O Terror of God! You are indeed a strong and mighty person! We, too, will change our names to match yours."

In this manner they proceeded onward making pleasantries. Amir gave them the names of Jahandar Qalandar and Jahangir Qalandar.

When it was noon Amir spread the wolves' skins under a shady tree and sat down to rest. He was overtaken by sleep and was soon lost to slumber. The boys went for a bath in the river that flowed by the tree. Suddenly a *dev* appeared from the forest, and upon seeing him, Bahlol said to Aashob, "Do you remember the formula for killing the *dev*, brother? Let us now go forward, you and I, and kill him." They consulted together and then shouted at the *dev* in challenge, "Here, O carrion eater! Where do you think you are headed? Do you not know that we are the Arm of God and the Sword of God and know all too well how to deal with your race?" After challenging the *dev* they went forth to skirmish with him. But as the *dev* kept advancing toward them without paying any heed to their words and did not turn, they took fright. They hastily woke up Amir Hamza and told him all that had happened.

Amir saw that a mighty *dev* was advancing on them. He cut off the *dev's* head with his dagger and then told the two boys, "Beware and be warned never again to try such capers!" After that, Amir headed onward in the company of the boys.

On the fifth day they saw a big ship being put to sea. Amir approached Khvaja Saeed Bazargan who owned the ship and was sailing to the world of humans. He agreed to take Amir and the boys aboard if Amir consented to marry his daughter. At first he would not consent but Khvaja Aashob and Khvaja Bahlol finally persuaded him to do so.

The boys rushed to Khvaja Saeed Bazargan and said, "Now you may marry your daughter to him and arrange for the wedding ceremony." The merchant married Amir to his daughter and Khvaja Bahlol and Khvaja Aashob to two other girls. Amir Hamza and the two boys slept with their wives that night.

In the morning when Amir woke up he found Aasman Peri sleeping by his side and discovered that the merchant was none other than Khvaja Abdur Rahman. Because Amir had divorced[8] Aasman Peri in anger, Khvaja Abdur Rahman had found a way of uniting them again, and made it permissible for Amir to sleep with Aasman Peri again.

Aasman Peri fell to Amir's feet and began begging and vowing her submissiveness to him. Abdur Rahman also touched Amir's feet and importuned him. Amir was then forced to return with Aasman Peri to Gulistan-e Irum along with the two boys, and there Aasman Peri held celebrations for six months.

One day Amir again said to Aasman Peri, "O Aasman Peri! Pray give me your leave now, as my heart has become oppressed from my sojourn in Qaf and I have suffered gravely from separation from my family and friends." Aasman Peri said, "Tomorrow morning I will send you off, God willing, but do tell me if you will ever come here again and offer me an opportunity to see your face." Amir answered, "O Queen of Qaf! Just as my heart longs for Mehr-Nigar in her absence here, it will crave you when I am back in my world and will long to behold your face." Aasman Peri was most pleased by Amir's words. In the morning when she ascended her throne, she sent for the four *devs* who always carried Amir's throne. First she gave them a reward and then had many gifts of Qaf loaded on another throne, and said to Amir, "Please ascend the throne in the name of God and prepare to depart."

Before Amir could ascend the throne, a great hue and cry suddenly broke out in a din like that of Judgment Day. When they looked they saw four hundred *devs* and jinns who used to attend Shahpal coming toward them in great anxiety. They were throwing ashes on their head and had torn their tunics in grief. Aasman Peri panicked at the sight of this and the world darkened before her eyes. She asked them, "What is the matter?" They submitted themselves to her, saying, "The emperor has departed from this world for the Eternal Kingdom!" From the shock of this terrible news Aasman Peri fell from her throne and gave herself to weeping and wailing, beside herself with grief. The whole of Gulistan-e Irum rang with lamentations and their mourning.

Aasman Peri yielded to Amir with folded arms. "Although you have stayed here already for seventeen years, please stay another forty days for my sake and bear the separation from your near and dear ones while I take my father's body for burial in Shehristan-e Zarrin. I shall inter him in our ancient burial grounds and commemorate the forty-day mourning ritual and grieve for his demise. Upon my return from there I will send you off and give you leave to go." Amir answered, "Very well! You may go and I will stay here and do what you ask me to do." Aasman Peri said, "Do not become sad in my absence and leave and inflict on me the wound of your separation. I am leaving Salasal Perizad here with you. If you ever feel restive ask her for the keys and visit the Forty Wonders of Suleiman to entertain yourself so that your heart does not feel oppressed and you remain in good cheer."

She then departed for Shehristan-e Zarrin with Shahpal's body.

Now hear of the Sahibqiran. He passed two days with great difficulty indoors, but on the third day he prepared to head outdoors as he could no longer suffer to remain within. Salasal Perizad said to him, "Until the Queen of the Skies returns after acquitting herself of her duties to the deceased, you may go and visit the Forty Wonders of Suleiman." He handed Amir a key and led him to the door of a building. Amir opened the lock and the moment he set foot inside, the door of that chamber closed behind him. After a moment the darkness subsided and he beheld a vast field. As he went onward and looked about, he saw a sumptuously decorated bejeweled throne. On that throne lay an apple that was half red and half green. Amir picked it up and smelled it and immediately fell unconscious and lost use of his senses. In his dream he saw a magnificent castle that was beautifully constructed. He went inside and entered a captivating garden where moonfaced damsels were promenading about. A comely maiden who was the envy of the stars was giving audience upon a luxurious throne. Upon beholding her, Amir immediately became enamored of her and pledged his life and soul to her on the spot.

That moonfaced beauty arranged a festive assembly in Amir's honor and waited on him hand and foot. Her father arrived in the meanwhile and saw Amir sitting beside his daughter. He saluted Amir and kissed his feet. Amir embraced him and said, "Dear friend, how did you recognize me?" He answered, "We had heard from our forefathers that the Quake of Qaf would arrive here at some time in the future to regard the Wonders of Suleiman and lay low many *devs* with his lustrous sword." Amir was greatly pleased to hear this. That man married Amir to his daughter and made him his son-in-law. The Sahibqiran passed seven years there and two sons were born to him in that period.

One day Amir was sitting with his beloved by the side of the pond when she said to him, "O Quake of Qaf! My anklet has fallen into the pond. I would be grateful if you could fetch it for me." As Amir dived into the pond, he suddenly started and discovered he was standing in the same chamber where he had entered this place, and found Salasal Perizad standing before him. Surprised at this turn of events, Amir looked around and said to him, "I would like to go into that chamber again, because my heart longs to see my boys." Salasal Perizad said, "Your honor! These are the Wonders of Suleiman. All this talk of your sons and wife is a dream. You were away for less than an hour. All that you saw was an illusion and a dream. One encounters such marvels in a *tilism.* Tomorrow you may go and visit the second chamber, where new marvels await you, and you will derive ever greater pleasure from visiting it." Then Salasal Perizad locked the chamber and escorted Amir back to the palace.

The next day, Amir opened the second chamber and went inside. After walking some distance he saw a woman's portrait propped upon a throne. As Amir picked up the portrait to look at it, he swooned and fell on the throne, having lost consciousness. In that state he saw a garden in which many beautiful women were gathered and the one whose beauty had made him lose consciousness was dancing amidst a group of women who were playing music and singing. Amir also saw a number of *ghols* standing in a corner of the garden. When they saw Amir they rushed at him wielding maces. Amir drew the Aqrab-e Suleimani and attacked them, unnerving and confusing their host. The shock also made Amir open his eyes and he saw there was neither garden nor *ghols* before him, but Salasal Perizad stood in the same chamber.

Amir marveled at this and returned to the palace, followed by Salasal Perizad, who took care to lock the second chamber. On the third day he visited the third chamber and went inside. After walking there for some distance, he lost his way and came upon a desert, a great wasteland where the sun was blazing. He wandered there for seven days and seven nights and on the eighth day he saw a *dev* of strange shape and form. He caught

Amir by his cummerbund and flew toward the sky with him, and when he reached the Milky Way, he flung Amir back to Earth. Amir's eyes opened then and he saw neither the desert nor the *dev* but instead Salasal Perizad waiting for him in the same chamber. Amir asked him for an explanation of that chamber and he answered, "These chambers are full of wonders. However, they do not pose any danger to your safety." In short, Amir visited thirty-nine chambers for thirty-nine days. On the fortieth day he asked Salasal Perizad to open the fortieth chamber for him so he could visit it as well. He answered, "I cannot open the door of this chamber, for I do not have the authority to do so. It is the Zandan-e Suleimani." When Amir insisted, he told him that he did not have the key. Then Amir snatched the key ring from him, found the key to the fortieth door, and went inside. Salasal Perizad rushed off to tell Aasman Peri that Amir had opened the fortieth chamber despite his objections and had gone in.

The narrator tells that when Amir entered the fortieth chamber he saw thousands of *devs,* jinns, and *perizads* languishing in captivity. All of them made obeisance to Amir and said, "O Quake of Qaf, have mercy on our circumstances and release us from this captivity!" Amir asked them, "How did you recognize that I was the Quake of Qaf?" They replied, "There are many here in this prison who were incarcerated by Prophet Suleiman himself, and he once stated that a human titled the Quake of Qaf would come someday to release those incarcerated here. We beseech you in the name of God to secure our release!"

Amir took pity on them and cut their chains and fetters and freed them from the prison. All of them kissed Amir's feet and went home after taking his leave. Suddenly Amir heard the sound of a horse's hooves and when he went to investigate, he saw a red colt with roseatte patches on his whole body, running about. When he caught sight of Amir he began prancing about and racing from one end of the chamber to the other. Then the colt rushed toward Amir and stepped on his foot. Although he was clad in armor, Amir felt severe pain from the horse's weight and rushed after the colt in anger. The colt entered a building and Amir followed in pursuit without a second thought. Because inside the building was utter darkness, Amir took out the *shabchiragh* jewel to illuminate his path.

He had hardly taken a few steps when he heard a voice call out, "I cannot bear my misery any longer, O my master! Come quickly to our rescue and release us from this hardship." When Amir stepped closer, he saw Arnais Dev and Laneesa sitting there, weeping and wailing in a most terrible state. Amir said to them, "I will come and rescue you after I have killed the colt that ran away after kicking me." Arnais and Laneesa said, "O Sahibqiran! He is our son! He committed that misdemeanor because he did not know who you were. Please pardon him." Amir was surprised by this and asked Arnais, "You are a *dev* yourself and your wife a *peri*. How did you beget a horse for a child?" They narrated the whole story of how Arnais had coupled with Laneesa in the form of a horse and said, "We have named our son Ashqar!" Arnais then called Ashqar, made him bow to Amir and kiss his feet, and secured pardon for him for offending Amir. Amir released them from their prison and said to them, "Wait for me here while I go and discover the other wonders of this place to see what else it has to offer."

A little farther along Amir found a building in which two *perizads* were hanging upside down and hitting their heads in misery. Amir took pity on them, too, and freed them. When Amir went onward he saw his wives, Rehan Peri and Qamar Chehra, sitting clad in chains and looking dejected and forlorn. Tears came to Hamza's eyes to see them in that state. Upon seeing Amir they, too, began crying inconsolably. Amir brought them out of the chamber along with Arnais and Laneesa. That night he slept with Rehan Peri and Qamar Chehra in Aasman Peri's bed and ravished them both to his heart's delight. As God had willed, the same night both Qamar Chehra and Rehan Peri were impregnated with Amir's seed.

In the morning Amir sent the two *perizads* away and they returned to their homes. Then Amir asked Arnais, "Can you now take me to my world?" Arnais answered, "I am at your service!" Amir sat with the two boys on the throne and both Arnais and Laneesa bore it heavenward and rose as high as the lights of the heavens. When a few hours remained until the end of day, they descended by the banks of a river. Amir saw a shining and luminous building. He discovered that this was the Shish-Mahal[9] of Prophet Suleiman. In the evening, the palace lit up by itself, becoming so resplendent that a hundred thousand lamps would have proved insufficient for the task. When a few hours remained until the end of night Amir and the boys fell asleep, and Arnais closeted himself with Laneesa. Ashqar, however, went outdoors for a romp in the forest, preferring this to sleep.

―――

Now a few words about Aasman Peri. After she had performed all the rituals and completed the forty days of mourning, she gave leave to the kings and princes of Qaf to depart, conferring on each a robe of honor and a gift according to his station. Then she headed for Gulistan-e Irum. In the middle of her journey Salasal Perizad presented himself before her and stated that the Quake of Qaf had released the prisoners of Zandan-e Suleimani and let them out of the prison. Aasman Peri responded to this news, "The prophecy made by Prophet Suleiman has been fulfilled! It was well that Amir did this!" Salasal Perizad then said, "Amir showed the same kindness to Arnais and Laneesa and released them as well." Aasman Peri replied, "It is well that he did that, too." Salasal Perizad next said, "Amir freed Rehan Peri and Qamar Chehra as well." Then Aasman Peri said, "He did wrong in setting free my rivals! Tell me, what happened afterward?" Salasal Perizad admitted, "That was all I witnessed before I left. I do not know what else transpired afterward." While they were having this conversation, another *peri* presented herself and added, "The Sahibqiran slept with Rehan Peri and Qamar Chehra in your bed and passed the whole night in pleasure-seeking with them. In the morning he sent them away and then departed for his world with Arnais and Laneesa carrying his throne."

Aasman Peri came into a towering rage upon hearing this and said, "I had resolved myself to send the Sahibqiran back to his world. Why should the Sahibqiran have slept with my rivals in my marriage bed if not to pour scorn on me and make me jealous? You will see how I repay the Sahibqiran for this deed and what terrors and calamities I unleash on his head!" With these words, she mounted a throne and took her intrepid army in search of Amir Hamza. Upon approaching the Shish-Mahal, she discovered that Amir was inside. As fate would have it, she found Arnais and Laneesa sleeping together in the very first chamber that she entered. Aasman Peri drew her sword and decapitated both of them with just one stroke.

Then she took the same bloodied sword to Amir's bedside and raised it over his head, resolved to murder him as well. But Quraisha, who had accompanied her, snatched the sword from her and said, "My hands are bound because you are my mother; otherwise I would draw my dagger this instant and disembowel you, putting an end to your life. How do you dare even think of harming my father while I still live and before my eyes, let alone kill him?" Then Aasman Peri withdrew from her plans, and after leaving a note at Amir's bedside, flew off to Gulistan-e Irum.

When it was morning, Ashqar returned from the forest and set to screaming and howling upon finding his parents murdered. His cries woke Amir, who soon encountered Arnais and Laneesa lying murdered and beheaded on the floor. Amir grieved for them immensely and said to Ashqar, "If I can discover the identity of the murderer, I shall avenge your parents' death. Cry no more and consider me now in the place of your mother and father."

Then Amir saw a note at his bedside, in which was written:

> I had resolved this time to send you back to your world and fulfill my promise to you, but it seems that you were not fated—either now or ever—to partake of food and water anywhere except Qaf. I do not approve of the two deeds you committed: You slept in my bed with my rivals, and then you tried to depart for your world without my knowledge. I wanted to murder you for your first offense like I murdered Arnais and Laneesa, but Quraisha intervened and I was unable to carry out my plan. In retribution for your second deed, however, I murdered Arnais and Laneesa. Now I will see how you return to your world. I would like to see who even dares to utter a word about conducting you to your world.

Amir was terribly shaken by the words in the note. He buried Arnais and Laneesa and sojourned in that place for seven days. On the eighth day, Amir said with tearful eyes, "How will I return now to my world and find release from Aasman Peri's clutches?" Upon hearing this, Ashqar said, "Do not grieve any longer, for I will take you to your world and will not fear Aasman Peri in the least. Climb on my back and be prepared to depart!" Amir asked, "What will become of the boys?" Ashqar answered, "Put them on my back as well."

Amir made two panniers and put Khvaja Aashob and Khvaja Bahlol in them on either side of his saddle. Then Amir took his seat and Ashqar took off carrying them all on his back. It is said that Ashqar took Amir toward his destination with lightning speed, bridging a thousands *farsangs* a day. Ashqar flew over the sea and when he landed and felt earth beneath his feet again, he sped faster than the wind's own charger.

A few hours still remained to the end of day when Amir reached the slope of the Koh-e Noor mountain and dismounted there with the boys. He soon saw the prophets Khizr and Ilyas coming toward them. They said to Amir, "It is certain that this time you will return to your world. Come with us, for our mother, Bibi Asifa Ba-Safa, has sent for you so that she might give you her leave to depart to your world." Amir and the boys climbed the mountain and saw a dome at the top. Flashes of light moved between the dome and the sky and lit up every inch of the mountain. When they went inside the dome, they beheld an old woman of luminous aspect sitting on a mat, prayer beads in hand, absorbed in worship of God. Her venerated presence struck awe in Amir's heart, and he greeted her with extreme reverence. Bibi Asifa pressed Amir's head to her bosom and said, "My child, I have been most desirous of seeing you. You shall soon return to your world." With this, she gave Amir a piece of rope that was no longer than a yard and quarter in length and said to him, "Give this lasso to Amar as a gift from me and tell him that I have made it with my own hands. If he so wishes he will be able to catch a *dev* with it and when he recites a benediction for Prophet Muhammad (praise be unto Him!) and blows on it, it will increase a thousand yards in length."

After that she said to Amir, "Tonight you will be our guest here." In the morning, when Amir had finished with his prayers, the holy Khizr said to him, "You will have to shoe your horse, otherwise he will not be able to cross the desert of Qaf or journey across the length of that harsh expanse." Khizr then clipped Ashqar's wings and made shoes of them, which he nailed to Ashqar's hooves. Amir said, "O holy one! How long will these shoes made of wings last?" Khizr answered, "They will last for the length of your life and won't come off. When the last wing falls from Ashqar's hooves, you should understand that your time has come to depart from this world to the Future State." Then he gave Amir a saddle and said, "Put this on Ashqar's back. It was made for Sikander himself." Amir then saddled Ashqar, expressed his gratitude to Khizr, and prepared to depart.

———

Now let me say a few words about Aasman Peri to keep you abreast of her news. Several days after she returned to Gulistan-e Irum from the Shish-Mahal, she donned a crimson dress, sat on the throne, and said to Abdur Rahman, "Give me some news of Hamza. Tell me how he is keeping himself." When Khvaja Abdur Rahman gave her Hamza's news, Aasman Peri became crimson with rage. She said, "How dare Bibi Asifa Ba-Safa, who is my subject, send my husband off to the world of humans against my wishes? Send for my throne this instant!"

Aasman Peri immediately mounted it and arrived swiftly as the wind to lay siege to the Koh-e Noor, where she ordered the *devs* to set up a cordon around it. Then with drawn sword, Aasman Peri went before Bibi Asifa Ba-Safa and said, "O Bibi, have you lost all regard for me that you decided to send my husband off to his world? Are you not aware that my terror has been impressed on every heart?" Upon hearing her harsh words, Bibi Asifa Ba-Safa said, "Watch your mouth, you wretch! Do not take it into your head that you have any power over me! I wish that your body would catch fire!"

The moment Bibi Asifa Ba-Safa said these words, a flame sprang up from Aasman Peri's body and it soon appeared as if her whole body had become a pyre. As she burned she cried, "Mercy! Mercy!" Abdur Rahman rushed to Quraisha and said to her, "Any moment now Aasman Peri will fully combust and you will be left without even the memory of her face to recall in dreams. Go and plead with Amir and prostrate yourself at his feet so that he may intercede with Bibi Asifa Ba-Safa for Aasman Peri." Quraisha rushed and threw herself at Amir's feet, whereupon Amir solicited Bibi Asifa's forgiveness for Aasman Peri. At Amir's request Bibi Asifa sprinkled Aasman Peri with her ablution waters, which immediately put out the fire, and thus Aasman Peri was saved. She swooned and fell unconscious to the floor, and the *perizads* carried her away to Gulistan-e Irum on her throne.

Amir stayed there that night as Bibi Asifa's guest. In the morning, she said to Prophet Khizr, "Take Amir to the Darya-e Khunkhar this instant." Amir took his leave of Bibi Asifa, placed the boys in the panniers on either side of Ashqar, and departed with the holy Khizr. They had gone some fourteen or fifteen *kos* when they came upon a sea whose other end could not be seen even with the eye of imagination. The holy Khizr said to Amir Hamza, "This is the Darya-e Khunkhar. All of you must close your eyes now and refrain from looking at its turbulent waters." Amir Hamza and the boys closed their eyes. The holy Khizr took seven steps forward and said, "Now you may open your eyes!" Amir opened his eyes and saw that the Darya-e Khunkhar was behind them and the holy Khizr, their kindly guide, had disappeared.

The narrator of the *dastan* tells that Amir went onward from there for forty days, and on the forty-first day he arrived at the banks of the Caspian Sea. Amir headed along its shores and on the tenth day saw a fort. The king, Samrat Shah Gao-Sar, was very pleased to hear of the arrival of the Quake of Qaf and came out of the fort to welcome Amir Hamza. At the feast given in his honor, Amir asked Samrat Gao-Sar, "Can you help me ford the sea?" He answered, "I will help you ford the sea provided you marry my daughter, Arvana." Amir declined, but the boys said to Samrat Shah, "Make arrangements for the wedding and leave it to us to persuade Amir and get his consent." Then Samrat Shah made preparations according to his custom and gave leave to his attendants to put together his daughter's dowry. The boys finally prevailed on Amir to marry Samrat Shah's daughter.

The night of their nuptials, when they went to bed, Arvana tried to hold Amir Hamza in her arms and kiss him and take her pleasure of him. Amir Hamza slapped her face so hard that her front teeth fell out. She went crying to her father who sent for the two boys and asked them, "Why did the Quake of Qaf behave in this manner toward my daughter?" The boys answered, "It is the custom of our land that on the wedding night a man knocks out his wife's teeth. Also, humans do not bed their wives until they have forded a full half of the sea's length."

Because Samrat was from the race of the *devs* himself, he believed that they spoke the truth. He immediately sent for a ship and provisioned it for the journey. The two boys returned to Amir Hamza and told him all that had happened. Amir could not help but laugh at the boys' antics and accompanied them aboard. When half the sea had been forded, Arvana wished to take Amir to bed again and expressed her desire for him. Amir Hamza tied her arms and legs and threw her overboard, drowning her and sending that poor creature to the depths of the sea of God's mercy. Afterward, he said to the skipper, "Speed the ship and take us to the other shore, or else I will kill every single one of you!" Terrorized by Amir's threats, the skipper obeyed him. The crew hoisted the sails and carried Amir across the ocean before long.

Of the King of *Ayyars* and the Peerless Dagger
Thrower Khvaja Amar Ayyar

Honey-tongued narrators have said that when eighteen months had passed that Amar had been living in the castle of Devdad, he asked King Antar Devdadi if he knew of another castle where he and his camp could pass a few days in peace. The king told him about the fortress of Talva-Bahar, which was situated on a mountaintop and was surrounded by water on three sides. Using another tunnel that led out from the castle, Amar and his men arrived near Talva-Bahar.

Amar hid four hundred warriors inside wooden chests and, disguising himself as a merchant and two other *ayyars* as girls, he loaded the wooden chests on camels and arrived at the fortress. When the news of the merchant's arrival reached King Jamshed Shah of Talva-Bahar, he sent his vizier Haman to find out what merchandise he had brought.

Amar had acquired details about Haman's family and easily fooled him by pretending to be his long-lost uncle. Homan brought Amar inside the fortress along with all the wooden chests.

Amar sent the *ayyars* dressed as girls to Homan along with other gifts. Haman presented those disguised *ayyars* to the king who appointed them as his cupbearers. Before long they rendered the king unconscious with drugged wine. Amar then let his warriors out of the chests who began slaughtering the dwellers of the fortress. The populace received reprieve by converting to the True Faith. King Jamshed and vizier Haman were also ennobled by converting to the True Faith.

When Hurmuz and Faramurz received news of Amar taking the fortress of Talva Bahar, they moved their army near it and sent the news to Naushervan.

Upon receiving the message from the princes Naushervan bitterly lamented that Amar's menace had not been eliminated. Bakhtak told the emperor that it was on account of the emperor's reliance on Buzurj- mehr's advice that he had always met with reverses and that Hamza had died long ago but Buzurjmehr falsely maintained that he was still alive. Bakhtak told the emperor that his skills in geomancy were superior to Buzurjmehr's and offered to be tested in a competition between the two. Buzurjmehr accepted the wager: the loser would be given into the power of the winner to do with him as the winner pleased. It was decided that a gravid cow would be brought before them and each of them would fore- tell the color of the unborn calf.

While Bakhtak predicted that the calf was black with a white fore- head, Buzurjmehr maintained that the calf was black with white legs. Buzurjmehr had correctly predicted all details but when the calf was brought out, the caul covering his forehead deceived everyone into believing that it was white.

Buzurjmehr was given into Bakhtak's power who wanted to kill him. His wife stopped him from that, and Bakhtak had to satisfy himself by lining Buzurjmehr's eyes with indigo and blinding him. Nausherван dis- covered the truth about the calf too late and severely punished Bakhtak.

Buzurjmehr then took the emperor's leave and went away to Basra after telling him that Hamza's return from Qaf was imminent and when that happened the heads of the kings of the East would be sent in the emperor's court, a horse would make a night raid on Nausherван's camp, and the following morning Hamza would hand him a resounding defeat.

After Buzurjmehr's departure, Bakhtak regained his influence in Nausherван's court. He finally persuaded the emperor to lead the cam- paign against Amar, and Nausherван marched on Talva Bahar with hun- dreds of thousands of troops and foot soldiers.

Nausherван's first assault on Amar's fort resulted in thousands of deaths of his men, and he retreated to reconsider his options.

Amar decided to teach Nausherван a lesson. He dressed himself as a juggler and disguised his *ayyars* Abu Saeed Langari and Aba Saeed Kharqa-Posh as beautiful women. They arrived near Nausherван's camp where Amar started beating the drum and the *ayyars* began dancing. Zhopin and Bechin fell prey to the *ayyars'* seductive gestures and praised the dancers so ardently before Nausherван that he sent for them and struck by their beautiful looks himself, appointed them his cupbearers. The *ayyars* soon started passing drugged wine to everyone in the court and they all fell unconscious.

Amar then drugged the attendants and guards outside as well. He shaved Naushervan's berad and whiskers after lathering him up with his urine, stripped him naked and painted his body and face. Then he took off the clothes of everyone including the princes. He disguised Bakhtiarak as a woman and left him in Bakhtak's lap and played the same trick on Zhopin and Bechin. Then Amar and his *ayyars* returned to their fortress. Naushervan was mortified to see his state when he woke up. He severely punished Bakhtak who had led him there and caused him to suffer those disgraces. Naushervan sent letters to the rulers of nearby lands warning them against Amar.

The ruler of Qirwan, Sher Shah Qirwani, colluded with Naushervan's messenger Samawa Ayyar to kidnap Mehr-Nigar. Samawa Ayyar infiltrated Amar's fortress and with the help of Mehr-Nigar's cook, Khalifa Bulbul, who had remained a fire-worshipper at heart, kidnapped Mehr-Nigar. However, upon learning that Samawa intended to deliver Mehr-Nigar to Sher Shah Qirwani instead of Naushervan, Khalifa Bulbul tried to stop him. Samawa killed him and then headed for Qirwan carrying Mehr-Nigar.

Amir Hamza appeared in Amar's dream and warned him that Mehr-Nigar had fallen into trouble. When Amar woke up and found Mehr-Nigar missing, he followed the traces left behind by Samawa.

Amar intercepted Samawa in disguise and tried to render him unconscious with drugged water. When Samawa saw through Amar's trick, they fought together and Amar captured Samawa. Amar then returned to his fortress with Mehr-Nigar and had Samawa killed.

Sher Shah Qirwani commended Amar's efforts and praised his cunning. He thought of offering his friendship to Amar. At that moment his commander in chief, Piran Maghrebi, advised against it and suggested that he lead the campaign against Amar. Sher Shah sent the message to Naushervan that the battle drums should be beaten proclaiming the name of Piran Maghrebi.

OF AMIR HAMZA'S ARRIVAL AT THE DOMICILE OF SAMANDOON HAZAR-DAST DEV, AND OF HIS FREEING ZEHRA MISRI FROM HIS CLUTCHES

The transcriber writes that the Sahibqiran started from the shores of the Caspian Sea and on the tenth day he approached a castle. He said to Khvaja Aashob, "Go forth and find out whether the castle is inhabited or not." Khvaja Aashob went into the castle armed with a dagger and found the place inhabited. In the bustling marketplace Khvaja Aashob made inquiries from a shopkeeper, but received no answer despite repeated requests. Then Khvaja Aashob grew furious and dealt him a blow of the dagger, cutting the shopkeeper in two.

The moment he killed the man, the other shopkeepers charged him from all sides. Upon hearing Khvaja Aashob's cry for help, Amir Hamza rushed to his assistance. Khvaja Bahlol, Khvaja Aashob, and Ashqar were all separated from him. Amir's charge propelled him into the palace, where those with whom he fought would not set foot for fear of offending the royal honor.

Amir found that Khvaja Aashob, Khvaja Bahlol, Ashqar, and another person were held captive there by Khalkhal Dev. It turned out that the other captive was the king of that land. Amir killed Khalkhal Dev and restored the king to this throne. The king ordered seven days of celebrations in Amir's honor, and on the eighth day Amir took his leave and departed.

On the twenty-first day after traveling from there, Amir saw a building with ramparts shaped like dragons. As its gates were locked, Amir broke them open with his mace and went inside and found a delicately constructed marble enclosure. He stepped inside this and found a refreshing garden. Amir sat down under a tree while the boys played. Khvaja Aashob and Khvaja Bahlol came upon a summerhouse and walked inside without a thought. They saw a baby *dev* sleeping in a golden cradle while a woman whose aspect was as beautiful as the sun rocked the cradle with a golden cord. When she spotted the boys, she said, "Get away quickly, for he has cried himself to sleep from hunger. If he wakes up, he will eat you alive."

The boys said to her, "We are in the company of the Terror of God! We have not the least fear of him or even his elder!"

The woman, who was none other than Zehra Misri, wondered if the man they had called the Terror of God was the Sahibqiran. She said to the boys, "Take a message to the man who accompanies you that Zehra Misri is imprisoned here!" Khvaja Aashob and Khvaja Bahlol took the message to Amir, who rushed in panic toward the summerhouse the moment he heard Zehra Misri's name, thinking that if she had ended up in Qaf, God alone knew what had happened to Mehr-Nigar. When he went inside the summerhouse, he saw that the woman was indeed Zehra Misri. Amir broke into tears then asked her what had happened to her, whereupon she told him her whole story and then said, "Now I am a prisoner of this filthy *dev*. If the Sahibqiran were to come here, I would soon find release because he has conquered the entire land of Qaf."

Amir said to her, "Do you recognize the Sahibqiran?" She answered, "Of course I recognize him, for I have been in his service for years." Then Amir removed his headgear and showed her his Ibrahimi ringlets. The moment she saw them, Zehra Misri rushed forward and fell at Amir's feet, crying.

The baby *dev* awoke from his sleep from the noise of her crying and saw humans standing all about him. He rushed toward Amir from the pain of his hunger so that he might eat him and fill up his belly. Amir caught him and tore him apart like an old cloth and then smashed his skull against the ground.

Samandoon Hazar-Dast Dev was already furious to see the enclosure's broken door. When he found his son lying dead, his rage knew no bounds. Samandoon Hazar-Dast picked up a thousand stones in his thousand hands and flung them all at Amir at once. Amir jumped behind the *dev*'s back with a single leap and, crying "God is great!," brought down the Aqrab-e Suleimani on his shoulders. It severed his five hundred shoulders but Samandoon escaped with his life. After a moment, however, he returned whole of body and attacked Amir as before. As before, Amir cut off his five hundred arms from the shoulders. The *dev* again ran away with his arms and soon returned whole of body and renewed his attack as before.

Then Amir began to pray, and the holy Khizr appeared and said to him, "O Sahibqiran, there exists a spring whose waters God has invested with the property to alleviate pain, cure injuries, and heal wounds. I will make it disappear so that the *dev* can be killed." Amir accompanied Prophet Khizr to that spring and beheld that it was the very Spring of Life. Holy Khizr stomped his foot on the ground and thus caused the spring to disappear. Then Khizr broke two leaves from a tree that stood by the spring and said, "Carry these leaves with you and put their sap into Buzurjmehr's eyes so that his sight is restored."

Amir Hamza put those leaves inside his headpiece and said, "Please do me the kindness of returning me again to that garden." The holy Khizr took him there and then disappeared. The next time Samandoon Hazar-Dast returned wounded to the spring and could not find it, he let out a terrible cry and fell dead.[10]

Amir meanwhile discovered some chambers in that garden, and upon opening them, found them full of all kinds of wondrous jewels. The boys said, "We must take some of these jewels from here." Amir smiled and said, "If you took them to the world and showed them off, my brother Amar would snatch them from you."

Amir Hamza spent two days in that garden. On the third day he put the boys into the panniers and Zehra Misri on the saddle and then headed onward. On the eleventh day he reached the deep sea and wondered how he could cross its waters since he had neither a boat nor a vessel. Amir was occupied with these concerns when the holy Khizr appeared and miraculously took them all across the sea. The next day Amir reached the place where he had killed Rahdar Dev. He found the door of the enclosure open and realized then that it must be Friday, as the gates opened only on that day. Amir recited a benediction for Prophet Nuh's descendant Saalim at his grave.

Amir started off from there and said, "By the grace of God Almighty! The frontiers of Qaf have ended today and I have been delivered from my troubles."

Amir and his companions proceeded on their way and passed by the mountain range, plucking and sharing the fruit from the trees. As he stood under a mountain, looking for some place to spend the night, Amir heard a voice call out to him, "Peace be with you!" Amir's eyes caught sight of a tree that stood before him. He saw that the fruits of that tree were shaped liked human heads and that it was from that tree that the greeting had come. Amir returned the greeting. Then the voice called out, "O Sahibqiran, my name is Waq and once upon a time Sikander himself rested in my shade for the night. Just as I hosted him once, I will host you this day and it will be a pleasure for me to arrange a feast for you. Pray stay here for the length of the night and enjoy the sights and the sounds of this place."

After this conversation, a fruit fell into Amir's lap, which Amir carved and shared with Zehra Misri and the boys. He found the fruit tastier than any other fruit he had eaten in the past and it fully sated him. Amir then lay down under the tree. The whole night the tree and Amir conversed together and the tree regaled Amir with his sweet speech. Amir asked the tree, "O tree, tell me when I will die." The tree answered, "When Ashqar's hooves lose all their shoes, you should recognize that it is time for you to leave the world."

When it was morning, Amir took his leave of the tree and started out again. On the eighth day they arrived at a city whose ruler was a woman named Shirin. She greeted the Sahibqiran and conducted him into the city and held a royal feast in his honor. When the Sahibqiran noticed that there were no men to be seen in the city and he asked her the reason. Shirin answered, "A male child is never born to the women of this city." Amir said, "How do the women become impregnated?" She answered, "When a girl reaches puberty, she goes to embrace a tree outside the city, which bears neither flower nor fruit. During the embrace she lets out a scream and is taken unconscious. She regains her consciousness after some time and at that moment the seed begins to grow in her womb and in due time she bears a girl child."

Upon hearing this Amir marveled at God's enterprise. He found every woman there a paragon of beauty. The boys said to Amir, "The women of this city are extremely pretty. We should take some of them along with us." Shirin said, "The women of this city cannot leave its precincts, for God has appointed a guardian over them. Even if she does leave the guardian brings her back." The boys replied, "This is all idle talk. Send them with us and no one will be able to snatch them from us." Shirin tried to convince them, but the boys did not listen to her.

So, with Shirin's permission they took fifty women with them. In the evening, Amir stopped to rest and spend the night. When he woke up in the morning he found that half of the women had disappeared. The boys then regretted not heeding Shirin's advice and having therefore unnecessarily put themselves in her debt. That night the boys fastened a rope around the waists of the remaining women, and tied the other end to themselves, thinking that they would be unable to disappear and would not be able to leave them as the others had earlier. Then they lay down to rest and were soon lost to sleep.

It so happened that the Simurgh's wife was the guardian God had appointed on those women. She plucked them all up and rose several yards above the ground. Now, the boys, too, were dangling from the rope with them, and they began shouting and screaming in fear. When Amir arose from his sleep, he saw someone taking away the women. Thinking that this was the work of some *dev*, Amir shot an arrow, which pierced the shoulder of the Simurgh's wife. She swooped down with the women and said, "O Sahibqiran! What crime did I commit against you that you shot me with an arrow? Is this how you return the kindness that my husband did you? I have been appointed by God to ensure that these women do not leave their city."

The Sahibqiran felt most embarrassed upon finding that it was the Simurgh's wife he had shot. He offered her an apology and prayed fervently and devotedly to God to make her shoulder well. Amir's prayer was received with favor in the Court of Heaven and the wound of the Simurgh's wife healed and no pain lingered. Then she took her leave of Amir and departed with the women.

AN ACCOUNT OF THE PRINCE OF *AYYARS*, KHVAJA AMAR BIN UMAYYA ZAMIRI

The emperor gave Piran Maghrebi leave to charge the castle and he headed for the fortress with his two hundred thousand troops. At that moment a dust cloud rose from the direction of the jungle and Naqabdar Naranji-Posh soon arrived with his forty thousand riders. In the combat between Piran Maghrebi and the Naqabdar, Piran was killed. Piran's army fell on the Naqabdar, and Naushervan's armies also came to their assistance, ready to battle and slaughter. The Naqabdar kept his advantage, however, and cut down the foe and then disappeared into the forest with his forty thousand troops.

Amar had the drums of victory sounded from the ramparts of his fortress and offered thanks to the Creator.

That same day, the king of the fortress of Tanj-e Maghreb, Misqal Shah, presented himself into Naushervan's service and offered him many reassurances that the next day he would win the fortress for the emperor. Then he got busy preparing a feast for the emperor.

Now hear of Amar. When he heard that Misqal Shah had ordered a feast for the emperor, he prepared a deception and during the feast attacked the enemy camp. Muqbil made Amir Hamza's war cries, Aadi pretended to be Landhoor, and Sultan Bakht Maghrebi called out Bahram's war cries. Then Amar rolled out *devs* made of paper to frighten Naushervan's army. They became convinced that Hamza had returned from Qaf with an army of *devs* and turned tail. Amar Ayyar looted the enemy camp and then ordered his army to head for Misqal Shah's fortress of Tanj-e Maghreb. He forged a letter to deceive Misqal Shah's vizier and captured the fortress. When Naushervan learned of Amar's deception he followed him and laid siege to the fortress of Tanj-e Maghreb.

Amar Ayyar gathered all his commanders and told them that as the eighteenth year was coming to an end without any signs of Hamza's return, they needed to tighten their belts and go with half their usual rations until there was some improvement in their circumstances. Everyone except Aadi agreed, who left after telling Amar that he would die of starvation if his already meager rations were halved. Then Aadi went and joined Naushervan's service, where he was fed to his heart's content and appointed to guard duty. While on guard duty, Aadi killed a woman in the act of ravishing her and left Naushervan's camp in fear of punishment and rode out to the forest. The next day he felt hungry and roasted the horse and ate it. From there he headed onward and came across a group of fakirs whom he astounded with his great appetite. Then Aadi moved on and arrived in a city where he started ransacking food shops to satisfy his hunger.

The commotion in the marketplace attracted the attention of King Me'aad Shah Maghrebi who offered Aadi employment and his daughter's hand in marriage if he consented to fight the followers of the True Faith. Aadi also agreed to the custom of the land which stipulated that when a spouse died, the surviving husband or wife was buried along with the dead. It so happened that in the act of sexual congress, Aadi killed his wife, who was no match for Aadi's bulk and size, and when she was taken for burial in the morning, the people also caught Aadi and tried to force him into the grave. While Aadi resisted them, Amir Hamza arrived on the scene and the boys brought him the news of the incident.

Amir Hamza met Aadi and revealed his identity and defended Aadi against the horde. King Me'aad Shah Maghrebi confronted Amir Hamza but was killed by his hand and his vizier, Aqil Khan, converted to the True Faith and sought reprieve for the populace. He sent Me'aad Shah's head to Naushervan while Amir headed for the fortress of Tanj-e Maghreb after learning from Aadi that Amar, Mehr-Nigar, and his companions were lodged there.

Amir Hamza went forward alone to check the fortress with Ashqar and saw Amar Ayyar installed in the fortress with great glory, and Naushervan's army besieging the place. Amir Hamza laughed at this vision of Amar's glory and sat down under the wall of the fortress spreading his wolves' skins. He addressed Ashqar in the language of the jinns, saying, "Go to the fields that are behind the fortress to graze as you please, but do not let anyone catch you." Ashqar then headed for the plains and did as Amir had instructed him.

Now hear of the King of Ayyars. That day he had gone to meet Mehr-Nigar and both he and the princess shed many tears of sorrow.

Mehr-Nigar said to Amar, "Today it has been full eighteen years since Amir departed." Amar said, "The evening of the day is yet far away. It is not at all beyond the power of the Almighty Lord to send Amir in safety and peace to you before the day is out. Take yourself to the roof of the fortress and take some fresh air."

Amar's suggestion pleased Mehr-Nigar and she did as he bid her. She went to the roof of the fortress and began admiring the bloom of the flowers and the grassy plain. It so happened that a flock of black-barred geese came flying overhead. Mehr-Nigar shot an arrow at them saying to herself, *If this hits a bird in the middle it would be an omen that I am destined to meet Hamza today, and I will see him and receive bliss from his sight and hold him in my arms after all this time.* Her arrow pierced the wing of a goose flying in the middle and the bird fell right before Amir Hamza. He slaughtered the bird and put it aside. Reading Mehr-Nigar's name on the arrowhead, he began kissing it with amorous fervor.

Amar witnessed this and became enraged at the man's actions. He walked up to him and said, "O wicked fakir! You do not know the majesty of the name written on the arrowhead that you so shamelessly kiss. Come, give me the arrow! I have forgiven you on this occasion since you are a mendicant, but if you show impertinence again in this manner, you will receive your due punishment." Amir Hamza replied, "Do not waste my time with this idle talk. Go and frighten someone who will believe you. A common *ayyar* like yourself will never frighten me."

Amar grew furious at these words and, untying the sling from his head and loading it with a carved and polished stone, let fly at Amir Hamza. But Amir Hamza dodged it. Then he threw it at Amar who realized that the fakir was no easy prey and that he could not prevail over him with violence. To obtain the arrow from him, Amar thought of tempting him with money. Amar approached Hamza and said, "I will give you five hundred rupees if you hand over the arrow to me!" Hamza did not consent to the proposal. Then Amar said, "Take a thousand rupees and give me the arrow!" Amir answered, "In Qaf I scattered such amounts to common folk on account of Hamza. I do not think you can impress me with your wealth with offers of such paltry sums!"

Amar sat down when he heard those words and asked, "How long ago was it that you saw Hamza?" Amir Hamza answered, "Just six months ago." Amar inquired, "Was there anything that Amir told you?" Hamza answered, "As I was leaving he asked me to send his greetings to his father and give him the news of his welfare." Amar asked, "Did he say anything else?" Hamza answered, "Yes, he also told me that should I meet his companions I should convey to them his fond wishes!" Amar asked, "Did he send any other messages for anyone else?" Hamza answered, "There is a message that he enjoined me to convey to Mehr-Nigar, his rosy-cheeked beloved and faithful lover!" Amar said, "Pray do not make delay and tell me what it was." Amir said, "I shall not tell you and go against his wishes. I shall only whisper it in Mehr-Nigar's ears." Amar answered, "How can Mehr-Nigar appear before you? She remains behind the veil and is a person of great dignity and majesty!" Hamza answered, "Very well, then! If she does not wish to hear it, I have no desire to convey it to her either."

Amar was thus forced to go before Mehr-Nigar. When he entered the palace he saw signs of celebration. Everyone was beside themselves with joy and seemed jubilant and happy. Amar inquired, "What is the cause for this jubilation? Has it been occasioned by some happy tidings someone has brought?" Princess Mehr-Nigar answered, "I shot an arrow at a goose to determine my lot of destiny and learn my fortune. That arrow pierced the wing of the goose, but the bird pierced with the arrow has fallen near the fortress walls. Pray fetch it from there and do me this kindness. I have often tried and tested this method of determining my fate and found it reliable and true. By all means Amir will arrive this evening, and for certain I will be reunited with him today."

Amar said to himself that it was for the best that Mehr-Nigar's attention was finally diverted. Mehr-Nigar again said to Amar, "Khvaja, the bird I shot with my arrow has fallen under the castle wall. Kindly fetch it yourself or send someone to bring it!" Amar answered, "A fakir arrived today and sat down under the wall. The bird pierced with the arrow fell before him and he slaughtered it and kept it. He is holding the arrow in his hand. He states that he has come from Qaf with a message from Amir for you, which he will whisper only in your ears in exact fulfillment of Amir Hamza's wishes. He will give me neither the arrow nor the message from Hamza."

Upon hearing Amar's words, Mehr-Nigar's anxiety grew ten-fold. She said to Amar, "Khvaja! For God's sake send that fakir into my presence without delay!" Amar brought Hamza into the palace and seated him in front of a curtain and said, "O fakir! Mehr-Nigar is sitting behind this curtain. Now you may convey to her Hamza's message." Amir said, "Hamza made me swear on his head that I should whisper his message in Mehr-Nigar's ear alone. If she wishes to hear the message, she must come before me, otherwise I will depart this instant." At this, Amir Hamza rose.

Unable to think of anything else, Amar went behind the curtain and brought out Fitna Bano, the daughter of Mehr-Nigar's nanny, draped in a mantle. He presented her to Amir Hamza and said, "O dervish, the rosy-cheeked beloved and Hamza's faithful lover is standing before you. Speak what you must and do not remain silent even a moment longer." Amir Hamza replied, "Let her show me her face so that I can ascertain whether it is Princess Mehr-Nigar." When Amar removed the veil from Fitna Bano's face, Amir Hamza said, "This is not Mehr-Nigar but Fitna Bano. Hamza gave me a description of her as well and informed me about her." Having no further ruse or pretext to remain concealed, Mehr-Nigar appeared before Amir Hamza herself and was forced to expose her face to him. Amir saw her miserable state, her wan face, her dry lips, her tearful eyes, and the grimy clothes in which she was dressed. Tears welled up in Amir's eyes also to witness her condition, but he successfully hid them from the others so that his identity was not revealed.

Amar said, "O dervish, this is Mehr-Nigar! Now say what you wish to say." Hamza answered, "I would still make the same condition I made before. I shall whisper Hamza's message into Mehr-Nigar's ear." Amar was enraged and sent for Muqbil and a few other commanders and said to them, "Stand ready outside the chamber with drawn swords. The moment the fakir emerges, kill him and cut him into pieces." Then Mehr-Nigar bent her head close and brought her ear near Amir's lips. Amir Hamza said in a whisper, "O life of Hamza, it is not some fakir but I myself." At these words, he removed his headgear and Mehr-Nigar saw the dark mole, the Hashimi vein, and the Ibrahimi ringlet. The moment she saw them, Mehr-Nigar let out a cry, Amir also exclaimed a sigh, and both were taken unconscious, for the ardor of their passion had made them lose possession of their senses.

When Amar looked closely at Amir's forehead he finally recognized that the fakir was Hamza in person.

The unconscious couple slowly regained consciousness before his eyes. Hamza embraced Amar and Muqbil and showed great favor to everyone. He broke into tears, and everyone cried copious tears of joy along with him. Jubilation spread within and without the castle.

The narrator tells that the noise of congratulations and felicitations and the music reached Naushervan's ears, and his *ayyars* told him that

Hamza's return had been announced, at which Bakhtak said, "Your Honor, it might very well be another one of Amar's tricks!" But Buzurjmehr said, "According to my calculations it is very probable that Hamza has arrived and that is why I have returned from Basra to meet him!"

———

Now hear of Ashqar Devzad. When he headed into the forest he beheld Nausherван's horses grazing there as well. This made him furious and he killed some of them with his hooves, and the others who tried to confront him were badly injured. The few who remained galloped toward their camp with Ashqar in pursuit. It was evening and the unnerved horses flooded into their camp, causing the tent ropes to snap and the ropes to drop from people's hands. People rushed to catch Ashqar, but he tore them apart with his jaws and disemboweled them with his hooves. He severed their heads with his powerful kicks and with his teeth he relieved their necks of the burden of their heads. Men fell on their faces to the ground and Ashqar killed thousands in the camp of the infidels. Nausherван's army thought that Hamza's forces had made a night raid on their camp. They armed themselves and, confusing their own army for the army of Hamza, killed and slaughtered one another until morning. When they looked around in the morning, they saw not a single enemy among the dead, and found not a single casualty except their own. When Nausherван beheld Ashqar, he was captivated by the sight of the majestic steed. He ordered that every effort be made to catch the horse. But Ashqar severely injured anyone who attempted to capture him.

Meanwhile, Amir Hamza said to Amar, "The whole night a commotion has been heard from Nausherван's camp that has continued until now. Find out what it is all about and the reason for the racket." At that moment an *ayyar* presented himself and gave a detailed account of what had passed in Nausherван's camp. Hamza said to Amar, "He is my horse. Go and say to him, 'O son of Arnais and Laneesa, the Sahibqiran has sent for you.' He will accompany you directly!" Following Amir's orders, Amar gave the message to Ashqar and the horse followed him quietly. Amir came down from the fortress and embraced Ashqar and praised Amar before him and said to the horse, "O Ashqar, Amar will take care of you and look after your every comfort."

The next day Aadi Madi-Karib arrived there with Zehra Misri, Khvaja Aashob, and Khvaja Bahlol. Amir sent Zehra Misri to Mehr-Nigar inside the fortress. Amir kept Khvaja Aashob and Khvaja Bahlol in his own company. Amir Hamza made Amar and Aadi embrace each other and renew their friendship. Then he said to Amar, "Aasman Peri will bring you many gifts from Qaf that will please you greatly!" The news made Amar very happy. He blessed Amir Hamza and in all love and sincerity offered to sacrifice himself to ward off any calamities from Hamza's head.

• • •

The third book is ended. God willing, the remainder of the narrative will be given in Book Four.

BOOK FOUR

The Beginning of the Fourth Book of the Dastan *of the Sahibqiran,
the Conqueror of the World, the Quake of Qaf, the Latter-day Suleiman,
Amir Hamza the Magnificent, Son of Khvaja Abdul Muttalib*

The warriors of the field of fables and the soldiers of the domain of legends thus gallop on the steeds of pens across the arena of the page to reveal that when Naushervan and Bakhtak and other nobles of his court learned of Hamza's arrival from Qaf, Bakhtak said to the emperor, "Hamza has returned from Qaf after eighteen years and did not pay his respects to Your Honor. He wishes to take the daughter of the Emperor of the Seven Concentric Circles by might. It would be most judicious to sound the drums of war and confront him, as he has returned worn and exhausted, and Your Honor has a force of intrepid warriors at your command." Duped by Bakhtak's words, Naushervan ordered the war drums beaten. Upon hearing this, the Sahibqiran, too, ordered the call answered from his camp. When the battle arrays were drawn, a Sassanid warrior named Koh-Paikar came forward to challenge Amir. After a long fight, Amir finally killed him.

The moment Koh-Paikar fell dead to the ground, Naushervan called out to his army, "Do not let this Arab escape alive!" The moment the orders were given, the army fell upon Amir Hamza, and the armies of the True Faith also charged forward bellowing "God is great!" The deafening clang of swords filled the field where forty thousand of Naushervan's men were cut down in the course of one hour. Naushervan's army beat a retreat, unable to withstand the blinding glimmer of the swords of the soldiers of the True Faith. Breaking with custom, Amir gave chase to the retreating army and kept cutting through swaths of them with his sword, following them up to a distance of four *kos*.

After God had sent him triumph and victory, Amir returned to the pavilion of Jamshed.[1] Preparations for a feast were made, and before long the spring of song bubbled forth, music enveloped them, and the place rang with the sound of festivities.

The narrator has said that after the festivities were over, Amir Hamza asked Amar what had passed with him in his absence. Amar related everything to him in detail. Amir Hamza sent for Khvaja Aashob and Khvaja Bahlol, and asked them what they wished to do now. They answered, "We would like to become merchants." Amir gave them gold pieces and bid them adieu and wrote them a note to the effect that they should never be interrupted in the course of their business.

Next, Amir asked Amar, "Did Landhoor or Bahram ever come to visit you in my absence and bring you any gifts?" Amar answered, "Many a time I wrote to them describing the vulnerability of my situation, but I never received a reply." Then Amar told him about the Naqabdar clad in an orange veil that would come to his aid with his forty thousand troops. Upon hearing this account, Amir became furious with rage and said, "From today onward, if I hear anyone even mention Landhoor or Bahram's name in my camp, I will have the speaker's tongue extracted from his neck and will visit a terrible punishment on him."

————

When the news of Amir Hamza's return reached Ceylon, Landhoor and Bahram were overjoyed. Landhoor said to Bahram, "We have been in this land some twenty or twenty-two years. There was no end to the terrors the infidels visited on Amar, yet none of us were able to bring him any aid. I am sure that the story of our indolence must grieve Amir no end. Come what may, we must present ourselves now before the Sahibqiran to kiss his feet and seek his forgiveness. If we fail to do so, people will brand us as ingrates." Bahram replied, "Very well." Bahram headed for China and Landhoor put in place a valiant force against his enemy, the Sagsars, and arrived at Amir's court within a few days.

After allowing Landhoor to see him, Amir censured him publicly. Landhoor recounted his adventures and offered many apologies to Amir, and he apprised Amir of Bahram's circumstances as well. Then Amir pardoned him and seated him by his side and restored him to the rank of his companion. Amir then asked Amar, "Do you have any news of where Naushervan has escaped to?" Amar folded his arms humbly and replied, "He has gone to Maghreb, whose king deputized one of his commanders with an army of five hundred thousand warriors to assist him." Amir then ordered, "Proclaim it to our soldiers that they should make ready to overwhelm Naushervan's army!" The royal pavilion was set up where Amir had indicated and all preparations were made for revels. The Sahibqiran and his worthy and venerable champions entered the court and all of them indulged in that assembly of revelry. The Sahibqiran was occupied with these matters when his *ayyars* brought intelligence that Muqbil Vafadar was on his way there, having taken captive both Prince Hurmuz and the ill-fated Bakhtak.

Be it known that the day the pitched battle was fought, Prince Hurmuz and the wily Bakhtak had sneaked away with five thousand troops in the middle of the war to seize Mehr-Nigar from the fortress. There Muqbil lay in wait for them with his forty thousand archers. He slaughtered the enemy force and took Hurmuz and Bakhtak prisoner. He now led them before Amir Hamza, who expressed great pleasure at the valuable work done by Muqbil.

The Sahibqiran said to Hurmuz, "If you will convert to the True Faith, you can have this throne and empire and rule it happily." Bakhtak, whose heart was fast sinking, told himself that Hurmuz was destined to receive whatever fate had in store for the prince, but his own survival surely did not seem at all likely. He made a signal to Hurmuz and the two of them pretended to convert to the True Faith and enter its fellowship. The Sahibqiran surrendered the throne to Hurmuz and made him the king of his armies. He appointed Bakhtak his vizier and counselor in all matters big and small. Amir was overjoyed and he ordered festive music to start playing.

Three days later, Amir was happily admiring the view of the green expanse that stretched around him when three beautiful peacocks descended from the sky. Amir dispatched Muqbil Vafadar and Amar Ayyar to investigate the occurrence, whereupon the peacocks disappeared into thin air. The narrator tells that those peacocks were in fact Abdur Rahman Jinn, Salasal Perizad, and Akvana Peri who had been sent by Aasman Peri disguised as peacocks to bring her news of Amir Hamza.

After some time passed, they presented themselves before Amir Hamza, in their true shape, and after making obeisance gave him news of Aasman Peri's arrival. Amir was delighted to see them and said to Amar, "Congratulations are in order because Aasman Peri has arrived with great fanfare bearing gifts from Qaf for you." Amar was most pleased to hear these happy tidings. The whole night was spent in festive assembly and in the morning Amir Hamza got ready and mounted his steed to go welcome Aasman Peri.

When Amir arrived at the Pavilion of Suleiman, Aasman Peri came with Quraisha to the entrance of the pavilion to greet Amir, and with a small laugh, addressed Amir thus: "You left us behind so we came by ourselves to visit you. We have also brought wedding gifts for Mehr-Nigar."

Amir said, "Give me the details now of all you have brought with you, and present everything to me." Aasman Peri answered, "I have brought the Pavilion of Suleiman, the Music Band of Suleiman, the tent of the Char-Bazar of Bilqis,[2] all kinds of jewels, and other gifts from Qaf." Amir was delighted with it all. He kissed Quraisha's forehead and embraced her, and he also embraced Aasman Peri and kissed her many times. All the *devs, peris,* and jinns who had accompanied Aasman Peri presented themselves and made obeisance to Amir, who looked upon them with favor and inquired after the welfare of each one of them individually. Then Amir said to Aasman Peri, "In Qaf, I often used to mention the name of Amar Ayyar to you. He has come with me, desirous to see you and make you an offering." Aasman Peri said, "Send for Amar Ayyar and present him before us."

As Amar entered that place, his senses took flight when he regarded the beauty and splendor of that unique and exquisite royal pavilion. But when Amar looked around, he saw no one but Hamza, and said, "Where is the queen of the heavens whose praises you used to sing? I would like to see the face of that beauty who kept your heart occupied in Qaf for a full eighteen years and snared you in her love." Amir answered, "Queen Aasman Peri is giving audience on the throne, O Amar. It is a thing to marvel at that you have not offered her your salutations!" Amar said, "I cannot see anyone to whom I may offer my greetings. My salutations are not so worthless as to be given freely to an empty throne and chairs." Aasman Peri ordered her attendants to put the collyrium of Suleiman into Amar's right eye and let him see the wonders that it would reveal. Be it known that when this collyrium is put in one's right eye *devs* become visible, and when it is applied to one's left eye one can see *peris* and *perizads*. When the collyrium was put into Amar's right eye, he instantly could see the faces of the *devs* who thronged about him. Amar was seized by terror at seeing them, and said to Amir, "Which one of them is the queen and your dear wife?" Amir Hamza laughed at Amar's words and Aasman Peri also shook with laughter. Then she ordered that Amar's left eye should also be lined with collyrium so that he could at last see her.

When his left eye was lined, Amar saw the *peris* and the *perizads* assembled there, and he also saw a woman whose beauty was as luminescent as the sun seated with great majesty and glory on the throne. Beside her was a girl whose face bore a striking resemblance to Amir and whose beauty struck its beholders with wonderment. Amar said to himself that the girl must be Amir's daughter. He approached the throne, made a salutation to

Aasman Peri, and said to the Sahibqiran, "Is this the Queen Aasman Peri for whom you wasted eighteen years in Qaf? May God protect us from the devil, I myself would not have spent even a single day there for someone so plain looking and put up with all those hardships. In fact I would not even let her carry the water bowl to my toilet chamber."

These words mortified Aasman Peri with shame, and tears welled up in her eyes. Amir said to her in the Jinni language, "Do not become sad at his words. He is a clown, and everything he said was in jest. Make him an offering of something, and then you will see how he undergoes a complete change." Aasman Peri did as Amir had told her and offered Amar a decorated robe of honor along with some jewels and gold pieces. Amar put the robe of honor on and made a bow and then said, "O Sahibqiran, I suspected from the start that you had found a moonfaced beauty in Qaf and that was why you were unwilling to return to the world of humans. Before I beheld this woman, I thought that Mehr-Nigar was the only paragon of beauty in the world and the very soul of charm. But after regarding this luminous sun of beauty, I realize that our princess cannot rightfully be judged even a ray of light compared to this one's resplendence. Before such a comely and charming face— whose luster and delicacy would shame the sun and would embarrass the glowing moon to show its face—Mehr-Nigar's charm cannot at all compete."

Aasman Peri was charmed and delighted by Amar's words. She laughed and said, "What a turncoat!" Then she showered Amar with jewels and gifts from Qaf that satisfied even Amar's insatiable greed. Thereafter, Aasman Peri sent for the commanders and chiefs of Amir's camp and offered each one a robe of honor commensurate with his rank, and lavished gifts and gold pieces on each of them. She said to Amir, "Order your attendants to make preparations for your wedding to Mehr-Nigar and to arrange all the necessities for the ceremonies. Although I have brought the wedding paraphernalia from Qaf I am not familiar with the rituals and ceremonies of your land. I will be on hand to facilitate and enliven the ceremonies." Amir Hamza spent three days with Aasman Peri and returned to his camp on the fourth day, unable to tear himself away from her sooner.

Then Amir went before Mehr-Nigar and broke his pleasant news to her, addressing her sweetly, "Aasman Peri has brought you all the accoutrements of marriage from Qaf, among which are many rare and delicate gifts, and she exhorts me to make no further delay in getting married but to do it as soon as possible." Mehr-Nigar lowered her head from modesty and did not answer. Amir Hamza then went before Prince Hurmuz and gave the same account to him with all necessary details. Next, he ordered the gongs to be struck to announce the impending ceremony. Amir then wrote a missive to Naushervan that read:

> In effect, you already gave me the hand of Mehr-Nigar, but due to the vagaries of time and the tide of events, I was kept from solemnizing the marriage. I am writing to let you know that yours truly is solemnizing his marriage with Mehr-Nigar and is hopeful that you will give your permission for it to proceed. It would be unimaginable for us not to receive the gift of your presence in this heavenly assembly and joyous gathering. It would not be too much to expect of your munificence that you would consent to attend this ceremony and thus honor your humble servant.

Amar Ayyar took Hamza's note to Naushervan, who read it and asked Amar, "I have heard that Aasman Peri has arrived there with much fanfare bearing wedding articles and mementoes from Qaf for Mehr-Nigar. Is the news true or false?" Amar answered, "The news is absolutely true." In the meanwhile a note also arrived for Naushervan from Hurmuz and Bakhtak that read: "Your Honor should not hold back permission to Hamza so that you are not accused of going back on your word. Even without your permission he will marry Mehr-Nigar and that would show Your Honor a dishonor." Naushervan gave his consent for the marriage to proceed, but declined the invitation to attend himself. Later, however, he changed his mind at the persuasion of his nobles and told Amar Ayyar that he would attend the ceremony disguised as a begger.

The narrator of the *dastan* tells that Amir Hamza was delighted to receive a positive answer to his missive and showed it to everyone present. He embraced Buzurjmehr, and then with his own hands he squeezed the juice of the leaves that the holy Khizr had given him. When he applied this to Buzurjmehr's eyes, they instantly regained their sight. Buzurjmehr congratulated Amir on the auspicious occasion of his wedding and the musicians struck up playing nuptial tunes. On the day of his wedding procession, Amir dressed in a royal robe and mounted Ashqar Devzad. Kings and princes from all over the world formed a procession with Amir Hamza's steed in the middle, and they went forth scattering gold and jewels over his head as the sacrifice of his life.

Amir's procession arrived with great fanfare at the Pavilion of Suleiman, where he alighted. The *peris* danced as Amir Hamza ascended the throne and sat beside Prince Hurmuz. Aasman Peri went with Quraisha and her attendants and adorned Mehr-Nigar with inestimable and precious jewels the likes of which none but the wives of the emperors of Qaf had ever seen, and beautified her with the seven adornments. Mehr-Nigar's beauty robbed Aasman Peri of her senses and faculties; she fell in love with her charm instantly. Before long Aasman Peri had thrown herself completely into the wedding ceremonies.

———

Now hear of Naushervan. He disguised himself like a mendicant, and carrying a stick in his hand, he headed to see the marriage ceremonies in the company of his seven nobles. Amar recognized Naushervan and offered to conduct him into the assembly so he could participate in all of the events, but the emperor would not accept. Then Amar offered to take him to a place where he could observe everything. Naushervan liked that proposition better and gladly agreed.

With a few hours left to the night, Khvaja Buzurjmehr read out the wedding sermon following holy tradition. As it was getting close to dawn, the female quarters buzzed with word of the arrival of the bridegroom. At the first of the seven doors to the women's quarters Amir was accosted by Aasman Peri who closed the door on him and told him that it would only be opened once he had paid the marriage money promised to Mehr-Nigar. Amir settled his pledge by offering Muqbil Vafadar along with forty thousand slaves in golden livery to Mehr-Nigar. At this, Aasman Peri opened the door. Then she closed the second door and asked him for another offering for Mehr-Nigar in return for the privilege to behold her. Amir did as Aasman Peri asked him and offered his sword, the Aqrab-e Suleimani, and his steed Siyah Qitas. In this manner Aasman Peri exacted a toll for Mehr-Nigar at all seven doors of the women's quarters and Amir paid without argument before he was allowed to set foot in Mehr-Nigar's private chamber.

Amir Hamza blossomed forth in smiles upon seeing Mehr-Nigar dressed in wedding costume, sitting among a cluster of moonfaced damsels who were lovely as *peris*. After the rituals were completed, Amir carried Mehr-Nigar to the bedstead. Like the frenzied Majnun he pledged his soul to his Laila and embraced her and sucked the jujube fruit of her lips. After some time had passed, a physical struggle broke out between the bride and the bridegroom, but Amir retrieved the desired pearl from love's sea after offering his bride many words of comfort and consolation, and then he fulfilled his desire with great facility and leisure. By the Grace of God a precious pearl[3] was conceived within the oyster of the sea of love.

In the morning, Amir took a bath and dressed and, smiling and joyous, arrived at the Pavilion of Suleiman. All his courtiers presented themselves to him and received great bliss from his audience. Festivities were held for the rest of the day. In the evening Amir shared his bed with Aasman Peri, and the next day it was Rehan Peri's turn to spend the night with Amir and for him to take his pleasure of her. The next night he slept with Saman Seema Peri and ravished her as well. In this way, Amir took his pleasure of a different woman each night for forty nights and tasted the finest pleasure that life can offer. And during each of those forty days, the kings of Qaf and the princes of the world engaged in festivities with Amir. Aside from pleasure seeking and reveling, all other matters were postponed.

One day, after the conclusion of the festivities, Amir mounted his steed to go to visit the Char-Bazar of Bilqis preceded by heralds and mace bearers. The moment he set foot outside, a *dev* who was the brother of Ra'ad Shatir whom Amir had slain in Qaf descended before him. Finding Amir by himself for a moment, he aimed a blow of his mace at Amir's head. Amir jumped from his saddle and foiled the blow and then, catching the *dev* by his waist, whirled him overhead three times and slammed him to the ground so hard that the *dev* recalled the days of his infancy and all his senses and faculties were dislodged from their stations. He tried to get up and escape, but Amir pressed his one leg underfoot and, holding the other leg in his hands, ripped the *dev*'s body in two with utmost ease like a piece of old cloth, and tore him up in two as if he were made of paper. The onlookers were shocked to immobility by this sight and marveled greatly. All the brave and valiant lords hung their heads in embarrassment at this unsurpassable feat, and Naushervan fainted at this display of Amir's might.

Later, having finished his romp, Amir Hamza returned to his court, where everyone expressed delight at his victory over the *dev*. Amar Ayyar restored Naushervan to his senses by sprinkling rose water and the perfume of orange blossoms over him, and brought him back to his senses. Amar then conducted him before Amir for his leave-taking, and the emperor announced his departure in terms suited to the purpose. Seeing Naushervan clad in the garb of beggars, Amir Hamza gently demanded, "O Emperor of the Princes of Seven Climes, renounce your idol worship and proclaim that there is only one True God. Then I will give myself in service to your most humble servants and will always remain faithful to you." Naushervan did not consent but forthrightly answered, "A change of religion is unacceptable to me! Moreover, it would be unbecoming to the traditions of my dynasty!" In the end, Amir was obliged to present Naushervan with gold and jewels and gifts from Qaf as offerings, and he bestowed Suleiman's robes of honor on the emperor's companions. Naushervan returned to his camp and ordered everyone to assemble and prepare to return to Ctesiphon the next day.

Aasman Peri, meanwhile, made Amir an offering of the gifts she had brought for him especially and then took her leave of him. Amir embraced her and said to her, "I am as happy and grateful to see you as I was once unhappy and discontented with you. You have put me into your debt. Whenever you send for me I will immediately prepare to come to you, provided I am not entangled in some battle here, and will make no delay." Then Amir embraced Quraisha and kissed her forehead and sent them both off with many gifts. Rehan Peri and Saman Seema Peri also took their leave of Amir and departed. The Sahibqiran bestowed all the lands of Maghreb on the King of Tanj-e Maghreb and made him the sovereign of those lands, but the new king appointed a deputy to rule in his stead and joined Amir as his riding companion.

The next day Hamza ordered his advance camp to move toward Mecca and designated Amar Hamza, his son by Naheed Maryam, the daughter of the king of Greece, as the commander of his camp in his stead. Amir then closeted himself with Mehr-Nigar to enjoy the sensual pleasures of life. Amir Hamza surrendered all offices of command and put his son Amar Hamza in charge of them completely.

One day, Amir's son Amar Hamza was busy drinking in the assembly with others when suddenly Aadi knitted his brow and said to Landhoor, "You giant, how did you find the courage to occupy my chair?" Landhoor answered, "You are already out of your depth after guzzling just a few cups, O monster-bellied one! If I sit in this chair it is with permission from the commander!" Aadi called out loudly, "I am sure that the commander has not asked you to warm my seat for me." Landhoor said, "O Aadi, it is not you talking but the wine." Aadi then rose from his place and punched Landhoor. The Khusrau laughed and said, "O Aadi, you should not let this incident drive you mad. Take stock of your senses and control yourself."

When Amar Hamza noticed the situation, he confronted Aadi and said, "Stop this drunken madness and wake up from your egotistical reveries!" Aadi answered him, "This is between Landhoor and me: You have no right to speak in an issue that concerns only the two of us." Amar Hamza rose from his station and punched Aadi so hard that he fell to the ground. Then Aadi started complaining loudly, saying, "If Amir's son feels he has license to humiliate us in this manner, we will not remain long in this court." All the commanders and champion warriors had taken exception to Amar Hamza's actions, and a great din arose from the assembly that brought Amir Hamza out of his bedchamber. When he was informed of the situation he admonished his son and said, "I am warning you never again to act in this manner against anyone here. Landhoor and Aadi would have sorted out the matter between themselves. You had no business interfering in their personal feud." His son flew into a rage and said, "If Aadi ever speaks to me with such impertinence again, I will cut off his ears and drive him away from the camp." Now Amir Hamza became angry and replied, "Hold your tongue! If you use such language again, I will pick you up and smash you on the ground and make your brains flow out of your ears. That will make you forget all your arrogance."

Amar Hamza was in the prime of his youth and his father's words rankled his heart. He shouted, "Who dares to touch me? There is no one who has the guts or the courage!" Furious, Amir Hamza led him by his hand into the arena. Father and son mounted their steeds and prepared for combat. Those present gathered around to see the fight between them. Amir asked his son to begin the combat, and Amar Hamza lashed his horse, but the animal refused to charge. Then Amir Hamza said, "O unwise man, learn comportment from this dumb animal." Amar Hamza left his saddle and Amir also dismounted and prepared for hand-to-hand combat. His son caught hold of Amir Hamza's cummerbund and exerted all his might trying to dislodge him, but was unable to do so. Then he let go his hold in frustration and stepped away, but now Amir caught him in a hold and lifted him over his head. Then he gently put his son down and kissed his forehead. Amir's son prostrated himself at his feet and sought forgiveness for his arrogance. Amir embraced him and said, "O light of my life, one rules with the support of one's champions. Regardless of circumstances, one must show them the utmost respect, and take every care that they feel gratified and honored." His son felt shame from his deed and mortification for his actions and returned to the assembly, where singing and dancing soon resumed.

The news gatherers report that after nine months a son was born to Amir by Mehr-Nigar, and his son Amar Hamza also became the father of a son. Amir Hamza named his grandson Sa'ad, but did not name his own son. He said to Amar Ayyar, "Take this news to Naushervan and request him to give a name to the child." Within a few days Amar reached Ctesiphon." Naushervan was greatly pleased by this auspicious news and named his grandson Qubad.

When both Qubad and Sa'ad reached the age of four, Amir Hamza gave them to the tutelage of Amar Ayyar. By the time the boys had turned five years old, all who beheld them prayed that the evil eye be warded off them and said, "We have never seen or heard of such comely and well-mannered boys. The signs of valor are already evident in their aspects and courage speaks in their faces and features."

———

The narrator tells that when Zhopin Kaus of Zabul heard the news of Qubad's birth, he wrote a note to Naushervan that read:

> If Hamza has allowed you to keep your throne until now it was because he had no son from Mehr-Nigar. Now a son has been born to him by your daughter. It is certain that he will overthrow and kill you and seat his son on the throne. In my opinion it would be most wise for you to seek Bahman Jasap's assistance immediately. It was my duty to alert you to the situation and now I have performed it.

After reading Zhopin's note, Naushervan said, "I have complete confidence that Hamza would never do me any wrong, as I have often been in his debt." Buzurjmehr answered, "Verily said and most just!" However, Bakhtak and other Sassanid nobles prevailed on the emperor to set out from Ctesiphon to meet Bahman Jasap, and thus planted the seed of fear and misgiving in his heart. Afterward Naushervan set out for Bahman Jasap's land. After listening to Naushervan's account, Bahman sent a letter to Hamza that read:

> Emperor Naushervan has sought refuge in my lands because of your tyranny. Therefore, I feel it is my duty to apprehend you and hand you over to Naushervan. If you have a claim to manhood, come here and test your mettle against mine.

Amir Hamza laughed heartily upon reading this letter and said, "Alas! God is my witness that I never wished to overthrow Naushervan or to treat him in this vile manner and enthrone Qubad. But now that he has gone over to Bahman to seek refuge and has complained about me, it has become imperative for me to depose him and seat Qubad on his throne." All his counselors and advisers piped up in a chorus, "Indeed, O Sahibqiran! There is no better manner of dealing with this situation. You must first hand over your own throne to Prince Qubad, and make him your heir and order everyone to make offerings to him. Then you may take the next steps." Amir Hamza enthroned Prince Qubad as his heir and headed toward Bahman's lands after forty days of celebrations. When Amir Hamza approached Kohistan and pitched his tents, Bahman sent his son Homan with a body of soldiers to take position on the mountainside so that Hamza would be foiled in his attempt to control the mountain. When Aadi tried to gain the mountain, Homan, who had already established himself there, started throwing stones at Aadi and his troops, making it impossible for Aadi to advance. In the meanwhile, Amar Hamza and Landhoor had arrived there with their armies and saw stones being thrown from the mountaintop and Aadi holding his ground with great courage and determination. Amar Hamza, King Landhoor, and Istaftanosh began scaling the mountain in order to dislodge the foe. Homan let loose a barrage of stones at them, but the three managed to climb up, using their shields to ward off the projectiles. Then they pulled out their swords and fell on the infidels, striking at the nation of mischief makers like bolts of lightning. Thousands of Guebers were dispatched to Hell, and with heads hanging in shame, they entered the chambers of God's wrath.

Homan escaped with his life, and in great disarray he went to Bahman and narrated the whole account of the skirmish to him. Bahman grew angry with Homan and said, "It was proved today that you are not my son; otherwise you would never have abandoned the field or run away from facing the sword. Moreover, you give me this account of your pusillanimity and cowardice so merrily." While Bahman was talking, a great dust cloud rose on the horizon and thousands of standards appeared from under its veil. It was announced that the Sahibqiran was approaching with great majesty and grandeur. Bahman said to Bakhtak, "I am very desirous of seeing the Sahibqiran, as his legend precedes him." Bakhtak answered, "If you mount your steed and stand along the way, I shall be able to show you Amir Hamza." Bahman mounted his horse and accompanied Bakhtak.

After his champions had passed, Amir Hamza himself came by riding Ashqar Devzad with great hauteur and ceremony. Bakhtak said, "This is Hamza of whom you have heard." Bahman was astonished to witness Amir Hamza's stateliness and magnificence, and said, "With *this* short stature he killed the *devs* of Qaf and prevailed over mighty champions of the world? How could even he—with all his valor—have routed the rebellious hordes of Qaf?" Bakhtak answered, "Once you get into the arena with him you will realize the truth behind his small stature and seemingly weak constitution." Bahman replied, "It would be improper to challenge him today as he has just arrived tired, worn, and exhausted from his journey. But, come tomorrow, I will inflict on him a humiliation he will never forget."

The next morning Amir wrote a letter to Bahman. After detailing his exploits in Qaf and describing his many victories over renowned champions of the world, he stated: "I have arrived here at your calling. You would do well to send Naushervan, Bakhtak, and Zhopin as prisoners to me and then present yourself to me with your treasury and ennoble yourself by converting to the True Faith. Otherwise, a most shameful defeat would become your lot."

Amir Hamza sent the letter with his son Amar Hamza. On the way to Bahman's court, Amar Hamza encountered Bahman's son Homan and defeated him in combat. Then Amar Hamza headed onward. Bahman was present in the court along with Naushervan, Zhopin, Bakhtak, and Buzurjmehr. After offering salutations to Buzurjmehr, Amar threw Hamza's letter before Bahman, but said nothing to him. After reading the letter, Bahman tore it up, thus portraying his resentment. Amar Hamza said, "Alas, my father forbade me from taking any excesses, or else I would have torn you up in the same way that you tore up that letter, and extracted your imprudent brains from your heedless skull." At a signal from Bahman, Homan rushed at Amar Hamza with his sword drawn, but Amar Hamza wrested the sword from Homan's hand with great alacrity, and slammed him to the floor. Homan's younger brother then charged Amar Hamza, but met the same fate. Seeing this example of Amar Hamza's courage and strength, Bahman greatly praised him and said without reserve, "I am not surprised at his bravery and might, for a lion's cub is born of a lion, and a valiant man's progeny will always prove brave." With these words, he put a robe of honor on Amar Hamza with his own hands, and kissed the young man's hands before giving him leave to depart.

Upon his return to camp, Amar Hamza recounted the whole story of his trip to Amir Hamza.

The following day Bahman took to the battlefield with his army. Amir Hamza also arrayed his force there. Amar Hamza kissed the leg of his father's throne to seek his permission for combat, turned his steed to face the battlefield, and issued a challenge to his adversaries, at which point Bahman signaled to Homan. He rode into the arena carrying a mace and raised it above his head to strike a blow against Amar Hamza, who foiled the blow. Amar Hamza lifted Homan clear off his saddle, whirled him seven times above his head, and slammed him to the ground. Then he tied Homan up and presented him to Amir Hamza, who gave him into Amar Ayyar's custody. Bahman sent his second son into combat and he fared the same as his brother. Bahman's side sounded the signal to announce the end of hostilities for the day and the king returned sorrowfully to his camp.

Amir Hamza, on the other hand, returned to his camp accompanied by trumpets of victory. All of his men presented themselves to make offerings to congratulate him on his victory. In the evening, Amir Hamza sent for Bahman's sons and said to them, "Convert to the True Faith and refrain from fire worship." They answered, "O Amir! We will convert to the True Faith the day our father does so. Pray show us this kindness and do not force us to convert this day." Amir Hamza set them free that instant and conferred robes of honor upon them. The brothers returned to their father, and after kissing his feet, told him what had happened, upon which Bahman praised Amir Hamza's conduct. The next day, he again sounded the drums of war and entered the arena, and Amir Hamza arrayed his army opposite his as before. Amar Hamza went forth for combat wielding his lance in his hands. That day Bahman himself came out to fight. Amar Hamza said, "It is not our tradition to deal the first blow, and I cannot violate this tradition. I will show you what I possess by way of courage and unleash my warring might after you have dealt me the first blow." Bahman brought his mace down on him with all the might he possessed, but Amar Hamza foiled the blow and said, "I give you two more blows, and then it will be my turn." Bahman dealt two more strikes with all his might and Amar Hamza foiled them both with great adroitness and effort. Then he wheeled around Prophet Ishaq's steed Siyah Qitas, and said, "Beware now, O Bahman! Summon all your senses to the ready. Now it is my turn to deal you the blow that will lay you flat!"

At this, Amar Hamza dealt Bahman such a mighty blow that sweat broke from every pore of Bahman's body. In that manner the two of them continued battling from morning to sunset until their maces shattered and their senses were disordered. As neither one was able to declare victory or subdue his adversary, both of them finally returned to their camps. Amir Hamza embraced his son and made many offerings in sacrifice for him. He asked his son, "What manner of combatant is Bahman, and how do you reckon him in power and might?" He answered, "If there ever existed a man worthy of being called a champion warrior besides yourself, it is Bahman."

The next day, Bahman fought Landhoor and the day after that he skirmished with Aadi but in both cases their combat ended in stalemate. Both Landhoor and Aadi acknowledged Bahman's might to Amir Hamza.

The next day, Bahman took Aadi Madi-Karib's six brothers captive. The fate of these champions falling prisoner to the enemy greatly grieved Amir Hamza. Amar Ayyar said to him, "If you should order me, I would go and secure the release of our warriors." Amir answered, "Nothing would gladden my heart more." Amar Ayyar then entered Bahman's camp in disguise. Bahman was quite overjoyed that night and ordered that the captive warriors from Hamza's camp be produced before him en masse. Then he asked Naushervan, "How do you recommend they be treated?" Naushervan said, "It would be best to put them to the sword." Bakhtak said, "I recommend that they be hanged!" Zhopin said, "I say that they should be killed for their meat. You see how plump they are. They should be fed to the hunting dogs." Buzurjmehr commented, "The command given by a ruler is unalterable. Do what would be considered just in the judgment of brave men, and act as the demands of righteousness decree." Bahman next asked his sons and brothers, "What do you counsel and advise in this matter?" They answered, "They should be decapitated and their heads displayed at the towers so that the enemy camp may find an example in their fate and terror may overwhelm their hearts." Bahman said to his sons, "I marvel at the depths of baseness to which your minds have sunk. It was Hamza who, when he had power over you, did you a signal favor. And now you advocate the murder of his companions? Do you not feel a single pang of shame, or does a sense of gratitude never make you pause and reconsider your thoughts?" Then Bahman conferred robes of honor on every captive man present there and released them all at once.

Amar Ayyar then revealed himself and said to Bahman, "Your actions are becoming to a brave warrior like yourself." Amar Ayyar then addressed Bakhtak, saying, "You were the one who counseled that Amir's commanders be hanged. I will change my own name, O villain, if I do not see to it that your ass is pierced by the point of an impaling stake." Bakhtak trembled at these words, made several bows to Amar, and said, "I uttered those words only out of the consideration that my words do not offend Bahman; otherwise, I would have suggested exactly what Bahman himself did in the end."

The commanders set free by Bahman returned to Amir Hamza and narrated their story to him. Amir Hamza praised Bahman and said, "I hope to God that he converts to the True Faith for verily he is a noble champion."

The two armies again flooded the battlefield the next morning. Bahman entered the arena and called out, "O Hamza, why do you not show your face in the arena and display your bravery in combat, instead of sending your champions to fight me?" The moment Amir heard this challenge, he took the reins of Ashqar Devzad and rode out to answer his call. Bahman asked him to deal the first blow. Amir answered, "It is not the custom of the followers of the True God to take precedence in combat. Deal me the blow you are most proud of." Bahman was greatly pleased by Amir's reply and said, "O Hamza, I know you are a renowned warrior. It would be best if I tried to dislodge you from the ground by lifting you, and you do the same to me. The one who is the lesser of the two must obey the superior and surrender his arms to him." Amir happily consented to this proposition and said to him, "I would like you to try to lift me from the ground." Bahman caught hold of Amir's cummerbund and spent every last bit of energy he had in trying to lift him up, but he was unable to move him even a fraction of an inch.

Amir called out to Amar Ayyar in the language of *ayyars*, "Tell our companions to put cotton in their ears." Amar Ayyar immediately carried out his orders. Amir then let out a mighty cry of "God is Great!" Many men in Bahman's camp lost their hearing from the violent force of his bellow, and even the beasts of the forest retreated deep into the woods. If Bahman had not blocked his ears with his fingers, his eardrums would have burst, blood would have issued from his ears, and he would have gone deaf. Amir then caught hold of Bahman by his waistband and whirled him seven times around his head before tying him up and giving him to Amar Ayyar as a prisoner. Bahman's army was ready to attack, but Bahman signaled them to desist. Sounding the drums to announce the day's end, Hamza returned to his pavilion in all safety.

Amir sent for Bahman and offered him the jewel-encrusted chair of champions and, showing him much favor, said, "O Bahman! You have the choice to prove your manliness and honor your word, or revert on it." Bahman said, "O Hamza, you well know that Naushervan and Zhopin approached me and sought my aid. I offered them support in the traditions of chivalry. Do me another great favor and forgive their offenses as well. For this kindness I will become your slave with all my heart and soul." Amir answered, "I will do so only on condition that they convert to the True Faith. If not, I will murder them with my own hands and they will never find reprieve from my sword." Bahman replied, "If you should order it, I would go and prevail on them to submit to you and follow the path of the righteous. Then in one gathering all of them could convert to the True Faith and surrender their authority to you." Amir sent Bahman away after giving him a resplendent robe of honor. Bahman went and gave a whole account of events to Naushervan and Zhopin, and then said to them, "Since I was unable to overpower Hamza, I know for a fact that no one else in this world will triumph over him."

Naushervan and Zhopin accompanied Bahman and other men of their court before Amir Hamza. Amir Hamza welcomed Naushervan, led him to his throne, and seated him there, treating him with great deference and respect. Amir taught the Act of Faith to Naushervan, Bahman, Zhopin, and Bakhtak. Then he ordered his musicians to play festive tunes, and for a full two weeks he held celebrations in honor of Naushervan and Bahman.

Of Amir's Departure for Mecca, and of His Taking Prisoner Shaddad Abu-Amar Habashi, and of His Converting to the True Faith

After these festivities were over, Naushervan said to Amir, "O Abul-Ala! Old age is upon me and I wish to enthrone Qubad and make him emperor in my place." Amir yielded to him. Then Naushervan enthroned Qubad and departed for Ctesiphon along with Buzurjmehr, while Amir Hamza went toward Kaus Hisar and ordered his camp to move quarters there. He occupied himself with pursuits of the hunt during the day and indulged himself in revels at night. One day he received Khvaja Abdul Muttalib's letter, which read:

> My dutiful son, Shaddad Abu-Amar Habashi has sacked our city and intends to destroy Mecca. Pray arrive here speedily, or else no follower of the True Faith will be left alive here and none will escape his tyranny.

Amir showed the letter to all the commanders of his army and then said to Bahman, "Until my return, I wish you to rule over my camp in my stead. Consider my companions and my sons as your own and treat them likewise. I shall depart on the campaign to Mecca and will triumph over the infidels with help from God Almighty. I shall soon return."

Bahman submitted respectfully, saying with folded arms, "It is not the place of a slave to occupy the seat of his master." Amir, however, prevailed on him to accept the trust. Afterward, Amir Hamza departed with Amar Ayyar for Mecca.

After passing all the stations of the journey, they came to Mecca, and Amir Hamza asked Amar, "What must we do now? What steps should we take to repel the foe?" Amar answered, "You must leave Ashqar Devzad in this wilderness to roam free, and proceed from here on foot."

Then Amir took Amar and they went on their way. When they approached the camp of the Ethiopians, Amar encountered an acrobat. They spoke together and Amar ingratiated himself into his graces. Amar Ayyar said to Amir Hamza, "I am headed for the court of the king of Ethiopia to do my work. When I send for one Faulad Pehalwan, you must present yourself speedily." After giving these instructions to Amir Hamza, Amar dressed himself as the master of a troupe of tumblers and took a procession to the entrance of the court of the King of Ethiopia, Shaddad Abu-Amar Habashi. Amar Ayyar said to the guards there, "Pray announce me. I hope to entertain the king and have brought many marvelous tricks to amuse him." The heralds announced the arrival of Amar Ayyar, and the king sent for him.

At the court, Amar displayed his many talents, which pleased King Shaddad. The king offered a reward to Amar, but he would not accept it. Shaddad said to Amar, "I offered you a reward, but you did not accept it. Tell me now what you wish to ask for." Amar declared with folded arms, "My uncle has a slave who has become a wrestler. He torments me night and day and rebukes and insults me. I wish you to warn and chastise him so that he will refrain from his audacious ways." Shaddad said, "Where is he? Send for him." Amar called out, "O Faulad Pehalwan! Present yourself!" Upon his call, Amir Hamza entered the court.

Shaddad was irked that Amir did not offer him any greeting. Shaddad therefore said harshly, "O slave-born tumbler, why do you torment your master?" Amir answered, "I am no slave! But *you* must indeed be one, and ingratitude your middle name." Amar said to Shaddad, "See, my lord! He even talks back to Your Honor!" Shaddad ordered an executioner to sever Amir Hamza's head but Amir immediately lifted him over his head with one hand and spun him hard. While turning him over his head with one hand, Amir delivered him a mighty blow with the other, and his soul soon left his body.

Then Shaddad sent another executioner to do the job, and Amir dispatched him to Hell along the same road. One after another, Shaddad sent forty Ethiopians to execute Amir, and he packed them all off to Hell. Then Shaddad ordered his champion warriors to behead the slave, but all of them kept away for fear of Amir. Shaddad drew his own sword and charged Amir himself. Shouting his war cry, Amir caught hold of Shaddad by his cummerbund, whirled him overhead, and slammed him to the ground. Then, drawing his dagger, Amir bore down upon him and declared, "Little did you know that I am Hamza. Even if Rustam himself were to confront me, I would humiliate him the same way." Shaddad responded, "O Amir, I took on this mission at the instigation of Naushervan. If you were to spare my life, I would never return." Amir said, "I will not let you go alive unless you convert to the True Faith." Shaddad was forced to convert to the True Faith and Amir then spared his life.

When the people of Mecca heard Amir's war cry, they gathered with Khvaja Abdul Muttalib who escorted him into Mecca.

Shaddad went to Naushervan's court and kissed the foot of his throne and said, "Your Honor caused me to be humiliated at Hamza's hands, and I suffered great distress at this." Having spoken, Shaddad took hold of Naushervan by his cummerbund and carried him out of his court. Observing that the hands of the royal slaves had moved to the hilts of their swords, Shaddad declared, "If anyone touches me, I will smash the emperor against the ground and he will die on the instant." Nobody interfered with Shaddad after this threat, and he took Naushervan prisoner to his land. There he constructed a cage and chained Naushervan's feet to its bars. Then he hung the cage in his court and put Naushervan on two rations of millet bread and water a day.

————

Now hear of Amir Hamza. After a few days' stay in Mecca, he sought leave of his father. Khvaja Abdul Muttalib said, "My dear son, I have now seen you after many years and my heart is not yet fully sated with the sight of you. If you stayed here another year, it would please me greatly." Upon that, Amir acquiesced to his father's wishes. Bakhtak, who had stayed behind with Bahman, had also heard that Amir would be spending another year in Mecca.

Bakhtak forged a letter from Naushervan addressed to Zhopin and Hurmuz. Giving it to a messenger, he instructed him to pretend that he had just arrived from Ctesiphon carrying Naushervan's missive. In that letter Bakhtak had written:

> Be it known to you that I sent Abu-Amar Habashi to Mecca to lay the city to ruin. The followers of the True Faith were slaughtered one and all, and the citizens of Mecca got retribution for their deeds. Shaddad took Hamza and Amar prisoner and brought them to his land, where he hanged them and put an end to their menace. You may slaughter the followers of the True Faith in Hamza's camp without the least worry,

showing them no reprieve or mercy. Afterward, you may hand over Mehr-Nigar to Bahman's custody.

By chance, the messenger crossed paths with Zhopin, who had gone out for an excursion. The messenger handed him the missive, and upon reading it, Zhopin went straight to Bahman and showed him the letter. After perusing it, Bahman said to Zhopin, "This is nothing but a trick played by you. I know you well and I will never believe a word you say." Zhopin swore that while he could not vouch for the veracity of the report the letter had come to him through a royal messenger. In the end, Bahman believed the news of Hamza's death. He said, "A thousand sighs, alas, that Hamza did not take me with him." Then Bahman said, "The will of God has prevailed. Now Hamza's two sons and his grandson will have my allegiance and I will put myself at their service."

Bakhtak said to Bahman, "To pledge your allegiance to someone of Hamza's caliber was perhaps acceptable. However, a mighty champion and powerful lord like yourself must not demean himself by serving under mere boys. Moreover, Naushervan has expressed a desire to accept you as his son-in-law and conferred that high honor upon you. Would it be seemly to serve under boys when you can have the title of Naushervan's son-in-law?" Hearing talk of such an association with Naushervan, Bahman could not resist the temptation. He said to Bakhtak, "If you are counseling me to act on your advice, perhaps you should also tell me a way to do it." Bakhtak answered, "Keep it all a secret for now until we have Mehr-Nigar secure in our hands." Zhopin said, "Today when I present myself at the court, I will tell Hurmuz and King Qubad that the anniversary of my father's death will be commemorated tomorrow and it would be a signal honor for me to have Amir's sons attend the ceremony with their commanders." Bakhtak replied, "That would indeed be an appropriate course of action."

When Zhopin presented himself at the court that night, he made his request to Hurmuz, Qubad, and Amar Hamza who accepted his invitation, and the next day they arrived at Zhopin's house along with their commanders. Zhopin offered them food and wine, and when all of them were intoxicated, Zhopin rose and declared to Amar Hamza and Qubad, "In the same manner that Your Honors have augmented my honor by your presence, it would confer great honor on me if Princess Mehr-Nigar, too, would condescend to set foot here." Amir's sons sent a message to Princess Mehr-Nigar.

Upon receiving this message, Princess Mehr-Nigar was conveyed to Zhopin's house. As Mehr-Nigar sat there among the women, she overheard someone say, "For the moment the princess is the picture of happiness, but soon she will learn the news and hear what mischief has been afoot." At once, Mehr-Nigar dispatched an attendant to send for Qubad, and she said to him, "Arrange a conveyance for me without delay. Some trouble seems under way and mischief is about to break loose." Qubad sent for the conveyance, and soon Mehr-Nigar departed. Zhopin and Bahman regretted the news and rued the loss of the great fortune that had slipped from their hands. Bakhtak comforted Bahman and said, "After losing her husband, she will not have too many avenues open to her. You will make her yours yet."

Following Bakhtak's instructions, Bahman wrung his hands remorsefully and said, "It is a shame that Nausherван's own son Prince Hurmuz must be passed over, and his grandson Qubad appointed heir to the throne." Amar Hamza commented, "What is that to you, Bahman?" Bahman answered, "This Arab lad has no right to rule this magnificent empire!"

When King Landhoor heard this speech, he grew irritated, and said to Bahman, "It is a shame that Amir Hamza put an unworthy wretch like yourself in charge of his affairs." A fight broke out in the assembly and outdoors and many Arabs and several of Bahman's followers were injured. Bahman's men carried him away from that place and saved his life.

It came to pass that news of these events reached Bahman's sister, Noor Bano, who had fallen in love with Amar Hamza. She left her house and joined the fight, and killed many infidels. She also killed her brothers who challenged her. After killing them, Noor Bano took the Arab commanders back to the fortress and ordered the moats to be filled up with water. The army of the infidels surrounded the fortress on all sides.

One day the infidels stormed the fort. Qubad said to his mother, "If I may have your permission, I would like to fight and kill them." Mehr-Nigar answered, "You are a mere boy. How can I allow you to go into battle?" Qubad then said, "My father triumphed over mighty champions in his boyhood. I am of the same blood. If you do not give me your permission, I will kill myself before your eyes." Noor Bano said to Mehr-Nigar, "There is no harm in allowing Qubad to go to battle. I shall accompany him and will be alert and ready to help and succor him." With a heavy heart, Mehr-Nigar gave Qubad permission to fight.

Qubad decorated himself with his arms and armor, and faced the infidels and challenged them. Seeing Qubad in the arena, Bahman said to himself, *How fortunate that Qubad has come to seek combat and got permission from his mother to battle. I shall take him prisoner and keep him in my custody. Pangs of motherly love will rob Mehr-Nigar of her peace of mind, and she will be forced to come to me.* Bahman attacked Qubad with his mace, but the boy blocked the blow with his shield and answered with a sword thrust of such finesse that Bahman was grievously injured and barely escaped with his life. Amir's son chased him for a distance of four *kos,* all the while cutting down Bahman's men.

A few days later, Amar Hamza and Landhoor presented themselves before Mehr-Nigar and told her that Bahman bore no blame in the matter; that it was Bakhtak and Zhopin who were the root cause of the mischief. Amar Hamza then said, "What must we do now? The infidels have besieged the castle and many of us are injured." Qubad declared, "Open the fortress gate and array the army in the field." The commanders forthwith positioned their troops, and the war drums were struck.

Bahman entered the battle arena and called out, "O Arabs, why do you sacrifice your lives for an idle cause? Hamza died a long time ago. Hand Mehr-Nigar over to me and go your own way." Hearing Bahman's scurrilous words, Landhoor sought Amar Hamza's leave to fight. He answered, "I give you to God's care." Then Landhoor and Bahman fought with maces so forcefully that their healed wounds opened up again. They were still fighting when the sun covered its face with the veil of night and both camps sounded the drums of retreat. The armies returned to their camps to rest.

In the morning a dust cloud rose from the forest and the *ayyars* from both camps rushed there to gather intelligence. They brought back word that Furhad-Akka had come with a large force of intrepid warriors to help Zhopin.

Farhad bin Landhoor took leave of Amir's son to go to face Furhad-Akka. Both warriors fought mightly but neither of them prevailed against the other.

The next morning a champion sought combat with Furhad-Akka. After skirmishing mightily, each of them returned to his camp at the end of the day.

———

Leaving the two armies engaged in battle, let us now hear an account of the Sahibqiran. One night in the realm of dreams, Amir saw that the infidels had conducted a night raid on the camp of the followers of the True

Faith and that many of his commanders had been carried injured from the battlefield. He started from the dream and described it to Amar Ayyar, who said, "O Amir, you never have dreams that prove false. If you permit me, I will go investigate and find out what has come to pass." Amir gave Amar Ayyar leave to go.

When Amar arrived there his camp rang with festive notes and each soldier took heart at the sight of Amar. Bahman said to Bakhtak, "You wretch! I thought you told us that Amar Ayyar and Hamza were both dead!" Bakhtak responded, "I know nothing of the matter. All I know is what Naushervan himself wrote in the letter." Bahman grabbed Bakhtak and hurled him toward Zhopin. As each man had life remaining to him, Bakhtak fell to the ground instead. Bahman felt great remorse and lamented his shameful deeds.

Amar Ayyar offered words of comfort to Qubad and Amar Hamza and returned to Amir Hamza. Then the Sahibqiran took leave of his father. He mounted Ashqar Devzad and, taking Amar along, departed for Kaus Hisar with a large entourage.

Now hear an account of the battlefield. A Turkic warrior named Sarkob had arrived with an intrepid and vast force to assist Naushervan's army.

In the meanwhile, Furhad-Akka rode his steed into the battlefield and sought combat. Amar Hamza's son, Sa'ad, asked his father's permission to answer Furhad's call. Amar Hamza said to him, "Light of my eyes, you are not of age to go into battle. Refrain from thoughts of fighting." His son replied, "Uncle Qubad and I are of the same age, and there is no accomplishment to which he has a claim where I am lacking. I find it most shameful that while he participates in battle, I remain a mere spectator; and where he wins laurels as a warrior, I stand idle."

Amar Hamza was forced against his wishes to give Sa'ad leave to fight. Sa'ad then entered the arena. Upon seeing him, the infidels said, "It is a strange nation where young boys take part in battles and face our champions without the least fear." Sarkob asked, "Who is this boy who has entered the arena?" Bahman answered, "He is Hamza's grandson." Sarkob exclaimed, "How can a boy like him compete against Furhad-Akka?" Bahman answered, "We will soon find out." While they were having this discussion, Sa'ad issued his challenge. Furhad-Akka galloped forth and dealt Sa'ad a blow of his mace and declared, "There! I struck and laid him low!" Sa'ad emerged from the cloud of dust created by the blow and dealt Furhad-Akka a blow with his sword that severed his mace-wielding arm. It fell to the ground along with the mace. Furhad-Akka attempted to turn his back and escape to his army when Sa'ad spurred on his horse again and dealt him another blow, severing his other arm as well and dispatching that warrior to the Future State. Sa'ad's *ayyars* cut off Furhad-Akka's head with great alacrity, decapitating his filthy corpse. Festive notes were sounded in Amir Hamza's camp, while Naushervan's camp rang with cries of lamentation. Sarkob said to Bahman, "Praiseworthy indeed are the parents who raised such a brave and strong son." Then each camp sounded the drums of retreat and the armies returned to their resting places.

In the morning, the warring armies had just arranged themselves in battle formation when a dust cloud rose from the ground in such abundance that it choked off even the wind. It was soon announced that Amar Ayyar and Amir Hamza were on their way there with a vast army. A wave of joy swept through Hamza's camp. Amir's arrival brought much needed relief to his followers.

Amir Hamza rode Ashqar Devzad onto the battlefield and called out to Bahman, "O Kohi, what wrong did I ever do you and how did I injure you that you have avenged yourself on me in this way? If you really are a man of courage, come out and face me!" Bahman said to Hurmuz, "I am unable even to look Hamza in the eye; I will not fight him. Now you are the master of your own fate. I will have nothing more to do with this business."

In the end, Sarkob went forward to encounter Amir and attacked him with his mace. After fighting with maces until midday, they drew swords and skirmished together for two hours. The glittering swords clashed and sparks flew without cease but neither received any injury by the hand of the other.

Amir Hamza said, "O Sarkob, we have tried all the blows. The only test that now remains is for one of us to lift the other person from the ground. If you succeed, I will pledge allegiance to you and never fight you again. If I succeed, then you must pledge the same." Sarkob acquiesced happily to the proposition. In the end Amir prevailed over Sarkob. After securing Sarkob with a rope, Amir handed him to Amar Ayyar.

As darkness was falling, Amir Hamza ordered the call of retreat for the day and sent for Sarkob, who willingly converted to the True Faith. Amir gave him a high rank among those present, and then held revels for three days and three nights.

On the fourth day, Amir ordered the drums of war to be sounded and entered the battlefield, and challenged Bahman. Bahman said to Hurmuz, "I will never face Hamza. Order the army and ready them to fall on Hamza as a body."

At a sign from Hurmuz, his entire army took rein. Amir drew his swords Samsam and Qumqam and confronted the infidels, plying the swords with both hands. For two hours Amir fought the whole army of the infidels by himself, showing his swordsmanship and proving his courage and mettle. Thousands of infidels died in the battle. Ashqar Devzad swam in a sea of gore, floating chest-deep in the blood of the infidels. At last Bahman said to Zhopin, "Amir is now growing exhausted from the fight. Foam flows from his mouth, and he is in a state of self-forgetfulness and is merely fighting reflexively. Amar Ayyar keeps hurling naphtha and fire at us and does not allow anyone to attack Hamza from behind. If you could separate Amar Ayyar from him, I would be able to kill Hamza."

At Zhopin's command, seven hundred elephants were released on Amar. Then, approaching Amir Hamza from behind, Bahman struck a blow to Amir's head with a two-handed sword that cut into Amir's skull to a depth of four digits. Immediately upon dealing the blow, Bahman ran away from Hamza exclaiming, "Friends, I put an end to Hamza's life!"

When Amir's friends heard Bahman's remarks they were overtaken by anxiety. Amir swam in and out of consciousness. He said to Ashqar in the Jinni language, "Take me from the arena and use any means to break the cordon." Amir clasped Ashqar's neck with both arms, and the horse carried him away. Ashqar made his way into the forest from the battlefield biting anyone who tried to bar his way and kicking the men who tried to approach him from behind. After galloping for several miles, the thirsty Ashqar spotted a river. He waded into the water to drink, and when he came out Amir Hamza fell from his back and the water ran red with his blood. Ashqar dragged Amir to the riverbank and saved him from drowning. A shephard named Siyah-Sher found Amir Hamza lying injured and took him home and nursed him back to health, for which Amir Hamza and his companions rewarded him richly.

After Amir's wound had healed, he returned to his camp. He gathered his army for battle and said to his companions, "Put a cordon around the enemy and attack them from all sides." Their army fell upon the infidels like a lion attacking a flock of sheep. Within a few hours countless infidels were dispatched to Hell.

As Bahman escaped from Amar Hamza, he gave him chase on Siyah Qitas. Bahman turned to confront him, thinking that Amar Hamza would be no match for him. Amar Hamza dealt him a full blow of the sword, which Bahman foiled although it killed his horse. Bahman then hamstrung Siyah Qitas, so Amar Hamza was forced to face him on foot. Amar Hamza dealt Bahman a blow that cut Bahman in two. He beheaded Bahman's body and presented the head to Amir Hamza to show proof of his courage, and told Amir that Siyah Qitas had been hamstrung. Amir lamented the loss of Bahman and the horse and said, "It is not every day that one comes across a noble horse, nor a warrior of such mettle as Bahman. Indeed they are rarities in this world."

Later, Amir's commanders likewise piled up the heads of enemy commanders before him, and thousands of infidels lay beheaded. Amir ordered the drums of victory to be sounded, and he returned to his camp. The followers of the True Faith sounded joyous notes upon their victory over the infidels.

When Amir Hamza had received his wound at Bahman's hands, a *perizad* was passing above the battlefield who took the news of the incident and the details of Amir's injury to Aasman Peri. This greatly distressed Aasman Peri. She took Quraisha, her *perizads*, and Khvaja Abdur Rahman and departed from Qaf for Earth at the head of an interpaid army of *devs* and jinns from Qaf.

Upon approaching the scene, she set up her camp two *kos* away and sent Khvaja Abdur Rahman to call on Amir. Amir was greatly surprised to see him and asked him about Aasman Peri and Quraisha and inquired about the reason for his visit. Khvaja Abdur Rahman said, "The queen and your daughter, Quraisha, are camped two *kos* from here with an powerful army."

Amir rode out with his commanders and warriors to call on them. He embraced Aasman Peri and kissed Quraisha's forehead and seated her on his lap. The *perizads* marveled at the grandeur of Amir's entourage and said among themselves, "It was on account of what he had left behind that Amir was so listless in Qaf and wished to return to his world." They said to Amir, "We have now seen your friends and companions, but we are most desirous of seeing Princess Mehr-Nigar." Amir replied, "Just as you wish to see Princess Mehr-Nigar, my friends are desirous of beholding you with their own eyes. Therefore I request that you either appear to them without your invisible guise, or else line their eyes with the collyrium of Suleiman." The *perizads* replied, "O Amir! We fear that if we do this your companions may become bold and try to take liberties with us." Amir answered, "Nobody would dare even think of it."

Thereupon the *perizads* lifted their veils of invisibility and presented their beauty to Amir's companions. When the warriors and champions of Amir's camp saw them, they were stunned and fell into a state of shock. When they regained their senses, they thanked Amir and said, "It is because of you that we who are made of clay were able to behold those made of fire." Amir retired to Mehr-Nigar's palace along with Aasman Peri, Quraisha, and the *perizads*, where they all derived joyous pleasure from one another's company.

Mehr-Nigar embraced Aasman Peri, kissed Quraisha's forehead and lips, and then received all the *peris*, hosting them in the finest traditions. For three days and three nights Aasman Peri engaged in feasting with her companions. On the fourth day Aasman Peri gave Mehr-Nigar the gifts she had brought for her from Qaf and returned to her abode.

After her departure, Amir asked his companions at court, "Do we know where the infidels have escaped to?" Amar Ayyar answered, "It is said that they have gone to Kashmir, where they have sought refuge with Jafar, the ruler of that land, who has pledged his support to them." Amar Hamza took seven champion soldiers, including Aadi Madi-Karib, Farhad bin Landhoor, and Istaftanosh, along with their respective armies, and headed for Kashmir. When he entered the lands of Kashmir, the infidels hid themselves for fear in a fort. Amar Hamza surrounded the castle from all sides and laid siege to it.

One day, an onager[4] entered Amar Hamza's camp from the forest and injured many men. Amar Hamza mounted his steed and gave chase to the animal in order to capture him alive. Upon reaching the side of a mountain, the onager quickly scampered up it. Amar Hamza followed but found no sign of the wild ass upon reaching the summit. Unable to find any trace of him, Amar Hamza sat down to rest under a tree. He hunted and killed an animal, and roasted and made a meal of it. Afterward he lay down under the same tree and slept. When it was time for *fajar* prayers[5] the same onager again appeared and Amar Hamza again exerted himself in capturing him. When the sun rose and its rays fell on every inch of the mountain, the onager disappeared again. Amar Hamza searched for him again and was unable to find him as before. He was forced to depart empty-handed after failing in his search.

Along the way back to camp he came across a most captivating city whose citizens were paragons of beauty. When he inquired the name of the city, he was told that it was called Farkhar, and that it was the residence of Zhopin's sister Gul Chehra. It so happened that Gul Chehra caught sight of Amir's son from her balcony. Instantly she fell madly in love and sent one of her eunuchs to bring him to her by any means possible. Amar Hamza declined the invitation. After a while the eunuch returned to him with the same message. Finally he convinced Amar Hamza and conducted him before Gul Chehra. She received him with great ceremony and fanfare and attended to him with great devotion.

Then she said, "I have burned with love for you for a long time. Today God granted my desire and sent you to me when I least expected it." Afterward, Gul Chehra ordered food to be laid out, and they shared a meal.

Next, they had a round of drinks. Soon both she and Amar Hamza were intoxicated and Gul Chehra sought congress with him. Amar Hamza said to her, "I already have your sister in my harem. I will not couple with you and break God's law." She presented all manner of excuses to attain her goal. Finally, the prince was forced to reply. "I shall ask the opinion of my commanders in this matter. If they give their consent, I will take you to bed." The shameless Gul Chehra immediately dispatched a messenger to send for Amar Hamza's commanders.

Now, an old man named Farkhar Sar-Shaban lived in that city and was held in reverence by all and sundry. When he heard that Hamza's son had arrived there, he sent for his two sons, Mehrdar Sar-Shaban and Dinar Sar-Shaban, and said to them, "You will find Hamza's son drinking wine with Zhopin's sister. Go and bring him captive to me. And if you are unable to take him alive, bring me his head. I wish you to display your true mettle in this endeavor." His sons headed for Gul Chehra's house carrying staffs. They accosted Amar Hamza and said, "You despicable thief, how dare you trespass on our land to hunt here and display your valor?" Amar Hamza did not answer them and held his peace. One of them attacked Amar Hamza with his staff. Amar Hamza caught hold of it and pulled the staff toward him, which caused his adversary to fall flat on his face. He then dealt the intruder a blow with the same stick that flattened him to the ground and caused him to give up all thoughts of fighting. His brother charged him next, swinging his staff. He, too, met the same fate. When they returned to their senses they went back to their father and told him what had passed with them. Farkhar Sar-Shaban laughed at their story and said, "I have business with Hamza, not with his sons. But it seems unlikely now that I would be able to overpower him."

The next day Madi-Karib and the other commanders presented themselves before Amar Hamza in Farkhar. When Gul Chehra told them of her passion for Amar Hamza, Aadi said to him, "Why are you bent on killing this poor creature before her time? Who has ever heard of someone torturing a lover in this manner?" Amar Hamza laughed at this speech and said, "How do you suppose I can commit an act that is forbidden?" Madi-Karib replied, "You are the master of your actions. I only expressed my views after taking pity on this woman's incessant crying and longing."

In short, when Amar Hamza fell unconscious after drinking, Gul Chehra became overwhelmed with desire and embraced him amorously. Amar Hamza knitted his brows and said, "O shameless wretch, what is this unseemly act? What disgraceful enterprise have you decided upon in your heart? I will never be able to reciprocate your desires in this vile act!" With these words, he slapped her in warning. Gul Chehra was frustrated in her desire and said to herself, *He is in love with my sister, while I burn from the fire of his love and long to have congress with him. As the saying goes, what I cannot have another must not enjoy either!* She drew her sword that same moment and beheaded Amar Hamza. Then realizing that Amar Hamza's commanders would kill her in retribution, she began shouting and screaming and raising an alarm, "Ah! Ah! Who was the enemy who killed Amir Hamza's son?"

Amar Hamza's companions came rushing inside, and upon seeing Amar Hamza lying dead, tore at their collars, threw dust on their heads, and gave themselves to ecstasies of sorrow. Aadi said, "It is neither a stranger nor an enemy who is responsible for killing Amar Hamza. It is all too likely that this shameless wretch was frustrated in her desire and killed him in her drunken rage." Aadi's companions agreed with his conclusion. They shackled that harradian and asked her, "Were you the one who killed him?" She answered, "I was overwhelmed by my passion. Now punish me as you wish and kill me to avenge his death!" They said to one another, "It is proscribed for a man to raise his hand against a woman. How could we kill her even if we wanted to?"

Meanwhile, Amir Hamza had a dream that his son was flailing in a sea of blood. He started from his sleep in fear and explained the dream to Amar Ayyar who immediately departed for Kashmir. When Amar Ayyar reached Kashmir, he discovered that Amir's son was in the city of Farkhar in the house of Zhopin's sister. Amar hastened to that woman's home, where Aadi and the others threw themselves at Amar's feet and told him everything. From there Amar Ayyar returned home beating his head and throwing dirt on it and said to Amir Hamza, "The prince lies injured in Farkhar at Zhopin's house, and he has sent for you urgently." Amir

Hamza departed for Farkhar riding Ashqar Devzad. Amar thought it best to give Amir Hamza something to eat to fortify him against sudden shock. Amar Ayyar said to him, "Let us rest a while in a garden and revive our spirits before we arrive at Gul Chehra's house." Upon his persuasion, Amir Hamza stopped in a garden where a flock of goats were grazing. Amar Ayyar slaughtered a goat and began roasting her, and Amir Hamza's mind was soon occupied fully in watching his proceedings.

When the shepherd of that flock saw smoke rising from the garden, he went to investigate and beheld two men roasting his master's goat. He rushed back to Farkhar Sar-Shaban, who was the owner of the garden and the herd that grazed there, and informed him that two men had entered the garden and were helping themselves to his property as if it were their own. Farkhar Sar-Shaban hastily entered the garden and confronted Amir Hamza who prevailed over him. When Farkhar Sak-Shaban learned that he had been defeated by Amir Hamza his grief at his humiliation was dispelled. Farkhar Sar-Shaban said, "Indeed none other than Hamza could have forced me down and pressed my back to the ground."

Amir Hamza converted him to the True Faith and won his heart with his generosity and munificence. Amar Ayyar signaled Farkhar Sar-Shaban to forbid him from speaking when he tried to bring up the subject of Amar Hamza's death. Amir sallied forth with Farkhar Sar-Shaban and his sons riding by his side. When Amir Hamza's companions caught sight of him, they broke into lamentations all over again. Amir asked, "What is the matter that the place is ringing with the cries of grief and lamentations?" Amar Ayyar answered, "Your son has died at the hands of Zhopin's sister." Amir said, "Take the deceased to his mother and bring that trollop there." Amar took Gul Chehra and gave her into the custody of Naheed Maryam, who immediately surrendered her soul upon hearing of his death. Amir's grief was thus doubled, and he went into forty days of mourning for his son and sent his corpse, along with the captive Gul Chehra, to Kaus Hisar to Amar Hamza's wife, who avenged the death of her husband by killing her sister with her own hands. Amir Hamza returned to Kavs Hisar after destroying the city of Farkhar. Hurmuz escaped to Ctesiphon but many of his men died at Amir's hand.

Of Hurmuz's Arrival in Ctesiphon and Learning of Naushervan's Captivity, and of His Departure to Secure His Release

The narrator has said that when Hurmuz arrived in Ctesiphon after escaping from the fortress of Kashmir, he learned that Shaddad Abu-Amar Habashi had taken Naushervan prisoner. When Hurmuz asked Buzurjmehr's advice, he said, "It would be impossible to secure the emperor's release without Hamza agreeing to undertake the mission." Hurmuz said, "Why would Hamza agree to it? He has no reason to undertake these hardships at our bidding." Buzurjmehr replied, "If you were to ask your mother to write him a letter, Hamza would be forced to undertake the mission out of regard for her honor."

Hurmuz told his mother what Buzurjmehr had suggested and she wrote a letter to Hamza that read:

> To my son and a part of my heart! A long time ago Naushervan was taken captive by Shaddad Abu-Amar Habashi. It is truly deplorable that in your lifetime someone should harm Naushervan and disgrace a magnificent emperor like him.

After reading her letter, Amir Hamza said, "Even though I have received nothing but harm from Naushervan's hands, I will continue to return his deeds with kindness. I shall secure his release. If he cannot desist from his evil acts toward me, should I desist from doing good? Even if he follows the course of injustice, I shall not stray from the path of integrity." Amir took Muqbil Vafadar with him and headed for Ethiopia, against Amar Ayyar's advice.

When they arrived in Ethiopia, they dismounted in a garden near the walls of the city and left their horses to graze there. Amir put on his night livery and, using a rope ladder, scaled the walls of the fort. When they entered, they saw Shaddad Abu-Amar asleep on a throne surrounded by flagons of wine and salvers of meat and dried fruit, while Naushervan was trapped in a cage hanging near the throne. Amir Hamza was challenged by the palace guards, whom he swiftly killed, and then he partook of the wine, meat, and fruit laid out there. Next he wrote a note addressed to Shaddad Abu-Amar Habashi and left it near him. It read: "I was here and have taken Naushervan, my mentor and my benevolent lord, from your prison after eating all the food lying here."

Then Amir took down Naushervan's cage and said to Muqbil, "You must remain on the alert and look sharp while I go in search of a fleet horse for Naushervan."

While Amir was gone, Shaddad Abu-Amar Habashi woke up and saw that Naushervan had disappeared with his cage and his guards lay murdered. He wondered who might have been the culprit. Suddenly he caught sight of the note, and upon reading it, grew enraged.

Shaddad mustered a four-thousand-strong force and set out in search of Amir Hamza. They soon came upon a garden where they saw Naushervan sitting in his cage. When Shaddad asked Naushervan for Hamza's whereabouts, he replied, "I only know that he has gone in search of a horse." Shaddad released Naushervan and went to look for Amir Hamza. On the way he saw Muqbil coming toward him. Taking Muqbil for Amir Hamza,[6] he arrested him along with Ashqar Devzad. Muqbil said, "I am not Hamza but Muqbil." Shaddad then said, "It seems that Hamza was lost in the desert and died from thirst."

In the meantime, Shaddad returned to his abode and drank himself to sleep. In the morning he set out for Kaus Hisar with Naushervan. Shaddad had decided that with Hamza dead he must kill Hamza's sons, and then he could take Mehr-Nigar and ravish her as his reward. While Shaddad was indulging in these vile thoughts, Amir Hamza had indeed wandered into the desert and become lost. He suffered terribly from loneliness, thirst, and the effects of the piercing sun. Wherever he looked, he saw nothing but desolation. His eyes swept the horizon and met neither shade nor water.

That night Amar Ayyar saw Amir Hamza in his dreams, wandering forlorn and distraught in a desert and looking bewildered and dizzy. The next morning he set out in search for him and after seven days of searching high and low Amar found Hamza, and saw that his eyes were bulging out from thirst and his tongue was a veritable bed of thorns. Amar shed many tears at the sight and revived him. After a while, Amir Hamza opened his eyes. After Amir had fully regained his faculties, he put on his accoutrements and returned to Ethiopia, where he found Muqbil and Ashqar tied up with ropes. At the sight of Amir Hamza, Ashqar broke his fetters.[7] Amir Hamza mounted him and made preparations to head into the city in the company of Amar and Muqbil.

The guards alerted Shaddad's son, Amar Habashi, of Amir Hamza's entry, and he intercepted Amir with a force of a thousand troops. Amir Hamza prevailed over him and instructed him in the Act of Faith and he sincerely converted to the True Faith. Shaddad's son then conducted Amir into the fortress and held a feast for him there for three days. Amir left for Kaus Hisar on the fourth day.

While Shaddad himself was on his way to Kaus Hisar with Naushervan, he sent a missive to Hurmuz that read: "I have killed Hamza and am bringing Naushervan to Kaus Hisar with me. You must arrive there with Zhopin and your army at the same time so that I can finish off the followers of the True Faith and lay claim to Mehr-Nigar and take her into my custody." Upon receiving that note, Hurmuz took Zhopin and departed with his entire army. Arriving at Kaus Hisar within a few days, he presented himself in Naushervan's service. Shaddad wasted no time in sounding the drums of war. He entered the arena astride his steed Shabrang, which was a matchless charger and a peerless mount whose horseshoes alone weighed one hundred and twenty *maunds,* and declared, "O Arabs! Hear that I am Shaddad Abu-Amar Habashi. I have killed Hamza and have Naushervan's permission to take Mehr-Nigar as mine. It is at the orders of the emperor that this army has arrived at your gates. You would do well to leave this place without injury to yourselves." Landhoor moved forward and spurred on his horse to encounter Shaddad, who dealt him a blow of his mace. Landhoor parried this successfully and answered him with such a powerful blow of his mace that Shaddad's horse sank deep into the ground, as if it had entered quicksand. But at the end of hostilities that day, Landhoor returned injured after a long battle. The next day, his son Farhad and several other champions were wounded by Shaddad. Finally, Farkhar Sar-Shaban confronted Shaddad and after fighting him for two days severed Shaddad's arm. Afterward the hostilities were suspended.

About this time, an *ayyar* named Galeem said to Naushervan, "If you were to order me, I would behead every Arab commander and dispatch them all to the Future State." Naushervan answered, "I would like nothing better!" That same night Galeem wormed his way into the Arab camp and entered Qubad's pavilion. Finding Qubad asleep, he cut off his head and left.

But Amar's *ayyars* who were on duty outside did not let him get away. They frustrated his escape and arrested Galeem. A great hue and cry arose when Qubad's severed head was discovered in his possession.

When Mehr-Nigar received the news, despair crushed her and raging grief burnt her heart to cinders. In the morning, Galeem was cut to pieces in retribution. When Naushervan received the news of his grandson's murder, he went into mourning as well. For forty days both camps remained in the state of mourning and indulged in crying and lamentation. When the mourning period was over, both armies again stood facing each other and battled mightily. On that first day of renewed combat, Shaddad and Farkhar were locked in battle when a dust cloud rose from the direction of the forest and *ayyars* brought news that Amir Hamza and Amar had come at the head of a large army. Farkhar Sar-Shaban suspended fighting and went to receive Amir Hamza along with the other commanders of his camp. Shaddad used this opportunity to escape. Sighting a pagan temple nearby, he tried to enter its confines to save his life. But Amir Hamza pursued him and put a noose around Shaddad's neck, gave the end of the rope to Landhoor, and said, "Pull it hard, O Khusrau!" Shaddad's soul flew straight to Hell when Landhoor pulled the rope.

Amir Hamza conferred Shaddad's horse Shabrang on Landhoor, making a gift of that peerless steed to him. In the meanwhile, Amar had arrived there, and he severed and raised Shaddad's head on a lance.

———

When Zhopin saw that the horizon was clear and Mehr-Nigar had been left alone, he decided it was an opportune time to overpower her and take her away. Entering Amir Hamza's pavilion with that plan, he killed the few guards who were standing at the door, gained admission to Mehr-Nigar's quarters, and entered her bedchamber. Mehr-Nigar fired a barrage of arrows at him. Figuring that Mehr-Nigar must abhor him, Zhopin dealt her delicate body a blow of his sword and was about to strike again when Amir Hamza arrived on the scene. Zhopin was cornered and, finding escape impossible, he attacked Amir Hamza. Amir parried his blow and returned it as Zhopin was trying to escape. Amir's sword cut through his skull, his neck, and his spinal column, and Zhopin fell dead in his tracks.

Amir Hamza found Mehr-Nigar at death's door and he dispatched

Amar to call Buzurjmehr there to witness her condition. While Amar was gone to fetch Buzurjmehr, Mehr-Nigar succumbed to her wounds and joined the company of the *houris* in heaven. Amir Hamza let out a cry and fell unconscious.

When Amir came to after an hour, he laughed and cried in turns maniacally, driving himself to the edge of his life. When Amar arrived with Buzurjmehr, he found Mehr-Nigar lifeless and Amir Hamza in a frenzy of grief. Amar was deeply troubled and said to Khvaja Buzurjmehr, "Pray do something to dispel Amir's frenzy and return him to his senses!" Khvaja said, "O Amar! Amir Hamza will get well by himself on the twenty-first day from today. Do not have any worries in this regard."

Despite his frenzy, Amir Hamza prepared biers for Mehr-Nigar, Qubad, and Amar Hamza, and departed for Mecca in an entourage of his friends and companions. Amir came upon a pleasant field as they approached Mecca, where he ordered graves dug for his family members, and he buried these three there. He camped at that place for the night as he did not wish to enter the city yet. It is said that after twenty-one days had passed, Amar saw Prophet Ibrahim in his dream and drank a goblet of pure wine from his hand. Prophet Ibrahim said to Amar, "My son, it is against reason to reduce yourself to such a pitiable state for the sake of a woman. In your life you will find thousands like her. Many women will enter your service who would be far superior to Mehr-Nigar."

Amir Hamza awoke and opened his eyes and asked Amar Ayyar, "Where am I? What happened to me? Tell me truly, what has my condition been?" Amar Ayyar gave him a detailed account of all that had passed, and informed Amir as to his condition since the incident. Amir Hamza then told Amar and his friends what he had seen in the realm of dreams. His companions responded, "Sire, you are the progeny of Prophet Ibrahim. It is only proper that he should appear to counsel you in your dreams. Who else would do so, if he did not? Every parent feels his child's pain." Amir said, "In any event, I gave my word to Mehr-Nigar. To keep it, I shall become a devotee at her shrine and spend the last breaths of my life there. All of you may return home now, and do not bother me with anything anymore."

Amar Ayyar counseled him against following this course of action, but Amir Hamza spurned his advice. He took leave of everyone and, delegating the throne to his grandson Sa'ad bin Amar Hamza, he sent him toward Egypt. Amar Ayyar beseeched Amir Hamza, "O Amir! Do not send me away. Allow me to remain in your company." Amir answered, "Muqbil's presence will suffice me. There is no need for you to stay here."

After everyone had left, Amir Hamza shaved his head, put on beggarly clothes, and spent his nights and days sweeping Mehr-Nigar's grave. Whenever sleep overcame him, he lay down at the foot of her grave.

Of the Arrival of Qaroon Akka bin Furhad-Akka and Kuliyat bin Galeem Ayyar, and of Their Taking Amir Hamza and Muqbil Vafadar Prisoner

The narrators of sweet discourse and the excellent stylists thus ride the galloping steed of the pen into the narrative's domain telling us that the news of Amir Hamza becoming a devotee at Mehr-Nigar's shrine spread far and wide. Seditious heads rose and recalcitrant souls stirred, and they all found the freedom to plan and plot Amir Hamza's murder. Thus it was that Qaroon Akka bin Furhad-Akka, who considered the might of Rustam an object of derision compared with his own, and who did not even fear demons much less human beings, resolved in his heart to kill Amir Hamza. He gathered a mighty army and started from his abode. On the way to Mecca he met Kuliyat, the son of Galeem Ayyar who had murdered Qubad, and joined forces with him. Traveling together, they arrived in the environs of Mecca in a few days.

They captured Amir Hamza and Muqal Vafadar by deceit and Qaroon Akka began inflicting pain and suffering on Amir Hamza.

Qarron Akka constructed a column one hundred and twenty yards high and attached bells to it at intervals, and hung Amir Hamza from the top. He made it his practice to whip Amir daily, sprinkle salt on him, wrap him up in freshly skinned hides, and hang him up from the pole of *uqabain* to avenge the death of his elders.

After some days had passed, he informed Naushervan of these circumstances. The emperor summoned his privy counselors and asked them, "What is your opinion in this matter? Shall I order Hamza's death or order his release?" All of them spoke with one voice, saying, "Now that even Mehr-Nigar is dead, you should not show any special consideration to Hamza out of the regard you had for the princess. You should humiliate him in the same manner in which he disgraced you." The faithless

Naushervan accepted their counsel as judicious, and departed for Mecca with his army. He arrived at his destination within a few days and showed much favor to Qaroon Akka.

A merchant conveyed the news of these events to Amar Ayyar who immediately headed for Mecca. In Mecca, Khvaja Abdul Muttalib summoned Amir Hamza's old companions and commanders by dispatching letters to them, and they, too, expressed great surprise at the news. Khvaja Abdul Muttalib also sent a letter with Umayya Zamiri, Amar Ayyar's father, to Aadi.

It happened that Kuliyat Ayyar caught sight of Umayya Zamiri hastening on his way. He arrested Umayya Zamiri and presented him before Naushervan, who bastinadoed him and demanded to know where he was headed. Trying to save his dear life, Umayya Zamiri confessed the details of his mission. After reading the letters, Naushervan had him killed.

It so happened that Amar Ayyar arrived in Mecca the very next day and immediately learned the details of his father's murder. Kuliyat became informed of Amar's arrival and ordered his *ayyars* to arrest Amar upon sight. Upon his orders everyone set out to catch Amar.

One day Kuliyat saw Amar walking alone outdoors and ran after him. They had gone for some distance in this manner with Kuliyat chasing Amar when Amar produced a flower steeped in a drug from his *zambil* and threw it to the ground. Kuliyat picked it up and smelled it. The moment he did so he fell unconscious, and Amar found his chance and cut off his enemy's head. At once, Amar went to the pole of *uqabain* and saw Amir Hamza and Muqbil Vafadar chained to it. Amar climbed the pole and removed Muqbil's fetters and stuck Kuliyat Ayyar's head on the pole of *uqabain*. He stuffed cotton in all the bells so that they did not ring.

However, Amar had not noticed one bell that was placed above Amir Hamza's head. Since he had not stuffed it with cotton, when Amar tried to bring Amir down his head struck the bell and it rang loudly. The infidels rushed there from all corners and began shooting arrows at them. Amar jumped down from the column and disappeared.

When the infidels reached the column they saw Kuliyat Ayyar's head displayed there. They went to Qaroon Akka to give him the news of Kuliyat Ayyar's murder. When Bakhtak heard this as well, he said, "None but Amar Ayyar could have done this." Qaroon Akka said, "If you were to advise it, I would kill Hamza!" Bakhtak shook from terror at Qaroon Akka's words and said, "Until Amar is captured, you must drive such thoughts from your mind!"

Now hear of Amar. He sent messages to Amir's champions and commanders to come to his aid.

Amir Hamza's commanders started to arrive in Mecca daily and his champion warriors all began gathering there.

Qaroon Akka departed with Hamza for his city, and after reaching his destination within a few days, began inflicting even greater pain and punishment on him.

Now back to Amir's camp: Sa'ad Amar Hamza also arrived in Mecca, and champion soldiers, kings, and princes came there daily until the armies were established as before. Qaroon Akka enclosed himself within the citadel and reinforced its ramparts and crenelations.

Khvaja Amar Ayyar was on the lookout for a chance to break into this citadel, and one night he managed to sneak into the fortress disguised as a merchant. He made friends with a clothier there and convinced him that they had been friends of old, and he thus began a partnership in his shop. Amar did his best to seek out Amir Hamza but could not discover where he had been imprisoned.

It so happened that around this time Qaroon Akka's sister, Farzana, saw Prophet Ibrahim in her dreams. He instructed her in the Act of Faith and gave her these auspicious tidings: "O Farzana! You and Hamza will become a pair and the Creator will grant you an illustrious son from Hamza's seed. Go forth and secure his release." Upon waking from the dream, Farzana immediately repaired to her brother's house and took Hamza back to her home after bribing and rewarding his guards. In the morning Qaroon Akka heard that Amir Hamza had disappeared. He sent his men in all directions to find some trace of him, but they returned empty-handed. Qaroon Akka said to his vizier, "If Hamza had returned to his camp, we would have heard the sound of festive music. Let us find where he is hiding through *ramal*." After making the calculations, the vizier began to laugh. When Qaroon Akka asked him the reason for his laughter he answered, "Hamza has been released by Farzana Bano. She has been biding her time in pleasure in Hamza's company." When Qaroon Akka sent one of his female attendants to Farzana's house to inquire about these matters, Farzana flew into a rage. She tore out her hair and wept, and then said, "It is a marvel that my honor should be considered so cheap that a vizier should accuse me of infidelity. Just because I did not agree to submit to his pleasure and fulfill his carnal desires, that vile man has maligned and accused me in this manner. When have I ever even seen Hamza? Whoever so wishes can take the trouble of searching for him here." The slave girl returned to Qaroon Akka and narrated all that Farzana had said to her. In his rage, Qaroon Akka put his vizier to the sword that very moment to avenge Farzana's name and honor. Then Qaroon Akka continued to search for Hamza as before.

Meanwhile, Hamza was able to make contact with Amar Ayyar through one of Farzana's slave girls and they planned their escape from that place.

Amar took Amir to a blacksmith's shop, where Amir picked up a hammer and began pounding away at a piece of iron to make himself a sword.

Qaroon Akka arrived there with Bakhtak and confronted Amir, who overpowered Qaroon and took him prisoner. Bakhtak ran away to inform Naushervan about these events and they escaped through a back door. When Qaroon Akka refused to convert to the True Faith, Amir Hamza ordered him to be killed. Amar severed his head and hung it upon the door of the castle and burned his body. Everyone occupied themselves with festivities, as their mission had been accomplished and their desires fulfilled.

———

Now hear of Naushervan. As he was making his escape toward Ctesiphon, he came upon an army led by two valiant and courageous brothers, Sar-Barahna Tapishi and Dewana Tapishi, who had come to assist the emperor with their armies. Naushervan himself set up camp there and received the brothers with great favor and showed them much honor and told them his tale of woe from beginning to end. The two princes pledged their swords in Naushervan's service. Bakhtak said, "Now Hamza cannot escape alive. Such champion warriors were never before pitted against him."

Now for news of Amir Hamza. He wedded Farzana Bano at an auspicious moment and enjoyed her for forty nights and forty days. On the forty-first day, Amir Hamza held court and discovered that the princes of Tapish had come to aid Naushervan. Amir headed onward to challenge them and battle lines were drawn.

First Sar-Barahna Tapishi rode into the battlefield, and after reciting martial songs, sought combat. Landhoor rode out on Shabrang and stood opposite him.

Until evening the two of them fought with their maces. Finally the drums were sounded to suspend combat. Amir asked Landhoor, "What is your estimation of Sar-Barahna Tapishi's prowess?" Landhoor answered,

"O Sahibqiran, I never saw even a *dev* of Qaf—let alone a human being on Earth—who could be said to be his equal." Amir laughed and then said, "O Landhoor, his body is made of steel. Spear, sword, and mace will have no effect on it; he will not die by those weapons."

The next day Madi-Karib fought with Sar-Barahna. Whenever Madi struck him with his mace, Sar-Barahna took it on his head without a single hair being harmed on his body. Madi-Karib tired of dealing blows, but Sar-Barahna remained unperturbed. Suddenly dust rose on the horizon from the direction of the forest and the *ayyars* from both camps brought news that Aljosh Barbari had come with forty thousand troops to aid Naushervan. When he finally arrived Naushervan saw that Aljosh Barbari was ninety yards tall. After sounding the drums to suspend combat, Naushervan returned with him to his pavilion and arranged revels for him.

The next morning, Sar-Barahna Tapishi entered the arena and cried out with great vigor, "O Hamza, why do you not come out to fight me yourself? Is this the proof of your courage?" Before Amir could go out to confront him, a dust cloud grew from the direction of the forest, and when the scissors of the wind cut it apart, everyone saw forty orange standards on the horizon. Amar said to Amir Hamza, "O Sahibqiran, it is the same Naqabdar Naranji-Posh who used to come to aid me in my hour of need!"

The Naqabdar soon arrived there and arrayed his army on one side and stationed his champions in battle positions. Addressing the infidel army, the Naqabdar declared, "Any Gueber whose claim on courage has made him vain must first fight me. Then he may fight the followers of the True Faith." Amir Hamza sent a message to the Naqabdar through Amar that his bravery, resolve, and chivalry were now plainly revealed to him but since Sar-Barahna had already challenged him and called him out by his name, he would answer the challenge. Amir asked the Naqabdar to make sure to call on him at the end of the day. The Naqabdar acquiesced to Amir's wishes.

Amir Hamza rode into the arena on Ashqar Devzad and said to Sar-Barahna Tapishi, "It is a waste of time to fight you with weapons. You and I must test our strength by trying to lift each other from the ground. If my feet rise from the ground I will submit to you, and if I lift your feet above the ground you must submit to me." Sar-Barahna agreed to it. Amir dismounted and Sar-Barahna joined him and began exerting himself to lift Amir Hamza by his waistband. He struggled at this until he sank knee-deep into the ground, but Amir did not budge. Sar-Barahna finally gave up in frustration.

Then Amir made his war cry. Most of the men in the infidel army fell into a faint, and many of them suffered burst eardrums. Amir Hamza caught Sar-Barahna Tapishi by his waist and lifted him up above his head on his very first attempt. He whirled him over his head seven times and then threw him to the ground. Amir Hamza tied him up, and gave him into Amar's custody.

Dewana Tapishi came charging at Hamza with drawn sword upon seeing his brother being taken prisoner but Amir Hamza overpowered him as well. With a heavy heart Naushervan announced the end of hostilities for the day and both armies went back to their camps.

Then the Naqabdar headed for Amir's pavilion. Amir received the Naqabdar with great honor and respect, and expressed his gratitude to the Naqabdar for coming to Amar's assistance during his absence. Naqabdar Naranji-Posh said bashfully, "O Amir, do not make me melt away with shame. I feel mortified that such a long time has passed since your return from Qaf and you have faced countless trials and tribulations in which I was unable to help you."

From the softness of the Naqabdar's voice Amir reasoned that it was a woman. He caught the Naqabdar's hands and led her to another pavilion, saying, "I can bear the excitement no longer, nor can I tell you the secret reason for my acting in this wise. Please forgive my offense and do not hold me to blame." Amir Hamza lifted the Naqabdar's veil without delay uncovering cheeks that were the envy of the moon and a face that was as resplendent as the sun. Amir Hamza fell unconscious, overwhelmed by this woman's beauty. Amar's eyes were also blinded and filled by the radiance of the Naqabdar's aspect. Amar sprinkled Amir Hamza's face with rose water and the essences of musk and orange blossom, and said to the Naqabdar, "Pray forgive me this license, but I request you in God's name to press your face against Amir's without delay so that when he inhales your perfume he is restored to his senses and receives comfort from the closeness of your body." With an embarrassed look Naranji-Posh, who had nursed the desire for such an opportunity for a long time and had lived in that hope, immediately pressed her face to Amir's and brought extreme joy to Amir Hamza by kissing and caressing him. Amir opened his eyes and Amar immediately brought wine. They had had two goblets each when all their shame and embarrassment left them, and Amir seated the Naqabdar in his lap and inquired about her past.

The Naqabdar narrated her story thus: "My name is Naranj Peri. A long time ago I left Mount Qaf and made my dwelling on Koh-e Silan. My throne was flying in the air the day you were fighting Gustham, and I fell into a swoon after beholding your face, which was the very picture of the sun's resplendence. When my vizier's daughter, Nairanj Peri, saw that I had fainted, she carried me back to Koh-e Silan. I learned that the moment my vizier's daughter took me to my dwelling on Koh-e Silan, you had departed for Mount Qaf with Abdur Rahman Jinn. I could do nothing else but pray for your safety and await your arrival. When I learned that you had vouchsafed Mehr-Nigar to Amar's care, and her father Naushervan had decided to snatch her from you by force, I delegated some messenger *perizads* to inform me at once if an army ever threatened to overwhelm Amar's force. Thus it happened that whenever I heard that Amar was in danger of being overwhelmed in a battle, I would arrive for his assistance without delay."

After hearing this speech, Amir Hamza kissed Naranj Peri's sugary lips and said, "My life, you slew the enemy with your relentless sword, and now you have put me to the sword of your chivalry and lofty conduct." He asked Amar Ayyar to read their nuptials, and he married Naranj Peri and spent the whole night in pleasure seeking.

In the morning, Amir bathed, changed, and held court. He ordered Sar-Barahna Tapishi and Dewana Tapishi to be brought before him. They acknowledged Amir Hamza as their master and converted to the True Faith. Afterward Amir Hamza retired to the women's quarters and occupied himself in pleasure-seeking with Naranj Peri.

One day the battle drums were sounded from the enemy camp, and Amir headed for the battleground. Aljosh Barbari fought with Sarkob the Turk that day and humiliated him on the battlefield.

In the meanwhile a dust cloud formed on the horizon and four brothers, Samoom Aadi, Sina Aadi, Qubad Aadi, and Me'aad-Raz Aadi, arrived from the Alburz to help Naushervan with four thousand fully equipped warriors of the Aadi tribe.

An onager suddenly broke into the encampment for the followers of the True Faith and injured hundreds of men. Amir Hamza turned his attention toward the beast and gave it chase. The onager escaped and Amir Hamza followed in pursuit, riding Ashqar Devzad. By late in the day the onager had traversed a great distance and Amir had crossed over the borders of another land. As soon as it was evening, the onager disappeared from his view, leaving Amir Hamza confounded and wondering where it had gone. When he was unable to find any trace of it, Amir hunted and roasted a wild animal, and after eating and drinking he fell asleep under a tree.

When Amir Hamza awoke the next morning, he again caught sight of the onager and again gave chase. The onager disappeared into a garden, and Amir followed him inside. He searched every corner of the garden, looking behind every bush and shrub, but the onager had vanished as if it had never existed.

Amir Hamza was challenged by the master of that garden, Qunduz Sar-Shaban, but Amir overpowered him and he converted to the True Faith. Amir hid his identity from Qunduz and told him that he was Amir Hamza's brother Sa'ad Shami, but Qunduz suspected that he was Amir Hamza in person.

Qunduz hosted Amir for a few days. One day Amir asked him, "What land is it whose borders I have crossed?" Qunduz answered, "This is the land of Kharsana, the kingdom of Fatah Nosh. He has a daughter who is a paragon of beauty. Kings and princes from every land have sought her hand, but she flatly refuses everyone's suit." Amir said to him, "O Qunduz, take me to the city of that princess." Qunduz replied, "Very well, I am bound to your service."

The next day, Amir left with Qunduz for the princess's city. They had gone some ten *kos* when Qunduz said, "Let us dismount to eat and take some rest." They stopped and roasted two goats. Amir was unable to eat a whole goat by himself, but Qunduz ate his goat and then ate the leftover roast from Amir's share as well. Then they traveled onward. After they had gone quite some distance, Qunduz said, "It is impossible for me to take another step for the pangs of my hunger." Amir wondered at Qunduz's speech and figured that Qunduz was a match for Aadi in his appetite.

Amir saw an encampment of merchants close by and went and met their leader, Karvan, who offered them food, and they joined his caravan, which was also traveling to Kharsana. Amir hid his real identity from Karvan as well, who was pleased to learn that he was Abdul Muttalib's son Sa'ad Shami, as Karvan was Abdul Muttalib's friend.

Amir Hamza offered to provide protection to the caravan from the bandit Faulad, for which Karvan offered him one fifth part of the profit from his merchandise. However, Amir refused it, much to the surprise and anger of Qunduz, who was only too willing to keep his share. The bandit Faulad was killed by Qunduz, who was reprimanded by Hamza, as Qunduz had not given Faulad a chance to convert to the True Faith.

In a few days they arrived in Kharsana. Amir Hamza passed his time in great comfort and pleasure and gave away so much in charity that all the mendicants of the city became men of means. Slowly the news traveled to King Fatah Nosh. Rabia Plas Posh, the king's daughter, also heard this news and said to herself, *The diviners often predicted that Hamza would arrive in this town someday and marry me. Perhaps the man in question is Hamza.* She said to her attendants, "Go and see who that man is who has surpassed Hatim in generosity." When the female attendants went and saw Amir Hamza at the caravanserai, they said among themselves, "This young man greatly resembles the portrait our mistress keeps with her. Indeed it seems that he is the subject of that picture!" All of them went before the princess and reported what they had seen. Rabia Plas Posh was delighted to hear this.

It so happened that Nasai, the son of the king of Farang, attacked Kharsana. Fatah Nosh enclosed himself in the fortress. Slowly the noise of this attack reached Amir Hamza's ears. Amir asked the people of the city, "What is the reason for all the commotion? What is afoot that we hear this noise and rioting?" Those who were in the know told Amir, "The king of Farang had asked for the hand of Princess Rabia Plas Posh for Prince Nasai, and the princess turned down the proposal. It is for this reason that the prince has attacked the city.

Amir decorated himself with his arms and armor, mounted Ashqar Devzad, and prepared to go to battle. When the magistrate of the city did not open the city gates to let them out, Qunduz killed him with a blow of his mace, which made Amir angry with him.

King Fatah Nosh learned that the stranger who distributed alms at the inn was heading out to fight the prince of Farang. Fatah Nosh immediately rode out to meet Amir and said to him, "O dear friend, I would like to help you in every possible way. I wish to attach my forces to yours, although they are much fewer than the enemy's hordes." Amir answered, "I have no need to take your army with me. You may go to the roof of the fortress and witness the spectacle there." Amir headed for the battlefield with Qunduz, and Rabia Plas Posh went to the roof of the fortress, and with unbraided hair she supplicated God, praying, "O Almighty God! Pray take this young man into your care, for he goes to do battle and takes on this hardship for the sake of strangers."

The Farangis thought that the two men coming out of the fortress had been sent to make a peace offering. As a precaution, they sent a rider toward them to discover their intentions. Qunduz had an altercation with the soldier, who attacked him with a sword, but Qunduz foiled his attack and dealt him a blow with his mace that made that Farangi soldier sink into the ground along with his horse. Upon witnessing this, Prince Nasai ordered one of his champion warriors to go and take both men captive without delay. Qunduz sent that soldier to the same land to which he had earlier dispatched the other trooper. In a short time, forty Farangi champion warriors lay dead at the hands of Qunduz.

The Farangis were terrified and said to one another, "These two men are not humans. They are from the race of jinns."

The king of Kharsana was greatly pleased by this scene, and when he learned that one of the two strangers who fought for him had introduced himself as Hamza's brother, he suspected that it was Hamza himself, hiding his identity.

To cut a long story short, when all forty champion warriors sent to fight him had been killed by Qunduz, the standard-bearer of the Farangi army himself came to fight Qunduz. Qunduz also attacked him with his mace, but the man caught his weapon and tried to snatch it from his hands. Qunduz called out, "O brother Sa'ad Shami, come quickly to my aid, or else my mace will be snatched from me and I will be overpowered by this infidel!" Amir Hamza roared so mightily that it shook the entire expanse of the desert. The riders of the Farangi army fell from their horses into ditches, and their horses, finding their saddles empty, ran toward the forest. The arm of the standard-bearer of the Farangi army grew limp, and Qunduz exerted himself and snatched his mace from his grasp. The standard-bearer drew the sword from his scabbard and dealt a blow to Qunduz, but Amir Hamza threw his companion out of harm's way and struck the standard-bearer with his sword, severing his arm at the shoulder. A great commotion broke out in the Farangi army and Prince Nasai fled from the battlefield. Amir Hamza and Qunduz followed them for a distance of four *kos* and slaughtered thousands of Farangis, sparing none who came within the reach of their weapons.

Upon witnessing this excellent victory, Fatah Nosh emerged from the fortress with his army and looted the goods and riches of the Farangis with great abandon. Fatah Nosh said to his men, "No one may take a single item from this loot, for all of it is the property of Sa'ad Shami. Beware and make sure that no one touches or appropriates it." Rabia Plas Posh opened the gates of the treasury with a view to offering a sacrifice for Amir's life, and distributed a great many riches among the destitute. There was not one beggar in the whole city who did not become rich that day.

When Amir Hamza returned triumphant and victorious to the city, Fatah Nosh conducted him in an entourage to the fortress and put all the loot before him. Amir embraced him and said, "Distribute this wealth among your men as their reward." Qunduz was shocked into silence upon hearing Amir's words. Fatah Nosh arranged a royal feast in Amir's honor and broke bread with him and joined him as his drinking fellow. Qunduz grew giddy with wine and picked a fight with one of Fatah Nosh's commanders, Yalan. Amir Hamza asked him to cease fighting and admonished him for conducting himself in that manner.

The revels continued for several days. One day Fatah Nosh took his vizier aside and said to him, "If Rabia is agreeable, no better match could be found for her than this man. Go and find out her intentions." The vizier broached the subject with Princess Rabia, who lowered her head and replied, "I shall obey the king's wishes in this matter."

Upon hearing Rabia's message, Fatah Nosh told Amir of his desire to make him his son-in-law. Amir Hamza agreed to his proposal with pleasure and enthusiasm, and the wedding preparations began immediately. On the day of the wedding, Amir remembered Amar and said, "It is a pity that Amar is not here today. Were he present, he would be gladdened by this event."

———

Now hear of Amar. The same day that Amir left the camp in pursuit of the onager, Amar had followed him. Amar had trekked past the same places that Amir had on his way to Kharsana.

God willed it so that Amar arrived at Fatah Nosh's doorstep two hours before the nuptials. He said to the guards, "Go and tell your king that my runaway slave, Sa'ad Shami, has sought refuge with him and hidden himself here. It is my desire that he be immediately arrested and brought as a prisoner to me." The guards went and conveyed Amar's message to the king's court in Amar's same words.

Amir Hamza asked them, "Describe that man's shape and guise to me and tell me how he is dressed and what are his mien and manners." The guards replied, "He is some thirteen yards tall and sports a red broadcloth cap that rises a full five yards from his head. The two feathers attached to his cap move by themselves independent of the movement of the air, and he is dressed in a felt robe. A hamper hangs around his neck, a bow is secured to his body, two feathers and a few arrows without arrowheads or tail feathers are stuck at his waist. He is carrying a paper shield on his back and wields a staff weighing eighteen *maunds*. Over his felt robe he is wearing a flowing gown that is so long and loose that a lion cub could easily hide in its sleeve." Upon hearing this description, Amir Hamza headed out of the court, and all those who heard the description marveled to the very limits of marveling.

Amar rushed forward and fell at Amir Hamza's feet, and Amir Hamza embraced him and showed him great kindness and favor. Then Amir Hamza led him by hand into King Fatah Nosh's court and introduced him to the king by describing Amar's trickery, his cunning, and his faithfulness. When it was time to read the nuptials, Amir said to Amar, "Quickly go and fetch some *qadi*[8] to conduct the ceremony, but make sure he is a follower of the True Faith and a believer."

Amar left the court, changed his garb, and disguised himself as a holy man by sticking a two-yard-long flowing white beard on his face. Then he put on a loose shirt that was so large that a baby *simurgh* could be carried in its sleeve, tied a turban on his head that was closer to a dome in its dimensions, and arrived in the assembly limping and carrying a staff several yards long. All those present, including Amir Hamza and Fatah Nosh, received Amar with great deference. Amir Hamza seated him at a higher station on his right and asked him to conduct the *nikah* ceremony. Amar followed his wishes and read the sermon in such sweet and warbling tones that the eyes of everyone in the audience filled up with tears and the entire assembly fell into a trance.

The king put a thousand dirhams before Amar, who said, "I would never accept such a meager offering, and will not take a farthing less than five thousand dirhams." Qunduz replied, "O mulla, if these thousand dirhams are of no use to you, then pray grant them to me. If they do not have any value for you, allow me to have them." Amar immediately stuffed the money into his shoe and disappeared after giving Qunduz a blow with his staff. After a while Amar again entered the assembly and put his foot over Qunduz's head and danced in such a clownish manner that whoever saw him broke into uncontrollable laughter. Fatah Nosh was greatly pleased by Amar's antics.

Thereafter, rounds of goblets of colorful wines were served and the guests began dancing in a state of giddiness. The king richly rewarded Amar Ayyar and spread joy throughout the whole assembly with his liberality and munificence. The celebrations were held for seven days and seven nights. On the eighth day, Amir Hamza said to Amar Ayyar, "Return to the camp, and I will follow you in a few days. I will spend a little more time here enjoying myself." Amar returned to the camp and Amir retired to the palace to seek pleasure with Rabia Plas Posh. After some days the keeper of the palace presented himself before Amir and gave him the auspicious news that Rabia Plas Posh was with child. Amir said, "I will stay here until my son is born and will not make any plans to go anywhere else." Rabia Plas Posh replied, "O Sa'ad Shami, what you propose is also my heart's desire. Now at last I have seen some happy moments and passed some days and nights of joy."

Of Amir's Departure for the Land of Fatah Nosh's Brother, Fatah Yar; of Amir Slaying a Dragon; and of the Birth of Prince Alam Shah Roomi

The narrators of sweet discourse and the scribes of legends thus relate that Fatah Nosh's younger brother, Fatah Yar, ruled a land neighboring Kharsana. Fatah Yar wrote a letter to his brother stating that he was desirous of meeting his son-in-law.

Fatah Nosh showed the letter to Amir Hamza. Amir said, "There is no harm in this visit. I will go and take on the hardship of the journey for his sake." So, Amir Hamza departed for Fatah Yar's land the following day. When Amir arrived, Fatah Yar received him and conducted him into the city. He seated Amir on a golden throne and was conversing with him when all of a sudden a commotion was heard without. Amir asked Fatah Yar, "What is this noise and disturbance?" Fatah Yar answered, "A dragon lives near this city, and when he exhales, a flame darts from his mouth for a distance of seven *kos*, burning everything in its path. When the dragon inhales, everything for a distance of seven *kos* gets sucked into his open mouth. This city has lived with this scourge for many years, and all things animate and inanimate have been marked by his shadow. The dragon has just exhaled, causing all this commotion in the city and setting all creation to great ferment and turmoil."

Amir said, "It is a shame that Fatah Nosh never breathed a word about this dragon to me; otherwise I would have rid you of this scourge many days ago and crushed the dragon's head. In any event, I would like you to appoint someone to lead me to the dragon's lair." Fatah Yar said, "I shall accompany you myself." Amir saddled Ashqar and took Qunduz and headed out. Fatah Yar took his army along and rode out with Amir. Everyone wondered in their hearts how that man would kill the dragon and overpower such a monster. When Amir saw that the dragon was about to inhale, he dismounted and went toward him. As he approached the dragon, Amir drew his dagger, rushed at the monster, and, pressing his dagger to the dragon's scales cut through them all the way to his spine, killing the dragon. Such a huge amount of smoke billowed from the dragon's mouth that it became dark for many *kos* around, and the sky resembled a ball of smoke.

When the air finally dissipated the smoke cloud, Fatah Yar went with his army and saw the dragon lying dead, heaped up like a small hillock. He kissed Amir Hamza's hands and arms, and thanked him for ridding him of that monster.

After spending a few days with Fatah Yar, Amir Hamza returned to Kharsana, at which time Rabia Plas Posh's pregnancy came to an end. At an auspicious moment, an illustrious son was born to Amir and a long awaited star appeared in the heavens of his expectations. Amir Hamza named the boy Alam Shah Roomi. Fatah Nosh flung open the doors of his treasury and the destitute received from it whatever was appropriate to their need. When Amir's son was forty days old, Amir took his leave of Fatah Nosh and Rabia Plas Posh, and said, "When this boy comes of age, you must send him to the camp of Amir Hamza." Fatah Nosh put Amir under strict oath and said, "Tell me whether your name is Sa'ad Shami or Hamza." Amir answered, "Indeed I am Hamza himself." Fatah Nosh was greatly pleased by that and Qunduz was also beside himself with joy. He began telling everyone proudly, "Verily, none but Hamza had the where-withal to overpower me." Rabia Plas Posh also offered thanks that she was the wife of Hamza, a legend of his time. In due course Amir Hamza departed for his camp with Qunduz.

Amir Hamza's camp, meanwhile, was engaged in daily warfare with Naushervan's forces. One day both armies had just arrayed themselves in battle formations when Amir arrived at his camp with Qunduz. His companions kissed his feet and told him of their campaign. Amir Hamza offered words of comfort to everyone.

Then Amir sent Qunduz into the battlefield. Qunduz and Aljosh were engaged in combat until evening, when the drums were sounded to suspend combat for the day and both armies returned to their resting places.

The next day, Aljosh entered the battlefield and called out, "O Hamza, come out and display your bravery and courage." Amir Hamza spurred on Ashqar Devzad and rode out to skirmish. Aljosh attacked Amir Hamza twice, but Amir did not return the strikes and stood quietly watching. When Aljosh attacked him a third time and aimed to kick him,

Amir caught his leg and spun him above his head. Aljosh grew limp and Amir slammed him to the ground and pinioned him, fastening his arms securely behind his back. Then Amir Hamza gave him to Amar's custody to be imprisoned.

That evening Amir had Aljosh appear in his court and asked him, "Tell me, what are your intentions now?" Aljosh answered, "For as long as I live, I shall remain your slave." Amir Hamza converted him to the True Faith and Amar put the hoop of slavery in Aljosh's ear and enrolled him in the ranks of Amir Hamza's slaves.

The narrators tell that in the midst of the revelries that night, a palace attendant presented himself and gave news of the birth of a son to Amir Hamza by Naranj Peri. Amir ordered the musicians to play festive tunes and conferred gifts and rewards on everyone. He ordered a gold necklace weighing one *maund* and put it around his son's neck and named him Tauq-e Zarrin.

Amir Hamza then rode with his companions into the battlefield. One of the warriors of the Aadi tribe who had come to aid Naushervan descended into the arena and sought combat by loudly challenging Amir Hamza's camp, whereupon Istaftanosh went to answer his challenge. At that time, a dust cloud rose from the direction of the forest. *Ayyars* from both camps exerted themselves to investigate it, and informed their respective armies of the arrival of the prince of Greece with a vast force he had brought to fight the champions of both armies. While the *ayyars* were making these reports, the Greek prince formed his battle arrays in between the two armies, and then rode his horse into the battlefield with great majesty and grandeur. He turned his face toward Naushervan's army and called out, "O Naushervan, send someone to fight me so that he may be acquainted with the mettle of the swords of brave men and may witness the courage and pluck of valiant warriors."

One of the Aadi warriors entered the arena and weighed his mace, aiming to bring it down on the head of the prince. The prince snatched the mace from his hands and, securing his hold on the Aadi's horse's saddle and martingale, lifted the horse along with its rider and slammed them both so hard on the ground that their bones were crushed. Shouts of "Bravo!" and "Well done!" rose from both camps at this show of might, and the tongues that had wagged before in making tall claims were silenced. The scribe of the *dastan* writes that in a matter of a few hours, well over a hundred Aadi warriors were killed by the prince. Naushervan's entire camp sank into disquiet and distress, and his fighters lost their hearts from fear. The prince challenged Naushervan's army, but none would come forward to answer his challenge.

The prince was obliged to turn toward the camp of the followers of the True Faith, and called out to them in a loud voice, "O Arabs, any man among you who dares to combat me should come forward."

The first to answer the challenge was Farhad bin Landhoor. The prince of Greece killed his elephant, and when he rode out against him on another elephant, the prince lifted Farhad bin Landhoor along with his elephant. Farhad returned injured to his camp. The next warrior to fight the prince of Greece was Landhoor. The prince proved his strength against Landhoor too and sought another warrior for combat. Then Sa'ad bin Amar Hamza fought him and they remained equal in combat. Finally, Amir Hamza himself rode out to face the prince.

Landhoor said to Amir, "O Sahibqiran! I believe that this prince is your son, for his features and physiognomy reveal that." Amir responded, "If he were my son, he would not battle with my companions." Landhoor answered, "Amar Hamza also fought with you. This prince also might desire to test his strength against yours."

In the arena, Amir brought his steed next to the prince's mount. The prince secured a hold on Amir's cummerbund and Amir caught hold of the prince's belt. They exerted themselves and, in the end, Amir Hamza bellowed his war cry and lifted the prince into the air. He was about to slam him to the ground when he heard a voice from the heavens and an angel brought him these auspicious tidings: "O Hamza, do not throw him down cruelly, for he is your own son." Upon hearing that voice, Amir Hamza put the prince down lightly on the ground and asked him, "What is your name?" He answered, "I am Alam Shah Roomi." He then kissed Amir Hamza's feet, and his father embraced him and kissed his face. They returned to Amir's camp and Hamza ordered festive music, most jubilant to have met the prince. He gave the prince the titles of Rustam-e Peel-Tan[9] and Sher-e Saf-Shikan.[10]

Amir then said to him, "You committed a grave wrong by humiliating my friends in the battlefield and fighting me." The prince answered, "Brother Amar Hamza was guilty of the same wrong that I committed. Your obedient servant was obliged to introduce himself thus." Amir Hamza introduced the prince to all his friends and companions and made the prince offer apologies to them. Considering that Alam Sher was Amir Hamza's dear son, everyone met the prince with great kindness, and for seven nights and seven days festivities were held to celebrate his arrival.

On the eighth day, when the drums of war were sounded in the camp of the infidels, Alam Shah answered the challenge. The narrator says that Rustam-e Peel-Tan killed fifty enemy warriors that day and slew many notable commanders with his glittering sword. Then Alam Shah charged the enemy ranks. The foe retreated and Alam Shah chased them for a distance of four *kos*.

Meanwhile, Naushervan said to Bakhtak, "We were handed a resounding defeat. Where should we go and what strategy can we employ?" Bakhtak answered, "The city of Khavar is nearby, and its ruler, Qeemaz Shah Khavari, is known for his bravery. The whole world rings with the renown of his courage and chivalry. If you were to take refuge with him and describe your troubles to him, he would exert himself fully in obeying your commands." Thus Naushervan headed for the city of Khavar. When he approached there, messengers alerted Qeemaz Shah Khavari of his arrival. Qeemaz Shah rode out with great magnificence to receive Naushervan and inquired of his welfare. After comforting and consoling him, Qeemaz Shah said, "If Hamza heads in this direction, he will receive the just deserts for his sins."

Of Amir's Departure Toward the City of Khavar in Pursuit of Naushervan, and of His Converting Qeemaz Shah, the Ruler of Khavar, to the True Faith

The storytellers have it that after Amir had finished with the festivities, he asked Amar, "Do you have any news of Naushervan's whereabouts?" Amar answered, "It is said that he has gone to the city of Qeemaz Shah Khavari." Amir said, "Order our advance camp to head for the city of Khavar." Nearing the city, Amir sent a missive to Qeemaz Shah that read:

> O Qeemaz Shah, know that Naushervan is my archenemy, and this time I am determined to punish him. Now I hear that he has sought refuge with you. It is incumbent on you to send him and the ill-starred Bakhtak to me as prisoners immediately upon reading this letter. Otherwise, you will find your place in the coffin instead of on the throne.

Amar carried Amir Hamza's letter to Qeemaz Shah's court. When Amar gave the letter into Qeemaz Shah's hands and he read it, he tore it up immediately and said, "I neither pay vassalage to Hamza nor do I have any awe for him that I would carry out his orders to arrest Naushervan and Bakhtak and send them to him." Amar answered, "O Qeemaz Shah, the Sahibqiran did not order me to do so, otherwise I would have ripped up your belly in the same way that you tore up that letter."

Qeemaz Shah turned to his slaves, who stood before him with folded arms, and said, "Catch this foul-mouthed messenger!" The slaves surrounded Amar on all sides. Amar drew a steel dagger from his scabbard and released countless slaves from the misery of attending to Qeemaz Shah. Then Amar slapped Qeemaz Shah, snatched his crown, and left after thoroughly humiliating him. Many ran to catch him, but Amar was not one to be caught and overpowered so easily.

Bakhtak said to Qeemaz Shah, "Perhaps Your Honor is unfamiliar with this attendant of Hamza. He is such a monster that the eyes of heaven have never seen his equal." Qeemaz Shah answered, "You will see how I treat him and his master and quench my sword in his blood."

The next day Qeemaz Shah marched into the battlefield to the sound of war drums, and Amir arranged his army opposite him. First to arrive on the battlefield was Qeemaz Shah's sister, Khurshid Khavari, who was a master lance thrower and unsurpassed in martial arts. She called out with great vanity and pride, "O champion warriors, come out and show me what you own in the name of valor."

Within an hour she injured several champions from Amir's camp. Rustam-e Peel-Tan could not hold back his fury any longer. He took to the field and descended into the arena like lightning. The prince caught hold of her lance, and despite her exertions, she was unable to wrench it from his hands. The prince snatched the lance from her and removed the poison from its tip, and then dealt her a blow of its shaft that threw her from her horse. When the prince dismounted and tried to fasten her up, he discovered that this warrior was a woman. He carried her off on his horse in his lap, and produced her before Amir and everyone in the camp. Amir Hamza asked her, "O woman, who are you and what is your name?" She answered, "My name is Khurshid Khavari, and I am the sister of Qeemaz Shah." Amir ordered that she be conducted to the mother of Rustam-e Peel-Tan and given into her care. That day Rustam-e Peel-Tan fought Qeemaz Shah's brother, his father, Nim-Tan Khavari, and Qeemaz Shah's elder son, Homan Khavari, who were all overpowered and taken prisoner when they sought battle with the prince.

Qeemaz Shah sounded the drums to announce the day's end and returned to his pavilion. Both armies went back to their resting places and took refuge from the hardships of the battlefield.

Amir embraced Rustam-e Peel-Tan and offered gold and jewels as a sacrifice of his life, and gave away even more in charity in gratitude for his safe return from the battlefield. Amir Hamza sent a message to Khurshid Khavari to inquire if she was willing and happy to accept Rustam-e Peel-Tan as her husband. She answered, "I would envy my own stars if I were granted such an illustrious husband and his company in which to enjoy life's pleasures." Amir Hamza engaged Rustam-e Peel-Tan and Khurshid Khavari in matrimony at an auspicious moment and then took part in the festivities.

For seven days and seven nights Rustam-e Peel-Tan remained in the palace, and on the eighth day he emerged to the sound of the drums of war and decorated himself with his arms and armor. Amir Hamza took to the battlefield and organized his army. Qeemaz Shah brought his horse into the arena and called out, "O Arab lad, come out and face me so that I can instruct you in the intricacies of combat."

Rustam-e Peel-Tan spurred on his horse and when he came within reach Qeemaz Shah dealt him a blow with his eight-hundred-*maund* mace with all his might. The prince escaped the blow by stopping it with his shield, but his steed was injured. The prince dismounted and cut off the legs of Qeemaz Shah's horse. The two of them changed horses and resumed fighting. Until noon the two of them fought with maces and then drew swords. When their swords grew blunt they wielded lances. They fought so mightily that their lances broke apart inch by inch.

Finally, Qeemaz Shah sounded the drums to announce the day's end, and the following day the armies again faced each other. Landhoor took Amir's leave and went to fight Qeemaz Shah. Qeemaz dealt him a blow of his mace that Landhoor parried with great effort and answered with his own mace.

Both warriors fought with such ferocity that the two armies constantly exclaimed "Bravo!" and "Well done!" With night falling, the trumpeters sounded the end of combat for the day. Amir asked Alam Shah Roomi and Landhoor, "How did you find Qeemaz Shah?" They answered, "If there is anyone who can be said to have a claim to power and strength after you, it is Qeemaz Shah."

The following day the two armies again faced each other in the battleground. A warrior had yet to enter the field from either side when a forty-yard-tall youth covered in steel came forward from the direction of the forest and stood between the two armies. He turned his face toward the infidel army and roared like a lion, "O Naushervan, send one of your champions to fight me." Naushervan sent an Aadi warrior to combat with him. The rider lifted the Aadi warrior up and slammed him to the ground so fiercely that every bone in his body was crushed and he never rose to his feet again. A second Aadi warrior came into the field and suffered the same fate. Then nobody dared to confront and skirmish with the stranger. After waiting for an hour for someone from Naushervan's camp to challenge him, he turned toward the camp of the followers of the True Faith and challenged them. Sarkob Turk took Amir Hamza's leave and confronted the youth, who threw Sarkob on the ground but allowed him to leave, saying to him, "Go and send me someone else to fight with me."

Qunduz Sar-Shaban next took Amir Hamza's leave and went to fight. That ferocious warrior caught Qunduz Sar-Shaban and separated him from his mount but left him unharmed and did not strike or injure him. The giant said, "Go back now and send me another man to fight." Qunduz returned and told Amir Hamza all he had undergone. Amir said to him, "From his face and features it seems to me that he is your son." Qunduz said, "If he is indeed my own blood, nothing will keep me from killing him and smashing his head with my mace for disgracing me in this manner before both camps and robbing me of my prestige."

Then Rustam-e Peel-Tan and Alam Shah Roomi went into combat against that desert warrior. The youth caught hold of Rustam's cummerbund and exerted himself to the last iota of his strength to lift the prince, but he did not budge even slightly from his place. Rustam caught hold of the mysterious youth, bellowed his war cry, and lifted him clear out of the saddle several handspans into the air. Then Rustam put him lightly on the ground and asked, "Tell me truthfully who you are and what your name is and of which place are you a native." He answered: "My name is Shaban Taifi, and I am the son of Qunduz Sar-Shaban."

Rustam-e Peel-Tan brought him along and produced him into Amir Hamza's service. After he had made Shaban Taifi kiss Amir's feet, he explained his particulars. Amir Hamza embraced him and showed him much affection, and then sounded the drums to announce the day's end and returned to his pavilion. Amir Hamza gave Shaban Taifi the title of the Latter-day Hamza and seated him on the throne of his son Amar Hamza, augmenting his rank before the whole court.

On the eighth day the two armies again faced each other. Shaban Taifi fought Qeemaz Shah Khavari, but despite remaining engaged in combat the whole day neither was able to overpower the other. Each soldier returned to his pavilion at the end of the day. The next morning the battle arrays were formed again. Qeemaz Shah came out onto the field and challenged Amir Hamza who rode Ashqar Devzad into the battlefield. Qeemaz Shah brought down his mace with all his strength, but Amir blocked it and then dealt a mace blow to Qeemaz Shah who stopped it with his head. Although Qeemaz survived the blow, sweat streamed from every pore in his body and all four legs of his horse were broken from the impact. Qeemaz Shah jumped from his horse and tried to hamstring Ashqar Devzad, but Amir quickly left his saddle to face Qeemaz. They fought until noon with maces and then they drew swords to continue the fight, but neither of them was able to achieve his end and secure victory over the other by any device.

Qeemaz Shah then praised Amir Hamza, who replied, "We have tried our weapons, and now only one thing remains. I will catch hold of you by your waist and you should do the same and we will both try to raise each other from the ground. The one who loses must pay allegiance to the other and give himself unto the other's service for the rest of his life." Qeemaz Shah accepted the condition. Thus speaking, Qeemaz Shah caught hold of Amir's cummerbund and exerted all his power and might to lift him, yet he was unable to raise Amir Hamza from the ground. Amir let out his war cry and lifted Qeemaz Shah above his head. After turning him seven times above his head, Amir threw him to the ground and pinioned him and gave him into Amar's custody.

Amir Hamza returned to his camp to the sound of festive music and ordered that all the Khavaris be brought before him. When Amar had done this, Amir Hamza said to Qeemaz Shah, "I won the wager and you are the loser. Therefore you must convert to the True Faith." He answered, "It is far more preferable for me to be killed than to convert to the True Faith. It is not the tradition of our forefathers to give up our ancestral faith." Amir was enraged and ordered Landhoor and Madi-Karib to kill him with their maces and dispatch the infidel to Hell. However, Qeemaz Shah remained unaffected by the mace blows showered on him by the two champions. Witnessing this, Amir Hamza became most sorrowful that a mighty warrior of Qeemaz's caliber should be lost to him for not obeying his commands. He said, "Give him into the custody of Madi-Karib." Qeemaz Shah asked, "How long will you keep me captive, and what will you achieve by imprisoning me?" Amir said, "I will not give up tormenting you. As long as you are alive, you will rot in prison."

At that moment Qeemaz Shah asked for water. Amir ordered sherbet made for him and had the Book of Ibrahim[11] recited over it. The moment Qeemaz Shah drank the sherbet, it melted his stony heart and he realized the truthfulness of the True Faith. He said to Amir, "Why do you not kill me?" Amir answered, "I am sorry for your plight, and I am rueful that a mighty warrior and a courageous and brave man like yourself should die in complete blindness to his own good." Then Qeemaz Shah laughed heartily and said, "O Hamza, I am now convinced that you are a great connoisseur of brave men and show mercy to the slaves of God. I am ready to submit to your every command since it would be against all wisdom to turn away from doing so. Tell me now, what is your pleasure?" Amir said, "That you should convert to the faith of Ibrahim." That very instant Qeemaz Shah ennobled himself with the True Faith, along with his father, brother, and son. Amir Hamza conferred robes of honor on all of them and, after conferring a Jamshedi robe of honor on Qeemaz Shah, seated him by his side on his throne and ordered revels to be arranged to celebrate the occasion.

Naushervan said to Bakhtak, "We must depart for another refuge and escape from their clutches." Bakhtak answered, "The city of King Kayumars is not far from here. That sovereign is an accomplished spearsman and is so intrepid and stalwart that fear of him used to drive Qeemaz Shah to retreat into the mountains to save his life. We must go to him."

Naushervan escaped with Bakhtak without loss of time and sought refuge with Kayumars Shah. Upon hearing the news, Amir Hamza decided to follow him to Kayumars Shah's dominion.

Rustam-e Peel-Tan said, "Khurshid Khavari is with child. What are your wishes with regard to her?" Amir answered, "Send her to her mother. You must depart with the advance camp." Rustam-e Peel-Tan sent Khurshid Khavari to her home to be with her family.

The next day Amir marched toward Kayumars Shah's lands accompanied by his whole army. Qeemaz Shah accompanied him, along with his brothers and sons.

After Amir Hamza's army had arranged itself in battle formations, Kayumars came into the battlefield wielding a lance and challenged the followers of the True Faith. Qeemaz Shah made a salutation to Amir Hamza and said, "If you were to order me, I would go to answer Kayumars Shah's challenge." Amir replied, "Go forth. I give you into the custody and protection of God."

After exchanging the challenge Kayumars attacked Qeemaz Shah with his lance. Qeemaz Shah did his best to foil the strike, but the point of the lance pierced Qeemaz Shah's foot, and since it was laced with a deadly poison, Qeemaz Shah returned to camp suffering from an unbearable burning pain. He fell unconscious immediately upon entering his pavilion. Amar put a bandage of *noshidaru* on his wound and went himself to face Kayumars Shah.

Seeing Amar's strange garb, Kayumars said, "O clown, has some madness seized you that you have come to face and fight me?"

With his cunning and alacrity Amar humiliated Kayumars and

snatched his lance. Amar presented the lance to Amir Hamza, who said, "Clean the poison from its tip and give it to Sa'ad Yemeni, who is a lance fighter and a spearsman beyond compare."

When night had fallen, an *ayyar* presented himself to Naushervan's service and said to him, "King Tassavuran has sent his daughter, who is unequaled in beauty and comeliness, to be given to you in marriage. Pray send for her and give permission for her to be brought into your presence." Naushervan was greatly pleased by these auspicious tidings and sent Buzurjmehr to bring her to him. Khvaja Buzurjmehr brought her into the camp and lodged her in the women's quarters, and her arrival afforded great pleasure to Naushervan.

The narrator states that this princess had once seen Hamza's portrait. She had become ardently enamored of him, and wished to sacrifice her life and soul at his feet. Some days after her arrival in Naushervan's camp, she found her chance and, dressed in night livery, she entered Amir Hamza's camp. She pulled out a peg from the back of Amir's tent and gained entry within. She drugged and kidnapped him in his sleep and carried him to a trench hidden from everyone's view. After diluting the effects of the drug in Amir's body, she disclosed her love for him and revealed to him the secret hidden in her heart. Amir asked her, "Who are you?" She answered, "I am Zar-Angez, the daughter of King Tassavuran. Now I am Naushervan's wife." Amir answered, "In the first place, Naushervan is my father-in-law, and in the second place, you have a husband. I would never inculpate myself in this manner with you. Such a deed is strictly proscribed in my religion and is considered a grave sin." Zar-Angez showered Amir with sweet words of love, but he paid her not the least attention and closed his ears to her words. When she saw that he refused her advances, she threatened him, saying, "O Hamza, I will kill you if you do not accept me!" Amir replied, "If that is written in my fate, then there is no help for it. But nothing that you do to harm me will have the least effect if it is not fated." They were still engaged in this exchange when the dawn arose. Zar-Angez left Amir imprisoned in the ditch and went back to her pavilion.

A great hue and cry rose in Amir's camp that morning. Seeing that he had disappeared from his tent, everyone began searching for him. In due time news of this reached the camp of the infidels, and they, too, were surprised. Kayumars Shah boasted to Naushervan that Hamza had decamped for fear of his poison-tipped lance. The two armies again faced each other in the arena. The camp of the followers of the True Faith appointed Rustam-e Peel-Tan as Amir Hamza's deputy and formed their forces in battle arrays. That day, Landhoor, his son Farhad, and Sarkob Turk fought Kayumars Shah and were wounded by his poisoned lance. As the shades of evening fell, the drums to announce the day's end were sounded in both camps and the armies went back to their resting places.

That strumpet visited Hamza again that night and told him that she was greatly distressed to see that three of his champions had been injured by Kayumars and that men who were the pride of his warriors had fared so ill at his hands. Amir said to her, "It is a shame that you have kept me a prisoner here. Set me free so that I may teach Kayumars the art of lance fighting." That harlot answered him, "Not until I have achieved my end will I set you free." Amir replied: "Whether or not you set me free, I shall never commit such a wrong as satisfying your carnal desire." In short, that night also ended and that licentious woman left Amir as before to return to her pavilion.

In the morning Kayumars again entered the arena and bellowed loudly, "He whose death is nigh should face me and enter the arena!" This time, Sa'ad Yemeni took the prince's leave to face him. Kayumars charged at Sa'ad and raised his arm to strike him, but Sa'ad foiled his attack. After they had fought and exchanged thrusts of their spears, Kayumars found his chance and injured Sa'ad Yemeni. It was soon evening and the armies again retreated to their resting places.

That wanton woman returned to Amir, proclaiming her desire to Amir in the language of tears and crying with her head lowered at his feet. It so happened that Amar Ayyar happened by that place in search of Amir and, hearing her words, confronted that whore, who immediately ran away at the sight of him. He asked Amir, "Who was she? If you order me, I will kill her and make her brains flow from her skull." Amir answered, "Do not harm her. Let her go, for she is a woman. Spare her because that sinful creature is Naushervan's wife and he is very enamored of her." Amar tried to open Amir's bonds, but the Sahibqiran broke them all by himself. Amar asked him, "Why did you not try these two days to secure your release? Why could you not break these chains before?" Amir answered, "Everything is fated to happen at a particular time. It was God's will that a worthless woman should make me her prisoner." Amir exited the trench and offered his gratitude to God for his release. He sent for Ashqar and his arms and armor, and rode from there straight into the battlefield. Upon sighting him, his friends ordered festive music played, and their hearts were pacified.

Kayumars came into the arena and called out loudly, "O Arab, where did you run off to in fear of me?" Amir smiled, spurred on Ashqar to face him, and answered, "O braggart, deal me your blow!" After they had fought for some time, Amir dealt Kayumars such a powerful blow with the shaft of his lance that Kayumars was stunned and darkness fell before his eyes. He fell from his horse and after pinioning him and securing his limbs well, Amir gave him into Amar's custody.

When Naushervan saw what had happened, he said to Bakhtak, "We must worry for our own fates now and escape from the clutches of the foe." Bakhtak said, "Let us depart for Gilan, whose sovereign is King Gunjal. He also has a daughter whose beauty puts the *peris* to shame, and the eyes of Heaven fail to find anyone as beautiful as she. She has a masterful command of the arts of lancing, swordplay, mace fighting, and other arts of war. Hamza stands nowhere in comparison to her." Naushervan departed that very instant and, traveling night and day, arrived in Gilan. He wrote a missive to King Gunjal describing the hardships he had suffered at Hamza's hands. After reading this letter, King Gunjal came out to greet Naushervan and conducted him to his court offering him words of comfort and solace.

While Naushervan was awaiting Amir Hamza's arrival in Gilan, Kayumars converted to the True Faith and received rewards and a high station in Amir Hamza's court. He invited Hamza to his city and hosted him there lavishly.

OF AMIR'S DEPARTURE FOR GILAN AND KING GUNJAL'S CONVERTING TO THE TRUE FAITH, AND OF AMIR'S MARRIAGE TO GILI-SAVAR, THE DAUGHTER OF KING GUNJAL

The narrator tells that Kayumars Shah's city had many pastures in its vicinity. The lure of the hunt kept Amir Hamza camped there for many days. He passed his days hunting and his nights in pleasure seeking, and his life there was an uninterrupted tale of cheer and comfort. One day he asked Amar, "Have you had any news where Bakhtak has now led Naushervan?" Amar answered, "He is in Gilan with King Gunjal." Amir said, "We must also visit Gilan and see the sights that land has to offer." The advance camp left the same day for Gilan, and the next day Amir followed with his army. After some days, he arrived near Gilan and set up camp in its vicinity.

Spies brought intelligence of Amir's arrival to King Gunjal and Naushervan had the drums of war sounded that same day. A warrior had yet to come forward from either camp on the day of battle when a dust cloud rose from the direction of the forest. The moment the skirts of dust were torn apart, they all beheld a mounted warrior striding forth with a lance in his hand and with an appearance to strike awe in the hearts of his beholders. He arrived in the arena at a leisurely pace, and after sweeping both armies with his glance, sought combat with the army of the followers of the True Faith. One after another, Shermar Sherwani, Taz Turk, and Kaus Sherwani challenged the warrior and were defeated by him.

In the meantime, the evening hours had crept over them and the combat was soon ended. Kaus Sherwani returned to his camp and the rider turned back toward the forest. Amir Hamza and Amar followed him to investigate the matter.

Hearing a sound behind him, the rider speedily disappeared into a garden. Amir followed him and watched the rider dismount near a pond.

Mace bearers, attendants, and servants—all of them women—rushed forward from all corners to receive the warrior. Amir said to Amar, "It appears that this rider is a woman." At that moment, the rider caught sight of Amir and sent a eunuch to Amir Hamza and Amar. The eunuch asked Amir Hamza, "Who are you, and why have you set foot here?" Amir introduced himself and Amar and said, "O attendant, what is the name of your princess?" The eunuch replied, "My princess is known as Gili-Savar." Then he returned to his mistress and told her the news.

The princess retired to the garden's summerhouse. She took off her armor and exchanged her manly garb for a womanly costume. She came forward to greet Amir Hamza and conducted him to the throne and treated him with great respect and honor. She offered Amir a crystal goblet filled with rose-colored wine. She drank one herself and after they had become inebriated, she removed the veil from her face and sat in Amir's lap, casting aside all modesty and shame.

When Amir's eyes beheld the gaze of that moonfaced beauty, her eyebrows shot out the arrows of her eyelashes and deeply pierced his heart. He involuntarily yearned for marriage with her, and openly stated his desire. As ardor and longing had already lodged themselves in her heart, she accepted Amir's proposal. Khvaja Amar Ayyar immediately tied them into the nuptial knot by reciting the wedding sermon and unifying the two hearts. Amir Hamza and Gili-Savar then retired to the bedchamber, where they took pleasure of each other and drank the nectar of nuptial delights.

News of the wedding reached King Gunjal, and he descended on them with four thousand troops and put a cordon around the garden. The princess said to Amir Hamza, "If you order it, I shall sever his head and dispatch him to the land of the hereafter." Amir answered, "He is your father, after all. You must never raise your hand to strike him. I will go to teach him a lesson for his arrogant ways." Amir then stepped out of the garden.

Upon seeing Amir, Gunjal said, "O Arab, did you consider my daughter to be like Naushervan's—someone you could marry by force? The same vanity has again possessed you. You shall see now how I punish you and take my revenge for your actions." King Gunjal drew his sword and rushed at Amir, who overpowered him, and King Gunjal converted to the True Faith.

One night Amir was lying with Gili-Savar in the garden when Zar-Angez, who had kept Amir her prisoner for three days in the trench, came into the garden armed with her bow and quiver. Seeing Amir asleep holding Gili-Savar in his arms, Zar-Angez was beset by terrible pangs of jealousy. She said to herself, *Hamza spurned me and married Gili-Savar, inflicting a great wrong on me. Now is my chance to kill both of them and show them no mercy.* She was taking aim when Gili-Savar woke up and, seeing Zar-Angez standing nearby, rose from bed. Zar-Angez climbed down from the roof of the palace and by the time Gili-Savar came out to confront her, she had galloped away in fear. Gili-Savar followed her on horseback. After they emerged from the garden into the open field, that strumpet turned around and said, "I ran away from the garden in fear of Hamza, not because I was afraid of you. I have no fear of you and deem it absolutely unworthy of my status to feel any dread or anxiety because of you." She shot an arrow at Gili-Savar, who cut it in flight with her sword. Gili-Savar then spurred on her horse, which flashed like lightning and came up to Zar-Angez. Joining her stirrups together, Gili-Savar dealt her a thrust of her sword that cut Zar-Angez in two; her body fell to the ground.

Amir had witnessed everything from afar. When Gili-Savar killed Zar-Angez, he called out, "What have you done, O Gili-Savar! Nausher-van will think that I killed her and will thus suffer terrible embarrassment and mortification." Gili-Savar answered, "What is done is done." Then Amir returned to the garden with Gili-Savar and rested there for the night.

In the morning Naushervan received news that Zar-Angez lay dead in the field. He sent *ayyars* to bring back her corpse, and after expressing much sorrow, said, "It seems that this wanton woman went to see Hamza, who then killed her. A thousand pities and great shame that I should see the day when a woman would leave my side to be with another man without any regard for my name and honor. Now I cannot show my face to the world." He then said to his slaves, "I have had my fill of reigning over the empire. Now I wish to travel from one land to another and pass the remaining days of my life in this manner." Naushervan ordered his saddlebags filled with a great quantity of goods, gold, and jewels and, taking a thousand slaves with him, he left the city in the middle of the night and headed for Tartary. Whenever people asked him who he was, he identified himself as a merchant and held back his true identity.

The next morning Naushervan's camp was in an uproar over his disappearance. Some suggested that Amir Hamza had killed him, others said that Amar Ayyar had kidnapped him. Buzurjmehr said, "If Hamza killed the emperor or Amar kidnapped him, who took the thousand slaves? Naushervan must have departed in shame for the deeds of Zar-Angez." Prince Hurmuz sent his men to all corners of the empire to find him. At the advice of the courtiers and nobles he ascended the throne to look after the affairs of the empire and took over Naushervan's duties.

————

Now hear of Naushervan. He went on his way, bearing the hardships of the journey and telling everyone he met along the way that he was a merchant. It so happened that a bandit named Bahram conducted a raid on Naushervan's camp. Most of Naushervan's slaves were killed and all his goods and wealth were stolen. Bahram also took Naushervan prisoner, and asked him, "O old man, tell me the truth. Who are you, and where are you headed?" Naushervan answered, "I am Naushervan bin Qubad." Bahram said, "Why do you lie, you deceitful old man? Where is the comparison between you and Naushervan? He is the Emperor of the Seven Climes. What business would he have selling merchandise?" With these words, Bahram had Naushervan thrown out by the scruff of his neck, and robbed him of every last farthing. Naushervan put on the garb of beggars and crept along his way, and on the fourth day he finally arrived in Tartary.

Finding a stranger in their city, all the citizens there asked him, "O dervish, whence have you come?" Naushervan replied, "I am Naushervan bin Qubad." Everyone who heard this considered him a liar and rebuked him, calling him names. Slowly the news reached the king of Tartary that a fakir had newly arrived in his land claiming to be Naushervan bin Qubad. The king had him brought into his presence and asked Naushervan to tell him about himself. Naushervan again repeated what he had told everyone. The king did not believe him and ordered that the false dervish be driven out of his kingdom.

In short, Naushervan was driven away as an impostor and charlatan whenever he gave people a true account of himself. In his travels, Naushervan finally arrived at the fire temple of Namrud. It was the custom of that place that any traveler who arrived there was given food for three days and on the fourth day he was sent on his way. If anyone wished to stay longer, he had to fetch wood from the forest for use in the fire temple. Thus Naushervan received food for three days and on the fourth day he was told either to leave or fetch wood from the forest.

Naushervan had never cut wood in his life; however, he was forced to comply due to the need to feed himself. The man in charge of the fire temple said, "This fakir has brought back very little wood, and therefore he deserves a like share of our food." That day Naushervan could not satisfy his hunger. When he went to the forest again the next day, he could not cut much wood at all and tried to steal some from other men's bundles. Someone caught sight of him stealing wood, and everyone there gave him a good beating. Naushervan suffered a double misfortune in receiving the beating and also having the wood he had cut himself taken from him. Naushervan returned with even less wood that day and, as a consequence, received even less food.

———

Now hear of Naushervan's camp. Hurmuz said to Buzurjmehr, "The emperor has not been found. Pray discover his whereabouts by *ramal.*" Buzurjmehr answered, "I have already made the necessary calculations and learned that Naushervan is at the fire temple of Namrud and is suffering great hardships. If no one goes there to aid him, he will never again be seen alive by anyone." Hurmuz said, "O Khvaja, pray go and bring him back." Buzurjmehr replied, "Not until Hamza goes to fetch him shall Naushervan ever return." Hurmuz said, "Why would Hamza ever go there?" Buzurjmehr replied, "If your mother were to write to him, Hamza would surely go and bring back Naushervan." Hurmuz then went and narrated the whole account to Mehr-Angez. The empress wrote a letter to Hamza requesting his aid.

Upon reading the letter, Amir Hamza sent Amar to Buzurjmehr to discover Naushervan's whereabouts. Buzurjmehr said to him, "Tell Amir that Naushervan is languishing in the fire temple of Namrud. If you depart on foot without delay, you would arrive there in time."

Of Amir's Departure for the Fire Temple of Namrud to Bring Back Naushervan, and of His Marrying Naushervan's Second Daughter upon Their Return

The narrator tells us that Amir cast off his royal garb and, wearing a sheet of cloth around his waist and putting on a habit of shreds and patches, set out for the fire temple of Namrud. Along the way, Amir learned that the bandit Bahram had looted Naushervan. Amir arrived at Bahram's castle and challenged him. In their encounter Amir prevailed over Bahram. Upon hearing his name, Bahram sincerely converted to the True Faith, conducted Amir to his castle, and feted him for several days.

When Amir asked Bahram about Naushervan, he answered, "O Amir, when he told me that he was Naushervan bin Qubad, I did not believe him and took for falsehoods everything that he told me. I can only guess that he has gone toward Tartary."

Upon hearing this, Amir Hamza left for Tartary and Bahram the bandit accompanied him. In Tartary they were told that their ruler expelled the man who claimed to be Naushervan as a liar and it was not known to them where the man went afterward.

As Amir and Bahram were leaving the city, they crossed paths with two men who were coming from the fire temple of Namrud. The men told Amir Hamza that an old man had arrived there from some place calling himself Naushervan bin Qubad.

Amir and Bahram headed for the fire temple. When they arrived there, the attendants brought food, and Amir shared the meal with Bahram. In the evening, the woodcutters came back to the fire temple carrying their loads of wood. After everyone else, Naushervan also arrived carrying a few sticks of wood on his head. Seeing his small load, the attendants gave Naushervan half a loaf of bread. Naushervan took the bread from the attendant without a word of protest, ate it in silence, and then lay down quietly in a corner. Amir Hamza's eyes welled up with tears upon seeing Naushervan's state and he said, "Indeed God is the One who dispenses honor and disgrace at will!"

In the meantime, the one in charge of the fire temple sent Amir a platter of sumptuous food. Amir said to Bahram, "Go and call Naushervan to join us, but do not tell him anything about me." Amir greeted Naushervan with respect and, seeing his miserable condition, involuntarily broke into tears. Naushervan said, "O generous youth, why do you cry after showing mercy to me?" Amir answered, "Your face greatly resembles my father's. Therefore I lost my self-control and began crying." Amir seated Naushervan by his side and fed him with his own hands while weeping quietly to himself.

After Naushervan had eaten to his heart's content, he said to Amir, "Tell me, O youth, who you are and where you have come from." Amir answered, "I am a soldier, and I travel from land to land. I would like to know who you are." Naushervan answered, "I am Naushervan bin Qubad and fickle fate has shown me this day." Amir asked him, "Why did you renounce your empire? What made you leave your land?"

Naushervan answered, "The excesses of an Arab named Hamza made me renounce my empire." Amir Hamza asked him, "What injustices did Hamza commit against you?" Naushervan replied, "He used to pay allegiance to me at first. Then he became enamored of my daughter and carried her away without my consent. Considering it a great disgrace, I went out into the world to roam from one city to another." Amir said, "I have heard that Hamza did not have any designs on your throne, and that it was you yourself who was his enemy, always seeking some way to kill him. Now you prevaricate and tell a contrary tale." Naushervan answered, "O youth, indeed it is true that Hamza never sought my death or my throne. It was Bakhtak, one of my viziers, who sowed enmity between us."

Amir Hamza now said, "Tell me, what would you give me and how would you reward me if I were to produce Hamza to you as a prisoner?" Naushervan's face lit up and he said, "Will my eyes ever see the day, by the grace of the gods Lat and Manat, that I will find that rebel in my power?" Amir answered, "I shall do you this service and produce Hamza to you a prisoner." Naushervan replied, "If you were to capture Hamza for me and do me this favor, O youth, I would give you in marriage my younger daughter, Mehr-Afroze."

Amir Hamza showed every kindness and favor to Nausharvan and did not allow him to cut wood the next day. On the fourth day, Amir and Bahram went out with the woodcutters and told Naushervan that they would bring wood for him too. They rested all morning while Naushervan scrounged the forest for wood, and in the evening uprooted whole trees and brought them to the fire temple. The attendants of the fire temple offered them the choicest foods, which they shared with Naushervan.

That night Amir asked Naushervan, "Who undertakes the expenses of this fire temple?" Naushervan answered, "My son, all these attendants are in fact my slaves and receive their stipend from my court. When I first arrived here, I gave them my name, but none of them believed it. They manhandled me so badly that my whole body swelled up from the beating I received at their hands." Amir said, "If you swear to renounce fire worship and hold God as unique and alone, and consider the faith of Ibrahim the True Faith, I will kill these attendants and destroy the fire temple. I will settle you on the throne and make all of them show obedience to you." Naushervan swore to everything that Amir had asked. Amir threw one attendant into the fire, dispatched many others to Hell, and razed the fire temple to the ground along with the idols that surrounded it.

When the attendants of the fire temple learned that Naushervan was in truth the emperor, they sought his forgiveness and were pardoned. Naushervan distributed the wealth stored in the temple to the needy and headed back home.

Then Amir said to Naushervan, "Let us go into our camp." Amir and Naushervan went to a baker, bought some bread, and sat down to eat it. Muqbil Vafadar happened to pass there, leading Ashqar to his water trough. The horse stopped when it recognized Amir Hamza's smell. Amar also passed by there at the time, and saw Amir and Naushervan having a meal with a stranger. Amar greeted Amir Hamza and said, "Welcome back and happy return!" When Amar called out Amir's name, Naushervan finally recognized Amir and learned the true identity of his companion.

Naushervan said to himself, "Hamza and I were together for so long, but I did not recognize him. There was no rebuke that I did not hurl at Hamza. He must harbor rancor against me." Naushervan got up and returned to his camp. The nobles of Naushervan's court were delighted to see him. Naushervan was seated on the throne and his courtiers and nobles made offerings to him.

Amir Hamza went into his own camp and met his companions. The next day Amir said to Sa'ad bin Amar Hamza, "Tie my hands with rope and lead me before Naushervan so that I can fulfill my promise to him." Sa'ad led Amir before Naushervan, who was dumbstruck by the spectacle and then asked, "Why have you brought Amir a prisoner here?" Amir answered, "I promised you that I would bring Hamza to you as a prisoner. Now you must fulfill your part of the bargain and convert to the True Faith without hesitation."

At that moment Bakhtak rose from his station and whispered into Naushervan's ears, "This is an opportunity to kill Hamza easily and give him his due punishment without making any great effort. If this moment passes it will not return, and Hamza will not be prevailed over by another man." Naushervan gave Bakhtak no answer, but Amir Hamza deduced that Naushervan was not being truthful with him. Amir untied his own hands and said to Sa'ad, "Get hold of this accursed Bakhtak and whip him as much as his wickedness deserves." Sa'ad immediately carried out Amir's orders. Naushervan retired to his palace when he saw Bakhtak being whipped, and whoever tried to come to the aid of the ill-starred Bakhtak lost his life at Amir's hands. Finally, Amir returned to his camp. The following day he sent Amar to Naushervan's court with the message that he had fulfilled his promise and wished Naushervan to do the same, that is, to give Princess Mehr-Afroze to him in marriage as pledged. Amar went before Naushervan and delivered Amir's message to him.

At first Naushervan did not answer Amar and said to his courtiers and nobles, "I promised Hamza that I would give him Mehr-Afroze in marriage. What do you advise in this matter?" All of them replied with one voice, "After marrying just one of your daughters to Hamza, Your Highness suffered anxiety that has driven you from land to land. God alone knows what terrors would visit you after marrying a second daughter to him." Naushervan answered, "Since I have given Hamza one of my daughters in marriage, I see no reason to make qualms about marrying a second daughter to him. I could have no worthier son-in-law, as none can compare with Hamza in capability." With this, Naushervan said to Amar, "Go and tell Hamza to make preparations for the wedding." The next day Amar recited the wedding sermon before Amir and Mehr-Afroze at an auspicious moment.

Bakhtak dispatched letters addressed to princes and kings everywhere soliciting them to advance and snatch Mehr-Afroze from the clutches of Hamza the Arab.

All the nobles of Naushervan's court consulted together and finally said to Hurmuz, "The emperor has lost his senses to dotage, but you are the master of your faculties. If you should so decide, Hamza would be killed speedily. Otherwise, this empire will be completely lost to you. Advise the emperor to go to Mount Alburz to seek refuge with the king of Alburz. If the emperor refuses, then you must send him toward Ctesiphon, ascend the throne yourself, and head for Mount Alburz to see what comes to pass there."

When Hurmuz put the proposal offered by the nobles before his father, Naushervan said, "I would like nothing better than if Hamza could be killed by this ploy and we could be rid of him." Naushervan's advance camp headed to Mount Alburz that very day, and the next day he followed and dispatched missives addressed to various sovereigns soliciting their aid.

Of Amir Hamza's Departure for Mount Alburz

The narrator records that Amar Ayyar informed Amir Hamza that Bakhtak had incited Naushervan to head for Mount Alburz. Upon receiving this news, Amir Hamza said, "Order our advance camp to move to Mount Alburz as well." When they arrived at the foot of Mount Alburz, they saw Naushervan already camped there.

Warriors and champions poured in daily from all corners to aid Naushervan. When Bahram Chob-Gardaan and Aadi Chob-Gardaan—who were paragons of bravery and courage—arrived with forty thousand troops to aid Naushervan, the emperor sounded the drums of war and led his army into the battlefield.

In the meantime, a rider came and stood between the two camps, seeking combat with the infidels. After proving his strength first against the infidels and then against the followers of the True Faith, he was overpowered by Amir Hamza. Then that warrior revealed that he was Alam Shah Roomi's son Qasim Khavari. Amir Hamza was most pleased to meet his grandson and returned with him to his camp.

In the meanwhile, a forty-yard-tall giant emerged from behind the ranks of the infidels on horseback and descended into the arena to challenge Homan Khavari. After overpowering Homan he wished to fight Qeemaz Shah Khavari, and prevailed against him as well. Finally Amir Hamza defeated him, and he revealed that his name was Qais Qeemaz Khavari and he was Qeemaz Shah Khavari's son. Then Amir sent for Qeemaz Shah and said to him, "May you have the pleasure of beholding your son!" Qeemaz Shah was greatly pleased by this news, and Amir sounded the drums to announce the day's end. He brought Qais Qeemaz

430 · *The Adventures of Amir Hamza*

Khavari back to his camp, where he ordered celebrations and organized an assembly of revelry and festivities.

The next day when the battle arrays were again formed Amir prevailed against both Aadi Chob-Gardaan and Bahram Chob-Gardaan. Amir Hamza converted them to the True Faith and Amar put rings in their ears to enroll them among the ranks of Amir's slaves. Amir conferred robes of honor on them, and cups of wine were passed around. Bahram Chob-Gardaan and Aadi Chob-Gardaan sent a message to their army ordering them to join the camp of the followers of the True Faith after making a night raid on Naushervan's camp so that they might earn divine blessings and earthly recompense.

THE HISTORY OF PRINCE BADIUZ ZAMAN BEING BORN TO GILI-SAVAR, THE DAUGHTER OF KING GUNJAL; AND OF THE PRINCE BEING PUT INTO A CHEST AND DROPPED INTO THE RIVER; AND OF QURAISHA, DAUGHTER OF AASMAN PERI, REARING THE PRINCE AT THE COMMAND OF THE HOLY KHIZR

The narrator records that when Amir Hamza departed for Mount Alburz, he sent Gili-Savar, who was with child, to King Gunjal, in effect leaving his family in trust with him. That ingrate Gunjal assembled all the servant girls and the midwife and made them swear that when Gili-Savar was delivered of a boy, they would immediately bring him the child. The attendants reasoned that since Gunjal was the grandfather, he must have foreseen something auspicious for the child, or else some clairvoyant must have alerted him to some fortunate or propitious hour. The moment the boy was born, they took him to Gunjal. That pitiless creature, who had converted to the True Faith for fear of losing his life, ordered the infant killed. The infant's nanny took pity on the child's comely face and, disobeying the king's command, said to Gunjal, "If Your Honor should order it, I will inter the boy alive in the ground." He replied, "Very well, do so!" The nanny put the boy in a wooden chest instead and put this into the river, committing him to God's care.

It so happened that Aasman Peri and Quraisha were visiting the riverside that day. The chest came floating down the river and reached the bank near them. When they retrieved the chest from the river and opened it, they found inside an infant sucking his thumb, whose beauty was the envy of the sun and the moon. Love flooded their hearts at the sight of him, and when Aasman Peri regarded the shining mark on his forehead, she said, "This mark is the sign of the friends of God. He has been committed into the grace of God." At that moment the holy Khizr appeared before them and said to Aasman Peri, "This boy is Hamza's son. You should raise him in the best tradition, send him to Hamza when he comes of age, and name him Badiuz Zaman." With that, the holy

Khizr disappeared, and Quraisha carried Badiuz Zaman to Qaf in her arms. They appointed *peris* as his wet nurses and raised him with great diligence and care.

When Badiuz Zaman reached the age of seven, Quraisha sent him to be trained in the arts of combat, and provided him with arms and armor once he had attained mastery in all arts of war. Whenever Quraisha went on a campaign, she took Badiuz Zaman along with her and introduced him to the realities of battle. When Badiuz Zaman reached his eleventh year, he asked Quraisha, "Who are my mother and father, and where are they? Tell me, what is the name of the city where they live?" Quraisha answered, "Both you and I are the children of the same father. He rules over the realm of men and his name is the Lord of the Auspicious Planetary Conjunction, the World Conqueror, the Quake of Qaf, the Latter-day Suleiman, Abul-Ala, Amir Hamza bin Abdul Muttalib. However, I have no knowledge of your mother's name and identity, and know not who she was or where she lived." Then Quraisha told Badiuz Zaman the circumstances that had brought them together.

Badiuz Zaman said, "Pray do me the favor of sending me to my father." Aasman Peri and Quraisha provided many gifts of Qaf to accompany him and ordered the *peris* to conduct him safely to the camp of the followers of the True Faith near Mount Alburz. At parting, they told Badiuz Zaman the names of all his relatives and explained to him how all his brothers had challenged and fought with Amir Hamza at their first meeting, and that he, too, must continue the family tradition and give himself to his father's service only after performing this ritual.

In short, Badiuz Zaman took leave of Aasman Peri and arrived after a few days near Mount Alburz. He saw the two armies facing each other on the battlefield and the warriors wielding their swords. The *peris* gave Badiuz Zaman the particulars of both camps. Then they hid themselves from human view to witness what would transpire next.

Badiuz Zaman stood between both camps and challenged the followers of the True Faith. Both camps marveled at Badiuz Zaman's comely youth, his fine garb, and his superior weapons, for they had never before set eyes on such a dazzling aspect or such attire and accoutrements.

One after another, Badiuz Zaman fought and prevailed over Kayumars, Qeemaz Shah Khavari, Landhoor, Qasim Khavari, Sa'ad bin Amar Hamza, and finally challenged Amir Hamza himself. Amir Hamza, descended into the arena and pitted himself against Badiuz Zaman, who raced his horse like lightning to reach the side of Amir and catch him by his cummerbund. Amir, meanwhile, secured a hold on Badiuz Zaman's belt. The two of them fought so mightily that their steeds were unnerved, and had they not dismounted, the animals would have broken their backs. When Amir was drenched in perspiration, he bellowed his war cry and tried to lift Badiuz Zaman from the ground and raise him above his head. However, Badiuz Zaman did not budge from his place. When Amir made his war cry a second time and made another attempt, he still achieved no results.

Bakhtak then said, "It would be little wonder if Hamza is defeated today by this youth and dies at his hands." The narrator has reported that Amir Hamza made several war cries that day and yet they did not perturb Badiuz Zaman in the slightest. Finally, Amir Hamza came into a rage and drew both Samsam and Qumqam from his scabbards to deal blows to Badiuz Zaman and strike that youth with his lustrous swords. Then Quraisha appeared before him, stayed his hand, and informed him that Badiuz Zaman was his son and her brother. Amir was greatly surprised and wondered who had borne him such a son.

Then Quraisha narrated to him the whole incident of the wooden chest and told him everything that holy Khizr had said. Paternal love stirred in Amir Hamza's heart and he pressed Badiuz Zaman to his breast with joy. He called out to Amar, "Regard that this illustrious boy is my son! He is a piece of my heart and the light of my life. The Almighty God has sent him to strengthen my arm." Amir Hamza returned to his camp to the notes of festive music and he ordered forty days of celebrations.

———

Now, the narrator states that Samandoon Hazar-Dast Dev had escaped Qaf[12] for fear of Amir and taken refuge in Mount Alburz, considering that place a safe haven. When he received word of Amir Hamza's arrival, he used subterfuge to infiltrate Amir's camp one night after two watches had passed. As he entered the camp, he beheld the pavilion of Sa'ad bin Amar Hamza, and upon going inside, he found Sa'ad deep asleep. He made him unconscious and carried him away to his sanctuary across he river. In the morning Amir Hamza received news that Sa'ad had disappeared from his tent. He said to Amar, "We must consult Buzurjmehr to find out what has passed with Sa'ad."

Buzurjmehr told Amar who had kidnapped Sa'ad and where he was imprisoned and told Amar that only if Amir went there alone would Sa'ad be found alive.

Upon receiving the news from Amar, Amir Hamza immediately took leave of his companions and waded across the river on Ashqar's back. When Amir arrived near the castle, the *devs* recognized him and alerted Samandoon, who left his castle with several thousand *devs* to face him.

When Amir saw Samandoon, he said, "O accursed creature, why did you put me to the inconvenience of this journey? You will see what an example I make of you." Samandoon ordered one of his *devs* who was held as a champion among them to arrest the human and speedily carry out his orders. Any *dev* who tried to capture Amir that day died at his hands. Then Samandoon pleaded with the *devs* but none of them dared approach Amir Hamza. Upon that Samandoon grew full of dread and hurled a several-hundred-*maund* rock at Amir, who foiled the attack and dealt Samandoon a sword blow that severed all seven of his hands in one blow, causing the hearts of the *devs* to burst with fear. Samandoon escaped and returned after a moment intact as before, and began fighting with Amir. And this same story repeated itself all that day until evening.

That night the *devs* retired to the castle and Amir fell asleep under a tree. The holy Khizr appeared to him in his dreams and said, "The Fountain of Life lies under the castle grounds. First, go and plug its source, and then fight the *dev*. Otherwise, you will keep fighting with him for the rest of your life and he will not be killed." Amir started from his dream and went to the castle that very moment and plugged the fountain that the holy Khizr had identified[13] with refuse and debris.

In the morning Samandoon emerged from the castle and arranged his army. As before, he hurled a thousand-*maund* stone at Amir's head. Amir foiled his attack and dealt the *dev* a sword blow that cut his neck in half and left it hanging from his torso. He turned tail and ran off, with Amir in pursuit. Amir saw that when the *dev* searched for the fountain and could not find it, he bashed his head against the ground and gave up his life. The *devs* who had accompanied him ran away pell-mell like rampaging camels. Amir cut off Samandoon's head and hung it from his saddle straps, and then fed his vile corpse to the beasts of the desert. Amir next began searching for Sa'ad bin Amar Hamza. His quest finally led him to a chamber where he found Sa'ad lying unconscious. Amir recited the prayer of Ibrahim over some water and washed Sa'ad's face with it.

Sa'ad regained consciousness, and Amir led Sa'ad out of the castle. The next day Amir seated Sa'ad on Ashqar and headed for his camp. When they reached the river, Amir said to Sa'ad, "Remain in the saddle because you do not know how to swim." Amir himself crossed the river holding onto Ashqar's tail.

They arrived at their camp to witness a pitched battle being fought. Amir Hamza threw the head of Samandoon Hazar-Dast toward the camp of the infidels and called out, "This was the same *dev* who kidnapped my grandson. I went to kill him and have brought back his head." The infidels were stunned to see the *dev*'s head and marveled greatly at its size, realizing that a *dev* who had such a giant head could be no smaller in size than a mountain. They realized, too, that it would be impossible for them to fight one who could kill so mighty a *dev*.

They were yet discussing this when a dust cloud rose from the forest. *Ayyars* from both camps rushed there to learn whether it was an enemy or a friend who had arrived. They learned that Bakhya Shutarban and Malik Ashtar had arrived with intrepid warriors and a vast army to assist Naushervan.

Naushervan sent Hurmuz and other kings to receive them.

THE DASTAN OF AJAL BIN ABDUL MUTTALIB, YOUNGER BROTHER OF AMIR HAMZA, LORD OF THE AUSPICIOUS PLANETARY CONJUNCTION

Narrators of sweet discourse relate that another son had been born to Khvaja Abdul Muttalib after Amir Hamza. Thus the oyster of nobility had revealed another pearl whom Khvaja named Ajal. Ajal had traversed twelve years of his life when Qalmaq Shah advanced on Mecca with his army to do battle with its citizens, who secluded themselves in their fortress. The news of their anxiety reached Ajal and he solicited Khvaja Abdul Muttalib for arms and a horse so that he could fight the infidels and slay every single man in his camp. Khvaja Abdul Muttalib laughed and replied, "Just consider your years and where you stand in your life, and then regard your ambition to fight a mighty commander like Qalmaq. I have eleven other sons, but it was only given to Hamza to fight with thousands of warriors and remain fearless before armies of hundreds of thousands of men." Ajal responded, "God is our savior. I am Hamza's brother after all." As Ajal's insistence to fight Qalmaq Shah kept growing, people said to Khvaja Abdul Muttalib, "Why do you hold Ajal back from fighting? He is full of courage and exceedingly brave." Forced by everyone to give his consent, Abdul Muttalib provided Ajal with a horse and suitable weapons. Ajal exited the fort with great magnificence astride his horse. Qalmaq Shah saw a youth on horseback and some foot-men coming toward him from the direction of the fortress and reasoned that he was headed there to plead for peace on behalf of the citizens of Mecca. Qalmaq dispatched a rider to meet them and find out his intention. Ajal exchanged words with the rider and overpowered him and took him prisoner. In this way Ajal took forty soldiers prisoner and, beside himself with rage, Qalmaq Shah faced Ajal himself and aimed his mace at Ajal's head. Ajal foiled the blow and landed his own mace on Qalmaq

Shah, the impact of which killed his horse instantly. Qalmaq Shah tried to hamstring Ajal's horse, but the youth quickly dismounted and, securing a hold on Qalmaq Shah's belt, raised him above his head. After spinning him around, he slammed him to the ground. Ajal climbed on his chest and pinioned Qalmaq Shah. Hearing of the incident, Qalmaq Shah's army prepared to charge Ajal with their full force, but Qalmaq Shah signaled to them to desist from it.

Ajal said to Qalmaq Shah, "Your life shall be spared if you convert to the True Faith. Otherwise, I will kill you immediately without the least fear of your army and warriors." Qalmaq Shah replied, "O Ajal, I will convert to the True Faith on condition that you grant my wish of finding me service with Hamza." Ajal answered, "The thing that you wish for you would have received even without asking." Qalmaq Shah then converted to the True Faith and Ajal embraced him and took him to his father. Abdul Muttalib conferred robes of honor on both Ajal and Qalmaq Shah and made them gifts of a great many jewels.

The next day, Ajal set out to see his brother. On the way he met Karib Madi, who was Aadi's son by Gustham's daughter and was headed in the same direction to meet his father. They traveled together and arrived at Mount Alburz.

Upon arriving at his destination, Ajal called out, "Any of Hamza's sons who has a claim to courage should come out to face me!" Ajal first tested his strength against Alam Shah. When fighting Badiuz Zaman, Ajal was overpowered, but he wished to test Hamza's strength. Amir overpowered him with great difficulty, then asked him, "Tell me truthfully who you are and give me the name and station of your father and grandfather." Ajal replied, "I am your brother, and the son of Abdul Muttalib." Amir embraced him, and his heart filled with fraternal love at the sight of his brother.

In the meanwhile, Karib Madi entered the arena and stood there like a fierce lion. Amir asked Ajal, "Do you recognize this man?" Ajal professed his ignorance. Karib Madi dealt Amir such a powerful blow of his mace that sweat broke from every pore in his body and darkness fell before his eyes. Nevertheless, Amir withstood the blow and caught Karib by his waist. Amir kicked Karib's horse out from under him and lifted the boy into the air, while the horse flew ten paces from the force of Amir's kick and its heart burst from the impact. Karib Madi said, "O Amir! Do not slam me on the ground, for I am your slave, the son of Madi-Karib." Amir put him lightly on the ground and embraced him. Then he called Aadi Madi-Karib and said to him, "Congratulations on your son!" He replied, "O Amir, he showed great irreverence toward you. Kill him and extract his brains from his skull." Amir replied, "I have forgiven him his trespasses and absolved him of them."

The next morning, Bakhya Shutarban came into the arena and challenged the followers of the True Faith. That day he fought Shaban Taifi but neither of them was able to overpower the other. The next day he fought Qais Qeemaz Khavari and their combat yielded no result. On the third day Badiuz Zaman finally overpowered him and took him prisoner.

When Malik Ashtar saw his uncle thus humiliated in the arena, he said to Naushervan, "Hamza's sons are truly mighty and brave. How easily did that youth capture my uncle!" Naushervan answered, "All of Hamza's progeny are cut from the same cloth." Malik Ashtar said, "Let the hostilities remain suspended for the day. I will fight him tomorrow so that none may get the chance to say that Malik Ashtar was able to capture Hamza's son because he was tired from earlier combat." The drums announcing the day's end were struck in Naushervan's camp at his orders, and he returned to his pavilion.

In the meantime, a messenger arrived from Kharsana and presented Amir with a letter from Fatah Nosh, who had written: "Marzooq Farangi has attacked us and we have received untold losses at his hands. Either come yourself or send Rustam-e Peel-Tan. Otherwise, you will lose the dominion of Kharsana and its people will lose their faith."

Rustam-e Peel-Tan then left for Kharsana but did not consent to take the army with him and claimed that he alone would rout the enemy.

He arrived there within a few days, reaching his destination with courage and resolve. He beheld the armies of Farang besieging the fortress, resolved upon taking it by force. Rustam immediately made his war cry and sought combat. Marzooq Shah Farangi sent his elder son to fight Rustam. His name was Malia, and he was a fifty-yard-tall giant. After killing Malia in combat Rustam drew his sword and fell upon the army of the infidels just as a lion tears into a herd of goats. A great unrest grew among the ranks of the Farangis and turmoil took over.

Marzooq saw that Malia's death had broken his army's spirits and robbed them of all courage. He went forward to challenge Rustam, but even that did not revive his army's spirits, and they retreated like a pack of foxes. Realizing that he would not be able to prevail over his adversary alone, Marzooq followed his retreating army with his companions. Rustam gave him chase for a distance of four *kos,* and with his sword he made heaps of dead infidels.

By that time Fatah Nosh had arrived at Rustam's aid with his army. He said to Rustam: "Now you have chased the enemy for four *kos* and inflicted grave losses on them. It would be against custom to follow them any farther. We do not wish to pursue them any longer." Rustam disagreed and said to him, "You should return to take care of the castle and strengthen its defenses lest the enemy, seeing the castle lying defenseless, should trick us and advance on it." While Fatah Nosh returned to his fortress and sent a complete account of the events to Amir Hamza, Rustam continued in his pursuit of the enemy.

In short, Rustam crossed into the frontiers of another land while chasing and killing the enemy. When it was night he fell asleep under a tree, and in the morning he rode off again in pursuit of Marzooq Shah's fleeing army.

———

Now hear of Amir. The day Rustam departed for Kharsana, Naushervan's daughter Mehr-Afroze was delivered of a son whom Amir named Mehr Shah. He ordered celebrations for forty nights and forty days and revels were held on a prodigous scale.

After the celebrations were over, Amir heard the drums of war from the enemy camp and ordered the Timbal of Sikander to be struck in reply. He ordered his camp to make preparations for battle and arrived in the arena with his forces. The hostilities had not yet begun when a messenger arrived with Fatah Nosh's letter. Amir read the letter and said to his friends, "Mark Rustam's childishness! He pursued Marzooq Shah all alone knowing full well that he had a large army at his command. He threw himself into this danger with open eyes. I must now go to his aid. All of you should pay your allegiance to Badiuz Zaman in my absence." Then Amir said to Amar, "I am taking five champion warriors with me. The rest of the army shall remain here under your command."

Amir took with him King Landhoor, Shaban Taifi, Karib Madi, Istaftanosh, and Qeemaz Khavari and headed toward Kharsana at great speed—making two and three days' journeys in a single day—and soon arrived at his destination. Fatah Nosh greeted Amir, conducted him into the fortress, and ordered festivities in his honor with all manner of dishes prepared for the occasion. Amir said to him, "I can barely swallow food, much less participate in festivities. I cannot rest easy until I have killed my enemy." The celebrations were canceled, and after resting there for the night, Amir headed in pursuit of Marzooq Shah's army.

Now hear of Marzooq Shah. When Rustam kept pursuing him for days, Marzooq reasoned that it was not Hamza but his son who had been following them because a retreating enemy was not followed for more than four *kos*, and wise and experienced commanders avoided such follies. Rustam had been following them, he decided, only on account of his inexperience, and with that realization, all fear and anxiety left him. He turned back to face Rustam. Marzooq Shah drew his sword and attacked the youth. Rustam parried his blow and struck Marzooq a blow that severed his hand. Marzooq pulled back his horse and called out to his army, "Kill him! Do not let him advance another step or escape!"

At his command, the whole army attacked Rustam, who took swords in both hands and fought back, piling up heaps of the slain. However, in the combat that ensued Rustam himself was wounded and his horse was killed. The infidels tried to take him prisoner, but no one could muster the courage to lay hands on him. Rustam finally climbed atop a rock and began shooting arrows at the infidels.

In the meanwhile, Amir Hamza arrived there with his warriors. Seeing Rustam lying wounded, Hamza and his companions fell upon the enemy host and attacked the ranks of the miscreants.

A great confusion took hold of the infidels after they heard Amir Hamza's war cry. Amir killed thousands of infidels. Marzooq Shah turned tail and shut himself in his fortress. Amir Hamza approached Rustam, and after putting bandages of *noshidaru* on his wounds, turned his attention again to the foe.

Marzooq Shah realized that Hamza would not be deterred from taking the fortress. Once inside he would conduct wholesale carnage, and Marzooq's wife, children, and family would all be murdered, finding no reprieve at Hamza's hands. Marzooq left the fortress with his sons and grandsons holding their swords in their teeth. Presenting his wife and children to Amir, Marzooq fell down at Hamza's feet and asked for reprieve. Amir said to him, "If you convert, along with your sons and family, to the True Faith and give your daughter in marriage to Rustam, I will spare your life and the lives of your family, and forgive all you have done." Marzooq immediately converted to the True Faith with his sons and promised his daughter to Rustam in marriage.

Marzooq escorted Amir Hamza and his companions into the fortress and arranged a marriage assembly. Amir sent Landhoor to fetch Rustam and wedded him to Marzooq's daughter. While Amir's son retired to the nuptial bed to indulge in pleasure seeking, Amir and his companions busied themselves in revelry.

After some days, Amir returned to Kharsana with Marzooq and arranged a meeting to establish peace between Fatah Nosh and him. The next day Amir departed toward Mount Alburz with his companions, and arrived there in the midst of the battle.

When he saw Amir Hamza had rejoined his camp, Malik Ashtar called out, "O Hamza, where had the fear of me driven you? Now your death has herded you back here, and you will taste the sweetmeat of doom from my hands." Amir answered him, "O warrior, champions do not indulge in idle boasting. Come, deal me the blow you take most pride in!" Amir defeated Malik Ashtar in combat, and he converted to the True Faith. Amir returned with Malik Ashtar to his pavilion to the sound of festive music and seated him on a golden throne. Amir sent for Bakhya Shutarban, who also converted to the True Faith without objection and wore the ring of slavery in his ear. Amir ordered him to be set free and provided him with a golden throne as well. After some time all of them sat down together to have a meal. Goblets of wine were passed in rounds and the dancers danced the whole night. When it was morning, it was announced that Zhopin Faulad-Tan had arrived to aid Naushervan, and had a vast army at his command. Amir remained quiet upon hearing this news and continued with the festivities.

One day Karavan, the leader of the merchant caravan, arrived at Amir Hamza's court. Amir seated him next to himself with great respect and honor and showed him much favor. Amir asked after his welfare and then said, "Tell me, why is your face so wan? Is it an illness or some trouble that afflicts you?" The merchant answered, "I am troubled by the sickness called the fever of love, which has reduced me to this state." Amir said to him, "Pray give me a detailed account so that I may learn it and do all in my power to bring you redress."

The merchant took out a portrait, showed it to Amir, and said, "This is a portrait of the sister of Hardam, the sovereign of Baru. Their father said on his deathbed that the one who wishes to marry her must first prevail over Hardam in combat. Fate ordained that I should visit Baru and pass under her balcony. No sooner did our eyes meet than the demon of frenzy claimed me for his own. Her love made me oblivious to food and sleep, and I have lost my forbearance from my passion. I do not possess the power to vanquish Hardam in combat, and thus I have come to you so that I may win that treasure with your help. I keep the portrait of this moonfaced beauty with me, and whenever I am beset by the pangs of love, I look upon it for a while to bring a modicum of solace to my heart and relieve my humors of their terrible frenzy."

When Amir Hamza's commanders looked at the portrait, they all said, "The poor merchant is right to feel thus afflicted by his beloved. Indeed no one would be able to control the fluttering of his heart in such a case." Amir Hamza fed the merchant and sent him away after promising that he would unite him with his beloved.

The narrator states that, upon seeing the portrait of Hardam's sister, Sa'ad bin Amar Hamza fell head over heels in love with her. He left the court and made preparations to depart for the land of Baru. Aurang and Gaurang were on vigil duty that night, and upon sighting Sa'ad, they said, "Where are you headed, O Prince?" Sa'ad answered, "If you wish to accompany me, come along without another word. Do not ask me anything, and you will find out in due course where I am headed and with what intention." Both brothers accompanied Sa'ad, and within a few days they entered the frontiers of Baru. There they sighted a magnificent garden and when they entered it and took a stroll, they saw a herd of goats grazing beside a pond. Sa'ad said to his lieutenants, "Catch four or five goats and roast them. Aurang and Gaurang carried out Sa'ad's orders, and before long the goats were roasted.

The shepherd was enraged at the sight of three men roasting and eating his goats. He approached them and said, "Do you not know that these goats belong to Hardam, the Angel of Death?" Sa'ad answered, "Do not waste my time with your jabber. Go and tell Hardam that Hamza's grandson has arrived and sends for him."

When the shepherd went and told this to Hardam, the king decorated himself with Prophet Daud's seven-piece suit of armor and headed for the garden wielding a mace in a state of raging frenzy. He went to where Sa'ad and his party were seated and said to them, "O youths, tell me who you are and whence have you come! Tell me truly what has brought you here." Sa'ad answered, "I am Sa'ad bin Amar Hamza, and I am the grandson of Amir Hamza. I have come here to arrest you. Take stock of my courage, for I have not brought along anyone except these two men." Hardam laughed heartily and said, "O Arab lad, there is a limit to idle talk. Has Hamza never heard of my renown that he sent a minor like yourself to face me?" Sa'ad said to him, "First, you should answer my challenge. Then you may worry about challenging Hamza." As Hardam prepared for combat, Aurang and Gaurang said to Sa'ad, "Your Honor! We entered your service longing for the day when we might sacrifice our lives for you. Let him fight us first. Then he may fight you." Sa'ad tried to keep them from fighting Hardam, but death had marked those two champions for its own. Aurang faced Hardam and was put to death with just one blow. Gaurang fared no better in combat with Hardam, and also met his death at his hands. Sa'ad was greatly grieved by their deaths and confronted Hardam to avenge his companions. Hardam struck a blow with his mace, but Sa'ad parried it. Then Sa'ad stood back and fired a hail of arrows at Hardam that cut holes in his seven-piece suit of armor. Hardam then caught hold of Sa'ad's belt, lifted him up, slammed him to the ground, and said, "Go and send Hamza to fight me, for I have taken pity on you and I cannot bring myself to kill you with my hands."

Hardam returned to his castle and narrated the events to his sister. She replied, "You acted as the circumstances demanded!"

After Sa'ad exited the garden and traveled for some two *kos*, he reasoned that it would be better to hide his name and identity from everyone. Thus resolved, he headed for the forest. After journeying many *farsangs*, he arrived in a garden, where he came across Hardam's niece. Her beauty drove all thoughts of Hardam's sister from Sa'ad's mind.

He asked her: "O light of the world, who are you?" She answered, "I am Hardam's niece." Sa'ad said, "Since you have shown favor to my state, pray allow me to light my eyes with your splendorous beauty and make the desolation of my heart a flower garden from the sight of your charms." She answered, "I would be happy to attend to you for the rest of my life, but you must give me your name and station in life and tell me the details of your pedigree." Sa'ad answered, "My name is Sa'ad bin Amar Hamza, and I am the grandson of Amir Hamza." Then Sa'ad gave her a complete account of how he happened to be there. That girl took Sa'ad to her home and happily gave herself to him in marriage.

———

Now hear of Amir. He became most anxious upon hearing of Sa'ad's disappearance. Landhoor said to Amir, "When the merchant was showing the portrait of his beloved, I noticed that Sa'ad seemed out of sorts. It would be little wonder if he departed for Baru with the intention of meeting that woman." In the meantime, news reached them that Aurang and Gaurang were also missing from the camp. Amir said, "Surely Sa'ad has left for Baru, and both Aurang and Gaurang have accompanied him."

Amir appointed Rustam-e Peel-Tan as the commander of the camp. Then Amir and Amar Ayyar headed for Baru. After some days they entered its frontiers and arrived at a garden where they saw the corpses of Aurang and Gaurang lying on the ground. Amir Hamza buried Aurang and Gaurang in that garden and wept many tears of grief at their fate.

They saw the very same herd of goats, and Amar slaughtered four of them and began roasting them. While they were leisurely having their meal, the shepherd rushed toward them and rebuked Amir. Amir Hamza said to the shepherd, "Go and inform Hardam that Hamza has arrived."

The shepherd went to Hardam, who picked up his mace and headed for the garden that very instant. Upon seeing him arrive, Amir decorated himself with his arms and armor and mounted his steed. Hardam laughed and said, "O Hamza, ever since I first heard your name, I have nursed the desire to see you so that I could fight you and test your bravery and courage."

After fighting and testing Amir's strength Hardam said, "Bravo, Hamza! I never saw a fighter more courageous than you. Pray remove the veil from your face and allow me to gaze on your consummate beauty, so that I may regard it with eyes of reverence and augment their light from its sight." Amir lifted up the veil from his luminous face and allowed his opponent to behold his dazzling beauty. Hardam saw that the sun itself shied away from the brilliance of Amir's beauty—although his face showed signs of age and was the visage of a man who had drunk fully of experience and wisdom.

Afterward they halted the combat. Hardam returned to his home and sent some fattened goats and flagons of wine to the garden for Amir's repast.

Hardam, meanwhile, praised Hamza to his sister and she was greatly pleased to hear his account.

The next day Hardam faced Amir for combat and challenged him with a mace. They fought until evening, when Hardam's mace broke. He said to Amir, "I would like to suspend combat until a mace can be made for me." Amir answered, "Very well! But do tell me truthfully what became of my grandson." Hardam answered, "O Hamza, I let your grandson go unharmed when he mentioned your name. But I have no knowledge as to his whereabouts."

Then Hardam went back to his house and sent Hamza some fat-tailed sheep and flagons of wine for his meal. Later that day, Hardam narrated the whole account of Amir's manliness to his sister and said, "There could be no better match for you in this world." Then Hardam sent for the blacksmith and persuaded him to make him a nine-hundred-*maund* mace overnight. By the time it was daylight, the mace was ready for Hardam. Having finished with his morning rituals, Hardam went into the garden and said to Amir, "I have already broken two of my maces and if this one is also broken by your own, I shall be in a great quandary. It would be so much better if you would simply put your mace aside. Indeed if you have a claim to bravery, you will assent to my request."

Amir granted Hardam's wish and agreed to receive the blows of Hardam's mace on his shield. This time, however, Hardam's mace made a deep impression in Hamza's skull after striking him powerfully. In consternation, Amir dealt Hardam a thrust of his sword, which cut through all seven pieces of Hardam's armor and injured him. Then Hardam drew a cold sigh and said, "I have spent my life in combat, but today is the first time that I have ever been wounded." Then the fight was suspended to allow both warriors to minister to their wounds. In a few days their wounds were healed and they renewed fighting.

Finally Amir Hamza prevailed over Hardam on the battlefield. Hardam converted to the True Faith with a willing heart. He took Amir Hamza and Amar to his house, where he arranged a feast in their honor and said, "It was my father's dying wish that I should willingly give my sister in marriage to the man who prevailed over me in combat and pressed my back to the ground. Now that you have been victorious over me, pray marry my sister and take her as your wife." With Amir's permission, Amar recited the wedding sermon. Amir then retired to the palace to indulge in pleasure seeking with Hardam's sister.

Sa'ad bin Amar Hamza learned that Amir had arrived there and taken Hardam's sister as his wife. He armed himself and headed toward the city of Baru on horseback to meet Hardam. When he arrived at its gates and made his war cry, Hardam went armed with a mace and found a warrior standing at his door. Sa'ad dismounted and grabbed both of Hardam's arms and heaved him up from the ground. He spun him above his head, slammed him to the ground, and sat on his chest. Hardam said, "Give me your name, O brave one, and tell me who you are." Sa'ad answered, "I am Sa'ad bin Amar Hamza." Hardam said, "Get off my chest so that I may take you to meet your grandfather!" Sa'ad went along with Hardam, and upon beholding Amir, he rushed forward and fell at his grandfather's feet. Amir embraced his grandson and kissed his head and face.

Hardam said to Amir, "There is something that astonishes me no end. I lifted up your grandson, Sa'ad, with absolute ease the first time I encountered him, but today he lifted me up as a mighty champion might pick up an infant. Tell me what is the difference between that day and today?" Amir replied, "Before, Sa'ad was afflicted with a corrosive love that disarrayed his senses, sapped his strength, and filled his heart with anxiety and apprehension. Now that he has recovered from it and has been restored to his natural strength, all those causes for anxiety and dread are completely dispelled from his humors." Amir made Sa'ad and Hardam embrace each other, and all of them sat down together to eat.

Amir then took his leave of Hardam's sister and headed back to his camp along with Hardam, Sa'ad, and Amar. They arrived to find Marzooq Farangi locked in combat with Naushervan's commander, Zhopin Faulad-Tan. Zhopin Faulad-Tan lifted Marzooq Farangi above his head and threw him to the ground, saying, "Go back, O Farangi, and send me someone else to fight, for killing you will win me no acclaim."

One after another, Malik Ashtar, Bakhya Shutarban, Qunduz Sar-Shaban, Landhoor, and Badiuz Zaman confronted Zhopin Faulad-Tan but no one was able to defeat him. Finally, Amir Hamza descended into the arena against him. After trying countless locks on each other and breaking the other's holds, Amir Hamza made his war cry and lifted Zhopin Faulad-Tan and spun him above his head. He then slammed him to the ground and sat down on his chest. Amar Ayyar quickly secured his limbs with his rope and took him prisoner.

Amir returned to his camp to the notes of festive music and retired to the women's quarters. The commanders of Amir's camp gathered and said to Amar, "Zhopin Faulad-Tan has humiliated and disgraced all of us in the arena. If he lives, we will never be able to look him in the eye. Were he somehow humiliated at our hands or killed, our sorrow would find an end." Amar answered, "Amir Hamza would never order the death of a warrior of Zhopin Faulad-Tan's caliber. Indeed he will value and favor him above all others. Those who put a value on valor never even dream of murdering brave men." When the commanders tempted Amar with money, he said to Hardam, "You should kill Zhopin Faulad-Tan with molten lead. If it grieves Hamza, I will be answerable to him, and will prevail on him to forgive the offense." Then Hardam poured molten lead into Zhopin Faulad-Tan's ear, which dissolved away his heart and liver. When Amir emerged from the women's quarters and sent for Zhopin Faulad-Tan, he was told that Hardam had fed him molten lead and killed him by deceit.

Amir expressed his displeasure with Hardam, who replied, "I did this at the behest of Amar Ayyar. It was at his bidding that I killed Zhopin with molten lead. I must not be blamed in this matter." Amir was greatly upset with Amar and said to him, "What harm did you receive from Zhopin's hand that you arranged to have him killed?" Amar answered, "O Amir! That dastard (deserving of smile beheading) merited such a fate in order to keep all creatures of God safe from his hands." Amir replied, "My hands are tied. Had it been somebody else, instead of you, who had ordered this, I swear by the God of Kaaba that I would have killed him." Amir Hamza gave Amar Ayyar seven lashes, and then said, "If you ever commit such an act again without my consent, I will make an example of you and punish you severely." Amar retorted, "If I do not lash you seventy times for this humiliation, I will consider myself a bastard not of my father's loins!"

With these words, Amar took himself straight to Naushervan and said to him, "O Emperor, I put myself to every hardship and pain in Hamza's service, and he rewarded me for it with seven lashes today for the sake of an infidel. He has humiliated me before all the commanders. If Your Honor wishes to have my allegiance, I am willing to yield it to you." Naushervan was greatly pleased to hear this and said, "O Amar, your rightful place is in my heart." Naushervan conferred a robe of honor on Amar and ranked him in honor above all his courtiers.

When Amir Hamza received these tidings, fear kept him awake at night, and he ordered his camp to maintain a state of great vigilance. Every night Amar made the rounds of Amir's camp with the intention of kidnapping him, but he quietly abandoned the plan each time he found Hamza awake. One night, however, Amir was unable to keep his eyes open, and he fell asleep. Finding Amir lost in slumber, Amar, who had been waiting for just such a chance, put a soporific drug in a tube and blew it into Amir's nose, rendering him unconscious. Then he tied up Amir with his rope and took him to the forest, where he secured him to a tree trunk in revenge for the lashes Amir had given him. Amar dispelled the effects of the drug, and when Amir came to he put his finger between his teeth in astonishment and marveled at his state and felt great shame.

Amar found a tree branch and hit Amir seventy times with it. Amir smiled and said, "You wily thief! I shall renounce my name if I do not shed your blood!" At this, Amir broke his bonds, and Amar ran away from him like a wild camel. Amir then reached for his bow and arrow. Realizing that Amir's arrow never missed its mark, and that he would certainly die and not escape Hamza's clutches, Amar rushed toward Amir and said to him, "O Amir, forgive me my wrongs!" Amir responded, "I have sworn that I would draw blood from your body and punish you." Amar said, "If that is your wish, then I am standing before you: Cut my neck without hesitation and sever my head." To fulfill his promise, Amir took out his blade and cut Amar slightly to open a vein and draw a little blood from him. Then he returned to his camp, taking Amar along with him.

Of Hakim Marzak's Entry into Amir's Camp at Bakhtak's Bidding, and of His Blinding Amir Hamza Along with His Commanders

The narrator of the *dastan* recounts that a man named Hakim Marzak was Bakhtak's bosom friend. He came to see Bakhtak one day and said, "If Naushervan were to order me, I would blind Hamza and all his companions, making them lose their sight by subterfuge." When Bakhtak communicated this to Naushervan, the emperor said, "A blind man needs aught but seeing eyes." He sent for Marzak and conferred a robe of honor on him, showing him much favor and showering him with gifts.

Marzak then went to Amar Ayyar and told him a tale of his helplessness and travails, and said, "If I could find a position in Amir's camp, I would earn my livelihood by administering medicine to the soldiers." When Amar presented Hakim Marzak to Amir and praised his accomplishments to him, Hamza showed him great favor and said, "You are welcome to stay with the camp, and attend to the sick men."

It so happened that Amir Hamza came to experience a dimness of vision. He sent for Marzak and described the symptoms to him, and Marzak prepared a collyrium and lined Amir's eyes with it. Amir's symptoms went away and his eyes lit up as before. He used that collyrium more than once, and richly rewarded and praised Marzak for it. Upon learning the qualities of the collyrium, Amir Hamza's friends also lined their eyes with it, and everyone sought remedies from Marzak for their many symptoms. All those who were cured by Marzak's hand made offerings to him.

Marzak now mixed the collyrium with blinding agents. He went before Amir and said to him, "The collyrium I have prepared this time contains an ingredient that has made it a perfect remedy, and you will never need to line your eyes again after a single application." Then Amir, along with his friends, applied the collyrium to their eyes.

Marzak saw that his work there was done, and that they had all been blinded. He went before Naushervan and said, "I have blinded Hamza and all of his companions." Naushervan asked him, "How are we to know that you tell the truth?" He answered, "Strike the drums of war and you will soon have your proof. Their whole camp has been blinded, and none will answer the call." Naushervan immediately ordered the drums of war to be beaten.

Upon hearing the enemy's call to war, Amir and his companions sent for water to wash their faces. Then they realized that they could see nothing, and all of them were blind. Amir said, "Go and look for Marzak!" But Marzak was nowhere to be found. Amir said to his friends, "It is a terrible calamity that we cannot see and the enemy has struck the drums of war. If we do not go into the battlefield, they will advance on our camp in broad daylight and steal all we have. We must arrange our fighting ranks." With this, Amir went into the field and ordered his army into battle arrays.

Witnessing this, Naushervan said to Marzak, "If they were blind, they would not enter the arena." That villain answered, "Send someone to fight them and you will soon learn the truth." Naushervan sent one of the Aadi champions, who entered the arena and challanged Amir's camp for combat. Hardam led his horse into the arena to face him and, swinging his mace, landed a powerful blow on him, which killed the Aadi warrior. One after another, Naushervan sent six Aadi warriors, and all of them were defeated.

Then Naushervan ordered his army to surround Hardam, cut off his escape route, and then kill him. When Naushervan's army attacked Hardam, he struck them with his mace, killing hundreds of infidels. They could not withstand his blows and at last turned tail. From a safe distance, they began showering Hardam with arrows. Since Hardam was wearing Prophet Daud's seven-piece suit of armor, the arrows were ineffective and the barrage of the archers caused him no harm. Finally, Bakhtak said, "Friends, Hardam is wearing Daud's seven-piece suit of armor. If you aim at his foot, he will presently fall!" The archers followed Bakhtak's advice, whereupon Hardam called out to Amir Hamza, "O Amir, now I need your aid. Come quickly to rescue me from the hands of infidels!" Amir took Ashqar's reins and said to him in the Jinni language, "Right now I am completely blind. Lead me wherever you see the infidels so that I may rout them!" Amir plunged into the enemy ranks astride Ashqar and slew many of them, making heaps from the corpses of the faithless.

Naushervan said to his army, "All the men in the enemy ranks are blind. Keep your spirits up, and seek out and kill every single one of them." At Naushervan's encouragement, his soldiers fought for some time but finally turned away. Amir returned to his pavilion in victory and triumph, and said to his companions, "It would not bode well for us to stay here until our sight is restored. We must head for some nearby city and seek treatment there for our blindness. Then we can worry about the enemy and prepare for the war with leisure." The champion Chob-Gardaan said, "Three days' journey from here is my city, Ardabil, which is well fortified. If Your Honor so wishes, you may retire there until your sight is fully restored to you." Amir's camp marched for Ardabil that same day.

Thinking that they were blind, Naushervan gave them chase and ordered his army to pursue them. Amir had stayed behind with four warriors and he attacked the enemy ranks. That day Amir's sword saw more action and he killed more infidels than ever. Finally, the enemy forces turned tail and fled, and not a single infidel remained behind. Amir entered the city of Ardabil in triumph and victory and finally was relieved of all his anxieties and worries. He fortified the city gates and filled the moats with water, cutting off all avenues for the enemy to enter within. He sent reinforcements to the battlements and began supplicating God Almighty to restore the sight to his eyes. Naushervan arrived and attacked the fortress, but when the fortified army inflicted many casualties on his soldiers, he put a cordon around the castle and camped.

Of Hashim bin Hamza and Haris bin Sa'ad Entering Amir Hamza's Service, and of Amir's Eyes Being Cured with the Holy Khizr's Help

The narrator has said that a son was born to Amir Hamza by Hardam's sister, who named the child Hashim. A son was also born to Sa'ad bin Amar Hamza by Hardam's niece, and she named him Haris. The two boys, who were granduncle and grandnephew by relation, had now reached the age of nine, and they felt great love and affection for each other because they were of the same age. They went hunting together and took meals in each other's company. It was Hashim's custom that when he hunted a lion, he always roasted and ate its heart, for which reason he had become known as Hashim the Lion-Eater. When the news reached them that Amir was camped within the fort of Ardabil, the two boys headed there from Baru with a large army. They arrived there in a few days to find the infidels besieging the city and their standards hoisted everywhere.

Hashim and Haris drew their swords and, without the least fear or anxiety, attacked the encampment of the dastardly infidels like lions tearing into a flock of sheep. They showed such excellent swordsmanship and fought so bravely that the infidels lost their nerve. Thousands of infidels became the prey of the crocodile of their swords, and were flung by them into the embrace of the denizens of Hell. Finally, the enemy fled from the vicinity of the fortress and camped at a distance that was many bow shots away from it. The armies of the True Faith reasoned that they had been sent aid from the Future State. They opened the gates of the city and welcomed Hashim and Haris inside. Both of them kissed Amir's feet, informed him of their names and pedigrees, and narrated to him the whole account of their lives.

Amir Hamza felt a strange and boundless joy that could not be described. Hashim submitted to Amir, saying, "It would be better if you returned with us to Baru, where your army can take rest and everyone can be comfortably accommodated." Amir ordered the timbal to be struck to announce their departure, and headed for Baru.

The army of the infidels followed them. When Amir entered the fortress of Baru with all his camp and entourage, the infidels laid siege to the place and set up camp.

Amir made tearful supplications night and day to God to restore his sight, and petitioned the Court of Heaven for a cure to his blindness. One day the holy Khizr appeared beside him and crushed a leaf and dropped a few drops of its liquid into Amir's eyes with his hands. Immediately, Amir's eyes lit up with vision and all the darkness and haze over them were cast away. Sight was restored to Amir's eyes and, ennobled by his meeting with the holy Khizr, Amir said, "I have been cured because of you, but all my friends are also handicapped by blindness." Then Khvaja Khizr gave Amir a few leaves and told him to squeeze their juice into his friends' eyes. After instructing him, the holy Khizr disappeared. Amir squeezed the sap of these leaves into his friends' eyes, and it revived their vision too.

Amar Ayyar said to Amir, "It is plain that all this was the doing of Bakhtak, whose idiocy has made him blind to all reason. I shall prepare a punishment for him, if you would so order, and avenge our suffering." Amir said, "He will receive his punishment in due time. It is not at all agreeable to me to cause grief to anyone." Amar remained quiet, but come evening, he dressed up as a cook and went to Bakhtak's pavilion and said to the guards, "Inform His Honor without delay that a cook has arrived at his doors from Greece who is a master of sweet and savory cuisine but is peerless in cooking the *hareesa*."[14] Bakhtak ordered him to come to his pavilion, but feared lest the cook should turn out to be Amar. Then he told himself that Amar had been blinded, and the person who had called on him must genuinely be a cook. Still, Bakhtak sent many *ayyars* to investigate the matter. The *ayyars* decided after conferring together that if the cook was indeed Amar in disguise, he would avenge himself on them for impeding him if they revealed his identity. They went back to the pavilion and told Bakhtak that Amar Ayyar was with Hamza in his camp. Bakhtak was satisfied and ordered Amar to make the *hareesa*. Amar made such a delicious stew that Bakhtak licked the entire bowl and went before Naushervan to extol Amar's talents. Naushervan appointed Amar as the royal chef.

One night Amar put a three-*maund* pot on the fire and filled it with water. In the middle of the night Amar drugged all the other cooks and entered Bakhtak's pavilion. He saw Bakhtak's eyes shut tight in sleep. Amar blew several *mithcals* of a soporific powder into Bakhtak's nostrils, whereupon Bakhtak sneezed and was taken unconscious. Amar rolled him up in a sheet and carried him to the kitchen, where he threw him into the pot of boiling water. Once he was fully blanched, Amar buried his skin and skull in the ground and covered the hole cleverly. Then Amar made a fine *hareesa* from Bakhtak's flesh and laid out the dish for the king's meal. The king offered portions of the dish to many of his nobles and ate it praising Amar's handiwork.

It so happened that while Naushervan was being served, the soup ladle brought up one of Bakhtak's fingers, which bore a ring given him by the emperor. Seeing the finger, Naushervan stopped eating and asked one of the cooks, "Whose finger is this? What is it doing in our food and why did you cook it?" The cook said nothing, but recognized the ring as Bakhtak's. Naushervan said to his attendants, "Go and see what Bakhtak is doing and bring him before me." When the men went into Bakhtak's pavilion they found his bed empty, and no one could tell them what had become of him. After conducting a search for him, they told the emperor that Bakhtak was missing from his pavilion. The emperor then realized that the *hareesa* had been made from Bakhtak's flesh. He became sick and vomited until he was beside himself with illness and pain. Amar made himself scarce and fled to Hamza's camp.

In the meantime, Buzurjmehr arrived in the court. Naushervan said to him, "I have saved you a share of the *hareesa*. Have some and enjoy this delectable dish." Buzurjmehr made an excuse and said, "I have already had my meal." Then Naushervan said, "I understand why you do not eat and make excuses for not partaking of the *hareesa*. You must have learned about the matter by *ramal* but did not care to inform me." Buzurjmehr answered, "It is against the custom of wise men to speak without being spoken to." Buzurjmehr's words fully convinced Naushervan that he had known of the matter. In his anger, Naushervan ordered Buzurjmehr to be blinded, and his eyes were lined with indigo. Then Naushervan put Hurmuz on the throne and went away to Ctesiphon.

———

Buzurjmehr now went before Amir Hamza and said to him, "My son, I have heard that the advent of the Last Prophet[15] (may God's peace and blessings be upon him) has been announced. Send me to Mecca so that I may take bliss in his sacred presence." Amir sent Buzurjmehr to Mecca.

Khvaja Abdul Muttalib greeted Buzurjmehr warmly and received him in the finest traditions of hospitality, and took him to kiss the feet of the Last Prophet. When Buzurjmehr came before the luminous aspect of the Prophet, he picked up some dust from under his shoes and applied it to his eyes, whereupon his sight was immediately restored, and by the grace of this act his eyes filled with the light of divine knowledge as well. This miracle of the Holy Prophet became renowned in every corner of the world.

Now hear of Hurmuz. After Naushervan departed for Ctesiphon and left him in charge, he conferred a robe of ministerial rank on Siyavush bin Buzurjmehr and made him his first minister. He showed him much regard and honor and gave him a seat to the right of his throne. He also appointed Bakhtiarak bin Bakhtak—who surpassed his father in deceit and evildoing—as his minister and gave him a seat to the left of his throne. Within a few days Bakhtiarak wormed his way into Hurmuz's graces and became so firmly entrenched that Hurmuz never did anything without first consulting him, and it seemed as if Bakhtiarak himself were the real emperor.

One day Hurmuz said to Bakhtiarak, "O minister of sound advice, we must think of some way to have Hamza killed with all his sons, relatives, and friends." He replied, "The Bakhtaris are known to be cannibals. If we can solicit their aid, I have no doubt that your purposes will be served." Bakhtiarak then wrote a letter on behalf of Hurmuz addressed to Gaolangi, the king of Rakham, in which he complained of Hamza and wrote that the Arab had wreaked havoc in his empire and held its citizens in his power, and was now headed to destroy his kingdom and inflict the same fate on him.

Gaolangi sent his son-in-law Marzaban Zardhasht with thirty thousand soldiers riding lions. When Marzaban arrived at Baru, Hurmuz greeted him and brought him into his camp.

Amir was apprised of these events. In the morning, Amir headed for the arena and arranged his army in battle formations. Marzaban sent a lion rider into the arena, who faced the camp of the Arabs and declared, "He who wishes to have his soul extracted by my hands should come forward into the arena to display his courage, for I am his Angel of Death." Amir's commanders said to their leader, "Our horses will shy away from even the spoor of the lion, for they have never before seen this beast. It would be better for us to fight the lion riders on foot, and it would be a wiser strategy not to send riders to encounter these blackguards." Amir said, "How will someone on foot prevail over a rider?" Hardam said, "O Amir, you well know that I always fight on foot. Pray order me to answer the lion rider's challenge and fight him." Amir said, "Go forth! I give you into the protection of God!"

When the lion rider attacked, Hardam swung his mace and dealt a blow to the lion rider that crushed him and his mount into dust. Amar Ayyar rushed forward and cut off the lion's head and threw it before the horses so that they could smell it. Amir said to him, "What purpose will it serve?" Amar answered, "I am familiarizing the horses with this smell so that they no longer fear the lions and do not shy away."

One after another, Hardam killed forty lion riders before the end of the day. Finally, Marzaban faced Hardam himself, delivering him a mighty blow. Hardam tried to pull the weapon from Marzaban's hands by winding the chain of his mace around it, but not only was he unable to do so, he began losing his grip on his own mace. Hardam immediately called out to Amir, "Hasten to my aid, O Amir!"

Amir spurred on Ashqar and bellowed so loudly that Marzaban's limbs went numb and he looked up to the heavens to see if they were crashing down on him. Hardam pulled his mace from his adversary's hands. Marzaban then dealt a blow to Amir. He struck two more blows in succession, but Amir stood his ground and did not budge an inch. Then it was Amir's turn. He swung his mace and landed such a powerful blow on Marzaban that many in the infidel army were deafened by the sound of its impact, and every pore of Marzaban's body broke with sweat. Then Marzaban realized that Hamza was a mighty champion and as strong and powerful as a rutting elephant. He turned tail and fled with Amir Hamza in pursuit. As Amir's steed caught up with Marzaban's, Amir dealt him a powerful blow of his sword that cut Marzaban's arm and knocked his weapon from his hands. With his mouth spewing blood profusely and his arm severed, Marzaban went before Hurmuz and said to him, "O Prince, Hamza is both stronger and mightier than I. If you wish to be delivered from his hands, you must depart to Qaza-va-Qadar[16] to seek refuge with Saryal bin Salasal, who is one hundred and forty yards tall, a great warrior, and a majestic and magnificent king."

Hurmuz consulted the kings in his court and they said with one voice, "You must follow the course that results in Hamza's death." Siyavush bin Buzurjmehr said, "I would not advise you to go there."

Bakhtiarak retorted, "Indeed he would say that, for one always tends to favor those of one's own faith." Siyavush kept his silence. The next day Hurmuz departed and headed with his army toward Qaza-va-Qadar.

Saryal greeted Hurmuz and conducted him to his castle. That night, when they sat down to eat, Hurmuz saw a roasted boar lying before Saryal, who offered Hurmuz a piece of its meat with his own hand. When Hurmuz tried to refuse it on some pretext,[17] Marzaban whispered in his ear, "Saryal will take offense if you do not eat that piece of meat." Against his will Hurmuz put the meat in his mouth but immediately spat it out. Saryal took offense at this and said to his companions, "Go and feed yourselves on Hurmuz's men, for the gods Lat and Manat have sent you all these goats as their gift. Go and sink your teeth into their tender flesh!" Saryal's people fell upon Hurmuz's army and began capturing and eating them. Trapped in this terrible scrape, Hurmuz became fearful and helpless.

Hurmuz cursed Bakhtiarak and his advice a thousand times and, addressing Siyavush, said, "O Khvaja's son! Indeed I would have saved myself this disgrace and embarrassment had I followed your advice. We must find a way to escape and use some strategy to flee from this place." Siyavush replied, "You will not be able to escape from here without Hamza's assistance. There is nothing I can do about it." Hurmuz said, "Why would Hamza come to my help at all?" Siyavush replied, "Since Hamza is a generous, munificent, and high-minded man, he will certainly rescue you if you ask him for help." Hurmuz said, "If you are of that mind, then go to him on my behalf and explain my plight to him." The next day Siyavush went before Amir Hamza and interceded for Hurmuz and sought his help. Amir said, "I would assist Hurmuz on the condition that he sincerely and truthfully convert to the True Faith." Siyavush returned to tell Hurmuz what Amir Hamza had said to him.

Hurmuz went before Amir in the middle of the night and cried copious tears while narrating to him his tale of woe. Amir instructed him in the Act of Faith and comforted and consoled him. He seated Hurmuz on the throne and ordered a meal and shared it with him. Hurmuz said, "O Amir, show me this favor: Send me to Ctesiphon in safety." Amir answered, "You are free to go where you wish and do as you please, but do not fall away from the True Faith now, or else you will dearly regret it and repent your decision." With these words, Amir sent Hurmuz away.

Saryal was enraged by Hurmuz's departure. He immediately sounded the drums of war and went to the arena with his whole army to do battle. Amir also organized his army into fighting ranks. Catching sight of Amir Hamza, Saryal came forward on horseback and challenged his army. Ceylon's Black Lion, King Landhoor, took Amir's leave and confronted Saryal.

The two fought with maces, but neither could injure his adversary. The armies retired after sunset to take rest at their appointed stations. The next day they formed battle arrays again. Qeemaz Shah came out to fight Saryal, who slammed him to the ground. Then Amir made his war cry and secured the release of Qeemaz Shah. Saryal mounted another horse and said to Amir, "O dwarf, why did you let my prey escape? Be quick and tell me your name and station so that you do not die unsung." Amir answered, "My name is Hamza bin Abdul Muttalib."

Saryal dealt a mace blow to Amir, who parried it with his shield. Saryal delivered a second mace blow to Amir, who parried that, too. When Saryal struck a third time, Amir caught his mace by its handle and, putting his bow around Saryal's neck, pulled Saryal to the ground. Amar Ayyar caught Saryal with a rope and tied up his arms. Amir returned to his pavilion to the sound of the drums of victory, satisfied and contented on all accounts. He asked Saryal, "What are your intentions now?" He replied, "Enroll me among your slaves and admit me as a faithful servant in your court." Amir converted him to the True Faith and conferred a robe of honor upon him. Saryal took Amir to his city, where he organized festivities in his honor.

After the festivities were over, Amir said to him, "O Saryal, take me to see the wonders of your land." Saryal replied, "Three days' journey from here is the Tilismat-e Jamshediya. You shall enjoy its sights." Amir said to him, "Tell me who constructed it and give me its complete history." He answered, "When Jamshed was nearing his death, he emptied the city of its denizens and installed wooden mace bearers and vigils at short intervals at its ramparts. Then he lay down in the grave he had constructed for himself. The other marvel is Jadu-e Jamshediya, also known as Damama-e Ilm. Sufaid Dev lives there,[18] whom everyone considers a man-eater." Amir said, "The terror I inflicted drove that *dev* from Qaf. Now I learn that he has found a refuge here." Amir left his army behind and headed for Jadu-e Jamshediya with Amar and Saryal.

When he arrived there, Amir heard a dreadful voice that struck fear in the hearts of all who heard it. Amir asked, "Whose voice was that?" Saryal answered, "It is the voice of the *tilism*." When they arrived at the gates and Amir tried to step inside to see its wonders, the soldier standing guard attacked him with their swords. Amir leapt aside to dodge the blow. Saryal now said, "I have heard my grandfather say that all men in this city are made by *tilism*. A bird made by *tilism* lives inside the dome that you see before you. When it sees anyone, it cries out. If you were to kill the bird, you would learn all the secrets of this *tilism* and then you would come to no harm." When Amir studied the dome, he saw a bird chirping there with a melodious voice. Amir notched an arrow in his bow, took aim, and fired with such a steady hand that the arrow pierced the bird and it fell to the ground with a thud. The moment it fell down the *tilism* was broken. Amir opened the city gates, went inside, and saw the man who had attacked him lying on the ground with his weapons. Amir secured possession of the place. When he opened the city's treasury in Saryal's presence, he found it filled with hundreds of thousands of snakes and scorpions, and he closed and locked it as before.

Then Amir said to Saryal, "I have seen all the wonders of Jadu-e Jamshediya. Now tell me where Sufaid Dev is hiding and take me to his dwelling." Saryal took Amir into the Bayaban-e Akhzar and pointed to a well and said, "This is where Sufaid Dev lives." Amir said to Saryal, "Exert yourself a little and remove the stone from the mouth of the well." Saryal tried but was unable to move the stone. Then Amir kicked the stone, shattering it into pieces.

Amir then lowered himself into the well with a rope, and once he reached the bottom he beheld a door covered by a stone slab. When Amir removed the slab, he saw Sufaid Dev sitting on a throne with lowered head in a state of anxiety, wonderment, and surprise. Sufaid Dev asked one of his minions who had informed him of Amir's arrival there, "Did you see the Quake of Qaf with your own eyes and recognize him?" The *dev* answered, "The Quake of Qaf was riding a horse and two men were accompanying him on foot. As to the Quake of Qaf, I recognize and know him well." Sufaid Dev said, "In the eighteen years that that man lived in Qaf he destroyed the domicile of the *devs* and drowned hundreds of thousands in the sea of death. It was my fear of him that forced me to make my dwelling here, but he has arrived here as well. It seems that the days of my life are at an end, for the signs of the diminishment of my power are becoming manifest."

Sufaid Dev had not yet finished his speech when Amir made his war cry. Sufaid Dev said, "O Quake of Qaf, I sent myself into exile for fear of you and left all my near and dear ones when I took myself to this corner. But you followed me here as well and have cornered me in this dark and narrow place. I shall do everything in my power to inflict on you a most painful death." At this, Sufaid Dev hurled a several-hundred-*maund* rock at Amir's head. Amir leapt to one side and the rock crashed to the ground. As Sufaid Dev bent to pick up another rock, Amir dealt him a blow of his sword from behind, carving through his skull and slicing his spine. Sufaid Dev fell on his face and cried, "Show me the kindness of dealing me another blow so that I may depart even sooner from this ephemeral world for the Permanent Land, and do not suffer the pain of my wounds any longer." Amir responded, "I know your race all too well. What you hope for will never come to pass." Sufaid Dev was thwarted, and he gave up his life by bashing his head against the ground. Most of the *devs* who had accompanied him were killed, while others fled and went their way. Still others asked for clemency, and Amir converted these *devs* to the True Faith and put them under his allegiance. Then he ordered them, "Return to Qaf and go to Quraisha and remain in her service."

Thereafter Amir emerged from the well carrying Sufaid Dev's head. He showed it to Saryal and hung it from his saddle straps. Then Amir mounted his horse and departed.

The narrators relate that Rustam-e Peel-Tan noticed that a long period of time had passed since Amir's departure and no news of him had been received. He decided that Hamza's companions would be idling their time to no purpose awaiting him there, and would do better to head for Jamshediya and visit its *tilisms*. He appointed Saryal's sons as his guides and headed from Qaza-va-Qadar with his army and arrived in the Tilismat-e-Jamshediya after a few days. Finding it destroyed, he realized that Amir must have razed it and headed onward after killing all the *devs*. Then Rustam headed to the second land.

When he entered the place with all his forces and broke down the dome, he saw Jamshed's body lying on a throne. He opened the treasury's chambers and killed all the scorpions and snakes that were there. Then he said to Saryal's sons, "We should now head for Bakhtar and see its sights." They answered, "The king of Bakhtar is Ahriman Sher-Gardaan, a magnificent and majestic lord. He is one hundred and twenty-five yards tall and his people and soldiers are all cannibals. It would not bode well to head there, as no one has returned alive from his dominions."

Rustam said to his friends and brothers, "Amir has gone to kill Sufaid Dev. It is certain that on his way back, he will visit Bakhtar to explore that land. If we advance now and vanquish Ahriman Sher-Gardaan before Amir's arrival, it will earn us great glory and we will be considered heroes and valiant champions." All of them replied in unison, "We shall do as you order us."

Rustam departed that very instant and arrived on the outskirts of Bakhtar in a few days. Ahriman laughed uproariously upon hearing these tidings. He took Marzaban, headed for Rustam's camp, and issued this challenge: "O herd of sheep! He among you who wishes to have his neck slit should come forward and face me!"

Qunduz Sar-Shaban took Rustam's leave to face Ahriman and was martyred at his hands. The cannibals swarmed over him, cut him up into small pieces, and ate him, bones and all. Aljosh Barbari in his turn attacked Ahriman with his dagger and landed a powerful blow that sank up to the hilt into Ahriman's body, but Ahriman did not feel a thing and no harm came to him. Ahriman tried to secure a hold of Aljosh Barbari to mangle him with his teeth, but Aljosh escaped with great effort and kept fighting. During the combat Ahriman finally prevailed over Aljosh Barbari and ate him alive.

When Rustam saw that two of his champions had been martyred he felt great consternation. He spurred on his horse and entered the arena to fight Ahriman himself. Ahriman dealt Rustam a blow of his mace, which he took on his shield. Rustam then answered with a sword blow that would have cut the cannibal in two and left him with no sign of life had it not missed its mark. Ahriman escaped the blow, jumped down from his horse, and caught Rustam's arms and pulled him till he ripped the skin from his abdomen. When Qasim Khavari saw that Rustam had been injured, he tore into the arena astride his horse, fearful that Rustam might die and his death would strike dread and terror into the hearts of his men. Qasim Khavari made his war cry and threw himself between Rustam and Ahriman, challenging the foe. The *ayyars* carried Rustam away to their camp.

Then Ahriman Sher-Gardaan asked Qasim, "Who was the man who was taken away, and who are you?" Qasim answered, "He was my father and Hamza's son." Ahriman said, "With Hamza there, why did he imperil his life and his father not help him?" Qasim answered, "Amir Hamza is not present in the camp, as he has gone to kill Sufaid Dev." Ahriman replied, "Since Hamza is not with you, it is useless for me to fight mere boys. It is not incumbent on me to fight you." At this, he retired to his dwelling.

While Ahriman headed off, Qasim returned to his camp with his whole army and found that Rustam had departed to meet his Maker from the injury Ahriman had inflicted on him. A terrible weeping and wailing rose from the camp of the followers of the True Faith. In the end, they performed Rustam's last rites and waited for Amir.

When Amir returned to Jamshediya from his hunting expedition, he saw signs that his army had camped there and said to Amar, "It seems certain from the signs that Rustam has been here. May God ward off the eye of affliction from him, for I suddenly feel a terrible anxiety and my heart is sinking." Amir Hamza then headed for Bakhtar himself. As he arrived in its environs, all his friends and sons came to him crying, bare-headed, and barefoot and fell at his feet. Upon hearing of the deaths of Rustam, Qunduz, and Aljosh, Amir dropped from his steed and rolled in the dust in ecstasies of grief, overtaken by terrible sorrow. When Amir's friends saw that he was beside himself with grief, they said to him, "O Amir, your friends and sons all grieve for Rustam, but you are suffering the most affliction and the hearts of those who behold your state bleed from pain. It would be better for you to head to the forest to divert yourself with hunting and the chase." They finally prevailed on Amir, and all of them headed for the forest.

It so happened that Marzaban Zardhasht was on his way to Rakham, after having taken his leave of Ahriman, when on the way he received news that Hamza was busy hunting with his friends and sons, and that the death of his son had wounded him deeply and made him oblivious to all concerns. Realizing that he would not find a better chance, Marzaban ordered a sorcerer to conjure him a horse from magic, complete with all the trappings. Then Marzaban stood the horse in a field and lay in wait with some companions on the path that led there. By chance, Sa'ad bin Amar Hamza happened to pass that way and was delighted to see the horse. He dismounted his steed and climbed into the saddle of the enchanted horse. Sa'ad gave the horse a cut with his whip and the horse took off like the wind. Sa'ad tried his best to rein him in, but the horse did not stop. Then Sa'ad drew his sword and beheaded the horse and both horse and he fell to the ground. Marzaban rushed out and tied up Sa'ad and took him captive. Then he went on his way to Rakham.

Arriving before Gaolangi, he presented Sa'ad to him and said, "This is Hamza's grandson and the king of the followers of the True Faith. I overpowered him and brought him here a prisoner." Sa'ad said, "O Gaolangi, since he states that he has overpowered me, order him to fight me before you. Everyone will find out who overpowers whom when we fight together." Gaolangi answered, "Yours is a fair request, and I would allow it!" He ordered Sa'ad's fetters removed.

Marzaban attacked Sa'ad with his mace, but he foiled the blow and, securing hold of Marzaban's arms, made his war cry and lifted him up over his shoulders. He raised him high above his head and slammed him to the floor. When Marzaban tried to rise to his feet, Gaolangi, who was a just man, killed him by dealing him a blow with his mace which forced his brains from his skull. Gaolangi heaped praises on Sa'ad, embraced him, sat him beside himself on his throne, and said, "My son, consider this place your home. I would gladly give you leave to depart, but I would like to detain you here, for Hamza will certainly head this way in search of you and take the trouble to come here to find you. I have long been desirous of meeting him. Because of your presence here my wish will be granted." Seeing Gaolangi's loving and affectionate nature, Sa'ad willingly agreed to stay with him.

Badiuz Zaman, meanwhile, was surprised to see Sa'ad's horse standing riderless and the enchanted horse lying dead nearby. He had the surrounding area searched, but no trace of Sa'ad was discovered. Badiuz Zaman felt at a loss and said to his friends, "My friends, a great calamity has overtaken us with Sa'ad's disappearance. I am duty-bound to search for him. Amir is not yet fully recovered from mourning Rustam. If he hears of Sa'ad's disappearance, his heart will bleed from excessive sorrow and grief. Let us go in search of Sa'ad and bring him back. It stands to reason that it is all the doing of that villain, Marzaban. Surely it is he— the most accursed being in the world—who is behind it."

Badiuz Zaman set out in search of Sa'ad. After many days he came upon a city and learned that its ruler was Taus Bakhtari, the son-in-law of Gaolangi. Badiuz Zaman said to his friends, "We must search for Sa'ad in this city. Perhaps Marzaban has brought him here and hidden him." He wrote a harsh letter to Taus Bakhtari.

Hardam Barui delivered Badiuz Zaman's missive to Taus. Upon receiving it, Taus Bakhtari tore up the letter, whereupon Hardam swung his mace and landed such a powerful blow on Taus that his throne became his coffin. The infidels surrounded Hardam.

Learning of this development, Badiuz Zaman rushed to Hardam's aid. After hundreds of infidels had been slaughtered, the remainder sought clemency, and Badiuz Zaman gave them reprieve. He made a heap from the heads of the dead infidels and placed Taus Bakhtari's head at the top of the pile. Then he and his men traveled onward, and after two days they arrived in another city whose sovereign ruler was Gaolangi's other son-in-law. Badiuz Zaman wrote a similar missive to him and sent it by the agency of Hardam. This ruler also died at Hardam's hand for the excesses he took with Badiuz Zaman's missive. Badiuz Zaman ordered wholesale slaughter of the city's inhabitants and reprieved the few who survived, and then headed onward.

In a few days he arrived in Rakham and sent this same message to Gaolangi with Hardam. When Hardam arrived at the court, he saw Sa'ad and Gaolangi seated together on the throne. He beheld Gaolangi's height and stature with marveling eyes and figured that God must have created giants of this size to cause the hearts of men to be seized by fear and dread. Seeing that Hardam was awed, Gaolangi said to him in a friendly tone, "Welcome, Hardam. Consider this your own house." Then Gaolangi said to him, "Although Badiuz Zaman killed my sons-in-law, I refrained from murdering him out of the regard I feel for Hamza. Although I had the power to do it, I did not avenge myself."

Hardam was greatly embarrassed by Gaolangi's fine manners and was mortified to have to hand him such a communiqué. He handed the letter to Gaolangi. After reading the letter, Gaolangi turned toward Sa'ad and said, "O Sa'ad, tell me if I have done you any wrong or submitted you to any torture for which your uncle has written me a letter that grieves my heart and causes me untold unease." Sa'ad answered, "He is unaware of all the kindnesses and favors that you have shown me as your guest. Had he known, he would never have sent you such a message." Gaolangi said, "What you say is indeed true."

He conferred a robe of honor on Hardam and informed him of the circumstances in which Sa'ad was delivered to him, the punishment he visited on Marzaban, and the reason he asked Sa'ad to stay with him.

Upon hearing Gaolangi's message, Badiuz Zaman said, "The army should be given orders to march. I will take Sa'ad away from him in the flash of an eye and will hear no excuses from him." When Badiuz Zaman arrived at the fortress with his army, Gaolangi said to Sa'ad, "I have now learned that Badiuz Zaman is a rank idiot and no better than a beast. You may take a seat in the tower and witness as I go myself to chastise him and teach him a lesson for his vanity." After these words, Gaolangi rode out of the fort astride a bull.

All of Badiuz Zaman's companions tried to keep him from fighting with Gaolangi, but Badiuz Zaman would not listen to them. As he readied himself to ride into the arena, Landhoor caught the reins of his horse and said, "It was for just such a day that we warriors entered your service." Badiuz Zaman could not dissuade Landhoor and the Khusrau went and faced Gaolangi. After Landhoor had tested his strength against Gaolangi, Malik Ashtar showed his strength and skill, and after him, Sar-Barahna Tapishi rode to the field with great magnificence. When Gaolangi swung his mace and landed the blow, Sar-Barahna Tapishi's head was pushed down into the cavity of his chest. Then Dewana Tapishi faced Gaolangi, who laid him low as well: Along with his steed, Gaolangi vanquished him. Gaolangi then dismounted his bull and carried both corpses before Badiuz Zaman and said to him, "O Prince, you had these two mighty warriors killed at my hands without reason, and you caused me to suffer grief and embarrassment before your father. However, what is past is past. Refrain from fighting me and do not think of making war against me. If you wish to have me killed, I have come before you unarmed. You should feel free to put me to death and behead me." Badiuz Zaman replied, "I am not some executioner who would first secure you before putting you to death. Nor am I a eunuch to act in this unchivalrous manner toward you. Go back and return here armed so that you can test my mettle."

Gaolangi was obliged to decorate himself with weapons, and mounted his bull to do combat. Presenting himself before the prince, he again expressed his reluctance to fight him. Badiuz Zaman, however, could not be persuaded as he thought nothing of Gaolangi's might. At last, Gaolangi dealt the first blow with his mace. Badiuz Zaman withstood it and gave Gaolangi two strikes. After Gaolangi had dealt the prince more blows and Badiuz Zaman had withstood them all, Gaolangi praised him highly and said, "His claim to fight me as an equal was justified."

Badiuz Zaman swung his mace and dealt such a mighty blow that Gaolangi's bull was killed from its impact and sweat broke out from every pore on Gaolangi's body. Badiuz Zaman dismounted and fought on foot with Gaolangi with maces, swords, and the lance until evening.

In the meantime, Amir Hamza received tidings that Marzaban had caught Sa'ad by deceit and that Badiuz Zaman had followed him to Rakham in search of him. Amir said to Amar, "Until I have finished my campaign against Ahriman Sher-Gardaan, I will not leave this place. However, I wish you to go with utmost haste to gather news of my sons and companions." Amar Ayyar set out like the wind and arrived in Rakham before long. There he witnessed Badiuz Zaman fighting with Gaolangi.

When he saw Amar's face, Gaolangi stopped the combat and tried to address Amar. But Amar jocularly said to him, "By the grace of God, you are too short, which is the reason I cannot hear you well. If I could sit on your shoulder, I would be able to entertain you with my words." Amar leapt up and sat atop Gaolangi's shoulder and said, "I have long received news of your valor but I am astonished that you deem it proper to fight Amir's sons during his absence and martyr his champions." Then Gaolangi gave him all the details.

Amar persuaded Badiuz Zaman to leave the arena, and then himself went with Gaolangi to his fortress. He kept Amar as his guest for the night and said to him, "I wish to see your *ayyari,* for people have praised your talents to me in glowing terms." Gaolangi sent for food and after sharing the meat and drink, Gaolangi said to Amar, "You have many great qualities, but one blemish. You shave your beard." Amar replied, "You would do well to pay me seven hundred dirhams as the tribute for your own beard or else your beard will not remain on your good face for long!" Gaolangi said, "I will consider you a man only if you are able to shave my beard." Amar replied, "Very well, I shall do so this very night!"

Gaolangi gave leave to the nobles to retire and sat alone on the throne drinking wine, so that he might pass the night in a state of wakefulness and not be tricked by Amar.

Amar saw Gaolangi sitting by himself drinking wine, and approached him in disguise and put a few *mithcals* of a drug in the king's wine flagon with great cunning. Gaolangi had consumed a few cups when he suddenly fell unconscious from the throne. Amar quickly shaved one side of his face. Then he restored Gaolangi to consciousness, made him a respectful bow from afar, and asked him to look into the mirror. When Gaolangi did so, he saw half his face shaved and was deeply mortified. He praised Amar and said, "Indeed you are the Prince of the *Ayyars* of the World. Verily you are an *ayyar* without equal. But now you must find some way to restore my beard to my face as before or else I will suffer great humiliation before my nobles." Amar shaved off the remainder of Gaolangi's beard and took out a false beard from his *zambil* and put it on Gaolangi's face and said, "This beard will stay on until you wash your face with warm water, and none will ever know it is false."

When Gaolangi looked in the mirror, he saw that his beard was as before. In the morning Gaolangi put seven hundred *tomans* inside a robe of honor and conferred them on Amar and then gave him leave to depart. Amar went to Badiuz Zaman and instructed him not to fight Gaolangi until Amir's return. Then Amar headed back to Amir Hamza.

After several days' journey Amar reached Amir's camp and gave him a detailed account. Amir was grieved to hear of the fate of Sar-Barahna

Tapishi and Dewana Tapishi. The next morning Ahriman Sher-Gardaan struck the drums of war and went into the arena. Amir formed battle arrays and confronted him. Ahriman landed a mace blow on Amir, but he withstood it and said, "Deal me two more strikes!" After he had landed his third blow, Amir killed Ahriman's steed with the very first blow he dealt. Then Amir dismounted Ashqar and faced his foe. They fought until evening when both armies returned to their camps. In this manner they fought for three days. On the fourth day Amir made his war cry and lifted Ahriman above his head. He spun him around over his head and slammed him on the ground. Then he called to Amar, "Tie him up!" While Amar took Ahriman from the battlefield, Amir drew his sword and attacked the enemy ranks. Those who sought quarter found reprieve and a new lease on life, and the rest were cut down by his relentless sword.

Amir's companions said to Amar, "Amir would never kill Ahriman. You should kill him to avenge Rustam's blood." Amar immediately poured molten lead into Ahriman's ears, and dealt with him thus. That blackguard was dispatched to Hell, and all felt relief at his death. When Amir returned and said to Amar, "Send for Ahriman and produce him before me," Amar answered, "He was made to pay for Rustam's blood with his life." Upon hearing those words, Amir fell silent.

The next day Amir Hamza said, "Dig a tunnel and blow up all the cannibals hiding in the fortress." A tunnel was dug and filled with gunpowder,[19] and Amar blew up the fort. Amir then marched out with his camp and arrived at Rakham within a few days.

Upon hearing of Amir Hamza's arrival, Gaolangi dressed Sa'ad in a robe of honor and sent him to Amir bearing gifts, and he also sent riches and provisions for Amir's companions. Amir embraced Sa'ad and was greatly pleased to hear of the many kindnesses and favors Gaolangi had shown him.

In the morning Gaolangi struck the drums of war and entered the arena, where he arranged his troops. Amir decorated himself with his arms and went into the arena as well. Observing Amir's height and size, Gaolangi took him for a common warrior and said, "O warrior, I wish to fight Hamza, not you. Go back and send me Hamza." Amir answered, "I am Hamza bin Abdul Muttalib." Gaolangi said, "O Amir, I thought that you would be as tall and mighty as myself. How did you lay low the tall and mighty *devs* of Qaf?" Amir answered, "I may be weak of body but my Lord is all-powerful. Come forward and strike your blow now." Gaolangi delivered three blows to Amir in succession, which caused sweat to break out of every pore of Amir's body, but he held his ground manfully. Gaolangi marveled greatly at Amir's might.

Amir landed his eleven-hundred-*maund* mace on Gaolangi, the impact of which killed Gaolangi's bull and rattled the king's nerves. Gaolangi tried to hamstring Ashqar, but Amir quickly dismounted and faced his adversary. Gaolangi struck him two blows of his sword, which cut through four inches of Amir's shield but also broke Gaolangi's weapon, as his sword broke at the hilt. Gaolangi threw away the hilt and secured hold of Amir's cummerbund. Amir took hold of Gaolangi's belt and the two tested their strength in this way until evening. Then Gaolangi said, "O Amir, the night is made for resting. Relax yourself and give me leave to go. What shall come to pass in the morning will come to pass." Amir replied, "I shall not turn back without a winner being decided in this fight." Food was sent for the warriors from their respective kitchens, and they sat down to eat together. After they had had a few goblets of wine, torches were lit and they continued testing their strength.

The narrator states that Amir and Gaolangi fought for twenty-one nights and days and remained at a stalemate. There was no strategem of war that they did not employ in their battle. Finally, on the twenty-second day, Amir Hamza said to Gaolangi, "We have exhausted all the maneuvers of our martial abilities. Now you should try to lift me from the ground, and I will try the same. The one who is lifted up must pay allegiance and submit to the other." Gaolangi happily consented, and replied, "O Amir, I easily pull out great and tall trees from their roots. You certainly do not weigh more than those trees!" Amir replied, "We shall presently test your claim and see who is humiliated."

Gaolangi exerted all his might and blood flowed from his fingers, nose, and ears. He grew near to fainting but was still unable to lift Amir up from the ground. Instead Amir sank up to his waist into the earth. Gaolangi said in a weakened voice, "O Amir, I have now completely exhausted all my strength." Amir replied, "Be on your guard now, for I am about to make my war cry." The king answered, "Cry all you wish! Make the surface of the earth tear open with your cries! I am not some little boy who will be frightened by it or feel any dread." Amir then let out his cry of "God is great!" which shook the ground for a distance of sixteen *kos*. Amir lifted Gaolangi up, and after spinning him around above his head, put him lightly on the ground.

Then Amir said to Amar, "Tie him up quickly, for he might find a chance to escape." Gaolangi said, "O Amir, why do you wish to secure me with ropes when I am tied up now by devotion to you?" Amir said, "If that is the case, then convert to the True Faith." Gaolangi sincerely recited the Act of Faith that very moment. Amir embraced him and told everyone the auspicious news of his conversion to the True Faith. Gaolangi took Amir, along with his sons and friends, to his own city, where they remained busy in celebrations for forty days.

Of Amir's Departure for Bakhtar, and of His Killing King Kakh Bakhtar

The narrator records that after the festivities were over, Amir asked Gaolangi, "Which other city lies beyond your own?" He answered, "It is the city of Bakhtar, which is ruled by King Kakh Bakhtar, a cannibal who is one hundred and sixty yards tall. Whenever he advances on my city, fear of him drives me to take refuge in the mountains with my sons. He is a magician himself and has sorcerers among his companions." Amir answered, "I am the mortal foe of sorcerers, cannibals, and infidels, and was born to crush their vanity into dust. Until I have annihilated them, I will find no rest." Gaolangi appointed his elder son, Rel Gaolangi, as his heir and accompanied Amir Hamza.

They arrived within Bakhtar's borders, and Amir wrote a missive to Kakh Bakhtar that read: "O Kakh Bakhtar, present yourself before me and convert to the True Faith and pay allegiance to me. Otherwise, I will kill you with impunity and visit such a terrible fate upon you that the birds of the air and the beasts of the ground will lament your fortune."

Amar Ayyar arrived at Kakh Bakhtar's court with the letter. After reading just a few lines, Kakh Bakhtar's face turned crimson with rage and he ordered that the messenger be arrested. Amar put on his cap of invisibility and before leaving the court, removed the crown from Kakh Bakhtar's head by knocking it off.

Kakh Bakhtar declared, "I shall exact retribution for that messenger's actions on his master in the arena, and shall kill Hamza at once."

When it was morning and Kakh Bakhtar took his place in the arena after striking the drums of war and leading his army into battle, Amir armed himself and went into the battlefield as well. Kakh Bakhtar said to Amir, "O weakling, I did not challenge you. It is Hamza whom I seek."

Amir answered, "Hamza is my name." The king said, "How did you conquer the world with that weak body? Is it because you are a sorcerer?" Amir answered, "I hold magic and sorcerers to be accursed. My God is all-powerful and mighty, who returns me triumphant and victorious from battle. Now deal me the blow you have!" Kakh Bakhtar swung his mace and struck Amir, who moved aside. The mace landed on the ground instead, causing a huge tract of land to sink upon impact and water to burst forth from the ground. Kakh Bakhtar landed a second blow, and Amir foiled that also. When he struck his mace a third time, Amir received it on his shield. When it was Amir's turn to strike, he laid the king low with a thrust of his sword. Kakh Bakhtar rolled on the ground like a slaughtered beast and died. His army fell upon Amir, who plied his sword with both hands against them. When only a few of them remained standing, they ran off and took refuge in the castle. Following Amir's orders, Amar blew up the castle by digging a tunnel underneath it and filling it up with gunpowder. All the cannibals became the fodder of the fires of doom.

Thereafter, Amir headed for the city ruled by a giant named Ara'sh and arrived there in triumph from his campaign against Kakh Bakhtar. Ara'sh emerged from his fort upon hearing of Amir's arrival. Amir saw that he was a massively built giant who was one hundred and eighty yards tall. He hurled his mace at Amir, but Amir jumped aside and the blow landed on the ground, creating a crater with its impact. As Ara'sh reached to pick up his mace and strike him a second time, Amir struck him with his sword. Amir had cut Ara'sh in two, and the giant forthwith gave up his life. Upon witnessing that incident, Ara'sh's army took refuge in the fort and was rendered helpless and powerless. Amar blew up that fort as well with gunpowder after digging a tunnel underneath. Ara'sh's lands and dominions were all destroyed, and the cannibals were all killed and found quarters in Hell.

OF AMIR'S DEPARTURE FOR NESTAN, AND OF HIS KILLING KING SANG ANDAZ KHUNKHVAR NESTAN

The transcriber has recorded that after routing Ara'sh, Amir asked Gao-langi, "What other city lies ahead?" He answered, "It is called the city of Nestan. The name of its ruler is Sang Andaz Khunkhvar Nestan. He is one hundred and ninety yards tall and his eyes glow like burning ovens. The passage that leads to his city is so narrow that two men cannot pass through it walking shoulder to shoulder. The path is surrounded by flames that emit heat so profusely that they make even mountains melt away like wax."

Amir paid no heed to his remarks and headed for Nestan. When he arrived there, his army was unable to bear the violence of the temperature and its incendiary power, and his men began dying from excessive heat. Amir took out the rope given him by the holy Khizr and threw it across the fiery passage. He asked his companions to advance holding its end and not let the least doubt enter their hearts. The narrator reports that nearly every man in Amir's army was burnt alive. Only one champion riding a camel and three hundred soldiers were able to ford that river of fire by holding the rope's end. The rest headed instead to the Land of Eternal Peace.

After much toil and trouble, when Amir arrived at the city, Sang Andaz Khunkhvar Nestan came out of the city with his army and brought his entire force to do battle. Amir saw that each of his soldiers had a bag full of stones tied to his neck. When they saw Amir, they started hurling them at him. Many of the three hundred men who had accompanied Amir this far were now stoned to death. Amir felt helpless finding himself in that unenviable plight. He drew his sword and assaulted the enemy ranks like a lion attacks a herd of goats. Amir plied his sword with both hands and started beheading his foes. Such a large number of Khunkhvar's warriors were killed that a veritable river of blood issued from the battlefield.

In the end, Sang Andaz Khunkhvar Nestan came forward and dealt Amir a blow of his sword, which Amir parried. When the king reached for his mace, Amir leapt forward and dealt him a powerful blow of his sword, which severed both his legs at the thigh. The king's stumps of legs fell to the ground. Then Amir dealt him a second blow of his sword and dispatched him to Hell. The king's men who had shut themselves into the fortress were burned when it was torched.

Amir now announced, "I once heard from Buzurjmehr that I would leave Zulmat[20] with only seventy companions and would vanquish all my enemies. Now there are seventy-one men with me. It remains to be seen who is the one to die next and whose name will be erased from the register of the living."

Then Amir Hamza said to Gaolangi, "O friend, tell me which city comes next as we advance from here." Gaolangi replied, "A few days' journey from here lies the land of Ardabil, which is ruled by two brothers, Ardabil Peel-Dandan and Marzaban Peel-Dandan. Farther ahead lie the *tilisms* of Zardhasht Jadu, where you will find everything a marvel to behold."

Amir headed for Ardabil and arrived at his destination within a few days. Ardabil Peel-Dandan and Marzaban Peel-Dandan led out their armies to do battle with him. Amir armed himself and went into combat with them. Ardabil Peel-Dandan attacked Amir without loss of time and tried to mangle him with his teeth. Amir drew his sword and struck a blow that sent Ardabil's head flying from his neck like a harvested ear of corn.

Seeing his brother dead, Marzaban Peel-Dandan rushed at Amir, who cooled his ardor with a single fatal blow and sent him to feed on the fires of Hell. After putting their army to the sword, Amir headed onward and arrived at the *tilism* created by the sorcerer Zardhasht. There Amir saw an enclosure without an entrance. It contained a dome from which emanated music and the sound of singing. Amir said to Gaolangi, "It seems that there are people within who sing and play this music that is so enticing and pleasant." Gaolangi answered, "There is no question of a human presence here. These *tilisms* are known to ring with such sounds." Amir said to him, "You are the tallest among us. Pray see what is going on inside and discover what is taking place." As Gaolangi looked over the wall of the enclosure, he cried out and jumped over to the other side as if he were unable to hold himself back. When Landhoor went and looked, he burst into uncontrollable laughter and jumped over as well. The same thing happened to others. In the end, only Amir and Amar were left standing there. Amar said, "If you were to order me, I would cover my face with a cloth and look inside to see what it is that makes everyone jump in without self-control." Amir replied, "Very well, but do so very carefully." Amar said, "I reason there is some beautiful woman inside the enclosure whose sight made our friends forgetful of themselves from love. I do not have amorous inclinations to become lovesick and forget myself in desire." Amar climbed the wall and, like his companions before him, burst into laughter and jumped over.

Amir Hamza was left alone and he began shedding tears and praying for his friends. He was near to giving up his life in grief for them when he was overtaken by sleep. In his dream he saw a throne descend from the heavens on which a holy man was seated who said to Amir, "Kill the white bird sitting on the dome with an arrow and you will conquer the *tilism*."

Amir woke up and saw that indeed a white bird was perched on the dome. When Amir shot an arrow at the bird, she fell to the ground. The same instant she fell, the *tilism* was broken. Amir's companions who had been caught in the enchantment returned to their senses and came out from under its spell. When Amir asked his companions their reason for jumping inside the enclosure, all of them replied that they had beheld a holy and luminous face whose sight made them oblivious to everything, and made them jump inside. Amir said to them, "Open the door of the dome so that we may see what is inside." Although everyone tried, the door of the dome did not yield.

Finally, Amir broke down the door and went inside and saw a casket hanging from the ceiling. When Amir brought it down, he saw the corpse of Zardhasht the sorcerer laid carefully within, and it seemed that he had just fallen asleep. Amir said, "There must be something else in the casket with him as well. We must search it carefully." When Amar Ayyar searched it, he found a book on magic. Amir burnt the sorcerer with the book, but Amar had first managed to remove several pages from it. Those pages helped spread the magic in the world that has continued to this day, and all those who practice it have learned it from the contents of those pages.

In short, after Amir had torched Zardhasht's corpse along with the book and was assured of their destruction, he reached the end of the *tilism* and said to his friends, "This place is full of peril and we may lose our lives here. We must not all sleep at once but take turns keeping watch." Amir appointed Aadi to do the first shift of the watch, Malik Ashtar to do the second, Landhoor the third, and himself the fourth and final watch.

When Aadi sat down to do vigil duty, he saw a deer. Aadi hunted him and started cleaning and cooking the meat. When the meat was ready, an old crone appeared like an unforeseen calamity and began grinding her teeth while looking at Aadi. He said to her, "O old woman, tell me who you are, why you have arrived here and why you grind your teeth when you look at me. You must truly tell me everything, or else I will punish you severely and murder you instantly." The crone answered with great humility, "My son, I am the wife of a merchant who was killed by a lion in the forest. Now I wander around without help or succor in great distress. Today is the fourth day since I last saw a morsel to eat. If you will give me some meat, I will pray for your well-being and will be indebted to you forever." Aadi felt pity for her and he reached out to serve her some meat from the pot. The old crone jumped up and slapped Aadi so hard that he fell unconscious to the ground. When he woke up after an hour and recovered from the shock, he found the pot empty. His watch having passed then, Aadi woke up Malik Ashtar and himself prepared to sleep.

Finding the pot empty, Malik Ashtar said, "O big-bellied fellow, you cooked the meat and ate it all by yourself." Aadi answered, "I was hungry, therefore I ate it all. If you are hungry, you may as well hunt and eat something and not suffer the pangs of hunger." After some time, Malik Ashtar also saw a deer and hunted and cooked him. When the meat was ready, the same crone appeared before him and sought some meat after reciting to Malik Ashtar her tale of woe. He, too, took pity on her and tried to ladle some from the pot when that crone jumped forward and slapped him hard. While he lay unconscious on the ground, she ate up the meat and disappeared.

When Malik Ashtar came to his senses, it was Landhoor's turn to do vigil duty. Seeing the empty pot lying on the fire, he said, "Why, Malik Ashtar, you cooked and ate the meat but did not offer us even a small slice!" Malik Ashtar answered, "The place abounds in animals and you may hunt and cook one for yourself."

Landhoor also hunted a deer and cooked the meat and the same crone slapped him unconscious and ate up all the meat and then disappeared.

When Landhoor woke up and was restored to his senses, Aadi and Malik Ashtar said to him, "We, too, were treated in the same manner." Landhoor said to them, "If you had told me, I would have taken caution and not been deceived!" Aadi and Malik Ashtar said, "What is past is past. Now hold your tongue and do not say a word of it to anyone. Let us wake up Amir and see how he fares with the crone." Landhoor said, "I cannot bear to see Amir deceived or suffer any hardship." Aadi said, "Amir will never be fooled or deceived by her." After their conversation, they woke Amir up to do his round of watch duty.

Amir also hunted and began cooking. The crone had now become well accustomed to stealing the cooked meat. When it was ready, she appeared before Amir to sing her usual song and narrate her old story. Amir got a whiff of rotten meat from her mouth and said to himself, *This is a tilism. There is no knowing what new calamity awaits me in the guise of this crone. Indeed she must be a witch, and it would be justifiable to take caution.* Amir held his sword in one hand and began serving the meat with the other. When the crone tried to slap Amir, he dealt her a blow of his sword and severed her head. Immediately upon hitting the ground, the head rolled away. Amir pursued it and saw that the head had rolled into a well. Amir was standing at the edge of the well when his companions reached his side. Amir said, "Tie a rope to my shield so that I may lower myself into the well." Amar Ayyar said, "I will undertake the mission." Amar Ayyar lowered himself into the well and beheld that the severed head lay on a golden platter before a fourteen-year-old beauty. The girl was crying and saying, "I told you not to go near Hamza, but you did not follow my advice and imperiled your life and put me in trouble as well."

Amar snared the girl with his rope and secured her with alacrity and cunning. He brought her out of the well and produced her before Amir, along with the head of the crone, and told him all that the beauty had said. Amir asked her, "Who are you, and who was that crone?" She replied, "I am Zardhasht's daughter, and the old woman was his mother." Amir asked her, "Are you alone or are there others besides you?" She answered, "I have two sisters who live in the *tilisms* with their armies. Upon hearing of our grandmother's murder, they will descend here and battle with you."

Amir Hamza gave her into Amar's custody and said to him, "Keep a strict watch on her and incarcerate her somewhere secure." They passed that night in peace, but the following morning sorcerers emerged from the well in waves and arranged themselves in battle formation. The armies were led by Zardhasht's daughters Gul-Rukh and Farrukh. They ordered their nanny, who was a renowned sorceress, to prepare her magic and to create a spell for them.

Amir sent for Zardhasht's daughter and asked her, "How do you think your sisters will fight me?" She answered, "They will employ magic and prevail over you with its power. Amir said to Amar, "Interrogate her yourself and ask her gently what that magic is and how it is created." Amar took her to his place and tried to extract the information from her by gentle persuasion but she would not reveal a thing. In the end, Amar tired of her and put her to death by smashing her skull. Then he presented himself before Amir who said to him, "Perhaps you could have extracted the secret and obtained the information from her by subterfuge." Amar answered, "O Amir, she was most cunning. As to obtaining information, I shall bring it for you from her companions." Amar then headed for the sorcerers' camp. On the way Amar encountered a sorcerer whom he killed and put on his disguise.

That night Amar went with several others to stand guard at the sorceress Farrukh's bed. A wizard arrived there in a state of great agitation and said to Farrukh, "Many days have passed since your nanny set out to prepare some magic against Hamza's camp. To date, we have seen no results." Farrukh answered, "The magic will be ready by evening the day after tomorrow. Then you will see what terrible destruction engulfs Hamza's camp. Not a soul will survive and none will find reprieve."

In the morning Amar returned with this information to Amir, who responded, "I wish we could find some way to turn the magic back on their own camp and use its destructive powers on their own forces." Amar replied, "That harridan is preparing her magic behind your encampment. I will go then to capture her and turn her magic against her own camp."

That day came to its culmination and the next day, late in the afternoon, Amar disguised himself as a wizard. Carrying a flagon of drugged wine, he went to the nanny and said, "Farrukh has sent me with the message that three days have passed since you started preparing your magic, and yet Hamza's camp shows no sign of its effects and are none the worse for it. She has also sent this flagon of wine for you." She answered, "The magic egg is now ready. It will show its marvels when the sun sets. Then everyone will see what terrors are let loose on Hamza's camp and how everyone is engulfed in calamity, and witness their end." She then put her mouth to the spout of the flagon and drank it all in big gulps, swallowing the wine in large swigs. As soon as the wine passed down her throat, she fell unconscious. Amar buried her alive in a hole and dispatched her to Hell. He took the magic egg and the bottle to Amir and said, "She has filled this egg and bottle with her magic, and now I am taking them to throw at Farrukh and Gul-Rukh's army and use it against their own camp."

Amar went into the sorcerers' camp and destroyed all their pavilions and supplies by releasing the contents of the magic egg, burning everything to cinders in just the flash of an eye. Then Amar poured out the contents of the bottle. This caused such a heavy rainfall that the entire camp of Gul-Rukh and Farrukh sank underwater and all the goods and provisions left in their camp were destroyed. Not a single one of them survived.

Amir occupied himself with hunting in the environs for a few days. One day he said to Gaolangi, "Let me know if some other menace remains and give me news of any new scourge." He answered, "All the evil that had manifested itself from Bakhtar to Zulmat has been put down." They set out for Rakham and arrived in that grand metropolis, where Gaolangi prepared festivities in Amir's honor on a most lavish scale and ordered his attendants and workers to provide all the apparatus for revelry.

When the festivities were over, they headed out of the city for hunting. Suddenly, Badiuz Zaman sighted a deer. He tried to make it his prey, but the deer galloped away with Badiuz Zaman in hot pursuit on horseback, and at last he took out his gun[21] to kill the animal. After running for some distance, the deer jumped into a pond. Badiuz Zaman followed him into the pond on horseback and Amir and his companions also rode into the water after them. The next moment, when they blinked their eyes they found themselves in a vast field surrounded by a strange forest. They searched for Badiuz Zaman in every direction but found no trace of him. Amir Hamza's eyes filled up with tears and he said to his companions with a voice full of sorrow and grief, "Finally, we are seventy. The seventy-first person was Badiuz Zaman, whom I was destined to lose." Amir's companions offered him words of consolation. Amir uttered not a word then except to express his compliance and cheerful submission to God's will.

Of Amir's Departure for Mecca, and of His Attaining Martyrdom in the Victorious Service of Prophet Muhammad; and the Culmination of the Dastan

The master narrators thus tell this wondrous tale that after Amir had found a measure of fortitude and his restive heart had attained a modicum of peace, Gaolangi said to him, "You had mentioned that you would take me to kiss the feet of the Last Prophet of the Times and allow me an opportunity to regard his holy aspect. Thus we should head for Mecca!"

Amir, Gaolangi, and the rest of their companions now headed toward Mecca. As they passed Qaza-va-Qadar, Saryal greeted them and took Amir to his dwelling and satisfied all the duties of a host. After many days, Saryal's father departed from this world. Amir performed his last rites and, offering words of consolation to Saryal, seated him on the throne. Then they continued toward Mecca. After traveling for a few days, they arrived in its precincts. Gaolangi along with all the companions of Amir Hamza kissed the feet of the Holy Prophet and renewed their Faith and earned great glory in the world.

―――

One day the Holy Prophet was present in the mosque when a desert Arab arrived with the news that infidels from Egypt, Greece, and Syria had banded together to advance on them with evil intent, and were bringing a vast army. The Holy Prophet first sent Amir Hamza with some men to Abu Qubais, then he headed there himself. When the infidels arrayed themselves, Amir gave Gaolangi leave to fight them. His challenge was answered by a massively built warrior from the infidel camp who made many great claims to his power and might upon entering the arena. Gaolangi lifted him above his head and spun him around for so long that he very nearly died from it; he was soon rendered completely powerless and helpless.

Gaolangi then slammed him to the ground, and the little life remaining to the infidel was flushed out of him. A second infidel warrior faced Gaolangi and fared the same. A few more infidels died at Gaolangi's hands, and then their companions were so terrified of him that none among them would come out to answer his challenge. Finally, the prince of India, Pur-Hindi, rode into the arena. He hurled his lance so powerfully at Gaolangi's chest that it exited from his back, causing him to give up his life to his Maker.

Amir suffered terrible grief at Gaolangi's death, and in his dismay he went and faced Pur-Hindi himself. Pur-Hindi said, "You dotard! Why do you volunteer your life? What idle thought stirs your fancy when even warriors in the prime of their youth avoid confronting me? But now that you are here, tell me who you are so that you do not die without anyone knowing your name and station and your corpse is not left exposed in the arena."

Amir answered, "O babbler, my name is Hamza bin Abdul Muttalib!" The prince said, "I had heard that Hamza had gone toward Bakhtar." Amir replied, "What you heard was right. I returned from Bakhtar not too long ago. Now deal me the blow you take pride in." Pur-Hindi aimed his lance at Amir, who caught hold of it at the handle and snatched it from his hands, rendering him defenseless. Amir threw the same lance at the prince's breast, and it shot through his heart and came out the other side of his body. Pur-Hindi fell from his horse and died that instant. Amir let out his war cry and fell upon his army, killing many an infidel and thousands of villains. Recognizing Amir, the infidels turned tail and fled en masse. The Holy Prophet returned triumphant and victorious to Mecca, and expressed his gratitude to God Almighty for his victory.

The narrator records that when Pur-Hindi's mother, a woman called Hinda, heard of his death, she gathered the kings and armies of India, Greece, Syria, China, Ethiopia, Zanzibar, and Turkistan, and amassed a mighty army to avenge her son's death, and headed to Ctesiphon. She sought redress from Hurmuz, who then accompanied her with his army. When these armies approached Mecca, and the Holy Prophet received the news, he said, "My uncle Hamza is capable of routing these armies all by himself." As the Holy Prophet had not uttered the words "God willing" with his claim, the Almighty God was not pleased. When the Holy Prophet faced the infidels with Amir Hamza and his companions, Hurmuz said to his men, "Do not fight these Arabs in single combat but fall upon them as a body and kill them at the same time. Otherwise, you will not defeat them." Hurmuz's entire force assaulted the followers of the True Faith as one, and Landhoor, Sa'ad bin Amar Hamza, and Aadi Madi-Karib—all Amir's dear companions—were martyred. Ali bin Abu Talib was showered by the infidels with arrows from all sides. One infidel threw a stone and broke a tooth of the Holy Prophet. Amar brought these tidings to Amir Hamza and communicated this heartrending news to his ears.

Amir put on his armor and mounted his steed and prepared to slaughter the infidels. While cutting through them, Amir Hamza drew near Hurmuz, who jumped from his throne and ran away. His army also stampeded off then, and none showed the wherewithal to put up a determined stand against Amir Hamza. He followed them for a distance of four *kos,* slaying infidel warriors along the way. Everywhere one looked the corpses of the infidels killed by Amir's lustrous sword lay piled in heaps. After killing them by the thousands, Amir returned to Mecca with the garlands of success adorning his neck.

Hinda had laid an ambush along Hamza's route to Mecca and was hiding with her army. She attacked him from behind and dealt a powerful thrust of her sword, which severed all four of Ashqar's legs. As Amir Hamza was taken by surprise, he fell to the ground when his steed collapsed. That accursed woman dealt a blow of her poison-laced sanguinary sword to Amir's immaculate head and decapitated him. She cut open his abdomen and plucked out and chewed up his heart, and then cut up his body into seventy pieces. Afterward, when her terrible folly became apparent to her, she feared the retribution Amir Hamza's daughter Quraisha would visit on her with the help of the *devs* and jinns of Qaf. That fear drove her to take refuge with the Holy Prophet. She shed bitter tears before him and repented her actions and converted to the True Faith.

The Holy Prophet said to her, "Take me to the corpse of my dear uncle so that I can see where that Lion of God lies." Hinda took him to see Amir Hamza's corpse and showed him to the place where he was martyred. The Holy Prophet gathered the pieces of Amir Hamza's body and said the funeral prayer separately for each part. It is said that Prophet Muhammad stood on his toes as he said the prayers. After the burial, people asked him why he had stood on his toes and Prophet Muhammad replied, "I stood in that manner because a great crowd of angels had inundated the prayer grounds and they all said the prayers seventy times for each part of his body." Thus the Holy Prophet informed everyone of Amir Hamza's holiness and lofty status.

When Prophet Muhammad turned back after burying Amir Hamza, Hinda presented herself before him. Prophet Muhammad turned his face away from her and showed her not the least favor. At that moment His Holiness received this divine message: "Dear friend! Hamza has indeed been martyred, but do look up to the heavens!" When His Holiness looked up, he saw Amir Hamza seated on a bejeweled throne in Heaven with *houris* and pages standing around him with folded arms. Then His Holiness smiled and said prayers of gratitude.

After several days, Quraisha arrived into the presence of the Holy Prophet with a huge army and asked for her father's murderer. The Holy Prophet showed Quraisha the lofty status attained by Amir Hamza and said, "O Quraisha, had your father not been martyred, he would not have found such a lofty station in Heaven, and God would not have promoted him to the rank of a holy personage. Thus you must obey my advice and shun all thoughts of revenge."

The narrator has said that that was the occasion when *Sura-e Jinn*[22] was revealed to the Holy Prophet and it comforted Quraisha's heart. Thus she was persuaded by the Holy Prophet to refrain from seeking revenge for her father's death. She did not speak another word about seeking vengeance but took her leave and departed for her land.

———

One tradition holds that it had displeased God that the Holy Prophet had not said the words "God willing" when stating that his uncle Hamza could rout the infidels alone and that this was why Amir Hamza's body was cut into seventy pieces and the Holy Prophet lost a tooth in the battle.

Yet another tradition maintains that Prophet Muhammad's wife, Ayesha (peace be upon her soul), was darning and patching her clothes when the Holy Prophet entered her room and the lamp was accidentally extinguished, and the thread came out of her needle. As the Mother of the Faithful sat worrying in darkness, the Holy Prophet smiled and, in the light that emanated from his holy teeth, she was able to thread the needle. The tradition holds that the Almighty God was displeased when the Holy Prophet said, "Regard, O Ayesha, my teeth are so luminous that you were able to thread your needle in their light, and my teeth performed the work of a lamp." This tradition holds that it was on account of the Holy Prophet's claim that his tooth was broken in the battle.

In the same battle, Prophet Muhammad's cousin, Ali bin Abu Talib, was wounded by an arrowhead that had lodged in his foot. The surgeon tried his best to remove the arrowhead but was unsuccessful. When Ali prostrated himself during prayers, the Holy Prophet said, "Draw out the arrowhead from Ali's foot." Then some champions removed the arrowhead with forceps, but Ali did not feel a thing. After he finished with his prayers, he noticed blood at his feet and asked, "Where has this blood come from, and when did I receive this wound?" His companions gave him a complete account, and then asked, "Your Honor, did you not know?" He answered, "By God, I did not know I was pierced by the arrow!"

May the beneficent God bless this translator[23] and transcriber as a sacrifice of Prophet Muhammad's (praise be unto him) martyred tooth and the wounded foot of Ali (may God have mercy on his soul); may He release him from dependence on everyone in this world and grant him His munificence by divine will; and may the truth and fiction of this tale be attributed to the inventors of the legend.

THE HISTORY OF THE LEGEND

LIST OF CHARACTERS,
HISTORIC FIGURES, DEITIES,
AND MYTHICAL BEINGS

SELECTED SOURCES

NOTES

THE HISTORY OF THE LEGEND

Musharraf Ali Farooqi

The *dastan* is an oral narrative genre, and the word itself means "tale" or "legend." The *dastan* of Amir Hamza has a rich folk history.

Storytellers brought the *dastans* to the Arabian peninsula via Persia as early as the seventh century C.E. It is related that a pagan named Nazr bin al-Haris of Mecca preferred Persian *dastans* to the message of Allah and turned men away from Prophet Muhammad's preaching. The Quran denounced him and others of his ilk, who preferred idle tales to life's realities.[1]

The hero of the *Dastan-e Amir Hamza* is based on Prophet Muhammad's uncle, Hamza bin Abdul Muttalib, who was renowned for his bravery. He was martyred in the battle of Uhad in 625 by a hired spearsman. But aside from the ancestral reference, there are no similarities between the Amir Hamza of this legend and the historic Hamza bin Abdul Muttalib.

The *dastan* relied heavily on familiar characters, icons, and legends to create scenes and situations. By using Amir Hamza's legend to describe the hero's bravery, using the names of idols and legendary villains of Islamic history to denote his enemies, using the rivalry between the Arab and Persian cultures to set up the conflict, using holy Khizr, the green-clad guide of legend, to be Amir Hamza's helper, and so forth, the story constantly evokes certain historical, cultural, and religious identifiers that allow it to narrate action without creating new histories and legends.

Like Amir Hamza, these characters, too, have no history beyond what is attributed to them by the story itself. The narrative discarded the real histories of the characters it chose, and sometimes even their legendary histories, and reassembled their legends.[2] To supernatural creatures such as jinns, which are part of the religious belief system, the story added *devs* and *peris*—creatures borrowed from the cultural belief system of folklore.[3]

But the name of Prophet Muhammad's brave uncle seemed to have stuck in people's imagination. Over time, folk legends continued to be grafted onto this legend. The seemingly contradictory claims about the origins of the story attest to this phenomenon.

According to one folk record, the *dastan* of Amir Hamza started as a commemorative account of the bravery and valor of the historic Hamza after his martyrdom, narrated by the women of Mecca. When Prophet Muhammad passed by the house of his uncle, he would stay awhile to hear these accounts of his bravery.[4]

Another source maintains that the legend was composed by the brother of the historic Hamza, Abbas bin Abdul Muttalib, who used to recite the legend of Hamza to Prophet Muhammad whenever the prophet grew nostalgic about the memory of his martyred uncle. According to the same source, two men compiled it into a book when Prophet Muhammad's followers were reviled in the time of the Umayyad dynasty (660–750). They composed this tale with help from historic and travelers' accounts as a rejoinder to the calumniators of Prophet Muhammad's companions and progeny. They recited it in the bazaars and in gatherings at coffee-sellers.[5]

Another legend has it that one of the caliphs of the Abbasid dynasty (750–1258) came down with delirium and remained incurable. Seven wise men—who were as wise as Aristotle himself—authored this *dastan*, and some of them were then deputed to read this story in the presence of the sick man night and day, until he was fully cured.[6]

Yet another tradition tells us that this story grew from the exploits of an early-ninth-century Persian adventurer named Hamza bin Abdullah, who belonged to the Kharjiite sect, which had rebelled against the Abbasid caliph Haroonur Rasheed—of *Arabian Nights* fame. Hamza bin Abdullah's legend, called the *Maghazi-e Hamza*, was supposed to be the origin of this story.[7]

The author of one of the Urdu versions of this *dastan*, Khalil Ali Khan Ashk, asserts that the tale was composed by "narrators of sweet speech" in the time of the Ghaznavid ruler Mahmud of Ghazna (971–1030).[8] Ghalib Lakhnavi, the original author of the present text, attests to Ashk's account, adding that the legend was composed because it described "all manner of humanity, and was an inspiration for plans of battle, capturing castles, and conquering countries."[9]

Other Indian narrators of Amir Hamza's legend give a different account. According to Ahmed Husain Qamar, one of the five authors of a longer version of *Dastan-e Amir Hamza,* this legend was first written by the Indian poet Amir Khusrau (1253–1325) in seven long manuscript volumes, and also by Emperor Akbar's poet laureate, Faizi (1547–1595).[10] Qamar also mentions that the Qajar king Nasiruddin Shah of Persia (1831–1896) sent for the seven books of Amir Hamza's legend from India and had them compiled at his court and published in two volumes in Persian.[11]

These are just a few of the more prominent names given as the sources of Amir Hamza's legend. What these seemingly contradictory accounts reveal is the legend's popularity over a long period of time, and the many sources from which it flowed down to the storytellers and their audiences.

If these accounts are accurate, the legend of Amir Hamza could have arrived on the Indian subcontinent around the tenth or eleventh century with Mahmud of Ghazna. However, the earliest known illustrated Indian manuscript of the legend dates from the late fifteenth century.[12]

It was the Quran itself that provided the first clue to the nature of the *dastan,* calling it "idle tales" aimed at escaping reality. Nearly a millennium later, the Mughal emperor Babur (1483–1530) condemned the *Hamzanama,* an early Persian version of the story. Discussing his chief justices, Babur wrote: "One was Mir Sar-e Barahna; he was from a village in Andijan and appears to have made claim to be a *sayyid.* He was a very agreeable companion, pleasant of temper and speech. His were the judgment and rulings that carried weight among men of letters and poets of Khurasan. He wasted his time by composing, in imitation of the story of Amir Hamza, a work that is one long, far-fetched lie, opposed to sense and nature."[13]

The phrase "one long, far-fetched lie, opposed to sense and nature" describes the development in this ideal. The "idle tale" has become even idler; it distorts reality, has a dynamic that does not follow the rules of cause and effect, and displays supernatural elements.

The Mughal emperor Akbar, disregarding his grandfather Babur's bias against the story, commissioned the celebrated illustration project of the *Hamzanama* around 1562–77. These miniatures reveal how contemporary reality was being woven into legends. We see anachronistic elements like firearms in these miniatures, as in this book. Other examples are seen in the details of clothes, jewelry, makeup, and cuisine in the story.

Amir Hamza's legend continued to spread in India. In the Indo-Muslim culture, the *dastan* literature played a vital role in the development of Urdu into a literary language. Four versions of *Dastan-e Amir Hamza* are known in Urdu. The longest version, printed between 1883 and 1917, combined many different traditions contributed by Urdu *dastan* narrators and comprised forty-six volumes and approximately forty-four thousand pages. It is considered the crown jewel of Urdu literature.

The true heroes of the *Dastan-e Amir Hamza* were the countless unknown and unsung *dastan-gos* (*dastan* narrators) whose imaginations made this legend grow and expand and leave a powerful imprint on world literature. Beside Urdu, it is known to exist in Arabic, Persian, Turkish, Sindhi, Malay, Javanese, Georgian, Balinese, Sudanese, Pashto, Bengali, and Hindi versions.

In nineteenth-century India, the popularity of *Dastan-e Amir Hamza* was widespread. *Dastan-gos* were employed at the regional courts and *dastan* narration was a greatly sought-after entertainment in public gatherings. Many *dastans* were also written and published during this period.

The tradition of *dastan* narration came to an end with the death of the last famous *dastan* narrator, Mir Baqir Ali, in 1928. The writing and publication of the *dastans* slowly ceased.

Over the next few decades, the vibrant Indo-Muslim civilization that had cultivated these legends underwent the catastrophic events of partition, and the communalization of the Indo-Muslim cultural heritage, which had begun as a project of the British colonial regime, was perpetuated for political gain by the new leadership of both India and Pakistan. Neither side was willing to commit to preserving the Indo-Muslim heritage. In this atmosphere, scholars, writers, and critics on both sides disregarded the *dastan* genre, and slowly the *dastan* literature was obliterated from the literary and cultural consciousness of the people of the subcontinent.

Recently, there has been reason for hope. The publication of the voluminous *dastan* study *Sahiri, Shahi, Sahibqirani* by Urdu's greatest living scholar, novelist, and critic, Shamsur Rahman Faruqi, was a landmark event in *dastan* scholarship. It bridged the huge gap in our knowledge of this genre and the many intricacies of this particular *dastan*. There is also a newfound interest in *dastan* narration. Mahmood Farooqi and Danish Husain in India are reviving *dastan* narration in a new format. Their performances have been great successes in both India and Pakistan, where new editions of the *dastan* are also being published. It suddenly seems possible that the *Dastan-e Amir Hamza* will soon reclaim its rightful place in the canon of Urdu literature.

NOTES

1. *The Holy Quran: English Translation of the Meanings and Commentary* (Medina: King Fahd Holy Quran Printing Complex, A.H. 1410), 31:6.

2. An example of this is the legend of the green-clad Khizr, who is tradition-ally considered a guide for the lost traveler. In the story, he was declared a prophet, shown to be the brother of Ilyas (Elias), and even had a mother, Asifa Ba-Safa. Moreover, he is shown killing the *devs* of Qaf to help Amir Hamza.

3. It should be pointed out that the concept of jinns itself was brought into the Islamic belief system from the Arab folklore tradition.

4. Haji Qissa-Khvan Hamdani, *Zubdat-ur Rumuz* (manuscript, c. 1613–14; Khda Bakhsh Library, Patna), 2.

5. *Kitab-e Rumuz-e Hamza* (Tehran: A.H. 1274–76 [1857–59]; British Museum Library), 2–3.

6. Ibid.

7. Suhail Bukhari, *Urdu Dastan: Tahqiqi va Tanqidi Mutaliah* (Islamabad: Muqtadira Qaumi Zaban, 1987); Suhail Bukhari, "Urdu Dastan Ka Fanni Tajziyah," *Nuqush* 105 (April–June 1966), 84–99.

8. Khalil Ali Khan Ashk, *Dastan-e Amir Hamza* (Lahore: Seth Adamji Publish-ers Bumbai Walay, n.d.), 2. Originally published 1801.

9. Mirza Aman Ali Khan Bahadur Ghalib Lakhnavi, *Tarjuma-e Dastan-e Sahibqiran Giti-sitan Aal-e Paighambar-e Aakhiruz Zaman Amir Hamza bin Abdul Muttalib bin Hashim bin Abdul Munaf* (Calcutta: Hakim Sahib Press, 1855), 2–3.

10. Ahmed Husain Qamar, *Tilism-e Hoshruba*, volume 6 (Kanpur: Naval Kishore Press, 1916), 924.

11. Ibid., 1373.

12. This manuscript is in the collection of Sitzung Preussicher Kulturbesitz, Tübingen, Germany. See Karl Khandalavala and Moti Chandra, *New Docu-ments of Indian Painting: A Reappraisal* (Bombay: Board of Trustees of Prince of Wales Museum, 1969), 50–55.

13. Milo Cleveland Beach, *The Imperial Image: Paintings for the Mughal Court* (Washington, D.C.: Freer Gallery of Art, Smithsonian Institution, 1981), 58.

List of Characters, Historic Figures, Deities, and Mythical Beings

Names starting with honorifics such as *Amir* and *Malik* should be looked for under the proper name. For example, Malik Alqash can be found at Alqash. Among these honorifics are the following:

Amir: Title used for a commander or leader. In this book the title is used for the hero, Hamza.

Bibi: Title used for a respectable woman

Hakim: Title used for a wise man, or someone with a knowledge of medicine

Khusrau: Title used for a majestic king. In this book it is used for Landhoor bin Saadan.

Khvaja: Title used for a man of distinction, usually conferred on dignitaries

Malik: Title of royalty. Also a title conferred on viziers, as in the case of Malik Alqash.

Mehtar: Title conferred on a chief or commander

Also note that the loyalties of characters change often. Their affiliations as described here are not permanent.

AADAM: Adam. In the *dastan,* he is given the rank of a prophet.

AADI CHOB-GARDAAN: Warrior in Emperor Naushervan's service

AADI MADI-KARIB: Bandit who is defeated by Hamza and joins his cause. He is Hamza's foster brother and a voracious eater.

AADIYA BANO: Wet nurse of Amir Hamza, Muqbil Vafadar, and Amar Ayyar; mother of Aadi Madi-Karib

AASHOB (OR JAHANDAR QALANDAR): Brother of Bahlol; an orphan whom Amir rescues from a *dev* in Qaf

AASMAN PERI: Daughter of Emperor Shahpal bin Shahrukh of Qaf

AATISH: Commander of Emperor Naushervan's *ayyars*

ABA SAEED KHARQA-POSH: Acolyte of Amar Ayyar

ABDUL AZIZ: King of Egypt and father of Zehra Misri

ABDUL MUTTALIB: Chieftain of the Banu Hashim tribe of Arabia; father of Hamza

ABDUR RAHEEM JINN: Minister of Rashid Jinn

ABDUR RAHMAN JINN: Vizier of Emperor Shahpal bin Shahrukh of Qaf

ABU JAHAL: Literally, "father of folly." His real name was Amar bin Hashsham and he was one of Prophet Muhammad's sworn enemies in the city of Mecca.

ABU SAEED LANGARI: Acolyte of Amar Ayyar

ABU SUFYAN: Abu Sufyan bin al-Harith was one of Prophet Muhammad's cousins and foster brothers. He remained his enemy until his conversion to Islam late in life.

ABUL-ALA: *See* Hamza

AFRASIYAB: An ancient sovereign of Turan celebrated in Persian legends

AGHA BULBUL: Courtier and executioner in the service of Amir Hamza

AHRIMAN: A *dev* of Qaf. Father of Ifrit Dev. Not to be confused with Ahriman, the force of darkness in the Zoroastrian religion.

AHRIMAN SHER-GARDAAN: One of the kings of the lands of Bakhtar

AJAL: One of Hamza's eleven brothers; son of Abdul Muttalib

AJROOK KHWARZAMI: Commander who attacks the dominions of Landhoor bin Saadan

AKHZAR FILGOSH: Sassanid commander in Emperor Naushervan's service

AKVANA PERI: Associate of Aasman Peri

ALAF POSH: Chief of Emperor Naushervan's gardeners

ALAM SHAH ROOMI (OR ALAM SHER ROOMI, OR RUSTAM-E PEEL-TAN, OR SHER-E SAF-SHIKAN): Son of Amir Hamza by Rabia Plas Posh

ALAM SHER ROOMI: *See* Alam Shah Roomi

ALI (OR ALI BIN ABU TALIB): Islam's fourth caliph; Prophet Muhammad's cousin and son-in-law

ALI BIN ABU TALIB: *See* Ali

ALJOSH BARBARI: Ninety-yard-tall giant who is Emperor Naushervan's supporter

ALQAMAH SATOORDAST: Commander in Emperor Naushervan's service

ALQASH: Vizier of Qubad Kamran and maternal grandfather of Bakhtak

AMAR AYYAR: A trickster and companion of Hamza; son of Umayya Zamiri

AMAR BIL FATAH: Name given to Amar Ayyar by Buzurjmehr

AMAR HAMZA: Amir Hamza's son by Naheed Maryam

AMAR HABASHI: Son of Shaddad Abu-Amar Habashi

ANIS SHAH: Ruler of Alania

ANTAR DEVDADI: Ruler of the Devdad fort

ANTAR FILGOSH: Commander in Emperor Naushervan's service

ANTAR TEGHZAN: Commander in Emperor Naushervan's service

AQIL KHAN: Vizier of Me'aad Shah Maghrebi

AQIQ: Commander in Amir Hamza's camp

AQLIMUN: Physician who treats Hamza when he is poisoned

ARA'SH: 180-yard-tall giant

ARBAB: Son of Antar Devdadi

ARDABIL PEEL-DANDAN: Co-ruler of Ardabil; brother of Marzaban Peel-Dandan

ARNAIS DEV: A confidant and mace-bearer of Prophet Suleiman; husband of Laneesa Peri and father of Ashqar Devzad

ARSHIVAN PERIZAD: Son of Landhoor and Rashida Peri

ARVANA: Hamza's *gao-sar* wife whom he marries in Qaf

ASAD ZARRIN-TARKASH: Nephew of Emperor Naushervan

ASHQAR DEVZAD: Hamza's favored mount. He is the son of Arnais Dev and Laneesa Peri, conceived when Arnais took the shape of a horse and coupled with Laneesa.

ASHTAR: Champion warrior in Emperor Naushervan's service

ASIF: Brother of Faridun Shah, the king of Greece

ASIF BIN BARKHIA: Minister of Prophet Suleiman

ASIFA BA-SAFA: Mother of prophets Khizr and Ilyas

ASRAR JADU: A *dev* from the Tilism-e Shehristan-e Zarrin

ATIQ: Commander in Amir Hamza's camp

AULAD BIN MARZABAN KAIKAUSI: Relative of Zhopin Kaus

AURANG: Prince of Lakhnauti; brother of Gaurang

AYASHAN MALIK: Warrior in Emperor Naushervan's service

AYESHA: Prophet Muhammad's wife

AYUB: Job

AZRA: Heroine of the romance *Wamiq and Azra;* the beloved of Wamiq

BABA SHIMLA: Name Amar invents for his teacher's turban

BABA ZUD-BURD: Amar Ayyar in disguise

BADI-UL-MULK: One of Amir Hamza's sons

BADIUZ ZAMAN: Amir Hamza's son by Gili-Savar, raised by Aasman Peri and Quraisha at Mount Qaf

BAHLOL (OR JAHANGIR QALANDAR): Brother of Aashob, an orphan whom Amir rescues from a *dev* in Qaf

BAHMAN JASAP: One of Emperor Naushervan's supporters

BAHMAN: Son of Salasal Shah

BAHMAN HAZAN: Emissary for Emperor Naushervan

BAHMAN SAKKAN: Emissary for Emperor Naushervan

BAHRAM: Bandit who robs Emperor Naushervan when he is in exile. Not to be confused with Bahram Gurd, the emperor of China.

BAHRAM CHOB-GARDAAN: Warrior in Emperor Naushervan's service

BAHRAM GUR: A legendary king of Persia known for his passion for the chase of the onager. Not to be confused with Bahram Gurd.

BAHRAM GURD: Emperor of China and son of the grand emperor. He is not related to Mehr-Angez, the daughter of the Emperor of China, or her brothers Kebaba Chini and Qulaba Chini.

BAHZAD: Legendary Persian miniaturist (1450–1535 C.E.) who was the head of the royal ateliers in Herat and Tabriz during the late Timurid and early Safavid periods

BAKHT JAMAL: Buzurjmehr's father; teacher and friend of Alqash

BAKHTAK: Emperor Naushervan's vizier; son of Bakhtiar by Alqash's daughter, Saqar Ghar Bano

BAKHTIAR: Nubian slave of vizier Alqash; Bakhtak's father

BAKHTIARAK: Son of Bakhtak

BAKHYA SHUTARBAN: Champion warrior in Emperor Naushervan's service

BARKHIA: *See* Asif bin Barkhia

BASHEER: Khvaja Abdul Muttalib's slave; father of Muqbil Vafadar

BECHIN KAMRAN: Brother of Zhopin Kaus

BILQIS: The queen of Sheba

BURRAQ: Legendary winged horse on which Prophet Muhammad flew to visit the heavens

BUZURG UMMID: Son of Buzurjmehr

BUZURJMEHR: Son of Bakht Jamal; vizier of Emperor Qubad Kamran and Emperor Naushervan

CHAMBELI: Wet nurse whose name is invoked by cowards

CHAND: A farmer

CHHALAWA: According to popular belief, a *chhalawa* is a demon that appears in the shape of an infant and can travel at breathtaking speed.

DAJJAL: In Islamic mythology the name given to the Antichrist. According to popular belief, he will appear riding an ass.

DANYAL: Prophet Daniel

DARA: King Darius the Third of Persia (died 330 B.C.E.)

DARAB: Keeper of the fortress of Kurgistan; brother of Sohrab

DARAB AYYAR: An *ayyar* in the service of Sabir and Sabur

DARBAN JADU: A *dev* from the Tilism-e Shehristan-e Zarrin

DARYADIL: Buzurjmehr's son

DAUD: Prophet David

DEV: A demon or a giant

DEWANA TAPISHI: Commander in Emperor Naushervan's service; brother of Sar-Barahna Tapishi

DIL-AARAM: Slave girl of Emperor Qubad Kamran; a lute player

DIL-AAVEZ: Khvaja Arbab's daughter

DINAR SAR-SHABAN: Son of Farkhar Sar-Shaban

DURDANA PERI: Mother of Rehan Peri, wife of Junaid Shah Sabz-Posh

DUR-DUR POSH: Hamza's son by Rehan Peri

EUCLID: Greek mathematician (325–265 B.C.E.)

FAISAL: A goldwright

FARAMURZ: Son of Emperor Naushervan by Mehr-Angez

FARHAD: Hero of the romance *Shirin and Farhad;* the lover of Shirin

FARHAD BIN LANDHOOR: Son of Landhoor bin Saadan

FARIDUN: Persian king who ascended the throne after killing the tyrant Zahhak

FARIDUN SHAH: King of Greece

FARKHAR SAR-SHABAN: Old man from the city of Farkhar

FARRUKH: Daughter of Zardhasht Jadu the sorcerer

FARZANA BANO: Daughter of Furhad-Akka and sister of Qaroon Akka

FATAH AYYAR: An *ayyar* in the service of Amir Hamza

FATAH NOSH: King of Kharsana; brother of Fatah Yar and father of Rabia Plas Posh

FATAH YAR: Brother of Fatah Nosh

FATIMA: Prophet Muhammad's daughter; Ali bin Abu Talib's wife

FAULAD: Rebel slave of the emperor of Greece

FAULAD BIN GUSTHAM: Son of Gustham bin Ashk Zarrin Kafsh Sasani

FAULAD PEHLWAN: Alias used by Amir Hamza

FIROZ SHAH (OR FIROZ TURK): Turkish warrior who attacks Landhoor's dominions

FIROZ TURK: *See* Firoz Shah

FITNA BANO: Attendant of Princess Mehr-Nigar and daughter of Princess Mehr-Nigar's nanny; Amar Ayyar's beloved

FURHAD-AKKA: Warrior who battles Hamza

FUTUH NIM-TAN: King of *nim-tans*

GALEEM AYYAR: An *ayyar* in Emperor Naushervan's service

GALEEM-GOSH: Creatures with large ears that they wrap around their bodies

GALEN: Prominent ancient Greek physician

GAOLANGI: King of Rakham

GAO-PA: A race of cow-footed creatures

GAO-SAR: A race of cow-headed creatures

GARSHASP: Legendary Persian warrior

GAURANG: Prince of Lakhnauti; brother of Aurang

GHOL: Commonly translated as "ghoul," this is an imaginary demon that appears in different shapes and colors and devours men and animals.

GHUR-MUNHA: A race of horse-headed creatures

GILI-SAVAR: Daughter of King Gunjal; wife of Hamza

GOSH-FIL: A race of elephant-eared creatures

GUL CHEHRA: Sister of Zhopin Kaus

GUL-RUKH: Daughter of Zardhasht Jadu the sorcerer

GUNJAL: Sovereign of Gilan

GUSTHAM BIN ASHK ZARRIN KAFSH SASANI: Renowned Sassanid warrior and Amir Hamza's mortal enemy

HAAM: Ruler of Antabia

HAAM DEVDADI: Commander of the king of Devdad's *ayyars*

HADEES SHAH: Ruler of Aleppo

HAMAN: Vizier of Jamshed Shah

HAMAN SHAH: Keeper of a castle

HAMZA: Son of Abdul Muttalib and uncle of Prophet Muhammad. Given the title Amir Hamza, and also called Abul-Ala, the Sahibqiran, and the Quake of Qaf.

HARAS FIL-DANDAN: Warrior who comes to aid Malik Siraj and Ajrook Khwarzami against Landhoor

HARDAM: King of Baru whose niece marries Sa'ad bin Amar Hamza and whose sister is given to Amir Hamza in marriage

HARIS BIN SA'AD: Son of Sa'ad bin Amar Hamza by Hardam's niece

HARUT: Harut and Marut were angels who severely censured mankind before the throne of God. They were sent to Earth in human form to judge the temptations to which man is subject but they could not withstand them. They were seduced by women, and committed every kind of iniquity. For this they were suspended by their feet in a well in Babylon, where they are to remain in great torment until the Day of Judgment.

HARUT GURAZ-DANDAN: Commander in Emperor Naushervan's service; brother of Marut Guraz-Dandan

HASHSHAM BIN ALQAMAH KHAIBARI: Warrior from the city of Khaibar

HASHIM BIN HAMZA: Amir Hamza's son by Hardam's sister

HATIM: Arab chief of the Tay tribe known for his generosity and munificence, and the hero of the romance *The Adventures of Hatim-Tai*

HINDA: Mother of Pur-Hindi

HOMAN: Son of Bahman Jasap

HOMAN KHAVARI: Son of Qeemaz Shah Khavari

HUD: Prophet Heber

HUMA-E TAJDAR: Daughter of the king of Yemen; Sultan Bakht Maghrebi's beloved

HUMRAN ZARRIN KAMAR: Vassal of Emperor Naushervan and commander of a fortress

HURMUZ: Son of Emperor Naushervan by Mehr-Angez

HUSAIN: Grandson of Prophet Muhammad and son of Ali bin Abu Talib by Bibi Fatima

IBRAHIM: Prophet Abraham

IFRIT DEV: Villainous *dev* of Qaf, head of the rebels of Mount Qaf

ILYAS: Prophet Elias. According to one legend he saves the innocent from drowning. According to another, he is the brother of the holy Khizr and has drunk from the Fountain of Life and will live to see the Day of Judgment. Ilyas helps people on water while Khizr helps people on both land and water.

ILYAS: King encountered by Mehr-Nigar when she runs away after Amar's harsh treatment of her

INDAR: Also known as Indra. King of the gods and regent of the visible heavens in Indian mythology. The court of Indar is synonymous with a place of amusement and pleasure.

ISFANDIAR: Persian king

ISMAIL: Ishmael

ISRAFIL: According to Islamic belief, the Angel Israfil will usher in the Day of Judgment by blowing his trumpet.

ISTAFTANOSH: Prince of Greece; one of Hamza's commanders

ISTEFUNOS: Prince of Greece; brother of Istaftanosh

IZRAIL: The Angel of Death, according to Islamic legend

JAFAR: Ruler of Kashmir

JAHANDAR KABULI: Commander in Emperor Naushervan's service; Jahangir Kabuli's brother

JAHANDAR QALANDAR: Name given to Khvaja Aashob by Hamza

JAHANGIR KABULI: Commander in Emperor Naushervan's service; Jahandar Kabuli's brother

JAHANGIR QALANDAR: Name given to Khvaja Bahlol by Hamza

JAIPUR: Son of Shahpal, nephew of King Saadan Shah of Ceylon, and cousin of Landhoor

JAMASP: Buzurjmehr's maternal grandfather. According to legend he preached the Magian religion after the death of Zoroaster and wrote a book on alchemy called *Jamasp-nama*.

JAMSHED: Ancient king of Persia. The name is often attributed in legend to King Suleiman and Sikander, and is invoked in this book in connection with Emperor Naushervan's court to convey the grandeur and prestige of his empire.

JAMSHED SHAH: Master of the castle of Talva-Bahar

JAN: According to legend, the father of all jinns and *peris* who inhabited Earth before the creation of Aadam. They were later banished to Jinnistan, "the Land of the Jinns," for disobedience to the Supreme Being.

JIBRAIL: Angel Gabriel

JINN: Creatures made of fire. According to Islamic tradition, Iblis (Satan) was a jinn. *See* Jan.

JUNAID SHAH SABZ-POSH JINN (OR JUNAID SHAH SABZ-QABA): Elder brother of Emperor Shahpal bin Shahrukh of Qaf

KAIKAUS: King of Persia. His name is invoked to connote the grandeur and majesty of Emperor Naushervan's court.

KAI KHUSRAU: King Cyrus. His name is invoked to convey the grandeur and majesty of Emperor Naushervan's court.

KAKH BAKHTAR: Cannibal king of Bakhtar

KAUS SHERWANI: Champion warrior in Amir Hamza's service

KARIB MADI: Son of Aadi Madi-Karib by Gustham's daughter. This version of the *Dastan-e Amir Hamza* does not mention the marriage between Aadi Madi-Karib and Gustham's daughter.

KARGAS SASANI: An *ayyar* in the service of Hurmuz and Faramurz

KARVAN: Leader of a merchant caravan that Amir encounters on his way to Kharsana

KARVAN: Vizier of the king of Egypt

KATARA KABULI: Commander of Hurmuz's *ayyars;* nephew of Zhopin Kaus

KAYUMARS: Sovereign who offers refuge to Emperor Naushervan

KEBABA CHINI: Son of the emperor of China; brother of Mehr-Angez and Qulaba Chini

KHALIFA BULBUL: Mehr-Nigar's cook

KHALKHAL DEV: A *dev* of Qaf

KHARCHAL: Vicious *dev* who takes over the city of Simin in Qaf

KHARPAL: Vicious *dev* who takes over the city of Simin in Qaf

KHIZR: A holy personage of Islamic legend who led Sikander the Bicornous to the Fountain of Life. He guides lost travelers on land and water. In the *dastan* he is the brother of Prophet Ilyas (Elias) and is given the rank of a prophet.

KHURSHID KHAVARI: Sister of Qeemaz Shah Khavari

KHUSRAU: *See* Landhoor. In this book the title is used for Landhoor bin Saadan, unless accompanied by another name.

KOH BAKHT HINDI: Brother of Sarkash Hindi

KOH-PAIKAR: Sassanid warrior in Emperor Naushervan's service

KULIYAT: Son of Galeem Ayyar

LAHOOT SHAH: A jinn; master of the Castle of Zamarrud Hisar; father of Laneesa

LAILA: Heroine of the romance *Laila and Majnun;* the beloved of Qais (Majnun)

LANDHOOR BIN SAADAN: King of India; a descendent of Prophet Shis

LANEESA PERI: Daughter of Lahoot Shah and beloved of Arnais Dev. She bears Ashqar Devzad, Hamza's legendary steed.

LAT: Pre-Islamic goddess of the Arabs; condemned in the Quran (53:19)

MADAR SHAH: Saint who lived near Ajmer and was venerated by charlatans

MAGHLUB FIL-ZOR: Warrior who aids Malik Siraj and Ajrook Khwarzami against Landhoor

MAHMUD SIYAH-TAN: Amar Ayyar in disguise

MAIMOONA: She-elephant of Landhoor bin Saadan

MIAN FATTU: Water carrier whom Amar Ayyar kills and then impersonates to enter the castle of Devdad

MAJDAK: Officer of Emperor Naushervan's court

MAJNUN: *See* Qais

MALIA: Son of Marzooq Farangi, a fifty-yard-tall giant

MALIK: According to Islamic legend, the porter of Hell

MALOONA JADU: Mother of Ifrit Dev

MANAT: Pre-Islamic goddess of the Arabs; condemned in the Quran (53:20)

MANI: Persian painter and founder of the Manichean sect, celebrated for the beauty of his house

MANSOOR AYYAR: An *ayyar* in the employ of Salasal Shah

MANWA: Son of a grass cutter

MARUT: *See* Harut

MARUT GURAZ-DANDAN: Commander in Emperor Naushervan's service; brother of Harut Guraz-Dandan

MARZABAN PEEL-DANDAN: Co-ruler of Ardabil; brother of Ardabil Peel-Dandan

MARZABAN ZARDHASHT: Son-in-law of Gaolangi

MARZAK: Agent of Emperor Naushervan; Hakim who blinds Hamza and his companions

MARZOOQ FARANGI: Warrior who raids the land of Kharsana and is routed by Hamza

MAYMAR DEV: A *dev* who constructed most of the buildings in Qaf and ordered the imprisonment of Khvaja Aashob and Khvaja Bahlol

ME'AAD RAZ AADI: Warrior of the Aadi tribe

ME'AAD SHAH MAGHREBI: King who ordered Aadi Madi-Karib buried alive with his deceased wife

MEHD ZARRIN KAMAR: Ruler of Antaqia

MEHR-AFROZE: Emperor Naushervan's younger daughter and Mehr-Nigar's sister

MEHR-ANGEZ: Daughter of the emperor of China; Emperor Naushervan's wife and Mehr-Nigar's mother

MEHRDAR SAR-SHABAN: Son of Farkhar Sar-Shaban

MEHR-NIGAR: Daughter of Emperor Naushervan by Mehr-Angez

MEHR SHAH: Amir Hamza's son by Mehr-Afroze

MIR BHUCHRI: *See* Pir Bhuchri

MISQAL SHAH: King of the castle of Tanj-e Maghreb

MISQAL SHAH MISRI: Companion of Amir Hamza. It is unclear if he is the same Misqal Shah who is the king of the castle of Tanj-e Maghreb.

MOHTRAM BANO: Qubad Kamran's cousin and wife; Emperor Naushervan's mother

MUHAMMAD BIN ABDULLAH BIN ABDUL MUTTALIB: The prophet of Islam

MUHLIL SAGSAR: One of the commanders who attacks the dominions of Land-hoor bin Saadan

MULLA: Teacher of Amir Hamza, Muqbil Vafadar, and Amar Ayyar

MUNZIR SHAH YEMENI: King of Yemen

MUQBIL VAFADAR: Companion of Amir Hamza; son of Abdul Muttalib's slave Basheer and a faultless archer

MUSA: Prophet Moses

NAHEED MARYAM: Daughter of Faridun Shah; Amir Hamza's wife

NAIK RAI: Vizier of Malik Shuaib

NAIRANJ PERI: Daughter of Naranj Peri's vizier

NAMIAN: An *ayyar* in Amir Hamza's service

NAMRUD: Nimrod. The title of King Suriyus, who is said to have cast Prophet Ibrahim into a fire. In the *dastan* he is mentioned as a god of the fire worshippers.

NAQABDAR: Literally, "the veiled one"

NAQABDAR NARANJI-POSH: Veiled rider who comes to assist Amir Hamza's armies in times of need

NARANJ PERI: A *peri* of Qaf who appears as the Naqabdar Naranji-Posh

NARIMAN: Famous hero of Persia

NASAI: Son of the king of Farang

NASNAAS OF SULEIMAN: Beast that resembles human beings and can speak the Arabic language. It is said that the beast has only one leg, one eye, one arm, and one ear, and hops when walking.

NAUSHERVAN: Emperor of Persia; son of Qubad Kamran and father of Mehr-Nigar

NIHAL: Princess Mehr-Nigar's childhood attendant

NIM-TAN: An imaginary being that has half a face, one eye, one arm, and one foot. There are male and female *nim-tans:* The male has the right hand, foot, and so forth and the female the left. When united, the male and female resemble one human figure; when separated, they run with amazing speed on their single feet and are considered very dangerous.

NIM-TAN KHAVARI: Father of Qeemaz Shah Khavari

NOMAN: Son of King Munzir; shah of Yemen

NOOR BANO: Sister of Bahman and daughter of Salasal Shah

NUH: Prophet Noah

PAIK AYYAR: An *ayyar* in Emperor Naushervan's service

PALANG-SAR DEV: A *dev* of Qaf and a minion of Sufaid Dev

PERI: A female fairy

PERIZAD: A male *peri*. The term *perizad* is also used to describe any creature born of a *peri*.

PIRAN MAGHREBI: Sher Shah Qirwani's commander in chief

PIR BHUCHRI (OR MIR BHUCHRI): Saint venerated by the transvestites

PIR FARKHARI: Companion of Amir Hamza

PIR JALILAN: Name of a saint, or a place named after this saint. No other information is available.

PIR-UL-WALI: Title of the Indian saint Khvaja Moinuddin Hasan Chishti (1142–1238 C.E.), in whose name food offerings are made

PLATO: Greek philosopher (427–347 B.C.E.)

POTIPHAR: Ruler of Egypt to whom Yusuf (Joseph) was sold in slavery

PUR-HINDI: Indian prince

PYTHAGORAS: Greek philosopher (569–475 B.C.E.)

QAILUM: Sassanid warrior in Emperor Naushervan's service

QAIS: Hero of the romance *Laila and Majnun;* the lover of Laila. His patronymic was Majnun, "the frenzied one."

QAIS QEEMAZ KHAVARI: Son of Qeemaz Shah Khavari

QALMAQ SHAH: Warrior who advances on Mecca and is defeated by Ajal bin Abdul Muttalib

QAMAR CHEHRA PERI: Amir Hamza's *peri* wife; mother of Qamza-Zad

QAMZA-ZAD: Son of Amir Hamza by Qamar Chehra Peri

QARAN DEOBAND: Commander in Emperor Naushervan's service

QARAN FIL-GARDAN: Sassanid warrior in Emperor Naushervan's service

QAROON: King Croesus of Lydia (reigned 560–547 B.C.E.), whose name connotes wealth

QAROON AKKA: Son of Furhad-Akka

QASIM KHAVARI: Son of Alam Shah Roomi

QATRAN MAGHREBI: An *ayyar* in Sher Shah Qirwani's service

QAUS: A shepherd

QEEMAZ SHAH KHAVARI: Ruler of the city of Khavar

QUBAD: Woodcutter to whom Emperor Qubad gives away Dil-Aaram

QUBAD: Son of Amir Hamza by Mehr-Nigar

QUBAD AADI: Warrior of the Aadi tribe

QUBAD KAMRAN: Emperor of Persia and father of Naushervan

QUFUL NESTANI: Ruler of the fort of Nestan

QULABA CHINI: Son of the emperor of China; brother of Mehr-Angez

QUNDUZ SAR-SHABAN: Owner of a garden who becomes Amir Hamza's companion

QURAISHA: Daughter of Amir Hamza by Aasman Peri

RA'AD DEV: Two-headed *dev* Amir Hamza encounters in Qaf

RA'AD SHATIR DEV: Nephew of Ifrit Dev and lord of the castles of Siyah Boom and Sufaid Boom

RABIA PLAS POSH: Daughter of King Fatah Nosh, the sovereign of Kharsana

RAE-BEL: Wet nurse whose name is invoked by cowards

RAHDAR DEV: First *dev* of Qaf killed by Amir Hamza

RAHMAN: Father of Vizier Haman

RAM: A Hindu god

RASHID JINN: King of the lands of Abyaz Min Muzafat, a dominion of Qaf

RASHIDA PERI: Daughter of Rashid Jinn

RAUF JINN: Minister of Junaid Shah Sabz-Posh Jinn

REHAN PERI: Daughter of Junaid Shah Sabz-Posh Jinn

REL GAOLANGI: Son of Gaolangi

RIZWAN: According to Islamic legend, the porter of Heaven

RIZWAN PERIZAD: One of the attendants of Aasman Peri

RUKH: Giant bird that is the enemy of King Tulu Gao-Pa

RUSTAM: Legendary Persian warrior and son of Zal

RUSTAM-E PEEL-TAN: *See* Alam Shah Roomi

SA'AD BIN AMAR HAMZA: Son of Amar Hamza and grandson of Amir Hamza

SA'AD SHAMI: Alias used by Amir Hamza

SA'AD TAUQI: Warrior in Amir Hamza's service

SA'AD YEMENI: Amir Hamza's companion

SA'AD ZARRIN-TARKASH: Nephew of Emperor Naushervan

SA'AD ZULMATI: Amar Ayyar disguised as a bearded forty-yard-tall giant

SAADAN SHAH: King of Ceylon; father of Landhoor

SAALIM: A holy man and descendent of Prophet Nuh

SAAM: Ruler of Antakia

SABIR: Son of Shahpal Hindi and brother of Sabur

SABIR NAMADPOSH AYYAR: An *ayyar* in Emperor Naushervan's service

SABIT SHAH: One of two masters of the castle of Rahtas Gadh; *see* Tahmuras Shah

SABUR: Son of Shahpal Hindi and brother of Sabir

SAEED BAZARGAN: Khvaja Abdur Rahman Jinn in disguise; the master of a ship Amir sees being loaded in Qaf

SAHIB-E HAL ATA: According to *dastan* scholar Shamsur Rahman Faruqi, this is from the phrase *"sahib-e hal ata"* and is a name signifying Ali bin Abu Talib. Chapter 76 of the Quran, the *Dahr*, or *Insan*, begins with this phrase. It means "has there not passed, or been?" Verse 8 of this chapter speaks of people who go hungry themselves while feeding others. Some interpreters of the Quran say that this verse refers to Ali bin Abu Talib, and it is therefore presumed that the whole chapter is about Ali bin Abu Talib in some way. Since the chapter starts with *"hal ata,"* Ali bin Abu Talib is occasionally described as the *sahib,* or the *tajdar* of *"hal ata."*

SAHIBQIRAN: Title for the Lord of the Auspicious Planetary Conjunction; given to those born under the conjunction of Jupiter and Venus. These planets were thought to be benevolent, and their conjunction was considered most fortunate. This epithet is also applied to a monarch who has ruled for forty years. In this book, the title is used exclusively for Amir Hamza.

SALASAL PERIZAD: Companion of Emperor Shahpal bin Shahrukh of Qaf, and messenger of Aasman Peri

SALASAL SHAH: Master of the fort of Salasal Hisar

SALEEM KOHI: Father of Susan Peri

SALEH: Prophet sent to the tribe of Samud. Some associate him with the biblical Shelah.

SALIM SHAIRAN: Queen of the land of Zulmat in Qaf

SAM BIN NARIMAN: Legendary Persian warrior; father of Zal and grandfather of Rustam

SAMAN SEEMA PERI: One of Amir Hamza's *peri* wives from Qaf

SAMANDAR KHAN: An expert in pyrotechnics; brother of Zaad Khan

SAMANDUN HAZAR-DAST DEV: A *dev* whom Amir Hamza fights in Qaf

SAMAWA AYYAR: An *ayyar* in Emperor Naushervan's service

SAMERI: Magician who was the contemporary of Prophet Musa. According to Islamic legend, he conjured a calf that had the power of speech.

SAMOOM AADI: Warrior of the Aadi tribe

SAMRAT GAO-SAR: King of the *gao-sars;* his daughter, Arvana, marries Hamza

SANG ANDAZ KHUNKHVAR NESTAN: King of Nestan, 190-yard-tall giant

SAQAR GHAR BANO: Mother of Bakhtak

SAQRA-E BARAHMAN: Chief of Sufaid Dev's minions

SAR-BARAHNA TAPISHI: Commander in Emperor Naushervan's service; brother of Dewana Tapishi

SARHANG MISRI: Chief of the *ayyars* of the king of Egypt

SARKASH HINDI: Ruler of Sindh; brother of Koh Bakht Hindi

SARKOB TURK: Warrior in Amir Hamza's service

SARYAL BIN SALASAL: Forty-yard-tall giant; the king of Qaza-va-Qadar

SAUDAI QALANDAR: Alias used by Amar Ayyar

SAYYAD: An *ayyar* in the service of Sabit Shah

SEHBA JADU: Chief sorceress of the Tilism-e Anjabal where Rashida Peri and Arshivan are imprisoned

SEH-CHASHMI DEV: Creator of the Tilism-e Anjabal

SHABAN TAIFI: Son of Qunduz Sar-Shaban, titled Hamza-e Sani, "the Latter-day Hamza," by Amir Hamza

SHABRANG: Horse of Shaddad Abu-Amar Habashi

SHADDAD: Cruel monarch who arrogated divine power to himself. He was the founder of the legendary Gardens of Irum. Reviled in the Quran (89:6–8).

SHADDAD ABU-AMAR HABASHI: King of Ethiopia

SHAHPAL: Brother of King Saadan Shah of Ceylon; Jaipur's father and Landhoor's uncle. Not to be confused with Shahpal Hindi.

SHAHPAL BIN KARBAL BIN TAVEEL ZULMATI: An alias used by Amar Ayyar

SHAHPAL BIN SHAHRUKH: A jinn; emperor of Qaf and father of Aasman Peri

SHAHPAL HINDI: Father of Sabir and Sabur; not to be confused with King Shahpal, who is Landhoor's uncle

SHAMIM: Vizier of Sabit Shah

SHAMSHEER-ZAN: Executioner in the court of Shaddad Abu-Amar Habashi

SHANKAVAH: Nubian who tyrannizes Faridun Shah's lands and is killed by Landhoor

SHARARA JADU: Mother of Ra'ad, the two-headed *dev*

SHATIR: Commander in the service of Prince Hurmuz

SHER SHAH QIRWANI: Sovereign of Qirwan

SHERMAR: Sherwani warrior in the service of Amir Hamza

SHIDAI QALANDAR: Alias used by Amar Ayyar

SHIRIN: Heroine of the romance *Shirin and Farhad;* Farhad's beloved

SHIRIN: Ruler of the city of women

SHIS: Prophet Seth

SHIS YEMENI: Amir Hamza's commander and camp guard

MIAN SHORA: Musician associated with the court of Asaf-ul-Dawla in Avadh who developed and refined the *tappa* style of singing

SHUAIB: Ruler of Mando

SIKANDER: Name often used for both Alexander of Macedon and the prince Sikander Zulqarnain (Alexander the Bicornous)

SIKANDER ZULQARNAIN: *See* Sikander

SIKANDER ZULMATI: Emperor of Zulmat

SIMURGH: Giant bird whom Hamza befriends in Qaf

SIMURGH'S FEMALE: Holy guardian of the women of the city of Shirin

SINA AADI: Warrior of the Aadi tribe

SIRAJ: Commander who attacks Landhoor's lands

SIYAH QITAS: Horse of Prophet Ishaq (Isaac); given to Amir Hamza by Angel Jibrail

SIYAH SHER: Shepherd who looks after Hamza when he is wounded in battle

SIYAVUSH (OR SIYAVUSH BIN BUZURJMEHR): Buzurjmehr's son

SOHRAB: Legendary Persian warrior; son of Rustam

SOHRAB: Brother of Darab, keeper of the fortress of Kurgistan

SUFAID DEV: Commander of Samandoon Hazar-Dast Dev

SUHAIL: A goldsmith

SUHAIL YEMENI: Commander of the king of Yemen who becomes Amir Hamza's companion

SULEIMAN: King Solomon. According to the Islamic tradition, he had power over men, jinns, and beasts.

SULTAN BAKHT MAGHREBI: Prince of Maghreb

SULTAN BIN ZAL SHAMAMA JADU: Fictitious name adopted by one of Naqabdar Naranji-Posh's *ayyars* in imitating the king of Turkistan

SUSAN PERI (OR SUSAN JADU): Daughter of Saleem Kohi and guardian of Maloona Jadu's *tilism*

TAAN-SEN: Court musician of the Mughal emperor Akbar

TAHMURAS DEOBAND: King of Persia. According to legend, he enslaved a demon and made him his mount. He was therefore titled *deoband*, "the demon rider."

TAHMURAS SHAH: One of two masters of the castle of Rahtas Gadh. *See* Sabit Shah

TAIFUS BIN MAYUS BIN SARBUS BIN TAQ BIN TAMTARAQ BAZARGAN: An alias used by Amar Ayyar when disguised as a merchant

TARAR KHOOBAN: Attendant of Princess Mehr-Nigar; Muqbil Vafadar's beloved

TASMA-PA: A race of beings that have leathery thongs for legs

TASSAVURAN: A king; father of Zar-Angez

TAUQ BIN HEYRAN: Robber and bandit who renounces banditry and becomes Amir Hamza's companion

TAUQ-E ZARRIN: Son of Amir Hamza by Naranj Peri

TAUS BAKHTARI: One of the rulers of the lands of Bakhtar

TAZ TURK: Champion warrior in Amir Hamza's service

TOMIAN: An *ayyar* in Amir Hamza's service

TULU GAO-PA: King of the *gao-pas*

UMAYYA ZAMIRI: A cameleer; father of Amar Ayyar

WAILUM: Sassanid warrior in Emperor Naushervan's service

WAMIQ: Hero of the romance *Wamiq and Azra;* lover of Azra

WAQ: Talking tree whose fruit is shaped like human heads

YALAN: Commander in the service of Fatah Nosh

YAQUB: Jacob

YEZID: The second caliph of the Umayyad dynasty; ruled from C.E. 680–683. Prophet Muhammad's grandson Husain and his family were put to death at Karbala on Yezid's orders. An archetypal villain.

YUSUF: Joseph

ZAAD KHAN: An expert in pyrotechnics; brother of Samandar Khan

ZAFAR: An *ayyar* in the service of Amir Hamza

ZAIGHAM: Commander for Malik Shuaib

ZAL: Persian hero who was the father of Rustam and the son of Sam

ZAR-ANGEZ: Daughter of King Tassavuran; wife of Emperor Naushervan

ZARAQ JADU: A *dev* who encounters Amir in Tilism-e Shehristan-e Zarrin

ZARDHASHT JADU: Sorcerer and author of a book on magic

ZEHRA MISRI: Daughter of the king of Egypt

ZHOPIN FAULAD-TAN: Warrior in Emperor Naushervan's service

ZHOPIN KAUS (OR ZHOPIN ZABULI): Warrior in Emperor Naushervan's
    service

ZHOPIN ZABULI: *See* Zhopin Kaus

ZULAIKHA: Potiphar's wife

ZURA ZARAH-POSH: Commander in Emperor Naushervan's service

SELECTED SOURCES

ENGLISH

Burton, Sir Richard Francis. *The Book of the Sword.* (New York: Dover, 1987).

Egerton of Tatton, Lord. *Indian and Oriental Armour* (London: Arms and Armour Press, Lionel Leventhal Ltd., 1968).

Fallon, S. W. *English-Urdu Dictionary* (Rpt., Lahore: Urdu Science Board, 1993).

Faridany-Akhavan, Zahra. "The Problems of the Mughal Manuscript of the Hamza-Nama 1562–77: A Reconstruction." Ph.D. dissertation, Harvard University, 1989.

Hosain, Shaikh Sajjad. *The Amir Hamza: An Oriental Novel.* Part I (Calcutta: Sarat Chandra Bysack & Co, 1892).

Khoneli, Mose. *Amir Darejian—A Cycle of Medieval Georgian Tales Traditionally Ascribed to Mose Khoneli.* Translated by R. G. Stevenson (Oxford: Oxford University Press, 1958).

Lyons, M. C. *The Arabian Epic: Heroic and Oral Story-Telling.* Vols. I–III (New York: Cambridge University Press, 2005).

Pant, G. N. *Indian Arms and Armour,* Vol. I, *Pre- and Protohistoric Weapons and Archery* (New Delhi: Department of Arms and Armour, National Museum, Army Educational Stores, 1978). Vol. II, *Swords and Daggers,* 1980.

Platts, John T. *A Dictionary of Urdu, Classical Hindi and English* (Rpt., Lahore: Sang-e Meel, 1994).

Pritchett, Frances W. *The Romance Tradition in Urdu: Adventures from the Dastan of Amir Hamzah* (New York: Columbia University Press, 1991).

Seyller, John. *The Adventures of Hamza: Painting and Story-Telling in Mughal India* (Washington, D.C., and London: Freer Gallery of Art; Arthur M. Sackler Gallery, Smithsonian Institution, in association with Azimuth Editions, 2002).

Steingass, F. *A Comprehensive Persian-English Dictionary* (New York: Routledge & Kegan Paul, in association with Iran University Press, 1995).

al-Thalibi, Abu Mansur Abd al-Malik bin Muhammad bin Ismail. *Lataif al-Ma'arif* (The Book of Curious and Entertaining Information). Translated and with introduction and notes by Clifford Edmund Bosworth (Edinburgh: Edinburgh University Press, 1968).

Walker, Warren S., ed. *A Turkish Folktale: The Art of Behçet Mahir* (New York and London: Garland Publishing, Inc., 1996).

URDU

Bilgrami, Abdullah Husain. *Dastan-e Amir Hamza Sahibqiran* (Lucknow, India: Naval Kishore Press, 1871).

Dehlvi, Syed Ahmed. *Farhang-e Asifya,* Vols. I–II (Rpt., Lahore, Pakistan: Urdu Science Board, 1995).

Faruqi, Shamsur Rahman. *Sahiri, Shahi, Sahibqirani: Dastan-e Amir Hamza ka Mutalaa.* Vol. I, *Nazari Mubahis* (New Delhi: National Council for the Promotion of Urdu Language, 1999). Vol. II, *Amali Mubahis* (New Delhi: National Council for the Promotion of Urdu Language, 2006). Vol. III, *Jahan-e Hamza* (New Delhi: National Council for the Promotion of Urdu Language, 2006).

Jah, Syed Muhammad Husain. *Tilism-e Hoshruba.* Vols. I–IV (Lucknow, India: Naval Kishore Press, 1883–90; rpt., Lahore, Pakistan: Sang-e Meel Publications, n.d.). Vol. V, Part I (Lucknow, India: Husaini Press, 1890; rpt., Patna, India: Khuda Bakhsh Library, 2000).

Jain, Gyan Chand. *Urdu ki Nasri Dastanen* (Lucknow, India: Uttar Pradesh Urdu Academy, 1987).

Kakorvi, Noor-ul Hasan Nayyar. *Noor-ul Lughat.* Vols. I–II (Rpt., Lahore, Pakistan: Sang-e Meel Publications, 1983).

Lakhnavi, Mirza Aman Ali Khan Bahadur Ghalib. *Tarjuma-e Dastan-e Sahibqiran Giti-sitan Aal-e Paighambar-e Aakhiruz Zaman Amir Hamza bin Abdul-Muttalib bin Hashim bin Abdul Munaf* (Calcutta: Hakim Sahib Press, 1855).

Majeed, Khvaja Abdul. *Jama-ul Lughat.* Vols. I–II (Rpt., Lahore, Pakistan: Urdu Science Board, 1999).

Qamar, Ahmad Husain. *Tilism-e Hoshruba.* Vols. V–VII (Lucknow, India: Naval Kishore Press, 1890–93; rpt., Lahore, Pakistan: Sang-e Meel Publications, n.d.).

PERSIAN

Hamdani, Haji Qissa-Khvan. *Zubdatur Rumuz* (MS, c. 1613–14; Khuda Bakhsh Library, Patna).

Kitab-e Rumuz-e Hamza (Tehran: A.H. 1274–76 [1857–59]; British Museum Library).

Mirza Muhammad Khan 'malik-ul kuttab.' *Kitab-e Dastan-e Amir Hamza Sahibqiran* (Bombay: Matba-e Sapehr-e Matla, A.H. 1327 [1909]).
Shiar, Jafar, ed. *Qissa-e Hamza*. 2 vols. (Tehran: University of Tehran Press, A.H. 1347 [1968–69]).

GERMAN

Egger, Gerhart. *Der Hamza Roman: Eine Mughal-Handschrift Asunder Zeit Akbar des Großen* (Vienna: Österreich Museum für angewandte Kunst, 1969).
Glück, Heinrich. *Die Indischen Miniaturen des Hamza-e Romanes im Österreichischen Museum für Kunst und Industrie in Wien und in anderen Sammlungen* (Zurich: Amalthea-Verlag, 1925).
Hamza-nama: Vollständige Wiedergabe der bekannten Blätter der Handschrift aus den Beständen aller erreichbaren Sammlungen. Codices selecti phototypice impressi, Vol. 52 (Graz: Akademische Druck- und Verlagsanstalt, 1974).

FRENCH

"Les artistes de la court d'Akbar et les illustrations de Dastan i Amir Hamzae." In *Arts Asiatiques*. Vol. II, fase 1–2 (1995).

DUTCH

Van Ronkel, Ph. S. *De Roman van Amir Hamza* (Lieden: E. J. Brill, 1895).

NOTES

1. *Ctesiphon: (Mada'in)* the collective name of seven cities that flourished in the reign of Naushervan in the seventh century C.E.

2. *henna from the palm:* The words used in the Urdu text are *duzd-e henna,* literally, "the thief of henna." It is a term used to describe the white parts of the hand that escape the application of henna.

3. *Khvaja:* a man of distinction. A title conferred on dignitaries.

4. hikmat: a high degree of wisdom. Also a lesser-known school of philosophy.

5. *Malik:* title of royalty. Also conferred on viziers, as in the case of Malik Alqash.

6. kalma: an act of faith consisting of the affirmation of the existence of one God and the prophethood of Muhammad.

7. maunds: A *maund* is a measurement of weight equivalent to a little more than 82 pounds, or 38.25 kilograms.

8. *Tabrizi* maund: a measure of weight equivalent to 3 kilograms.

9. *Jamshedi robe of honor:* a royal gift consisting of eleven pieces of cloth; usually conferred on viziers as a mark of honor.

10. *God forbid . . . harm:* The term *enemies* is substituted for a person's name because of the superstition that just mentioning the name of a person in the context of a calamity will bring the calamity down on his head. Thus, if person A is unwell, his friends will ask, "Are the enemies of A unwell?"

11. *Mount of Wisdom:* A pun is intended here in Urdu as well. The word used is *khar-e hukma. Khar* means "ass" as well as "great." So the literal translation of the term would be "ass of the wise men" and "wisest of the wise," both of which are conveyed in the term *Mount of Wisdom.*

12. *seven treasures of Shaddad:* In classical literature, not seven treasures but seven gates of Shaddad's city Irum are mentioned. It was the emperor Khusrau who was known to have seven treasures. In the *dastan* tradition these references are typically mixed up.

13. *Seven Climes: (Haft Aqlim)* an approach used by classical Islamic geographers to divide the Earth into the Greek system of zones or climes.

14. ayyars: tricksters or spies. In the *dastan* the word *ayyar* is mostly used with Amar's name. Amar is an *ayyar*, a most cunning fellow unmatched in slyness. While his resourcefulness derives in part from divine gifts, his slyness and craftiness are native.

15. *the prince Naushervan:* The name *Naushervan* is constructed from the composition of the two words *nosh*, meaning "drinking," and *ravan*, meaning "flowing," used in the context of the water spring.

16. *dulcimer:* a type of stringed instrument, harp, or psaltery played by hand without making use of any plectrum or bow.

17. *chain:* a chain hung outside his court by Emperor Naushervan, which allowed petitioners a direct and personal audience with him.

18. *Kaaba:* the holy shrine in Mecca toward which all Muslims turn when saying their prayers.

19. *Mount Qaf: (Koh Qaf)* according to Islamic legend, the huge mountain in the middle of which the Earth is sunk, as a night light is placed in a cup. It binds the horizon on all sides. Its foundation is the emerald *Sakhrat*, the reflection of which gives the azure hue to the sky.

20. *collyrium of Suleiman: (Surma-e Suleimani)* according to legend, a powder that makes one able to see the hidden treasures of the Earth. The collyrium of Suleiman in the *dastan*, however, makes one see jinns, *devs, peris,* etc., who otherwise remain invisible to the human eye.

21. *carbuncles:* any of several red precious stones such as the ruby.

22. *lost Yusuf:* A parallel is drawn between Yaqub (Jacob) being reunited with his son Yusuf (Joseph) and Khvaja Abdul Muttalib with his son Hamza.

23. fateha: a prayer read on an offering. Generally the first chapter of the Quran, *Sura Fateha*, also known as the Exordium, is read on offerings. See also note 57.

24. peras: sweetmeats made of curds.

25. tola: a traditional Indian unit of mass, now standardized as 11.66 grams.

26. *burqa:* a robelike veil for the whole body, which also covers the head, supplied with an opening for the eyes.

27. khagina: a dish similar to an omelet but containing more spices, and sometimes mince as well.

28. shir-maals: a kind of bread made of flour kneaded with milk and sugar.

29. nihari: a kind of meat curry or mulligatawny traditionally prepared for breakfast.

30. *five vices:* The five defects in a horse as described in the sharia are: *hashri*, a stallion who is violent and impetuous with the mare; *sitara-peshani*, having a star on the forehead; *kamari*, a horse weak in the loins; *shab-kur*, having night blindness, or suffering from a disease known as *rataundhia;* and *kuhan-lang*, being unable to budge from its spot.

31. *sharia:* the code of social life modeled on the teachings and traditions of the Prophet Muhammad.

32. Sahib-e Hal Ata: This phrase signifies Ali, the fourth caliph of Islam. Chapter 76 of the Quran, called *Dahr*, or *Insan*, begins with this phrase. It means "has there not passed, or been?" Verse 8 of this sura, or chapter, speaks of people who themselves go hungry but feed others. Some interpreters of the Quran say that this verse refers to Ali, and it is presumed that the whole sura is about Ali in some way. Since the sura starts with *hal ata*, Ali is occasionally described as the *sahib*, or the *tajdar*, of *hal ata*. For this information I am indebted to Shamsur Rahman Faruqi.

33. *Second of the Five Holies:* The Five Holies are usually listed as: Muhammad, first; Fatima, second; Ali, third; Hasan, fourth; and Husain, fifth. However, in this instance, Ali is listed as the second.

34. *a seven-year-old boy:* The *dastan* follows the classical tradition of heroes acquiring prodigious strength at a very young age.

35. *Erebus of Hell:* the darkest region of Hell.

36. *thousands ... lying murdered:* The exaggeration in numbers is sometimes used in the *dastan* to emphasize some aspect of the scene—in this case, the sheer havoc caused by Hamza and his companions.

37. *amir:* a commander or leader. In this book this title is used for Hamza, the hero of the story.

38. *horse-shinty: (chogan)* an eastern game of which polo is the modern form.

39. *ringdove perched on a cypress branch:* The poets traditionally considered the ringdove a lover of the cypress tree. The event suggests the image of a lover (ringdove) coming to his beloved (cypress tree) in distress. It is also significant that the ringdove as a citizen in Naushervan's land has come to seek redress at the emperor's court.

40. *court of Jamshed:* An ancient king of Persia, Jamshed (often confused in legends with Alexander and King Solomon) is invoked here to suggest the grandeur of Emperor Naushervan's court. See also note 46.

41. *Abul-Ala:* This is one of the titles used by Amir Hamza.

42. *Maghrebi wrestling:* The Greek style of wrestling is most likely intended by this reference.

43. *Mehtar:* a commander.

44. *tent of the prophet Danyal:* A tent on which magic had no effect.

45. *hava-mohra:* some kind of conch shell.

46. *Throne of Kai-Khusrau:* The name of the mighty Persian emperor Kai Khusrau (King Cyrus) is invoked here to suggest the grandeur of Emperor Naushervan's court and his throne. See also note 40.

47. *Turan:* the ancient Iranian name for Central Asia, literally meaning "the land of the Tur." According to legend, the nomadic tribes who inhabited these lands were ruled by Tur, who was the emperor Faridun's elder son.

48. *Rustam's Throne:* The most celebrated champion of the Persian court occupies the traditional seat of Rustam, the ancient warrior and hero of the *Shahnamah*. This seat has been given to Gustham bin Ashk Zarrin Kafsh in view of his might and valor. It is this chair that Hamza occupies in Gustham's absence when Naushervan offers him a seat of his choice in his court.

49. do-tara: a stringed instrument with two wires. Here and on p. 100, Amar is seen playing the *do-tara* when the instrument will be bestowed upon him much later. See the Translator's Preface for explanation of these apparent inconsistencies. See also note 60.
50. ambarcha: a neck ornament that has a cavity for storing amber.
51. *Sahibqiran:* Lord of the Auspicious Planetary Conjunction. Someone born under the conjunction of Jupiter and Venus was given this title. Jupiter and Venus were thought to be benevolent planets, and their conjunction was considered most fortunate. This epithet is also applied to a monarch who has ruled for forty years. In this book the title is used exclusively for Amir Hamza.
52. *simurgh:* a legendary bird.
53. *moon's partridge dove:* The partridge dove is famous in Persian and Urdu poetry for the beauty of its gait.
54. *Khusrau:* a title used for a majestic king. In this book it is used for Landhoor bin Saadan, unless accompanied by another name.
55. *Shah Mohra:* a precious stone, said to be found in a serpent's mouth or a dragon's head, that is reputed to have curative properties.
56. *salve of Daud: (Marham-e Daudi)* a legendary ointment that is known for its miraculous healing properties.
57. *"over which* fateha *has been said":* to cause blessings to be invoked upon a dead relative. This is done by having the opening chapter of the Quran, the *Sura Fateha* or the Exordium, read over the deceased for forty days after his death, and by distributing alms and food. See also note 23.
58. dev-jama: a garment of animal skin with the hairy part outside. Also refers to a lion's skin in which the warriors clothed themselves.
59. zambil: Amar's *zambil* is perhaps based on *Zambil-e Suleiman,* a wallet or leather bag in Suleiman's possession which produced anything he wished for. (It was also called *Amban-e Suleiman.*) In the Turkish version told by Behçet Mahir we find that Amar's pouch was made from the skin of the sheep that Prophet Ibrahim had sacrificed to Allah instead of his son. Thus that sheepskin had been waiting there for Amar since the time of Prophet Ibrahim.
60. do-tara: See note 49.
61. *"You shall run ... tire":* It is interesting to note that earlier Khizr also gave the same miracle to Amar. In the Turkish version of Behçet Mahir, Amar could run as fast as the wind because he did not have any kneecaps. Also in this version, Izrail, the Angel of Death, was unable to catch him and take his soul because Amar ran faster than Izrail could fly. When Izrail asked Allah's advice, the Almighty God told him to place a golden pickax and a silver shovel in a newly dug grave and to catch Amar when his greed for the gold and silver lured him there. Izrail acted on Allah's advice and successfully captured Amar's soul.
62. mithcals: measures of weight.
63. *Sikander's rampart: (Sadd-e Sikander)* according to legend, a rampart built by Alexander the Bicornous to hold back Gog and Magog.

64. Koh-e Besutoon: the great mountain through which Farhad, the legendary lover of Shirin, had to cut a channel as a precondition for winning his beloved.

65. *Bardwani:* of or pertaining to Bardwan, a city in Bengal.

66. *old woman of Ctesiphon:* According to legend, an old woman who lived near Naushervan's palace whose cooking wafted smoke into the emperor's palace. Naushervan offered to give her another place to live but she refused, and he did not use coercion to have her moved despite his discomfort due to the smoke.

67. *Gueber:* a derogatory term for Zoroastrians.

68. noshidaru: a confection that is supposed to be a sovereign antidote against all kinds of maladies.

69. *"Your Honor ... I will not pay":* a conversation conducted in an Indian regional dialect (Abdullah Bilgrami, *Dastan-e Amir Hamza,* 1871, p. 235, lines 8–13, 15–16, 21–23).

70. mashas: traditional units of weight used in India, approximately equivalent to one gram.

71. *King of the Four Climes:* an allusion to the sun, which shines on the four corners of the globe.

72 maiyoon: a ceremony of Indian Muslims in which a few days before the wedding the bride is sent into seclusion and no man is allowed to approach her, so her thoughts may become focused on her bridegroom.

73. *One hundred and seventy-five gods:* The *dastan* mixes social and cultural references, which explains the presence of Brahmins in a Zoroastrian funeral procession.

74. *squib:* a firecracker in which the powder burns with a fizz.

75 *Anno Hegirae ... Anno Domini:* Anno Hegirae is used to indicate the time from the first year of the Muslim calendar (622 C.E.); Anno Domini is used to indicate the time from the birth of Jesus of Nazareth.

BOOK TWO

1. *avis of Naushervan's soul:* In the Indo-Persian literary tradition the soul is likened to an avis or bird. When the corporeal self dies the soul flies away. A state of extreme fear or agitation is said to cause the soul to begin fluttering inside the cage of the corporeal self. In this instance, however, Amar Ayyar makes a wordplay on the allegory by threatening to pluck the avis of Naushervan's soul.

2. *The westbound bird:* an allusion to the sun, for its movement from east to west in the sky.

3. maghreb *prayers:* the fourth set of prayers said by Muslims daily, occurring after sunset.

4. *Potentate of the First Heaven:* an allusion to the moon. In Islamic mythology the skies were divided into regions named first heaven, et cetera.

5. *salve of Suleiman:* The invention of this salve is attributed to Prophet

Suleiman (Solomon); it is supposed to have miraculous healing properties. See also note 56, Book One.

6. dastan: an epic, romance, adventure, or story. It is an oral narrative form.

7. zuhr *prayers:* the second set of prayers said by Muslims daily, occurring in the afternoon.

8. *catechu, and kohl:* Catechu is an astringent; it is the extract of *Acacia catechu,* produced by boiling the wood in water and evaporating the resulting brew. Kohl is a dark gray ore of lead usually used to outline the eyes.

9. *Samsam, Qumqam, Aqrab-e Suleimani, and Zul-Hajam:* names of legendary swords that belonged to Prophet Suleiman.

10. *Naqabdar:* literally, "the veiled one."

11. tilism: The word as used here means an enchantment or an enchanted region. It also refers to a device or a combination of devices that have magical attributes.

12. *Koh-e Besutoon:* In the earlier instance, the term was used to describe the great mountain through which Farhad, the legendary lover of Shirin, had to cut a channel as a condition to winning his beloved. In this case, it is a fixture of Qaf. See note 64 (Book One).

13. *gave up the ghost with just one cry:* This is the first time we see Sufaid Dev being killed. However, because of multiple *dastan* traditions intervening in the text, he appears alive on two subsequent occasions, and is killed each time. See note 6 (Book Three) and note 18 (Book Four).

14. *Badi-ul-Mulk:* Badi-ul-Mulk never appears in this story. See A Note on the Text.

Book Three

1. *Zandan-e Suleimani:* a prison built by Prophet Suleiman.

2. *signet of Suleiman:* also known as the Seal of Suleiman. The signet worn by Prophet Suleiman. It is said that because this ring had the Most Great Name inscribed on it the jinns obeyed the prophet.

3. *color of Mars:* Red is the color most often associated with the planet Mars. As Mars is also the God of War, wearing red clothes signifies the sanguinary mood of the wearer.

4. *a giant crane:* the species of gigantic crane *Ardea argala,* known as "the bone swallower."

5. *Some transcribers ... a false tradition:* Here two versions of the event are mentioned as described by the *dastan* narrators of the time: In one Hamza divorces Aasman Peri and in the other he does not. It is not specified in this passage which one is chosen by the author of this narrative. We find out later that it was the one in which Hamza divorced Aasman Peri. See note 8 below.

6. *He killed him ... draw another breath:* In this passage Sufaid Dev dies at Landhoor's hands, but in Book Four we discover he is alive; he is ultimately killed by Amir Hamza. See note 13 (Book Two).

7. *Khvaja Nihal:* Earlier, Amar was shown to have killed Khvaja Nihal. In this

passage we see Khvaja Nihal alive. This disparity exists, perhaps, because of the various, often conflicting, narrative traditions of the *Dastan-e Amir Hamza* used by the author to compose his own version. See also A Note on the Text.

8. *Because Amir had divorced:* See note 5 above. In this passage we finally learn which tradition the narrator chose to build his story. See also A Note on the Text.

9. *Shish-Mahal:* Mughal architectural term for a room decorated with mirror mosaics. The term can also be described as "glass palace."

10. *fell dead:* In this passage Samandoon Hazar-Dast Dev dies, but in Book Four we discover he is alive and is ultimately killed by Amir Hamza in similar circumstances.

BOOK FOUR

1. *pavilion of Jamshed:* The name of Jamshed, an ancient king of Persia, is often confused in legend with that of Prophet Suleiman. In this instance, the Pavilion of Jamshed is interchangeable with the Pavilion of Suleiman. See also note 2.

2. *Pavilion of Suleiman . . . Char-Bazar of Bilqis:* These are enchanted pavilions and tents, according to the *dastan*. They have more than one story, multiple chambers, and interconnecting passages or spaces.

3. *a precious pearl:* an allusion to the act of conception. Earlier in this passage the same imagery was used to describe the act of coition.

4. *onager:* a wild ass.

5. fajar *prayers:* the first set of prayers said by Muslims in the morning.

6. *Taking Muqbil for Amir Hamza:* In the *dastan* tradition Muqbil and Amir Hamza share a likeness of features.

7. *Ashqar broke his fetters:* Ashqar Devzad breaks his fetters by himself when aid arrives. Throughout the *dastan*, the champions of Amir Hamza's camp similarly are able to set themselves free when their friends arrive at their imprisonment to save them.

8. qadi: in Muslim culture, the person who reads the wedding sermon and solemnizes the nuptials.

9. *Rustam-e Peel-Tan:* literally, "elephant-bodied Rustam." It should be noted that the word *peel-tan* connotes great physical strength and is a title reserved only for the greatest of champions. The title does not signify that the person is of an elephantine size.

10. *Sher-e Saf-Shikan:* the Rank-Destroying Lion.

11. *Book of Ibrahim:* the Holy Book that Prophet Ibrahim received from God.

12. *Samandoon Hazar-Dast Dev had escaped Qaf:* In Book Three, Amir Hamza is shown to have killed Samandoon Hazar-Dast Dev. Here the narrator recounts another tradition, according to which Samandoon Hazar-Dast Dev escaped Qaf and the deadly encounter with Hamza. However, the manner in which Samandoon Hazar-Dast Dev is subsequently killed in this passage is similar to the one in which he is killed in Book Three.

13. *holy Khizr had identified:* In this passage it is Hamza who plugs the Fountain of Life. In Book Three, however, it was Khizr who stopped it, which resulted in Samandoon Hazar-Dast Dev's death. See also note 12 above.

14. hareesa: a kind of stew made of crushed wheat boiled to a thick consistency, to which is added meat, butter, cinnamon, and aromatic herbs.

15. *the Last Prophet:* This is a reference to Muhammad bin Abdul Muttalib, the Prophet of Islam (ca. 570–632 C.E.).

16. *Qaza-va-Qadar:* In this instance the term *Qaza-va-Qadar* is a geographical location. It should not be confused with the Islamic concept of predestination also described by this term.

17. *When Hurmuz ... on some pretext:* Some Zoroastrians interpret their religion as advocating the avoidance of pork and beef, and it is perhaps on account of this that Hurmuz avoids eating pork on this occasion.

18. *Sufaid Dev lives there:* In an earlier passage in Book Three, Sufaid Dev was killed at Landhoor's hands. See note 13 (Book Two) and note 6 (Book Three).

19. *filled with gunpowder:* The use of gunpowder in the times described by the *dastan* seems anachronistic. It should be noted that the *dastan* genre did not observe verisimilitude too strictly. The incorporation of contemporary reality in artistic creations was evident in the Indian visual arts of the time as well. Several illustrations of the *Hamzanama* (another name for the *Dastan-e Amir Hamza*) commissioned by the Mughal emperor Akbar in the mid-sixteenth century also depicted characters wielding and firing firearms.

20. *"I would leave Zulmat":* The reference to Zulmat (literally, "the Land of Darkness") is also found in the *Iskander-Nama* ("The Romance of Alexander"). However, in the *dastan,* Zulmat is often depicted as a land populated by sorcerers and magicians.

21. *he took out his gun:* See note 19.

22. Sura-e Jinn: the seventy-second chapter of the Quran, which mentions the jinns.

23. *this translator:* This is a reference to Ghalib Lakhnavi, the author of this version of the *Dastan-e Amir Hamza,* who called his work a translation. See also A Note on the Text.

About the Translator

MUSHARRAF ALI FAROOQI is an author and translator. He has translated works by the contemporary Urdu poet Afzal Ahmed Syed and is currently working on the Urdu Project (www.urduproject.com), an online resource for the study of the Urdu language and literature.

A NOTE ON THE TYPE

The text of this Modern Library edition
was set in a digitized version of Janson, a typeface that
dates from about 1690 and was cut by Nicholas Kis,
a Hungarian working in Amsterdam. The original matrices have
survived and are held by the Stempel foundry in Germany.
Hermann Zapf redesigned some of the weights and sizes for
Stempel, basing his revisions on the original design.

MODERN LIBRARY IS ONLINE AT
WWW.MODERNLIBRARY.COM

MODERN LIBRARY ONLINE IS YOUR GUIDE TO CLASSIC LITERATURE ON THE WEB

THE MODERN LIBRARY E-NEWSLETTER

Our free e-mail newsletter is sent to subscribers, and features sample chapters, interviews with and essays by our authors, upcoming books, special promotions, announcements, and news. To subscribe to the Modern Library e-newsletter, visit **www.modernlibrary.com**

THE MODERN LIBRARY WEBSITE

Check out the Modern Library website at
www.modernlibrary.com for:

- The Modern Library e-newsletter
- A list of our current and upcoming titles and series
- Reading Group Guides and exclusive author spotlights
- Special features with information on the classics and other paperback series
- Excerpts from new releases and other titles
- A list of our e-books and information on where to buy them
- The Modern Library Editorial Board's 100 Best Novels and 100 Best Nonfiction Books of the Twentieth Century written in the English language
- News and announcements

Questions? E-mail us at **modernlibrary@randomhouse.com**.
For questions about examination or desk copies, please visit
the Random House Academic Resources site at
www.randomhouse.com/academic.

Printed in the United States
by Baker & Taylor Publisher Services